SANJAY CHOPRA is an airline pilot and the author of two collections of short stories. His stories have won the Invisible Ink, the Millennium writers and Southport awards in the UK and the USA. In the words of his readers, 'He is a storyteller like those of the old days, yet his stories are as modern as tomorrow.'

During a school project on 'The most memorable day of my life', NAMITA ROY GHOSE wrote about a Russian girl on the day WW2 ended. She got her first rejection slip from the teacher for making things up. Ever since, Namita has established her storytelling skills through her scriptwriting, screenplays poetry, fiction, legendary advertising campaigns, and as a renowned advertising film director. A Creative Director with HTA, she left after 13 years to start her own film company, White Light, one of India's top ad film outfits. A social activist, she is the founder ofVanashakti, an NGO that works to protect the environment. Namita has done pro bono work on issues like domestic violence, child welfare, sexual harassment and forest preservation. She is an avid traveller, a photographer, foodie and teacher.

The Wrong Turn

Love and betrayal in the time of **Netaji**

SANJAY CHOPRA **NAMITA ROY GHOSE**

Om Books International

First published in 2017 by

Om Books International

Corporate & Editorial Office
A-12, Sector 64, Noida 201 301
Uttar Pradesh, India
Phone: +91 120 477 4100
Email: editorial@ombooks.com
Website: www.ombooksinternational.com

Sales Office
107, Ansari Road, Darya Ganj,
New Delhi 110 002, India
Phone: +91 11 4000 9000
Fax: +91 11 2327 8091
Email: sales@ombooks.com
Website: www.ombooks.com

Disclaimer: This is purely a work of fiction. While it takes place against the backdrop of the Indian freedom struggle and World War II, the story and characters depicted here are fictitious. Any reference to or use of historical characters is also fictional.

ISBN: 978-93-86316-96-7

Printed in India

10 9 8 7 6 5 4 3 2 1

Contents

ACKNOWLEDGEMENTS

Sanjay Chopra is grateful to:

Priyanka Mukherjee for her invaluable contribution.

Bauji, my grandfather who introduced me to the magical world of stories;

Meena and Satish Chopra, my parents and Pammi and Subhash Arora, my in-laws, for their love and blessings;

The sage, Daisaku Ikeda who taught me that 'where your ability ends, your faith begins';

My muse, my wife Tisca;

Another muse in the making, my daughter Tara;

And Namita Roy Ghose for believing in this story.

Namita Roy Ghose is indebted to:

Arobindo and Gouri Roy, my parents who gave me the gift of life;

My mentor Dr Daisaku Ikeda who gave me the belief;

My husband Pronab Ghose who encouraged me endlessly;

My godfather Gora Mukherji who taught me the love of story;

Rajesh Ashar, who helped with machines and their malfunctions,

And Sanjay Chopra for the journey.

The co-authors are beholden to:

Peter Fay for *The Forgotten Army;*

Sugata Bose for *His Majesty's Opponent;*

Leonard A. Gordon for *Brothers against the Raj;*

Hugh Toye for *Subhash Chandra Bose: The Springing Tiger;*

Patralekha Paul; Samay Pandit and Saki.

I started wanting to tell the truth but the result was fiction.

— *Katherine Ann Porter*

In India's pantheon, there is space reserved, high ample and honourable space, for those men and women who, when certain accidents of time and space gave them the opportunity, seized it and went out to do battle for India's freedom.

— *Peter Fay*, Historian, Author of *The Forgotten Army*

PROLOGUE

High, on the thermals, the black ravens floated, their bright, glassy eyes scanning the gorge below. The grass that had grown tall and wayward, crowded with the wild flowers of summer, lay bruised and flattened by the blind upturned faces, the out-thrown hands, the sprawled, ungainly legs of the dead. They lay, muddied, bloodied, shrouded in a great silence that hung over the valley. A tattered tricolour, its orange, white and green singed by fire, lay draped across the face of a young woman, like a veil hiding the ugliness of death. The mist — common in the early morning in these parts of the woods near Kohima — had begun to move in ragged, wind-swept patches as the pale sun rose higher, softly illuminating the road that would have led to Delhi.

He could see them now, soft gentle mounds, in the hundreds, curiously peaceful despite the violence of their passing, stretching all the way to the tree line. Through the swirling fog, damped down, distant sounds began to seep through — the flat crack of gunfire...a muted scream...the rude cawing of a bird.

He stared, bemused, at the useless gun in his clenched hand, the great bloom of blood on his thigh. Then his eyes snapped into focus, as complete awareness flared up in those big, dreamy eyes. A low, strangled wail of despair, the cry of the damned, was torn from his dry throat. Slowly, he sank to his knees in the killing field, a supplicant, a penitent.

LONDON, 1991

Fog shrouded the two big Crimean War cannons in the forecourt. The morning forecast had said a maximum of 5°C. Bleeding hell, thought James Cartwright, as he pulled off his ancient overcoat in the freezing lobby of the National War Museum on Royal Hospital Road, Chelsea, winter's really dragging her feet this year. It's the middle of effing February but there's no let up, is there?

He shuffled down the grey stone corridor, set in the back of the building away from the tourist beat, to his lair, the Archives Section, rubbing his big gardener's hands. He really needed to buy a new overcoat — a nice Harris on sale at Marks and Sparks — but with the recession, who could afford anything good these days.

Molly Underworth, big, placid Molly with her blood-red nail varnish and bottle blond bobbed hair to cheer up any winter's day, had already put the kettle on.

'Freezing, isn't it?'

'Aye, it is. Nothing much to cheer us up, I'm afraid. They say there's been another bit of rioting in Birmingham and Blackbird Leys and Kates Hill, up Oxford way.'

'And Cardiff too. My Aunt Myrtle in Bristol said it's all that unemployment and lay-offs.'

'Yes, Iron Maggie better do something soon or she'll be out on her ear,' growled Cartwright.

'Well, here's something to cheer you up. New *cha* from the Indian store near the station. Good strong Assam, he said. Which reminds me. Your friend from Calcutta is back.'

Cartwright raised a bushy eyebrow. Molly wagged one red-tipped finger towards his table. On top of the small, neatly sorted heap of mail sat a letter in a plain, unremarkable envelope. A large, bulging dog-eared box file sat beside.

'Aah, our esteemed correspondent,' said Cartwright, easing his bulk into his capacious, creaking swivel chair. The letter was addressed to the National War Museum in an elegant, flowing cursive type and had an Indian stamp on it. He pulled out the single-page letter and looked at the date.

'Yes, there it is...on the bloody nail, dated 23rd January from our mystery man.'

A thin, pale-eyed man with a precise centre parting and a nose pink from the cold, entered the room, blowing on his fingers.

'Morning, Cartwright. Morning, Mrs. Underworth.'

'Good morning, Sir,' chirped Molly, beginning to make up a tea tray.

'And what mystery man might we be referring to, Mr. Cartwright?' asked the gentleman on his way to the inner office.

'Oh, this is a bit before your time, Sir. There's this bloke, anonymous, from India…'

The gentleman paused. 'Before my time, eh?'

'Been writing, every year, mind you, since…oh…' Cartwright opened the box file. Inside lay identical-looking letters, a dusty big bunch, all in the same handwriting. 'Oh, since 1950, I think.'

'1949, Sir, that was the first one.' Molly chipped in.

The pale gentleman sat down in the spare chair and slid the box file towards him. 'You don't say. That's um…some 40-odd years,' he murmured. 'And what is the subject of his correspondence, may I ask?'

'Oh, he keeps blathering on about the same old rubbish, Mr. Jones. How a little dust-up with the British Army in some godforsaken place called…ummm…Kohyma.'

'Koheema, Mr. Cartwright,' Molly whispered.

'Thank you, dear. Anyway, this bloke declares that it was the toughest battle us British fought.'

Mr. Jones gave a superior twitch of a smile. 'Benighted heathen. Can't be knowing about Waterloo and Dunkirk, can he?'

Cartwright picked up a few more of the letters. 'Strange though, Sir, this guy writes in pretty decent English, really knows his stuff. He's got dates and data bang on the nose. Been doing a bit of reading myself. This Brigadier Whyte he keeps talking about. Looked him up, I did.'

'Why you do that for? It's history, done with, forgotten,' chided Molly.

Cartwright shrugged his shoulders. 'Ah, it's all history in here, isn't it, Molly? Archives Section, that's us. I don't know, he's kind of intriguing. Persistent bloke…keeps harping on about this Whyte who was in India during the war. And you know what? This Whyte actually existed. He was a bleeding hero. Helped us beat the Japs in that Kohima place.'

Mr. Jones' colourless eyes narrowed. All his life, as a Fellow in Cambridge, later as a drone in MI6, he had dreamt of one day coming across some unknown or forgotten nugget of history, a secret he could claim to have unearthed, which would enable him to crawl out of the dusty backrooms and unregarded corridors of Official Secrets, and shine. Something about this whetted his appetite.

'You don't say. So what does our mystery writer want?'

'He wants this Brigadier Whyte's file to be made public. Something about some secret recordings. He wants all the files on something called the INA and someone called Bose to be made public. Apparently, that's going to reveal the truth, that our chaps would have lost at Kohima, and lost India in the bargain.'

Mr. Jones smiled, a thin, mirthless smile that failed to lift the corners of his pinched lips. 'I thought we lost it, anyway.'

Cartwright drained his tea, brushed the dampness from his moustache. 'Aah, we did, didn't we? Like everything else…lost the whole Empire along with the bathtub. Anyway, who's going to know the bloody truth of it after all these years?'

Molly started to clear up the tea things. 'And who on earth cares?'

Cartwright dropped the letter inside the box file, rubbed his big hands. 'Go on, dear, put it away with the other bits and bobs.' He settled down ponderously to the order of the day.

Mr. Jones lingered. As Molly went to clear up, he laid his perfectly manicured forefinger on her wrist. Up close, in the central heating, the lavender perfume she wore was a bit overpowering. He wrinkled his nose. 'Hold on there, I'd like to give it a go-over. Maybe there's something we are missing. Worth a dekko.'

Molly shrugged. Cartwright, without even looking up from his papers, shrugged too.

'Ain't even given a return address, the silly coot.'

Mr. Jones didn't hear him. Carrying the box file with its curious contents, murmuring something unintelligible, he made his way to the inner sanctum.

KOLKATA, JANUARY 23, 2013

The sabziwalla, a stout Bihari from Monghyr, places the small plastic bag of vegetables inside the basket. The basket is ingeniously suspended by a plastic line, hanging down from the dark green, cast-iron railing of the second-floor balcony of Supriya Debi's flat. Her old, cracked voice wafts down, disembodied, through the thick winter fog of this January morning, whining about the gola-kata price of veggies these days. The sabziwalla shivers, waiting for the old lady's maid to send down his payment in the basket.

Under the dark, lowering skies, the narrow, winding gully, crowded by ramshackle houses on either side, snakes away into the fog. It is in an old part of North Kolkata, still untouched by predatory builders. Sounds float out of the fog — the thin squeaking of a tubewell being pumped, a young girl practising scales, her voice just that one irritating octave off-pitch, the Bengali morning news announcing some scam and a possible arrest. As the sabziwalla pushes his cart back onto the street, he almost bumps into a shadow that looms out of the fog. It's an old decrepit man, somewhere in his late eighties maybe, once tall, now bent, swathed in a much worn, ragged shawl. The man stumbles.

'Sorry, sorry, Dadu.'

The old man peers at the sabziwalla through thick, really old-fashioned, wire-framed glasses, held together by some Johnson tape; then muttering something under his breath, he hobbles away, his eyes downcast, his shoulders hunched, hugging the side of the alley.

Smog blurs his outline, turning him into a floating wraith. From an unseen balcony above, some unmindful cleaning woman chucks out slop from a bucket, narrowly missing him. He flinches, breathing in deeply, then crosses to the other side of the alley and limps away. On the corner, where Telipara Lane opens out to Shyampukur Street, stands a rusty postbox, drowning in lurid posters for some anti-haemorrhoid cream. The old man shuffles up to it and pulls out a letter from underneath his shawl. He holds it up close to his rheumy, fading eyes. The letter is addressed to the National War Museum in an elegant, cursive handwriting, in a plain unremarkable envelope. He gives it a little shake and then drops it into the box.

On Shyampukur Street, at Dulal da's chayer dokan, the local tea shop tucked away in a garage, cheek by jowl with Pinge's Tuition Hall, the usual suspects have already gathered. In the smoky, dim interior, they sit huddled, smoking their unfiltered cigarettes, reading the day's newspapers — Dulal da, the dyspeptic eponymous proprietor, who once owned a jute mill rendered defunct by one strike too many; Balai da, retired insurance agent with a penchant for Nazrul Geeti; Ganesh babu, ex-Professor and HoD of Chemistry at a small upstate university, unmarried, living with his widowed sister; Bhombol da, a retired sales executive with Bata and now the neighbourhood homeopathic doctor. All of them are greying or balding, past their prime, the promise and expectations of their dreaming years curdled into apathy and pot bellies and the endemic cynicism of Bengalis. They sit in a loose group, sparingly sipping on the small Irani glasses of sweet, muddy tea that Haru, the tea boy, has served them. The thick, oily smell of shingara, those fried dumplings dear to all Bengalis, clings to the still air.

'Arre, no, no, no, what are you saying, Dulal da? The Congress will never come into power in Bengal,' Balai da says with a lugubrious shake of his head.

'Too much water under the Howrah Bridge, heh heh.'

A shape darkens the doorway for a moment. The old man stands there, catching his breath. The huddle of men look up and then, with habitual disregard, carry on talking. He too is a regular of the tea shop but evidently not part of the hallowed circle. The old man coughs, a hard, rasping sound, maybe just a stubborn winter cold, maybe a deeper malaise. Then, slowly, he limps into the shadows and takes up residence at a lonely, corner table. He taps on the cracked Sunmica top with his knuckles…two short, sharp, peremptory knocks. Haru looks up and nods. He pours out a hot, steaming stream of tea from the large blackened kettle on the hob into an Irani glass and picks up a plate of shingara.

Outside, the fog blankets the dilapidated buildings and second-hand bookshops. A sudden gust of cold wind shakes the blue plastic sheeting insulating the windows, making the old man shiver. A young man, light grey intelligent eyes behind horn-rimmed glasses, wearing the uniform jeans and kurta of a Bengali intellectual, steps through the doorway.

Dulal da greets his latest client with obvious fondness. 'Good morning, Sudipto babu, so how are things with our favourite young journalist?'

Sudipto rubs his hands. 'Freezing, Dulal da. Haru, my boy, one cha, nice and hot, chop, chop.' He gestures towards Balai da's opened paper. 'So what's the latest on that chit fund scam?'

Balai da shakes his head in disgust. 'That Madan fellow…caught red handed! Shameful!'

Bhombol da scratches his stubbly grey beard. 'Mark my words, what India needs is a military dictatorship. Like Pakistan. A strong hand at the helm.'

'No, Dada, strong hand-shand won't work any more. What we need is a strong foot — to give one tight big kick up everyone's ass.'

There is muted laughter, a shake of heads, a scratching of bellies around the table. The sound of drumbeats and shouted slogans from the main road breaks the moment of reflection. Ganesh babu looks up with exasperation. 'Now what? Abaar ki?'

Dulal da gets up and pokes his head round the door to look down the street. 'Ah, of course, today is 23rd January — Netaji's birthday.'

Ganesh babu throws his hands up in exasperation. 'O re baba, those bloody clowns will be out on the streets, left right, left right, marching around in those khaki shorts, causing traffic jams.'

The old man slumped in the corner, a shadow shape, slowly stirs.

'Oops, I better hurry up then,' mutters Bhombol da, starting to gather his things. 'I have to go all the way to the Dalhousie area today. The bank is really giving me a royal run around over my pension cheques.'

Sudipto too starts to take out change to pay Haru. 'But Ganesh babu, if Netaji had been there today, this would have been a different country. He had such vision, such plans.'

Ganesh babu looks at him curiously. 'Really? And how would a youngster like you know about Netaji? That's all ancient history.'

'I'm a journo, I make it my business to know. And anyway, he's still relevant today. It's not just me. Every Bengali, every Indian, should know what Netaji could have done.'

Balai da, who has been engrossed in his paper, suddenly slaps one page. 'What a coincidence, here we were just discussing Netaji and see, there, a big article on him. Something about Imphal and... Kohima.'

The old man sits up. The Irani glass rattles against his plate.

Ganesh babu is sceptical. 'Written by some party bigwig's chamcha. The Communist party used to hate him when he was alive. But now they blow conch shells and clean up the crow shit on his statue once a year and make a big hoo-ha.'

Balai da shakes his head. 'No, actually it's written by a Thomas Jones...a Britisher, I think. It's about some battle. Here, you read it.' He hands the paper to Sudipto.

'Ummm...secret files made finally public by Thomas Jones. About a battle between the British and the Japanese and...Azad Hind Fauj, Netaji's army. Happened in 1944. For two weeks, the future of the British Empire hung in the balance. Etc. etc...wow, look at this. Recently, U.K.'s National Army Museum conducted a poll on Britain's greatest battle fought over the last 400 years. Waterloo, Aliwal, D-Day/Normandy, Rorke's Drift and Imphal/Kohima were selected but to everyone's surprise, the twin battles against Japan-Azad Hind Fauj fought in Kohima and Imphal in India were voted the greatest ever.'

Sudipto looks up, his eyes shining. Then he goes back to reading.

'Most Indians are not aware that one of the bloodiest, and most crucial battles of World War II was fought on their soil, which, if Japan had succeeded in winning, would have changed the fate of the Allied Forces and maybe the course of Indian history.'

Ganesh babu is still sceptical. 'Tch tch, just a gimmick to sell newspapers.'

Sudipto is indignant. 'How can you be so offhand about this, Ganesh babu? Look here, it says…' Suddenly, his hand is jolted. The old man, who has crept up silently, snatches the newspaper out of his hands.

'Hey, what the…' But he falls silent.

A demented spark lurks just under the surface of the old man's milky eyes. He clutches the crumpled paper to his chest. His other hand, shaking, palsied, is raised to fend them off… part in imperious command, part in trembling entreaty. Slowly, he backs away, shaking his head, then turns towards the murky light coming in from the street and holds up the paper. He reads silently, his lips moving imperceptibly, whisper of sound and breath. Balai da makes a silent but universally rude gesture, tapping his index finger against his temple; Bonkers, lost his marbles, it says. Haru stifles a giggle. The fog has thickened again and inside the tea shop, there's a hush. Then the old man sighs, looks up. The rheumy eyes peer at them over the thick wire-frame spectacles. A ghost of a smile appears on his seamed face. When he speaks, his voice is hoarse, strained, almost as if he hasn't used it for a really long time.

'Finally...finally.'

He turns to the confounded faces around him. 'It's all true...it happened. The British were going to lose India that day. They won… but there is so much more to the tale.'

Something about his voice, the ring of some conviction draws the others in. Bhombol da turns back from the door, abandoning the joyless prospect of solving his pension problems. The old and the young, unconsciously, all turn to him, like children to a Pied Piper of tales. They can sense that there is some secret, some revelation about to unfold.

The old man whispers, 'What men they were…the men who fought and died on that day. It wasn't British military prowess that defeated them that day but…'

Sudipto, fact-sensitive reporter that he is, interrupts 'That day? History says it was a campaign stretching over months.'

The old man turns sharply and hisses, 'Yes...but it was all lost on just that one fateful morning...lost...'

He suddenly sways; his frail body seems to tremble. Sudipto quickly holds his arm, painfully thin under the shawl, and eases him into a chair. 'Haru, get some water.'

Sudipto pulls up another chair and sits down close. 'How do you know all this, Sir?'

The old man takes a long sip, the water shivering from the trembling of his gnarled fingers. 'Because I was there...I...I stood witness...'

The unasked question hangs in the damp, cold air as they all stare at him. Haru quietly squats on the ground, curling up at the old man's feet. The old man gazes at something far away. His lips move soundlessly. Then, with a curiously dignified gesture, he settles his threadbare hair, his rumpled shawl. He sits up straight in the chair and takes a deep breath.

'To a great betrayal. To treachery most profound. In a place called Kohima.'

Outside, the Netaji Jayanti procession winds its way down Shyampukur Street towards Bidhan Sarani. The shouted slogans, garbled, unintelligible through the cheap PA system, and the singsong rhetoric of 'Zindabad! Zindabad!', slowly fade further and further away. Inside the tea shop, it is quiet except for the occasional rickshaw bell.

'There were two of them...fellow officers in the Azad Hind Fauj, brothers in arms, two men...like chalk and cheese.' The cloudy, rheumy eyes close for a second as he begins.

'Debraj Mookerji. He was the golden boy, scion of zamindars, and heir to a fortune. Cambridge-educated, bileth-pheroth barrister, and a club-trotting playboy. Privileged, spoilt, too good looking for his own good. But everyone loved him, you know...his Ingrej friends, women...women of all persuasion, broke their hearts, he did. They all fell in love with him...even his enemies.'

ACT I

CALCUTTA, 1943

That year, the monsoons arrived early in Calcutta. When the *SS Duchess* docked at Kidderpore that evening in June, the rain made halos of the half-dimmed blackout lights. As the passengers were herded down under protective umbrellas by the ship's staff, Debraj Mookerji — Deb to friends and family — elegantly attired in a bespoke Holland and Sherry suit, fedora at a rakish angle, stepped on to the gangway, pulling on expensive kidskin gloves. Tall, mid-twenties, with a springy shock of dark hair tamed by Brilliantine, a fine-boned face and light, slightly feline, grey gold flecked eyes, he moved with an athlete's, or perhaps a dancer's, lazy, self-assured gait down the gangway. With his colouring, his unconscious air of privilege and entitlement, you could have almost mistaken him for an Englishman.

'Your car, Sir,' the purser fussing around him purred as a gleaming black Rolls Royce Wraith swished up, the rain gliding down its sides in silken rivulets. A liveried driver hurried up with an umbrella and took the set of matched bags from the ship's purser.

'Oh, that's a jolly surprise. The pater's sent his new toy, I see,' drawled Debraj. As he strolled towards the Rolls, the quiet of the night was broken by two cars racing on to the pier amid a cacophony of horns, flashing headlights.

A squeal, a shout, 'Deb! Over here!'

A gaggle of inebriated party goers spilt out — a sturdily built young Englishman, along with a man in British naval uniform, a pale, slender blonde in a clingy, quite flagrantly daring gown and a foppily dressed Indian with two giggling Anglo-Chinese girls, twins in identical red dresses and red high heels, clinging to his arms. They swooped down upon Debraj, dodging the rain, brandishing opened bottles of champagne, laughing, kissing, hugging, and backslapping.

'Andrew! James, my man,' Debraj greeted the two British men with obvious affection. 'Natasha, how absolutely delish. Didn't know you were going to grace the black hole with your lovely presence. I would have returned so much earlier had I known I would be seeing you again here,' he murmured as he kissed the tips of the blonde's outstretched fingers. A feint at the Indian man with a smiling, 'Barooah, my dear fellow, long time.' And finally, a slightly ironic bow to the twins, Li and Lee. They piled into the cars.

Natasha cuddled up to Debraj as he leaned back in the cushioned luxury of the Rolls, the smell of expensive leather mingling with the rummy fragrance of the Cuban he lit up. Lazily, he looked out at the city of his birth and childhood. Like the streets of London, where he had spent the last many years, Calcutta glistened in the rain. Unlike London, though, the air was stifling, almost equatorial.

'God, it's sticky. Forgot how hot it could get!'

'Not glad to be back, darling?' Natasha whispered. 'What on earth made you come here, my sweet? You said you were off to New York after your London gig. I distinctly remember you telling me that. Broke my heart, you did.' She slapped his arm playfully.

'Nonsense. That heart of yours is made of Sheffield steel. Anyway, they said Calcutta is the golden city of Empire and I thought it would be such fun to give you a nice homecoming present.'

She laughed, the throaty growl of a contented cat. He leaned forward and kissed her hungrily.

Past the Raj Bhavan, modelled after Kedleston Hall in Derbyshire, past buildings bearing the mark of over 300 years of British occupation, they crossed the Maidan and the Victoria Memorial, the angel atop the giant marble rotunda, rotating. Outside, on the streets, through the watery glass, Debraj saw his own people. It startled him, the abundance of brown faces, faces so different from Billy and Codgy Cooper and Jameson, his merry band of fellow students and old Albert, the porter at his digs. He would miss the lads now that he was back here. As he would miss the pub crawls and Sunday rugby games and the pretty Army girls always ready for a night of carousing while the air-raid sirens plunged the city into darkness.

The other car drew level. The twins tipsily leaned out of the windows, squealing, the rain on their upturned red painted lips. He smiled but there were blue shadows around his eyes, lines round his mouth — of tiredness, a tad too much good living, and maybe a trace of ennui, of done this, seen that.

And then they were driving through the great iron gates of Mookerji Mansion, the ancestral pile, down a long driveway with ancient trees standing sentinel, up to the sweep of wide marbled steps, the bougainvillea curling up around the East Wing. As he stepped out of the car, the doors of the mansion flew open, spilling warm light on a pretty girl in her teens. She paused in mid flight, then rushed helter-skelter down the steps. An old man in a valet's uniform tried to keep up with her, holding aloft an umbrella to shield her from the drizzle. She ran to Debraj and jumped up into his arms, sending him staggering.

'Dada, oh my dearest, gorgeous brother, you're finally back… I've missed you so, so much!'

'Debi, my god, you've grown heavy. Let me look at you, pumpkin!' Debraj held his sister's face in his hands. Her long hair was swept neatly back, her face had become lean, with their mother's legendary bones already showing through the last traces of puppy fat. She had grown tall, more angular, more contained in these few, short years. The thought that she was no longer a child dawned upon him and he felt a wave of sadness. He had missed her growing-up years, those rites of passage that had mysteriously transformed a tomboy into this child-woman. He had missed so much. He looked past her, towards the open door, hoping. They were not there. He had not really expected either of his parents to grace his return home, of course, but still, he had hoped.

Debi suddenly noticed the other cars driving up, the rest of the company, and clambered down, her face red. As his friends milled around, opening, closing car doors, Debraj turned to them. 'You guys carry on. I think I'll catch up with all of you a little later.'

A groan but then they acquiesced. Andrew smiled at Debi who looked down, not meeting his eyes. Debraj noticed the exchange, puzzled. Debi had known Andrew for years. She had been the pesky appendage to all their afternoon shenanigans in the garden after school.

Andrew would tease her mercilessly but she took it all, proud to be a part of their older boy's world. Maybe she's just feeling shy, maybe this also is part of her growing up, he thought. Andrew and the gang left with a scrunching of gravel and pip-pips of horns. Debraj put his arm around Debi and turned towards the great house.

'Chhoto babu!!' Khogen da, the valet, limped up, his lined old face crinkled into a thousand happy creases, his eyes brimming with unshed tears. 'You are home, Chhoto babu!'

Debraj felt his own eyes start to burn as well. 'Ah, Khogen da, it wasn't all that long, now was it? And look! I've returned as a barrister! We'll do all sorts of good work now, won't we? We'll make this city a better place, you'll see.'

'Hmph, let's make this house a better place first.' Khogen da muttered, with the familiarity of an old family retainer. The liberties that Khogen da took with Debraj were quite unheard of. But it had been Khogen da who had brushed his hair and helped him into a shiny pair of 'naughty boy' shoes for his first day as a full and proper student. And when he had spent that first day as a full and proper student depositing a box of chalk dust on his teacher's head as a prank, it had been Khogen da who had pleaded with the coughing, indignant gentleman not to report Debraj to the headmaster.

They went into the great hall lined with ancestral portraits.

'Your room is made up. I have drawn a bath for you, Chhoto babu.'

'Capital, Khogen da. Feel terribly grubby. A good, hot bath and then I'll be ready to boogie the night away.'

Debi's face fell. 'Dada! Don't you want to spend your first evening back together?'

'We have all the time in the world, pumpkin. I'm feeling stir-crazy. Been cooped up on that ship. Need to stretch my legs, get out a bit. Tomorrow morning, I'll be all yours. How does that sound?'

She nodded, her head down, then ran up the stairs.

Debraj whizzed through the red light at the intersection of Red Road and Outram Road. A dimly lit tramcar trundled past, bells ringing in alarm, almost blindsiding him but he ignored it. In fact, he found it so much easier to ignore all the inconvenient things in his life. The magnificent Rolls he was driving was obviously the apple of his father's eye and the close shave would have got the old man's knickers in a twist. He grinned. What mattered most right now was winning the race. Andrew's Studebaker was not a patch on the Rolls but she was a fast little thing and could top out at 80 miles per hour. In a short race, the Studebaker had the advantage. But what was life without taking chances?

So when Andrew had proposed the race at the poker game at the 300 Club earlier in the night, his bubbly raised mockingly, it had been game on. Debraj had had a winning streak, the jazz band had played his favourites and Natasha had been quite generously welcoming. She had pressed her long, lithe body against his drawing hungry looks from the shadowy men at the long mahogany bar. He had felt…proprietorial. Sometimes, though, he wasn't sure whether this was prompted by real desire or just habit. Natasha had crossed the seas in the middle of a bloody war to be with him. But how did he actually feel about her? Lovely distraction, not a doubt about it. But would it ever go anywhere, given her background? As usual, he had ignored the prickly questions and had pulled her closer. 'Your voice, your body is...' he had murmured in her ear.

'Groovy?' she had murmured back, the American slang sounding exotic in her husky Slavic-accented English.

The race was deemed to have started the moment they left the table. Breathless, they squeezed into the two cars fetched by the valets. Debraj had got off first but Andrew had caught up swiftly, jabbing at Debraj's tail as he wove in and out of the Friday night traffic on Chowringhee. Pedestrians skipped back as the two cars roared past.

Neck and neck, they skidded onto Casuarina Avenue, tyres squealing and smoking in protest. Andrew accelerated in the turn, taking him by surprise, forcing Debraj to fall behind or go into the railing. He grinned, his teeth white in the darkness. Did Andrew not know him at all? He gunned the engine, coaxing every bit of power from the Rolls and used her bulk to force Andrew to give ground. He drew level with Andrew, keeping him pinned to his right, himself inches from the railing. Andrew always claimed that Debraj had the home field advantage on Calcutta roads. True. And he did know that just ahead, where Casurina Avenue turned onto Hospital Road, there used to be a whopping big speed breaker.

This was exactly what Debraj was counting on. He hit the brakes at the precise moment.

Andrew's car, with all its occupants, hit the speed breaker at full speed. It reared up and landed heavily. A carefully manicured hand in lace cuffs shot out and clutched the windowpane in terror. The Studebaker transformed from a racing cheetah to a buffalo wallowing in mud. Debraj coasted past, smiling in the rear-view mirror, and whizzed down Lower Circular Road, whistling 'That Old Black Magic'. The race had worked up his appetite and he headed towards Trincas. He could almost smell the sizzling ham steak that was the chef's particular speciality. A perfumed arm slipped around his neck. She was breathing heavily. 'That was just...'

'Groovy?' he said with a wink.

She laughed shakily and ran her red-tipped finger down his cheek. He couldn't have left Natasha behind now, could he?

The doorman at Trincas beamed as Debraj alighted. 'Welcome back, Sir.' Within minutes, he was ushered to his table right in front of the stage. He rapped the table twice. His favourite whisky arrived, and a flute of champagne for Natasha. He leaned back with a deep sigh. A burst of laughter made him turn.

Andrew and James had just walked up to the bar with some of the Indiamen — men who had come to serve the Crown or seek their fortunes in companies like Burma Shell. Debraj excused himself and strolled over to them.

'Okay, mates, this round's on me. Just won a little wager, haven't we, Andy?'

Andrew punched him, hard enough to make Debraj wince a little.

'Ow, don't be such a sore loser, man.'

'Tricky bugger, aren't you? You knew about that speed trap.'

'A soldier should always know his ground, my friend.'

'Soldier? All that muckin' in the trenches? That's for the likes of you. Me? I'm the sodding master of the universe.' Andrew held up his swizzle stick like a sceptre.

Debraj's eyes danced. 'Oh, I would have thought you like muckin' around, Andy. Being a good old country lad from Shropshire making eyes at the sheep.'

Andrew flushed. 'My folks go back to the Norman invasion, you ignoramus.'

'And mine to Kurukshetra. But that's before your time, isn't it?' Debraj's smile was a little flinty. Really, Andy could be such a tosser sometimes. He turned away. 'What's with Benny?'

Benjamin Railer, a shy, bookish man standing behind Andrew was biting his fingernails convulsively, staring fixedly across the room at a gorgeous red head. Debraj recognised her with a start. Rosamund Bailey, daughter of Sir Edmund Bailey. She had been a skinny, freckled, carrot top in school but had turned into a green-eyed smasher.

Andrew accepted the distraction with a small frown. 'He's besotted. Been dithering about asking Rosamund to dance.'

A wicked spark glinted in Debraj's grey eyes as he scanned the room. He thumped the lovelorn Benjamin on the shoulder. 'Go on then, Benny. Ask her!'

Benjamin was terrified. 'She'll probably slap me.'

Debraj laughed. 'She's far too well bred. At worst, she will politely decline. Are you really going to let the fear of rejection deter you from a taste of heaven?'

Benjamin stared at Debraj, his mouth open. 'My god! You're right!' And he marched off, chest puffed out, to ask the girl of his dreams whether he might have a taste of heaven, please.

Andrew shook his head. 'Always happy to stir the pot, eh?'

Debraj gave an innocent, angelic smile. 'Look at Benny making his lust-fuelled approach now.'

'I think it may be love.'

'Piffle. Benny's just plain randy.' Debraj chuckled. 'Now, watch this... approaching at 8 o' clock... Company man...red faced... bearing down on Benny... Our amorous friend is tapped on the shoulder... Will he challenge him to a duel?'

'Who the hell is that?!'

'Her fiancé, I think!'

'What? You knew she was engaged, you heartless dog!'

Debraj sipped his drink. 'Read about it. I think I may have saved Benny from a dreaded disease...nincompoopitis!'

They all guffawed. As a chastened Benny shuffled up, the boys closed ranks around him, consoling him with a chilled Martini.

When Debraj returned home in the wee hours, the great house was silent. He had a splitting headache. The night had palled after a while. And he felt bone tired after his journey. He went to pull the bell ringer, paused. The main door had been kept slightly ajar. He entered, closed it. Inside, the central chandelier glowed, throwing the rest of the hall into darkness. Midway up the great staircase, a soft rattle at the main door made him pause in the shadow of the landing. He waited for the bell to ring. Was it his father? The rattle again. He hurried down and opened the door. A thin, almost frail figure stood in the opening, blowing a kiss at a car that was reversing and driving away with a crunch of gravel. The diminutive figure stepped into the hall, swaying a bit.

'Ma?'

She stumbled, stopped, limned by the golden light of the chandelier, adjusting her midnight blue tanchoi sari. Heirloom diamonds at her throat and ears glittered coldly. It was Bubbles Mookerji, Lady Mookerji, famed hostess, compulsive gambler, one of the three famed Lahiri sisters, legendary for their beauty.

'Who's that?' she rasped in her brittle smoker's voice, a frisson of alarm making her voice sharp.

Debraj stepped out of the shadow. She blinked, owlish. 'Debu! Of course! You were supposed to land today, weren't you?'

He went to her, his arms held out, ready to be welcomed, hugged, patted, kissed. But she stood, immobile, her face a prison wall, her hands empty, the lips slack, staring at her son, her handsome, tall, so impeccably turned out stranger of a son, and cleared her throat. Debraj's hands dropped, awkward, as if he had committed a social gaffe. 'Well, here I am.'

'Right, of course. Right. I'm such a silly billy. I must have mixed it up. How are you, darling?'

'Fine, Ma. How are you?' The question came out louder than he had intended, echoing around the great hall. The flash of décolletage as she pulled up the sari pallu to cover herself, coupled with the sweet fumes of inebriation that he could smell, now that he was closer to her, affronted him deeply. Whatever, whoever it was that she had dressed up for, wherever she had been, it had been deemed more important than welcoming him home. And that's the way it had always been. Some card party, or charity gala or whatever, something had always been more important, more demanding of her attention than being his mother.

'Fantastic, dear, fantastic. Just had the most wonderful evening at the Surrey's. You know them, don't you? The Su..Shu..Shurreysh...' her tongue thickened, slurred, ran out of steam. She stumbled as she walked past him. 'A tiny little nightcap before I head to bed. I'll see you tomorrow, darling.'

Bubbles Mookerji, famed for her patronage of the arts, her collection of heritage Baluchari saris, and her lavish parties — his mother. Her parties were legendary for their extravagance, requiring the staff to slave for days in preparation. But Khogen da said that she was never happy; she would sweep in and go tsk tsk, the prawn bisque is too sweet, the Martinis too warm and the napkins in the Blue Room aren't the right blue. But Debraj and Debi had adored her as she would sweep down the stairs in her glittering best, always a late entrance, the heads of the guests looking up, like so many flowers turning to the sun, to watch her slow, regal passage down the grand stairs. Hidden in the upstairs landing, their faces pressed between the bannisters, her children would giggle as she flicked her fan open and then, under its cover, gave them her secret conspiratorial smile and crinkled those slanting, brown naughty eyes. They would tuck into the guilty pleasures of the grown up chocolate confections their mother sent up from the dining room as a special treat. The sounds of laughter and music and the subterranean hum of voices would float up to them, their lullaby, as they were tucked into bed by the nursery maid.

He didn't wish her good night, just watched her make her way with the exaggerated casualness of the tipsy. In spite of the late hour, he didn't feel like being alone. Debi's room down the corridor was in darkness. He made his way to the cavernous kitchen quarters. All was silent, the servants long gone to their honest night's comforts. Suddenly, he heard shuffling footsteps. It was Khogen da, still wearing his valet uniform, his sparse hair standing up. He yawned and without a word, put a pan on the stove and poured milk into it. Debraj sat down at the massive marble-topped table, loosened his tie. Khogen da knelt down, grunting a little from the bad knee, and reached to take off Debraj's shoes. Debraj flinched. 'Come on, Khogen da, I'm not a child any more. You don't have to do that.'

'You will always be a child to me, Chhoto babu. Now give over.'

Debraj gently made him sit. Through an open window, a cool, wet breeze came in. It was going to rain again. Debraj opened the kitchen door and sat on the threshold, like he used to as a boy. The fresh air cleared his head. It was his first day back, and so much had happened but he felt flat, empty inside. Khogen da appeared at his elbow with a steaming silver tumbler. 'Here, drink this.'

Debraj cupped its warmth and sipped. 'Mmm, you've put...?'

'Nolen gur. Last year's date molasses. From the Chandernagore estate. I saved up a bit. A spoonful, just the way you used to like it.'

Debraj nodded, remembering all those times, when he was laid up in bed with measles or a childhood fever, how this used to be Khogen da's panacea for all ills. An overflowing spoonful of the thick, golden syrup, smoky, smelling of the dusty winds of winter, mixed in a glass of hot, soothing milk. And only Khogen da knew that hot, liberally buttered toast with sugar sprinkled on top was Debraj's comfort food, faithfully served up whenever the young lad was down in the dumps. And every monsoon...

'Khogen da, we must have khichuri and hot telebhaja, now that it's raining. And that spicy jhaal-muri. And...oh, I've missed all that food!'

'We'll make anything you want. But day after. Tomorrow, we'll all be too busy running around with your welcome party.'

'Welcome party? What party? No one's told me about any party.'

'Oh my, my. They've invited all your family and friends and Madam has asked Altaf Bhai, the new bawarchi, you don't know him, very famous cook, to make barra English dinner.'

'Of course, England-returned son to be feted with a stodgy English dinner. Worst food in the world, Khogen da, boring and bland and...anyway, when do you think they are going to tell me about the impending festivities?'

'I suppose they will tell you at breakfast tomorrow when you meet Boro babu, your father.'

'Yes, my father, who has not bothered to meet the prodigal son.'

'Well, he did ask after you when he came home — must have been 11. He had already dined at the Club and on finding you had left for the evening with the Rolls, news which did not please him much, I can tell you, his face was like thunder, he said he would meet you tomorrow. Now off with you, you must be sleepy.'

Debraj yawned prodigiously.

The cup of tea was cooling on the damask cover of the breakfast table in the morning room as Sir Harindranath Mookerji, Harry to his inner circle, frowned and clicked his tongue over the morning news. It was all uniformly bad. Faizlul Huq, Bengal's chief minister, had warned of an impending famine. And now, the first wave of starving, bag-of-bones villagers had started arriving in Calcutta. Cities were going to come under rationing. A shortage of coal was going to affect electricity supply. Rocketing prices, labour unrest... he flung the paper down and rang the bell.

'Thunder and damnation, how's a man to do business in such a benighted land,' he growled, his multiple jowls quivering. A large, heavy-set man with fleshy lips crowned by a luxuriant salt and pepper moustache, he came from a long, illustrious line of aristocrats and landed gentry. He had inherited a considerable ancestral fortune, studied in England, had been quite a prolific hitter for one of the better known county cricket teams, and was an unabashed Anglophile. He took the good things of life for granted and partook of their pleasures freely.

A manservant hurried in. 'For heaven's sake, what do I need to do to get a decent cup of tea in my own house!' he shouted at the hapless man.

'Maybe start drinking coffee, Baba.'

Sir Harry swung around. Debraj, bathed and fresh but with telltale bags under his eyes from the night's excesses, placed a packet of coffee on the table. 'It's called instant coffee. All the rage. Has a kick like a mule.'

'Ah, it's you. Where were you last night?'

'And a lovely good morning to you, too.'

He bent to touch his father's feet in the traditional gesture of deference. Sir Harry accepted it somewhat reluctantly, and patted his son's head the way you would pet a dog or a horse, with absent-minded affection.

'There, there, that's enough, don't go much for these old-fangled ways, you know. So how are you, boy? How was the ship's passage?'

'Bumpy. Terrible weather round the Cape. And the passage through the Indian Ocean was hairy. Jap and German subs on the prowl. Had to take huge detours and forced to double back once to avoid running into them. They are attacking anything they can find — merchant ships, passenger liners, freight. And then last couple of weeks, we were trying to outrun the monsoons, which were sweeping in early, I believe. But, on board, it was party time, barring the blackouts.'

'Hmm, you seem to be on perpetual party time.'

Debraj stiffened. His rebellious streak, carefully kept under wraps but which had got him into any number of scrapes over the years, made him clench his jaw. But he leaned back even more nonchalantly, lazily picked up the papers and opened them with a precise flick of his wrists. Sir Harry continued, 'I mean, how do you think I feel, coming home to find you have gone traipsing off with my new Rolls to meet your motley crew?'

'I wouldn't know. If I were a father, maybe I would be inclined to be there to greet my son so he wouldn't have to return to an empty house after five years.'

Sir Harry's brow beetled. 'You will show respect, Debraj.'

'When have I ever not?'

There was a strained silence, the clinking of cups. Khogen da walked in with breakfast for Debraj. Sir Harry asked him without raising his head, 'Where's Madam? And Debi?'

'Chhoto didi is not feeling well. And Madam is yet to summon her maid.'

'There you are, our loving family. Incidentally, I think your mother has planned a little get-together for you tonight. Welcome back and all that nonsense. Do call your friends, if you like.' A pause. 'Haven't bumped into her — your mother — yet, have you?'

'Alas, very very briefly, yes. She wasn't inclined towards much conversation. The last I saw her, she was heading for another nightcap.'

Sir Harry stiffened, then his shoulders slumped. 'She's getting worse by the day. Impossible. And running up debts like there's no tomorrow. In fact, Deb, I need to talk business with you. Being a barrister is all very well but the Mookerji finances need some tending and...'

He was interrupted by the entrance of his wife, waving a long ivory cigarette holder, her eyes hidden behind dark glasses, wearing a rich wine Chinese silk robe and, incongruously, rabbit fur slippers on her tiny feet.

'Oh, come on Harry, stop being a plebe. Talking business with the poor boy at his first breakfast home. Let him enjoy himself, poor babe.' She kissed the top of Debraj's head as she passed and clapped her hands, calling out, '*Bawarchi*! Khogen! Munshi ji! In the small parlour, please, chop, chop. We need to plan today's entertainment. You will be coming, darling, won't you?' she asked Debraj as she swept away.

Debraj laughed out loud. This was more like the mother he had been used to all his life. A butterfly, flitting, so fragile, hard as nails and incandescent at the same time when she wanted to be.

That evening, dark, scudding monsoon clouds, swollen with rain, hung low over the city of British Calcutta. The handsome, broad façade of Mookerji Bari, with its Doric columns, glowed in the pale evening light. Strong winds whipped the top of the trees, sending the leaves flying, thrashing the top of the palms lining the long driveway.

Inside, by the light of gleaming, much-polished chandeliers, there was a flurry of activity. An army of servants scurried around, some carrying food in silver tureens, some arranging flowers in outsize Chinese vases, the scent of arum lilies overpowering in the humid staterooms, some rolling out Persian Farsh and Kilim carpets. Preparations were afoot for Debraj's welcome-back party.

In his bedroom, filled with the memorabilia of a privileged boyhood, Debraj was getting ready. His evening attire, a midnight blue Barathea bespoke ensemble hung from a teak valet stand. In a time when England was reeling under wartime shortages, his wardrobe, in spite of the understatement of its lines, announced, rather obtrusively perhaps, his position and wealth. Khogen da was laying out a selection of ties. 'Black, Brown And Beige' by Ellington played softly on a gramophone. Debraj snapped his fingers lazily and half hummed along with it.

A sudden gust of wind rattled one of the French windows, throwing it open, sending the curtains flying. Khogen da rushed to the window to secure it. As he smoothed the curtain down, he paused, looking out at the cloud-filled twilight.

'A storm is coming, Chhoto babu…'

'It will pass, Khogen da. Don't worry.'

'I *am* worried. Remember, Neelu…Neelkantha…my son?'

'Of course, intelligent boy.'

He remembered that long-ago night…he must have been five or six, walking into the kitchen, hungry for a snack, and seeing Khogen da, standing at the door, crying and laughing as he gazed at a letter in his hand. The child he had been then was mystified that this grown man, so dear to him, was shedding tears, yet was full of joy. 'Khogen da, what's happened?' he had asked. 'The most wonderful thing. I have become a father. Ma Durga has blessed me with a son.'

'What's he doing now?' Debraj asked the old man on that June evening. 'He's…he's joined the INA…Azadi korbe…wants to fight for the freedom movement.'

'INA? That's that army thing…'

'Indian National Army. Azad Hind Fauj they call themselves.'

'It's banned, isn't it? Run by that Bose everyone's talking about?'

'You have heard of him?'

'The British press is full of him, how he's a traitor and enemy of Empire. All in a huff, they are.'

'Nobody dare speak of INA…or of Netaji. The police are hunting them down. If they find Neelu… Chhoto babu, please don't tell anyone. If your father got to hear about this, it would…'

The door was flung open. Startled, Khogen da swung round.

'Dada, are you ready?'

It was Debi. She was dressed in a pale pink spangled sari, looking stunning, her hair caught up fashionably in a braided style, her eyes lined with kohl.

'Goodness, where's my pumpkin? What have you done with my

baby sister? Look at you! You were...what...10 when I left? And now...gosh, you are going to break a lot of hearts!'

She smiled but something, a flicker of some unease, a hint of some inner turmoil, haunted her pale face. He noticed the fingers knotting the edge of her sari convulsively.

'What's wrong, little one? From the time I've come, I've been feeling something's wrong. Is it Ma? Is it her drinking? It's getting worse, isn't it?'

She shook her head at each question.

'Is it Baba? Are you ill? Khogen da said...'

'No, no, it's...I'll talk to you...after the party. See, what I got you.'

She held out a box, embossed, leather. Inside, nestled a pair of gold cuff links, emerald studded, in the shape of horseshoes.

'For luck.'

'Thank you, bless you, pumpkin, they're very handsome.'

She glowed.

'But now, tell me what's bothering you.'

She shook her head mutely. Debraj gestured imperceptibly to Khogen da, who left the room.

'Come on, out with it Debi.'

'No Dada, let's enjoy your homecoming... I don't want to spoil the party for you...for Ma and Baba.'

'Fat lot they care.They won't even notice if I arrived at the party in a...in a grass skirt with a policeman's helmet.'

She giggled at the vision, then sobered up again.

'Haven't seen either of them since the morning,' he muttered, struggling with the knot of his tie. She came to him, pushed his hands away, fixed the knot neatly.

'I think Ma has some gala opening of that new painter of hers.'

'And Baba? Obsessed with making money, being more British than the British...'

'Don't be so bitter.'

'No? They were never there for us. Always, something else that was a bit more pressing. When I broke my leg, they were at the races and sent me with Munshi ji to get it plastered. Your birthday, your sixth, she forgot to come back because she had a winning streak. All we had was an endless succession of nannies and tutors and finishing schools and being dumped at the Club to keep us amused. They must have heaved a sigh of relief when they shunted me off to Cambridge. Baba doesn't give a rat's arse about...'

Debi covered his mouth with her hand.

'Hush...he's with Goopta babu in the library.'

Debraj shook his head impatiently.

'That snake...never liked him. Why Baba has to be so hugger-mugger with a low life like him, I don't know. He's just a damn butcher prettied up in a suit.'

The man earning such censure was at that moment ensconced in the dimly lit, wood-panelled library with Sir Harry. Shri Gangadhar Goopta was known in the city for having risen stratospherically in life. Born in the slums of Taltola, close to S.N. Banerji Road, he had started earning his keep by the age of 13, expertly slicing cuts of meat in a butcher shop outside Sir Stuart Hogg Market. Inside the market, he had encountered members of society who had always been out of reach for those of his station — wealthy, perfumed ladies who sometimes braved the milling crowds, holding lace-trimmed handkerchiefs delicately to their pinched nostrils, to procure items unavailable anywhere else; genuine oolong tea and Italian porcelain, paints and powders smuggled in from France in defiance of the strict British shipping laws and sold inside the high-ceilinged, red-bricked building. The young boy had made himself useful to them, getting them their gewgaws and bibs and bobs, gaining their confidence through small acts of confidentiality. They learned to trust him. He was quiet, discreet and cultivated an appearance of tragic, genteel poverty. He gradually moved on to larger things to procure, went further and further afield. As he grew into manhood, he mysteriously acquired a string of riverside godowns where shrouded boats would land in the darkness before dawn. The word spread. He was your get-it guy when it came to forbidden pleasures, for which the privileged were willing to dig deep into their silk-lined pockets. G.G., they called him, his initials scrawled in their leather-bound little notebooks.

In time, he found himself invited to their smoking rooms and libraries. But never as an equal, never to the top end of the table. The rest of his story was blurred, and the topic of some cynical speculation amongst the bridge players at Calcutta Club and elicited hushed whispers and titters in the Fort William Ladies Association, that met at Flury's on Saturdays for scones with clotted cream. Somehow, along the next ten years, he amassed some serious wealth and under the social patronage of men like Sir Harry, got a foothold in the world of commerce and industry.

Sir Harry dabbled in a diverse number of businesses, most of which were not terribly profit inducing. Mr. Goopta, on the other hand, though of much humbler parentage, was particularly talented at spotting the main chance. A small, rotund, oily man, with a shiny billiard-ball pate, a man of very few scruples and overweening ambition, he fancied expensive but ill-fitting suits which couldn't hide his less-than-illustrious origins. Mr. Goopta sat before Sir Harry that June evening, his head bent, gently servile, his disproportionately large hands with many astrologers' rings on the podgy fingers clasped together like a choirboy's. Sir Harry splashed some Scotch into a tumbler.

'Fancy a Scotch? Remarkably smooth and smoky. Debu brought it.'

'No, Boro laath, I don't partake of such matter, my Lord.'

'Of course, you don't, men like you…you wouldn't know the difference between Malta and a malt, would you?'

'As you say, Sir.'

'You really must polish up those social skills, G.G. So, how's the timber-contracting business coming along? Raking in the old dinero?'

'Very well, Boro laath.'

'Well, that's what I wanted to talk to you about, G.G. I find myself in need of another rather substantial loan! Without that, I'm afraid the estate will go under.'

'Oh, Sir, we can't have that, Sir. What about that contract for…'

'Uh huh. Made a bad call.'

'The banks surely…?'

'The banks seem to think my British affiliations won't be a guarantee for much longer. It's this bloody poppycock about Swaraj and self-rule catching on amongst the plebs. All these Gandhis and Boses trumpeting on about a free India…damn it to hell! It's bad for business.'

'Well, we have to go with the flow, Sir… Make hay where the…'

'Nonsense, the future of this country lies with the British. Now tell me, how much can you cough up?'

'I already hold a great many promissory notes from you, Sir…a great many.'

'I know, I know. If there's anything I can do for you, my good man?'

'You have done so much for me, Sir… I'll be eternally grateful. Were it not for your patronage, I would not be sitting here.'

'Now, G.G., that is not entirely true…'

'Please, Boro laath, it is no secret that I am the first of my family to have made a fortune. Butcher I was, and butcher I would have remained, if you hadn't taken me under your wing. The money is yours to do what you want with it. We have a lot invested in the estate.'

'Well, that's mighty white of you, G.G.'

'Of course, there's the matter of my only daughter…she has grown up, without a mother. I've done the best I could. I have such high hopes for her…her future…an alliance that would serve both our enterprises…'

'Ambitious little rat, aren't you G.G.? We'll see, we'll see…'

A servant came in: 'The guests are arriving, Hujoor.'

Sir Harry growled, 'Hujoor, Hujoor…how many times do I have to tell you not to call me that! It's so…provincial. A simple "Sir" will do. Got it?'

'Yes, Hujoor.'

Downstairs, in the formal drawing room, about a hundred of Calcutta's well-heeled were gathered. Looking at them, no one would think that there was a great war being waged in most other parts of the world, that thousands were dying in concentration camps, that men and women were giving their lives to wrest freedom for their country, that famine in Bengal was killing millions mere miles away. Champagne flowed. Artfully decorated canapés and hors d'oeuvres were passed around by silent, brown, invisible men. Chatter, laughter, whispered nuggets of gossip swirled around Debraj as he mingled with the guests. He spied Debi in a corner by herself, looking out of a window, clearly tense. He excused himself and walked up behind her.

'Boo!'

She jumped like she had been shot.

'No point fretting, pumpkin. She'll make an entrance when she wants to.'

'Who…?'

'Ma. Isn't that who…'

'Yes...no…I…' Suddenly, tears welled up in her eyes.

Debraj took a step towards her, his heart jumping at the thought of some unknown hurt, beyond mending. 'Debi, what is it?'

Then a murmur went though the room, a ripple.

Bubbles Mookerji, decked in diamonds and emeralds, topped by a regally swept-up hairdo, made her signature late entrance through the door, fanning herself languidly with a black lace Spanish fan. Her eyes were feverishly bright, her colour a little high, the dark line of her lipstick a tiny bit smudged. She drawled in her raspy, smoker's voice, 'Hello, darling ones. Sorry, I'm late. Debu, sweet boy. Come and give your mother a kiss.'

Debraj walked up to her and pecked her rouged cheeks.

'Mother.'

'Get me a drink, darling. I'm parched.'

'Are you sure, Ma?' Debraj hissed under his breath as he pecked the other cheek offered to him.

'Don't be impertinent, child.' She floated away, snapping her finger at a passing bearer. Debraj stood alone in the middle of the room, marooned. He looked around…at people he barely knew who smiled at him, at his father deep in conversation with Goopta at the other side of the room, at the overdressed young woman beside them simpering at him. He looked around for Debi, for the comfort of some mooring, a safe shore.

Then they were there, his trio of British mates — Andrew, James and William. Somewhat flushed with drink, laughing a little too loudly, they arrived, his friends, to lessen the tedium of this insufferable evening. He had known them from childhood, especially Andy. The two of them had studied in the same prep school, scraped their knees playing football against the Armenian boys, got caned for insubordination together. They had shared their first hunt in the Sunderbans, and lost their virginity one summer night up in Darjeeling with the Gudrung sisters. They now sauntered towards

Debraj, a sense of familiarity and ownership in their body language, calling out to known faces in the crowd.

'Good evening, Ma'am.' Andrew bowed to Bubbles and kissed her hand. She nodded her head at him regally, tapped his shoulder with her fan. Over her shoulder, Andrew spotted Debi, standing to one side, a tentative, uncertain smile on her face, her hand half raised in greeting. He gave her an imperceptible nod and a lazy smile. The three reached Debraj, clapped his shoulder. Andrew spoke under his breath.

'Gawd, Dave, this is a bloody wake.'

'Hey, go easy on them, chaps,' Debraj muttered back, 'After all, it's the prodigal son returning to the bosom of the Mookerji clan etc. etc...'

'Yes, Mook but tonight you belong to us, hear me? You're one of us, and no one can say different,' slurred James, a little belligerently.

'Shut up, James. So when can we scarper?' Andrew said as he swirled the ice cubes in his glass.

'I don't know when I'll be able to get away. Family stuff, Andy.'

'Ah, family...country...it can all wait. Tonight is your night. The Pimms are waiting, the Rolls needs a spin and the ravishing Natasha awaits your pleasure.'

'Your pleasuring...nyuk...nyuk and there's that Armenian bombshell...' James giggled, made a little obscene gesture with his finger. Debraj frowned at him.

'Shut your gob, James. When are you going to grow up?'

'Ah, too big for the likes of us, are yer?'

A peremptory 'Debu' came from across the room. Sir Harry was calling. His father took his arm in a proprietorial manner. 'Circulate, son. I know you would rather spend the evening with your chums but there are other important people in this room. People waiting to meet you.'

'Yes, Sir.'

'Remember Goopta? We've been doing a bit of...you know... together. You should get to know each other better. And this is his daughter. Sorry, what is your name, dear?'

The overdressed girl beside Goopta curtseyed and said in a high, voice, 'Kumudini, Hujoor.'

Sir Harry grimaced. Debraj remained impassive. Goopta turned eagerly to Debraj.

'B.A. Honours, Chhoto laath, she also sings and plays piano, young master.'

Debraj turned away impatiently, 'I wish you wouldn't call me that. Now, if you'll excuse me, I have...'

Sir Harry interrupted him imperiously, 'Debu, I needed to discuss a matter of some importance...'

Debraj gently removed his father's hand from his arm. 'Tomorrow, Baba? We do have all the time in the world.'

He looked around for his friends. James and William were at the other end but there was no sign of Andrew. He suddenly felt claustrophobic. The stifling smell of the hot house flowers, the cloying perfumes — he turned abruptly and stepped out through the nearest French window. Outside, the air was clean, washed by the rain, the scent of wet earth and grass, and broken leaves. A fitful moon flickering behind gusting clouds sent shadows and silver light racing across the lawn. Debraj took a deep breath. 'What are you doing here, Deb?' he muttered to himself. He rubbed his eyes. Then squaring up his shoulders, he lit up a cigar. He pulled in the smoke gratefully, looking around the dark garden, the lily pond in which he and Debi had grown koi fish as children, the old sycamore tree where Khogen da had built him a tree house. It had stood at the far end where the gazebo used to be. Was it still there? He stepped onto the wet gravel to find out. Sure enough, there it was. And underneath it, the white, ivy-covered, glass-walled gazebo. Strange, there was a light on inside, and shadowy figures. He hesitated, not wanting to break into someone's secret assignation but a strangled shout made him pause.

Inside the gazebo, Debi stood crying, pleading with Andrew who was pacing up and down angrily.

'Andrew, please, you can't do that... I won't...'

'How can you be so stupid!! You...you...'

A sudden clear patch of moonlight revealed Debraj as he stepped hesitantly through the gazebo entrance. Andrew stopped in his tracks. Debraj paused in puzzlement.

'Oh, it's you two. What's wrong?'

Debi, her face buried in her hands, swung around at the sound of his voice. Her mouth flew open. She rushed to him.

'Dada, oh thank god, I'm… I'm…'

Andrew turned on her furiously. 'Shut your gob, Debi!'

Debraj recoiled at the venom in his friend's voice. 'Hey Andy… don't talk to her like that. What on earth's wrong with you!'

Debi blurted out, 'Dada, I'm going to have a baby.'

Debraj staggered back. 'WHAT?! Debi, you're just 15.'

Debi wailed, a child's cry of helplessness and incomprehension. Debraj shook her by the shoulders, none too gently. 'Who's the bloody bounder, tell me.'

'I love him, I love him… Andrew…' she pointed to him.

'Andy, you know who it is? Tell me, man, who's this guy?'

'Tell him, Andrew, tell him, I dare you,' she gulped, wiping the snot from her nose with the back of her hand, defiant now.

'What's she talking about?'

Andrew put his hands up, placating. 'Dave, calm down…we didn't mean to…it was an accident…after the Tolly Ball…'

'You? You…did Debi!'

Debraj felt like throwing up. He desperately tried to regain control. 'I… I'll kill you… She's a…my baby sister, for heaven's sake… It'll kill my father…'

'They don't have to know, you know,' Andrew said in a low voice. Debraj didn't pay any attention. He stared at Debi's swollen eyes, her tear-blotched face. He squared his shoulders, took a deep breath.

'Andy, you have to do the gentleman's thing here, you know. My family's pretty liberal, I can convince them…'

Andrew smiled in relief. 'Thanks Dave, I'll organise everything… I know a good reliable doctor who can…'

'Doctor?! What the…what are you…saying?' Debraj's face twisted in incomprehension.

Debi, her face suddenly hard, stepped forward. 'He wants me to get rid of it.'

Andrew was furious again 'Obviously. What else can we do, you stupid cow?'

'Well, you could marry me.'

Andrew gave a short bark of a laugh, turned away. Debraj stepped up, calm now.

'She's right. Of course you're going to marry her, man. That's the honourable thing to do. Don't worry, we'll cook up some nonsense to explain why everything needs to be so rushed. You two could pretend to be so madly in love that you can't bear to wait. Maybe you'll just elope. Or you could say you have to go back to London, family and all that so you want to tie the knot.' Debraj laughed out loud. 'We'll think of something together, like we always have, eh?'

'I cannot marry Debi.'

'But, Andy, I don't understand. Why not? Surely you can see it's the only way.'

'Dave, you can't be serious...don't put me in this position.'

'Don't put you? Andy, you're my friend...you're my best friend... Of course you're going to make this right.'

'No, Dave, damn you, I'm not doing it!' Andrew shouted, his voice shaking. And, out of nowhere, a terrible rage filled Debraj's heart. This was not the hot anger towards an unfair foul on the polo field, nor the quick flare of temper when he saw toadying and ass licking. No, this was a visceral anger, an ice-cold rage that snaked up from the pit of his stomach, a spreading darkness, clawing at his innards. His voice was very quiet, very silken, when he finally spoke again. 'Tell me, Andy, the real reason you won't marry my sister.'

Andrew hunched his shoulder and turned away. 'You're off your rocker.'

'SAY IT,' Debraj roared. Debi's hands started to shake.

Andrew swung around, his fists balled. 'Eh, don't you dare take that tone with me!'

'I'll take whatever tone I want with you. Why won't you marry my sister? The truth, Andy.'

'She's...we're...you're from a different background, old boy.'

'Are we, then?'

'Well yes, she...she's a darkie.'

Debi gasped. Hot angry tears welled up. Andrew turned away.

'My old man would disinherit me. I could never go back to England, Dave.'

'England!!?? To your piddling little farm? You're just a sodding farmer, Andy. She's worth ten of you! We come from a long line of aristocrats…'

Andrew spat on the floor. 'Screw you, and your aristocracy, Mook. You're brown, I'm white, you're native, I'm British — and I fockin' rule you!'

Debraj snapped. He lunged at Andrew, and with the full force of his pent-up rage, slammed into him, beat him to the ground. Debi screamed. Andrew, always a dirty fighter, rammed his knee into Debraj's groin, gouged, bit. As they grappled, blindly hitting each other, Sir Harry and Goopta charged into the gazebo.

The guests milling in the drawing room heard the shouts. They crowded the French windows, murmuring, 'What on earth, isn't that…' In the distance, lit up in the tiny stage of the gazebo, they could see the two men pulling Debraj back. They saw Sir Harry say something to Debi, who ran out of the gazebo and disappeared towards the house, sobbing. They witnessed Andrew lunging at Debraj but being restrained by Goopta. James and William ran out to the gazebo. Andrew shrugged off Goopta's hands and stormed off, followed by his friends. And finally, they saw — 'with my own eyes, dear' as Mrs. McCauley would tell the Bridge Club the next day — they saw Debraj arguing with his father and being slapped hard by him. Tongues would wag. Rumours would fly.

Bubbles took a long sip of her drink, then clapped her dainty hands together. 'Okay darlings, show's over. Just young people letting off steam. Shall we proceed for dinner?'

Debraj scooped up some ice cubes to put on his already swelling eye. A small but deep cut on his forehead had streaked his shirtfront with blood. A stone-faced Khogen da stood by with wet napkins. They were in the library. Sir Harry sat glowering in his wing chair, nursing a large whisky. Goopta stood in the shadows.

'I'm going to thrash Andrew and you won't be able to stop me next time, Baba.'

'And all you will achieve is to find yourself behind bars.'

'Who's in the wrong here, Baba?'

'Doesn't matter. You can't go around assaulting high-born Englishmen.'

'High born? He's just a jumped-up squire's scn. And what of Debi? What of the life of a child that this high-born Englishman of yours has ruined?'

Goopta spoke softly from the shadows, only his clasped hands in the light. 'We will handle it, Chhoto laath. It is not for you to worry about anymore.'

Debraj turned on him with a snarl. 'Shut up, Goopta, this is none of your business. What the hell is he doing here, anyway?

Sir Harry took a meditative sip. 'This and that. We have much to be grateful for...to G.G. here,' he murmured.

Debraj prowled, short restless moves, like something caged. 'You know the Police Commissioner. Tell him Andrew took advantage of a child. Put him behind bars.'

Sir Harry squirmed in his cavernous chair. 'It's not so easy.'

Debraj suddenly stopped as the awful realisation hit him. 'You're actually going to just bury this thing, aren't you?'

'I have to. We are not in a position to handle a scandal right now.'

'Scandal?! The whole town will know about this evening's fracas by tomorrow morning. How does it matter? What's important is Debi.'

'No, what's important is our family name, our honour.'

Debraj smashed his hand down on the table, making the ice bucket and the glasses jump and rattle. 'Screw your honour. She's your own flesh and blood. Take a stand for once, Baba.'

His father looked at him with an expression that almost resembled pity. 'Such foolishness, Goopta. What are we to do with this boy?'

Goopta stepped into the light, and with some familiarity, sat down in a chair opposite Sir Harry. 'Your father is right, Chhoto laath. Confronting the enemy head on is not always wise. There are other ways to take care of the young man.'

'Shut up, Goopta, no one asked your opinion.'

Goopta spread his hands. 'I am only saying, to actively harm one of the sahib folk is not very prudent. These are treacherous times. You will be branded as a traitor.'

'But we are the Chandernagore Mookerjis.' Debraj was almost pleading with the two older men, trying to batter down the wall of their cynicism, of expediency. Surely provenance would mean something to them.

Goopta was implacable. 'What you think you can do, eh? It will be her word against his. *Your* word against his. He will say she lured him, tricked him…'

'How dare you!'

'Shut up and listen to him, Debu.'

Goopta carried on as if the interruption had never happened. 'He will say you offered her to him. He will drag in your mother, her not very secret assignations…'

Sir Harry stood up with a jerk. 'Enough, Goopta. It will be us against Empire, Debu. The Brits would never support us over their own kind. That would be the end of us…all the privileges, the patronage, the flow of advantage — gone.'

Debraj stared at his father, his voice very close to breaking. 'She is a child.'

'Don't give me that poppycock, I'm not losing everything because she couldn't keep her legs together. G.G. will take care of it.'

Debraj stared at his father. He saw the impeccably cut suit, the pomaded hair, the pink, carefully manicured nails, the polished black shoes and the haughty expression of a man born to rule. He looked every inch an Englishmen — except for his heart. Inside, he was just a servant, a stooge, a prisoner of his own fears who glorified his servitude and called it honour.

The tyres spun, throwing up gravel in the driveway. A muted roar and the gleaming Rolls hurtled out through the tall iron gates of Mookerji Mansion, skidded on the turn, and shot off towards the Maidan. Debraj at the wheel, the incipient black eye and the cut above the eyebrow giving him a rather sinister air, bombed the big car down the straight stretch of Red Road, shouting out in frustration, slamming the wheel with his fist. Damn, damn, damn them all to hell. The bitterness of his thoughts made him almost miss the roadblock. It loomed out of the darkness, wooden barricades, sand bags, a police checkpost. He slammed on the brakes, going into a skid on the rain-slick road. A quick bit of footwork and he brought her to a squealing stop, her headlight just kissing the barrier. The police, alarmed, had scampered out of the way but now converged on him, guns drawn.

'Out of the car, now!'

He was shoved unceremoniously against the side of the car, roughly frisked. 'Sala, daru piya. This bastard's drunk.'

'Eh, where you coming from?'

'From Mookerji Baadi, residence of the most esteemed Sir Harry Mookerji, most loyal servant of the King Emperor.'

Suddenly, they let go and snapped to attention. A convoy of unmarked jeeps was approaching the police checkpost. As it squeezed through the narrow gap of the barricades, Debraj saw shadowy figures inside, hard-looking men with guns. The centre jeep slowed down, almost stopping as it passed Debraj. A man in plain clothes, an Anglo, sat in the passenger seat, smoking. A scar running diagonally across his face, across his lips, gave him a lopsided, almost clown-like grin. The man turned slowly to look at Debraj. They locked eyes for the briefest of moments. The man took a long slow drag of his cigarette, spat out a stray fleck of tobacco, then turned away, losing interest. The jeep swung through the checkpost and they were gone.

The policemen turned their attention back to the young man with the fancy clothes and fancy car, and the black eye. One policeman muttered something to the other. The first cop gave Debraj a measuring look. 'You are Sir Harindranath's relation?'

Debraj's face twisted into an ironic smile. 'Of sorts.'

'Your good name?'

'Oh, I don't have much of a good name, gentlemen. And there's absolutely no reason why you shouldn't arrest me. No one gives a pig's **** who I am.'

'Enough. No more of this speeding-sheeding. You rich boys think you can get away with murder.'

The golden city of the British Raj was well into its weekend revelry as Debraj drove up. The nightclubs on Park Street overflowed with the men who ruled the Empire's jewel in the crown — bureaucrats, army officers, political mandarins, loyal servants of the Crown and King. On their arms, were the women — with copper waves and blonde curls and jewelled snoods and bright lipstick and shimmering Vera Maxwell evening dresses — bright splashes of colour in a sea of drab khaki. On this street, the war itself seemed a million miles away.

The brown faces were few and far between, usually trapped in the kitchens or serving the patrons or parking their fancy cars. Debraj, in his Montague Burton's and his glossy bespoke shoes, however, almost blended in as he tossed his keys to a valet for parking.

He strode into The Blue Fox and upto the bar. The bartender, with a sideways look at his eye, his bruises, inclined his head politely. Debraj rapped the counter twice…two short taps. The bartender suddenly broke out in a smile. 'Mr. Mookerji, welcome back, Sir, didn't recognise you for a moment there.' A whisky glass was slid towards him. He took a deep breath and swigged it back. He tapped the bar twice again, lit up a cigar.

On the stage, Natasha was well into her act. 'I've Got You Under My Skin', she crooned in a throaty, intriguingly accented voice. She spotted Debraj, blew him a kiss, swaying sinuously. Debraj leaned back against the bar, took a deep breath. No sign of Andrew, James or William. He was disappointed but also somewhat relieved. In his headlong rush to get here, he had not thought through what he would do when he caught up with them. Wouldn't do to create a scene. The rumour mills were sure to be working overtime tonight over the evening's brouhaha. He'd threatened his father that he would pulverise Andrew and in his rage, he'd meant it too. But after the somewhat sobering encounter with the police, he realised he actually was quite, quite powerless. The frustration left him exhausted, sick to the stomach. He rapped the bar again.

A bunch of British servicemen jostled up to the bar. They were guffawing, red faced, sweating in the tropical heat. A burly Sergeant caught sight of Natasha.

'Oh, mother of god, look at that honey bun…'

'Hey, Sarge, thought you had a thing for brown ass. That darkie you did last night…'

'Burnt meat, fellas. Your dick would shrivel up, it's so black inside.'

There was a cackle of mirth. Debraj swore, swung around at the guy. But a strong arm pulled him back. It was Navin Barooah, with the twin sisters today dressed in identical blue, twittering behind him.

'Uh huh, Deb. You don't want to tangle with this lot.'

Debraj shook off the restraining hand, and smoothed his jacket. Navin shepherded him to a corner table, clicked his fingers at a passing waiter.

'Heard about your little dust-up with your mate Andrew. What actually happened?'

'News travels fast. And he's not my mate.'

He took a deep slug from his drink but nothing could dull the acid of anger he felt. Restless, he got up to leave.

'You need a new high, my pet,' one of the twins purred. 'Come with us.'

Outside, it had started to rain again. They all piled into the Rolls, everyone a little unsteady on their feet, the twins giggling. They drove east, leaving behind the lights of Park Street, through narrow bylanes, across the railway line, into a strange netherland on the outskirts of the city.

Debraj gunned the big car over the cobbled uneven roads, drumming the wheel with his hands, trying to work off his anger. He tried to shake off his dark thoughts, wanting to be able to drown himself in the evening's promised pleasures but they kept swirling back, clinging to his mind like the leeches which frequented these areas.They were in the middle of the wetlands, the flat, dark marshes going on for miles, which were home to local Bheel fishermen and thousands of Hakka Chinese immigrants. One of the twins tapped his arm. Debraj swung off the main road to enter Tangra, Calcutta's Chinatown, a walled enclave full of bustle, and shops selling silk and leather and exotic Chinese dishes and medicinal herbs to cure one of all manner of malaise. They parked in a narrow lane.

Debraj slipped some coin to a Chinese boy leaning against a handcart, and told him to look after the Rolls. It stood out, like some alien spacecraft in those seedy surroundings and he didn't want it stripped by the time he came back. Led by Li — or was it Lee — they stepped out into the strange, fantastical world of Tangra. Wattle and daub shanties stretched in all directions along higgledy-piggledy, muddy lanes. Chinese signs glowed redly in the smoky, greasy air. The stench hit him. Tanneries lined the wetlands, and the effluence of sulfur fumes and caustic lye was overwhelming. The twin pulled him by the hand and led him towards a traditional Chinese dentist's shop. A sliver of light escaped from the dusty, crudely curtained window. Lee — or was it Li — knocked on the door gently. A stooping old Chinese man opened the door a crack, waved his hand at them.

'Dentist doctor closed.'

'Uncle, wait, we are Dao.'

The Chinese man took in their expensive clothes. He bowed low.

'Come, sheng waiting for you. House always wait for Dao.'

They stepped in. It was dark inside but Debraj could make out pictures, hand-drawn pink gums, dragon calendars and an ancient dentist's chair looming in one corner. 'What's this place? What's Dao?'

The Chinese man smiled. 'It mean seeker...seeker of truth.'

Li/Lee explained. 'Most afeem addas double up as a respectable business during the day. Mr. Lung's son is a dentist.'

'Afeem? You mean this is an opium den?'

Li/Lee giggled. 'Why do you think we are here?'

Inside, up some rickety stairs, down a dimly lit corridor, they came to a blue door. A rich, sweet aroma, ripe and dark enveloped them as they stepped in. In the semi-darkness, they saw figures — men, women, some curled up in foetal positions on narrow bunks, some sprawled on divans, drawing on pipes, the air thick with smoke. Debraj coughed, breathed in the pungent air. Mr. Lung ceremoniously handed Li/Lee a brass bowl. Inside, nestled small soft black pellets, perfect little globules of oblivion, to pull a man into blessed forgetfulness, into a few hours of sweet mindlessness.

They lit up. Naveen offered Debraj the thick bamboo stemmed pipe. He pulled on it greedily and waited for the promised euphoria to descend. Naveen and the twins each drew on the pipe and then curled into each other's bodies, seeking corners and warm niches to wrap themselves in, a symbiotic entity with three lips and six arms, breaths intermingled. He wanted to be part of their magic circle and yet, the thought of drowning himself in that shared, humid flesh filled him with sudden loathing. He wanted something clean, unequivocal, something with some compass to anchor his whirling, vertiginous thoughts, his feelings of betrayal and impotency.

He stood up, almost fell. An immense weariness, a fathomless lassitude filled his bones. As he picked his way with exaggerated care through the sprawled, inert bodies, he thought, we all are seekers of the truth. He felt an odd kinship with them — these dreaming slaves, in thrall to something or the other — drugs, money, power, sex and ultimately, the white men who ruled them all.

Downstairs, the old man sat hunched near a lamp, reading from a Chinese newspaper. He looked up briefly, at the young dishevelled man, weaving gently, his hands held out protectively, as if he were blind and wanted to ward off some danger. He shook his grey head and softly said, 'You should sleep.'

'I am not in the least bit sleepy.'

'The afeem has taken you in its arms. Give yourself to it.'

'I'm fine. Just…' Debraj tailed off, his mind suddenly white.

The old man got up, politely opened the door and bowed as Debraj stumbled out.

Coming out into the steaming heat of the sulphurous night, he was disorientated. The ramshackle lanes zigzagged out, all looking the same in the dim lamplight. The car…where had he parked his car? One sign, a chrysanthemum on a white ground, looked familiar but then again, he wasn't sure. He swayed towards it but there was no car in sight down the lane. His knees buckled. He slid down to the ground, came to rest on a stone doorstep. He laid his head on the cool, rain wet slab, smelling of earth and salt water, and, inexplicably, started crying, his tears mingling with the rain.

When he came to, what time was it, where was he, he wondered, tottering to his feet. It was still night, dark. The lane was deserted, quiet. He looked down at himself. Mud caked his fine clothes. The black eye from the evening's fracas felt pulpy, tender, half shut. The cut above his eyebrow had started to bleed again. He picked himself out of the gutter, muttering to himself. As he lurched towards the end of the lane, he heard footsteps, staccato, echoing. He swung around, almost losing his balance. A couple of men, wrapped in shawls, brushed past him. Debraj called out after them, 'Hey, one moment.' They ignored him, long strides, men in a hurry. He shouted after them, his voice hoarse from the opium, 'Bastards…'

They stopped, their faces shadowed, the light behind them and turned slowly — big men, something menacing in their studied, deliberate stance. They took in the sight of Debraj, his expensive, ruined clothes, his addled state. One put a restraining hand on the other's arm.

'Chhor de, chutiya angrez ka gand chatnewala laath saab hai... let him go, just some bastard British-ass-licking good-for-nothing. Don't waste time... Nishonko will be waiting.'

They strode away, turning into an ill-lit alley ahead. Debraj shouted, after them, 'I'm not a laath saab, you, come back here...' He followed them into the alley, then stumbled to a stop. Illuminated by the soft red glow of a sign saying Shandong Silk Works, stood a small knot of men. They fell silent as the two men walked up and knocked on the heavy red painted door of the silk works...three sharp raps followed by two slower ones. The door creaked open; a large Pathan — what was a Pathan doing in Chinatown — poked his head out. He looked down the lane. Debraj pressed himself back into the meagre cover of a doorway. The Pathan let the men in, then shut the door. A Chinese rickshaw puller, curled up on the seat of a lone rickshaw parked further down the alley, stirred, went back to sleep.

'Something afoot, old boy,' Debraj muttered to himself. And then that devil-may-care grin, the grin which had always got him into trouble, lit up his face. His head felt a little clearer. He brushed himself off, as best as he could, tried to slick back his hair, then strolled up to the door. He knocked, three short, two long, stood back. The door opened a crack, and he was pulled in.

The Pathan patted him down roughly, gave his clothes a quizzical look, then pointed him down a long corridor, lit by an overhead line of feeble, bare bulbs. At the end, a steep set of wooden stairs led into a surprisingly large warehouse. Silks, rich maroons, purples and midnight blues were stacked in shelves running along the sides, their luminous colours lit by the low, dusty light.

The place was teeming with some fifty odd people, a motley band of Bengalis, Sikhs, Biharis, roughly dressed, some in tattered remnants of British uniforms. They stood, or sat on packing cases littering the floor, conversing in low, urgent tones. The air hummed with an intense, electric urgency and Debraj felt a flush of excitement raise the hair on the nape of his neck.

No one paid him much attention as he edged towards the back of the room. In his expensive suit and bespoke shoes, he should have stuck out like a sore thumb but the mud camouflaged him somewhat. The only other people in western clothes were two middle-aged men, pot bellied, oily hair neatly combed. What was it about them that bothered Debraj? The fact that they weren't looking at anybody? That they were scribbling into a notebook? Or that they wore identical black shoes? Very few Indians wore covered footwear; heat, humidity, and unavailability made sandals the norm. And identical?

A voice, raised, distracted him. 'He's here.' It was one of the two men he had encountered in the street. A ripple went through the room. And then a tall, sunburnt, lanky young man, probably his age, walked in, accompanied by the Pathan keeper of the door. He had a thin, sensitive, almost ascetic face, large, darkly lashed eyes. He stepped on to an upturned crate at the head of the room — reminding Debraj of the Speaker's Corner in Hyde Park — and started speaking, in a quiet, measured voice.

'So, Gandhiji told the British to quit India. Did they? Did they listen to him? No. All those lovely ideas about non-cooperation… did they work? No. We're still writhing under their boots. They're still our overlords.'

A low growl went up from the audience. Debraj enthusiastically clapped, 'Attaboy!' The lean young man looked up. One of the men from the street caught sight of Debraj, frowned in recognition. The young man on the crate shook his head, carried on.

'Britain has declared that it is fighting a World War for freedom. Whose freedom? Certainly not ours! They say their fight is for democracy. Democracy for whom? Millions on this continent are forced to live as slaves, so that a few living on a tiny island far away can enjoy their democracy! It is OUR blood spilt on their battlefields, OUR wealth they loot and take back to their King.'

A long pause. He looked at them, at Debraj, his eyes piercing. Debraj felt himself nodding in agreement.

'But Netaji has given us an alternative. A real shot at getting rid of the British. Action, not words. That's Netaji's promise. And that is what has brought young men like us here today, what has lit a fire in all our bellies. It has made you leave the ranks of the British and come to join the Azad Hind Fauj, the real Indian National Army! So here we are, my brave brothers! We have all gathered here to do what is right, to be part of the great fight!'

The young man's eyes flashed with emotion but his voice was steady as he continued.

'Indians…thousands of Indian POWs captured by the Japanese forces in Malay and Singapore, thousands of Indians from the Punjab regiment of the British Indian Army, thousands of Indian expatriates in Burma and Malay…right now, they are all joining the INA and pledging to fight alongside the Japanese against the British.'

There was a stirring amongst the assembled men. Debraj exclaimed to his neighbour, a burly Sikh, 'Hey, so that's who you are! You're those INA boys we've all been hearing about. You're the ones the British are after.'

The men turned to see what the commotion was about. The man from the street stepped up and whispered something to the speaker. The young man gestured sharply at the Pathan doorkeeper. The Pathan and the neighbouring Sikh grabbed hold of Debraj and started pushing him out. Debraj struggled, shouting, 'Hey, hold on, I'm one of you…'

But he was dragged ignominiously up the stairs and down the corridor to the main door. As they reached the door, three sharp knocks and two slow ones were heard, the familiar call sign. The Pathan let go of him, leaving the Sikh to hold him, and turned to open the door.

A man stood in the darkened doorway, his face in black shadow. Behind him stood a Chinese rickshaw puller. As the man in the doorway stepped in, he moved into the light. Debraj caught a glimpse of him, over the Sikh's shoulder, and there was instant recognition. It was the hawk-faced man in plain clothes with the livid scar running across his face, last seen in the police jeep at the Outram Road checkpost earlier that evening, so long, long ago. He realised it was the cops, that it was a trap, a raid. A moment to gather himself and then he was galvanised into action. He violently shoved the Sikh away, who taken by utter surprise, stumbled, fell over his own feet and back into the Pathan, who lost his balance and carromed into the cop, who in turn grabbed at the Pathan. All of them fell, coming down in a tangle of arms and legs and shouted curses. Debraj spun around and ran down the corridor, shouting 'Bhago…run… police…bhago!!' He grabbed an iron rod leaning against the wall as he sprinted, smashing the overhead bare bulbs as he went, plunging the corridor into darkness.

The rest of the force who had been hiding outside came charging through the red door, falling over each other and the three flailing around in the dark. Outside, a dog started howling. The cop with the scar, still trying to disentangle himself, screamed. 'Spread out! Cover the back! Now! Not a single one must get away!'

Debraj charged inside the warehouse. Pandemonium reigned. Men were scattering in different directions. The speaker was roaring out instructions. 'Take the canal path! Move!' To the man Debraj had met in the street, 'Nawaz! Through Mama Chang's kitchen! Now!'

Debraj took in the scene with a glance. He turned and toppled a big crate across the door, put the flimsy latch on. Just in time. There was a hammering, shouted command. 'Police! Open up in the name of his Imperial Majesty! You are all under arrest for treason. Open the door, NOW!'

Two shrill blasts from a police whistle, from inside the room, suddenly pierced the hubbub. Inside the room? Debraj swung around. The two men in the identical black shoes stood back-to-back, brandishing guns. 'Police! Don't move! Stay where you are!'

Someone started blowing out the lamps and the basement darkened. There was a shout from Nawaz. 'Back door, Major!!' There was the flash of gunfire, in the darkening room. One of the plainclothes policemen yelped, clutching his arm. They dived behind one of the crates, firing blindly. Bullets whistled and ricocheted in the enclosed space. Debraj ducked. In the gloom, he saw the speaker, his own gun out, heading for the rear. Debraj lunged and brought him down with a rugby tackle behind a shelf. The shelf teetered, spilling its burden of slithery, rich silks. The young man entangled in maroon, somehow swivelled round, snarling, and jammed his gun against Debraj's forehead, all in one smooth, feline move. They froze, motionless in the middle of the sound and fury of the battle raging inside. The young man was flat on his back, Debraj straddling him, poised above him, the gun's barrel smack between his eyes. Then Debraj just sat back and laughed, his face boyish with excitement, adrenaline lighting up his face. He threw his hands up in mock surrender and climbed off the young man. There was another rattle of shots and shouts from the rear.

'The back is blown. The cops are swarming all over it. And the front is not going to hold much longer. Come with me,' Debraj shouted above the din. He pointed to a catwalk in the shadows. Iron stairs led up to it. The faint light of the night sky could be seen through a dusty skylight. The young man stared at him for a long moment, then brought down his gun and jerked his head at Debraj. They crawled on their stomachs, veering off to the right and headed up into the shadows. The basement was, by then, shrouded in darkness. Screams echoed in the rafters as they felt their way up. Flashes of gunfire lit up the room, revealing bodies, outflung arms, lying tangled and tumbled in the silk bales, which had fallen and rolled out like great rivers of blood. The acrid smell of gun smoke filled the air. The young man looked down at the carnage. His face was like stone.

'Come on, there's nothing we can do here now.'

They broke open the skylight, crawled out on the tiled roof. From that vantage point, they could see the chaos below. The police were desperately trying to round up the fleeing men who had scattered in a dozen directions. Police dogs were barking wildly and sandals and discarded shoes littered the wet street. A body lay, face down, on the cobblestones. Creeping along the tiled roofs, going house to house, they moved steadily away. Slithering down a drainpipe, they managed to reach the street but, within seconds, they were spotted. A whistle shrilled out, the dogs bayed. They ran, arms pumping, breath whistling, turning into blind alleys, scrambling over walls. Suddenly, they were back in front of Mr. Lung's dentist shop. Debraj whirled round, got his bearings. He grabbed hold of the young man's arm and pointed. The man hesitated, then followed him.

They arrived panting in the lane where the parked Rolls stood, waiting magnificently alone. There was no sign of the Chinese look out. As Debraj started to head towards the car, a couple of policemen led by the scarred cop burst out onto the street ahead of them. Debraj and the young man lunged into a doorway, breathing hard. They waited. Then Debraj nodded, peeled off his Montague Burton jacket and tossed it away. He pulled up his collar, rolled up his sleeves, mussed up the other man's hair. Then, grabbing his arm, he stepped out and started walking, singing loudly, drunkenly. The young man caught on. He too lurched against Debraj, his head down, weaving towards the car, the three cops. The cops looked away. Chinatown was famous for young Turks who came late night — to score a hit or try Mama Chang's famous hot and sour momos. Some came for more illegal diversions — to bet on the savage cockfighting in hidden basements or for the more gentle pleasures of the flesh. The police got a nice fat weekly payoff and left such philandering young men alone.

They passed the cops, reached the car. Debraj fumbled for his keys. A moment of panic — was it in the jacket he had thrown away — and then found them in his trouser pocket. He slid in behind the wheel, gestured to the young man to get in. The man looked at the car with a broad grin and started to climb in. But at the last minute, he turned to look at the scarred cop down the street. They locked eyes. The cop roared out the alarm. The young man slammed the door. 'Go, go, go,' he screamed at Debraj. The car started with a purr and they were off, with a police jeep hot in pursuit.

They barrelled down dark roads, tyres screeching, the headlights dancing on the bumpy road, beacons crisscrossing the darkness. Debraj felt more alive than he had felt in a long time. Despite the large quantities of whisky he had imbibed and the opium hit, he felt a great clarity of mind and drove calmly. But as they approached the railway level crossing, Debraj saw the barrier was down. He heard the lonely wail of an approaching train whistle. He looked back. The police jeep's bouncing headlights were alarmingly close. He grinned as they approached the level crossing. The barrier was down. The headlights of the oncoming train sliced through the darkness on their right with another primordial howl. It was very close. The young man pulled out a gun, checked the chamber, turned to lean out of his window. But instead of slowing down, Debraj slammed his foot down on the accelerator.

'What the hell!? Slow down, you idiot!' the man shouted. Debraj just gripped the wheel and kept going. The young man's eyes widened as he realised what Debraj was about to do. He braced himself against the dash, his eyes narrowing. As they crashed through the barrier, both of them screamed at the top of their voices, in sheer terror and exhilaration. The car landed on the tracks, bucked like a horse. The train thundered towards them. Then the Rolls gathered her mighty heart and surged ahead with inches to spare. The rush of the train's passage buffeted them and then they were clear. The police jeep swivelled to a muddy halt, cheated of its prey. The scarred cop got out, slammed his fist on the bonnet. 'Get the Outram Road outpost… find out who that man in the Rolls is. And set up roadblocks at all exit points. Grand Trunk Road, Jessore Road, the train stations, the docks. I want that Nishonko Mitro. I want his bloody head.'

Outside the tea shop, the skies have cleared a bit. The late morning sun has burned the fog off and it has turned less cold. The old man pauses. Sudipto leans forward. 'His name was Debraj Mookerji? You sure of it?'

'More than anything in my whole life,' the old man muttered.

'This Debraj Mookerji? He just happened to be in the wrong place at the wrong time. If he hadn't come…'

The old man shakes his head. 'If? So many ifs. Every moment, you stand at a crossroad. You make a choice. You take the right or the left…and the path is created, the destiny made. If…'

He takes a sip of water, starts speaking again.

'And then there was Nishonko Mitro, known as Nishachar, or Night Walker, for he came and went under cover of darkness…invisible, like a shadow on a moonless night…but Netaji trusted him. See, he was the one who went behind the lines, deep into enemy territory, looking for deserters from the British Army in India to swell the ranks of the INA. A good soldier, followed orders. He was willing to sacrifice everything for the cause…for Netaji…for India's independence.'

A sickle moon hung over a dark country road somewhere in eastern India. It was a hot night, the relentless heat of an Indian summer just before the monsoons. The heavy, velvety silence was broken by the occasional chirping of cicadas and the faraway howl of some night creature. On a dirt track in the woods, invisible from the main road, a pre WWII jeep stood parked, camouflaged by branches. Nishonko leaned against the hood. His face was calm, almost serene. And blackened. As were his hands, which cradled a gun. It had a curious carving of a springing tiger on the worn, shiny, mahogany butt. He tapped it lightly with the side of his thumb, an unconscious gesture of controlled impatience. Large, almost limpid, dark eyes, stared intently into the forest. A soft birdcall floated out of the woods. He let out two soft birdcalls in response, then crouched, his gun cocked. From the trees, a shadowy figure stepped out, hands raised. It was a Sikh soldier in British Army uniform. Nishonko slowly uncoiled. He stood a head taller than the Sikh, himself a man of no mean height and width.

The Sikh whispered, 'Major Mitro? Nishonko Mitro?'

'Password. What's the password?'

'Sorry, sorry. Chaalis Chor. Forty Thieves.'

A small smile creased Nishonko's granite face.

'Where are the rest of your men?'

'In a clearing half a mile from here.'

'Okay, let's go.'

They flitted from shadow to tree shadow, not a snap of a twig to mark their passing. Silent as a ghost, Nishonko circled the clearing and came up behind a man standing at the edge and gently put his gun to the back of the man's head. He leaned in and whispered something. The man nodded gingerly, cupped his hands and gave the same soft birdcall. A mashal was lit. Its flickering light revealed a ragged group of men, sitting around the clearing, all in British Army uniforms. They clustered around Nishonko as he handed out cigarettes, shook his hand.

'Don't travel together. Separate. It will be easier to become invisible in the city. When you get into Calcutta, make for this address. Memorise it, then destroy it. You will get a bed, food, instructions and passage money. Wear dhotis and kurtas. And no drinking. It makes for loose talk. All the best.'

Driving back that hot, muggy June night in 1943, Nishonko felt a great sense of peace. He had done good work today, as Netaji would say. That's what he had said the last time they had met —

that momentous cold January night in 1941 when Netaji had so magnificently outwitted the British and escaped from house arrest, fooling the government agents who were guarding him, getting away from under their very noses. Nishonko had been deputed to provide distraction. The memory brought a rare smile to Nishonko's face as they sped through the night towards Calcutta. It had been a truly hazardous undertaking, meticulously planned. For the young Economics student freshly arrived from Shantiniketan, awestruck in the presence of the great leader, the opportunity to be a part of such a historic event, however marginally, had been a seminal moment, a prime point. In those brief months that he had known Netaji, he had learned to love him, to revere him with a fierce intensity that he felt for no one else. Netaji knew that both his parents, freedom fighters, were prisoners of the British, no chance of parole or reprieve. He had encountered them in Presidency Jail while he was serving out his own sentence. With that special solicitude for comrades rotting in British prisons, he had promised the serious-faced boy, his hand resting squarely on his thin shoulder blades, 'I will throw open the prison gates before long so that India's worthy sons and daughters can step out of the darkness of prison cells into the light of freedom, joy and self fulfillment.' Big words, pompous in a lesser man but spoken with that clear transparent light of truth he saw in Netaji's eyes, they gave him surety. Netaji had arranged for the young man to become a part of his family's extended household. He didn't pity Nishonko. Instead he gave the 17-year-old with the big dreamy eyes clarity, goals and a sense of pride in being Bengali, being Indian. 'I will be your family. I will come back for you. I promise you that. In the meantime, will you do some work for me?'

So Nishonko, lonely child of Swadeshis, freedom-fighters, growing up under the benign shadow of Rabindranath Tagore in his peaceful university town, had taken up Netaji's mandate with an unquestioning fervour. When they told him to put his elbow over a guttering candle flame, a simple test of fortitude, he had not jerked his arm or even sighed, though the smell of burning hair was acrid in the small room. When he had been arrested on some trumped up charge, the police had put a tiny beetle found in horse droppings and put it in his navel and tied a bandage over it. Then they had tied his hands and stood around laughing as the insect bored in. There was nothing you could do except roll and roll on the ground, the pain excruciating. But he had not opened his mouth or even whimpered.

He became an active azadi, a freedom fighter. He took to martial training like a seal to water. Guerrilla warfare, subversion, sabotage were what this quiet, intense, fiercely private boy excelled at. He had burned down station buildings, cut telegraph wires, blown up railway lines, looted government seed stores, wrecked post offices. Netaji had not forgotten him. Secret letters, coded missives arrived, sometimes by way of Kabul, sometimes from Tokyo, passed from stranger to stranger, hidden in the spines of holy books and the hollow heels of shoes. Written in that neat, fastidious, slanting hand, they brought fragmented news from far off places with exotic names — Hindu Kush, Samarkand, Moscow, Berlin, Rome. Lucid, inspiring letters, they spoke of homesickness, frustration, resolve, courage — and gave detailed instructions. The letters were shared by the family, read out aloud, the words written down in a notebook like litany, a talisman, to be repeated by the flickering glow of a bonfire in some jungle encampment. He spied, he sabotaged, he recruited, he organised, he helped to build up a secret army. And he survived, for the day when his mentor would return to lead them to victory, to independence.

And now, in 1943, the time was near. The previous year, a conference of Indian expatriate patriots in Bangkok had sent Netaji an invitation to lead them in South East Asia. Netaji had undertaken an extremely hazardous 90-day journey by German and then Japanese submarines. Landing in Sabang, he had arrived in Tokyo the month before. He was there to garner support for his armed struggle and Japanese recognition of India's independence movement.

With Netaji accepting the leadership of the Indian independence movement in East Asia, the stage was set for action. Malaysia had fallen, Singapore had been wrested from the British by the Japanese. Netaji was in Tokyo, trying to persuade the Japanese High Command to take on the British with the help of the INA.

Dawn was flushing the sky as his jeep reached the outskirts of Calcutta two days later. He knew the police and government agents would be on the lookout at the main entry points of the city. He cleaned the remnants of the black soot from his face and hands at a roadside tea shop on the truck route. In the lean-to, roofless toilet, he changed into labourer's clothes, which he had stolen off a clothesline from one of the villages they had passed through. He had a flair for disguise, a chameleon-like quality, which allowed him to blend in with his surroundings, become invisible. In the hitched-up dhoti, worn like a sarong, the slightly frayed vest and a red-checked gamchha, tied around his head, he became the lie, the illusion. He hitched a ride in a truck heading towards Sealdah Market, with produce.

Disembarking, he was immediately lost in the thousands milling around the wholesale market and the sprawling adjacent station. Two bus rides later, he was in Dhakuria, walking up a tiny alley to an unremarkable green door in an old two-storey house. He had taken off his gamchha, rolled his dhoti down and put a shirt on top of the vest. With his jhola, and his studious glasses, he was transformed into one of the thousands of young men studying in Calcutta University and staying in cheap digs on the outskirts of town. He entered, went up narrow stairs.

A pretty young girl, dark skinned, with long oiled hair, a maid from the Sunderbans, was sweeping the small inner courtyard. She looked up, broke into a smile of unabashed delight.

'Arre, Anando babu, where did you disappear? We missed you.'

Nishonko paused, spoke without looking at her. 'To my *village.*'

'Is there anything I can get you? Some water…or food? You look tired.'

Nishonko hurried to open the lock on his door, slipped in. It was a hermit's room. Small, spartan, it had a rolled-up bamboo mattress on the floor in one corner and a tin trunk which doubled up as a desk in the other. Books stacked in neat piles on the ground doubled up as tables. On the wall hung pictures of Netaji, Tagore, Swami Vivekananda, Deshbandhu Chittaranjan Das — the great men of Bengal. The only personal things in the room were a studio photograph of a young couple, black and white, their faces closed, blank, facing the impersonal black box of the camera, and another photograph, blurred, hazy, the sun in the lens, of a little girl with pigtails, looking up at the camera with the curious, challenging look of the very young. In her skirt, held up like a basket, were mangoes, stolen or retrieved after a storm, who knew. There was nothing else of the man in the room, nothing that a police raid would unearth. The anonymity, the complete lack of evidence of human interaction made the room look like a prison cell.

He closed the door behind him, bolted the green shuttered windows. Then he jumped, caught hold of one of the rafters holding up the tiled roof and hauled himself up. Hidden in the eaves, artfully concealed, was a long wooden box. Inside lay arms, ammunitions. He cleaned his gun, oiled it, polished the carved leaping tiger on the butt and put it away. Another fake beam held maps, documents, cash. In it, he placed hand-drawn maps of terrain, stolen passports, lists. He then took out some fresh clothes, a new bar of soap and went down to the communal tap in the corner of the courtyard to bathe. The maid watched him from an upstairs window, saw the lean brown body sluiced in water, the loin cloth round his middle turning dark, the strong long-fingered hands running through the wet, dense black hair. She wondered about the scars across the back and the chest, like little puckered mouths, and the long slash of healed flesh on the back of the beautifully shaped calf. She smiled. If he knew she was watching, he would actually blush, as if caught out in some indiscretion. He was different from the brash boys she knew, and his shyness, his thoughtful serious expression, the rare smile that would suddenly make him look years younger — it all made her feel weak at the knees. So many times she had thought of tapping on his door at night but there was an unbreachable sense of reserve that kept her away.

The next two nights, Nishonko slipped into the Bose house on Elgin Road, where he had once, so long ago, been given refuge. He spoke to the inmates, giving them an update of deserters from the British Indian Army willing to join their cause. The monsoon was early this year and arrangements had to be made to transport as many of the men as possible across the border into Burma. Passage by sea was fraught with danger and too expensive.

He was invited to the evening meal, and with deep contentment had the simple khichuri, kedgeree the Ingrej called it, unable or unwilling to pronounce the words they had appropriated for themselves correctly. A spoonful of ghee was poured on top of the hot, steaming plate, melting, releasing its earthy aroma. It took him back to the small, unpretentious house in Bolpur where he had grown up with his parents and Annada mashi, the large, ample woman who was cook, housemaid, and gardener rolled into one and who had actually brought him up. His parents, writers, intellectuals, deeply committed to the idea of self-rule, had been too absorbed in their calling to lavish much love on the lonely, introspective boy who would crouch at the foot of a chair, listening to the talk swirling around, the debates, the diatribes. When they were arrested during a protest rally, he didn't even know about it till a month afterwards. He moved around the empty house for days, curling up in his parents' bed at night. Annada mashi was a rock, a refuge through those dark days. And she would cook khichuri with raw papaya from their garden tree and large creamy potatoes, and she would sit on the ground, fanning him with a palm leaf fan, telling him stories of Krishna and Radha and their immortal love, while he ate silently. He thought sometimes of finding out how she was, where she was but with the same single-mindedness inherited from his parents, he had become totally immersed in his mission.

He left Elgin Road humming a Tagore song softly under his breath. The hour was late, the streets deserted. It was raining, the wind swaying the tops of the trees, a soft rushing sound like the beating of wings. He enjoyed the soft drumming of the raindrops on his bare head, the wind whipping his face. He felt cleansed, reborn. Soon, he would meet Netaji again. The first guerrilla regiment of the INA's First Division had been stationed in Burma for almost a year. He had remained in India and done what was required of him but he couldn't wait to be at the INA Headquarters in Singapur. He would be at the centre of things, actually making history. No more hiding in the shadows, no more running from the minions of law and order.

And he would meet her. It had been — what six, seven years? — since he had seen her last. He would meet her and renew their bond, forged in childhood. He remembered their time together as if it was yesterday. The only friend in those solitary growing up years, she was his shadow; running together through the kash fields, the drumbeats from the Durga temple echoing in their heads; jumping into the brown pond from the thick branch of the gulmohar tree they had made their diving platform, noses pinched between clenched fingers; stealing guavas, chased by the Mallick Baadi gardener with the fierce handlebar moustaches. She brought lightness and air into his life and he couldn't wait to see her, enjoy the way she laughed with her head thrown up to the sky, her lips wet, or the way she nibbled on her knuckle when lost in thought.

Immersed in these pleasant memories, it took him a couple of seconds to register the man standing in the doorway of the sweet shop he had just passed. He stopped, cupped hands to light a cigarette, and looked covertly over his shoulder. He felt a prickly sensation down his neck. It was the same man he had seen earlier in the evening, astride a cycle, smoking outside the Bose house gates. He glanced down the street but the man seemed to be the only one tailing him. Nishonko grinned to himself. He loved this cat-and-mouse stuff, the pitting of wits and the gulling of the enemy. He walked faster, heard the footsteps hurry up. He slowed, they slowed in rhythm. Near Jadu Babur Bazaar, he hopped into a northbound tram. From the corner of his eyes, he saw the man run to board the second-class compartment. He was a thin, dyspeptic man, like a government clerk, nothing like a policeman or a spy. He skittered to the back, slipping into a seat, not looking up. The tram was almost empty. At Park Street, Nishonko suddenly made a dash for it. He jumped down from the slowing tram, slipped across its front and pelted across the broad avenue of Chowringhee. He looked back. The thin man had scrambled down to give chase when two cars, a big Rolls and some other foreign car came tearing down the Chowringhee stretch, racing each other. By the time they turned onto Casuarina Avenue, with a squeal of brakes, people's heads turning, Nishonko had melted into the back alleys. 'Bastard rich boys,' the thin man cursed under his breath as he gave up in disgust.

At the briefing the next morning at the underground headquarters of the Bengal Volunteers, made up of those who had managed to stay out of prison, Nishonko reported the incident to Tiwari.

'Are you sure no one else followed you?'

'To the best of my knowledge, Sir.'

'You better lie low for a few days.'

'Sir but what about taking the recruits across the border tomorrow?'

'Drop out of that, Major. Don't want you leading the police to the crossing point. The whole operation would be in jeopardy.'

'But, Sir, there's no one on my tail. I…'

'Just follow orders, Major.'

As Nishonko turned away, bitterly disappointed, Tiwari called out to him. 'There's a new batch coming to the Tangra warehouse today. Get over there, and give them your pep talk. Just keep your head down for the next few days. Maybe, head to Ranchi or Monghyr till this blows over.'

'Yes, Sir.'

That night, as he sat hunched, his head swaddled in a black shawl, in one of the Chinatown soup joints, tucking into a fiery Talo mian, he scanned the people walking by. No one paid him any undue attention, no one turned away sharply if he chanced to look at them. A Chinese coolie eating at the next table gave him a gap-toothed, betel-stained smile. He took the usual precautions, the roundabout route, doubling up on his steps. Except for a somewhat persistent Chinese rickshaw puller, no one else took any interest in him. As he knocked on the red iron door — three short, two long — and greeted the Pathan, rebellion flared in his heart. He had so looked forward to getting out of India and joining Netaji in Singapur. So much was happening there; everybody was on the brink of history and he was stuck here, twiddling his thumbs. But he was a good soldier. He composed himself and stepped into the warehouse.

'So that's how they met, Debraj Mookerji and Nishonko Mitro. Events had moved inexorably to draw them to that crossroads of history. What would have happened if one, any one of those random events had not happened, if one domino in that headlong rush had stopped? Would there have been a different ending? Or would it all have turned out the same way anyway?'

The old man rubs his eyes, rests his head in his hands. The others stir, drawing in breaths that they had unconsciously held for some time. Balai da gestures to Haru to get some more tea. Reluctantly, Haru gets up.

'Dadu, wait until I get back.'

The old man nods, a tiny smile crinkling his cloudy eyes. He takes off his glasses and wipes them, his gaze far away.

In the Rolls speeding away, Nishonko and Debraj whooped, laughing, two schoolboys on a prank. Nishonko knew there would be police roadblocks on the main roads so he told Debraj to take the bumpy back roads through the jheels, those vast water bodies which made up Calcutta's eastern boundaries, their still black surfaces, serene mirrors reflecting the turbulent sky, the scudding clouds, the elusive moon. They stretched for miles, with just a few villages, black silhouettes, to break the calm. Nishonko knew his way around these parts, where the water was just underneath the surface, a quagmire waiting to trap the unwary traveller and where the Rolls, heavy beast that she was, would be on safer ground. They travelled without lights, met no one. After all the noise and shooting, the night was calm, silent. The Rolls' engine hardly made a sound. Both the men were also silent, lost in their own thoughts, Nishonko only murmuring brief directions. Only when they were almost near Dhakuria, did Nishonko speak.

'How did you find us — our meeting? Who told you about it?'

Debraj blinked at him. 'Er, well, no one. It all happened because Li…a friend…took us to an opium den…'

'You expect me to believe that? Turn right here. You just happened to know the code and Inspector Haley.'

'Who's Haley?'

'That cop with the scar.'

'Oh, I have absolutely no friggin' idea who he is. He was there at the Outram Road police checkpost when I…oh it's a long story. I just saw him in that doorway and it all fell into place.'

'And he just happened to turn up?'

Debraj tensed. 'What are you getting at?'

'How were you there at the precise moment the raid took place?'

Debraj drove carefully, looking straight ahead, trying to figure out what to say and, as always, decided that the truth was the least tiring option.

'Look, here's what happened.'

By the time he finished, the big black car was coasting along the road next to the Lakes. Debraj didn't know if the young man believed him or not but he had put away his gun and was sitting back in his seat. Debraj knew his way around these parts a bit. He had come here often as a boy to sail his toy boats and for the rare picnic when his mother would sit under a silk-lined parasol, nibbling at tiny watercress sandwiches and drinking something pink and frothy from a tall, fluted glass while their nanny kept a strict eye on them. Debi had fallen in once and his mother had gone into hysterics but when Debi was fished out, none the worse for the ordeal, it was he who had been roundly blamed by everyone for not looking after his little sister.

'Turn left at the corner.'

He came out of his reverie. They were driving past open fields. Firelight from small bonfires lit up people, thousands in makeshift tents, sleeping on open ground, just sitting, thin, emaciated men, pot-bellied children with vacant eyes. They passed a small group, wailing, beating their chests. A young woman, skeletal, lay on a white sheet on the ground in the centre of the grieving circle.

'Who are these people?'

'Refugees from the villages, fleeing the famine.'

'Famine? What famine?'

'Where on earth have you been?'

'Away. England.'

'It's the biggest man-made famine in history, all engineered by your good friends, the British administration and Mr. Churchill. They are just sitting on stocks, thousands of tons of rice, while village after village starves to death.'

'They are not my friends.'

'Stop at the corner.'

They rolled silently to a stop on a dark street near a dark house. Nishonko cupped his hands, gave his soft birdcall. He was answered from the right. A man, wrapped in a shawl, stepped out from the shadows of a peepul tree. From inside the car, Debraj saw it was the man who had confronted him on the street. Behind him, half seen, was a big Sikh and a small, wrinkled, peg-legged man.

'Nawaz, how did you get out of that mess?'

Nawaz spoke in a low, urgent voice. 'Never mind, Major, you have to move. It's not safe here any more. They got Bismillah and Balbir. Maybe some of the others. Someone will break before the night is out. Get your things and let's get out now.'

'The Behala safe house...?'

'No use. That's also blown. We need to join the others.'

Nishonko shook his head.'The border roads will be watched. Command will have to come up with an alternative route for them.'

'We've burnt our boats here,' Nawaz muttered.

Nishonko nodded, a sudden boyish grin lighting up his face.

'You're right. We should head for Singapur.'

The Sikh spoke, a deep rumble.'Then we go by sea.'

'Yes, that's the only way out, Mohan Singh.'

'What do we do with his lordship?' Nawaz jerked his head towards the car.

They all turned to look at Debraj who had got out and was lighting up a cigar.

'We can't leave him here. They'll get to him. The car won't be hard to trace,' Nishonko muttered

'So junk it, and junk him, ' Nawaz muttered back.

'He saved my life.'

'How do you know he wasn't the stool pigeon? He had no earthly reason to be there. You know nothing about him.'

'He was there for the opium. So he says, and strangely, I believe him.'

'Come on, Major, don't go soft on us now. We have to get rid of him. He's just extra baggage.'

'Then we're no better than them. No, I have a better idea.'

Nishonko walked over to Debraj. 'What's your name?'

'Debraj Mookerji...but Deb will do.'

'You have two choices, Deb...go home, get arrested for treason and they'll hang you for sure. Your family shall be destroyed, your land forfeited. Or come with us. Join the INA. We could do with a man of your talents.'

Debraj looked at the tip of his cigar. 'Hmmm...Hobson's choice. And what is your name, my friend? And where are you headed?'

'Nishonko Mitro. To find a ship that will take us to Singapur.'

'Singapore? That's a bit...far, what?'

'It's where the INA HQ is right now. It's where a whole army's being trained to throw the British out of India.'

'Do I get to tell my family the glad tidings?'

'No, there's no going back. You are a fugitive now...like all of us.'

'What happens if I decide to take my chances? My father has some connections with the authorities. He might make them understand.'

Nishonko shrugged. 'Well, what you need to understand is that you are a liability, a bit of a loose end. And we can't have loose ends hanging around.'

There was a brief silence as Debraj took another drag on his cigar.

'And the car?'

'We'll junk it once we get to a ship.'

'Pity, just broke her in.'

Nawaz spoke up.'A small sacrifice for the cause, Debraj saab.'

'Ah, I was never one for causes. The good thing is it should get my father truly incensed.' A bitter smile twisted his mouth. 'I wish I could at least talk to Debi before leaving. She will feel so... abandoned.' He looked at his cigar.

'You think we could pick up a box of good Cuban cigars on our way at least?'

Nawaz shook his head in disgust, 'Laath saab!'

The pretty maid, her long hair tied in a thick braid, slept, the deep slumber of the darkest hour of the night, at the back of the house. It took a while for the soft scratching on her window to wake her.

'Who is it?'

'Anondo.' A hoarse whisper.

Her heart leapt. She hurriedly draped her sari round her, opened the door. Nishonko stood there.

'Can I come in? I've lost my key.'

'Why are you whispering?' she whispered.

'Mustn't wake the landlord. Wait here. I need something from my room.' He tiptoed up the wooden staircase, crept into his room. From the darkness of his window, he could make out the anonymous van parked at the corner of the street in front of the house, the lone plainclothesman smoking a bidi. He started packing, scrabbling up papers and some meagre clothing. He took the photographs of the couple and the young girl in pigtails carefully from the wall and put them in his pocket. He stuffed everything else into a leather bag, picked up a battered camera, which had seen many battles. He left the books, the portraits, the mattress. Finally, from inside the fake wooden beams, he retrieved the hidden arms and ammunition and bundles of cash. A last look around, then he snaked his way down.

'Are you in trouble, Anondo babu?' she whispered from the foot of the stairs.

He shook his head, finger to his lips. He went to the back door, peered out. The rectangle of pale moonlight framed his tall, lean form.

'Wait,' she whispered, then handed him a small bag. It contained some bread, two hard green guavas, a packet of puffed rice. He looked at it, at her. He bent down and kissed her forehead. Then he melted into the night. She sat down, her eyes suddenly tearing up. Somehow, she knew she would never see him again.

Though it was still an hour before dawn, the Kidderpore docks were buzzing. Large steamers, primordial hulks, their outlines blurred by the mist rising from the grey roiling water, rumbled in and out of the harbour. The air was heavy with the aroma of spices and tea being loaded but the biggest cargo was coal, hundreds of tonnes transported daily in baskets by an endless stream of thin, brown, sweating bodies to feed the hungry maws of the Allied war machine. The British were sucking all their colonies dry to keep their precious Empire afloat.

One of the coolies, his skin tarred with coal dust, limped through the maze of alleys between the cargo stacks. As he reached the riverside, Nawaz and Mohan Singh stepped out of the shadows.

'Kabootar!' Nawaz hissed.

The peg-legged man joined them, shook his head. 'The police are all over. There are checkpoints at all the gates. They're going through every ship.'

'Damn it, where the hell do we find a ship?' Mohan Singh growled.

'We need Ah Ping.'

As dawn broke, villagers heading for the fields for their morning ablutions along Behala Road saw a most surreal sight — a huge black car, like a ghost ship, sailing silently down the country roads, its chrome glinting in the pale sun. Debraj sat at the wheel, silent, smoking. Nishonko, beside him, thought of the strange turn of events that just might take him to Netaji, and smiled.

'Turn in,' he said as big iron gates loomed up on the right. Inside, behind a large ramshackle warehouse, through the trees, they could see the gleam of the river. As they drove round, a large Chinese junk docked at a jetty came into view. It was dirty, dilapidated but looked fast, as if it could outrun the lumbering boats of the Coast Guard. A large Chinese man walked down the gangplank, scratching his belly. He spat on the ground.

'Salaam, my good Sirs. And how can I help you so early in the morning?'

'The usual, Ah Ping, safe passage to Singapur and your silence.'

'And it will cost you the usual, agreed?'

Nawaz grunted, nodded. 'The royal sum of 100 taka, yes?'

Ah Ping nodded, his multiple chins wobbling. 'Per head, my friend.'

'What!! But that's...Ah Ping, that's bloody highway dacoity!'

'Not at all, my friend. I take a great risk. My cargo, my precious cargo, will be seized, my lovely ship impounded, my hide flayed and my balls stuffed in my mouth if that white-skinned mongrel of a Harbour Master gets wind of this. I ply my trade, illicit as it is, with his most courteous understanding. So, if he knows I'm harbouring fugitives — and fugitives, you most definitely are — Mama Ping will find herself widowed and bereft before the night is out. So, no argumenting please, it spoils my mood.'

Nishonko and Nawaz went back to the others.

'Okay, who's got what? Let's pool it in.'

Kabootar gave a gap-toothed grin and emptied out his pockets. Except for a wicked-looking knife, he had nothing. Mohan Singh too came up empty handed.

Nishonko muttered, 'I have enough to pay for just two of us.'

'Okay, we'll draw lots.'

Debraj, who had been leaning back, his eyes closed, now seemed to wake up. He uncoiled his body, stretched, yawned.

'Captain Ah Ping — a most intriguing name, I must say – how would you like to own a treasure beyond compare, in exchange for passage for all of us?'

Ah Ping looked at the young man sprawled on the front seat, took in his ruined but expensive attire, saw the lazy smile and wondered who this man was, what crime he had committed to bring him to this back of beyond, end of the world staging point in search of an escape.

'Indeed, Sir, what is this treasure you speak of?'

'Oh, merely this practically brand new, single owner, magnificent Rolls Royce Wraith,' he said, sweeping his hand down the flanks of the car. 'Fancy a spin, old boy?'

Ah Ping gulped. Greed turned his mouth dry. He walked slowly to the car. She was dusty, mud spattered but still the most beautiful creature he had ever seen. In that drab grey dawn, she shone like a pearl. He tenderly rubbed her bonnet with the back of his sleeve, sighed when the black sheen of the swooping line of the hood was revealed.

'You are sure, young Sir, that you wish to part with this beauty?'

'Well, won't be needing it where we are going, will we? In exchange, dearest Ah Ping — does it mean anything? Ping?' he said, putting his arm round the Chinese man's shoulder, 'In exchange, you will give us food worthy of a king and clean sheets and your best staterooms, separate rooms for each please. You will give spending money for all the carousing we will do in Sin city and of course, you must ensure that the weather behaves itself because I've had it up to here with storms at sea. Most uncomfortable.'

Ah Ping giggled, his jowls and belly quivering. 'You are most entertaining, Sir.'

Nawaz and Mohan Singh looked at each other. Kabootar looked at Debraj with almost abject devotion. Nishonko smiled. 'Staterooms? Why don't you ask him for lifeboats while you're at it, you idiot?'

Within the hour, the Rolls had been loaded into a truck, camouflaged and driven away. Watching the car being manhandled onto the truck, Debraj just wished that his father could have seen the dirty grubby hands of the Chinese crew on his 'Pearl'. Would have served the old bugger right.

The stench hit them as soon as they went below decks. It was a ripe mélange of every foul cargo the junk had ever carried.

Ah Ping showed them two cubby holes with four fold-down bunks and a hammock, where cockroaches and bugs had already taken up residence. They preferred the open deck but Ah Ping told them to stay below, keep their heads down, just in case. By noon, the *Flying Eagle* had cast off and taken the tide down the Hooghly, past small fishing villages, brick kilns and grey jute factories. Naked, brown children ran along the earthen bunds, waving at them. In time, they hit the broad estuary, thousands of rivulets, dividing, sub-dividing, spreading out, an endless flat grey tapestry, stretching right to the horizon, till they slipped through the place where the sweet waters of the river melded into the salt of the sea.

ACT II

PASSAGE

Back at the tea shop, they all looked up. Conch shells by the hundreds had started to blow, filling the cold air with the breath and boom of the sea. It was noon, and all over Calcutta, women blew sea shells to mark the hour of Netaji's birth. The group stirred, rubbed their faces. The old man paused also, licking his dry lips. He rapped twice on the table. Haru hurried to get him another cup of tea.

'So the laath shaheb and the azadi, the lord's son and the freedom fighter, set forth. Fate had thrown them together, joined their destiny. And each day brought them closer to their tryst with fate.'

Debraj stood alone, leaning against a tar-encrusted large bale of coiled rope, the freshening salt breeze coming off the Bay of Bengal, ruffling his hair. An unlit cigar dangled from his mouth. He stared out to sea, the horizon a thin blue line in the light of the rising moon. What wouldn't he give to slide into the steaming comfort of a hot tub, Khogen da standing by with a soft, fluffy pristine white towel, the bathroom redolent of the vetiver lotion he had picked up from that apothecary in Bond Street. Just a couple of days and his whole world had turned upside down. At what point had it all begun to unravel? What madness had possessed him to go into that warehouse, what twist of fate had thrown Naveen and the Chinese twins into his path? What was he doing here, where the hell was he headed? When would he be able to return?

He heard footsteps, soft, above the sound of the creaking wooden planks. It was Nishonko. He leaned on the railing, a few discreet feet away from Debraj. There was a brief silence. The river flowed.

'I wanted to say thank you...back there, for saving me.'

'Funny, if any one had told me this was the way last night would end, I would have…'

He shook his head. 'You know, last night I found out that my best friend, Andy, a good, decent English squire's son, had got my kid sister pregnant and was refusing to marry her. Called her a darkie. I wanted to kill him, thinking the shame would kill my father. But it was my father, the great Sir Harry Mookerji, who, after years of servitude, thinks the sun shines out of the King's arse…my father slapped me and told me to back off. He said if I killed Andy, the British would hang me and ruin the family.'

He drew a ragged breath. Then, in a whisper, 'I don't know why I'm telling you all this.'

Nishonko laid his hand on Debraj's shoulder, gave it an awkward pat. There was silence, broken by the sound of the waves slapping against the hull, the distant cry of a sea bird. Debraj struggled for control.

'He told Goopta, they do business together — he's a snake — told him to take care of Debi. That's my sister. Fifteen years old. And I might as well have killed Andy, you know — because here I am, on the run, anyway, ruining my family name, accused of treason… for what?'

'Have you ever killed a man?'

'What…no…of course not.'

'It's harder than you think. But you can have your revenge, Deb. There's so much you can do…to get rid of the British forever.'

'You know, I don't hate them. For god's sake, some of my best friends are British. I admire their humour, their language, their literature, their liberalism, their education, their sense of fair play and a man's right to…'

'How naïve. The British sense of fair play and the rights of man? Come on, these don't apply to the millions they have colonised. We're slaves in our own land, Debraj. You, privileged as you are, you think any of it belongs to you? It belongs to Empire. That's why Netaji is fighting to build the INA.'

'Hey Nishong…Nisho… I'm going to call you Mitro…you're obviously a good man, very passionate about your mission. Me, I'm a bit of a waster. The dark horse, the black sheep, you know.

Not really cut out for saving the country and all that heroic blarney. Singapore, they say, is a great town for having a good time – or used to be. I'm just hitching a ride till I figure out what to do.'

Nishonko nodded curtly, then turned away. 'Of course, good night.'

Debraj turned to look at his retreating back. He raised a hand to call him, then let it drop.

Debi, her face white, rushed into the library in Mookerji Mansion, where Sir Harry and Goopta were standing and talking in hushed tones. Bubbles stood at the window, looking stricken, the jerky movements of her thin fingers betraying her turmoil.

'What's happened to Dada? Khogen da said the police were here.'

Sir Harry glowered at her.

'Your Dada is apparently a hard core INA terrorist…or some such insane claptrap. They've combed the whole house looking for clues. Preposterous! If they find him…'

'Do not worry, Sir, I will take care of it. I have contacts.'

'Tell me, Goopta, what have I done to deserve this?! Haven't I given my children every privilege, the bloody world on a platter? How do they repay me?! One's a fugitive from justice, the other's a…a…'

Goopta made a soothing gesture. 'I'll take care of that also…'

Debi whirled on him, her eyes flashing, her mouth set in a hard line. 'What will you take care of, Goopto babu? I won't do it. Ma, tell him!'

Sir Harry smashed his fist on the table. 'Not a bloody cheep out of you, girl. You will do exactly what I tell you to do.'

'Maybe, Sir, just a thought, maybe keep the infant. Who knows… it could be used…against young Mr. Wyeth at a future date.'

'No Goopta, it'll just be another bastard left behind by the British — a bloody half-breed, a calumny on my ancient family's name. Just get rid of it.'

'Yes, Boro laath.'

'I can't believe you…you're evil.' She ran out, sobbing, slap bang into Khogen da's arms. The old man had been lurking outside, grim-faced. She clung to him, sobbing. He led her towards the sanctuary of the kitchen. Inside, Bubbles turned to Goopta.

'Find him, please. Bring him back.' Her voice sounded even more broken than usual.

'Yes, my friend, return him to us.' Sir Harry sounded very tired.

Dawn broke, a pale, wet light suffusing the sleeping trees and the green expanse of the lawns. The great mansion lay silent. From far away, came the chug-chug of steam barges on the Hooghly. A door opened softly in the first-floor corridor, throwing a shaft of warm light onto the gloom of the passage. Debi stepped out of her room. She was dressed in a simple cotton sari, her hair tied back in a no-nonsense bun. Though her eyes were swollen from the night's weeping, her face was grave, composed. She looked down the length of the passage, then picked up a small suitcase and tiptoed out. At the head of the sweeping marble staircase, she paused. She walked back to a door, put her hand out to knock, stopped. She whispered, 'Ma?' A shade louder. 'Mama?' There was no reply. Somewhere, in the hall, a grandfather clock struck the hour, its sombre tone echoing round the emptiness. She turned, wiping her eyes and hurried down the stairs. Khogen da waited at the foot of the stairs, anxiously looking up, a small tin trunk clutched in his hands.

From an upstairs window, through a gap in the French lace curtains, Bubbles watched the two hurrying down the water-logged, empty driveway. Something collapsed in her face, rendering it barren, a desert. Difficult tears coursed down her rouged, ravaged cheeks, smudging the kajal, making her look ancient. She took a long, shuddering breath and turned to pour herself another drink.

The fifth day, out at sea, in the middle of the Bay of Bengal, they hit a nasty storm. It had been dogging their heels, the thunder growling low, the thick black plumes of rain sweeping across the darkening sky. Ah Ping's men had battened down everything but when it hit, even he, seasoned mariner, chanted loudly to his gods as he cowered in his cabin. The candles were blown out in seconds, the incense tossed in the howling wind. Through the night, the storm snarled at them, lashing, ripping at their rigging. But the junk, though she took in water, was a veteran of these waters and many monsoons. They trimmed the sails as best as they could and just hung on for dear life. Only at dawn, did the banshee wind suddenly die down but the rain still pelted down and the sea rolled in big oily swells. Nishonko came staggering down the deck, drenched. Looking into one of the cramped cabins, he paused. Inside, both Mohan Singh and Nawaz were being violently seasick. Mohan Singh, in particular, was clutching a bucket, his face a pale shade of green. Debraj was ministering to them cheerfully, helped by Kabootar. He swirled an evil-looking concoction in a glass, holding it gently to Mohan Singh's lips.

'Come on, Mohan Singh, bolt this down. Hellbrew, it's called... an old Scottish barman taught me the trick. But you'll be right as rain. Come on, just a teeny sip...there you go...no, no — hold it down, dammit!' He pinched Mohan Singh's nose but to no avail. Mohan Singh groaned and threw up all over Debraj. Debraj's face fell but then he shrugged good-naturedly and wiped Mohan Singh down tenderly. 'Ah well, we'll make some more. Kabootar, my dove, get some more hot water, there's a good lad.'

Kabootar picked up the blackened kettle and scuttled out, with a lopsided grin at Nishonko. A small, irrepressible smile hovered on his normally serious face.

'Florence Nightingale, I presume.'

Debraj balled up the wet towel and chucked it at Nishonko who ducked. But then a roll of the ship brought them all crashing and sliding into each other, whooping and laughing, cracking up. Till Mohan Singh retched again and they all scrambled to get out of his way.

Next morning, it was as if the storm had never happened. The sun shone blithely from a blameless sky. The ocean was a postcard blue. The motley crew, their hair tousled, stiff with salt, faces shadowed by stubble, sat leaning against one of the bulkheads, bare-bodied, drinking tea, sharing smokes. They looked like castaways. Nishonko had his battered camera out and was taking pictures. Mohan Singh, none the worse for his turbulent night, hammed for the camera but Debraj covered his face.

'Mitro, my dear man, stop waving that thing in my face. Why do you want pictures of us in a state of semi-nudity?'

'Because you don't know it but we are creating history. And I…I'm the chronicler of the truth.'

Debraj rolled his eyes, felt his stubble. He rapped twice on the bulkhead to draw Kabootar's attention. Kabootar, squatting in the shade oiling his moustache, sat up instantly, alert.

'Kabootar ji, a little hot water and some soap and your knife, if you please?'

Kabootar jumped up. 'Ji, sahab.'

Nawaz, who had been watching all this with an ironic smile, sneered, 'Tu Kabootar ya laath saab ka kutta? Are you a pigeon or his lordship's pet dog?' There was a small uncomfortable silence, the camaraderie broken for a moment. Then Mohan Singh cleared his throat and spoke gruffly.

'Ah Ping says we should touch Singapore in another 10 days if we don't run into another bad one.'

'Can't wait to stand on solid ground,' muttered Nawaz.

'Can't wait to meet Netaji!' breathed Nishonko.

Debraj scratched his stubble. 'What's so special about this Netaji of yours? I mean, look at you Mohan Singh, you seem like a reasonable chap. Why are you fighting for this man?'

'I'm fighting for freedom and I like what Netaji promises.'

'Fair enough but what precisely does the man promise?'

All three spoke together, their voices quiet with conviction. 'He promises, "Give me your blood, and I'll give you freedom."'

'Whoa, all this talk of blood…kind of macabre, isn't it? Anyway, what's wrong with the Congress? Aren't they also fighting for freedom?'

'Nah! They're weak, ineffectual, dithering around, afraid to take action,' snorted Mohan Singh.

'Gandhi? Nehru? Surely, they…'

'Are fighting, are concerned. But they are both looking back, not ahead. They are silent about the revolution that is needed – the revolution which will destroy the old decaying feudal structure once and for all and build the new society, the new political structure that India needs.'

'Hmm. And Netaji is effective…why?'

'When the Quit India Movement began…you do know about the Quit India Movement?'

'Yes, Mitro…I'm not that illiterate.'

'Well, it put the wind up the British but they weren't *really* worried. They had the Indian sepoy. The good old Indian sepoy who was loyal first to his regiment, to the Army he belonged to. And they knew they could rely on the Indian sepoy to fight all their battles.'

'But now the British are shitting their togs,' chortled Mohan Singh. 'Netaji…he's ignited a storm. Done the impossible. He got into the Indian Civil Service and then rejected it. It was such a slap in the face for the British. And then he hoodwinked the British Government and escaped from house arrest from right under their noses. He's the only one who cocked a snook at the British Empire, who had the guts to go to Europe in the middle of a World War and get Britain's enemies to support our cause.'

'And now he's ready to raise the flag of independence abroad.'

'He's made the Indian soldier...Indian. He's given him a new identity. He told them, this is not *your* army, you belong to the *real Indian* Army. And we need you to free India.'

'Only Netaji has been able to rekindle the spirit of nationalism amongst the sepoys and weld them into an effective fighting force.'

'And the British are finding out they can't rely on their "Indian" Army any more. And without Indian soldiers, they can't hold India *and* Africa *and* Europe. It's the INA that has forced their hand.'

'So the British are pissing their pants.' Mohan Singh grinned.

Kabootar came back with the shaving stuff. As he began to work up a lather, he started to whistle a tune. The men smiled and started to clap. Then they all broke out in a soldiers' marching song:

Hup two three
When the lal gand see
Oh when they see
The mighty INA
Coming with Netaji
They will shake in their boots
They will shit in their togs
They will beg for their lives

They will die, the white dogs
When they see
Oh when they see
The INA marching
The INA charging
The INA winning
With Netaji!

The men catcalled and cheered as the song came to an end. There was a little silence.

'And what do you do in all this, Major?'

'I go behind enemy lines and help the soldiers make up their minds. I train them. You could help me.'

Nawaz snorted. 'Oh come on, how's a laath sahab like him, a blue blood, going to do dangerous work like that? Look at his hands... soft as a woman's.'

'Precisely. Because he's from a high-born family, he will have an advantage. He's been to England, he knows their ways. If he told the jawans why the English are not to be trusted, he can turn them. If he told them about Netaji, they will listen.'

'Oh, whoa, whoa, hold on to your knickers, I've never met the man, I don't understand what he's trying to do. And Nawaz is right, I wouldn't know how to go about it.'

'I could teach you.'

Nawaz shook his head in disgust and left, taking Mohan Singh with him.

Nishonko looked after them, his face grim. He turned to Debraj. 'Seriously, I could train...'

He stopped. Debraj was looking thunderstruck, his jaw slack, transfixed by something behind him. Nishonko turned. At the rail, stood an exotic Anglo-Burmese beauty, drying her long black hair in the sun. Nishonko turned back and shook his head at Debraj.

'Uh huh, that's strictly off limits. It's Ah Ping's...umm...niece, I think. You don't want to tangle with that.'

Debraj smiled, a boyish, feckless smile that had made many a woman's breath quicken.

'Quite the ladies' man, aren't you?' Nishonko murmured.

'Ah, women…one of life's great pleasures, yes? Well, alongside good Cubans. And the more, the merrier.' He shrugged expressively, stole another look.

Nishonko shook his head. 'One good woman…that's all a man needs.'

'Monogamy? Booooring. Think of it — each one so bewilderingly different, so uniquely captivating. How can one woman, in spite of her no doubt inestimable virtues, ever encompass such myriad delights? And even if you found that…*that* one, how would you know she's the one?

'Oh, you would.' Nishonko smiled to himself.

'Ah…what do we have here? A lady love, no less, for our stern revolutionary. Spill the beans, old chap.'

Nishonko looked at Debraj. He had never told anyone about her before but something about this laughing young man with his clear, grey eyes made him want to share.

'I've known her since childhood. We grew up together. It was an unspoken understanding between our parents that we would marry. They were friends but, even if they didn't want it, I've always known we would be together.'

'Is she beautiful? She must be — to make a man like you swear such loyalty.'

Nishonko pulled out a photograph. 'That's her…Jhilik.'

The picture was the blurred portrait of the girl in pigtails, looking up at the camera. Debraj peered at the picture, frowned.

'My apologies, Mitro but isn't she a tad young for you?'

Nishonko looked up, startled. A beat…then both burst out laughing.

'Where have you hidden her away?'

'Far away from your roving eyes.' He laughed. 'You…we will meet her — sooner than I hoped.'

But before he could say anything more, Debraj, who had kept stealing glances over his shoulder, stood up, wiping the foam from his face.

'Excuse me, old chap, can't keep the fair sex waiting. Terribly ungallant and all that.'

'Debraj, hold your horses.'

But his words fell on deaf ears. Debraj was already heading jauntily towards the woman.

While the junk sped southwards, helped along by fair winds, up north, in Tokyo, Hidaka Tojo, the Prime Minister of Japan, rose from offering prayers to his Shinto shrine. He had hoped for calm but the prospect of meeting Bose again filled him with a strange mixture of exhilaration and deep unease. The man's energy and passion were bracing but Bose was pushing him to sanction an immediate military thrust into India — with the INA fighting shoulder-to-shoulder with the Japanese Imperial Army. Preposterous idea. The INA was tiny, untried. Any way, India did not figure prominently on Tojo's list of priorities. And Bose's plan would not offer any immediate benefits to Japan. There had been some military setbacks for his own forces that he would rather meditate on. But Bose was an irresistible force, a tsunami of hope. Even the military elite in Tokyo had been affected by his rousing words, his certainty. His message was clear. Indians outside India were going to organise a fighting force, which would be powerful enough to attack the British army of occupation. When they did so, a revolution would break out, amongst the civilian population as well as the Indian soldiers of the British Indian Army. The British Government, thus attacked from both sides, would collapse and India would regain her liberty. Presumably. As he kneeled on the tatami mat, Tojo shook his head. He shouldn't have assured his support openly. It would be better to wait, to observe. But Bose was in a hurry. He was everywhere — holding press conferences. And then there were those broadcasts over Radio Tokyo, a whole series of them, rousing Indians all over South East Asia. The man certainly had nerve. He was pitting his will against vastly superior military forces. And yet he had the calm composure of the Buddha. Soon, they would meet again and who knew where the winds of war would carry them?

The winds of war had carried Brigadier Whyte all the way from the dank, subterranean corridors of MI6 and the SOE in London to the hubbub of Istanbul's Blue Mosque to this cool, green-shuttered room in Fort William in Calcutta on the trail of Bose. The original order to assassinate Bose, issued by the SOE in 1940, when he escaped to Europe, was still in play. He had come to this humid, crowded, smelly city to sniff out Bose's whereabouts. Something was brewing in South East Asia and Whyte's superiors needed him to get on top of it fast. He prowled up and down underneath the slow turning wooden bladed fan, pipe clenched in his teeth. He felt another one of his blinding headaches coming on — it was the heat of this blasted city but also because of the rage that knotted his jaw. Haley, the plainclothes policeman with the scar stood at stiff attention, his chin jutting out.

'How in the dickens did you manage to lose him? I thought you had him in the bag and ready to be milked! I ought to have you cashiered for this!'

'Yes, Sir.'

'It's beyond belief, the incompetence of you half-breeds!!'

'Sir, they had help.'

'Did they? And who might that be?'

'Debraj Mookerji, Sir Harry Mookerji's son.'

'Then haul his sorry ass here now.'

'He fled with them.'

'Brilliant! Where do you reckon they are headed?'

'It will be the Burmese border, Sir. Very porous, now that our forces are withdrawing from Burma.'

'I want to know everything about this Debraj character.'

'I have just the man for it, Sir. If I may.'

Haley hurried out. Whyte resumed pacing, his freckled forehead knotted. He pushed his fingers through his ginger hair, trying to find the epicentre of his headache. Haley came back, ushering in a small, balding man in an expensive but badly fitting suit. Grease ball, thought Whyte. The man had an unctuous smile and beringed fingers that wrung each other in a washing gesture.

'This is Mr. Goopta, Sir, a close business associate of Sir Harry.'

Goopta bowed to Whyte, looking down at the checkered marble floor, obeisant, obedient.

'So what do you know of this Debraj fella?' growled Whyte.

'Oh, a great deal, Sir, a great deal.'

The subject of their deliberations lolled in the shade of the topsail of the *Flying Eagle*, his bare body tanned a golden brown in the middle of the Andaman Sea. Beside him, his ample girth sprawled in a deckchair, sat Ah Ping. They had fishing lines out. The ship was becalmed, rolling gently, some 60 nautical miles off the coast of Malay. The Anglo Burmese beauty, incongruously named Felicity, leaned over Ah Ping's shoulder, fanning him with a palm leaf fan. Sweat beads shone on her upper lip and ran down the generous valley of her breasts. Debraj steadfastly focused on his line, giving it an occasional twitch. Ah Ping gave him a slow sideways look, then wagged one podgy finger at the girl. She straightened languidly, then walked away towards the back of the junk to fetch water. Both men watched her, squinting in the sun.

'Talking of women…' Ah Ping drawled.

'Were we?' said Debraj.

'Aren't we always?'

Debraj smiled.

'How do you think you should land one you desire avidly, Mr. Debraj?'

'Well, I would give them slack and let them run till they themselves want to be reeled in.'

'You do not believe in taming her forcefully, pulling her in against her will?'

'Oh, the fish never tastes the same that way.'

'Were we talking fishing?'

'Weren't we?'

There was a short companionable silence.

'She's not really your niece, is she?'

'And if she was, what would you do, Mr. Debraj?'

'Oh, I would never go for another man's catch. Just not in the code, dear chap.'

There was a pull, a shiver on Debraj's line. He sat up hurriedly. 'Ah, we have a nibble. Come on darling, take a bite, come to Papa.'

ACT III

DAYS OF TRAINING

'And then...then there was Aditi,' the old man whispers. He stops, takes a deep breath, rubs his eyes on the edge of his shawl. Is it just a sign of weakness, the incontinence of old age that explains the moistness in his eyes? He sits, looking at his hands, turning them gently. Then he sighs, a wind through tall grass.

'Aditi. Do you know what "Aditi" means in Sanskrit?'

He doesn't wait for a reply.

'It means freedom, limitless, boundless. Unbroken. She is the goddess of the sky, the mother of the sun, she is both the past and the future. Our Aditi...she too was the primal centre of all our gravitational fields. Aditi, pet name Jhilik. Quicksilver, restless, like a kaal baishakhi, that sudden summer storm, sweeping into your life and sending everything flying.'

The usual afternoon rain had swept through the city of Singapur, that day in July, washing the trees clean, leaving a rich, loamy fragrance clinging to the wet, heavy equatorial air. The bicycle wheels spun through the puddles, as she furiously pedalled down the cobbled road, narrowly missing a hawker's cart, a rickshaw, an army truck. In the distance, a voice could be heard, booming, speaking in Hindustani.

'I accept the baton with humility and pray that Khuda, the Almighty, will give me the necessary strength to discharge this duty. The British are losing ground everywhere in East Asia. The way lies open...to Calcutta and beyond. The day our brave band of warriors sets foot upon our homeland, the whole country will rise up in armed revolt.'

Her white kameez was mud spattered, the sash of the dupatta tied determinedly around her middle. Her face, with wide-spaced, kohl-lined eyes, had hectic spots of colour on the cheeks. The full mouth with a child's obstinate pout was set in a determined line. She wove through the traffic, almost falling, skidded and scrambled off, throwing the bicycle into a ditch. The voice was louder now.

'The weary eyes of millions of Indians are fixed on us here...on the Indian National Army, the army of independent India, the army of Azad Hind Fauj. Let us organise an army to fight the British.'

Her unruly hair had come undone, tumbling round her face, which blazed with excitement. She pushed her way through the throng, 60,000 strong, all craning to see, straining to hear the voice. Their faces were rapt, eyes shining. She managed to squeeze her way to the head of the crowd. And then, she saw him.

He stood, dressed in a simple khaki military uniform on the balcony of Singapur's green-domed municipal building, flanked by its majestic Corinthian columns. The springing tiger emblem adorned his shoulders. The INA flag hung behind him, its tricolour muted in the pale shafts of sunlight coming through the parting clouds. The sky was reflected in his glasses, turning them into two suns. It was Netaji! Tears welled up in her eyes as she heard him speak, at the rally in the Padang in Singapur that historic day.

'I can offer you nothing but hunger, thirst, privation, forced marches and death. If you join our movement, do so after great consideration, for ahead lies a grim fight, requiring great suffering and sacrifice. The motto of the INA, this great army of liberation is Ittehad, Itmad aur Qurbani — faith, unity and sacrifice. When we reach the Lal Quila of ancient Delhi and hold our victory parade there...'

Thunderous cheers interrupted him. He waited, a gentle smile, for the applause to die down, then continued.

'No one can say who amongst us will be there, who amongst us will live to see India free. Whether we live or die, that is of no consequence. The only thing that matters, the only truth is that India shall be free.

'For an enslaved people there can be no greater pride, no higher honour than to be the first soldier in the army of liberation. I will be with you in darkness and in sunshine, in sorrow and in joy, in suffering and in victory. If you follow me, in life and in death, as I am confident you will — I shall lead you to victory and freedom.'

Another roar of applause shook the air. The man beside her wept openly, pounding his closed fist on his chest.

'The British will never quit India until we throw them out. I call upon every true Indian to join hands with us. To the millions of Indians in South East Asia, I say let us have total mobilisation for a total war. Give me your blood and I will give you freedom. Will you come with us, will you walk this historic road with me?'

A roar rose from the crowd, scattering the birds over the Padang, sending them wheeling over the expanse of green that stretched from the steps of the city hall toward the sea.

'Chalo Delhi!!' thundered Netaji.

The crowd roared again.

'Jai Hind!' roared their leader.

'Jai Hind!' shouted Aditi, her eyes ablaze.

It was late when she reached the old colonial bungalow surrounded by palms on the quiet side street off Clemenceau. The streets had been packed, people beating drums, dancing to the Hindustani song composed by Mumtaz Hussain, with which Netaji had been welcomed a few days ago. She had wheeled her bicycle through small bonfires that had sprung up. Her mind was in a whirl. By the time she walked in through the big wooden door, her feet mud-stained, the amah had already gone around with the brass pot of smoking charcoal to drive off the mosquitoes.

'Where have you been, Jhilik? I was getting really worried about you!'

She turned. An older woman, her hair beginning to grey, stood in the small stone-flagged inner courtyard, her face creased with anxiety. Aditi ran up and hugged her.

'It was wonderful, Chhoto mashi. He was magnificent…the crowd was chanting "Asia ki Aftab" — Light of Asia — and they were singing and showering him with petals…'

'You went to the rally? I told you…'

'Oh Chhoto mashi, how could I not go? This is the most important moment of my life! We are standing at the crossroads of history!'

'Jhilik, you will not get involved in all this nonsense. I'm your aunt, your guardian. You will listen to me.'

'Too late, Chhoto mashi. I volunteered for the Rani Jhansi Regiment.' She did a little victory jig.

Chhoto mashi was incensed. 'Bose's preposterous idea of women fighting in the trenches!'

Aditi's mouth set in a hard line. 'Why is it preposterous? The real Rani of Jhansi took up arms against the British, died fighting on horseback. Netaji said she was like Joan of Arc. Netaji said she is a shining example of…'

'Netaji said! Netaji said! Listen to yourself, child! You are in some la la land. You…we lost your parents. I can't lose you. Don't you understand?'

'It is for *them* that I must join. Don't *you* understand? After what they did to Baba…'

'Precisely! Your Baba got caught in the wrong place at the wrong time. If he hadn't gone to North Calcutta that day during the rioting…'

'He went because he was a doctor. There were people trapped in that narrow alley, wounded, bleeding, women, children. He couldn't just let them die. If the police had let that ambulance out, he could have saved some lives. But…'

'But the British gunned him down instead. The British do that, Jhilik. And they won't hesitate to gun you down if you go against them. What do you know about war, child?'

'Don't you see, Chhoto mashi, I have to… I want to do the things he would have done. To save even one life. To heal. He would like that.'

Chhoto mashi stared at her, at the stubborn jaw, at the slightly trembling lips. She shook her head.

'He would like you to be safe, my child. Safe from harm.'

In a quicksilver change of mood, Aditi grinned and grabbed an umbrella from the hatstand. She held it like a parade ground rifle.

'I'll be safe. They'll train us. And I'm joining the medical arm.'

'With Geeta Rangarajan?'

'You know her?'

'She's an old friend.'

'Well, then you know, she's a doctor, like Baba. The Japanese were simply aghast at the idea of a woman's regiment. They refused to supply arms and ammunition. But she stuck it out and found barracks and equipment. Come on, Chhoto mashi, stop looking so glum. It will be such an adventure.'

'What will I do with you, you impossible child? Go and have a bath. Look at you, covered in mud.'

The *Flying Eagle* had berthed at the farthest end of the docks in Singapur. The Japanese had renamed Singapur Syonan-to, meaning 'Light of the South'. Signs of the occupation were on display everywhere. Flags with the red circle hung from official buildings. The dreaded Japanese military police stood at all important points, surly, suspicious, ready to smash anyone down with their gun butts, merely for failing to show the proper respect.

Nishonko, Nawaz and Mohan Singh, sunburnt, stubbled, in their rumpled, sea-worn clothes, were scrutinised by a couple of hard-faced Japanese soldiers. Only after Nishonko showed them some papers were they allowed to pass. As they pushed their way through crowds of stevedores, coolies and passengers, Nishonko looked around.

'Where's Debraj? Kabootar?'

Nawaz grimaced and pointed. In the distance, they saw Debraj bidding farewell to Felicity, bending low to kiss the tip of her fingers. Ah Ping stood by, watchful, his arms crossed over his belly. Kabootar loitered at the bottom of the gangplank, picking his teeth with his knife.

'I say we leave him behind,' Nawaz said, tetchy.

Nishonko put his fingers to his mouth and let off a piercing whistle. Debraj looked up, saw the gang and waved nonchalantly to them.

'Why would you want to introduce a man like that to Netaji, Major? You mark my words, you are going to regret it.'

'I most probably will but we can't just dump him. Give him a chance to prove himself. Netaji says every man has to be given the chance to show what he is made of.'

Debraj strolled up to them.

'Tally ho, gentlemen, Dame Fortune beckons. What now?'

Nishonko turned to the others.

'Carry on to the camp, get accommodation for all of us. I'm going to report to Netaji without delay. Debraj, you come with me.'

Debraj gave a mocking salute.

'Yes, Sir, Major, Sir.'

They stepped out onto the hot, humid street. As they wove through the traffic in a rickshaw, both Debraj and he drank in the sights, sounds and smells of this nascent city, two young men on the brink of adventure and discovery.

The Chinese orderly shouted, 'Make way, make way,' as he pushed the stretcher with a bleeding accident victim through the rush of nurses and patients, down the corridor of the Singapur General Hospital. He swore as he almost crashed into a bunch of young women standing nervously at the side, Aditi, amongst them. An older nurse hurriedly shooed them into a room. She looked sharply at one of the girls who had turned pale.

'Pull yourself together. You're in the Rani Jhansi Regiment now. We don't faint at the sight of a little blood. Anyone with any nursing experience?'

Aditi raised her hand.

'My father was a doctor, I used to help him in the clinic with emergencies.'

'Is he here…in Singapur? We could use trained doctors.'

'He passed away, Ma'am.'

'Well, we've all lost somebody, haven't we, to this terrible war.'

Another girl, dark-eyed, ebony skinned, with a lithe dancer's body, her black hair in a plait, raised her hand.

'Meenakshi Menon, Ma'am. I worked as a nurse at Divisional Hospital in KL.'

'Good. You two kit up. Today looks like it's going to be murder.'

In a cramped storeroom, surrounded by mops and cardboard boxes, Meenakshi and Aditi changed into the uniforms — white slacks and shirts. Aditi adjusted the cloth cap and bashed it a bit to set it at a fetching angle. They looked at each other and giggled.

'Well, it's better than I'd expected.'

Meenakshi nodded. 'Yes but a skirt would have been prettier. Not that you don't look pretty.'

'You too. I'm Aditi Sen.'

'Call me Meena.'

The senior nurse stuck her head round the door and barked at them. 'If you've finished admiring yourselves, we need the bedpans in the surgical ward to be collected.'

They looked at each other, rolled their eyes and rushed out.

'Some more of your excellent coffee, Gaffar?' Bose said gently. 'Planning campaigns is thirsty work.'

Gaffar Khan, the bearded aide de camp, hurried up to clear the coffee cups from the table around which the company was gathered in the Meyer Road bungalow. The large sprawling house was the de facto nerve centre of the freedom movement. The late afternoon sun flooded into the spacious living room, through tall windows opening out to a tropical garden, falling on the man who stood there, slowly cleaning his glasses. With his round, fair face, the high sloping forehead, his serene expression and the kind, slightly myopic eyes, he looked more like a philosopher or someone's favourite uncle than a military commander.

'Netaji! 18,000 have enlisted!' Ahmed Hassan was grinning like a boy as he walked in.

There was a burst of cheering. Two senior officers in INA uniform thumped the table, setting the cups rattling.

'It's your speeches, Sir — at the Cathay Theatre, and later, with the INA soldiers, and of course, your stirring words at the Padang.'

'They were singing in the streets till dawn.' An elegant lady in khaki, her hair cropped short, spoke in a soft voice.

'Even those who were unconvinced, the fence sitters, they have all been swept off their feet. Thousands are joining the Indian Independence League, pledging their support,' Hassan continued.

Netaji nodded, lit up a cigarette. 'Good. Our work has begun.'

'It will be uphill work, Sir. The Japanese top brass aren't too keen,' Colonel Gokhale demurred.

'Well, they've heard us out. Now we wait,' Lieutenant Commander Giani said.

'And while we wait, we work. Systems, structure, logistics, supply lines — everything has to be built. By the time we enter India, we must have an administrative machinery in place. Otherwise, there will be chaos.'

'And we will have to start building an air force, a navy.'

'For starters, all those recruits will need military training,' Giani chipped in.

Netaji smiled. 'Absolutely. Along with their political education. The men must be clear why we are fighting this battle. The power of the idea, the power of what it symbolises — that's what will keep them going when the going gets rough.'

'Funds, we need funds.' Ahmed added, drily. 'Fighting a war requires deep pockets. Once we get moving, we don't want to depend on Japanese handouts.'

'Correct. We will need our own bank. Can you get on to that, Professor Murthy?' Netaji told the grey-haired man, sitting in one of the armchairs, his head buried in a book.

Gaffar whispered something to Netaji. He turned with evident delight. 'Where is he? Bring him, bring him.'

Gaffar returned with Nishonko.

'Nishonko, dear boy, it's been so long. Let me look at you.'

Nishonko touched his mentor's feet.

'They told me you were expected. What happened in Calcutta?'

'Well, we had a little run in with Lalbazar and had to skip town in a hurry. This is...' But before he could introduce Debraj, Netaji turned away to the others.

'Friends, let me introduce Nishonko Mitro, one of INA's true warriors. Faithful to a fault, a great man to have on your side when the chips are down.'

'I believe you have single-handedly gone behind the lines and turned hundreds of jawans to our cause. They call you Nishachar?' The lady smiled at him warmly.

Nishonko flushed with embarrassed pride. 'Just doing my duty, Ma'am.'

Netaji took him by the arm. 'Look at him. This is the face of the India we want to create. Idealistic, young, committed, disciplined. Nishonko, you've heard of Colonel Gokhale and Lieutenant Colonel Giani. This is Professor Murthy, Economics Chair at Presidency. And this dapper Oxonian here tucking into the scones is Dr. Hassan. And last but not least, Geeta Rangarajan. She's doing a magnificent job with the medical arm of the Rani Jhansi Regiment.' He noticed

Debraj, waiting patiently near the door, not in the least bit overawed as he took in his surroundings.

'And who is your young friend?'

'Sorry, Sir, this is Debraj Mookerji. He was… I recruited…'

Debraj stuck out his hand. 'Delighted to make your acquaintance, Sir. I've heard so much about you.'

Netaji shook it warmly. 'Most of it rather unflattering, I presume. They don't approve of me back there, do they?'

'Well, yes, they are all rather nervous about your little sojourn in Germany — you know, meeting up with old Hitler and Mussolini and all that. Fascist is just one of the politer words being bandied about.'

Nishonko turned red. 'Debraj! I'm sorry, Sir…I thought I would bring him…'

Netaji laughed, shaking his head. 'No, let him be. It's very refreshing to hear the honest truth. And what else do they say about me, young Debraj?'

'Oh, that you…' He paused, then with a self-deprecating smile, 'Do you mind if I wade into some of that delightful coffee there? Our journey here was singularly bereft of any such civilised pleasures.'

'Oh, I'm so sorry, how rude of me not to offer. Gaffar, please, could you? Milk? Sugar?'

As Gaffar Khan poured, Debraj helped himself to some muffins. Nishonko politely declined, furious with him. Netaji waited until Debraj had had his first sip.

'You were saying…?'

'Yes, well they also say that Germany and Japan make strange bedfellows for a man who talks about freedom and equality and self-rule.'

'Well, you know what they also say — that hoary chestnut — my enemy's enemy is my friend. Anybody who can help us throw off the British yoke is our ally. Taking their help — it's like a pole vaulter using the pole to clear the bar.'

Debraj took his coffee and sat down in one of the armchairs. Even in his stained, rumpled clothes, his unkempt hair, the stubble, he had an unconscious grace, an air of self-possession and entitlement.

'And wouldn't you be just exchanging one imperial bully for another? The Brits may be terrible but they're angels compared to the Japs. Their atrocities in China positively churn the stomach. The stories about the Death Railway boggle the mind. And what happens if the Japs don't win, which may well happen, given they are rather stretched across far too many fronts?'

'Perspicacious…and what is your background, young man?'

'Oh, I'm sorry, how remiss of me. I'm Sir Harry Mookerji's son and heir, lately from Cambridge.'

Netaji chuckled. 'Oh, that's my alma mater too. That's two of us against you, Ahmed. And what did you major in?'

'Law, Sir.'

'Just what this band of merry men needs. We have economists, writers, philosophers, soldiers, doctors — eminent men fighting for an eminent cause.'

'Not the rah rah jingoistic mob they make you out to be?'

'I hope not. Ahmed, you think we are jingoistic?'

Hassan brushed crumbs off the front of his shirt, wiped his mouth. 'Well, I believe jingoism refers to excessive belief in the superiority of one's own country over all others — a rather extreme form of nationalism. And by that very count, I would beg to point out that it is the British who are jingoistic, not us. I mean, we don't even have a nation, do we? And it is they who believe, in the name of their empire, that they have the god-given right to rule over us poor heathens.'

'Well put, Ahmed, as always. So, young man, do they have any nice things to say about us? Or are we beyond redemption?'

'My apologies, Sir, if I have been a tad impolite. Of course, they also say that you are very good at speeches, that you have the gift of the gab.'

'Do they also say that he is the only man who has a vision…a plan…about what a truly free India should be?' Nishonko interjected, sharply.

'That it will be truly equal, truly secular?' Hassan said with a smile.

'That he…'

Netaji shushed them. 'Gentlemen, please…let this remarkable young man make up his own mind. Debraj, Nishonko has invited you to join our little adventure, yes? So why don't you spend a little time with us and see how things go? Nishonko, you will organise things?'

Debraj shrugged. 'Absolutely, Sir. Free bird, you know? Footloose and fancy free.' He stood, bowed elaborately, almost mockingly. Netaji bowed back.

'And try to keep an open mind, young man. Maybe I can earn your trust one of these days. If the wily, cunning and infinitely resourceful British have failed to corrupt me, maybe the Japanese will not have much luck either.'

Debraj nodded, still with a mocking smile. He ruffled Nishonko's hair as he turned to leave the room. 'Coming, Mitro?'

Nishonko bristled. 'Wait outside for me.'

Netaji called out to Debraj's departing back. 'And just to put your mind at ease, young man, the Japanese actually need us as much as we need them. They just don't know it. And when we enter India, the government will be run only by Indians. We have their assurance. And even if they lose the war, as long as we have our little revolution, Britain at least won't be in a position to lord it over India any more — or help the other colonial masters to do so. Makes sense?'

Debraj waved cheerfully and stepped out, without answering, without turning. Netaji drew Nishonko aside.

'Tell me what happened. How did you find him?'

Debraj walked out into the garden. Alone, he looked around, then drew in a deep breath. 'What the hell are you doing here, mate?' he muttered to himself. He felt around in his pockets, then dug out a stub of his favourite Cuban and a wad of crumpled notes, the last of the payment for the Rolls. 'Damn it, this is not going to last forever. Maybe I should have just carried on with Ah Ping to Shanghai.' He looked around, a quiet despair clouding his face. A fountain burbled quietly in the garden. A peacock strutted at the far end, incongruous, bobbing its head. He looked at it, then smiled his devil-may-care smile. He took off his shoes, rolled up his trousers and stepped onto the grass. The peacock gave him a disdainful look, then minced away. He walked up to the fountain, got in. He splashed water on his face, his hair, wiggled his bare toes in the cool water. He sat and leaned back to feel the weight of the sunlight on his closed lids.

Debraj and Nishonko stood in the fumes left behind by the truck which had dropped them at the gates of INA Training Centre No 4. The journey had been a sullen one, Nishonko still angry with Debraj and showing his displeasure by shutting him out. Debraj had made a few efforts at conversation, then given up. He had nodded off, bushed from the long sea journey. He stood now, his heart sinking as he looked at the entrance. *'Abandon hope, all ye who enter here,'* he thought, a long-forgotten lesson surfacing in his sleep-addled mind. The Centre was basically a large muddy field on the banks of a smallish river near the Malayan border. It was a bleak place, deeply pitted by cart and jeep tracks, hotter and more humid than Bengal. A few Malayan-style bamboo huts, which served as the headquarters, were surrounded by a sea of drab tents where the recruits lived. A row of crappers, basic structures of bamboo and sackcloth, steamed in the heat on one side, the stench hazardous for anyone standing downwind. Civilians — clerks, labourers, merchants, shopkeepers, men who were not from military backgrounds, not known to be particularly martial, were dispatched here for training alongside professional soldiers. The place was teeming, choice curses shouted out in stentorian voices, hundreds of men in ragged ranks, being pushed to the extremes of physical endurance. Nishonko went into the quartermaster's tent, leaving Debraj alone.

'Look what the cat dragged in.'

Debraj turned. His fellow passengers, in clean uniforms, were strolling towards him. Debraj waved at them, immensely glad to see familiar faces. Kabootar ran up to him, beaming, glad to have him back.

'What are you doing here?' Nawaz demanded.

'Waiting for Mitro.'

'That's Major Mitro to you.'

'At ease, old chap. I'm not part of your army…yet.'

'And you never will be. If I had my way…'

'What would you do?'

'I'd make a man out of you,' Nawaz said, his lip curling.

Debraj gave him a slow, level look, then smiled his mocking smile. 'Go ahead, here's your chance. Where do I sign up?'

Nawaz's eyes narrowed. He jerked his thumb towards a queue of men in front of the quartermaster's tent, waiting to enlist. Debraj looked at the motley group. For a moment, he looked undecided, lost. Then he squared his shoulders and stepped up. Mohan Singh slapped his back and gave a bellow of a laugh.

'What's amusing you so much?' It was Nishonko. When he heard that Debraj was ready to enlist, a reluctant smile broke out.

'Sign up in the officer's category. The training is more intense but I have a feeling you have what it takes.'

Nawaz sniffed. 'Major, he'll never last the course. He's going to be under Pandey ji.' All of them broke into loud guffaws. Debraj looked on bemused, aware that the joke was somehow on him.

Debraj crouched behind the bushes, trying to get his breath back. God, they were still only halfway through the damn obstacle course. He was winded but not as jelly-kneed as some of the others, thanks to all that tennis he had played at the Club on pound-a-game bets. If his mates could see him now — head to toe plastered with mud and elbows and knees raw from crawling in a rice field for the last hour — they would probably die laughing. He took off his helmet and rubbed the quarter inch of hair on his head. The slick, pomaded style carefully created by the master barber of Bright and McIver Gentlemen's Hairdressers was gone. And what would Sir Harry think of his son, heir to the Mookerji millions, polished in the hallowed halls of Britain's premier universities, now holding a captured British Enfield rifle, rubbing shoulders in cramped trenches with sworn enemies of Britain, fighting the very British he revered. And Ma? She might pour herself another pink gin and introduce mud streaks as the next fashionable thing at her theme parties. The extreme incongruity of that made Debraj laugh out loud. A squelch of mud and a thin young man from his unit surfaced next to him, panting and wheezing through mud-clogged nostrils. They grimaced at each other.

'Move before Pandey ji catches you!'

He lunged out of cover. And there, right in front was Pandey ji, the dreaded drill sergeant, glaring in his direction.

Pandey ji was a veteran of the British Indian Army, taken prisoner when Singapur fell to the Japanese. Indian POWs with military experience joining the INA were assigned to train raw recruits who had flocked to Bose's call, who were high in spirits but low on fitness. Most armies took about a year to train a soldier. But Netaji did not have the luxury of time. So seasoned veterans like Pandey ji had condensed the initiation into a couple of months, making it an agonising crash course in the discipline of war — a whirlwind of jungle drills, obstacle courses, cross country hikes, shooting practice, radio communication, handling machine guns, setting up tents, digging trenches, cleaning latrines — it was endless! He pushed them relentlessly, over the brink, demanding more of them than they thought they could give. The recruits all hated him but were slowly beginning to feel a little proud of themselves. In a perverse way, Debraj too was actually beginning to enjoy the grind, the punishing physical labour, the steady strengthening of his body and polishing of his skills. During a break, he stared at his palms. He remembered Nawaz's jibe about his hands on the boat. They were like leather now. The blisters had hardened, the nails chipped. They looked like the hands of the sharecroppers who worked the sugarcane fields in the family estate in Chandernagore. But before he could wallow in nostalgia, another roared command from Pandey ji jolted him to his feet.

Pandey ji was Debraj's special nemesis. The drill sergeant, a dairy farmer from the Hindi heartland, had a deep contempt for the privileged. And in Pandey ji's jaundiced eyes, Debraj epitomised everything loathsome of that despised breed. He assigned the dirtiest jobs to him. He even had a pool going on how soon Debraj would quit.

Of all the weapons they trained in, the bayonet sickened Debraj the most.

'Crouch, thrust, rip his stomach out, yell HAMLAA! Louder! If you can't beat him, scare him to death.' Pandey ji demonstrated in vivid detail as they charged straw dummies.

'Won't the bayonet stick in his guts?' Debraj asked.

'Yes, pretty boy. When it gets entangled in the intestines, blow off a shot and knock your rifle loose. Why are you looking so green, milkface?'

Over those first excruciating weeks of training, there was no sign of Nishonko. He was busy with something or the other in Singapur.

Debraj was dying to get a leave pass and visit him for a weekend. Singapur had been a city famous for its nightlife and no-questions-asked attitude. Even when he was in England, he'd heard of the raunchy entertainment available across the river at the nightclubs and dives. The city was full of women, the spectacularly beautiful Anglo-Burmese, the petite Straits Chinese, Thai stunners...he was itching, quite literally, to make their acquaintance. But each time he applied for leave, it was rejected, and they assigned him night sentry duty. Instead of lying back with a flute of champagne and taking in the latest cabaret, he spent the night standing in full kit and rifle in the pouring rain, shouting challenges at shadows. He half suspected that the suggestion for this 'special' treatment came from Nishonko himself and, coincidentally, the night duties stopped when he stopped asking for leave. Where the hell was the man?

Chhoto mashi, sitting in the verandah beside the tiny courtyard, was immersed in the morning newspapers over a steaming cup of Darjeeling. Aditi, looking tired and grubby in her uniform, came dragging her feet down the verandah. She bent and kissed the top of her aunt's head.

'Morning, Choto mashi.'

'Morning, my child. Tea?'

'Chhoto mashi, why is your front door open all the time? Anyone can walk in and rob you blind.'

'There's very little to rob in this house, my dear. It's perfectly safe.'

Aditi flopped down into the cushioned softness of the armchair and flung her shoes off, wiggling her toes. She leaned back with a deep breath, letting the calm of the early morning courtyard, the soft warble of tropical birds wash over her. 'Ohhh, I really need a bath.'

'Rough night?'

'Hmmm, a knife wound, a young Chinese boy with a third-degree burn. The Chinese patients are so much easier to deal with. They do what they are told and take the pain without any fuss. But the drama the Indians create! And they ask the most intimate questions — are you married, why aren't you married. Then they try to set you up with some moronic nephew.'

'They're just trying to help, Aditi. And you are getting on, you know.'

'God, Chhoto mashi, don't start. I'm pooped.' Her voice wavered.

'Jhilik, you alright?'

'Subedar Surat Singh… I don't think he'll make it.' Sudden tears welled up in her wide eyes. 'He's just a boy…keeps asking for his mother in his delirium.'

'It's hard, isn't it — when you lose one of them? Specially the young cut down in their prime.' She paused, her face shadowed. 'And this…this is just the beginning. When the big march starts…'

'But it will all be worth it, won't it? At the end, we will be free. Losing Ma, Baba…it will all mean something.' She rubbed her eyes fiercely, pulling herself together.

'You…you're all I have left, Jhilik. I couldn't bear to lose you also.'

Aditi jumped up, hugged her aunt. 'Oh, come on, stop being such a mope. I'm almost 18, I can take care of myself. Please, stop fretting. We're going to win! Netaji will take us back to India and we'll march upon Delhi!'

Chhoto mashi tried to hold her a little longer but she was off, half marching, half dancing down the verandah, singing, 'Kadam Kadam Badaye Ja' — Step by step, Forward let's march, the INA's marching song. She shouted out, 'Amah, can you draw some water?'

Steam rose from the old claw-toothed tub in the large stone-flagged bathroom as the wizened amah poured another flagon of hot water in. The early morning light fell pale on the honey brown slope of Aditi's shoulders, as she slid off the white cotton robe. She touched the water, testing its warmth, then slid in. She leaned back, soaking in the heat, softly humming a love song by Tagore under her breath. The steam beaded her skin, turned the tendrils of hair on her bare, unprotected nape into black rivulets. Hers was a tender, still tentative beauty, waiting. She leaned out, soft lapping of waves, and picked up a hand mirror. She stared back at herself, gravely, her eyes dilated with the awareness of being on the brink of things…everything lambent with possibility. A knock on the door. She started, her reverie broken, suddenly shy. The amah poked her head round the door. 'Baby, Mausi calling. Guest man here see you.'

In the verandah, a khitmatgar, the manservant of the house, brought in a tray with mint tea.

'Do you like mint tea? Or would you prefer Darjeeling?' Chhoto mashi looked up at Nishonko. 'It's been such a long time.'

'Anything will do. Lovely house.' Nishonko sat down, looking around. He was dressed in mufti, his hair combed neatly, his face composed but his eyes shining, unable to contain his anticipation.

'How are things with you, Mrs. Swaminathan?'

'Oh, as good as they can be. I've been looking after my late husband's spice business well enough but it's Jhilik who has brought back life into this lonely house.'

'She is lucky to have you...after her parents...'

'How are your parents?'

'Still behind bars.'

'So many lives shattered. Do you really think it's going to end soon?'

'It will end...before the next monsoon. One way or another, we will know. Know who we really are.'

'Nishonko da!'

She came flying down the verandah, her hair damp, face glowing, kohl put on hurriedly. The mynah in the courtyard cooed. Nishonko stood up slowly.

'There she is!' Chhoto mashi said.

He shook his head, overwhelmed. His words stumbled out in a confused rush. 'Jhilik, m...my god, you're...it's b...been years.'

She laughed, an easy friendly laugh, unselfconscious. She was happy to see him. 'That's Sister Aditi to you now — of the Rani Jhansi Brigade. We're being trained for the frontlines, for the field hospitals.' Her voice had that remembered huskiness, as if it would break any moment. His heart squeezed.

Chhoto mashi left discreetly, murmuring an excuse.

'Oh, so much has happened and it's so good to see you, Nishonko da.'

'You don't need to call me that.'

'But you've always been Nishonko da...my friend and elder brother.'

'Yes, of course, but that was when we were growing up. But you're no longer a child.'

'Shall I call you…Nishachar? The Phantom, isn't that what they call you?' Her eyes danced, teasing him.

'How do you know that?'

'Oh, I've heard tales of your deeds, how you have brought men to the INA.'

'So they speak well of your…friend?'

'My best friend. I feel so puffed with pride.'

'I'm glad that I bring you pleasure.'

His intense gaze made her swallow. She looked away, moved to the edge of the courtyard, to the frangipani that grew there.

'How long are you in Singapur?

'I don't know…waiting for orders.' A beat. 'Can we — would you like to go out, have something to eat?'

'Oh no, there's too much happening at the hospital, so many….'

'I'm sure you can make time. You can't be all that critical to the hospital.' His tone was a little stiff, a thin line appearing between his eyebrows.

'I am. The senior sister thinks…'

'Make the time, Jhilik. Who knows when we will meet again.'

Her face fell, the light dying out of her eyes. 'Yes, Nishonko da, sorry.'

'Shall I call for you? At the hospital gates? Tomorrow? Five?'

She nodded mutely at every question, agreeing to everything, chastened.

The first crack in Pandey ji's armour came the day of the ravine crossing. It had been another hot, wet, miserable day. The slush was up to their knees, the leeches hungry, the flies a menace. Pandey ji had set a punishing pace, whipping them on with the choicest curses in his extensive vocabulary. For Debraj, he had an extra treat — carrying the unit's rations. The load made Debraj unsteady on the jungle trail, his boots slipping and sliding. When they came to the ravine, Debraj made the mistake of stopping to let the other men pass.

'Hold, hold. Who told you to stop, mama's boy?'

'Sorry, Sergeant, I just…'

'Sorry-worry, no use. Get on that bridge, you shit-eating apology for a soldier.'

Debraj looked at the 'bridge' — a frayed, rope and jungle vine woven contraption, swaying gently above the foaming rapids and sharp-toothed rocks waiting a hundred feet below. He grimaced, his stomach hollow. An image appeared behind his clenched lids. High up on a gulmohur tree, in the garden at home, the slender branch stretching out, Debi stranded at the other end, crying, unable to climb down. Khogen da telling him gently, 'Don't look down, keep your eyes on Debi and tell her not to feel afraid. Keep telling her that. And remember, the branch is like a nice broad road, like the road to school.'

Debraj opened his eyes, a small smile at the memory. He grabbed the rope handle, took a deep breath and looking straight ahead, walked steadily across. A small cheer went up as he reached the other end, stilled by the glowering look on Pandey ji's face as he ordered the next recruit across. The man started across, his face white. Debraj gratefully eased the backpack from his aching shoulders. The other recruit was by now halfway across. And then he froze.

Pandey ji roared, 'Get your sorry butt across, you son of a gadha.'

But the man stood motionless, dangling precariously. Then Debraj stepped in. Talking companionably, asking him which village he came from, the name of his daughter, he kept up a steady prattle, all the while coaxing the man to keep moving. As he reached the other end, Debraj grabbed him and hauled him up unceremoniously. He looked across the bridge. The next recruit, a bulky Mussalman, was also a bit hesitant.

'Arre, Khan sahab, what did you have for breakfast? Surely you are not afraid of this piddly bridge?'

'I'll tell you what I had for breakfast. I had your mother... eat my Hyderabadi seekh kabab,' said Khan, stepping onto the ropeway.

Debraj and the men roared with laughter. Pandey ji nodded slowly, a flicker of grudging respect in his eyes.

But the real change came from the day on the shooting range. Evening was falling as the recruits were finishing off their rifle training on an open field near the river. But as Pandey ji came driving up the rutted track, he heard a cheer go off. His forehead beetled. The recruits were crowding around someone, their practice forgotten. As he shoved his way through them, he found Nawaz on the ground, taking careful aim. Nawaz had a reputation as a marksman. His target was pock-marked with bullet holes, closely clustered round the centre with four already in the bull's eye. In the fading light, he drew, fired, hit the bull's eye again. Another lusty cheer went up.

'Excuse me, Sergeant, may I?' Debraj stepped up from behind Pandey ji, examining his rifle, a Lee Enfield 303. He looked unsure, hesitant.

Kabootar called out from the crowd. 'So who's going to wager on Debraj saab? Odds of 20 to one, best of ten shots. Step up, step up.'

The men eagerly called out their bets. Nawaz was a sure shot. He had hit five out of ten already. This guy was fumbling with the gun, the butt held too high. This would be a walkover. Pandey ji knew he should interrupt the contest but the temptation to teach Debraj a salutary lesson was too strong. He hung back, a grim smile creasing his leathery cheeks. Debraj squinted down the barrel. The light was dull but the white circle of the target stood out. He pulled the trigger, the shot went wide, not even remotely close to the target. Boos and cheers went up.

'One down, nine to go. Any more bets?' Kabootar waved money around. '20 to 1, going once, going…'

There was a clamour of voices, hands reaching out. Debraj settled the stock once more into the crook of his shoulder, drew breath, squeezed. A flat crack echoed out over the trees. This time, he managed to hit the outer rim of the target.

'Arre wah wah, at least he hit something, boys.' Guffaws, ribald jibes were directed at the unflappable Kabootar.

'Two down, eight to go!' The evening light was dropping fast, the target hard to see. Debraj glanced at Kabootar. The tiniest of smiles crinkled his eyes. Kabootar gave an imperceptible nod. Debraj took a fresh sighting, fired. And wonder of wonders, yes, it was a bull's eye. A few groans, a couple of boos broke out.

'A fluke, a fluke!' a voice called out.

'One out of ten, seven to go,' intoned Kabootar.

Debraj's eyes were dancing now, the devil-may-care grin was back. He drew, fired, didn't wait, smoothly pulling back, aiming, firing, not even waiting to see the result, shooting now in a continuous rhythm.

The overlapping echoes of the shots punctuated the air, sending the nesting birds flying up in dark flurries against the reddening sky. Then there was silence. Debraj stood up slowly. The smell of cordite hung in the air. A few of the men slowly walked out to the target. There was a muttering as they peered, counted, recounted. Then one of them called out, 'Eight.'

Kabootar called out, 'Eight out of ten. Debraj *saab* wins, 20 to one.'

Pandey ji pulled Debraj's arm roughly, ordered him to step aside. 'How in hell did you manage that?'

'I'm sorry, just pulling everyone's legs. Kabootar, all bets are off. Gentlemen, you can keep your money.'

Kabootar groaned, shook his head, walked off disappointed while the rest marvelled at what they had witnessed.

'Sorry Pandey ji, sorry Nawaz but I've had a fair bit of practice. Shikar trips as a kid, picked up my first gun then. And I trained as a cadet at Cambridge, represented the alma mater at the All England Rifle Championships…'

'Sorry? No sorry. Do you know what this means?' Pandey ji chortled, slapping his thigh. 'Our Company now has its own "marksman" with 90 per cent accuracy. That's worth a ten-rupee increment for me…and one step closer to my next promotion.'

From that day on, he changed. But Nawaz? Nawaz couldn't forgive him for showing him up so publicly. It rankled deeply, intensifying that instinctive distrust that had surfaced that night in Chinatown. Now, it began to fester.

Nishonko knew nothing of Debraj's trials and triumphs as he drove his jeep up to the gate of the Singapur General Hospital that evening. He parked, looked at his watch. Five minutes to go. He drummed his fingers on the wheel, impatient. Then, on impulse, he ran across the road, dodging through honking cars. An old lady stood at the street corner, selling flowers. As he dithered about what to buy, she looked up from her prayer beads. With a toothless grin, she asked, 'Old love or new?'

He paused, smiled. 'A bit of both.'

'Oh, you are lucky. Then you would do well to mix. Maybe, this bunch of red carnations. And the virginal white of this baby's breath?' She cackled and made up a pretty little bouquet. He looked across the road, worried she would come and not find him. He quickly paid the old crone and ran back to the jeep. The minutes ticked by. He paced around now, unable to sit. What if there was some other gate, unknown to him? What if she had forgotten the date? He looked at his watch again, a little angry now. And then, there she was, pushing her bicycle tiredly, walking slowly, her shoulders slumped. His heart did a funny lurch. Even at the end of a shift, even in uniform, she could make him breathless, dizzy.

'Jhilik!'

She looked up, took a moment to focus. Up close, her eyes were red rimmed.

'You're late.' He kicked himself immediately for coming out with that first, that accusing tone. He wished he could take it back.

'I'm sorry, I just...' Her voice trailed off. She looked down at the ground, a chastised child.

'You forgot, didn't you? I've been... I thought you weren't coming.'

'No, I... it's just that...'

He held up the bouquet, his hands awkward, unused to this gentle art of wooing. 'I brought you flowers.'

She looked at them, at him. Then her face crumpled, the full mouth trembling, her eyes filling up.

He was flummoxed. 'What the...'

'Surat Singh...Subedar Singh...he just...right there, in my arms... he died.' She broke down, her shoulders shaking. 'I couldn't save him, why couldn't I save him?'

He had no clue who she was talking about or the depth of her loss. He reached out, patted her shoulder, a small, almost formal gesture, looking around a little embarrassed. The crowds flowing in and out of the hospital gate gave them curious looks, this beautiful, grieving girl and the intense-looking young man. But grief was to be expected in front of a hospital, was it not? Hopes died, loved ones were lost. She stood, knuckling her eyes, her body unconsciously leaning towards him, wanting to be held, to be comforted, to be shielded, even for a moment, from the horror of war and the implacability of death. But Nishonko, poor Nishonko, growing up learning to hide his emotions, to be self contained, Nishonko was too inhibited, or maybe too young, too untried, to give her shelter. He pulled away, the gap between them widening. She swayed back, regained her balance.

'Come on, Jhilik, pull yourself together. You can't be so weak.'

She wiped her nose with the back of her sleeve, like a child. 'Sorry, Nishonko da.' She started to wheel her bike through the crowds. He looked at her, at the useless bouquet in his hand, chucked it on the seat of the jeep and hurried after her.

They walked by the riverside, down the deserted towpath, she lost in thought, he giving her an occasional glance. Once, he opened his mouth but the words to break through the intangible wall would not come. Finally, she broke the silence, her voice hoarse. 'What are your plans?'

'We're off in a couple of weeks, I think. The Malay border. The Chindits are kicking up trouble, so...'

'Will it really happen, Nishonko da? Will we really go back... one day?'

'Jhilik, I promise you, we will. If it's the last thing I do, I will take you back. And then we can all pick up the pieces of our lives. We...you could go back to Shantiniketan. Would you like that?'

She shivered. The wind was coming off the water. 'No. There are too many ghosts, too many memories there. I want to learn medicine...like Baba...I want to save lives, make a difference...'

'And what about...marriage?' he murmured, astonished at himself that he could actually speak the word.

She laughed.

He looked at her, his heart shrinking. Was she laughing at him? 'You find that amusing?'

'Oh, Nishonko da, you don't have to worry about me. I'm no longer that little girl you had to protect. Marriage can wait. There's so much I still want to do. Travel, see the world...'

'It's my duty to worry about you.' It came out pompous.

'God, Nishonko da, you're so serious...'

'And you, Jhilik, you are so...so...' he gritted his teeth in frustration. She dropped the bike and started to prance around him, laughing, a quicksilver change of mood, eyes flashing.

'*So*...? Come on, tell me. I'm *so* whimsical...*so* feather brained... *so* idiotic...*so*...'

Nishonko, unversed in the ways of women, was taken aback by the sudden counter-attack. 'No… I meant…'

She carried on in a rush, whirling round and round. '*So* harum scarum, *so* higgledy-piggledy, *so* aagdoom baagdoom…'

His hand shot out, grabbed her arm. 'Jhilik! Stop it! You're making a scene.'

She stopped mid whirl, panting, staring at him, her eyes wide. He glared back at her.

'Nishonko da, you're hurting me.'

He dropped his hand, turned away. His fingers, the force with which he had held her, had left red weals on the soft skin of her arm. She rubbed it, grimacing. Then, lips set mutinously, she picked up her bicycle. He turned away, looking out over the river, the barges passing, their sirens hooting.

'Jhilik, please…please don't change. You are the only thing left that I can hold onto — my only centre of gravity, the only bit of my past I can still call my own. Do you understand? Jhilik?'

There was no answer. He turned but she was already in the distance, riding away.

He called out, 'Jhilik, I'm sorry.' But the shriek of gulls wheeling on the wind, drowned out the words.

The closest Pandey ji came to saying sorry was the night he invited Debraj to his tent to share his bottle of rum. Debraj, weaned on scotch and champagnes, could barely swallow the fiery stuff with its distinct after-taste of turpentine. But he did it gamely, his face straight. Pandey ji knocked back a couple of quick shots, drumming his chest with shouts of 'Hari Om'. Another couple of shots later, with his nose turning distinctly red, Pandey ji became mellow. Turning down the Hindi film music crackling out of a radio sitting on his campaign trunk, he sat back with a contented sigh.

'You never behaved like an officer candidate. Never asked for any favours. I like that.'

'Would you have ridden me less hard if you knew?'

Pandey ji let out a belly laugh, and a copious burp. 'Not a chance. I would have made it even harder for you!' Then his face sobered. 'Do you know why I'm so hard on the men?'

Debraj waited. He would be told, whether he wanted to hear it or not. Pandey ji was in that mood.

'What brought you into this army, my boy?'

'My good friend Nishonko. Major Mitro. And a completely fortuitous sequence of events.'

'Ah, you use such big big words. Me, I'm a simple soldier. Been one now for 30 years. Been all over the world with the British Army. I've fought the Afghan tribes in the Hindu Kush, charged German trenches in France in World War I and gone up against the Japanese in Singapore. I must have been in 50 units and seen hundreds of commanders. Never seen anything like this one. He shows unbounded love and the men return it with fierce devotion. He is not just some general. He's a true leader...he's Netaji. So when I train men for him, I make sure they are bloody good.'

'I hear he gives great speeches.'

Pandey ji grinned. 'Even I was suspicious of men who go buk buk, talk too much. But this one is different. This army is different.'

He dwelt on that for a moment.

'Instead of trained men, battle-hardened men, what do we have? Children! Beardless youth with silly dreams in their eyes, who get sozzled on a bottle of beer. Never thought they would shape up, never thought they had it in them. But I've seen these kids charge British machine guns with nothing more than a rifle in their hands, getting cut to ribbons. I've seen these chhokras, these wet-behind-the-ears idiots, delirious with joy at being given the honour of planting the flag on a hill.'

He cleared his throat, his eyes suspiciously red. Debraj refilled their glasses, bracing himself for the explosion in his throat.

'Cheers to the chhokras, Pandey ji!'

Pandey ji was right. Although they hadn't seen any combat yet, his entire unit seemed to be high on something. They were a mixed bunch — farmers, clerks, students, drifters. There was an anaemic Tamil Brahmin who jumped at loud sounds, a Bengali poet who always seemed to be humming under his breath, a strapping Sikh who couldn't move out of his own way. The unit had its gamblers, drunks, loudmouths and its lovers. But they had one thing in common...what the sergeants called 'josh'. It was, in their opinion, the essential quality of a warrior. But was it enough to take on the British with their tanks and heavy guns? No way, thought Debraj. He was beginning to doubt the soundness and, maybe, even the sanity of this bunch of high-spirited youngsters. About their enigmatic leader, he was still undecided. Their brief encounter had whetted his appetite but he wasn't sure, in spite of what Pandey ji had shared so emotionally, what Netaji could actually deliver. He was to find out the next day.

The klaxon went off early, summoning them to the parade ground. As Debraj stepped out pulling on his fatigues, brushing off the caked dried mud, a hand fell on his shoulder. He turned. To his delight, it was Nishonko, a wry smile on his lean face.

'Mitro! Where the hell have you been?'

'Here and there. You're looking good.'

'What brings you here?'

'You'll see. Now get your sorry butt onto the parade ground.'

There were a thousand men, both soldiers and officers, lined up, eyes snapping with excitement, necks craned, an animated buzz in the air.

Debraj walked up to Pandey ji. 'What's up?'

'He's coming.' Pandey ji turned, stretched himself to his full height. Then, in his most powerful voice, the voice that had inspired terror in thousands of men across the world, he roared, 'Company... attenhut!'

A thousand pair of boots hit the gravel in a resounding crash, a thunderclap of sound that made the hair on Debraj's neck suddenly stand.

A convoy of jeeps, short Willys, drove in through the camp gates. The man who stepped out of the leading jeep must have been cramped from the journey, for he stamped his feet as he alighted, making a small gravelly sound in the uncanny silence hanging over the ground. Debraj recognised the high forehead and finely drawn mouth. It was Netaji. He was in uniform — tunic, jodhpurs, boots polished to a high gloss, heavy cross belt. On another man, it may have seemed a bit theatrical. But somehow, Netaji carried it off with aplomb. Drums started to beat out a tattoo, deep tympani, rattatatat snare. A trumpet sounded, its raw brass note thin and tenuous in the morning air. The rest of the band fell in with a jangle of brass and cymbals and swung into a brisk martial beat. Debraj found his feet tapping to the piper's tune. Netaji got on to the makeshift stage. He smiled at them, a schoolboy-like delight spreading across his face. When he spoke, it was in simple and direct Hindustani, a mixture of Hindi and Urdu.

'A few days ago, I had the honour to be in Burma to take part in the independence celebrations. The last Mughal emperor, Bahadur Shah, was exiled to Burma in 1858 after a show trial. We Indians cherish the memory of Bahadur Shah because under his sacred flag, freedom-loving Hindus, Muslims and Sikhs fought side by side in a confrontation that English historians called the Sepoy Mutiny but which we Indians call the first war of independence. As the Emperor used to say, "So long as ghazis, heroic warriors, are imbued with the spirit of faith/The sword of Hindustan will reach London's throne."

'London's throne has kept us in chains for centuries. The British have disarmed our people since 1857. The right to bear arms has been denied us. They insult us by making us carry wooden guns, toys. They deny us our basic rights — the right to assemble, the right to speech, the right to breathe free air, the right to feed our children.'

Netaji's face turned somber.

'Right now, as we speak, Bengal is reeling under a terrible man-made famine created by the British administration. It is their moral responsibility to ensure two square meals a day for all its subjects. Instead, they are deliberately decimating Bengal. More than three million have already died. Three million. Women, children, babies, the old. Dying in the villages, at train stations, on the streets and the pavements of the great city of Calcutta, like dogs, scrabbling for one fistful of rice to feed a family of eight.'

Debraj remembered the spectral figures seen by firelight that night in Calcutta. The first flickerings of rage were lit.

'The calamity could have been avoided easily. It started in March this year but it has not even been acknowledged in Parliament. The

British are only interested in feeding their own soldiers. They have been warned repeatedly that if supplies are not shipped to Bengal, untold thousands more will die. But they have neither sought nor accepted any aid to bring relief.'

He cleared his throat.

'I offered help. Rangoon Radio broadcast my proposal to send 100,000 tons of rice from Burma to Bengal from a nearby port. I made no pre-conditions. Just a humanitarian offer that could harm nobody, only save innocent lives. But the British nervously suppressed this offer. They just censored the news. And do you know what Mr. Churchill said? He said he felt no sympathy for Indians whom he regarded as a beastly people.'

The soldiers stirred, their anger flowing like a hot wind through a field of rice, shaking the ranks.

'And this policy of denial doesn't end there. They have confiscated boats, bicycles, bullock carts — any transport within 50 miles of the coast, denying people even the means to find food. They call the Japs barbaric. What is this but the planned, deliberate murder of a whole people? Our people. Are we to stand by and do nothing? Tell me, are we to follow the path of ahimsha as yet another child dies, without even having the strength to whimper, because his mother's milk has dried up, like the rest of her, turning her into a living skeleton?'

His voice rang out now.

'The weapon of violent non-cooperation has been used since 1919. The time has now come to meet force with force. The enemy has put us to the sword. He must therefore be fought with the sword. The sword of the warrior is as necessary for justice and righteousness as the holiness of the saint. Who is this warrior?'

A vast silence hung over the ground. The river gurgled as the tide swept in, the trees sighed.

'Who are these warriors?' he asked again, softer.

A single voice replied from somewhere within the serried ranks.

'Main hoon. I am.'

Another voice, then another, called out, like echoes of gunfire.

'Yes, you, the warriors of the Azad Hind Fauj. There are close to half a million Indian soldiers in the British Indian Army. They are our brothers. And they help the British to keep India in chains.

But when they see *you*, the REAL Indian Army, their eyes will open. When they see *you* take up arms for our freedom, their hearts will no longer remain in bondage.

'It is time we Indians fought for ourselves. It is time we shed our blood for our freedom. Because, believe me, without shedding blood, neither we, nor our future generations, will value independence. Without shedding blood, we will consider freedom a handout, not an inalienable right. Without shedding blood, we will always be slaves — now to them and later to the forces of chaos. The hour has struck and every patriotic Indian must advance towards the field of battle. Only when the blood of freedom-loving Indians begins to flow will India attain her freedom. Blood is our rite of passage. Give me your blood! I will give you FREEDOM!'

A roar from the men, a thousand voices raised together in pledging their allegiance to this man. He had asked them to do the impossible but had done the impossible himself first. He himself had made the greatest sacrifice first before asking them to give up anything. Even Pandey ji, hard-bitten veteran that he was, had forgotten his parade ground restraint and was clapping deliriously. Debraj felt his hair stand and he shivered, though the day was becoming warm. He suddenly had a prescience, a feeling in the marrow of his being, that this was where his life had been heading all along.

'JAI HIND!' their leader roared.

'JAI HIND!' the recruits roared back.

'Are you Indian?' Bose challenged them.

'YES!' they yelled.

'Are you men?'

'YES!'

'Then this is where you belong! Anybody who is a real Indian and a real MAN'— he paused to let them contemplate that one for a second — 'will be with us on the front lines. History may say that we are in the wrong...that violence is wrong. Maybe. But men who do violence to us, to our wives and daughters, our sisters and mothers, to our villages and towns, should not they be stopped now, with violence if need be? You can wait a month, a year, a decade but 300 years of sitting on our hands? Are we sheep?'

A growl, like cannons going off far away, rolled out of the throats of a thousand men.

'Our symbol.' He pointed to the INA insignia of the springing tiger on the flag behind him.

'Do you know what it stands for, this fierce tiger?'

He didn't wait for an answer.

'It is to remind us of Tipu Sultan's gallant resistance against the British. Tell me, does the tiger worry about the opinion of sheep?! Does the tiger behave like a kitten, go miaow?'

A roar of laughter. By now, he had them completely.

'Field Marshal Terauchi, Commander of Japanese forces in South East Asia, has said he wants the INA's role to be limited to field propaganda units. I have told him any liberation of India secured through Japanese sacrifices is worse than slavery. I have insisted that the INA will be in the vanguard of the offensive into India. He has agreed on one condition — that we deploy one regiment as a test of efficiency and morale before he sends the rest of INA into action. The First Division of the INA is made up of three regiments, a total of 10,000 great warriors. From them, the best soldiers will be selected to form a special guerrilla regiment, which will be sent into Burma. We have been training all of you rigorously. How many of you are ready to be amongst them?'

Another roar, like rolling thunder! Debraj found himself yelling with the rest. He saw Nishonko, taking pictures with his trusted camera, a smile on his saturnine face.

'The time is coming. We will meet again soon.'

Netaji nodded at Pandey ji who bellowed out, 'Company, dismissed!'

But the men stood, no one willing to leave. Netaji walked amongst them, greeting one here, clapping the shoulder of another, asking a question of a third. Debraj waited in line. When Netaji, accompanied by the senior commanders and Nishonko, came up to him, he smiled warmly.

'Debraj! So you decided to join our merry band.'

'You remember me, Sir.'

'You are hard to forget, young man.'

'Well, that little speech of yours was rather unforgettable, if I may be so bold, Sir.' Debraj let out a long breath. 'So, I think I'll trot along and we'll see what this whole fuss is all about. And I must confess, I'm rather intrigued to see how it all ends.'

Netaji smiled. 'Aren't we all?'

In the mess, afterwards, Netaji ate with the men. They were all there, all communities sharing their meal. The British had segregated them, separating the so-called martial races from the rest. Netaji would have none of that. Looking at Debraj laughing with Kabootar and some of the young chhokras at another table, Netaji turned to Nishonko.

'So how is young Debraj there shaping up?'

Pandey ji spoke up. 'Little impulsive but good officer material.'

'And thinks on his feet, the way he got us out of that police trap, Sir,' Nishonko added, proudly.

'Excellent shot. Ninety per cent accurate,' Pandey ji said proprietorially, as if he was personally responsible for Debraj's prowess on the range.

'Hmmm, a man of many parts,' Netaji murmured.

Nawaz growled from the bottom of the table, 'And secrets too.'

'You don't like him, yes?'

Nawaz shrugged. 'Oh, he's just a little too slick for my liking. I mean, what do we really know about him, Sir? He's too...British. When it comes to the crunch, where will his loyalties really lie?'

'We will see, we will see.'

The jeep's tyres swished through the puddles reflecting the blue neon-lit sign of the former Charles Club, now named the Pegu Club after its more glamorous counterpart in Rangoon. A once vibrant cosmopolitan city with a carefree nightlife and live music and exotic food, Singapur had been transformed by the Japanese occupation into a wary city, a city under curfew, stifled by harsh rules. Anything Western was anathema to the Japanese. To remove the influence of the city's former imperial masters, the Japanese had set up schools, forcing people to learn their language. Every morning, children had to stand facing the direction of Japan and sing the Japanese National Anthem. The local Chinese and English newspapers carried very little local news. Most of what was reported was the Japanese version of the war and pro-Japanese speeches. Tuning in to foreign broadcasting stations was done at great risk. You could be severely punished or even killed if you were caught. In cinemas, only Japanese movies and propaganda films were shown, making fun of the British. Going to the cinema had its own dangers. The Japanese police could suddenly appear and take away young men to work on the Death Railway. However, compared to the Chinese who bore the brunt of the Japanese crackdown, things were much easier for the Indian and Malay population, who were allowed certain liberties. Some places of entertainment, especially those frequented by Japanese officers, were allowed to stay open. The tony Pegu was a rage with the city's privileged.

Debraj got off, shot his cuffs. The cuff links were gold, emerald studded, horseshoe shaped, Debi's gift, held on for luck. He was freshly bathed, his hair slicked, his body lean and hard in a rather natty suit.

'Ah, the sweet perfume of civilisation!'

Nishonko stuck his head out. 'We can't afford this, Deb.'

'Yes, we can. I hocked everything I had for one glorious weekend on the town. You promised me, Mitro.'

'You are such a reprobate.'

Inside, they were greeted by a scattering of laughter, the tinkle of glass; soft lights gave everything a sheen, the silken patina of privilege. Debraj took in a deep breath. It was heady stuff after the weeks of deprivation. This was his world, this was where he belonged. He boogied up to the bar, rapped on it twice to get the bartender's attention. Nishonko, a little awkward, lugging his battered camera, trailed behind.

'Two Pegus, please!' Debraj laughed at his own joke, swivelling around to check out the room, his nostrils flaring with anticipation.

'No, Deb, not for me.'

'Nonsense, the night's young, we're single and available, we're off to fight for freedom, the ladies are waiting to give us a hero's send-off…'

'No, really, Netaji doesn't like all this.'

'Bollocks. You chaps have put him on some blasted pedestal. He's not some tight-ass, holier than thou plaster saint. He's very real, rooted.'

'So you think you know him? You just met him. I've known him for ages. He respects discipline, self control. He's...'

'Not a policeman. Not a dictator. He actually wants us to be free, in the truest sense.'

He stopped. A thick-set Japanese man, in his mid-thirties probably, drinking alone at the end of the bar, smiled at him and tipped his glass in a toast.

'You agree? See, Mitro, he agrees.'

Debraj walked over to the Japanese man and shook his hand.

'Good evening. Debraj Mookerji, at your service. You're the first live Jap I've had the pleasure to meet.'

'Harada Saito, of His Divine Majesty's Imperial Army.' He bowed from the waist. 'You are right, your leader is indeed a very complex, intriguing man.'

Nishonko jumped up, startled. He had heard of Saito. They said he would be the man to command the Japanese forces when they actually went into battle. He was the youngest Brigadier in the Japanese Army, with a fearsome reputation as a unconventional tactician. He saluted smartly but Saito seemed more preoccupied with Debraj. As the two sat down at the long mahogany bar, Nishonko hung back, quietly shooting. As the evening wore on, the Pegus flowed and the laughter rang out. Soon, they became the centre of a bunch of revellers. Nishonko found himself further and further down the bar, on the fringes of the group. Debraj had an Eurasian girl hanging on to each of his arms. One of them whispered something into his ear. Debraj listened, then shook his finger at her.

'Naughty, naughty. The last time, I did that, I got into a whole lot of trouble. But I don't mind carrying on to a new watering hole. Who's game?'

A chorus of suggestions, contradictions, pouts and agreements followed. Generous tips were tossed on to the polished bar as they swept off. Debraj, halfway down the room, turned to look for Nishonko. Nishonko was sitting hunched, looking at them, his expression guarded. Debraj waved to him.

'Come on, what are you waiting for?'

Nishonko shook his head, waved him away. Debraj paused, then strode back and, to Nishonko's surprise, hugged him.

'Catch you up.'

Then he ran back and with a whoop, twirled one of the girls around and danced her out. Nishonko looked around the room, got up. He looked at his watch. It was too late to go to Aditi's house. He sighed, then tapped the bar twice for a drink.

'Ouch!'

The light seared his eyes. He squinched them shut. He tried to sit up but his head felt like a wet bag of fertiliser. He sagged back, drifted off. After a while, maybe a few seconds or a few hours, he came to. He tried to open his eyes. This time, it was a tiny bit easier. He looked around slowly, keeping his movements to a bare minimum. He was sprawled on a sofa in someone's house...a beautiful, old traditional house, a profusion of exotic blossoms arranged on sills, large windows leading out to a garden. He had not a clue where he was. He stood up very carefully. The house was quiet, no one around.

'Hello? Anyone?'

Round a corner, he came upon a spartan room with tatami mats, sliding doors leading to a minimalistic bathroom. Debraj caught sight of himself in the mirror. Dishevelled hair, shirt undone, mauve blue shadows under the eyes. He drank thirstily from the tap. Bits of the evening started to come back. They had gone to Raffles, then gambling in one of the junks parked mid river. Things were hazy after that; somewhere there had been a dwarf lady, two naked girls in a pillow fight and someone had fallen into the river. How he came to be here, he had not the foggiest. Then through the windows, he saw a figure out on the patio. It was Saito — in a white robe, moving calmly, fluidly through a series of movements, using a bamboo staff, like a spear, like a fan, like an oar, in a beautifully controlled rhythm of movement and stasis. Mesmerised, Debraj sank down on a large stone bench. The cool touch of the rough stone, the sighing of the jacaranda trees ringing the garden, the perfume of some hidden flower — a great sense of peace descended. Saito finished, bowed to an imaginary opponent, then came towards him.

'Tea?'

Saito had clapped his hands. A manservant had appeared silently from nowhere and led Debraj to a hot tub. Naked, the steam swirling around him, Debraj had felt the wet heat cleansing him of all thought and toxins. Now Saito kneeled in front of him and poured the tea in a simple ceremony, the ritual imbued with a profound courtesy. Debraj, in a clean white robe, his wet hair slicked back, felt reborn. He accepted the cup with an awkward bow and sipped. The unfamiliar flavour, with its clarity, redolent of earth and leaf, so different from the muddy brown over sweetened British cuppa he had grown up with, was startling.

'One hears such horror stories about your people, your barbarism and cruelty, what you did in Shanghai, the rumours about the Death Railway. And yet there's so much beauty in your ways.'

'Debraj san, is that not true of all people? Darkness and light, side by side, violence and compassion, goodness and evil? Each of us is capable of killing, yet each worthy of redemption.'

'I don't know. The stupid mistakes, the regrets, the wrong turns? Can one really be redeemed? Like last night, dumping my friend Mitro? Unforgivable.'

'A serious man but very young. I get the feeling he has had a rather one-dimensional life.

'Well, I don't really know much — in fact, anything — about him. He's rather tight-lipped about his past.'

'Maybe, he doesn't know who to trust?'

'I do hope he can trust me. I have become rather fond of the solemn, intense young Major.' He chortled. 'He is so disapproving of my flighty ways. Lost his temper with me at our meeting with Netaji.'

'Netaji. And do you trust him?'

'Do you?'

Saito sipped his tea, his face impassive. 'No one man has elicited such conflicting emotions. Britain has declared him Public Enemy number 1. And yet he has done extraordinary things. His escape to Germany right from under their very noses. His incredible 90-day journey to South East Asia. And now, he's building an army to take them on. He is a visionary…'

'Or a madman.'

'And yet you have decided to throw in your lot with him? Make history with him?'

'It's history…if you win.'

'Your Netaji and our General Mataguchi have planned well. The time is right. Now it is up to the Sun Goddess.'

'Sorry, I'm not much into leaving things to goddesses to sort out.'

'That is my faith. What do you believe in? Why do you think you have come to Singapur?'

'Oh, long story. It will take many pegus to tell the tale.'

'Debraj san, why this city, why now, at this crossroads of time, when Netaji is getting ready to create a new age? What is it you are meant to do?'

'Well, put that way, the only reason I go anywhere is to have a cracking good time. And this city, in spite of all your curfews, has very naughty ways that I thoroughly approve of.'

'Even you don't believe that, my young friend. This façade of yours…'

'Ah Brigadier, it's too early in the morning for such deep stuff. Let's plan my last afternoon of freedom, shall we?'

'Of course.' Saito bowed politely, his impassive face hiding any disappointment he may have felt.

The sun is high overhead. It is past noon. The fog has burned off, turning the sky a pale blue. In the tea shop, Balai da stands up. 'This is taking much longer than I thought. I have to go. Diabetic, no. Need to take my shots.' He stretches, gets up. Sudipto looks at his watch, exclaims.

'Damn it, my boss is going to kill me.' He pulls out his cell phone.

'Sir, yes, Sudipto, I'll turn it in by the evening. Positive. But I'm onto some thing new…something quite interesting. May I come by later and brief you?' He listens, nods. The old man looks at him.

'This story…you think people will want to hear it?'

'I find it fascinating. Netaji is a personal hero.'

'Do you know what Richard Tottenham said when Netaji offered rice during the famine? He said, "We are of course particularly anxious to discredit Bose in every possible way." Such a huge empire and so scared of one man.'

Sudipto laughs. 'Well, naturally. Who else got together nearly a million Indians from Malay, another 60,000 from Thailand and close to 800,000 in Burma? In just months? They say that if the monsoons had not come early, he would have reached Delhi for sure.'

The old man slaps the table, sending the Irani glasses tinkling. 'Rubbish. You've lapped up that old British horseshit, just like everyone else. You think a master strategist like Netaji, and a son of the soil wouldn't take the monsoons into his calculations? Utter bilge. The monsoons weren't the cause of the defeat.' He pauses, his face stricken. Then, once more he collects himself. 'Where was I? Ah yes, in the jungles of Malay. That's where they sent us first to engage the enemy in advance of the Imphal campaign.'

A monkey, its teeth bared in panic, went scampering and swinging across the jungle canopy, raising the alarm. Other monkeys joined in, their chattering spreading in circles, sharp, scolding, peremptory. But no hunter or big cat appeared. Slowly, the sound ebbed out, rippling away. The forest clearing stood empty, baking in the humid tropical heat of post monsoon. Then, a soft birdcall echoed out. Another answered. The leaves of a giant fern trembled and from under its dark shadows, a figure stepped out, in camouflage, a chimera amongst the dappled greenery. Face painted, hair matted in mud, only his round, googly eyes moving, he swept the clearing with darting looks, frozen in position. Then he raised a closed fist and gestured sharply. Other shadowy figures in camouflage stepped into the clearing. The figure walked over to the leader of the group and saluted.

'Major Mitro, there's a British camp just east of the ridge…six miles tops.'

Nishonko nodded. 'Good, Captain Nawaz. Get to a vantage point and just observe. Don't confront any one.'

'What are we looking for?' Debraj, also in camouflage, chewed on a stalk of grass.

'The unhappy ones,' Nishonko answered. 'The ones without their heart in it, the ones lagging behind.'

Nawaz spat on the forest floor. 'There were Gurkhas. Don't approach them. They're mercenaries.'

Nishonko nodded. 'Identify and isolate the vulnerable ones. Find out their habits, when they take a shit, when they go on guard duty, what they had for lunch. Approach them in secret. Persuade them, make them believe. Then make them into your eyes and ears. They will give you leads to other guys.'

'Oh, I thought we were going to fight. No charging the enemy lines, with blood-curdling yells of HAMLAA?' Debraj scoffed.

Nawaz gave him a stony look. 'You think it's going to be cushy?'

Loud rustling in the undergrowth made them all turn, guns cocked. But it was just Mohan Singh, all large feet and big boots.

'Mohan Singh! How many times do I have to tell you to use the call signal!'

'Sorry, sorry, Major Sir.'

'What did you get?'

'There's an encampment south of the river...part of the Madras Regiment.'

'Okay, let's split up. Lieutenant Mookerji, Lance Naik Kabootar Singh, go with Captain Nawaz. Mohan Singh, Corporal Shikdar, with me.'

'Yes, Sir.'

'And under no circumstances get caught. They will torture you and wring out the last bit of intel from you, then shoot you in the head for treason.'

The British encampment sprawled on the riverside looked peaceful from the ridge where Debraj and Nawaz lay hugging the ground, hidden in the wild oleanders. Nawaz scanned the camp through field glasses. Debraj fidgeted beside him.

'What do you see? Can you make out anything?'

'Quiet, Lieutenant.'

'Let me have a look.'

Nawaz lowered the glasses, then turned slowly to Debraj. 'Let me have a look...??'

'Sorry. Let me have a look, Sir!'

'Keep your voice down, Mookerji.'

'Damn it, we're too far away, Captain. Let me go in.'

'No, you heard the Major, wait and watch.'

He went back to keeping tabs on the movements below. Suddenly, he stiffened. 'What the...!' He brought down his glasses, snapped his head around. Kabootar crouched near the tree line where they had left him but Debraj had disappeared. Nawaz brought his glasses up again. He could see him clearly…the crouching figure snaking its way down the slope. It was Debraj, heading towards the camp on his own. 'Behenchod, fucker, wait till I get my hands on you, bastard!'

Through the field glasses, he watched Debraj crawl through the long grass up to the camp perimeter. He expected an alarm to go off any second. The open ground just before the fence would be the problem. Nawaz held his breath but saw Debraj was timing his moves to the sentries' movements. Slither, slither, then hugging a rock or a clump of grass, then another almost imperceptible movement and finally he was at a gap in the rusting sag of barbed wire. The sentry was mere yards away but facing the other side. Debraj suddenly stood up, turned around and unbuttoned himself and started to pee. Nawaz gasped at the effrontery of it. Debraj shook himself off, stepped in nonchalantly through the gap and made his way casually towards a tent, buttoning himself up. He peeked in, then stepped in.

Nawaz let out his breath. This was what set Nawaz's teeth on edge about the INA. A career military man, he hated the lack of proper military discipline, the rank amauteurism. Netaji would take in anyone who wanted to join his army. Hierarchy, protocol — all this had taken a backseat in the rush to get ready for the campaign. He grunted and trained his field glasses on the tent that Debraj had entered. A British officer stepped out of the tent. It took the tense Nawaz a few seconds to realise that the man was Debraj.

'What the hell?'

Debraj was transformed. Cleaned of the mud and camouflage and kitted out in an officer's uniform, he blended in perfectly as he walked through the lines, his confident bearing and looks fooling even a keen observer.

Back on the ridge, Kabootar smiled, tipped his helmet over his eyes and went to sleep. Nawaz, his eyes glued to the reckless Debraj, saw him bump into an Indian soldier, as a tired platoon returning from a patrol, marched past him. Debraj swivelled around arrogantly, and snarled something into the man's face. Nawaz swore under his breath. Why the hell was the idiot drawing attention to himself? Bloody show-off!

In the camp, Debraj shouted in his best clipped accent, 'Lazy, good for nothing badmash, watch your step, bloody monkey!'

His eyes swept haughtily over the platoon. Most of the Indian soldiers stoically looked into blank space. But in the eyes of two of them, he spotted the flare of anger, the set jaw of rebellion. Debraj's lips curled in a smile.

'You two, fall out. Platoon, carry on.'

The two soldiers stepped out grimly. Debraj led them into a nearby tent.

Nawaz waited, drumming his fingers. After about 20 minutes, all three stepped out, nodded at each other, split up. Debraj looked towards the ridge, and snapped off an ironic salute.

'The orders were to wait and watch. Which part of wait and watch didn't you understand, Mookerji?' Nawaz was seething.

'Sir, you waited and watched. I followed the rest of the orders.' Debraj looked straight ahead.

'We'll see what Major Mitro has to say about that.'

'It worked. Isn't that what counts?'

'You could have jepoardised the whole mission.'

'So, shoot me, Sir.'

That night, back at camp, Nawaz made his displeasure evident.

'He's impossible. Went against direct orders. Completely untrustworthy.'

Nishonko nodded but hid a small smile. In spite of being exasperated by Debraj, he felt a sense of kinship, a secret admiration for Debraj's rebellious ways.

'I understand. But remember what Netaji says — that every man has one gift, and a leader must train himself to recognise it. This is Debraj's gift — his flair for being unpredictable, for doing the unexpected. Nurture that Nawaz, use it. And he did get back good intel on their troop movements.'

'Unpredictable? I would call it unreliable. I sincerely hope you don't regret this gift one day.'

Nawaz strode off to join the rest of the men, his back stiff.

Later, after they had eaten their rations, Nishonko and Debraj sat at the campfire, smoking. Kabootar squatted in the shadows, whittling the usual piece of wood.

'Go easy on Captain Hussein, Deb. He's a decent soldier and there's much you can learn from him.'

'Come on, Nishonko, the man's a...stick in the mud. Everything by rote. No creativity, no taking chances. We aren't going to win this war by playing by the rules.'

'Still, take it easy. There's nothing to be gained by making an enemy of him, is there?'

They were interrupted by the dark curly-haired Corporal who had accompanied Nishonko on his sortie, with mugs of hot, sweet tea.

'You're Debraj Mookerji, aren't you? You may not remember me but I used to come to your Durga Pujo, the festival of the Goddess, as a kid. My father worked for you...Khogen Shikdar.'

'My god, Khogen da...you're Neelu, aren't you?'

'Yes, Sir.'

'He was speaking about you...the night I... How is he? I didn't get a chance to say goodbye.'

'So you haven't heard?'

Debraj tensed. 'Heard what?'

'Debi, your...'

'What about her? Spill it man!'

'She ran away from home. Baba helped her...'

'She what? Is she well?'

'Don't know. I haven't had news from home a long time. The police are after him...but they have just disappeared.'

'So she decided to go through with it,' Debraj muttered to himself. He didn't know whether to be happy or mad. She was a plucky thing, a strong girl in spite of all that cloistered upbringing. She would land on her feet. Khogen da loved her like his own. She would be safe, she would be safe.

'And here you are fighting for azadi also. What a strange place this world is, right, Mitro?'

Nishonko looked up; he had been lost in thought, not paying attention to their exchange. 'Yes, whatever.'

Debraj nodded at Neelu, who, after a glance at the brooding Nishonko, saluted and left.

'What ails you, Mitro, my friend? You have been moping like a sick monkey. Come on, tell Papa.'

'It's…it's just…we have to win, Deb. I promised someone we would win. And I'm not going to stop until we are free. I'm ready to die for it…as long as she doesn't stop believing in me.'

'She? Is it after all only an affair of the heart that troubles you? The friend you spoke about? The great Major Mitro, laid low by a mere girl?'

'Deb, you won't understand…'

'Oh, I wouldn't be so sure. What is it? She's in love with someone else? No? Good. You are in love with someone else? No? Good. You want to marry her, yes?

'She may not…'

'Have you asked her? Told her, "I worship you, I adore you, please be mine."'

'Don't be silly. Women don't fall for drivel like that.'

'Listen to a veteran. Buy a ring, go down on your knees and tell her. Don't beat about the bush. Frontal assault, Major…works sometimes.'

'You think so?'

'I know so.'

The bell was tolling for the vespers in the tiny church near Chhoto mashi's house as Aditi walked her bicycle wearily past its little green-painted iron gate. The heavy oak doors stood ajar, the deep sound of the organ floating out, a counterpoint to the shrill chattering of birds returning home. She felt a need this evening for the serenity of this place with its cool stone-flagged floors, the smell of guttering candles clinging to the air, the smooth silken feel of the wooden pews polished by generations of kneeling penitents and seekers of solace. She was born a Hindu but had studied in Christian schools. Her parents had been open-hearted, celebrating all faiths equally in their little white-painted house on the outskirts of Bolpur. She suddenly felt a rush of longing, of loss, wash over her, shaking her to the bones. When would she actually get over their deaths, she wondered. She entered the church, purified herself at the font, knelt. Tears pricked the back of her eyes.

He had left for Calcutta that fateful day, without saying goodbye. He had taken the early morning train, and she had not woken up when he had placed his hand on her curly mop of hair. She was used to these absences and knew he would be back in a few days. She looked forward to those trips for there would always be some little thing he would bring back, infinitely precious, a bird's feather or a blue glass bottle or a little terra cotta lamp on his return. There was no news for a couple of days, and then word came that her father had gone missing during another riot in Calcutta. There had been some shooting, some people had got hurt and her father, kind, careless man, above all a good doctor, had gone rushing in with an ambulance to give succour. But the police had blocked the narrow lane leading to the quadrangle and when he had tried to back the ambulance out, they had apparently warned him. But no one seemed to know exactly when it had all gone wrong. When the news came, her mother had gone white as a feather. She had looked like someone had slapped her hard. They had hunted far and wide, from one hospital to another but when his body was finally discovered, black and bloated, the eyes blanketed by flies under a pile of corpses in the Metiaburiz morgue, her mother had turned away and let out a small whimper. It was the last audible sound that Aditi would hear from her. She had covered her face with her sari, denying the awful truth and never spoken another word. Aditi, still a child, had not been able to break through that terrible wall of unspeaking, unspeakable grief. She had felt abandoned, somehow at fault. The magic circle of her parents' love for each other, for her, was closed to her from that day on. Her mother had withdrawn behind a veil, and that morning, when Aditi had found her, 'Ma, wake up, Ma,' she had said over and over again, her mother had been curled up on the floor of the bathroom, clutching her father's jacket to her like a blanket, the bottles of sleeping pills scattered like forgotten toys. Why had she done the unthinkable? Why had she not wanted to stay alive for her child?

Along with the incomprehension had come guilt. The young girl just couldn't get it out of her bruised mind that she should have done something to save her parents. Maybe, she should have stopped her father from going that day to Calcutta. Maybe, she should have stood guard over her mother through those dark nights of silence. But she had fallen asleep and her mother had slipped away.

Sitting in the pew, her fingers twisting, she tried to obliterate that time from her memory. But the scenes just kept running behind her eyes, a relentless diorama. Her parents' friends, the Mitros, took the silent child in for a while. But they were swadeshis, freedom fighters, busy with their marches and protests and politics. The only one who took care of her was their son, her Nishonko da, her big brother Nishonko, a lonely, quiet, very private boy. He had been there for her, a watchful shadow, guarding her, making sure she ate and bathed. He was the one who would soothe her at nights when she awoke, gasping, sweating, knotted up in the damp sheets, fighting the demon dreams. He was the one who drew her back to her studies, accompanying her back to school at Shantiniketan and picking her up each evening. They would walk down the dusty red roads, he naming the birds winging home. He helped her with her sums, taught her the inner workings of poetry and scansion. Slowly, he healed her, coaxed a tiny smile out of her when they made Annada shriek with that frog in her bed. He had been her rock and when Chhoto mashi arrived in Bolpur to take her away to Singapur, she had howled, clinging to him, not wanting to let him go. So he had tied a small string of beads around her wrist and she had done the same to him, cheap red plastic beads with a golden thread, promising each other that they would be together, friends, forever and forever, promise me Nishonko da. And then the years had slipped away, and she had struggled to be her father's daughter. It had made her become a nurse, so she could try to heal, to reclaim the lives that had been stolen from her. And he, he had become an azadi, fighting for his country's freedom. An honourable man, a worthy man.

And now that they had met, what had she done? She had fought with him, caused him hurt. Why had she said those things to him? And then with that famous little flash of temper with which she used to argue with him about everything under the sun, she silently asked him *Why did you have to say all those things to me?* So much had changed. He had become…harder, peremptory. Something about him made her feel prickly. But again, remorse came flooding back. His parents were in prison, he was in the middle of a war, where was her compassion? Why did everything have to be so mixed up?

'Where are you, my child?'

She turned, startled. It was Father Unnikrishnan, his dark face creased with concern, his pastor's robes crumpled as always.

'You were very far away.'

'I'm sorry, Father, I was just...how are you?'

He sat down in front of her. They talked of simple things, the church raffle, the biscuits to be baked, the planning for the Christmas decorations. They would have to keep everything low key in view of the Japanese this year but how about candles and hydrangeas? The Japanese couldn't take exception to that, could they? And maybe, no dressing up as Santa Claus though the children loved that. And for a while, Aditi forgot.

The first units of the Special Bahadur group arrived in Burma with the British in headlong flight. The Japanese 15th Army had practically chased them over the border into India. Nishonko decided to split up once more as they headed towards the hills. Smaller units would be able to move faster, cover more ground. They were here not only to recruit but also mop up the British rear guard. They also needed to map the route, establish supply points, figure which villages would be hostile and which tribes friendly. He thought of taking Debraj under his wing but then decided that working alongside Nawaz would push him harder. The animosity between Debraj and Nawaz had only deepened but Nawaz, tight-lipped, had given him rope. In fact, Debraj and Kabootar had evolved into a great team.

There was that day when they smuggled themselves onto a work detail digging trenches for the British. During a break, they started a heated argument between themselves.

'That Netaji is the reason we are stuck in this godforsaken place.' Debraj spat on the ground.

'Arre bhai, Netaji is our only hope.' Kabootar was truculent

'Arre Langda, you want to be shot as a traitor?' growled Debraj.

'We're all going to die any way. I would rather be shot freeing my own country than be shot for licking the gora gand,' said Kabootar with a dour smile.

A grizzled mountain of a Pathan spoke up. 'He's right you know...the only reason the British can hold onto India is because we are helping them.'

Debraj and Kabootar exchanged looks. After the day's work, before slipping back into the forest, they drew the Pathan aside.

That night, camped in a cave, Kabootar, who was on guard, shook the other two awake. A silhouette, hulking, filled the cave entrance. As the man stepped into the cave, the firelight revealed the big Pathan, with a trickle of men behind him. They came bearing arms, ammunition. They saluted Debraj, much to Nawaz's chagrin.

Of course, not all their sorties met with such success. Another day, the duo, with fake bandages and on crutches, had joined the queue in a field hospital. As they talked surreptitiously to some of the wounded, a Gurkha had noticed them and whisperd something to a British officer. The officer had ordered them to step out of the line. Debraj and Kabootar had taken to their heels, unwinding bandages, using the crutches as battering rams, scampering, laughing, a volley of shots and shouts following them, while Nawaz, seething, cursing, gave them covering fire from the tree line.

'That was stupid,' he told Debraj over the campfire that night.

'Oh, it would have been brilliant if it had worked.'

'If…too many men have been fooled by ifs.'

'We're the special Bahadur Group, Sir. We should milk all the ifs we can lay our hands on.'

Kabootar walked into the light of the campfire, three dead jungle fowl slung over his shoulders. Silently, he sat down to clean them.

'Ah, a veritable feast. Good going, Kabootar.' Debraj started building up the fire for roasting the birds.

'Why is he called that?' snapped Nawaz.

Kabootar looked up briefly, went back to cleaning.

'Because, back in Lucknow, he used to raise kabootar, pigeons,' said Debraj.

'From childhood, Sir. I loved them — their gentleness, that soft cluck they make. They trust you, silly creatures. You can hold them in your hands, their tiny hearts fluttering against your palm. All it needs is a quick twist, swift, merciful and they're gone.' Kabootar's voice was almost a lullaby.

Nawaz looked spooked. 'Pagal hai. You're a nut. Is that how you got these birds?'

'These? No, these are very canny, they have to be hunted and trapped. Pigeons? I would find it very hard to kill a pigeon.'

'Men... would you find it hard to kill a man?' Debraj asked

'If they are beimaan, traitors, it's easy.'

'Beimaan or not, I don't know if I would knowingly be able to kill a man.'

'When the time comes, you will. That's what it means to be a soldier,' grunted Nawaz.

'I know. But frankly, Captain, I'm not looking forward to the business end of it, the torn limbs and people you care about falling...'

'Nobody does...but it has to be done. Just don't chicken out when it's your turn. It's one thing to lunge and gut straw dummies under Pandey ji but quite another thing when it's real flesh and crunching bone and the sound of the intestines squelching as you pull out the bayonet. And that metallic smell when the blood gushes out...'

Debraj waved his hands at him. 'Whoa, whoa, not before dinner.'

Nawaz grunted, shook his head contemptuously.

Mookerji Mansion was blanketed in silence. The scraping of the chairs as they sat down to dinner, echoed in the great house. It was a sparse repast, Sir Harry picking at his food, Bubbles chain smoking, her plate untouched. He had lost weight, his shoulders slumped in shame, the skin on his face mottled, sagging.

'Anything? Has Goopta any news at all?' The cigarette smoke was a cloud around her.

'He says he's looked everywhere but there's no sign of either.'

'She can't disappear into thin air.'

'Neither can he. Roberts, that commissioner fellow, he thinks Debu has skipped the country. They can't find any traces of the car. He hasn't been through any of the checkpoints.' He paused. 'I was looking forward so much to him coming home. We were going to turn our fortunes around, together.'

'Are they very bad, our fortunes?'

He shivered.

'You are not well?'

'If...when...the children come back, there might not be much left of their inheritance.'

'Goopta will help out, surely.'

'Goopta...has been pressing for payment. He has become quite rude and obstreperous.'

'Darling, he always was obstreperous. What about all our other friends?'

He sighed, shook his head. 'Won't take my calls.'

She mashed out her cigarette angrily in a silver ashtray. 'I know. Not a single invitation for weeks now. And everyone is suddenly so busy. And that cow, Mrs. Dagleish, she looked through me at the Tolly.'

'I'm sorry, my love. I'm so sorry.'

'It's okay, Harry. We'll get through this.'

Near Tantabin, they were hot on the heels of a band of Chindits, the guerrilla units of the British Army. As the Chindits scampered up a woody hill, falling over themselves to reach the safety of their bunkers, Lieutenant Sridhar hollered, his voice shrill. 'Run, sahibs, run...run all the way to London! Platoon, fix bayonets!'.

His sergeant's voice was urgent. 'Sir, they've reached cover. There's no use going after them.'

Sridhar didn't hear him. He felt the blood hammering in his head. Position 3421 was his! 'Platoon...HAMLAA!!' Pumped up with adrenaline, he leapt forward. The sergeant and the men hesitated. For crucial seconds. Sridhar charged uphill, a lone figure, arms pumping.

Nishonko, a 100 yards away, swore. 'Get back, you bloody idiot!'

But Sridhar, ears singing with battle lust, carried on. Within seconds, he reached the outer accordions of barbed wire. He threw himself flat and fired a long burst and turned to look back. Only then did he realise that he was alone, stuck on his own. 'Damn it!' A machine-gun opened up from the British bunkers, kicking up dirt inches from his face. Damn, damn, damn. He whirled, ran, feinting, dodging. And then a hammer blow on his spine, another to his legs. He was thrown up, a rag doll, and landed, crashing into the barbed wire. Entangled in it, unable to move, he lay there, spread-eagled.

The machine gun from the British position fell silent. Neither side moved. The only sound was a soft moan from Sridhar.

'How do we get him out, Sir?' Mohan Singh whispered to Nishonko.

Out of nowhere, Nishonko remembered a lesson from the Mahabharata. So that's why the Pandavas froze and didn't send more warriors to rescue Abhimanyu.

'They're using him for bait. They want us to try to get him.' He turned to the men. 'Give me your grenades.'

'Sir, you can't go in there by yourself,' Mohan Singh was alarmed.

'Just give them!' Nishonko hissed. He took the grenades, locked the pins and tied them into a bunch. Using all the tree cover he could find, he moved uphill. The British held their fire. Someone would come to get the wounded man. Then they would get him too. And then the Indians would send another...and another.

Nishonko got to within 20 yards of where Sridhar was impaled on the barbed wire. The ground in between them was open, no rocky outcrop or trees to shield him.

'Major, don't do it,' Sridhar rasped out, his face grey with pain in the dim light filtering through the canopy of trees. Nishonko saw the telltale crimson tide spreading from under Sridhar. He saw the light glint off the barrel of the machine gun in the British bunkers. He tried to keep his voice even.

'Sri, tere liye jamun bhej raha hoon. Got some berries for you.'

Sridhar nodded. The bunch of tied grenades, a lethal cluster of black fruit, arced through the dappled air and landed at Sridhar's side. He grabbed them and held them close to his torn chest. 'Go!' he rasped out.

Nishonko broke cover and sprinted down, catching the British by surprise. They opened fire but he slid and scrabbled to safety, unharmed. Sridhar, gritting his teeth, tied a single twist of cloth around the pins of the grenades and hugged them close to his body.

The hours passed. Dusk started to fall. Sridhar lay inert, life slowly ebbing out of him. He heard footfalls, looked up through a haze of red. Ten British soldiers were cautiously creeping up on him, circling him.

'Sergeant said get him alive, he's an officer.' They moved in, prodding his limp body with their gun butts. 'What's your name?'

Sridhar smiled. 'Ittehad, Itmad, Qurbani,' he whispered and pulled out the pins.

About three miles down the trail, Nishonko and his unit heard the multiple blast, the rumble echoing in the blue tinted hills. They took off their helmets and stood silent for a moment. Nishonko looked up wearily.

'Okay, let's keep moving.'

Debraj and Kabootar came looking for Nawaz at the end of that day's sorties. While Nishonko was chasing Chindits, Debraj had been concentrating on recruiting Indian soldiers.

'Captain, we are running out of supplies. Too many men to feed. We should head back.'

'What's the latest count?'

'About 300, by our reckoning.'

'That's...impressive. You do seem to have a knack for this.'

'Wow, that's high praise, coming from you. You're a hard man to please.'

'Oh, make no mistake, Lieutenant, I don't like you or your fancy ways. The Major might think the sun shines out of your arse but you don't fool me.'

Debraj got to his feet, his face suddenly pale.

'Why? Because I studied in England? Because I know a few British? It makes me less Indian? Who is a real Indian? Your forefathers came from across the Hindu Kush. Your Muslim brethren are negotiating right now for a separate state. What gives you the right to say you're more Indian than me? What gives you a patent on loyalty?'

Both of them were on their feet.

'Because I know who I am. I'm no good at pretty speeches and fancy stuff. But when I bleed...'

He whipped out a knife. Kabootar stood up quietly, his hand resting lightly on his knife. Debraj shook his head at him imperceptibly. Nawaz nicked his finger. Red beads of blood oozed out.

'This khoon...I spill it for *my* land. You?! You don't know where you belong — strutting around, a make-believe sahib, hankering after...after...'

'Freedom...isn't that what we all are hankering after? I want a free India as much as you do, Captain. I also want to go back — to my family, to my life. Yes, I've been a fake sahib. But can't I now try to be a real Indian?'

Nawaz let out his breath. He shook his head, the red haze slowly dying out of his eyes. 'I'm sorry, that was...uncalled for.'

Debraj saluted awkwardly, gave a shaky laugh. 'My apologies, Captain. Spoke out of turn.'

'You're right, we should be heading back.'

He turned abruptly and left. Debraj and Kabootar slowly sank down to the ground. Kabootar drew patterns on the ground with his knife.

'The Captain...he's a good man at heart. Lost his brothers, his father, at the Quissa Khwani massacre in Peshawar. It's a burden he has carried for 13 years. We have all suffered betrayal by the British, Debraj sa'ab.'

Debraj nodded. He knew the taste of that for sure.

The staff lined up in the big entrance hall of Mookerji Mansion looked up at Bubbles Mookerji as she swept down the grand staircase, regal in a silk sari, diamonds flashing, her eyes hidden behind a pair of studded dark glasses. Her spine was ramrod straight, her chin jutted out imperiously as she stepped down to the bottom of the staircase. She walked by the servants, scarcely giving them a look. Parul di, an old retainer who had entered the Mookerji household as a young personal maid for Bubbles when she got married, stumbled forward and fell to her knees in front of Bubbles.

'Boro ma...e ki hoye gelo? My lady, what on earth has happened? Apnara Mookerji Baadi chhede ki korey jaben? How can you leave Mookerji Mansion? Bhogoban e ki korlen? What has God done?'

Bubbles paused, her face softening a fraction. She put her manicured, beringed thin fingers on Parul's shoulder.

'Parul, this isn't up to God any more. From now on, all of you are in Mr. Goopta's hands.'

'But without you, without his Lordship, the young master and Debi di, what will happen to us? You are our family.'

'The house, the estate...everything...' Bubbles' voice cracked a bit but her iron control, bred into her by generations of strong-willed ancestors, pulled her back from the brink of breaking down. 'Everything belongs to Mr. Goopta. You may serve him, if you so wish. He will pay you all your...' She waved her hand dismissively.'Whatever you need.'

'Boro ma, please take me with you ...'

Bubbles raised a peremptory finger. 'Parul, Sir Harry and I no longer have the means to retain any of you. Do you understand what I'm saying?'

Parul wailed, beating her chest. Bubbles looked down at her, her face impassive, her eyes hidden. She looked at the other servants, trained to be poker-faced, though some openly sobbed. A long look around the great hall, at the grand chandelier under which generations of Mookerjis had welcomed the rich and famous, at the wall of illustrious and some black sheep ancestors, at the hand-carved bannister at the top of the stairs from which her children had peeked, at the...she stopped, drew a deep breath.

'Our chapter here is over. I wish you all well. Tomra shobai bhalo theko.'

She rustled out. In the driveway, the head gardener's son had finished loading a few suitcases into an ancient car. Inside the car, Sir Harry Mookerji sat hunched in the back seat, his face twisted. Bubbles got in. Once inside, Bubbles let out her breath. Her shoulders sagged, she looked even thinner and paler than usual. A soft whimper came from her, unbidden. The car rumbled off, the dogs running after it, barking, right up to the massive iron gates. The boy stood alone, looking at the car as it turned at the gates and disappeared.

Upstairs, in the panelled study, Mr. Goopta turned away from the big windows where he had been observing the departure of the Mookerjis. He walked up to a marble table laden with bottles, humidors. He straightened a decanter, humming something tunelessly under his breath.

'Would you like a whisky? The previous owner, poor soul, was something of a collector.'

The man in the big wingchair opposite Goopta rubbed his fingers over his meagre moustache and nodded. Thin, angular, dressed in a khadi kurta and Gandhi cap, he looked dyspeptic and vaguely dissatisfied.

'As I was saying, with your considerable resources, you should do well in the Congress party. Become a party functionary and in time...'

'Mayor of Calcutta? Sounds good — Mayor Gangadhar Goopta.'

'Anything is possible. You are a businessman, Mr. Goopta... it makes sense to keep your options open.'

'Yes, Mr. Chakroborty, I've always believed in keeping all my doors open...especially the back door, heh heh.'

The car bearing the Mookerjis, Sir and Lady, stopped in a cul de sac in a maze of small lanes somewhere in the Maniktala area. It was a poor part of town, shabby genteel houses, windows uncurtained, naked children with swollen bellies and runny noses rolling around a ball fashioned out of rags. When the driver opened the car door in front of the green-painted door with the two meagre steps leading up to it directly from the street, no one stepped out. The ladies of the neighbourhood, sunning themselves in the balconies overhanging the street, drying their oiled hair, looked down curiously. Few visitors came in cars here. When a tiny foot in a diamante encrusted, high-heeled slipper set foot on the cobbled ground, they craned out even further, expectation running in a ripple of murmurs from balcony to half-shuttered windows. When Bubbles stepped out fully, the murmur swelled, the sound of gossip mills starting up. She stood, in front of the modest little house, a marooned exotic bird, transfixed, her eyes very far away. Then with a sigh, a squaring of her shoulders, she turned to peer inside the car.

'Come, Harry, we are home.'

When the 100-odd men led by Nishonko marched wearily into the INA base camp, the quad was curiously empty. When Nishonko walked into the mess tent, he found it packed, the men all clustered at the far end. Pushing his way through the crowd, he discovered the reason. Netaji was there, sharing a meal with the men! He must have flown in. Eagerly, his fatigue forgotten, he stepped up. Netaji looked up, smiled. Nishonko felt his heart go lighter. He saluted his leader.

'Mission accomplished, Sir.'

Netaji noticed the dark shadows of the last few days smudging those intense big eyes.

'Bad one?'

'Lost some good men.' Nishonko's voice was hoarse.

'How many did you get to join our cause?'

'About 60, Sir.'

'That's splendid, that's...'

A burst of cheering outside made them all pause.

Through the gate, they came marching, singing, accompanied by loud whistles from the camp personnel, Debraj and Nawaz, followed by a large motley band of grinning men, waving like conquering heroes. As Debraj passed the mess tent, a little swagger to his gait, he did a double take. He straightened up abruptly, and pulled off a flustered salute. The men behind him milled to a halt, looking curiously at the bespectacled man in the military uniform who stood there, a quiet smile on his face.

'Sir, didn't expect you here. '

He turned to face the men he had led back.

'Company attention!'

The men fell into line. Debraj looked at them with a big wide grin. His voice rang out over the quad.

'Comrades, the moment all of you have been waiting for. The man you have been yearning to meet. The leader who you have pledged to follow in our just war against the British. Men, I give you Netaji!'

There was a muted roar, a few whistles. Netaji saluted the bleary-eyed, mud-stained, ragged crew with deep respect.

'Welcome to the Azad Hind Fauj. We are so proud to have you with us at this historic crossroads. How many of these great patriots are here today?' Netaji asked Debraj.

'Close to 500, Sir,' Nawaz stepped up and took his place at the head of the ranks, beside Debraj.

'546, Sir, to be precise,' Debraj interjected, still grinning from ear to ear.

A strained look crossed Nishonko's face as he watched from the sidelines.

'Wonderful. Debraj, right?' Netaji said with a twinkle.

'Lieutenant Debraj Mookerji, Sir!'

'Thank you, Lieutenant. Will you see to the arrangements for these brave men? They must be hungry after their long march.'

'Yes, Sir. Company, fall out. The Grand Hotel it ain't but the mess serves up a decent dal chapati. Kabootar, wake up the khansama and the matey. Let's get these boys fed.'

Netaji saw the easy camaraderie, the respect the men obviously had for the young man. He turned to one of his adjutants.

'Make sure the men get decent rations. And let's see if we can increase their pay a bit.' He turned to Nishonko. 'A good month's work, Major. You make a great team. It was a good day you decided to bring young Debraj on board, yes? What do you think of kicking him up to Captain? He has a way with the men and it's extraordinary what he's managed to accomplish in such a short time.'

Nawaz, standing on the fringe of the group, drew in his breath angrily. Nishonko's face tightened. 'But he's very new...and young, Sir.'

'But gifted. The INA mustn't be tied down by the old way of doing things. We are conducting a revolution, are we not? And time is of the essence. We will need to speed up everything if we are to win this difficult battle.'

As Netaji left, Nawaz strode up to Nishonko.

'Debraj...ya Yuvraj? Is he a crown prince or what? Looks like you can become a Captain in the Indian National Army nowadays if you have the right connections and the right accent.'

Nishonko stood still, his jaw clenching, his forehead furrowed in anger. He too felt that the promotion was premature and Netaji should have consulted him in private before announcing it so publicly. But then his training took over.

'Captain Hussein, look to the men. Give Lieutenant Mookerji a hand. And don't ever question Netaji's decisions again.'

Nawaz's face went red. He stiffened, then saluted.

'Yes, Sir!'

Late, that night, Debraj sat in the mess tent, drinking alone. The mess, with its packed earth floor, its rough-hewn wooden tables and smoky kerosene lanterns, was a far cry from the perfumed salons and candle-lit club lounges where he had been used to taking his tipple all his life. The adrenaline rush of the last few weeks was coming down and he felt flat, stale. He didn't feel like company and was tired of the rah rah and rhetoric he himself had been spouting. He had been told of his promotion and, for a few minutes, had felt warmed by a sense of achievement. But how was it important? A Captain in an unacknowledged, ridiculed, hodge-podge, patched-together army? How was this a leg up for a Cambridge-educated lawyer with millions in family inheritance? And who was there to share the moment of triumph with? His parents? Where the hell were they? He had tried to find out but it seemed they had left Mookerji Mansion. He had written to them but had no idea if the letter had reached them. And Debi. It was as if the earth had swallowed her whole. How was she coping with bearing a child, all alone, no one to soothe her fears and teach her the ways of motherhood? Maybe she was stuck in some godforsaken village, no medical help, just rural midwives, no money. He swigged back the rough rum that had now become his staple and rapped on the table. There was Kabootar, of course, his faithful shadow, who had grinned from ear to ear when he heard the news but...

A hand placed two glasses of rum on the table.

'Good evening, Captain, thought I would find you here.'

'Hey Mitro — sorry, Major, good to see you.'

Nishonko sloshed water into the glasses, then held up his in a toast.

'Congratulations, you've obviously made an impression on the High Command.'

'And you obviously think it's ill judged.'

'No, no, who am I to...'

'I thought it wouldn't go down too well — you know the jumped up, fake, British-ass-licking laath shaheb...no military training.'

'It's not that...'

Debraj just laughed, his lips twisting a bit. 'It's okay, I know Captain Hussein calls me that. I thought we were at last getting along, you know but then...'

'You'll just have to win his trust.'

'I'll have to kill a man for that.'

'What do you mean?'

'To prove I'm one of you... that I won't cross over and betray you one of these days.'

'Don't worry, you'll do it when the time comes. You won't even think about it.'

'Betray you? I saved your life, Mitro.'

'No, I meant kill...'

They drank in silence, immersed in their own uneasy thoughts. Far away, the small pip pip of a sentry's whistle sounded, warning all trespassers to beware.

'I took your advice, you know. I'm going to ask her. I'll buy a ring when we get back.'

Debraj was puzzled. 'What?? Oh, your mysterious lady love. Well done. When do I have the pleasure of making her acquaintance?'

'Soon Deb, soon.'

Shopping in Singapur was no fun, thought Aditi. There was hardly anything to buy. The prices of everything had skyrocketed during the occupation. Rice, just rice, and not very good rice had gone from $5 for 100 catties to $5,000. And you could only get 11 lb of rice per month for an adult and half that for a child. Most people in Singapur were living on sweet potatoes and yams. The amah had become very good at spicing them up with their Bengali condiments, inventing new ways of cooking tapioca with other vegetables but after having them for all three meals in a day and for dessert, Aditi was sick of them. Chhoto mashi was well off and they had not faced any severe privations but Meenakshi, who lived on her own and the Chinese and Malay staff had a really hard time. Chien Win, the Chinese gardener, was suffering from rickets and needed something non-starchy to sustain him. Of course, all the scarcity meant a flourishing black market. It was possible to get things, specially stuff to delight an 18-year-old — at a price.

Aditi and Meena walked down the long open verandah of the Singapore Gymkhana Club, with its rattan chairs and bamboo blinds painted the regulation green by the British. It was one of the last establishments that retained its former air. Singapur was free of the colonial yoke but the legacy lingered — in the Georgian buildings, the English gardens, the croquet and club rituals, forged during decades of occupation in tropical climes. Afternoon tea, another of those rites, was on as the two traipsed in with their shopping bags. Heads turned to watch their passage, one honey brown of skin, the other ebony, both striking in cool white muslin which moved in the breeze blown from the standing sentinel fans.

'You should have bought those peep-toe platforms, they were much more fun,' Meena told Aditi.

'But tricky to walk in and they hurt.'

'God, Aditi, must you be so pragmatic?'

They spotted Chhoto mashi at a far table. Meena stopped in her tracks. Her hand flew to her mouth.

'Oh my god, do you know who that is? With Chhoto mashi. That's Geeta Rangarajan.'

'The one who…Rani Jhansi Geeta?!' Aditi was agog.

Chhoto mashi turned to them with a smile as they hurried up.

'There you are. Geeta. My niece…'

'Are you really Geeta Rangarajan?' Aditi interrupted, her eyes sparkling.

'Yes, I am. And you are…?'

'Aditi. Sister Aditi Sen.'

'Meenakshi Menon.' Meena stuttered with excitement. I've dreamt of meeting you, Ma'am.'

'Every one at the hospital is in awe…'

'Girls, girls, contain yourselves.' Chhoto mashi was laughing at their unbridled excitement.

'Yes, Ma'am, we are in your regiment, Ma'am.'

'Delighted to hear that. Come, sit. Tell me, how do you find the training?' Geeta asked in her soft voice. The two looked at each other, not sure whether to confide in such an important person or not. Then Aditi burst out.

'It's so frustrating, Ma'am. They gave us rifles, old ones but no automatic weapons. They gave us arms training but with no ammo. And they taught us jungle drill in a gymnasium and how to handle explosives but all on paper. We haven't got anywhere near the action. Apparently, the Japanese officers think it's a waste of time to train women. It's all about bedpans and drips and paperwork and…'

'Thank goodness for that,' Chhoto mashi muttered under her breath.

Geeta looked at her, quizzically. 'You don't approve of our cause, do you Suchandra?'

Chhoto mashi shook her head vehemently. 'No, frankly I abhor the idea of losing young, promising lives like these. I know you and Netaji have it all planned out but the thought of endangering Aditi's life makes me…'

'Chhoto mashi!' Aditi was pink with embarrassment. She turned apologetically to Geeta. 'I'm sorry, Ma'am, she just…'

Geeta shushed her gently. 'It's okay, she has every right to worry about you. I can't guarantee her you won't get hurt.'

Chhoto mashi's mouth set in a hard line. 'Can you guarantee that we will win at least?'

Geeta shook her head, still composed. 'Can anyone?'

Aditi jumped up, pushed back her chair, and stamped her feet in a child's tantrum. 'I don't need guarantees. I just want to get going. I want to fight back. I'm so tired of waiting. Sometimes I think I'm going to explode!'

Chhoto mashi turned on her fiercely. 'Tell me, how do you intend to fight back? What exactly will you do when you come face-to-face with men trained to kill? Will you be able to kill someone, Jhilik? With what? Your pretty smile? Your soft little hands? Will you scratch their eyes out?'

Aditi was taken aback. 'Chhoto mashi, I…' she stammered.

The words tumbled out of Chhoto mashi in a harsh, strained voice. 'Grow up, Jhilik, war is ugly. War is piss and blood and diarrhoea and leeches and intestines spilling out into the mud. War is fear eating away your insides like acid and rotting rations and bloated corpses and widows handed a flag to make up for the man they have lost. War is…'

Aditi, standing open-mouthed, suddenly stepped forward and hugged her aunt, clinging to her, rubbing her back. 'Shhh…shhh… it will be okay, Chhoto mashi, I'm there, shhh…'

Chhoto mashi dashed the angry tears from her eyes. 'Oh, all this makes me so mad…'

Geeta leaned forward and touched her shoulder. 'We are close… so close to freedom.'

The advance through the Shwedong lowlands in Burma was taking forever. Debraj looked at the flat, dank expanse of marshland stretching on both sides through the field glasses. 'How in hell are we going to cross that? The trucks will never make it through that porridge.'

Nishonko and he had driven ahead of the main unit. Now they stood up in their jeep at the edge of the watery expanse, trying to figure a way through.

'Remember when we came through the marshland on that Chinatown night? The trick is to not move in a straight line but zigzag and find the path of least resistance. Think of each stretch of high ground as an island. We hop from island to island. It's not the marsh I'm worried about, it's the open fields beyond...that's where we'll make contact.'

There was that word again — contact. That's what everybody ever spoke about... "First unit that encounters the enemy...radio back contact"..."Keep your formation even after making contact." Contact, contact...the word was making Debraj nervy. His experience of violence up till now had been the canings they got at school when they were caught whistling at the St. Mary's Girls or the occasional dust-up at a pub on a Saturday night at Cambridge. He was the company's best marksman but the only time he had actually shot something was on those shikars in his teens, and the prey had not shot back. Now he was about to 'contact' men whose only aim in life was to kill him. He gulped thirstily from his water bottle.

Nishonko gave him a sideways look. 'You okay?'

Debraj grunted. 'Uh huh.'

'It's natural to feel fear before your first battle. I'd be worried if you didn't.'

'It's not fear. I'm worried how I'll perform under fire, if I'll freeze.'

'Ah! The old performance anxiety!'

'Shut up! You know what I mean.'

'I do. You *will* freeze the first time you're fired upon. Everyone does. Men freeze because they can't figure out what's going on. That's not the same as fear or cowardice. It takes a few battles to figure out what is going on and what to keep doing with your hands and feet even when your brain freezes.'

'How do I not freeze?'

'Well, the thing that cripples most people is thinking. Thinking "I need a plan". Won't help you when you're under fire. By the time you come up with a plan, you will have a bullet up your arse.'

'So...?'

'Trust your instinct and rely on your training.'

'That's it? That's all you can give me — trust my instinct? That's your big secret?'

'That's the secret. Your instinct is not wild any more. It's trained. Trust it. And I've seen your training reports. This soldiering…this actually may be something you're good at. Let's head back.'

The landscape ahead of them was a waste land crisscrossed with the black burnt-out remains of rice fields. The British had razed the crops as they retreated to make sure they couldn't be used to feed either the Japanese or the local villagers. Debraj's unit, a group of men as green as him, was covering the left side of the fields, with Nishonko on the far right. Debraj was on his own now. The good thing was he had Sergeant Pandey with him. Pandey ji, never a man to be rushed, took his time to set up the mortar and machine gun on the lee side of the half-burnt huts. 'Ready, Sir,' he said finally, satisfied with his arrangement.

Then he turned his back and started urinating noisily into the bushes. 'Right, you lot,' he called out to the soldiers over his shoulder, 'Empty your bladders! I don't want you wetting your pants once the firing starts! Sir, I suggest you do the same.'

Debraj shook his head, licked his dry lips. 'Carry on, Sergeant.'

Pandey ji saluted formally. 'As you wish. On your command, Sir!'

Debraj gave the pumped fist signal for advance. The platoon fanned out into the open field.

Debraj was sure the others could hear his heart thumping like a drum. *These might be my last few minutes on earth. Is this it? Is this where I die? Where will I get hit? Not in the legs, please God! Will they send my body back in a bag? Who would really mourn? Ma? Baba? 'That's what comes of defying the British,' the crones at the Cricket Club would cackle. They would just burn his body beside some unknown river…*

'CONTACT!!' Pandey ji's voice bawled out: 'Through the grass at 10 o'clock!'

Debraj's head jerked up. Sweat gushed into his eyes. The blurred figure of a man rose up, through the tall grass, a mere hundred yards ahead. He could make out the florid face, burnt red by the tropical sun. Another and then another swam into his clouded vision. The red-faced man's rifle seemed to come up ever so slowly, as if moving through molasses. Someone shouted something, the spit flying but he couldn't hear anything except for a faint pop pop sound. From his left, there came a sudden tearing sound. He felt a heavy hand push him down in the grass. Upside down, he saw Sergeant Pandey firing from the hip, spraying the line of men in front. He saw the red-faced man fall, then another, like marionettes, loose-limbed, ungainly.

With a whoosh, like coming out of a tunnel, everything snapped back into focus. The pop pop he'd been hearing became the deadly stutter of machine guns. Another British soldier, snarling, came charging at him through the grass. Come on, FIRE! *That's the enemy. You're supposed to hate him. But do I hate this man coming at me? He's closer. Does he have a girl? Or a plump wife back home? Kids? A dog?*

DON'T THINK! JUST SHOOT!

What happens if it doesn't fire, grab the gun, pull the trigger, keep it low to compensate for the upward swing.

He saw the charging soldier jerk and go down. And now he could hear himself roaring. 'Radio, Major Mitro! 3rd platoon has made CONTACT!'

On Nishonko's order, the mortar teams opened fire. With a banshee howl, the bombs arced overhead and landed on the edge of the jungle where the rest of the Wales Rifles were. The air filled with acrid smoke, blanketing out the ruined field. Under its cover, Nishonko's company charged forward, with blood-curdling screams. Debraj too flew, at the head of his platoon, a wordless, atavistic howl coming unbidden from his corded throat. The volley of bullets from his gun flew true and straight. His hands were steady.

The shakes came much later, just as Nishonko had said. It was the body's delayed reaction to all that adrenaline pumping up his heart and frying his brain during the heat of battle. Sitting on the hard ground, where they had struck camp and fires had been lit, the men's wounds being tended by the field medics, his hands started trembling uncontrollably. He tried to hide it, hoping no one would notice. But then his whole body started to shake, the sweat on his neck turning icy cold in spite of the heat coming off the bonfire. He tried to contain the shivering but it was as if he was in the throes of malarial fever.

'Just let it come...no shame in it. Happens to everyone.'

Nishonko was looking at him from across the flame. 'After a while, you learn to ignore it. Here.' He handed Debraj a battered, dented flask. 'Have a slug...you'll be fine.'

As Debraj took the flask, he saw the faint tremor in Nishonko's hand. Then the harsh, pungent aroma hit his throat, making his eyes water. The country brew was rougher, fiercer, more primitive than any drink he'd had but he was grateful for its heat, its steadying hand on his hammering heart, the afterglow. He drew a deep breath, felt his body start to calm down.

'I killed...I don't know how many men I killed.'

'Hmm...and we lost ten of our brothers. Ten men whose widows will shatter their marriage bangles. Ten men whose brothers will have to think of ways to break the news to their mothers. Ten men whose blood ebbed out in a burnt-out rice field in a land not their home. And there'll be many more before the job is done, before we can say mission accomplished.'

'Men died on the other side too. We took lives.' Debraj's voice shook.

'Steady, man, steady. Remember, we are fighting a just cause. Hold that thought. In our holy books, there is a difference between vadh and hatya — slaying and murder. The goddess Durga had to slay the demon Mahishashura, because he represented evil. Evil must be slain. That is the burden of those who wish to create good.'

'By that token, you can justify any killing. Who decides what is good, or that someone is evil?'

'You think what Netaji is doing is evil? That it is evil to set millions free?'

'No, I don't mean that. But the means...' Debraj took another slug of the numbing country liquor. 'It's all so confusing.'

'If you are to command men in battle, shake off these regrets. They will sap your will and paralyse you. We soldiers can't afford such navel-gazing, such self-indulgence.'

'But Mitro, what does that make us?'

'Men of the Azad Hind Fauj who are willing to sacrifice anything to set India free. Are you one of those men?'

A deep shuddering breath. 'I suppose so.'

'Here's to the mission, my friend!' Nishonko held the battered flask up and took a long swig.

Debraj stared into the fire, silent.

Back in the tea shop, the old man draws a deep breath, a bitter little smile flitting around his seamed lips.

'First blood. A rite of passage for brothers in arms.'

His gaze is distant, eyes clouded with memories of a time and a place none of the motley crowd around the table can know or can imagine.

'Dadu, cha debo? Would you like another tea, old man? On the house?'

The old man shrugs, then looks at his hands, turning them over slowly, gnarled hands, bent by arthritis, that have done so many things over a lifetime.

'So much lost. The years just went by.' He clears his throat. 'So they fought, the two, side by side, watching each other's backs. And the camaraderie that can only be born in the trenches slowly deepened. So different they were… yet joined by invisible threads that kept pulling them inexorably together, intertwining their fate.'

He falls silent again. After a minute, the listeners start fidgeting. They wait politely till Haru arrives with the promised tea. The old man pours some into a saucer, blows on it.

Sudipto urges him gently, 'Tar porey? What happened after that?'

The old man turns to look at him. 'You are a writer, yes?'

Sudipto nods. 'A reporter.'

'Will you write about this?'

'Depends. If it has any news value.'

'And you want to know how it all ends?'

'Doesn't everybody?'

The old man shakes a crooked finger at him.

'But some stories never end…no nice full stops, no final turning of the last page. You think you can tie up the loose ends but they keep unravelling. Life is never neat. It's all higgledy-piggledy, aagdoom-baagdoom, chaotic, refusing to be put into neat little boxes, refusing to be labelled. The hero turns out to have feet of clay and the man waiting in the wings suddenly holds centre stage.'

'Arre moshai, oshob philosophy chharoon, aagey baroon.' Balai da's tone is tetchy. 'Get a move on, Sir, enough with the philosophy.'

The old man nods grimly. 'Tar porey…'

They were in Kanbalu, Burma, in that hour before dawn, waiting in position, crouching in one of the ditches. It was cold and the damp mist chilled their bones. Debraj had plotted out markers meticulously on the map the day before with Mohan Singh, figuring out distances and obstacles and lines of engagement across the open stretch of field. The markers would serve as their guideposts in the heavy morning fog which he planned to use as cover, a tactic which had proved successful a few times already. All they needed was sun up and a breeze. The slight heat would thicken the mist and the easterly breeze would slide it their way, hiding them across the open ground, allowing them to creep up and take the British camp by surprise. Except there was no breeze.

'Come on, dammit,' Debraj whispered fiercely. Nishonko had gone off to Kawlin, leaving him in charge of the op. He couldn't screw it up. Not on his first command. Then, a whisper of a wind stirred. Reluctantly, a few wisps of the mist moved.

'Yes!'

But it was still patchy, shifting and parting, not the thick curtain he'd expected, hoped for. It would not hide them from the enemy lookouts. And soon it would be light and the window of time would pass. Mohan Singh crept up.

'I think it's a no-go, Sir. The mist isn't thick enough today.'

No-go, eh? Dammit if he was going to allow his first operation in command to fail. If he called it off, they'd say the laath shaheb had chickened out. Think! There was a chance, a slim one. He was all about taking chances anyway… from the polo field to the roulette tables to women. It was just before dawn, that deathwatch time when the human body is at its lowest ebb. The enemy lookouts would be tired, maybe even asleep. They wouldn't be seeing too well in the grey light anyway. There was a good chance that he and his squad could cross the fields unseen. But it had to be done now. He gave the signal to advance.

They moved fast. But halfway across, the last tendrils of mist began to evaporate. He could make out the vague shape of the temple and the lone palm tree that he had marked on the map the previous day. He hesitated, stood up to peer ahead into the half light, trying to…

Ratatatat!!

The first burst from the British machine guns hadn't even registered properly in his brain, when he felt as if someone had struck him with a giant hammer on his legs. There was no pain, just a sudden slam of shock in his thighs, jolting up his spine, making his jaws clash. His mouth filled with the warm, metallic taste of blood as he bit his tongue. Another volley of gunfire. He was flung into the air like a rag doll and then slammed down on his back, the wind driven from his lungs. His ears were buzzing, a strange, hollow, underwater sound. He tried to roll into a sitting position but his legs wouldn't listen to him. Bemused, he looked at them, sprawled awkwardly, at an odd angle on the stony ground. The left one was flayed and blood pumped out from a series of openings in his shredded khakis. As he watched, thick, dark red blood squirted out from the other thigh in bright arterial bursts. Kabootar was suddenly at his side, shielding him with his body. He was shouting something at someone, his lips stretched in a snarl. A face swam into a focus. A medic, a young, bespectacled boy with terrified eyes and trembling hands. Kabootar was ripping away the pant leg, already sticky with blood. The medic stuck his thumb in the puncture to locate the ruptured artery. Debraj howled, almost whiting out with the hot, searing pain.

Kabootar grabbed him by the hand. 'Easy, easy, you're going to be okay. Jaldi kar, sala! Move it, man!' he screamed at the medic.

He stammered. 'Yes, yes, j-j-just a minute.'

As Debraj tried to suck in air desperately, the medic hurriedly squeezed a tourniquet around the leg. Kabootar stroked Debraj's face, pushing the sweat-wet hair from his eyes. His fingers, tender as a mother's, came away stained with blood. The firing was still rattling all around them, kicking up puffs of dirt, ominously close. The medic, crouching, his eyes darting, jabbed an injection into

Debraj's leg. A grenade burst close, showering them with pebbles, some as big as clenched fists.

'Come on, we'll do the rest at the dressing station. Move him now!'

Kabootar and the medic scooped up Debraj, his legs dangling uselessly. They ran low, dodging bullets. The sudden movement was too much for Debraj. He passed out mercifully as the two carried him over the rough ground to the safety of their lines.

Nishonko came running into the field dressing station, a makeshift tent pitched near the river. The Japanese doctor, bent over the stretcher, straightened up. Nishonko saw Debraj lying there, still as marble, his skin like putty, grey green, blood everywhere. His heart did a funny lurch, something he had not felt ever since his parents had been arrested.

'How bad is it?'

'We can't do anything for him here. I've patched him up the best we can but...' He shook his head. 'He has to be moved to a hospital, to Rangoon. I've held the convoy back.'

'Rangoon? That's a good 10 hours away! What about something closer?'

'He needs surgery. Only a big hospital can handle this. It's the only chance he's got. He'll lose those legs otherwise.'

Nishonko nodded reluctantly. He wished they could move him to Singapur. At least Jhilik was there at the hospital. Kabootar and the orderlies loaded Debraj's stretcher into the last of the three ambulances parked outside. Nishonko held Debraj's hand tightly. 'You hang in there, Deb. You don't let go, you hear me? That's an order, Captain.' He covered him with a rough army blanket and slid out of the ambulance. He went up to the driver.

'That's a very badly wounded officer there. And a damn good man. Try not to jolt him too much.'

'Yes, Sir.'

He hastily scribbled a note and handed it to the driver. 'And give this note to the doctors at the hospital. It's got all his details.'

'Yes, Sir.'

'Stay off the main roads. The British shouldn't attack a medical convoy but you never know. Where's your helmet, soldier?'

The driver quickly brought out his helmet from below his seat and rammed it on his head.

Nishonko rapped the mudguard. 'Move it!'

As the ambulances rolled away, Kabootar took a swift look around. No one was paying attention. He sprinted forward, limping. As the last ambulance slowed down at the gate, he swung himself onto the floorboard and slipped into the passenger seat. Hell if he would leave the Captain to go off to some strange place alone. They could cashier him but he was going to make sure the Captain made it to hospital.

'Major told me to go along,' he told the driver, tersely.

The metalled road ended after two hours. From there the ambulances went on to a rough track, lurching and rolling, gears whining. There were only two ambulances left. The first one had broken down, its axle a victim of the vicious potholes. They had loaded all the stretchers into the remaining two. Their overloaded suspensions groaned. It was impossible to drive close to the trees. The sides were slushy with thick mud. He drove down the middle, tiny under the vast sky.

The planes came from behind, flying low and fast. They were British Hurricanes, looking for targets. From the air, the two ambulances, covered in mud, their red crosses barely visible, looked like regular army trucks.

The ground exploded around the ambulances. There was a deafening roar and the ambulance juddered violently. And then fire bloomed in the ambulance ahead. It had been directly hit. Kabootar swore.

'Head for the trees!' he screamed.

The driver wrenched the wheel but he was too late. The second Hurricane caught them dead in its sights. Machine gun fire lashed the ambulance. The driver lost control and crashed the ambulance into a tree. He was thrown violently forward and was catapulted out of the shattered windshield. He died on the spot. He hadn't been wearing his helmet.

Sparks sprang from the wrecked engine. Fingers of flame started licking up. The Hurricanes swooped once more over the wreckage strewed on the road. There were no signs of life. They wagged their wings and climbed up steeply, banked and disappeared into the clouds. Silence descended over the plains.

Slowly, from the surrounding fields where they had thrown themselves flat on the ground when they heard the first roar of the planes, villagers, rice farmers, emerged. They scampered on to the road to see if there were any survivors. The upturned ambulance lay shattered, its wheels spinning. The patients and the orderlies inside were all dead. The driver's body sprawled, broken, across the road. They were about to turn away when someone heard a faint groan from inside. They rushed back. They found Debraj, flung to one side, moaning. The fire was spreading, they had to hurry. They pulled him out, ungentle in their haste. Then, with great care, they laid him out on a pallet made out of coconut leaves and carried him to their village.

Kabootar, crumpled against the front door, stirred, then tried to sit up. Smoke billowed in black, noxious clouds through the shattered windshield. The world looked upside down. For a couple of moments, he couldn't remember which battle he was in. Then everything swam back into focus with a snap. He realised he was in the ambulance, which was lying on its side. The fire was creeping closer. He heaved, pulled himself out through the shattered windshield, lacerating his arms, choking. Then he was out, spilling onto the pitted road, now slick with escaping fuel. He hobbled, staggered to the back. The door was wide open, bodies cut in two, riddled with bullets. But no Captain Mookerji. The wind suddenly quickened, the smoke swayed and changed direction. An ominous sound of crackling and banging came from the wounded ambulance. He tottered to the roadside ditch, just made it to cover when the whole thing went up with a big whoosh. He coughed, retched, then lay back in the mud. Sleep, blessed unconsciousness, came.

Birds circled in the sky, riding the thermals, looking at the burnt remains of the two ambulances. Slowly, they started to swoop lower. The note that Nishonko had given the driver drifted in the wind, a burning scrap, an ember, finally just a smudge of soot.

The village headman, whose wife was also the midwife, had very limited medical supplies – a few bandages and iodine paste, and some herbal painkillers. She patched him up as best as she could but whispered to her husband that the man needed hospital. But the only transport they could drum up belonged to Htway, the village headman's younger brother, who was also a local big time smuggler. His truck was about to do a fast run to Singapur, avoiding all the big cities. The villagers bundled Debraj into the truck, packed him with straw amidst the sacks of vegetables hiding the sacks of contraband so he wouldn't be rattled around too much. It was a 48-hour run and he had already lost a lot of blood.

It was on the road that the effect of the morphine started wearing off and the pain kicked in. Debraj felt his body being torn apart. Each wave of pain opened the floodgates, so that his uniform turned black with sweat. He begged and cursed God in the same breath. God! What did God look like? His fevered mind spun around. Christ, spread-eagled on a cross, long, girlish hair and painted blue eyes lit by hundreds of candles. Where? Midnight Mass in St. Paul's in Calcutta? Christmas lunch at the Club the next day, a bicycle wrapped in gaudy paper. No, no, wait, that time in Coventry, with…with that...Nora, wasn't that her name, blonde hair tumbling down her back, green eyes, spread-eagled on the flagstones, softly screaming, God, god, yes, yes, don't stop, don't stop. Kneeling on the cold stone floor of that ruined country church, amidst the dust of centuries, in that sacred place, under the eyes of a beatifically smiling Mother Mary, they had sinned, God, don't punish me, please, I can't bear it, oh god, Ma. Ma Durga. Dugga Dugga, the goddess on a roaring lion, the incantations at the pujas in the ancestral home, the early morning bath with the chill of autumn in the water drawn from the well, the whirling dhakis, drummers with scarlet plumed drums, dancing dervishes, frenzy and sweat, pounding rhythm, the incense smoke making the eyes water, the ringing bells and cymbals, the shrill ululation from a hundred throats sending a shiver down his back. Delirium raged through his mind, setting it adrift…the smoke from the sacrificial fire hid the goddess' face and the goddess' face peeled to reveal Debi. Her face beckoned but then swam away and now there was Nishonko, roaring, 'HAMLAA!' Whoosh in and out of a tunnel. The axe rose and fell. The sacrificial beast fell to its knees, its head rolling on the ground, its legs still shuddering. The boy's cheeks were wet with tears. In the jolting truck, Debraj was crying and singing and praying. No sound came, for his swollen tongue had almost blocked his throat. Mercifully, he passed out.

It was late night, the roads empty, when the truck finally reached the gates of Singapur General Hospital. The driver, Lwin, Htway's assistant, got out, stretched. It had been a long, hard drive with just two stops. Thankfully, his passenger had remained comatose. He was unfamiliar with this part of the city and had had a hard time finding the hospital. He was also sleepy and bone tired and still had to deliver his precious cargo. He had absolutely no intention of explaining the deeply wounded, maybe dead, passenger inside his truck to the authorities. So he opened the tailgate and pulled out the unconscious man and left him propped against the pillar of the front gate. He then walked into the lobby and told a sleepy orderly about a wounded man lying outside the gates. By the time the orderly had wheeled out a stretcher, Lwin had melted into the night. The orderly called for help and they wheeled in the wounded 'John Doe' without any papers, any identification, into the hospital.

A junior nurse ran up to Aditi in panic. 'Sister, there's a wounded man here.'

Aditi, in the middle of wheeling another patient to the ward, turned on the young Tamil girl, shaking her head impatiently. 'There are many wounded men here.'

The junior nurse ran alongside, trying to keep pace. 'I've given him morphine.'

'Good girl.'

The junior nurse tried to stop Aditi. 'But I have to pin the empty vial to his shirt so he doesn't get overdosed.'

'Yes, yes, so do it.'

The junior nurse blurted out, 'But he has no shirt. And I think he's dead, he's not breathing.' The young girl's voice quavered, on the edge of panic. Aditi stopped, looked down the corridor. At the far end, under the cold glare of naked lights, a lone stretcher on wheels stood outside the EMS. She saw a sprawled form, the ominous stillness. For a moment, she hesitated, looked at the patient she had been wheeling. She took a snap decision — this one could wait.

'Pull yourself together. Take this one to 102.'

She hurried down the stone-flagged corridor, her canvas shoes squeaking in the silence of the late night shift. As she came up, an involuntary gasp escaped her set lips. The man lay there, in tattered, flayed khakis. Through the rips in the blood soaked trousers, now turned black, through the loose torn bandages, she saw the huge ugly gaping wounds, the terrible damage. The hair was matted with dried blood, the face almost white, drained, the bare body like marble, tinged with blue. A boyish face, very young, and a soldier, going by the khakis. Where had he been fighting, she wondered. She reached for his pulse, held on grimly till she found a faint, thready beat. She called out for an orderly, rushed to get the man hooked up to an oxygen tank. She was quick, efficient, economical in her movements and calm. She remembered what the junior nurse had told her and after a moment's thought, took out a lipstick from her pocket and wrote a big M on the man's forehead. She pinned the morphine vial to his pillow and the two of them ran with the stretcher down the corridor.

Miraculously, the pain eased. He could breathe. Where was he? White walls, blur and streak of lights. Through the slit of his puffed eyes, he saw people in white rushing around, heard the echoing voices, the urgent commands coming from a long distance. A high ceiling with rafters, like a church, whirring ceiling fans. They passed sails, billowing. Was he on the boat with Ah Ping? Ah no, they were white mosquito nets hung from the heads of a long row of beds, shrouds for the dead. Where was he? Was he dead? And then, he saw her. An angel in white, with wide-open eyes, unruly curly hair. Her lips were moving but she made no sound.

'He's come to.' Aditi leaned over him, shone a torch into his eyes. She got a blink from him. 'His eyes are dilating. What's your name? Can you hear me? Nod if you can hear me.'

'Forget that for now, sister. We can identify him later.'

The doctor, a large, fat Straits Chinese with multiple chins and a beautifully shaped bald head, pulled on surgical gloves. His face was grave.

'Start prepping him. We need to operate fast. I have no idea how long he has been wounded but he's been exsanguinating and is going to lose those legs if we don't hurry.'

Debraj screamed, 'NOOO!' But no sound came, only a gagging warble, his throat almost closed from the swollen tongue. The angel leaned in, pried open his mouth.

'He's bitten his tongue, Sir.'

'Intubate him.'

Gentle fingers started wiping him down. The sudden sting and icy coolness of the alcohol made him shiver. Aditi looked down at him. He was mumbling something incomprehensible. She leaned in close to make out what he was trying to say. His eyes, up close, were a curious light grey-green with gold flecks in them. Tiger, tiger, burning bright, in the forests of the night, the words came unbidden. He suddenly gripped her hand, mouthed something desperately, then slumped, his eyes closing wearily. She felt for his pulse, looked at him for a long moment, and whispered, 'Don't worry, you're safe now. I won't let you die.' She kept holding his hand as she continued to prepare him for surgery.

A sharp pain on his cheekbone jerked Kabootar awake. He sat up, wildly flailing his arms. A raven, black as sin, its eyes opaque and beady with calculation, hopped away a few feet and waited, its head cocked expectantly. Kabootar swore at it, picked up a round largish stone and chucked it. The raven retreated, then flew away, losing interest. Kabootar stood up with a groan. He looked at the scattered wreckage of the two ambulances and it all came back to him. His body sagged, seemed to lose its fight. He had not been able to keep the Captain safe. What was the point of all this fighting and hardship and giving up everything if one couldn't protect the things that mattered? He felt immense weariness, a numbing lassitude overtake him. He would have sat down on that dusty road and never got up again if the sudden barking of a dog had not roused him. He looked up, the sun in his eyes. Hazy, like a mirage seen in the dunes near his village, the dog stood at the roadside, beside a small man. Kabootar peered at him. It took a few moments for his sight to adjust. It was actually a boy, watching him warily from a distance. Kabootar beckoned to him, then swayed. The sun wheeled in the sky. He sank to his knees. The boy whistled sharply, waved to someone behind in the fields. A man came, a farmer, thick-built. The two, shadowed by the skittish dog, walked up to the man with the blood-stained face and hands and the wooden leg, crouching like a beaten animal on the ground.

'Can you walk?'

Kabootar nodded, mute.

'Come with us. Our village headman will talk to you.'

Kabootar grunted, lurched to his feet. The boy was instantly at his side, supporting him. The simple act of kindness made Kabootar's eyes water. He put out his hand, rested it on the boy's scrawny shoulder. And thus, they limped their way homewards.

'Sir, we lost all the wounded. The convoy was attacked from the air.'

Nawaz's face was grim as he reported to Nishonko. Nishonko's mouth tightened.

'Bastards. And Captain Mookerji?' he asked, tersely.

'Gone, Sir.'

'What happened?' he asked in a strangled voice.

'Both ambulances were gutted, burnt. All the dead are cinders. No signs of any survivors.'

Nishonko turned away, trying to control himself. He felt sick to the stomach. If only he hadn't sent Debraj in that ambulance, he might be alive today. He shouldn't have taken the risk.

'And Lance Naik Kabootar Prasad has gone missing. The men think he went with Captain Mookerji's ambulance. In which case, he's also probably dead.'

'Stupid! Stupid! No bloody sense of responsibility. Always flouting orders.' Nishonko's voice shook with anger. 'What the hell am I supposed to tell the CO? We're losing too many men.'

'Not your fault, Sir. He was too inexperienced, too raw, too cocksure. Shouldn't have taken the chance of attacking like that. *Laath shaheb*, always showing off.'

Nishonko's face darkened. 'Are you referring to Captain Mookerji?'

'Yes, Sir.' Nawaz, righteous in his anger, failed to notice Nishonko's simmering rage. 'He shouldn't have been given so much responsibility so fast. He was...'

Nishonko smashed his fist down on the table, splintering it. 'He was my friend. He was a good man, an honourable man. And a far better soldier than many of us. Careful of your words, Captain. They betray a smallness of heart. For goodness sake man, he's dead. If only... if only I hadn't pushed him so hard.' His voice trembled.

Nawaz kept his head down. He had never seen the Major lose control like this. But inside, he was seething.

Netaji smashed the shuttlecock into Hassan's corner and jumped with glee. He loved his game of badminton and took a childish pleasure in winning.

'Well placed!'

Colonel Gokhale and Brigadier Saito came striding down the verandah of the Meyer Road house.

'Thank you, Colonel. Good evening, Brigadier. Ahmed here is new to this sport and still not au fait with its nuances. But soon he will beat me, eh Ahmed? What brings you here, gentlemen?'

'I wanted to report the progress the Bahadur regiment have had in the advance campaign. We've suffered some losses but have managed to...'

Netaji interrupted him. 'How many?'

'Close to hundred men.'

Netaji sat down heavily on a courtside bench. 'I thought we told them not to engage the enemy just now.'

'They couldn't help it.' Saito interjected. 'Some British units got cut off or were left behind in the retreat. They are putting up quite a tenacious rearguard action. It's giving our troops and especially your boys, who are untested, a good stab at actual combat. It's invaluable military experience. But, of course, it has a cost'

'Of course. But it still hurts. Do you have a list of the...'

'Yes, Sir.' Gokhale handed over a sheet.

Netaji ran his eyes down the handwritten lines, the roll call of the lost, his face bleak.

'That young man, Mookerji. Remember him, Geeta? Gone. There was a promise to him, a spark, a great hunger for life.'

Geeta, sitting quietly at the edge of the court, nodded. 'I liked him. He brought with him a certain air of hope, of possibility.'

Netaji got up, shaking his head. 'Hope. That's all we're living on. Waiting and waiting, while these young lives are snuffed out before their time.'

Saito clicked his heels. 'Just a bit more patience, Sir. Your cause is true. Your men are true. You will prevail.'

Netaji laughed, a harsh sound. 'The whole world thinks otherwise. They say Netaji is sleeping with the enemy. The whole world calls me a traitor, a lackey to your empire.'

Geeta's normal soft-spoken tone rang with conviction. 'But when we march upon Delhi, they will know the truth.'

Gaffar walked in silently, carrying a tray with cold glasses of pomegranate juice. The soft tinkling of ice against crystal echoed in the long pause as Netaji looked at his hands, turning them over and over.

'What is the truth, Geeta? That I'm a patriot or a power-hungry megalomaniac? They say, Netaji, he's a dictator, he's a...'

'Geeta san is right. Once you breakthrough, once you form your own democratic government, you will be vindicated. Your countrymen will acknowledge what you have fought so hard and so long for.'

'My countrymen? My own countrymen block me, betray me at every turn. Oh, they do not approve of what I'm up to. They set spies on me. Some have much to lose if we win. They will thwart me at every turn. They will betray me, given a chance.'

He looked out at the empty badminton court, the evening light falling, the sound of birds returning home filling the air. Gaffar picked up a glass and carried it to Netaji. 'Sir, your pomegranate juice.'

Netaji looked at him. A little smile broke out on his lips.

'You are a good man, Gaffar. Thank you for taking care of me so kindly. All of you.' He turned to look at them. 'All of you. Thank you for being here, my comrades. I have brought down all your spirits with my little outburst and for that I must truly apologise. Come, let us go inside before the mosquitoes decide to join us for the evening.'

The orderlies had gone down the corridors of the hospital with their incense burners to drive off the mosquitoes from the wards. Night had brought quiet, the sounds of distant traffic and the voices of the muezzin calling the faithful now hushed. Meenakshi was exhausted. Her feet hurt and she was dying to get out of her sticky clothes and take a long, long bath in the outdoor bath-house. She would stand under the open night sky, the stars wheeling above, the cold water cascading down her upturned face, her bare back. The evening breeze, laden with the scent of frangipani, would soothe her and wipe out the day's witnessed pain and suffering that clung to her like smoke. Oh, bliss! Sometimes, she wondered if she really was cut out to be a nurse. The illness, the indignity, the helplessness of the human beings lying spread-eagled, their lives ebbing away, filled her, not with compassion but with guilt and rage and a powerlessness she hated. The inability to make a difference so many, many times left her feeling exhausted. Aditi was different. Aditi actually cared. Aditi thrived on being around the sick, the incontinent, the maimed. Meenakshi entered the General Ward, looking for her. Through the mosquito nets, draped like sails, she saw her, standing alone beside a bed in the far corner. God, she looked knackered. Meenakshi walked up to her, whispered.

'Coming? I'm heading home. There have been troubles in the city. The Kempeitai — I hate those Japanese military police, so bad tempered— they're patrolling the streets. You shouldn't be late. There's a curfew.'

'I'm going to stay and watch over this one.'

Meenakshi peered at her patient. It was a man, bandaged heavily, and, by the looks of him, unconscious.

'What's happened to him?'

'Wounded. Both legs. Spine. Bit his tongue. Burns. Lost buckets of blood. He's been out for days.'

'Aditi, you can't keep looking after every wounded man who comes in here, personally. If he's been like this for days, one more night won't matter.'

'Tonight is critical, Meena. I can feel it. He needs someone to watch over him.'

'You're going to collapse at this rate. Come home. Get some rest.'

'Just this night, Meena.' Her calm voice, the stubborn set to her chin, made Meenakshi realise that further discussion was pointless. Reluctantly, wanting to help this strange, intense girl whom she had grown so fond of in these few weeks, she offered to stay in Aditi's stead. But Aditi would have none of it. She shooed Meenakshi away, giving her a hug and pushing her out. Then she went back and continued her lonely vigil. Sometime later, as she gently changed his dressings, smelling them to check for signs of putrefaction or dreaded gangrene, he stirred. Eyes closed, he waved one hand blindly in the air, seeking something, someone. He was mumbling, snatches of meaningless sounds, the tongue still sluggish, though healed. She thought she caught the word Debi. Maybe he was Hindu and was invoking some goddess he believed in. He wasn't Muslim, he wasn't circumcised. Maybe Anglo-Indian, given his colouring, his light eyes. He called out again, a strangled shout, a slurred sound. She caught the wildly flailing hand, grasping at nothing, and held it tightly in her own.

'Shhh, it's alright. You're safe.'

She began to croon, a soft wordless lullaby with those lilting rhythms all mothers know instinctively, the rhythm and cadence of a heartbeat. Her lips, with that childish pout which could set stubbornly when crossed, now breathed and hummed the comforting sound that all children know from the moment of their birth, the song to put them to sleep as the cradle is rocked. It calmed him down. He slept.

The truck carrying chickens — to Kabootar's disgust, for if there was one bird Kabootar despised, it was chickens — the truck deposited him at a corner of the bazaar. Dawn was still an hour away but the market which was normally abuzz at that hour, was shuttered. Thiha, the driver didn't particularly like this gimpy, taciturn man who had spent the last few days in his village, trying to cadge a lift. Hwat had instructed him to take him to Singapur so Thiha had grudgingly complied. The gimp had not spoken much, except to constantly harass him to hurry, hurry, and even begrudged his stopping to relieve himself at the roadside. So Thiha just pointed in the direction of the hospital and spat on the ground to send him on his way. Kabootar too was glad to be rid of the foul-smelling truck, the incessant clucking that had driven him bananas and Thiha whose loud, unchecked and unconcerned farts throughout their journey had turned even Kabootar's cast-iron stomach. He limped down broad pavements, empty and lit fitfully, going steadily south. Then, round a corner, through large rain trees, he saw the lights of the hospital. Fear and hope rose in equal measure, made his breath falter. His head swam. He stopped, clung to some iron railings. The ministrations of the village midwife had taken care of the obvious wounds. But unexplained stabs of pain would make him double up now and then. What drove him on to find the Captain, he couldn't explain. He just knew that Debraj Mookerji was his responsibility, to guard and protect.

Sent away by his parents when he was merely a child to a grand uncle's house as an unpaid hand, because they could not afford to feed another mouth, specially another mouth with a lame leg, Kabootar had grown up with no moorings or sense of belonging. His bed was in the stable, with the animals, his meals the leftovers from the communal kitchen. He had never expected love, never received respect. His only companions were the kabootars, the homing pigeons he trained by hand to become couriers. Only once, just once had he looked for friendship — from a girl child who had been brought from another village to be the hand maiden of the new daughter-in-law. But it ended badly, with Kabootar given such a thrashing, it broke his other leg and left him scarred in places no one could ever see. When the leg healed, he stole the grand uncle's heirloom pocket watch and a diamond stud and hopped onto a freight train in the middle of the night. He hopped off at Lucknow and found a calling in the training of pigeons and horses and hawks and pet monkeys. It was from Lucknow that he learnt of a new army that was taking in whoever was willing and able to fight the white overlords. But it was when he met Debraj that he felt accepted unconditionally for the first time in his life. His limp, his lack of education, his scrawny body — none of that mattered. Debraj had called him friend and embraced him as an equal. And he would go to the ends of the earth to find him. If he wasn't already...but he stopped that thought from burgeoning and walked through the empty streets.

The streets, even for this early hour, were curiously deserted. Normally, Chinese people could be seen through uncurtained windows, smoking and playing mah jong. But today everything was shuttered, silent. Only Japanese military vehicles seemed to be on the roads.

What Kabootar didn't know was that only the previous morning, seven Japanese ships, comprising over 39,000 long tons, had been blown up and sunk in Singapur Harbour. The attack, code-named *Operation Jay Wick*, the brand name of a popular lavatory deodoriser, had been carried out by an Allied commando unit known as Z Special Unit, led by Lieutenant Colonel Ivan Lyon. The group of Anglo-Australian commandos had sailed from Western Australia to Singapur in an old Japanese fishing boat, the *Krait*, named after a Malayan snake. Once within striking distance of the harbour, the commandos took to folboats and paddled into the docks under cover of night. Using limpet mines, they sank the Japanese ships, including several tankers, and then slipped away to their rendezvous with the *Krait*, finally returning successfully to Australia. This was the first major sabotage since the Japanese had captured the island. The loss of ships in such an important place was an enormous blow to Japanese prestige. The Japanese could not conceive that a force could have the audacity to penetrate and attack this deep. They therefore concluded that it must have been an internal operation, carried out by Chinese guerrillas. The Kempeitai had gone on a rampage, hunting down suspected collaborators, hauling truckloads to Changi Prison to wring out confessions. Kabootar knew nothing of all this but he was a survivor, a creature of instinct who knew that he had to stay out of sight. He stuck to the night shadows and dark places. As the first pale light turned all the windows of the hospital into pink mirrors, he climbed its steps wearily and entered the empty lobby.

The yawning man behind the desk said there was no patient named Debraj Mookerji. Kabootar left, only to slip in through the EMS entrance along with a wheeled stretcher in a borrowed white coat. He padded through the grey corridors, peering into wards full of somnolent figures, dozing nurses. In one room, an old man sat upright, quietly tearing off all his tubes and his hospital robe. Naked and shivering, he stared at Kabootar, who stared back. When Kabootar turned away, the old man sat down, looking out of the window at the sun beginning to rise. There was no sign of Debraj. Kabootar felt his heart falter. There was only one large ward left but it had many beds and an empty nurses' table at the entrance. Knowing he might be discovered any minute, he swiftly limped from bed to bed, trying to pierce the veil of mosquito nets. Then he heard the rattle of the nurse's chair. He dropped to the ground and crawled forward. The last bed in the corner remained. He peered over the edge of the chipped green regulation iron cot. And there he was, sleeping like a baby. Beside him, on a chair pulled close, a young nurse dozed, her tousled head cradled on one arm resting on the edge of the covers, her other hand curled around Debraj's fingers. Kabootar squatted at the foot of the bed, leaned back with a sigh and closed his eyes.

As the first sunlight fell across the bed, Debraj opened his eyes. He slowly looked around, down at his hand, saw it was clasped in a sleeping nurse's hands. He saw the top of her head, the nape of her exposed neck. With a soft sigh, he drifted back into sleep. A few moments later, Aditi sat up with a jerk. Guiltily, she looked at the patient, saw he was sleeping peacefully. She checked his pulse, his temperature, smiled, stretched. That's when she noticed a pair of legs in khaki, sticking out from underneath the bed. She inched her way forward and discovered a man in filthy khakis, a white intern's coat, asleep, sprawled against the hospital bed. She gingerly poked the man with her finger. No response. She pushed harder and then nervously skipped back a couple of steps when he hobbled upright, blinking, disoriented.

'Who...who are you, you can't be here.'

Kabootar took a couple of seconds to focus. Then he pointed to Debraj. 'Captain saab...hum unka orderly hoon. I'm his orderly. I have been hunting for him. I'm not leaving him.' He paused, then added, 'Major saab ka orders.'

Aditi was flummoxed. 'How did you...okay, you can keep him company. But outside. Please.'

Kabootar looked at her defiantly but seeing the set of her chin, the air of unconscious command, he knew she was a formidable opponent. He retreated.

She called out, 'What's his name?'

'Debraj Mookerji.' He turned back, his face suddenly vulnerable. 'My sahab, he will live?'

Aditi saw him, saw the deep weariness in the pitted, seamed face, the fresh cuts and lacerations, heard the fear and concern in the gravelly voice. She smiled gently. 'And what's your name?'

'Lance Naik Kabootar Prasad.'

The oddness of it brought a little giggle, instantly suppressed.

'You better get yourself patched up in Emergency, Lance Naik. And don't worry. Your Captain will be okay.'

She led him out, her hand gentle on his scruffy shoulder.

Chhoto mashi was just sitting down to her morning cup of tea when Aditi came in, her eyes puffy from lack of sleep, her face a little gaunt but light of step. She hugged her aunt and collapsed into a chair, stretching her arms.

'What a night!'

'Good or bad?'

'Wonderful. That nameless man, remember? The very badly hurt one? He's turned the corner. He's going to make it. That's one soldier we managed to save.'

'So he is a soldier?'

'Yes. A very funny, odd man, his orderly, identified him. He's a Captain.'

'Well, I'm glad to hear that. Now run off and grab some sleep. You look terrible.'

Aditi smiled and stretched like a cat.

'I'm not sleepy at all. And Chhoto mashi, the main door was left ajar again.'

Debraj woke from a deep sleep. He lay still, eyes closed, savouring the feeling of a new day about to start. Soon, Khogen da would come in with his bed tea, the napkin snowy white, the steam curling from a porcelain pot so thin that you could see the amber liquid swaying gently inside. The day's paper would have been ironed and folded precisely and Khogen da would ring his little brass bell politely to waken Chhoto babu. Debraj stretched lazily, luxuriantly. His hand hit a cold iron bar and a sharp pain shot through his back like a red hot skewer. His eyes flew open. Above him, an ancient fan clicked and clacked crookedly. The ceiling was high, white but nothing like his bedroom. He turned his head slowly, took in the saline stand, the adjacent hospital bed, the sea of mosquito nets. His heart knocked against his ribs as he looked around wildly. Where was he? Then recollection flooded back. He saw Kabootar squatting at the foot of his bed, dozing.

'Good morning, Captain. And how we are feeling today?'

A plump, middle-aged Malay nurse was at his elbow, holding up a thermometer. She unceremoniously popped it in his armpit. He looked around desperately.

'Where's she?' His voice came out a whisper.

'Who please?'

'The... the...' He gestured, mimicking Aditi's unruly cloud of hair.

'Off duty. Now you are having me. Since you are up, how I give you a proper sponge down?'

'Sponge? You mean, you...' Debraj was horror-struck.

'Dearie, I'm seeing more naked men than the hoores of Sodom and Gomorrah. Just lie back and enjoy it, I say.'

Before he could stop her, she moved the sheet off him. His legs were exposed. Debraj's face went white. Both were bandaged heavily from toe to groin.

'What happened to my legs? God, what have you done to them?'

Kabootar, who had woken up with the commotion, put a calming hand on Debraj's shoulder.

'You caught a few bullets, Sir. And then the ambulance got hit.' His voice faded to a murmur as he leaned in close. Debraj listened, his face stony, his hand clutching the sheet, the knuckles white.

As Aditi pulled on a fresh uniform and belted herself up, she absent-mindedly hummed a Tagore love song under her breath. Her errant curls, always earning her Matron's sharp censure, had come undone as usual. She took a jewelled comb, one of the few things she had kept of her mother, from a lacquered box and ran it through her hair. Halfway, she stopped. She stared at herself in the mirror, looking for the flaws and imperfections, impervious to her own beauty. She stared at the long column of her throat, the collar bones flaring out like a bird's outspread wings. She considered her nose, slightly tip tilted, then wrinkled it in disapproval. Lips, too full. Eyes, almost too wide apart. Then, with an impatient shake of her head, she got back to taming her unruly hair. But just before leaving, she pulled out a couple of strands to frame her face. Then a pinch of her cheeks to get some colour into them, a bite of the lips. She pulled her cap to a more fetching angle and ran out. Meenakshi, waiting outside looked at her, her eyebrows raised. Aditi just shrugged.

'Whhhat?'

From the head of the corridor, she knew something was wrong. A knot of nurses had gathered at the door of the General Ward, peering in, fingers held up to mouths nervously. They whispered to each other, their faces tense.

She ran down, her heart in her mouth. 'What is it?'

The plump Malay nurse turned to her. 'It's that patient of yours. He's gone berserk, throwing things…refusing to let anyone come near him. We've called the doctor. Even his man can't control him.'

Aditi pushed her aside, moved through the cluster of twittering females. The plump nurse tried to stop her but Aditi was already in, moving swiftly along the side of the room. Debraj was at the far end, backed against the iron headboard, the sheets bunched around him, the saline stand upturned. The other patients cowered in their beds while two orderlies and Kabootar circled him from a few feet away, trying to calm him down. Debraj had ripped out his IV needle and was holding it out like a weapon, shouting, 'Don't you come near me…stay away from me…'

Aditi called out in a commanding but quiet voice. 'It's okay. Let him be…let him be.'

Everyone turned towards her. Kabootar fell back, pulling the two orderlies away.

She called out, her voice soothing 'Debraj, it's okay, no one will touch you. That's your name, right? Debraj?'

He turned and stared at her out of wild eyes. Then slowly, the glare of madness died out, a candle flame, guttering, then gone. He swallowed convulsively.

'Yes. She said I might never...' He touched the bandages on his leg, his eyes like sinkholes. Fresh blood had seeped through, deep scarlet against the pristine white.

Aditi turned, gave the plump nurse at the doorway a long, level look. 'She is wrong. You *will* walk.'

He looked at her, beginning to shake. She was at his side by now. She touched his shoulder with infinite gentleness. She could feel him shivering violently. He reached out to her blindly. She took the needle from his slack fingers and held it away. The orderly quickly took it from her outstretched fingers and stepped back. She moved in, held him tight.

'You'll walk, I promise you. And when you do, you get to dance with me, how's that?'

'That's good, that's...' He gulped. 'Promise I'm not going to turn into a crip...' He strangled on the words. Tears welled up. He was a child, entreating her to somehow make everything alright. She smoothened his hair down.

'I promise.'

As the liner docked at Singapur port, blue turbaned, red-jacketed coolies ran up to the gangplank to greet disgorging passengers. They scrabbled to take the luggage of a particular passenger, a small, rotund man in an expensive silk suit, dark opaque glasses that hid his eyes, a pencil moustache and shining balding head. Strutting a bit with the penguin gait of the flat-footed and the newly fat, he waddled down the gangplank. A thin, nervous, bespectacled underling with a prominent nose hovered near his elbow, laden down with bags and a portmanteau, swatting at the importunate coolies.

'Shoo, shoo, g..g..get away you sc..sc..sc..avengers, you badmaash log, off with you.'

As he dithered, he almost bumped into the man in front, treading on his heels. The man turned with a grunt. 'Arre, Noshir bhai, careful, my little man.'

'S..s..sorry, Mr. G..G..Goopta, so sorry.'

Goopta it was, looking prosperous, almost transformed. Gone the hand-washing, diffident man from Calcutta. Money, the promise of power had made his skin pink and shiny. He stepped onto the dock, brushing his jacket sleeve fastidiously with his podgy beringed hand. A group of men, Chinese, Burmese, stood in a row in front of two cars, bowing formally, repeatedly. Goopta strolled up to them, smoothing his moustache, a little unconscious, self-congratulatory habit he had picked up of late.

'Hello, hello Mr. Lim. So glad to finally seeing you facing-facing. Now where's this wonderful plantation of yours we have heard so much about?'

'Ah, Mr. Goopta, you will see it soon enough. And much more.'

'Call me G.G.'

'Yes, Mr. Geegee. We are looking forward to our most fruitful association. But now we take you to bungalow and some refreshments, yes?'

Goopta nodded. He got into the first car, gesturing to Noshir bhai to follow. Mr. Lim went to pour out a glass of champagne but Goopta waved him away.

'Ah, Mr. Lim, I don't partake of such matter.'

'Some malt whisky perhaps?'

'No, no, please, I have seen too many illustrious men lose their wits because of this malt-sholt. I am a god-fearing man, you understand.'

'My apologies, I did not mean to offend you.'

'I am hard to offend, Mr. Lim. Thick skin.'

Goopta looked out of the window. The city, such a British city, and yet thoroughly tropical, with its palm trees and masses of flowers growing wild at every rain-fed street corner, passed by in a kaleidoscope. They passed rickshaws, hand-drawn carts, Tamil spice shops, Chinese tea rooms and Thai massage parlours. It was a melting pot of a city and, with the departure of the British, rich for the picking. Goopta was happy that Whyte had dispatched him here, 'to keep an eye on that INA fellah,' as he put it. Not only would it further his newly acquired political ambitions but there were opportunities here, fortunes to be made. What did they say — two birds with one stone? Or was it a bird in the bush? All these Ingrej sayings, very confusing. He turned to Mr. Lim.

'So tell me, when do I get to meet the new masters of Rangoon… most particularly the man of the moment…your esteemed Netaji?'

'Ah Mr. Goopta, you mean *your* esteemed Netaji? For isn't he a compatriot, a hero to all of you?'

'Is he? Is he?'

The Meyer Road house was still shrouded in darkness, the staff still fast asleep. A heavy, earthy dampness hung over the garden, the east verandah. The sky was a gun metal grey with a sliver of deep scarlet low on the horizon. Netaji had woken up before dawn, as was his habit, and had a bath and purified himself. He now sat down, cross-legged, facing the coming of the sun, on a bamboo mat and composed himself for prayer. The worn rosary of beads and a small, much-thumbed copy of the *Gita*, which were his constant companions, sat on the small trestle table in front of him. This was his most private moment, when there were no distractions, only calm and silence, to commune with his innermost thoughts. Never one to make a public display of his religion, he sought this solitude to seek the truth. A low murmur, sonorous, came from his lips. He prayed.

Gaffar, when he came on duty, found Netaji, deep in study. He came, on soft feet, and placed the fragrant steaming cup of tea beside his leader. Netaji gave him a benign smile. 'Good morning, my friend. Did you sleep well?'

'Yes, my leader.'

'I had an idea while praying. Music. We should compose some stirring regimental songs for the men to march to. Music can inspire the way no words can. Music is the voice of the Almighty. Would you agree, Gaffar?'

'I wouldn't know, Sir. Your god, my god, they are not the same.'

'Aren't they? Ah, Gaffar, this cup of tea that you have made with such consideration for the start of my day's journey, is this not the work of God? This morning sky, with its benediction and its promise, which god made it, yours or mine?'

'I'm not sure I understand what you mean, Sir.' Gaffar stood, stiffly.

Netaji clapped him on the shoulder. 'It's alright, my friend. I understand you.'

The same morning sun stole across the bed and woke up Debraj. He had been moved to a small room but it had a single window, which opened out onto a magnificent rain tree full of squawking parrots and squabbling sparrows. But this morning, the bird chatter was superseded by the strains of a Tagore song in Bengali playing on a little turntable on the dresser. Debraj's brow furrowed in irritation. Those plaintive notes and ploddy beat, while very popular in Calcutta, had always made him go to sleep. A music teacher had come for a summer to teach Debi as part of her proper Bengali upper class upbringing but she had driven him to distraction with her dogged tone deafness. He had thrown up his hands in disgust and quit but not without Debraj running for cover whenever the familiar notes were struck on a harmonium. And now someone had decided to invade his space and his peace of mind, with the same stuff and he couldn't even get up to shut it off. Fuming at his helplessness, he rang the bell. The plump, jolly Malay nurse came in.

'Yes dearie?'

'Please, this terribly lugubrious music, do you think you could turn it off?'

'You must be feeling better. You are again using those long, long words. Anyway, you'll have to take it up with Sister Aditi, dearie.'

'Ah, is she responsible for this? Tell me, what is the point of trying to fix my legs if she ends up deafening me in the process?'

She chortled loudly. 'You are definitely better.'

He fished out a bunch of yellow lilies from the vase by his bed.

'Here, please, Sister, give her these with my compliments and request her, bribe her, to stop this?'

She chuckled. There was a knock on Debraj's door. It was Aditi.

'Ah, *there* you are. May I take the liberty of offering you these lovely flowers?'

'Hmm. Well, I do love lilies.'

'Really? How perspicacious of me.'

The plump Malay nurse laughed as she walked out. 'There he goes with the big, big words again. Told you, he was better.'

Kabootar came in, squatted near the door.

'Very perspicacious, Captain, considering I brought them for you on my way here.

'You did?'

'To cheer you up.'

Debraj was crestfallen for a moment but then brightened up.

'Oh good, so will you please, please change the music to cheer me up?'

'Not a snowball's chance in hell.'

'Oh, come on. Can't we have a little Duke or Dizzy instead of this...this...'

'I don't know who they are, this Duke but I will get them. In return, you will have to get off that bed and stand.'

'I can't do it, Sister. I know your intentions are noble but there's no way I'm going to be able to stand.'

'Just try. One second. That's all.'

'No angel, not even for you.'

Aditi's mouth tightened. 'You're such a coward.'

Debraj's jaw fell open. He looked at Kabootar who was very busy whittling a piece of wood.

'Hey, you take that back. Do you have any idea what I've been through? I almost died!'

'Oh, you poor thing.' Her eyes flashed. 'Is pretty boy feeling sorry for himself?'

Debraj was livid. He wanted to get up and...no woman had ever spoken to him that way. And this chit of a girl with her untidy hair and her provincial ways and her funny accented English...how dare she.

'You wouldn't understand the first thing about pain, girl.'

'Oh, I know plenty about pain, Captain. I deal with it every day...men with great holes in their sides...a child, screaming, not understanding why her whole arm is hanging by a single piece of skin...a good man, a doctor, trying to save lives, the back of his head just not there.'

She stopped, her voice shaking. Then she gulped, got herself under control.

'I'm sorry. That was rude of me.'

Debraj slowly unclenched his fists. Why did she do this to him, make him want to shake her hard till her teeth rattled? Exasperating creature. She was standing there, head down, the lilies limp in her hands. She looked away, then with sudden decision, chucked the flowers into the bin, muttered something and walked out of the room.

Debraj slumped back. He felt exhausted, sick to the stomach. He looked for Kabootar but he had disappeared. Gosh, he had been a bit of a cad. But preposterous, her trying to blackmail him into standing. His legs were… a hot gush of tears, blinded him for a few seconds. Suddenly, he missed his wayward mother with a deep sense of loss. Where was she? And Baba?

The weather was turning colder in Calcutta. The maid-cum-ayah had not come that day. Bubbles sighed, then turned Harry on his side. He had become quite, quite thin, the lines of his face once more like the young man she had first seen at the Fort William Gala. So handsome and imposing he had been, with his trim little moustache and his riding crop. Their wedding had been a glittering event, the talk of town, what a handsome couple. And then, what went wrong? When did they lose their way? When had the separate bedrooms come, the separated evenings? Now all they had was this room and only each other for company. And nothing left to say to each other. Harry was mumbling again, a disjointed stream of muttered words, a burbling of whispered figures, counting on his fingers, convulsively, starting over and over again. The local doctor, with unsteady hands, the cheap liquor fumes on his breath making her gag, had said something about clots. All she knew was the great Sir Harry was a ghost, a child she had to feed and bathe and clothe. And curiously, she found she loved him again, a different love but love nevertheless. 'Bubbles?' He paused, his hand frozen in mid air.

'Yes, dear.'

'Have you sent the car?'

'Where dear?'

'Ah Bubbles, what will I do with you? So scatter-brained. Debu is coming home today. Have you forgotten?'

'How could I, dear?'

'Send the Rolls. He will enjoy her.'

'He will. I will.'

It was evening in Singapur and the end of her hospital shift. Aditi unchained her bicycle. The air had the damp smell of coming rain. Chhoto mashi would be telling the amah to put down the khus khus and close the windows. She would ask Aditi about her day. But Aditi didn't feel like talking. She hadn't acquitted herself very well that day. Losing her temper with the soldier...so childish. Insulting him was not going to help him to walk. But he made her so mad, she wanted to slap him. Oh, god, there she went again. Temper, temper Chhoto mashi would chide. But he was going to walk if it was the last thing he did. He just didn't know it yet.

'Missy Madam.'

Startled, she almost dropped her bike. Kabootar had sidled up to her elbow.

'Kabootar ji, you gave me a start. What is it?'

Kabootar leaned forward and murmured something. She looked at him quizzically, her head tilted, her lower lip caught between her teeth, frown of concentration.

'Where?'

Kabootar pointed towards the bazaar road.

'And you know what to get?'

He scratched his head.

'Because I don't have a clue who they are.'

Kabootar shrugged delicately. We'll see, we'll see, he seemed to suggest. She took a deep breath, then smiled. Her eyes were shining. Suddenly, it had become an adventure. A mission, Nishonko da would have called it.

'Okay, let's try.'

The door let off a tinkling sound from the tiny bell hung outside. The old Anglo-Burmese man in the white serge suit, his moustache neatly clipped, looked up. It was a nurse, with a ragamuffin lame man, in khaki, both looking ramshackle and not at all the kind of persons he would welcome to his establishment. He was known the length and breadth of the Peninsula as a true connoisseur, a man of rare good taste who had a most exclusive collection of music. People would come from far away, music buffs, to browse through his collection. When the British were here, God rest their souls, business had been brisk but now the clientele was a mixed lot. He cleared his throat.

'Sorry, we are closing shop, chalo, chalo, out, out.' He crossed his arms and gave them his most intimidating look.

The gimp paused, turned away but the nurse stood her ground.

'A few minutes of your time, please. Do you happen to have something by the Duke?'

One grizzled eyebrow went up. My god, what a voice, that husky, half broken, slightly wounded quality. What a blues singer she would make!

'Say again, Miss?'

'Sorry, did I get that right? I thought he said Duke.'

'Duke is correct, step right here please.' He led her to one of the old wooden shelves, stacked with 78 rpm records. With infinite care and respect, he slid out one, gave it a little wipe with his sleeve, handed it to her. 'A perfect gem, this one. Do you perhaps sing, Miss?'

She gurgled with laughter, a sound that made his seamed face smile. 'Only in the bathtub.'

'Lucky bathtub.'

She gurgled again, her head back, her teeth shining, eyes crinkled. 'And Dizzy?'

He was confused. 'Beg your pardon, Miss? Are you okay?'

She let out another peal of laughter. Kabootar too was mesmerised. He had never heard her laugh with abandon, had never realised how beautiful she was when free and without burden.

'No, no, I meant someone called Dizzy. I'm not familiar with all these names and this music. You will have to guide me.'

He looked relieved. 'Ah, you mean Mr. Gillespie. A capital choice. Allow me to help, Miss.' He took out the record reverently from the sleeve he had already picked out and placed it on a turntable. The rich, fat notes of 'It Don't Mean A Thing If It Ain't Got That Swing' melted out, filled the old music store and escaped out into the twilight. Aditi's eyes widened. She had not heard anything like this before. Aditi had learned dance in Shantiniketan as a child, a staid, mannered, genteel style. But this, this rhythm which slipped and slid, seemingly out of control, yet insistent, hinting at forbidden pleasure, this set her heart racing. She swayed, her fingers trying to catch the playful twists and leaps of this most intriguing sound. The old man dusted off a wooden stool, pushed it towards her.

'Come, sit, enjoy.'

But she was on her feet, clicking her fingers, her feet tapping, shifting, dancing, her shoulders moving. He leaned back, savouring the pleasure the old have in watching the very young, being young. Kabootar quietly watched her too, framed in the plate glass window, with its gold painted curlicue sign, her cloud of hair shimmering, golden in the store's lamplight, dizzy with delight.

The next evening, sedate in her nurse's uniform, her face scrubbed of all emotion, she walked into Debraj's room, all business. On the turntable, a record was playing. Debraj, his bandaged legs dangling from the side of the bed, clicking his fingers to the music, smiled beatifically. It was 'Prelude To A Kiss.' He greeted her with a broad grin. 'Ah, my angel in white. Listen to this. Pure genius.'

But she didn't smile back. She merely took out the thermometer and shook it, her face grave and composed.

'Oh, come on, are you going to sulk now? You look like my great aunt Sati Devi who lost her knitting and sued the family cat.'

Her lips twitched but she repressed it and held out the thermometer.

'Open your mouth, Captain.'

'Shut yours and just listen.'

'How did you get it?'

'Kabootar, my man. One in a million. How he even figured out what to buy, I have absolutely no clue. So, tell me, isn't this divine?'

'It's not so terrible, I suppose, in spite of being English music.'

'No, my sweet mulberry pie, it's American.'

A giggle escaped. 'You talk so funny.'

'Now, that's more like it…'

In a quicksilver change of mood, the sun going behind a cloud, her face turned solemn. 'You know, we're fighting for freedom. My father was...my friend's parents are still languishing in prison. Isn't it a betrayal to listen to this…to enjoy this?'

Debraj wanted to scoff, to mock her. But then he saw the traces of some subterranean sorrow, darkening the pools of her eyes.

'Can one not believe in freedom, even fight for it, my dear, but also enjoy something of beauty?' He was gentle.

She frowned. 'Freedom…it should also mean the freedom to choose, shouldn't it? Even something as basic as what kind of music we like.'

'And you don't like this music?'

'Well…'

'Come on, I've been seeing your feet tapping away quietly.'

She looked down at her feet, in plain white scuffed pumps, indeed tapping away with a mind of their own. She broke into a chortle. It was a most unladylike, unselfconscious sound, and he was startled. He stared at her, then started laughing. Almost spontaneously, she held out her hands. Unthinkingly, he took them. They were blood warm, buttery, not passive. She pulled. He hesitated, then slowly lowered his legs to the floor, touched ground. She cupped his elbows, the mouth open in silent urging, as if encouraging a toddler to walk. He stood, teetered. He couldn't feel anything. Then he could. The rush of pain made him gasp. She held him, took his weight. He was a good six inches taller than her but her arms were firm, her feet steady. Slowly he regained his balance, sweating with the effort. She was very close to him, her arms now around him. Slowly, like the tide going out in the river, the pain ebbed, became a little bearable. He looked at the determined bite of her lips, the stubborn tilt to her head, the delicate angle of her jaw set in a hard line and smiled crookedly, understanding what she had done. She gently lowered him onto the bed, let out her held breath. He still held on to her, his hands clasped loosely around her tiny waist.

'Sister Aditi, you really are an oddity.'

She was puzzled, not understanding him.

'Odd…oddity…Aditi.'

She realised his arms were around her and stiffened for just a heartbeat. Then, gently, she slipped out and placed his hands on his bandaged thighs.

'Has anyone ever told you, you speak the silliest nonsense? Come, rest now.'

He lay back gratefully. As she covered him, he said, 'Will you come tomorrow? See me?'

She hesitated for a moment, not sure, unlike herself. Then she nodded briskly. 'Yes. Yes, of course. You are my patient, my responsibility.'

'I didn't mean that.'

'No?'

She tucked him in, picked up the turntable arm. The music hung in the air, the notes faded away. Then, in an off-hand voice, 'Who's Debi?'

'How do you know that name?' His eyes flew open, his voice was sharp.

'You were calling out to her in your fever…you were crying.'

'She's someone very dear to me…and I failed her.'

The words came out of nowhere. She regretted them, the moment they tumbled out of her lips. 'Were you in love with her?'

He frowned, looked away. 'The whole world was in love with her…and Sister, has anyone ever told you it's rude to pry?'

Her face turned white. She turned away, almost stumbling, hurrying for the door.'I'm sorry, so sorry, I didn't mean to…'

'Aditi, wait, it's okay, it was…'

But she was gone, the door empty, yawning.

She ran down the corridor, almost colliding with the Head Nurse. Her face was flushed, the mouth set in a grim line. The Head Nurse called out to her but she was already at the end of the corridor, turning the corner, skidding, a flash of white heels. She ran into the staff bathroom, bolted the door shut. Then she turned and slammed her hand on the wall. Stupid, stupid, STUPID. What was wrong with her? She stared at herself in the speckled mirror, then rubbed her eyes hard, willing the tears not to come. But they came, spilling over, catching in the hollow of her upper lip, angrily dashed away. She drew in a shuddering breath. She would tell Head Nurse to assign someone else to the Captain. No, she wouldn't, that would make her a coward. But how would she face him again? He must think her such a flibbertigibbet. But she must. She had promised him she would get him back on his feet and damned if she was going to back down.

As she walked home, wheeling her cycle, Meenakshi ran up to join her.'What's happened?'

'What do you mean?'

'Oh come on Aditi, your face is like an open book.'

'Got chewed out by the Head Nurse. Behaviour unbecoming a member of the Rani Jhansi brigade.'

'What did you do?'

'Ran down the corridor and almost knocked her down.'

'That sounds positively criminal.'

'Men are such beasts.'

'And which particular unlucky male of the species has earned himself such stern disfavour?'

'I'm trying so hard and he just makes it so difficult...'

'Is this your Major we are talking about?'

'A perfectly normal question and he begins to...no, he's a Captain.'

'The man who came to see you a month or so ago? The tall, really intense, one? Looked like a Major to me.'

'Who are you talking...oh, you mean Nishonko da.'

'Whom were *you* referring to?'

Aditi was silent.

'Aaah. The wounded soldier. No wonder you have been going around with this...this...goofy look on your face for the last few weeks.'

'Don't be silly. I'm just trying to...I don't know what I'm trying any more. It's all so impossible. He may never walk. The war is coming. He'll be gone soon, he...'

Meenakshi gave her a sidelong look. Aditi's face was drawn. She tucked her arm into Aditi's as they made their way down the quay path, two girls, two women, ebony and ivory, on the cusp of two worlds.

'And Nish... What did you say his name was?'

'Nishonko. He's an old childhood friend. A true friend. He looked after me, when my parents...were no longer there. We promised to be there for each other, ever and after, when I left India, but that was all kid stuff, make-believe. I think our parents...they kind of hoped we would be together. But people change — and they're gone — so we don't have to be tied to some silly pact we made, do we?'

'Have you told him — that you feel this way?'

Aditi was silent for a moment. 'I can't, he's scary.'

'Really? He seemed... attractive.'

'He is, oh he is, very...but there's something hard inside him... like a cold, black rock touched at night. Something unyielding and dark. He was always silent, remote, even as a boy. He's a great leader, he's done wonderful things for the movement. Netaji really likes him but...' She shivered.

The jungle clearing in the foothills of Burma was pretty. Wild flowers grew in profusion. The sunlight slanted through the tall trees, dappling the undergrowth. A stream tumbled over rocks at the far end. As Nishonko held up his fist, the platoon shuffled to a halt. They were tired, thirsty. It seemed as good a place as any to take a breather. He knew they were close on the heels of the retreating British but they needed to fill up their canteens. On his signal, the men eased heavy rucksacks off aching backs and unslung their arms quietly. The grass was rich and spongy on the edge of the clearing and they flopped down gratefully. Nishonko signalled to a young soldier silently, pointing at the stream. The soldier, barely out of his teens, lanky, large footed, and the platoon's favourite for his finger-snapping renditions of Hindi film songs, gathered up the men's canteens and headed across the clearing. Two others followed him, wanting to have a quick wash. Except for the screeching call of a bird, the clearing lay silent. Nishonko was dying for a cigarette but he couldn't afford to have the smell carry on the wind. Suddenly, he heard a small metallic click. His head swung up, the hair on his neck prickled. The young soldier had frozen in the middle of the clearing, staring down at his feet. The right one was on a steel plate hidden under grass and moss. The two other soldiers had also frozen, one poised on one foot, like a crane. It was a contact mine, maybe one of many.

Nishonko hissed, waving back the other two soldiers frantically. The young boy stood alone in the middle, frozen, sweat popping on his forehead. The sun shone, the bird called out again, the stream warbled. Nishonko knew there was no way out of this. The boy was going to have to move that foot sooner or later. And the moment he took his weight off the pressure plate, he would be blown. The platoon couldn't stay here forever and they didn't have anyone to defuse the mine. He took a long breath, then stepped on to the path of bruised flowers left by the soldiers. Up close, he saw the boy shaking, his teeth chattering.

'Santosh, that's your name, right?' The boy blinked. 'Now listen to me carefully. Throw those canteens to the men.'

The boy gulped. He bunched up all the canteen straps in his fist, whirled them round and round and tossed them into the air. Nishonko's mouth opened, then shut. The boy's foot had almost come off the mine. The canteens spun and floated through the forest canopy, turning end on end. They all looked up, their mouths agape. The canteens landed in the undergrowth on the edge of the clearing. Nishonko turned to Santosh. Amazingly, the boy was smiling. Nishonko smiled also, grudgingly. Then he stretched his hand out. The boy looked at his hand, uncomprehending. Nishonko waited, his eyes gentle, his outstretched hand steady. Then the boy understood. It was an unwritten rule, one drilled into every INA soldier. Slowly, he unstrapped his gun, his ammo, the grenades on his belt and handed them to Nishonko who passed them, without looking back, to Neel who had come up silently behind him. The boy took off his helmet, rubbed his short-cropped hair, which was sopping wet. He turned his face up to the sun, breathed in the sweet, fragrant air of the forest, closed his eyes. The men waited, the forest waited. The boy opened his eyes, looked at Nishonko, who was still standing quietly, his hand outstretched. He handed over his helmet, his rucksack. Still, Nishonko waited.

'I've given everything, Sir.' His voice was a whisper. Nishonko touched his own chest lightly, his eyes infinitely kind. The boy looked down, then started to shake his head.

'I'm sorry, it has to be done. I'll make sure they get everything.'

The boy was now crying openly. His downy moustache was wet with snot. He took out his ID, pictures of a young girl, family… all traces of who he was. He carefully put it all, one by one, into Nishonko's hands. Nishonko started to back off. The boy patted his pockets, then exclaimed.

'Wait.' He pulled out an amulet and held it out to Nishonko.

'Give this to Netaji. For luck. Tell him I'll be waiting for him in Delhi.'

'I will.' He quietly gave the order to move. Reluctantly, the men picked up their kits. Then Neel called out softly but it carried in that silent jungle clearing.

'Company. Present arms!'

They came to attention. Neel swivelled, faced the boy. In unison, they all crisply saluted their young comrade. Then, without looking back, they melted into the jungle. Nishonko was the last to go. As he left, the boy started to sing in a high clear voice, 'Tu Meri Chand…'

Hunched at the campfire that night, Nishonko went through the boy's possessions. There was a picture, of a young girl, in front of a temple, flowers in her hair. She had a plain but strong face, a level look at the viewer. Was she the boy's sister? Or was it an early picture of his mother? Or could it be a village girl he was betrothed to? She didn't look anything like Jhilik but in some strange way, maybe in the calmness of her gaze, this unknown girl reminded him of her. What was Jhilik doing right now? Had she eaten, alone? Was she already in bed, the lamp turned low? A vision of her, her skin golden in the lamplight, the long, curved slope of her back as she bent to touch his feet suddenly flared in his mind but he backed away hurriedly from the thought, guilty at the pleasure it had evoked, suppressing it.

'You can't blame yourself, Major.' Nawaz sat down, stirred the fire. Nishonko looked up puzzled.

'About the boy. No point brooding.'

'Oh, I don't, Captain. I do what needs to be done. Making the hard choices. That's what soldiers do.'

'Yes, but I also know every time we lose a man, it tears you apart.'

'You really think that you know me?'

'We have fought together. You get to know a man.'

'Do you? Is it ever possible to really know what's in another person's heart? To get through all the walls and defences we build to stop people from getting in?'

'Break down those walls. Share the burden. Otherwise it gets too heavy.'

'There is one I would share it with. But she is too young… too weak. She will not be able to bear the weight of the blood and the daily list of dead or missing in action.'

'Try her. War brings out strange things in people. Talk to her.'

'Deb said the same thing.'

'Well, for once I agree with him.'

It was visiting hours at the hospital and the halls were crowded. She felt dread as she walked down the long corridor to his room. She veered off at the last minute but, halfway down the corridor, stopped. Coward, she hissed under her breath. What's the worst that can happen? He'll bite your head off. You won't die. Deep breath, a squaring of the shoulders, and she turned in a rush and swept into his room. Her face was grave, reserved, her eyes lowered. Then she forced herself to look up. The bed was empty. He was sitting on a wheelchair, his bandaged legs stretched out. Kabootar stood by, a mother hen, fussing over him. Her face lit up. She hopped with excitement.

'You got up!'

'Well the Mookerjis can't be accused of forgetting their manners. Though it may be a little while before I can stand up and do the honours.'

In her joy, she hugged Kabootar, whose seamed face turned red with delight and embarrassment. In the melee, her cap got knocked off. That unruly hair tumbled down, a soft cloud, framing her glowing face, strands and tendrils caught up in those parted lips. Debraj stared at her with a very queer, intense expression on his face. Aditi came to a stumbling stop.

'What…what are you doing?'

'I am thinking, Sister Aditi, that you are such a hodgepodge, such a bundle of contradictions.'

Defensive now, her face clouding over, she tried to settle her hair, gather her dignity. Kabootar slipped away quietly.

'Yes, I know, I've been told that before. I'm so harum scarum, so higgledy-piggledy, so…'

'So aagdoom baagdoom…' he added, quoting from a childhood nonsense rhyme.

She recognised it, started to grin.

'You are such a contrary creature, Sister.'

Her face fell. She stared at him, rebellious, uncertain, frightened of herself, braced against the storm. He watched her, watched all the conflicting emotions, some he could read, some unknowable, chasing across her face, like the shadows of passing clouds across an untravelled landscape, a dapple of sun and dark, shifting. Who was she, this girl still in her teens, with her delicate waist and her steely mind, this little country bumpkin with her fearsome intelligence, her strange aloofness coupled with an unfathomable passion — waiting, waiting to be ignited. Everything about her was in hiatus, a held breath, waiting to exhale. Even when she stood, one foot was slightly lifted, as if about to take off, poised to flee. Who was she? And did he really want to know? All his liaisons had been quite simple, undemanding. This was unfamiliar territory.

'Come here.'

'Why?'

'So you can help me to my bed, Sister.'

He knew he was playing her, some part of him wanting to be cruel, so he could keep his distance, not get sucked in. Yet, another part…

She pushed his wheelchair towards the bed, businesslike again, in control.

'Why is it so important for you to make me walk?'

'Captain, it's important to heal whoever comes here.'

He understood she had retreated behind her wall. He reached out, touched the back of her hand lightly. A tiny shiver and then she recovered her composure.

'I'll get an orderly. Please, just sit. Don't go anywhere.'

'Yes, Ma'am, I wasn't planning to.'

She left, unsmiling. He sat back. He could have any woman he wanted but this one, so outside his orbit, intrigued him. She was opaque, a puzzle. And he loved solving puzzles. The more enigmatic, the more challenging, the more he was pulled in. It would be fun, taking apart the pieces and putting them back together again.

'How's Aditi?' Geeta was having tea with Chhoto mashi.

'You tell me. I hardly get to see her. She's at the hospital 24 hours.'

'Really? I didn't know there was such a rush.'

'Well, there's some special patient apparently. It's become an obsession with her, trying to save him.'

'Can't be. We don't distinguish between patients.'

'Some Captain…Debraj something. He's been wounded and there's a chance he won't walk again. So…'

'Oh dear, did you say Debraj? Could it be…we all thought him dead. How did he land up here? I must tell Netaji.'

'Oh, another of Netaji's boys, is he?'

'Yes. Very…charismatic.'

'No wonder. She hasn't been herself.'

'Hmmm. A bit of a ladies' man, from the rumours one hears.'

'And she is still such a child.' Choto mashi frowned.

'Nonsense. She's a woman, Suchandra. How long do you think you are going to mother her?'

'As long as I can,' Chhoto mashi said, fiercely. 'She has won a fragile peace.' 'Was it very bad, when she lost her parents?'

'Became a ghost. She went around that empty Bolpur house, clutching her mother's worn sari for days. The servants couldn't take it away from her. She said it smelt of shiuli mala, the garland of tiny white flowers her mother used to wear in her hair. No one could get through to her. Only a neighbour's son, not much older than her, only he could get her to eat. Only he could get her to break her self-imposed silence. She came to me, broken but the bones of her grief have begun to heal, however crookedly. She is the child I could never have, given to me as a gift in the twilight of my life. I will shield her for as long as I can.'

'That's what all mothers say but still their children scrape their knees, fall off trees, fall in love with the wrong men and break their hearts.'

'All we can do is be there when they fall, and try to catch them.'

Nishonko came back to base camp bone tired, irritated, muddy. The sortie had been useless. Their truck had broken its axle, they had slogged cross country only to get bogged down in some bad marshland, some idiot had fallen into the river and lost all their rations and they were forced to march back through the night. In the communal camp bath, where the shower was actually just a perforated, rusted drum, he soaped his body, nut brown from the sun and puckered with all the battle scars of his 22-year-old life. He was sluicing off the hard, army issue soap when Neel came running into the bath house.

'Major, Sir, urgent call from HQ.'

'Oh, blast, tell them I'll call back.'

'You'll want to take it, Sir. I think it's Netaji.'

Wet-haired, bare feet, Nishonko rushed into the command tent and scooped up the receiver.

'Major Mitro here.'

The line was full of hissing static but his leader's voice came through, sonorous, deep, and all his tiredness just dropped away.

'How are you, Nishonko, my boy?'

'Waiting to see you again, Sir.'

'Well, you'll have to wait a whole lot longer. Twenty officers are being sent to Tokyo for training. Your name came up.'

'Sorry, Sir, did you say Tokyo?'

'Yes, my boy. I wanted the entire first division of INA to take part in the offensive. Japanese High Command came back saying our officers would need to get trained by them. So, are you up for it?'

'Absolutely, Sir, thank you, thank you for trusting me.'

'Thank you for trusting me, Nishonko. And, by the way, a bit of good news. Remember Debraj?'

'Yes, good man. Quite a loss.'

'Well, he's actually alive.'

'Come again, Sir?'

'He's alive. In hospital, apparently.'

'That's the best thing I've heard in weeks. Rangoon?'

'No, Singapur. They're not sure he will walk again.'

Static on the line. A moment of silence.

'How did he get to Singapur? I'll meet him as soon as I get some furlough.'

'Sorry but you will have to leave right away. I shall see you in Tokyo. I'm to meet Tojo by month end. Think he's keen now to get the operation underway.'

'That is good news, Sir.'

'And Nishonko, keep this under your hat. Eyes, ears everywhere.'

'Of course, Sir.'

Nishonko walked out, beaming. It was a huge step. And the fact Netaji had chosen him, had called him personally, made his heart full. And Debraj was alive! He felt like calling Aditi. He suddenly realised she was the only one with whom he would want to share something like this. Well, it could wait. He would come back, take her for dinner maybe. He would buy her something nice in Tokyo. What did she like? It was strange, he knew so little about her. But he would get to know her. They had time.

October was already halfway over. The nights in Singapur had turned a little cooler. When Ahmed Hassan left at midnight, Netaji was still hard at work, his customary coffee by his elbow, the smoke spiralling up from a parked cigarette. On an average, he put in about three hours of sleep. Often, the next morning, Hassan could tell how late Netaji had worked from the cigarette butts in the ashtray. That night, he sat down to write the proclamation of the Provisional Government of Free India. When they set foot on Indian soil, a political organisation would have to be in place to take over governance of the reclaimed territories. Once the British were thrown out, the Provisional Government would make room for a permanent government as decided by the Indian people. In drafting the proclamation, he drew on Indian history and elements of the Irish and American declarations of independence.

'*Having goaded Indians to desperation with its hypocrisy,*' he began, '*and having driven them to starvation and death by plunder and loot, British rule in India has forfeited the goodwill of the Indian people and is now living a precarious existence. It needs but a flame to destroy the last vestige of that unhappy rule. To light that flame is the task of India's Army of Liberation.*'

As the grandfather clock out in the hall tolled away the hours of the night, he wrote in a continuous flow, no corrections or superscriptions. His thoughts were already clearly formed, enunciated in his mind. He had been planning this for a long time. As dawn was breaking, he started the final paragraph: '*In the name of God, in the name of bygone generations who have welded the Indian people into one nation, and in the name of the dead heroes who have bequeathed us a tradition of heroism and sacrifice, we call upon the Indian people to rally around our banner and strike for India's freedom.*

'The Provisional Government is entitled to and hereby claims the allegiance of every Indian. It guarantees religious liberty, as well as equal rights and equal opportunities to its citizens. It declares its firm resolve to pursue the happiness and prosperity of the whole nation equally and transcending all differences cunningly fostered by an alien government in the past.'

Debraj felt restless. He had slept the whole afternoon and now, in the evening, felt cooped up. Aditi had been completely avoiding him the last few days. The Malay nurse, he kept forgetting her name, had taken over, her rather rough, matter of fact ministrations very different from Aditi's careful hands. He was irritated by Aditi's absence, her recalcitrance, her refusal to meet him halfway. To hell with her, prissy Miss two shoes. He rang his bell but no one came. Where was everybody? He struggled to ease himself out of his bed and managed to collapse onto his wheelchair.

Outside, the cold, antiseptic smell of the floor cleaners made him sneeze. He could see the nurses' station at the far end, light spilling out of an open door. But he didn't fancy talking to any of them. He felt a cool current of air coming from somewhere. He swerved and headed for its promise of freedom.

A verandah led out onto a small walled garden. Crickets chirped. The oversweet fragrance of some nocturnal flower, the damp smell of earth filled his lungs. It was turning dark, twilight softening the outlines of the little stone cherub perched under a drooping willow. He, suddenly thirsted for a stiff drink and a cigarette. He thought of Nishonko, how he would never light a second cigarette from his match, calling it sniper bait. 'One strike, the enemy can't draw a bead. But you pass the flame to another cigarette, he's got you in his cross sights and poof, your head bursts like a watermelon as you bend down to cup the light.' All of a sudden, he missed Nishonko, missed his dry, reserved manner, his down-to-earth words. He missed Pandey ji and even the ever-disapproving Captain Nawaz. He missed the male ribaldry and the clean, single-mindedness of soldiers engaged in battle. He realised that none of them had tried to find out how he was, that the knowledge had been secretly rankling inside. Did no one care? Or, maybe, they didn't even know where he was.

A shadow darkened the doorway. A figure in white, a nurse, stood there, shoulders hunched, indistinct in the twilight.

'Hello,' Debraj called out, softly.

She straightened up, stepped into a spill of light. It was Aditi. He was absurdly happy to see her. She drew in a deep shuddering breath. 'What are you doing out here?'

'Following doctor's orders, doing my evening constitutional. Where's everybody?' He was glad to have her back.

She shook her head, as if trying to clear it. 'One of the operations up north, it went wrong. We've all been busy.'

'Are you okay?'

A long sigh of bone tiredness. She absent-mindedly started peeling off surgical gloves. He saw they were soaked in blood. He noticed that she still had a surgical mask curled around her throat. Without looking at him, she started to talk, in a flat monotone.

'They tell us it's useless, you know, to waste time and supplies on the ones who are too…damaged. It's so tough to get medicines, morphine. We are always running short. So who deserves them more? The ones who can continue to fight…or the ones who have already fought so hard and sacrificed so much? We make that call every night. We play God.'

He wheeled his chair to her, reached out his hand. She took it absent-mindedly, slowly sliding down the stone wall till she was resting on the stone flags, propped against his bandaged leg. He cupped his hand on the nape of her neck. She leaned back, accepting the solace.

'They accept our "professional" judgement silently, no complaints. But their eyes Debraj, their eyes. What happens if we are wrong? Maybe, if we had held on a little longer, given him some more penicillin, maybe…'

'Who did you lose?'

'Too many. Anwar Qasim. A big bull of a man, a laugh like a big drum. Told me to give the morphine to the bachchas, the kids. Went so gently into the night with his god's name on his shattered lips.'

She started to cry softly, hot fat drops. He leaned forward and enfolded her, burying his face in the springy, curly, cloudy mass of her hair. She smelled of hay, spring water, oranges and lye. They remained like that for a long moment. Then, she stirred, turned her face up to his. He stared at her, at the wide apart eyes, the dark bruises of weariness like smudged kohl underneath. She stared back. His hair had grown back, curly. He had not been shaving and his cheeks, hollow, thin, were shadowed with the beginnings of a beard. The irises of those grey, gold flecked eyes were wide open, dilated, like a cat's. The scar across his forehead, still healing, was a livid pink. She reached up to touch it with her fingertips. He held them, brought them to his lips. Then they kissed, chaste at first, the merest brush of lip against lip, then exploring, feeling their way, then the shock of hunger, and finally the plunge into the wet, secret recesses of each other. It was her first kiss.

Above, in the patch of night sky seen from the walled garden, fireworks went off, pin wheels of light. But they were oblivious, drowning in each other.

Chhoto mashi looked up from her book, startled by the loud crackle and popping. Was it gunfire? She stepped out of her front door to see what on earth could be happening. On the streets, people were cheering, soldiers hugging each other.

'Ki baypaar? What's happening?'

An Anglo-Indian man turned to her and shouted, 'They've proclaimed a new government!'

'Wait... Who?'

'The Provisional Government of Azad Hind Fauj... Netaji announced it today. No stopping us now.'

The proclamation of the Provisional Government had been read out in Hindustani, Tamil, and English that afternoon. Netaji had addressed 50,000 Indians in the Padang in Singapur. His voice choked with emotion, he had taken a vow.

'In the name of God, I take this sacred oath — that, to liberate India and the three hundred and eighty million of my countrymen, I, Subhas Chandra Bose, will continue this sacred war of freedom till the last breath of my life.'

A few days later, the Provisional Government declared war on Britain and USA. Nine states of the Axis and pro-Axis powers, including Japan and Germany, gave diplomatic recognition to the Indian Provisional Government. Personal congratulations came from Ireland.

The old man sits back in the tea shop chair, his milky eyes full of remembered excitement.

'History was being made. Everyone was charged up. Finally, it looked like the months of waiting were going somewhere. Netaji went on a whirlwind tour of East Asia, attended hundreds of meetings.'

Sudipto too jumps up, paces around, his eyes shining. 'It was an extraordinary time. Look at it. In less than four months, Netaji had galvanised the entire freedom movement of overseas Indians. More than 2 million Indian civilians — maybe three million, as Netaji claimed — came together. There were capitalists, labourers, professionals who had migrated, financiers from South India. And we also had novelists, poets, artists, missionaries, mystics and anti-colonial visionaries.'

'We? You are behaving as if you were there.' Ganesh babu is supercilious.

'In a way, we were. It was the beginning of *our* freedom movement,' Sudipto says with a smile.

The old man stares at him. 'How do you know all this, boy?'.

'Studied it in some depth. There's loads written about all this — by the British, the Americans, *Time* magazine. And a lot was recorded on film and in photographs. There's a wealth of material on Netaji. Sadly, most of it is under wraps, with the whole controversy about his death. But my grandmother…we were intimately connected with the freedom movement.'

'Arre, we all were,' Ganesh babu protests. 'My great uncle on my mother's side, Anirban Haldar, you must have heard about him, he was a freedom fighter also.'

Dulal da scoffs. 'Ganesh babu, everyone is now saying they were freedom fighters. No offence, okay, your Anirban uncle…'

'Great uncle.'

'Whatever. He must have been a good man but nowadays, any Tom, Dick, Hari is saying he fought for independence. Reason being? Government is giving concessions to freedom fighters. So all and sundry making applications. It's a racket, baba. Who will know for sure? I can say my pop was on the Dandi March. You prove he wasn't.'

'So how do we know Grandpa here, was there or not?'

'Oh, I was there alright,' the old man grunts.

'I am just saying.'

'Shall we stop interrupting him and let him get on with the story? Too many intervals.' Dulal da drums his fingers on the table.

They met in one of the teahouses. Tokyo was a desolate place, bombed out, a smoking ruin. But this particular establishment had somehow escaped the terrible toll. The teahouse owner led them to the back, to a peaceful little garden with black rocks floating in carefully raked 'seas' of sand. The sound of running water falling and turning on water wheels was soothing. Nishonko found himself relaxing as he picked up the tiny translucent bowl of tea and sipped from it.

'Mmmm...no milk?'

Netaji smiled. 'Murder, that's murdering good tea. It's the British who did that, wanting cream in everything. Now, a good Oolong, that's nectar, not to be tampered with.'

'I suppose I could get used to it.'

Nishonko sipped again and felt calm descend. It had been so long since he had spent any private time with Netaji that he had forgotten how he could put you at ease.

'And how is your training going?'

'They are a strange race, Sir. Very martial, militaristic, driven by ideas of honour code. Extraordinary discipline. And incredibly obsessive about detail. They have had a long history of battle, internecine mostly. They came very close to being invaded by the Mongols but they believe Kamikaze, their divine wind, saved them, not allowing the hordes to cross the sea. So, in an ironical, almost poetic twist, they have named their suicide air missions kamikaze.'

'You seem to admire them.'

'Not really, they are insular to a fault, and it is difficult to make friends because no one speaks English.'

'Now that is indeed ironic, English having to be our lingua franca.'

Nishonko grimaced. He poured out more tea, breathing in the earthy forest smell. 'But they have a great sense of beauty and tradition that lies at the core of their belief that they are a nation ordained by divinity to rule.'

'Very good, Nishonko, very observant. I'm proud of you. They are such a tiny country but they can teach us many things about the art of war.'

'But, Sir, this is not to question your judgement but they do seem exhausted, running out of steam and pretty thinly stretched.'

'You are right, my boy but as long as they help us through this campaign, we will achieve our aim. I have come here to parley on equal terms with Tojo. I have demanded they hand over the Andaman Nicobar Islands to us.'

'Tall order, Sir.'

'Well, they accepted our Provisional Government. This Government should govern the liberated zones within India and exercise jurisdiction over abandoned Indian property all over South East Asia. That's our right — just as it is our right to issue our own currency and have our own air force. I have also demanded full control of intelligence operatives to be sent to India.'

'That's…it takes my breath away. You know, we just focus on fighting, gain a mile, lose two, put one foot in front of the other, go from one mission to another, while you — you think of things — most of us can't even imagine things that far ahead.'

'But you, you do the truly hard things. You put your life on the line every day, you take the burden of another man's blood on your hands. You live with the bad food, the hard ground as your bed, the leeches and the loneliness. Your parents, how long have you not seen them?'

Nishonko's face contracted involuntarily. He had not thought of his parents for a very long time. It was, as if being in prison, they had ceased to exist. He tried to remember their faces but all he could picture was the old studio photograph of them, which he carried with him. What did his mother look like now? Had her hair turned grey? Did she still sing her favourite Tagore songs the way she used to while watering her garden at dusk? Did she even have a garden to water? And his Baba, already a little bent, a little absent-minded even before going to prison, was he well? Did he still roll those hand-made cigarettes, spitting out that fleck of tobacco as he lit up? The memories had come rushing back, pouring out of the floodgates, opened up by his teacher. Memories but curiously no feelings. He remembered them but with detachment, no real pain. He looked up. Netaji was watching him through his round glasses.

'It's been a long time, Sir. I don't even know whether they are in the same prison.'

'They are there. I send them news when I can. Your father's health has been indifferent.'

'My mother?'

'We are negotiating for her release. Her age, the fact that she is a woman. But the British — they are very single-minded in their tyranny. They want to keep people like your parents firmly behind bars, as an example that they can do anything they please.'

Netaji looked at the calm, opaque face, the lack of any emotion. He sometimes felt sadness at these arrested lives. He had asked so much of them, so many sacrifices to be made. But Nishonko, especially, seemed to have become somehow removed, remote. But it made him an efficient soldier, an effective commander. Suddenly, his thoughts flew to that other boy, the one who had survived. Debraj, that was his name. He wondered how he was doing.

'When shall we be going back, Sir?'

'Soon. We will need you before we embark for Burma.'

'Is that where it will happen?'

'You haven't heard it. Singapur, Rangoon, they're all crawling with spies, carpetbaggers, out for the main chance. The British are desperate. They know something big is going down. They just don't know exactly where and when.'

'My lips are sealed.'

'Good. Wish me well. I meet Tojo tomorrow.'

Gaffar Khan, who had been keeping vigil outside, handed Netaji his overcoat. It was already end of October and Tokyo was quite cold. He signalled to the bodyguards huddled against the wind outside the gate. They formed a phalanx around their leader and whisked him away. Nishonko walked back through the ruined streets. He wished he could be part of Netaji's personal circle, so that he could learn, the way he used to at Elgin Road, at his feet and witness the creation of history up close. Maybe, that was why Netaji had sent him here, so that he could play a more concrete role in the days to come. The thought filled his heart with a sense of deep satisfaction.

Prime Minister Tojo was seated in his tokonoma, a private alcove with Shinto prayer scrolls and delicate ink water colours on the wall. Tojo, though dressed in a simple indigo cotton kimono, looked every inch the daimyo, the traditional Japanese noble that he was. The close cropped hair, moustache and round spectacles were instantly recognisable. His likeness had been printed on millions of recruitment posters in the West. His face was the symbol of the inscrutable enemy.

To Netaji's surprise, kneeling across from him was General Renya Mataguchi. Netaji had thought he was meeting Tojo alone.

'Ah Subhas, I trust you have met the General.'

'His name is legend.' Netaji bowed deeply. Mataguchi's handshake was firm, a soldier's grip.

'So Renya, tell us about your plans regarding India.' Tojo leaned back on the tatami mat.

Mataguchi unfurled a large map. 'Tojo san, the lance of the armies of Nippon is ready to pierce India here and here. This arc, 400 miles across, will close in on the British. With the fall of Imphal and Kohima, the British will be on the retreat.'

'Excellent. But time is of the essence, Renya. It's no secret that our campaigns against the Americans in the Pacific have faltered somewhat. Maybe we've underestimated them, thought them to be a soft, effete people. But they are going for the throat of Japan itself. Many of our esteemed colleagues fear the tide is turning against us. They have begun to whisper in the Emperor's ear, *Tojo is losing his grip*.'

'Bastards!' Renya's voice was high.

Tojo shook his head, smiling. 'Just politicians. But I need a big victory, Renya, a spectacular one. You understand?'

Mataguchi nodded. Tojo had been the toast of the Japanese nation when they were winning. But now, there was a shadow over him. There was talk of finding a new prime minister. Tojo was telling him that it was probably his last chance to redeem himself.

Tojo broke into his thoughts. 'Now this whole India exercise started as a minor distraction...a side show, an experiment. But now ..'

Netaji saw that Tojo was looking straight at him. In a flash, he understood why this meeting had been initiated. Tojo's next words confirmed his impression.

'What Subhas has been proposing is dramatic but not preposterous. Others don't agree but I'm convinced that this campaign in India is the key to our future. Mind you, this is not a normal military campaign where we are trying to win territory. We have no interest in capturing Indian lands. We have no ambitions to rule India. But, if our joint spearhead results in Indian civilians and troops rising up in revolt, I'm convinced that Britain will sue for peace. Subhas wants freedom for his people... I want to get Britain to the negotiating table. If I can do that, it will force their cousins, the Americans, to parley too. Then I can extract the most favourable terms from them. The lynchpin to this enterprise is you and your INA, Subhas. It's our last chance at turning things around in this war.'

So there it was. Tojo had declared how crucial the India campaign was to the Japanese. He wanted Bose to understand that no favours were being granted here. They were equal partners.

'Negotiations, Sir? With the gaiko, the baijo?!' Mataguchi's derision for the whites, the outsiders was scathing.

Tojo laughed. 'Ah Renya, you have the warrior's disdain for negotiations. I don't have that luxury. Today, getting favourable terms is akin to victory.'

'But the strategy of the Kirimomi Sakusen, the driving charge, got us Singapore, Malay and the Philippines. They are on the run everywhere. This will work. You'll bury your critics, Sir.'

'Hmm. Do you have a good man there, Renya?'

'I have a brilliant young man there. Brigadier Saito. Best man for the job.'

'Good to have the young to lead. But young men can be impatient. They don't appreciate how war can be like a game of cards. One wrong move and the whole strategy can become undone. They seldom have any regard for the sweep of history.'

'This one is different, Tojo san. He gets it. He understands.'

Tojo bowed. 'I have faith in your judgement, Renya.'

Mataguchi bowed back. 'I promise you, daimyo, I will not let you down!' Tojo looked up with a start. Mataguchi had just addressed him as his lord. He paused, then reached across and grasped Mataguchi's shoulder. It was the traditional gesture of a lord acknowledging his samurai. Mataguchi realised that Tojo had tacitly admitted him to his inner coterie. His star would now rise or sink with Tojo.

Netaji too understood. The question that had bothered him from the beginning had been answered today. *What was in it for Japan?* Simple — their survival depended on it. He stood up. 'I too pledge to do my best to support you. You hold the future of Japan in your hands.'

'Come, come Subhas, I'm but a small man.' Tojo made himself seem diminutive by bowing low.

'It all depends on the light, Tojo san. If the light is with you, even a small man can cast a very large shadow.'

'Ha! Well put, my friend! Let's keep the light on our side then.'

Tojo saluted them both.

'The light on our side!'

When the large, rather ostentatious car drove up to the entrance of the mansion on the outskirts of Singapur, Goopta, fastidiously dressed, got out. A Chinese manservant opened the big, brass-studded door and bowed deeply.

'Welcome, most honoured gentleman. You are expected.'

Goopta, smoothing down his laboriously cultivated, pencil moustache, gestured with a quintessential Indian jerk of the head that said enough with the blandishments, chal, get on with it, man. Inside, a group of men, Burmese, some Indians, merchants by the look of them, a sprinkling of Chinese, some Muslims in traditional garb, greeted Goopta with varying degrees of bonhomie. But he was the perfect guest, smiling, nodding, patting backs, bowing, a compliment here, a facetious comment there. Finally, he found himself centre stage, the men in a semi-circle around him.

'Gentlemen, thank you for inviting me to this noble gathering. We have common interests, the most common of which is making money, lots of it, heh heh.'

There were smiles and nods, a guffaw from a red-faced Burmese gentleman sprawled in one of the armchairs.

'I represent certain parties who want to be partner in all the post-war opportunities waiting for picking.'

'Parties or the Party? I believe you are rather intimately attached to one in particular,' the Burmese gentleman with the exaggerated sense of humour chortled. Goopta gave him a blank look, then carried on as if the interruption had not happened.

'As I said, I'm allied to certain interests who are wanting very much to have stake in the future prosperity of this part of the world. Timber, shipping, construction, oh, the prospects are quite mouth-watering. The thing, of course, will be to make sure we are all on the winning side.'

There was a pause. No one spoke for a few seconds. These were not men with much loyalty. They had no political philosophy other than expediency.

Goopta smiled, understandingly. 'Precisely. Who will win, who knows? So we take control over who wins, isn't it so, gentlemen?'

The gentlemen in question nodded eagerly. Now, that was an idea!

'From whom we stand to gain most?'

'Definitely not that man Bose!' a man in a white fez burst out. 'All those ideas about egalitarianism and equality and all that brotherly Hindu-Muslim bhai bhai bullshit — it's not going to fly. Muslims and Hindus, they can't co-exist.'

'Oh, come now, Omar,' piped up a thin, intelligent-looking Chettiar man. 'We have co-existed for centuries, my dear man.'

'No, correction please, we Muslims have reigned over you. Do you forget who were the rulers before the British came?'

There was a bit of an uproar at that.

'No, I don't. Our civilisation goes back much longer than the advent of some blood-thirsty desert bedouin who came to pillage and rape. We are the majority, like it or not. It will be called Hindustan, that's what Netaji promises.'

Goopta watched Omar intently, letting the argument play out.

'Precisely. The man will create a Hindu state, which will never allow other religions to have an equal say. And that includes your church, Mr. Fonseca, and your fire temples, Mr. Sodabottlewala.' Omar growled.

'Well, I don't really agree with Mr. Omar here,' the gentleman called Mr. Fonseca said with a smile. 'Bose has a real chance of winning, of pulling off the impossible. We would do well to not underestimate him.'

Goopta was delighted. The lines had been drawn, the sides taken, the men who would do his bidding identified.

'Gentlemen, gentlemen, not to lose sight of our priorities. For the purpose of business, we have to control the outcome. If Bose wins, we must be able to dictate our terms. If he loses, we should make sure we don't sink with that particular ship. But to do that, we must know what he is up to, eh? I'm told he is planning big campaign. Where, when, this is not clear. Who can provide us with information from the inside? Information, gentlemen. That is real power. Who is on his staff that can become our eyes and ears? Who can be *ghumaoed*, turned, made into our creature?'

He left them with the thought as they were led in for dinner by the Chinese major domo. Goopta hung back till Omar caught up with him. He fell into step.

'So what is it you deal in Mr. Omar?'

'Perfumes, spices, oil, any thing really, Mr. Goopta. We have built a far-flung network.'

'And it is a family business?'

'Indeed. From my grandfather's time. And you?'

'Like you, I take what comes. My enterprise however is entirely built by myself, yours truly.'

'You have sons?'

'My only grief. I have a daughter whom I love to distraction but alas, the business brain, she does not have.'

'That is indeed unfortunate. To know everything you have toiled for will go to another man's son.'

'Well, I take my pleasure in the chase, the planning and the pursuit of wealth. She will be rich and taken care of but I intend to enjoy the fruits here and now. Tell me, Omar, what we were discussing earlier. Do you know of such a person?'

'I may have just the man for you.'

Gaffar laid out the evening clothes carefully on the bed. Netaji would be back any minute from the Ramakrishna Mission. This was where he went at the end of a hectic day at the Indian Independence League office at Chancery Lane. Ever since he had come back from Tokyo, it had been a whirlwind. The trip had been an unqualified success. His speech at the Greater East Asia Conference had held the entire assembly in awe. They had been swept off their feet by his passion, foresight, vast knowledge and conviction. Tojo had reiterated his full support and announced the transfer of Andaman and Nicobar islands, as a token of his commitment. General Sugiyama, the army chief, had agreed to regard INA as an allied army. Netaji had pushed through his advantage and put in requests for equipment to build a navy and an air force. But — and this was the most astonishing thing — he had said that he regarded all Japanese support as loans to be repaid and undertook to pay for civilian recruits in the INA from his own funds. From the time he had returned, he had been attending meetings non-stop at Supreme Command HQ to discuss strategy, or dropping in at the training camps or drumming up support. The Ramakrishna Mission was his oasis of calm. At day's end, he would change into a silk dhoti and meditate for an hour or two alone. He would then emerge rejuvenated, serene.

'And who are we meeting tonight, Gaffar?' Netaji asked as he entered the living room. Gaffar consulted a pad.

'Gangadhar Goopta. Timber merchant, ship-owner, landowner, recently joined Congress, looking for…'

'Yes, yes, I get the picture.'

Goopta was ushered in. Today, he had decided to dress in khadi and Gandhi cap.

'Namashkar, Goopta babu, welcome.'

He was unctuous and bowing, as he walked into Netaji's presence. 'Ah, Netaji, I am too much honoured, to be in your presence. Thank you for giving time in the middle of your so, busy schedule.'

'And what brings you here?'

'Mutual interests, I hope. I am anxious to form an association that will benefit both of us, in the event you eventually win.'

'Oh, we will win, do not doubt that.'

'Then we should discuss business.'

'The only business we are interested in right now is the business of liberating our country. How can you help us?'

'Well, there is small matter of…how you call it? Quid pro quo?'

'Ah, quid pro quo. You know, I was speaking to a few eminent Chettiar and Tamil businessmen the other day. They were asking me whether total mobilisation means contributing 10 per cent or 5 per cent of their assets. I asked these people, who think in percentages, whether we should tell our soldiers to fight and spill only 10 per cent of their blood and save the rest. In the end, of course, I gratefully accepted 100 per cent from the enthusiastic and 10 per cent from the reluctant. But the niggardliness of a few is far, far exceeded by the generosity of many others. There are stunning instances in which millionaires chose to become fakirs. At one meeting, with 15,000 Indians in Penang, we raised 2 million Straits dollars in a single day. Remember, Gaffar?'

Gaffar nodded, politely. Goopta looked up at him, his eyes disinterested. 'You are Gaffar Khan?'

Gaffar nodded, surprised.

'Are you related to Omar Ibrahim?'

'I have met him once. He's an eminent businessman.'

'Ah, must be my mistake. He was speaking of you highly.'

Gaffar was puzzled. The meeting with the gentleman in question had been very brief, after the Friday prayers, and on the part of Mr. Ibrahim, singularly disinterested and dismissive. He wanted to ask this Mr. Goopta what Mr. Ibrahim had said about him but he had already turned away and was listening to Netaji. Netaji was asking him about Calcutta, the weather there, how the Durga Puja had been that year, innocuous things. Every time Goopta tried to steer the conversation to Netaji's plans, Netaji would deftly sidestep the question and veer into some distraction. Gaffar quietly suppressed a smile as Netaji stood up and adroitly ushered his visitor towards the door, speaking of looking forward to doing business with him.

'When can we meet again to discuss specifics?'

'In good time. Meanwhile, why don't you come to one of our fundraisers, meet some of the brave men who are fighting for our cause. In fact, there are some from Calcutta you might know.'

'Really? And would there be one called Nishonko Mitro?'

'Ah, you know Nishonko Mitro?'

'Well, I have heard of his exploits.'

'Really? Where did you hear about him?'

Goopta was flummoxed for a couple of seconds but he quickly recovered. 'Oh, here and there. Rumours. I know someone who knows someone in the police. He said this Mitro character escaped the police dragnet and fled with another man, no one knows where.'

'Hmmm, did they? Well, this Mitro is not here but there are others you should meet. They will inspire you. I will arrange for Gaffar to invite you.'

'Oh, I shall look forward to that.'

Waiting in the porch for his car to come to the door, Goopta found himself fortuitously alone with Gaffar for a few moments. Gaffar stood to attention, courteous but impassive. His beard, dyed henna, was jutting out, maybe a bit imperiously. He had handled the likes of Goopta before and he wasn't particularly fond of the breed. Goopta spoke without looking at him.

'So, you have known Netaji a long time?'

'Long enough.'

'And you think he will win this round?'

'It is what we pray for, Sir.'

'And your god will be happy if he wins?'

'God is great.'

'And your god will approve even if your Netaji robs you of your promised land?'

Gaffar's head snapped around to look at the small man. He was busy twirling the end of his moustache to make it curl like a scimitar.

'Netaji will never rob us of anything. He is a good man, an honourable man.'

'Absolutely, salt of the earth. But maybe you should ask him what he feels about Partition. I'm sure you know Mr. Jinnah's views. It would be most salutary to know where Netaji draws the line. Ah, here he is.'

The car purred to a halt. The chauffeur held the door open. Mr. Goopta placed his beringed fingers on Gaffar's arm.

'Thank you for a very pleasant evening, Gaffar ji. And do look up Mr. Omar, when you have the time.'

Kabootar was sitting in the verandah outside one of the wards, when a commotion outside made him get up. A motorcade was drawing up. He shook Debraj, who was dozing in his wheelchair, awake.

'Captain, Netaji…he's here.'

Netaji entered. The patients out in the verandah, including Debraj on his wheelchair, craned their heads to see. Netaji went down the ward, speaking, encouraging, drawing laughter out of even the most wounded men. The ward was silent, just the murmur of his voice heard. He finished with the last bed, stepped out on to the verandah where the men, bandaged, bent over crutches, limbs and eyes missing, stood to attention, their gazes fixed ahead, as if for a ceremonial inspection. Netaji walked down the line, greeting them, his eyes soaked with respect. Debraj was thinner, paler, his gaunt face hidden behind a bushy beard but Netaji recognised him immediately.

'My boy, how are you doing? They told me we nearly lost you.'

'Scraped through, Sir.'

'Excellent. How soon are you going to be operational?

'Should be back in the field in a few weeks,' Debraj answered.

'At least a month, Sir,' Geeta interjected from behind. 'His wounds are…'

Netaji shook his head. 'Not good enough. We need him before that…even if he has to be wheeled out. Can we do that, Geeta?'

'If you really need him, Sir.'

'Begging your pardon, Sir but I'm not being carried out on a dratted wheelchair. On my own two feet, if I may. Won't be able to face the men like this.'

'I don't want you out in the front, Captain.'

Debraj's face fell.

'I need you for something equally important. I need you to get out there and talk to Indian prisoners of war and convince the fence sitters to join the INA. These soldiers have been deployed overseas to defend Britain's imperial interests. So they have been insulated from all the civilian and political discontent back home.'

'What do you want of me, Sir?' Debraj's tone was a little stiff.

'You, the sight of you — in a wheelchair, on crutches, I don't care which — when they see our young, brave warrior, wounded in battle, back from the dead, it will give them pause. What do you think?'

There was a whisper of hesitation, a flash of rebellion in Debraj's eyes. This man was responsible for his being stuck in this awful place, maybe crippled for life. Why the hell should he actually help him? He owed him nothing. He wasn't sure he even believed in half the things this man professed. But if Netaji won, that would be his ticket to freedom. He would be able to go back home, pick up the pieces of his life. And all he had to do was chat up some soldiers.

'Well, I could haul myself around on a pair of crutches, I suppose.'

'Perfect. And while you're about it, attend a couple of fundraising events. Can you do that, Debraj? For me? I sorely need that charm of yours.'

Debraj nodded, albeit a little curtly.

'Good man. And Geeta, who is the Sister you were mentioning — the one who nursed him back to health?'

Geeta gestured to Aditi who had been standing inside the ward to step forward. She came, her eyes shining, and saluted crisply.

'Sister Aditi Sen, Sir!'

Netaji looked at her, the firm set to her mouth, her lucid gaze.

'Good job, Sister.'

She glowed.

Outside in the driveway, Geeta turned to Netaji. 'He's nowhere near ready, you do realise that?'

'I don't have the luxury of waiting, Geeta. We'll get only one small window of time. I need him. Badly. With your permission, can we borrow Sister Aditi…you know, to rehabilitate him? Take him to the meetings? She has something special — something those battle-hardened men will not be able to resist.'

That night, dinner was a relaxed affair. They had enjoyed the simple but well-cooked meal. Ahmed Hassan was in attendance along with Professor Murthy and Giani, and Geeta came in towards the end. She had started recounting the afternoon hospital visit but Netaji refused to discuss work while eating. Dinner, for him, was a hallowed time.

Instead, he held forth on a variety of fish recipes and different ways of cooking spinach and bitter gourd.

'Every home in Bengal has a different way of cooking it and the recipes are closely guarded secrets.'

Geeta laughed. 'Even in our extended family, each aunt will cook rasam differently. But whatever twist we use, we all swear that Amma's, our mother's, rasam is supreme.'

Netaji nodded, his eyes far away. 'Yes, the payaish cooked by my mother, for the Bengali New Year, nothing else in the world tasted like that.'

There was a pause. Each mind drifted to the people at home. They were all exiles, homeless in a way, adrift. Until freedom came and they could go back to the shores which had nurtured them, they had only memories and the cherished rituals of their banished lives to sustain them.

'Kali Puja is coming.' Netaji's voice was soft.

Gaffar was quietly at their elbows, offering hot steaming coffee redolent with the fragrance of freshly crushed beans. They sipped, tasted that special pinch of spices he put in which gave it an exotic twist.

'Where did you get him?' Giani asked when he withdrew.

'Yes, I have been fortunate. He's the perfect aide. Ran into him in Kabul. Came out of nowhere when I came back and basically took over my life.'

'He is privy to everything, isn't he?'

'Yes, we have seen much history unfold.'

'You trust him?'

'Implicitly.'

It rained heavily that night, the kind of gushing equatorial shower common to Singapur, bringing with it a welcome drop in the temperature. A cool, wet breeze came in through the open windows. Netaji was pensive that evening, deep in thought. Maybe the dinner time conversation had brought back memories of Germany, of love put on hold. Or was he thinking of Elgin Road and its inmates? He sat by himself, smoking, staring at a map spread out on the table.

'Anything else, Sir?'

Gaffar Khan stood at the door.

'Thank you Gaffar, I'm fine.'

Gaffar cleared up the table. 'Are you done with that, Sir?' He pointed to the map.

'We won't be done until the dream of an undivided India comes true.'

Gaffar paused, then started to roll the map up. 'What about the idea of Partition, Sir?'

'What about it, Gaffar?'

'Should we not have separate states for…'

'No, Gaffar, what is the point of ripping the country, neighbours, and families apart, tearing hearts and minds asunder? What is the point of uprooting people from the land they have tilled for generations? An undivided India, Hindu and Muslim side-by-side, will be a strong India.'

Gaffar, his back to Netaji, clenched the map. 'With Hindus in the majority, Sir?'

'Equal, Gaffar, equal. Isn't that what we have been fighting for?'

'In an ideal world, Sir. But…'

'But what, Gaffar? Is it such an impossibility? Have you been listening to those hotheads in the League?'

'No, I…' Gaffar stopped. 'I'm sorry, Sir. It is not my place to ask you anything.'

'Of course it is, Gaffar. If I can't convince you, you who are so close to me, how will I convince the millions of others who are hell bent on ripping the land apart? Ahmed, Giani…they are Muslims. Do you think they are sacrificing their lives to create a divided India?'

Gaffar was silent, his head down. Netaji looked at him, shook his head. 'Good night, Gaffar. We'll speak again.'

The so-called recovery room was actually just a big, draughty spare room on the first floor of the hospital, tucked away under the eaves. It was filled with odds and ends, spare beds and rolled mattresses, large drums and tarpaulin. Aditi was with Debraj, making him work on his legs. He was in agony, sweating, gasping with the effort. She was squatting behind him on the ground, using her hands to push and pull the wasted muscle.

'Come on, one more time, Captain, push against my hand.'

He did and let out a muted scream, then abruptly shoved her away and collapsed on a nearby torn mattress.

'To hell with this… I can't take this.'

She looked at the massive scars running down the leg, the mutilated knee and felt only pity. But pity wouldn't get him out of here.

'Fine, suit yourself.'

She started getting her things together, her mouth set in a hard line. He shook his head.

'That's it? That's all you're going to do? Sulk?'

'Well, I'll also be reporting to Geeta Ma'am that they should forget about you.'

'Who the dickens are you to decide what I can and can't do?'

'Oh good, then you tell Netaji that you won't be going on his precious...'

'You're such a…' He bit on the words.

'Go on, call me names. Not going to make you walk.'

'Can't you see how hard it's for me? I don't know how many men would have survived that journey.'

'Sure…but it's pointless if you are going to be so pathetic and feel so sorry for yourself. You want to get mad at somebody? Get mad at your self. Stop being a cry baby.'

He gasped. No one, no woman, not even his own mother had ever spoken this way to him. If she had been a man, he would have got up and beaten him to a pulp. He glared at her, his fists bunched. But she stood her ground, her arms crossed, staring him down. His own eyes dropped. He looked at his legs, mutilated, wasted, and felt a wave of disgust and self pity wash over him. Tears pricked his eyes but he held back with a supreme effort of will. She was not going to have the satisfaction of seeing him weak.

'Okay, let's try again.' He tried to smile but it came out lopsided.

'Let's,' she said, unsmiling, dropping her things on the ground. She held out her hand. He looked at it, the nails cut short, shorn of all feminine adornment, then pulled himself up, shunning her help. A shaft of pain almost blinded him, making him sway but then it passed.

'Alright, let's take it from the beginning.'

As Gaffar finished his salat at the Masjid Omar Kampong Melaka mosque, dusk was settling over the golden dome. Gaffar sighed, took off his head covering. He did not feel at peace. His mind was full of troubled, conflicting thoughts. Battling with his deep sense of loyalty to Netaji was his conviction that his brethren would never get a fair deal in post-Independence India, regardless of who ruled it. The street was deserted. The clock across the river struck the hour. He was late. Netaji would be home soon. As he began to walk briskly, a big car with a sweeping hood drew up alongside. The setting sun glinted off its chrome embellishments. The window slid down. A podgy hand with many rings came out through the window and gestured to him to approach. He tentatively stepped forward. Inside the car, leaning back against the plush upholstery sat Goopta, a fat cigar clenched in his mouth. Another man sat in the shadows behind him.

'Ah, Gaffar ji, wonderful bumping into you. I told Mr. Omar here, that looks like Gaffar.'

The other gentleman leaned forward also and touched his hand to his forehead in a ceremonious gesture. 'Salaam alaikum, Gaffar bhai.'

'Alaikum salaam, Omar sahib.'

'Would you like a lift? You are going to Meyer Road?'

Gaffar looked at his stopwatch. He got into the car, leaned back.

'Thank you, you are most kind.'

Debraj was sweating profusely, rivulets running down his scarred bare body. It was another, hot humid afternoon in the recovery room. He held on to the pitted, peeling wall grimly, slowly trying to do squats, gritting his teeth each time he had to push up. Aditi leaned near the only window, trying to find some comfort in the hot, sluggish air that came in, watching him. His body, had become stronger. The khakis he wore hung loosely round his hips, revealing the hard slab of muscle down his sides. He's beautiful, Aditi thought. It was followed by a hot flush of guilt and embarrassment. What was wrong with her? Ever since that kiss that night, she had been intensely, painfully aware of him, the way the down on his arm moved in the breeze, the unconscious curling of those long, strong fingers as they turned the pages of a book, the dampness of his hair at the nape of his neck. She had thought about the kiss, over and over again, the blood warmth of the inside of his mouth, the clutch of his hand in the small of her back, the sense of falling endlessly. Neither had spoken about it. She had avoided close contact ever since, scrupulously treating him as a patient. But just looking at him sleeping, his arm lying across his eyes, made her breathless. She had no idea what to do with these alien sensations, how to handle it. Now she stole another look, saw his shoulders sag on an expelled breath.

'Take a break, you look exhausted.'

'Fat lot you care,' he muttered under his breath.

'Are we feeling sorry for ourselves again?'

'You wouldn't understand.'

'Try me.'

'Can't we get out of here? I hate this place. People dying, the bad dreams, that stench of illness and floor cleaner — how can anyone get well here?'

'Where would you go?'

'I don't know...back to the camp...get a room...some digs... anything.'

'What about...'

She paused, terrified of what she was going to say, the consequences. He looked at her, the way she held herself, almost rigid, the consternation on her face. He wanted to hold her, bury his face in her hair, taste the salt of her lips. But after the kiss that day, she had gone behind her wall, become all Sister Sen and efficiency and thin-lipped in disapproval.

Then in a rush, she blurted out, 'What about Debi?'

He was silent, then curt. 'What about her?'

'Wouldn't you rather...don't you want to...I just thought...'

'Debi is my little sister. She was dishonoured by my...by a Britisher. And betrayed by my parents. And abandoned by me. When I left Calcutta, she too disappeared. No one knows where she is, whether she's alive or... I lost her, Aditi. And I have to live with that knowledge every day.'

'I'm so sorry... I thought...'

'What did you think? That she must be my secret paramour? That I've got her tucked away in some sleazy love nest? That I could just shack up with her any time I wanted? That I could…'

'Why are you so angry?'

He took a deep breath, steadied himself.

'I'm sorry, I'm just mad at myself, at this stupid helplessness and feeling so goddamned useless. I know the hospital is trying its best to look after me but I just want to go someplace I can call home, be normal.'

'Fine, I'll get you out of here. I'll speak to Geeta Ma'am.'

'Will you? Oh, bless you, you angel.'

He took two unsteady steps towards her. She rushed to support him but he scooped her into his arms, holding her so tight, she couldn't breathe. He looked at her — was that fear in her eyes — and almost let go. But now she was reaching for him, her arms snaking around his neck, squeezing the dark, damp hair on his skull, her mouth hungry, open.

It was a big old decrepit bungalow near the marshy Strand. It had been built on pillars, rooms leading out of rooms to more rooms, with big shady verandahs. It was crumbling, completely bare but spacious, and all he could afford. Inside, leading off the hall, was a large high-ceilinged room, with sunlight pouring in from a skylight, splashing the floor and walls. Pigeons roosted in the rafters. Aditi came through the oversized doors on her bicycle, turning, wheeling, sending the pigeons scattering in a slow flurry of white feathers, a few errant ones floating and circling with the dust motes in the air. Her voice rang out, laughter bubbling up.

'It's lovely! Kabootar ji, look, it even has pigeons for you.'

Kabootar came, wheeling Debraj on his wheelchair, grinning. Debraj looked around, his eyebrows raised.

'And centuries of pigeon shit. Plus, I don't know if you noticed but… there's no furniture!'

'Who needs furniture!'

She laughed and pushed the cycle across the unpolished wooden planks of the floor. It wobbled forward on its own, teetered, then fell, one wheel spinning. A picnic rug was rolled out and spread in the middle of the room. Kabootar carried in a basket and a bottle of wine. She unpacked the little record player and put on one of his precious records. The mellow notes of 'Sophisticated Lady' bloomed. Debraj looked up, surprised. Aditi was on her feet, twirling, snapping her fingers, moving to the music. As she strutted and turned, her feet quicksilver, she stepped into the column of light coming from the high skylight. Debraj gave a tiny, involuntary gasp. She was on fire, her honey brown skin limned by the sun, her hair flowing free, her head thrown back in abandon, dancing, dancing. And the music played.

'They say into
your early life
Romance came
And in this heart of yours
Burned a flame
That flickered one day
And died away...'

And so romance came to Aditi Sen and Debraj Mookerji.

ACT IV

LOVE IN THE TIME OF NETAJI

Over the next few weeks, as he began to heal and the weather cooled a bit and the skies became marvellously clear, they took long drives to explore the countryside. Kabootar chauffeured them, chaperoned them, tilting the rear view mirror to the sky when they would reach for each other in the back seat. On Debraj's insistence, she bought, with great trepidation, a one-piece swim suit, and in a hidden cove on the East Coast, they floated in the quiet lukewarm waters, aquamarine and green, the salt making her eyes water, as she helped him to get his strength back. They lay on the sand, afterwards, side by side, bodies on fire but discreetly apart, the sun a pink shimmer behind closed eyelids. Slowly, the scars on his legs lost their raw mottled look, became sunburnt. His mind too healed, becoming clearer each day with her luminous presence in his life.

Soon, sooner than either would have liked, he went to work. On his first outing, to the POW centre at the Selarang Barracks, men had lined up behind the barbed wire, watching him being driven in, their hostile stares making his throat go dry. A grizzled veteran had stood, his tattooed arms crossed on his barrel chest, barring the entrance to the camp. But when he saw Debraj get down, his crutches making a hollow sound on the stone floor, he had scratched his cropped head and stood aside. Debraj had spoken long with him. He was obviously the ring leader, and by the time he heard Debraj out, he was introducing him to the men like an old friend. That day, hundred men gave up their misplaced allegiance to the crown and swore fealty to the INA and Netaji.

At a fundraiser, no sooner had he entered, he was surrounded by a bevy of businessmen, eager to experience his close brush with death vicariously. Aditi stood to one side, her eyes shining, as Debraj spoke, with fluency and wit and most of all, conviction. As he finished with an impassioned appeal to support the movement, she heard a murmur behind her.

'Impressive. He's very convincing, isn't he?' It was Netaji, leaning against the door, his face thoughtful. She went to touch his feet but he stopped her, gesturing towards Debraj.

'Go, stand by him.'

She stepped forward. They made a striking couple, embodying hope, a promise of the future. He smiled at her but she could tell that the effort of standing and talking had taken its toll. She took him home and left only after he had drifted off, with Kabootar keeping vigil.

They sat at tiny cafés, over cups of coffee. She found its taste bitter but exotic, a glimpse into an unknown world. Watching her biting into a meringue, licking the sugar off her fingers, he smiled at her evident delight.

'Did you ever have Nahoum's cheese sumboosucks?'

'Sum what?' she said, her mouth full.

'Or their almond rings? And what were they called…um… nankhatais?

'What's Nahoum's?'

'Where have you been? Everybody knows Nahoum's! It's this incredible confectionery shop in Calcutta. It's like a cave of delights. My mother used to take us, me and Debi, when we were small. It was our Saturday treat.'

'Do you miss her? Your mother?'

'She used to buy roses, dozens of them, from this old man in front of New Market. And she would put one between her teeth and pretend to be Theda Bara.'

Aditi didn't want to ask him who Theda Bara was. He probably thought her a country bumpkin and she was constantly mortified to realise she knew next to nothing about his world.

'You never talk about your mother. I know nothing of your life before we met.'

She pulled her hand away from his clasp, wiped the fingers on a napkin.

'There's nothing to tell. There's no exciting story, no adventures abroad. I'm just an ordinary Bengali girl. My parents are gone. I live with my aunt. Boring stuff.'

'No, no, you don't run away and hide behind that wall of yours, Aditi Sen. Tell me, what do you miss about home, about Calcutta?'

'I hardly knew Calcutta. I lived in the country…in a place called Bolpur, near Shantiniketan. Have you heard of Shantiniketan?'

'Of course, Tagore's university. I have a friend who was there.'

'Oh, there were so many people around *Guruji*.'

'I wonder how he is.'

A shoeshine boy scampered up to them. 'Shine sah, shine sah?'

He taught her to dance, the fox trot, cha cha cha, leaning on his cane in the cavernous house, five, six, five, six, seven, eight, impatient because of his limp, wanting to show off his prowess as a dancer, to sweep her off her feet.

Kabootar, too, taught her things. How to whittle and tease a flying bird shape out of inert wood. How to turn under a flock of tumbler pigeons which would wheel in the air and dive, plummeting and stopping inches from the ground and then flying up again on the terrace of Debraj's house so that she could feel them fluttering brushing her face and arms as they tumbled.

He patiently showed her how to drive the ramshackle temperamental jeep, which would buck and stall like a difficult horse — until he taught her not to fight it but to use its unique rhythm. She would drive alone, at night, glorying in the freedom, her foot hard on the pedal, her mouth open to suck in the wind, hair flying like smoke behind her. Twice, she had got hauled up by the military police and had to be rescued by Debraj, whose wounded hero status helped to bend a few rules.

On Diwali, Netaji invited them for dinner. Tiny earthen lamps had been placed everywhere, at every doorstep. Everybody was there, Geeta, Ahmed Hassan, Gokhale, Mohammed Giani. Gaffar had got fireworks from a Chinese shop. Aditi had dressed up for the evening in an emerald green sari, sweet white champa flowers entwined in her dark hair, her honey-brown skin accentuated by the gold of an heirloom necklace. She was a goddess that night. Debraj couldn't take his eyes off her. He was distracted, not really paying attention to the conversation during dinner. Netaji noticed and smiled. There was something about young love that made you forgive things. And they were so, so young.

Later, as he dropped her off, he clung to her, his hand insistent on the small of her back, on that little swell at the bottom of her arched spine, pulling her to him, hard against her. His kiss was insistent, demanding everything. She wanted to melt, her senses dissolving. It felt like she was underwater, weightless, suspended. But at the bottom of the ocean, she found her feet and pulled away. She couldn't give in, what if, maybe, who knew, could she, would he — and the moment was gone.

'It's been a long day. You should rest.'

'Stay.' It was a whisper, more entreaty, than command.

'I can't. I mustn't.'

Another night, neither wanting to sleep, they strolled through the grand lobby of the Fullerton, his limp still pronounced. Two attractive Anglo-Burmese women walking by in open fronted skirts smiled at him, dipping their long, elegant necks. Debraj paused to look at them.

'Exquisite…the most beautiful and intelligent in the world…'

Aditi, a couple of steps ahead, smiled. Then, not finding him at her side, she turned. He was still standing, leaning on his cane, admiring the two women. When he turned, she was already halfway across the lobby.

'Hey, wait…'

'The most beautiful and intelligent in the world? Really?'

'What…oh…them. Well, of course, they are.'

Her head went up.

'But you, Aditi Sen, you could be the one woman in the world for me.'

She stared at him, a long, level look. Then she was sprinting towards him. He braced himself as she launched herself into his arms. A stumble, a wince but he held her, turning her round and round. She looked at him, grinning, her arms round his neck.

'How do you know this, Captain?'

'A friend once told me that, when the time came, when I met the one, I would know.'

'What a good friend. I'd love to meet him.'

'Hmm...' He set her down. 'And how do you assume it wasn't a woman friend?

'Was it?'

He saw the flash of her temper, again, like distant lightning, heralding a storm. He loved seeing her all riled up, the fire in her eyes. But her possessiveness, her fragility disturbed him. He had known many women but always there had been the freedom to walk away. Now, when he felt, for the first time, no desire to be free, her insistence on fealty made him feel chained. She looked at him, troubled. Again, the sense that she had somehow put her foot in it clouded her mind. It made her feel awkward, inadequate. Nishonko da was right. She was such a harum scarum. She wished she could talk to him about Debraj, he was a man, maybe he would understand. Or maybe not She suspected that his feelings too ran deep, that their old, comfortable friendship was lost. Why did men have to be so difficult?

Debraj watched her as she straightened her clothes, her eyes far away. He reached for her hand. The fingers were a little cold. He rubbed them, carried them to his lips. Now, she looked up, her lips red from biting them.

'Do I disappoint you, Debraj?'

'You could never disappoint, Aditi Sen.'

'And then the news came.'

In the tea shop, the crowd has thinned. The mundane and the ordinary business of feeding and earning a living and getting pension cheques have pulled some away. Only Dulal da and Haru, Sudipto and Ganesh babu are left from the motley crew. The old man looks more awake, more alive than when he had come in in the morning.

'It was December.'

Sudipto nods. 'That's when the go-ahead came, isn't it?'

'Excellent. Your knowledge of the times is admirable.'

'Well, for us unenlightened ones, Dadu, please what go-ahead?' Dulal da is caustic.

'Oh, from the Japanese HQ, my dear man. That is what all of us had been waiting and waiting for.'

Nishonko was really homesick for the camp food in Singapur, the simple dal chapati, the humble vada, which he used to criticise so abundantly. The Japanese food in Tokyo was too insipid, too little, too alien. The wartime shortages had begun to really pinch Tokyo and breakfast sometimes consisted of just balls of rice in a tiny bowl of watery soup. How the Japanese soldiers fought so viciously, so unflaggingly, on food like this, he could not comprehend. He was just sitting down in the mess when one of the trainees came running in.

'Sir, HQ on the line.'

The line was faint but the message unmistakable. Nishonko's eyes shone with excitement.

'Wonderful news, Sir. I'll get the men onto a flight as soon as possible. Maybe a couple of weeks, on the outside. Yes, mum's the word.'

He thought of calling Jhilik and telling her the good news, that he would be seeing her soon. He realised how much he had been missing her. And maybe he would meet Debraj. He missed Debraj's easy laughter, his sunniness. Maybe, he would introduce Debraj to Jhilik. Or, he laughed to himself, maybe not.

Early that morning, Debraj was at the rifle range. He felt rusty. His eye was off and he desperately wanted to do something concrete, to work off the frustration gnawing away inside. All the talking and the receptions were palling. It was much of the same thing, repeated ad nauseum. He knew he was faking it, that none of it was real. He was just coasting along, pretending that he was actually going somewhere. So he had come to the range. It was empty that early and the targets were indistinct shapes in the haze. Debraj lined up, then drew and fired, drew and fired. Within minutes, he found his rhythm, the actions once more second nature. He was actually beginning to enjoy himself when he was disturbed by a shout. He missed, cursed, spotted Kabootar running up to him, shouting something.

The jeep scattered gravel as it scrunched to a halt in front of the Indian Independence League Headquarters. Netaji and Saito, accompanied by hurrying bodyguards, strode down the hall, their footsteps echoing in its emptiness. It was early, the offices yet to open but the situations room was packed. They waited, their faces expectant. The messages they had received had been urgent. Netaji went to the head of the table.

'I have summoned you all to tell you that…no, I'll leave it to Brigadier Saito to do the honours.'

Saito bowed formally and stepped forward with a smile. 'Prime Minister Tojo has given us his approval!'

A roar went around the room. Debraj, hurrying in, was startled at the thump of tables, the applause. 'What did I miss?'

'Netaji has done it. We have the go-ahead for the campaign.' Ahmed Hassan was jubilant.

Debraj looked around with a queer expression on his face. 'Already? And when are we planning to go into battle?'

'Soon. You will all get to know the exact date soon enough.'

'The staging point?'

'That too will be revealed in due course. In the meantime, keep it under wraps. We can't afford to tip our hand to the British.'

They met near the wharves, which were usually crowded during the day with stevedores and sailors. Goopta believed that the best place to be invisible was in the middle of many people, in constantly shifting currents, the anonymity a perfect cover. He walked up to one of the chop chop joints, set up on a cart, surrounded by the riverside people and stood in line behind Gaffar, his face buried behind a newspaper.

'Anything special on the menu?'

Gaffar started. He hated these open meetings, preferring the privacy of closed doors. He growled softly under his breath.

'The order has come. I think they are going to move the parcels soon.'

'You are not sure?'

'I could not accompany him.'

'How many parcels? I must have more specifics. My master will not be happy with such vague vague things.'

'He has become secretive.'

'I would not expect him to be otherwise. You must use more ingenious means. You must make him trust you.'

'He does.'

'Obviously not enough.'

The wood-panelled back-room at Fort William in Calcutta was wreathed in cigar smoke. Murky light filtered in through blackout curtains, picking out the men gathered around the long table. Some were in uniform, some in woollen suits. Winter had come to Calcutta early and the big, draughty room was cold.

'They're late,' growled General Campbell.

'The bloody nerve of them, wanting self-rule, when they can't even keep to the bloody time! Heathens!'

There was a soft knock on the door. An Indian orderly poked his head in through the narrow crack. 'They're here, huzoor.'

A group of men, some in the Congress uniform, bare feet in sandals, some in traditional Muslim sherwanis and neatly trimmed beards, stepped into the carpeted room, looking distinctly at unease.

'Ah, gentlemen, a bit tardy of you, what? Have a seat.' General Campbell drummed softly on the table.

The Indian contingent settled down, amongst much scraping and pulling of chairs and tidying of dhotis and shawls.

'Chop chop, haven't got the whole day, you know. What's the news from Singapore?' General Campbell snapped.

'Well, our people in Singapur say that Japan has agreed.' The man who spoke had the big, dark bruise of a devout Muslim on his forehead.

'Yes, we have heard the self same thing,' said a thin man in khadi, who looked like he was one of the ringleaders.

'Vicious, yellow bastards', growled a grizzled British veteran in uniform with a black eye patch that gave him a piratical air. 'Horrific, what they did to our boys at Arrakan…slaughtered them wholesale.'

'And on top of that, they've got the INA mustering. Their sepoys and jamadars are...'

'*Their sepoys?* Those are *our sepoys.* They're stealing our troops, the sneaky bastards.' The man in the eye-patch was livid.

'Any numbers on the deserters?' growled General Campbell.

'Hundreds...maybe thousands,' the leader of the Muslim contingent offered.

'Intel says it could be as high as 16,000.' The man who spoke was half concealed in the shadows. He now leaned forward. He had the pale colour of a redhead, his orange eyebrows and lashes giving him the look of an albino.

'Whose intel is that, Mr...um?' Campbell asked, his eyebrow cocked.

'Whyte, Brigadier Alan Whyte. From British Intelligence.' Whyte's voice was low, the voice of a man used to being listened to.

'And money and support are pouring in. Netaji has become a very rich man suddenly.' The thin man in khadi was bitter.

'How in dickens is he doing it? I thought your bunch were supposed to have discredited him.' Campbell turned accusingly to him.

'All that is irrelevant right now. Where are they going to go in? And when? That's what I need to know,' Whyte interrupted.

'Don't know yet but we will,' the thin man replied, stiffly.

'Well, you better ask them to hurry, put some jaldi into it.'

Whyte scraped his chair back and stood up. He started to pace down the room, passing close behind the Indian contingent, speaking in a gentle, meditative tone, made the more threatening by its complete lack of inflexion.

'Don't want to have to report to Mr. Churchill his precious jewel in the crown is about to be snatched away, now, do we? Or to tell your esteemed leaders that they are going to have their stab at greatness whisked away from under their very noses. There's just too much at stake here, gentlemen. You don't want to be caught with your dhotis round your ankles, do you? Get your Party to up the ante. Get someone to bump him off. Find something on one of his key people and use it as a lever. We need to move. As the General here said, chop, chop!'

The Indian contingent had gone red in the face. Whyte's calm tone of voice, the not so veiled insults...it was intolerable. The presumption of the man!

The man with the beard spoke up loudly. 'And who will provide the money, Sir, for such operations?'

Whyte laughed mirthlessly. 'Money! No wonder this country was such a walkover. Everything comes down to money. Everyone can be bought here. All you have to do is find the right guy and pay him off.'

He turned to General Campbell.

'General, I will leave you to deal with the petty cash. Meanwhile, can you get me up to the Burma border? That's the closest I can get to them, right? I need to be hands-on, check out the lay of the land myself.'

Twilight had already descended when Aditi came cycling helter-skelter down the road towards the bungalow. The bicycle lay on the empty, overgrown driveway, the wheels clattering on the gravel as she ran in, skidding on the steps, shouting out Debraj's name. The big, bare room was empty. On the floor, dozens of candles, all shapes and sizes, burned, softly flickering in the twilight. She ran through the rooms. Empty, empty. Where was he? Then, out in the back patio, a dark shape against the darkening sky, he sat hunched on the parapet, smoking. She ran to him, pulled him by the hand. His face looked drawn. On his breath, were the sweet, cloying fumes of alcohol.

'You've heard the news?' Her eyes were shining.

'Slow down…what news?'

'Netaji has got approval, the battle will start soon.'

'How do you know?'

'I… I… I overheard.'

'You mean you were eavesdropping?'

'Whatever. How does it matter how I heard? Aren't you excited?'

'No, my love.'

'Oh, how can you say that? It's the most tremendous news ever. We're going to march upon them and destroy them and take over India!' She was practically fizzing with excitement.

He leaned back on the parapet. 'You bloodthirsty hellcat. And what about us?'

'What about us?'

'Won't you miss our time together?'

'Debraj, how can you…this is what all of us want!'

'Do we? I just want to be with you, hold on to these days, these... I don't want to die in some godforsaken jungle, my insides spilling out on to some burnt out rice field, far away from you, knowing we could have lived our lives together. I don't want to be a hero and lose our only chance to be happy for someone else's war.'

She put a finger on his lips, trying to stem the words. 'Hush, you mustn't speak like that. It's our war, Deb.'

'Is it? When did it become your war, Aditi?'

'The day my parents were taken from me.'

'I've also lost mine. But I have you and all I want to do is take you somewhere far away, away from all this. Is that so bad a thing to want?

'Are you scared, Deb?'

'Aren't you?'

They fell silent, only the lonely call of a cicada breaking the stillness. Then, she reached out, as if stepping across a vast, fearful chasm, and touched his face. She traced her fingers across his forehead, stopping to move aside the damp hair there, sweat muddled. She lingered on the hollow cheeks, the jaw clenched in silence. Then back to the caves of his eyes, touching the closed cave of his mouth, she pushed her finger into its moist depths. He gasped, a tiny sound, suppressed, not wanting to frighten her. Slowly, she slipped into the forbidden space between his outstretched thighs. She cradled his head, that beautiful carved head she had stared at through all those dark nights at the hospital and pulled it between her breasts. He could contain himself no longer. A low moan escaped through his clenched teeth. Yet, he sat still. She was glad, glad to be given the freedom to make her own way, glad he didn't overwhelm her with insistence. Now, she held the column of his throat, stretched upwards, the head thrown back, as if offered in sacrifice. The pulse at its base throbbed underneath her fingertips. She was aware of some seismic shift deep inside her, a tearing apart of the fabric of her being. Heat crept up her legs, her back, pooling in the valley between her thighs. Now, she was drowning but she didn't want to find her feet. She wanted to be adrift, a paper boat at the mercy of forces beyond her control, her knowing. She whispered his name, her voice cracking. He reached out for her now, placed his cupped hand on the swelling mound. For just an instant, she stiffened. Then, with the arch of her back, she told him of her surrender.

'Are you sure?'

She nodded, trembling.

He rose to his feet, picked her up in his arms and carried her in. An old, second-hand four-poster bed stood alone in the middle of a vast room, swathed in net curtains. An oil lamp burned beside it on a windowsill. By its flickering light, he set her down gently. She lay back, honey gold, luminous, the hair spreading like mist under her. He looked at her, the tiny, tiny waist, the shyness in the unconscious way she laid her hand across her eyes, her head turned away slightly.

'Do you want to wait...'

Her eyes flew open.

'For what, Debraj? You're right. We don't have the luxury of time... any day, you could be called up...'

'But you're so young...so...'

A laugh gurgled out from her lips.

'I'm almost 18, an old maid.'

He laughed too. The tension drained out of him. He reached for her now, with joy. When he uncovered her breasts, the sight of her chocolate brown nipples, erect, proud, filled him with tenderness. He tasted her and she tasted like nothing he had experienced before, a constellation of smells and textures, spice and sea water, fever warm and subterranean cool at the same time, her body an uncharted landscape on which he now laid total claim. She too was on fire, impatient with his patience, reaching for him. She marvelled at the velvety texture of his manhood, felt breathless at its engorged power. She cried out exultantly when he entered her, not even knowing she was meant to feel pain, taking him inside her as naturally as she took in air.

Outside, the night cries of wild animals hung in the air. Beyond the overgrown garden, the muddy river whispered past, the foghorns of the steamboats echoed. Kabootar sat, leaning against the outside doorway, carving with his knife. Did he hear the gasps of delight, the urging, the merging, the shouted name, the whispered plea, the final exhalations and cry? He looked up once, staring into the dark, then went back to carving, the bird taking wing in the curve of his palm.

They lay in bed, in the afterglow, her hair spread across his chest, her bruised mouth lying in the crook of his neck, touching each other, feeling their bodies cool down. He looked at her, her body innocent of shame, golden brown, damp from the labours of love. He lifted the damp hair off the back of her neck, licked her shoulder, salty and musky, the fragrance of their coming hanging in the air.

'Did it...hurt?'

'No, silly.'

A moment of silence, a shift of her weight.

'Have you been with many women?'

He smiled. There she went again. 'It doesn't matter how many women I have been with. With you, I'm...it's as if this is the first time.'

She slid down, nuzzled one of his nipples. So strange that he had pale pink ones, so much prettier than her own dark aureoles. Under her probing tongue tip, it hardened, opened like a tiny flower. He shivered.

'How is it, my darling oddity, that men have not beaten their way to your doorstep?'

'Oh, there have been some.'

'Tell me their names and I shall murder them in their sleep.'

She giggled, her chortle of delight rippling across the skin of his stomach.

'Alas, they were pimply boys and a shy music teacher.' Her face grew serious suddenly.' There was one. I think he loved me. But I could not love him back, poor thing.'

'Lucky thing, otherwise he would be dead.'

She stopped him with a kiss, then with a frisson of daring, straddled him.

'Shhh...now lie back and don't move.'

At dawn, when the sea breeze began to blow inland, bringing the smell of brine and deep sea, she left him, the fist under his cheek, the body curled up in deep slumber. Kabootar was nowhere to be found, so she took the jeep and drove through the empty streets, wet with night rain, the smell of fresh grass and wood smoke in the air. She felt bone tired but wide awake, a nagging sense of guilt and yet a sense of relief filling her limbs with a pleasant lassitude. She drove, taking detours, not wanting to arrive home. She wanted to be in limbo, unmoored, for a little while longer. She could smell the trace of their love-making on herself, a trace she would always carry now. There was no undoing this night, this act, this union of flesh and juices and impulses and hearts. From the moment she had run out of the house earlier in the evening, after Nishonko da's call, saying he was coming back, through the pell-mell cycling through the streets, she had known, hadn't she, that this would be the night. She looked at herself in the rear view mirror, her hair mussed, a pink telltale blotch on her neck, the lips swollen. She thought back, her fingers clenching on the wheel, the way she had screamed out his name in that moment of sweet surrender, and felt no regret. And yet, there was a premonition, a fear she could not name. She hoped she would be able to slip into the house unnoticed but Chhoto mashi was up, watering her plants. Aditi tried to silently walk by but Chhoto mashi called out. 'Morning, Jhilik.'

'Oh good morning, Chhoto mashi.'

'Long night at the hospital?'

'I really need a bath.'

'Have a tea with me. I hardly see you these days.'

Aditi sat down, keeping her distance. She was suddenly conscious of the telltale evidence of her transgressions. She breathed in the clean mountain fragrance of the tea, staring at the amber liquid. A tiny unconscious smile played on her lips.

'Any news from Nishonko?'

Aditi looked up, her face paling. 'Why do you ask?'

'Just...we haven't seen him in such a long time.'

'Yes, he had called. Yesterday. He's coming back.'

'Oh. Where has he been?'

'In Japan. They have received a go-ahead from the Japanese HQ. But please don't tell any one, it's meant to be a secret.'

'Oh dear, so soon. And are you two planning to get married?'

'NO!'

Chhoto mashi looked up, her eyebrow raised.

'I mean...why...do I need to get married?'

'Well, I thought, before you all march off to battle, and if you are serious about Nishonko?'

'No, I'm not. I mean, there's never been anything. In any case, there's far too much happening'.

'With a certain Captain? I hear you spend all your time in his company.'

Aditi flinched and her mouth took on a rebellious twist.

'I hope you know what you are doing, child. This man doesn't have a terribly savoury reputation. He is a bit of a bounder, by all accounts.'

'You haven't even met him.'

'People are talking, Jhilik. And Nishonko? What would he make of all this?

'It's none of his business.'

'Isn't it? Isn't he the only real friend you have from the past?'

'He...you mustn't tell him.'

'It's a small town, Jhilik. Word gets around. How are you planning on keeping it from him?'

Aditi stood up abruptly with an angry shake of her head. 'Just let it be, Chhoto mashi.'

She marched into her room, fuming. Why couldn't everyone mind their own business? She bolted the door against the world and threw herself on the bed. She knew she wouldn't be able to sleep a wink but as soon as she collapsed on the clean, hand-washed sheets, she sank into a deep slumber.

When she awoke, the late afternoon sun splashed onto her bed, across her back. She stretched, luxuriously, running her hands over her body, across her breasts, those dark brown aureoles he had pinched between his fingers the night before. She touched herself in all the secret places, tracing the journey he had taken, tenderly feeling the soreness of her womanhood. She inhaled the undersea fragrance of her subterranean depths, making her head swim. Suddenly, she was on fire, crying out with desire, wanting to be consumed. She whispered his name, like a litany, a prayer against all the bad things that could happen.

She bathed, and in fresh clothes, hair wet, rushed back in the jeep. But when she drove up to the bungalow, he was not there, not even Kabootar to answer her peremptory knock. She sat forlorn on the steps, her heart again hesitant. Was it forward of her, to come looking for him so soon after? Did a man need space, time? Had she been too wanton? Would he lose interest now? She had not had a mother or a close friend in those growing up years, to answer the questions all girls ask, to be guided in the ways of the heart. She waited, hoping he would come, dreading it if he did.

Debraj had been summoned by Netaji early in the morning to visit another potential donor. They travelled light, accompanied by only one bodyguard, a large young Bihari named Samir and Gaffar at the wheel.

'You handled that meeting well, Debraj. Mr. Chidambaram was impressed.'

'Learnt from you, Sir. You seem to know the right thing to say, every time.'

'I think it's about getting into the other person's shoes, seeing things from their point of view. '

'Sure but sometimes, you don't really like the other guy and have no desire to get into his smelly, sweat-stained shoes, if you get my drift, Sir.'

Netaji laughed. 'You are certainly honest, Debraj. A very attractive quality. Don't lose it.'

'I'm not so sure, Sir. Can get you into a whole lot of trouble.'

'Especially with the ladies, eh?'

Now it was Debraj's turn to laugh. That was the good thing about Netaji. You didn't have to pretend stuff. He was a man's man, not some pontificating tightass.

'Is there a particular one who infuriates you the most?'

Debraj had the grace to look sheepish. 'There's one…drives me up the wall sometimes.'

There was a small silence.

'Is there anyone who infuriates you, Sir?'

Netaji smiled but it was a smile laced with such a sense of loss, that Debraj's heart lurched. He started to stammer his apologies but Netaji waved them away.

'The cause we serve — she's a hard mistress. Consumes you. She will not take dallying around. So we just shut down that part of our heart, put a lock on it and didn't let it weaken our resolve.'

'Is it really worth all that, Sir?'

'To live for one big thing, one thing that you can look back on, at the moment when Yamraj comes calling and you have to cross that dark river to the other bank. To say, I did my best and I did not hold back. Now that's worth it.'

'I don't know I could do it, Sir.'

'None of us do, Debraj. Till we do it.'

He bent to pick up the bag lying near his feet. There was a sharp whingggg and a crack. The jeep windshield shattered and shards of glass rained down on him. Gaffar swerved, the jeep almost turning turtle. But he managed to grind to a halt, narrowly missing a big gulmohur tree. Someone was screaming. Debraj shoved Netaji out of the jeep unceremoniously, tumbling him to the ground, on all fours, his glasses flying off. He crouched behind the jeep, shielding Netaji with his body. Gaffar scrambled out of the driver's seat, his hair glittering with tiny glass particles. He started to shoot, randomly, not sure where the shots had come from. Through the gap, he saw Samir sprawled on the back seat, bleeding, screaming.

'Go around, I'll cover you.' Gaffar muttered.

Debraj tried to peer out but was met with another volley of shots. He ducked, grimacing.

'Go. Otherwise, we'll be pinned down here.' Gaffar hissed at him. 'I'll take care of Netaji.' He pushed his gun through the shattered windshield and laid down covering fire.

Debraj crabbed across the rough ground and eased himself into a nullah running alongside.

Gaffar reloaded, fired, reloaded. His eyes fell on Netaji who was scrabbling on the ground, still looking for his glasses. All Gaffar could see was the top of his head. Netaji had lost his cap in the melee and the balding dome of his head, the high forehead was bare, vulnerable. Gaffar stared, his face impassive. Then, Netaji looked up at Gaffar, putting on the glasses he had finally found. The long moment stretched. There was a bubble of quiet. Gaffar stared into the other man's eyes, hidden behind round glasses reflecting the vast sky. A sudden burst of gunfire from the other end made him duck.

'Got him.' A shout.

They climbed a rocky outcrop. Beside it ran a ditch with rain water spill. They found Debraj leaning against a slender tree trunk, panting. He had his gun trained on a lone man sprawled in the ditch, clutching his leg, which had taken a shot. The man was dark skinned, oily haired, thin and rangy, with a meagre moustache. He was dressed in nondescript clothes, an old khaki pair of trousers, a soiled, mud-stained shirt, sandals. His gun lay on the ground, surrounded by spent shells and a small leather bag. As Gaffar bent to pick it up, the man looked up at him. A tiny flicker passed over his eyes but the next moment, he looked away. Gaffar hauled him upright roughly, not looking at him and searched his pockets. He dug inside the bag, rooted around, then came out empty-handed.

'Nothing. He could be from anywhere,' he growled.

Debraj hobbled forward. 'You understand Hindi?'

The man kept his head down, sullenly staring at his feet.

'Who sent you?'

Netaji sat down on a rocky outcrop and lit a cigarette. 'It's obvious. Seems we are making our friends back home nervous. The curious thing is, he knew we were coming down this road. Chidambaram confirmed the meeting only last evening.'

Debraj slammed the sniper against the rock face and thrust his gun against his bleeding cheek. 'How did you know we were coming? Talk, or you'll get a bullet in the other leg.'

The man looked at Gaffar, standing impassively at one side, turning his gun slowly in his hands. Gaffar shook his head slowly at him. 'He's not talking.'

The man turned away and spat on the ground, his face insolent. Rage flared in Debraj's eyes. He pistol-whipped the sniper across the face.

'Talk, you bastard.'

The man's mouth was a bloody gash. He snarled, then spat out a gob of bright red blood. Debraj hit him again, his mouth stretched in a snarl.

'Debraj! Enough.' Netaji stood up, dusted off his hands. 'We'll deal with this back at HQ. Samir needs attention. Gaffar, take him.'

Gaffar shoved the man forward up the ridge, towards the hidden road below. Debraj slowly brought his gun down, letting out his pent breath. He took one step but his legs gave way. Netaji caught him. 'Easy, take it easy.'

They stood side by side, Debraj swaying, riding the pain. Gaffar had disappeared from sight. After a minute, they made their way slowly up to the ridge.

Suddenly, a shot rang out.

From the top of the ridge, they saw Gaffar standing by the jeep. The captured sniper lay sprawled on the grass verge, his face turned up to the leaden sky.

Gaffar called out, 'It's okay. He was trying to make a run for it.' Debraj hobbled down to the jeep. The sniper was dead, a large ragged round hole in the middle of his forehead. Debraj gave Gaffar a sharp look.

'You could have gone for his legs. We needed him alive, man.'

'I just…reacted.'

'He was running…away?'

'Yes.' A pause. 'What are you trying to say?'

'Nothing. Except why is he lying on his back if he was running away? And how come you've got him slap bang in his forehead instead of the back of his head?'

Gaffar's face darkened ominously. He took one threatening step towards Debraj, who though tall, was no match for the big Pathan.

'Gaffar.' The low command came from Netaji.

Gaffar stopped, blinked slowly. Then he rubbed his eyes, as if coming out of a mist.

'Sorry, Sir, it's just that he tried to kill you and I lost my head. Saw red. Forgive me, Sir.'

'Well, now we'll never know who fed him the information. Let's get Samir to a medic fast.'

Debraj got in at the back, cradling the unconscious Samir while Netaji brushed the glass shards off the front seat. Both were distracted. Gaffar slipped behind the wheel and shoved the small leather bag he had got from the sniper under the seat.

At the hospital, after they had dropped off Netaji and got Samir admitted, Debraj flopped down on a bench in the foyer. His legs were shaking, and he felt like throwing up. Though the target had obviously been Netaji, it had been too much of a close call. Ever since being wounded, he had not faced any combat and while the adrenaline rush was there while the fireworks went off, he hated the aftermath, the sick feeling in the pit of his stomach, the metallic taste of terror lingering on his tongue. Mitro had been right. It never really went away, the fear. You just got better at hiding it. He missed Mitro, the calm of his friend, the sense of reassurance he emanated. Where the hell was he? He had just dropped off the map. If he got some furlough, they could go out for a drink or two, hit one of the nightclubs. He smiled. He could of course ask Aditi to join them. Mitro would love her, he was sure. Or maybe not. Maybe, they could just have a boys' nightout.

Gaffar yanked the small leather bag from under the seat and stuffed it into his pocket and strode into the hallway of the spacious bungalow on the riverside. Noshir bhai, Goopta's general factotum, hurried up to greet him politely.

'Where's he?'

'In the l..l..ibrary. Please wait here, M..m..mister Gaffar, I will inform him of your a..a..arrival.'

Gaffar headed down the corridor. Noshir bhai tried to keep up, flapping his hands in consternation but Gaffar brushed him aside. He unceremoniously slammed open an imposing pair of double-panelled teak doors. Goopta looked up from a winged armchair in which he was ensconced. A Chinese girl, very young, with alabaster skin, knelt before him, massaging his tiny foot. Goopta looked most put out by the interruption.

'Gaffar, what the hell are you doing here? Told you not to come here in broad daylight, didn't I?'

'Get out. Out! Out!' Gaffar shooed the girl and Noshir from the room and shut the door on them. He turned on his heel and stood looming over Goopta, his arms akimbo. 'What the hell are you trying? Are you trying to get me exposed?'

'Now why would you think that, my friend?'

'You sent that sniper. Don't deny it.'

'What sniper?'

'I'll wring that fat neck of yours. Netaji now suspects that someone close to him is passing on information. I was just supposed to tell you his whereabouts, his movements, the point of entry into India, not be party to assassinating him.'

'Oh dear, did they succeed?'

'No, your pet killer made a hash of it.'

'Why do you insist that I had something to do with it? I'm a mere businessman, a facilitator of things. What connection could I possibly have to some low life who tried to do away with the illustrious Netaji?'

Gaffar reached into his pocket. For a second, Goopta tensed. But Gaffar just pulled out the small, leather bag. Then, very slowly, he pulled out money, a frayed ID card, and lastly a letter. Staring at Goopta, he unfolded the letter and held it up very close to Goopta's nose. Goopta blinked, then went very still.

'Recognise it? Just in case anyone wants proof of what you have been upto. My little insurance, Goopta ji, in case you have notions of betraying me.'

Goopta sighed, then smiled. 'I'm just a cog in the wheel, Gaffar bhai. Just like you. I merely carry out orders. Nothing personal.'

'As long as those orders don't involve killing Netaji. I will do what's best for my people, I will supply the information that you need but you must not harm him, do you hear me?'

'You are such an optimist, my man. I, on the other hand, am an incorrigible realist. And we have a saying in Bengali that goes something like — you can't dip your foot in the puddle and protest when it gets muddy. Politics is like business, my dear fellow. Somebody always ends up having to pay the price. And if you have this little leverage on me, rest assured I have enough on you.' He reached out and tinkled a little bell. Noshir rushed in.

'Y..y..yes, Sir.'

'Those excellent photographs of our guest here, that I gave you for safekeeping, Noshir?'

Noshir smiled with great satisfaction.

'S..sa..safe, Sir.'

'So, you see Gaffar bhai, we are rather at a stand-off here. Thank you, Noshir. And now if you'll escort Mr. Khan to his vehicle.'

Gaffar glowered. He had come thinking he held a trump card but somehow this little leech had turned the tables on him. He shoved the letter back in his pocket. Goopta looked up at him through his lazy, half-lidded eyes, then waved his many-ringed podgy fingers at him.

'Go on, run along now, and send back little Ah Kum so she can carry on with her good work. And Netaji? I'm afraid no power on earth can guarantee that he won't come to a sticky end. All his own fault, you know, putting everyone's backs up.'

Netaji lit the incense carefully and snuffed out the match. He sat cross-legged on his prayer mat and tried to compose himself for meditation. But his thoughts were unquiet that evening. Images of the shattered windshield, the tremor of air, that soft whistling sound as the bullet missed him by inches, the sniper's mouth a red gash… it kept coming back, ambushing his thoughts, scattering them to the winds. What disturbed him most was not that he had escaped death narrowly but the sickening feeling that there was one, maybe very close to him, who had betrayed him. Would he ever again be able to look upon those faces — he ran them through his mind, the men and women who could have known — without wondering what if. What would it take to betray him? Money? Revenge? Despair? Fear? Just plain tiredness? Of course, he was a target, that was inevitable. British Intelligence had long ago put a price on his head. There was a standing order to kill. Their agents would be swarming all over the region, each trying to worm their way in. He knew the immense value of intelligence. He had placed his own secret agents long before in Calcutta and had established a wireless link with Bengal. Japanese High Command had of course dispatched their spies to India but they had failed singularly. That's why he had wanted to control the intelligence ops out of Penang and Rangoon. Already, well trained groups of men had been sent off to India in a Japanese sub. They would be landing on the Kathiawar coast with weapons, money and sophisticated wireless equipment by month end. He had given their leader a letter, handwritten, to be delivered in person to Woodburn Park. His thoughts slipped sideways into memories of home, concerns over the well-being of the people he loved and revered. For a few moments, a great wave of home-sickness enveloped him. A sense of loss, of the unfairness of it all, threatened to overpower him. He thought of the child and the woman, in a small house in a small town in Germany, winter in the air, waiting for some word from across the seas. His throat closed with despair. But he shook himself and forced his mind back to contemplation, to philosophy and reflections on duty. Slowly, his mind calmed. He found a serene centre and felt, finally, at peace.

As he opened the gate, Debraj frowned. On the step, outside the main door, a covered figure lay crumpled. In the dusk, he couldn't make out who it was. Kabootar? No, too small. Then his heart started hammering. It was Aditi! She lay on the doorstep, curled up, her face covered by the tumble of her hair, her hand lying upturned. He reached out, touched her arm. She was cold to his touch. His hand was shaking as he moved the hair off her face ever so gently. Her eyes were closed. It felt like someone had squeezed his heart. He called out her name softly, urgently. And then she took a deep breath, stirred, snuffled like a child and sleepily tucked her head under her arm. He sat back, giddy with relief. Unbelievable! She had actually gone to sleep on his doorstep. He picked her up, carried her in, laid her down on the four-poster bed. She curled up with a little mewling sound. He covered her, then lay down behind her. He looked at the long rounded curve of her back, the deep valley of her spine, the little knob of bone just above the dimple at the base. He felt himself swell, so swift, it was like being struck. Unable to stop himself, he ran his hand down her flank, then cupped the core of her. She stirred now, sentient, awakened. Her eyes flew open as he moved against her from behind. She felt his need, and tried to turn towards him. But he restrained her, kept moving against her slowly. She moaned softly, thrashing but he controlled her, deliberately not letting her see him, so the only way she would know him would be through the friction of their bodies, still clothed, through the chance gaps and missed corners of flesh. She understood and moved against him, a dance, giving when he pushed, pushing when he retreated, moving out of reach, teasing. It was leisurely, slow lovemaking, very different from the night before. They took their time, holding back, the heat building, building, so when the storm broke, it was like the skies opened, a deluge, the pent energy released, her cry keening, high, a gull out at sea. They lay spent, their breath slowing down.

'I thought I had lost you. You were lying there so still.'

'I must have drifted off, waiting for you. I thought you were avoiding me…'

'Aditi, my mad, impossible Aditi, do you have any idea how unique you are? How bloody fantastic you are to be with?'

Later, they sat at a corner table, at one of the few nightspots still allowed to function by the Japanese, sharing a bottle of wine. Debraj had told Aditi about his day's adventures and she had gone pale and clutched his hand, and now they sat, fingers intertwined, their heads close together. The music stopped, there was a scattering of desultory applause. Aditi excused herself. He watched her go, marvelling at how her walk itself had changed, from the awkward coltish strut of a girl to the sway and tilt of a self-aware woman. He leaned back, lit up. Life, to Debraj Mookerji, in that moment, seemed perfect.

The band struck up again and a woman's silky voice began to croon. Debraj stiffened. A gilded pillar obscured his view of the singer. Debraj shifted in his chair, craned his neck. The woman came into view. She was long limbed, dressed in a glittery white gown, her hair smoothly swept up in a pale blonde chignon. It was Natasha! He ducked back, swearing under his breath.

Aditi came back, trailing her fingers down the back of his hand, playful, her eyes heavy with the wine, swaying to the music. 'Dance?'

'Uh huh.' He shook his head, leaned back in his chair.

Natasha sang a song of doomed love, swaying sinuously, clicking her scarlet-tipped fingers. When she finished to enthusiastic applause, Aditi turned around in her chair to clap.

'She's gorgeous, isn't she?'

He fidgeted, stole a look over her head. He felt guilty, he didn't know why. He hadn't done anything wrong, had he? He just wanted to meet Natasha. Don't Debraj, leave it alone, just get up and leave. And the quisling other voice in his head, why not, Aditi doesn't own me, I owe it to Natasha, she might know something about Ma and Baba. But Aditi will be hurt, oh, come on, she should grow up. But why keep it a secret? But who knows what secrets she herself has? And so he went back and forth, a yo yo of contradictions, agonising as the set wore on. Aditi was lost in the music, her eyes closed. He muttered an excuse, slipped out.

Natasha walked down the ill lit corridor to her dressing room, fanning herself. It was hot backstage and she had a bad headache. As she flopped down in front of her dressing table, she looked at herself in the mirror. God, she looked a wreck. She had heard so much about Singapore but with the British gone, the pickings were thin. She leaned forward to fix the deep red lipstick on her mouth and let out a small shriek. Reflected in the mirror, stood a man, leaning on a cane, backlit by the lamp behind him. She swivelled round to face him, her hands flying up to her creamy décolletage. Then he stepped forward and she gasped. It was Debraj, a glass in his hand, smiling at her lazily. She ran to him, full tilt, threw her arms around him, sending him staggering back, spilling the wine.

'Oh, my god, it's you, it's… I can't believe it!'

She kissed him, her red mouth smudging against his. He kissed her back, he couldn't help it, my god, she was as provocative as he remembered her, her mouth a hot furnace, her body wrapped around him like a vine. But the wild rush he expected wasn't there. He held her bare arms, pale, white, the veins blue in the crook of her elbow, and gently disentangled himself from her.

'Steady, old girl,' he said.

'You just poof…you disappeared. Not a word.'

'I'm sorry but I had to skip town in a bit of a bother.'

'They said you were a bad man, that you killed people.'

'Lies. Do you know what happened to my parents? To Debi, my sister?'

'No Dave, I stayed away. The police came. They asked many, many questions. You have a smoke?'

He reached into his pockets and offered her a crumpled pack.

'They made things hot. Brought up permits and all kinds of silly rules. So I left.'

'And...Andrew?'

Her face took on a haunted look. Suddenly, she looked years older.

'He...he was found in a ditch with his throat slit. Some say it was dacoits...but it was also whispered that it was actually the work of your father.'

'That's ridiculous! My father, whatever his faults, was never a murderer. Come on, Natasha, you know him.'

'I don't know what to believe, Dave. How are you here?'

In the restaurant, Aditi looked at her watch. Where on earth was Deb? She felt her head swim a bit. Oh dear, too much wine. She picked up a piece of ice from the silver bucket and rubbed it on her temple. What was keeping him?

Natasha moved in close again, clinging to the lapels of his suit.

'But now we are together again, no?'

'Natasha, things are different. I have nothing...no money, no home.'

'But you have me, Dave. I'll take care of you.'

'Ah, I wish things were that simple.'

He held her hands at arm's length, and backed out of the room towards the door.

Aditi looked around restlessly, finally got up. She made her way outside. A large, sleek-looking maître d', waiting like an attentive penguin, she thought with a tiny giggle, stood in ceremonious splendour at the lobby. She asked, he pointed, and she found herself walking down a poorly lit corridor behind the stage. Again a premonition, a little shiver made her almost turn back but she shook herself and turned the corner. Three dull green painted doors, all closed, stretched to the end. It was deserted. She stood for a moment, undecided, not at all relishing the prospect of knocking on them and having to answer to strangers. Finally, she turned and was turning the corner when she heard a door click open behind her. A slant of light cut through the gloom and fell across the uncarpeted floor. Debraj stepped out, facing the door. She gave a sigh of relief, opened her mouth to call him. Then a woman's hand snaked out, held the front of his shirt.

A white woman, the singer, stepped out and clung to him. Aditi stood frozen, her face stricken.

Debraj held the woman's hands in his own. 'I like you, Natasha Marinsky, I do...'

Aditi backed away. Then she turned and bolted.

'But I can't be with you, love.'

He turned at the sound of the running footsteps but the corridor was empty. He kissed Natasha on the forehead, hurried away.

When he got back, there was no purse, no Aditi, only an empty glass. He asked the penguin maître d', who just shrugged eloquently. He went out and found the jeep parked but still no Aditi. He drove home but it was silent, empty, echoing. He started to worry. She may have had a bit too much to drink. Kabootar drove up to her house and rang the bell. The amah opened the door, shook her head. Debraj, waiting in the passenger seat, slammed his hand on the dash in frustration. Where the hell was she? He drove around the streets, aimlessly, looking for her, getting angrier by the hour.

He went to the hospital. Maybe she had been called in for an emergency. It was like her to just run off into the night without saying anything if there was a patient in distress. But she was not there either. He sat in the foyer, and drifted off to sleep. It was there she found him, next morning, when she walked in for duty. She had gone home and bolted herself in, with strict instructions to the amah not to reveal her whereabouts. She instinctively went to wake him up but stayed her hand and went in.

She was with Meenakshi, dressing a patient when he came limping in.

'Aditi, what the hell is wrong with you?'

'Please leave, you're disturbing my patient'. She was calm, controlled, a little pale.

'What happened last night? Where did you disappear?'

'I was tired.'

'Did I do something wrong?'

'You tell me.' She was suddenly angry, the colour coming in like the tide, her voice high.

'Oh, stop behaving like a...'

'Child?'

'No, I was about to say shrew.'

She turned away, shaking her head, refusing to react to the barb. 'Is there anything you wanted from me?'

'The fundraiser this afternoon. I need you there.'

'I'm busy.'

Meenakshi, who had been a silent but attentive witness to the verbal tennis match, decided to take a hand in the proceedings.

'No, you're not. You aren't even on the duty roster.'

Aditi was irritated at her interference, dropping the scissors she had in her hand into the dressing tray. The clatter made all of them wince. She spoke to Meenakshi without looking up.

'Tell him to take his blonde — whoever she is — and go to the stupid fundraiser.'

Debraj threw up his hands.

'Ah, so that's what all this natak…this drama, is all about. Come on, Aditi, she's…'

She swung around, stopped him, a sharp chopping gesture of her hand.

'It's of no interest to me.'

Debraj took a step towards her, beseeching. 'Will you let me explain, for heaven's sake!'

Meenakshi stepped in again. 'Yes, let him explain.'

She pushed both of them out, raised her eyebrows at the elderly patient who shook his head at the timeless vagaries of love.

They stood in the garden, not looking at each other. She was demolishing a flower she had picked, petal by ragged petal, he was lighting up a cigarette, tapping it with jerky movements. They both started speaking together.

'I trusted you so…'

'I would never do…'

They stopped, looking helplessly at each other. She was very close to tears, the flood stemmed with a furious bite of her lip and clenched fists.

'Forgive me, I should have never left you and gone. But she's from my past and I wanted answers.'

'Your past…it will keep haunting us, won't it?'

'As does yours.'

They fell silent. An ambulance siren wailed in the distance, and the subdued hubbub of lives dying and life being reborn floated out.

'What time is your fundraiser?'

'4.30.'

'Ask Kabootar ji to pick me up from here.'

She turned on her heel, left.

Netaji caught sight of Debraj and Aditi as they entered the high-ceilinged room, the INA orchestra playing in the background. He was in uniform, leaning on his cane. He looked tired, drawn. She too was in uniform, a pale figure, hanging back.

'My dear boy, are you well? You look pale. Sister, are we overstraining him?'

'Oh, he's doing exceedingly well, Sir.' Her tone was curt, her manner brusque.

'Come, let me introduce you to someone. You will have your work cut out with him, I can assure you.'

Aditi remained where she was, her arms crossed behind her back, almost at attention. She watched him limping towards a group of businessmen — his limp always became pronounced when he was tired. Their drive to the meeting had been a silent one, Kabootar driving, she relentlessly sitting in the front seat, looking steadfastly ahead. He had tried to talk, his tone stiff but apart from a few murmured reactions, she had shut him out. This was her way of punishing him but she felt raw, whipped herself. She didn't know how to bridge that awful chasm that had appeared between them, how to erase that haunting picture of him and that woman from her mind's eye. She stared at his back as he walked away, aching and hollow inside.

Netaji took his arm, and led him to a group of men. One man, short, bald, his back to them, was holding forth.

'A logging contract for at least 20-30 years, if not forever…that's what I'm looking for. There are hundreds of acres of deep forest, virgin forest. We should get at throwaway price, no? In a few years,

God willing, India is free, there will be so much building…houses, factories and such. And we, with cheap supply of wood, we would be sitting on a gold mine.'

'If I may interrupt?' Netaji was at his elbow.

The man turned. It was Goopta. He looked at Debraj, went completely still.

'Let me introduce Captain Debraj Mookerji, son of Sir Harry Mookerji. From Calcutta, like you. Perhaps you know him?'

Goopta was staring fixedly at the carpet with an absent-minded look on his face. Then he looked up with a contented smile, a cat with a bowl of cream. 'Of course I know him.' He gave Debraj an ironic bow. 'My dear Chhoto laath, what a pleasure.'

Debraj took almost five seconds before he recognised Goopta. It had been a few months but it was as if Goopta had become someone else. He had taken on a shine, a patina, of money, success, power, all the things that make small men walk big. Even his language seemed to have changed, the timbre of his voice deeper.

'You! What the hell is this snake doing here?'

Heads turned. Debraj's voice had been loud, outraged. Netaji was startled. But Goopta was unperturbed, unruffled.

'Oh, please disregard his rudeness, he is like a son to me. If I may have a private moment with him? We have a little history to catch up on.'

Netaji stepped away, frowning. The rest of the group dispersed, people shifting away from the epicenter. Debraj turned blindly away, almost stumbling. Aditi, her face set, quickly stepped forward and steadied him, earning a sharp, searching look from Goopta. He called out to Debraj's retreating back.

'Your father, he suffered a stroke when you left.'

Debraj stumbled to a stop. Goopta waddled towards him, stroking his moustache, his eyes glittering with anticipation.

'Of course, not entirely your fault. He tried to tell you the night of the party, that he was in shock to me, deep, upto his neck but you didn't listen. The shock of losing his entire estate, even the Chandernagore ancestral property, the jomidar baadi, alas proved too much. He is quite gaga, I'm afraid. Missing his marbles, isn't that what they call it?'

Debraj swayed. Aditi held on to him, her mouth fierce. His voice was strangled as he turned back. 'My…mother?'

'Oh, still the legendary beauty, and still hitting the bottle. But that you know.'

'Where do they…?

'In some little hovel in Maniktala. I let them have it — out of the bigness of my heart. I did make sure they get some basic rations but those medical bills, tch tch…'

'Why…why did you do it, Goopta?' Debraj's voice was hoarse, as if he had run up a hill.

'Why? To help them out, naturally. Wouldn't want the Lord and Lady Mookerji begging on the streets.'

Aditi spoke up, her voice strong, calm. 'Debraj, you can walk away.'

'And who are you, dear?'

'I'm Sister Sen and Captain Mookerji is in my care.'

'Captain, is he? And a cripple, yes?' He smiled at the cane.

'Why are you punishing him?'

'To show him that he, his kind, their time is over. Your jomidari ways, Chhoto laath…aar cholbena. Your high and mighty airs, you can lump them. You stuck your aristocratic nose up at my little girl. But you'll see…we are running things from now on. There's a new order, a new class on the rise. Men like me who will create the new India.'

'Shut up, you carpetbagging, opportunistic scum! It will be Netaji's India, Netaji who will lead.'

Netaji looked up from the other side of the room, troubled. Something was brewing, something bad. He whispered to Ahmed Hassan, who hurried towards the island of people marooned in the centre of the carpet.

Goopta snapped his finger at Noshir bhai who quickly conjured up an ashtray with a genie-like air. Goopta mashed out his cigar in it, taking his time. Then he turned to Debraj with a barely concealed sneer.

'We shall see, we shall see. You have no idea, pretty, foolish boys like you, what the truth is, do you? Playing at swadeshi, at independence, with your silly parades and made-up battles. You don't have a clue about the deals being made, the tide of the times, the powers behind the powers behind the powers, the puppet masters pulling the strings. Such chhelemanushi…utterly childish!'

Debraj trembled with the effort to hold his rage in. Aditi put a restraining hand on his arm. 'Deb…easy.'

Goopta gave her another veiled look, the malice seeping through the slits of his eyes. She recoiled at the venom she saw there. Then in a mercurial change of mood, Goopta smiled disarmingly.

'However, Deb, as your very pretty nurse so nicely calls you, Deb, you can have your share of all this. My offer for dear Kumudini's hand is still open. Out of respect for your great family name, and my enduring affection for your father. Of course, you won't get your legacy back, that would be too much generosity on my part, even if you were my son-in-law but I could easily find some use for that expensive bileth-pheroth education of yours.'

Debraj's face darkened, scarlet, his rage volcanic, simmering just before erupting. 'I wouldn't wipe my arse with your offer, you greasy son of a bitch.'

Noshir bhai started stuttering in protest at this grievous insult to his employer but Goopta waved him away. Instead, he turned towards Aditi and with a faint but unmistakable air of impropriety, placed his podgy fingers on the bare skin of her arm and stroked it.

'See, Sister, how he insults me. Fortunately, I have thick skin. Water off duck's back.'

She flinched, jerked her arm away, her skin crawling. Debraj took one threatening step forward, his fists bunched. Goopta took two steps back, hurriedly, bumping into Noshir, who was twittering around just behind his shoulder. Goopta gave him a baleful look, then turned to Debraj once more. The crowd had started to drift towards them, gravitating to the scent of conflict and salacious gossip. Ahmed Hassan came up and courteously requested Goopta to join Netaji.

Goopta bowed. 'Of course, mustn't keep the great man waiting.' He turned his back on Debraj, then over his shoulder, almost as an afterthought, he tossed off his last barb.

'And oh, forgot to tell you about the last member of your most illustrious family. Your sister, Debi, the little goddess.'

In spite of himself, in spite of knowing that Goopta was manipulating him, trying to destroy him, Debraj couldn't resist the bait.

'Where is she?' he growled.

'In hiding but myself, Goopta, your faithful servant, no one can hide from me. She has given birth to an illegitimate son, your good friend, the late Andrew's legacy…'

'You bastard!'

'No, no, Chhoto laath, you are mistaken, it is the child who is the bastard.'

It was Aditi who stepped up with a calm look now, her clear eyes brooking no argument.

'Stop. You should leave now, Sir.'

Goopta laughed, a small bark of a laugh but it sounded very loud in the silence that had descended over the room.

'Ahhh, I know that look. Diddled his way underneath that white little skirt of yours, hasn't he? Always had a way with women…'

Debraj smashed his fist into Goopta's face. Goopta reeled, staggered back, tripped over a table, sent a lamp crashing. Noshir screamed, Aditi tried to pull Debraj off but all Debraj's pent up frustration just boiled over. He hauled up Goopta, and hit him again. Goopta went down on his butt and scrabbled backwards to get away. Gaffar, who had been watching, motionless, finally strode up and shoved Debraj away. He turned to help Goopta up. Goopta's face was a mask of rage, blood trickling down from his nose, one eye already swelling up. Gaffar looked at him, gave an imperceptible shake of the head. Goopta spat, slowly staggered up. Netaji was at his side, helping him.

'My deepest apologies, Goopta babu. Come, please let us have your wounds attended to.' He muttered to Gaffar. 'Get Sister to the library.'

In the library, Goopta sank into a chair. 'You better rein in your dogs, Netaji, or they will be the death of you.'

'They are not my dogs and you did provoke him.'

'As he did me.'

Aditi came in, reluctant, hesitant. But her training took over. Quickly, efficiently, with Gaffar helping, she patched him up. He stared at her balefully through his rapidly closing eye. He said nothing, taking her ministrations without a word of thanks. She shivered. When she was done, she gathered up her things and left.

Netaji too had excused himself. Gaffar and Goopta remained in the room.

'Shall I ask Noshir bhai to get the car?'

'That khanki'r bachcha, that whore's son, he's going to pay.'

'We have far more important things to think about, Goopta ji, than your little personal vendetta. You will become persona non grata in the Netaji camp, you do realise that? If you weren't so bent on rubbing that man's face in the ground, you might have forged an alliance with Netaji tonight. I had worked so hard towards that and it's all come to nothing.'

Goopta took a deep, shuddering breath.

'You're right. That was weak of me. I'll find a way to punish him later. But it makes your presence that much more important. You have to get closer to Netaji than ever before. Something big is coming, I'm sure of it. All the signs are there.'

'Then don't pull the rug out from under me at the first opportunity. If I'm going to worry all the time about you lot betraying me, I can't do anything.'

'Set your mind at ease, Gaffar bhai. Free hand, I'll tell them.' He put his hand out, then winced.

Gaffar actually smiled. 'You know, you are going to have a really bad black eye tomorrow.'

Debraj stumbled out into a courtyard behind the house. He slammed his already bruised fist against the wall. Goopta had ambushed him and he had walked into it, lamb to the slaughter. The news about his father had thrown him badly. Sir Harry, the man in charge, the authority figure he had fought all his life, the father whose approval he had sought and never got, that superhuman being had disintegrated. It was as if someone had ripped the centre of his life out and left a large hole. He wanted to howl but no tears came. He heard footsteps and knew it was Aditi.

'Please, no sanctimonious lectures.'

She stood silently, patiently, waiting for the storm to pass.

'I need to go back to Calcutta. I have to find my parents. Debi.'

'You will be arrested.'

'I'll slip in somehow. I shouldn't have left.' He groaned in frustration. 'What am I doing here?'

'Fighting to create something good…something that will make up for all that we have lost…'

'Oh, how noble. In the meantime, my parents are starving, Debi is alone with a..a…child and…'

'You can make sure that the child inherits a world in which he will be free.'

'They should call you Mother Mary.'

She flinched but held her ground.

'We have to win, Debraj!'

'And what happens if we don't? What happens if all this, these grand plans, these complex geo-political manoeuvres fail? Maybe it's all too big for the likes of me. Maybe I just don't belong.'

'You do, all of us do. We have a mission.'

'Oh, that terrible M word again. You sound just like a friend of mine, parroting all this stuff. How can you be so goddamn sure? All of you?'

'We just have to believe.'

'Believe? Believe? I don't know what the hell to believe in anymore. All I know is that everything that mattered to me…it's gone…lost!'

'Maybe that's the point. That you have to lose everything to find out who you really are.'

'Oh, I can think of better ways of figuring that out. All I know is that if I hadn't come on this little adventure, none of this would have happened.'

Aditi was silent. Then, in a barely audible voice, she spoke. 'But then, we would have never met.'

He looked at her, faltered in his anger.

'That was quite a show you put up there.'

Debraj swung around. Netaji was standing in the shadows at the edge of the courtyard. Debraj had no idea how long he had been standing there, how much of their argument he had heard. He automatically saluted him, stood to attention.

'Sir!'

'Conduct unbecoming of an INA officer, Captain Mookerji.'

'Yes, Sir.'

'Don't forget, wherever you are, you not only represent the INA, me but also India, the dignity of our land.'

'Yes, Sir.'

'There must be disciplinary action.'

Aditi couldn't keep quiet any longer. 'But Sir, if you had heard what that man was saying and…'

Netaji silenced her with a tiny gesture of his hand. 'If we cannot rise above the foolishness of other men, how will we forge a country? How other men treat you, behave with you, that's their karma. How you react to it is your own. Your wounds, your loss, these are mitigating circumstances, Captain. But I want you to apologise publicly to Goopta.'

Debraj's eyes flashed in anger, his nostrils pinched white. 'Please Sir, punish me if you must but not that.'

'I will and I must. Because only then will I know that you are a bigger man than what you have demonstrated tonight. And I know you are.'

Debraj looked at him, his jaw clenched in rebellion. Netaji returned his look steadfastly. And then the fury drained out of Debraj.

'I *will* find out where my parents are — as soon as the campaign is over.'

'And I'll help you with all the resources at my disposal. Thank you for trusting me, Captain.'

'Okay, let's go and do it.'

'Follow me.'

The two men left. Aditi let out her breath. Strange creatures, men. All the emotion and logic she had marshalled had not made a dent and then Netaji had to just look at him and tell him he was a better man and it was done.

Goopta was about to leave, Noshir fussing around him, when Ahmed Hassan came into the library.

'Netaji would be honoured if you came into the reception room, Mr. Goopta.'

'I do not relish being insulted again, Ahmed ji. I'm sure a respectable man like you will appreciate my sentiments.'

Ahmed bowed politely. 'It is to make amends that he invites you.'

As Goopta entered the room, Netaji walked straight up to him and joined his palms.

'Mr. Goopta, let me apologise profusely for the insult and injury done to you in my home. You are a guest and therefore, according to Indian tradition, you are a god to us. Unfortunately, angry, importunate words were exchanged and in the heat of the moment, a young man, wounded grievously and having given so much to this cause, lost his temper — and his manners — and put his hand upon you.' Then in a loud voice, he commanded, 'Captain Mookerji, step up, please.'

Goopta's piggy eye which was still open, widened. This was truly unexpected. All eyes turned to Debraj as he stepped in. He saluted Netaji, then did a crisp about turn and came to Goopta, leaning on his cane, looking every bit the gallant, wounded soldier. He looked at Goopta, his face impassive, his head held high. Then he spoke.

'Mr. Goopta, gentlemen. All of you came here this evening to see how you could contribute to the cause of Indian independence, to stand beside Netaji and take your rightful place in these historic times. You came looking for belief and hope and to know that whatever you do, however small it may be, you would make a difference.'

Across the room, his eyes met Aditi's. He used the pause, let the silence speak.

'I too came here for that reason. I came here to share the stumbling journey I have made. I left my country, became an exile. I lost my home, my family.'

A murmur went round the room, nods of sympathy.

'I almost lost my limbs, my life, in this battle for our freedom. But I have not lost hope. I am here tonight to tell you that I will persist, I will persevere because Netaji is my leader.'

A burst of applause. Goopta was filled with admiration. What a clever, clever man this Netaji was, what a worthy opponent.

'But unlike Netaji, I sometimes falter. I become weak, I lose my way. And in such a moment, I did the unthinkable. I laid hands on a comrade, a fellow traveller. And for this, I...'

He paused, looked straight at Goopta. Goopta swelled visibly, relishing the coming apology. But looking at Debraj, he found no fear, no cringing, no shame there. Instead, his light grey eyes were curiously alight, glittering dangerously. Goopta was confused, then grim. He began to realise he had been manipulated.

'For this, I abjectly apologise to you, Mr. Goopta. Please forgive me, if you can. I will receive a soldier's punishment at the hands of my Commanding Officer but if there's anything you want me to do, in reparation, I will do it gladly. I am a proud soldier of the Indian National Army and I will do what I must to wipe out this disgrace.'

He stood, quiet at last, a look of calm on his handsome face. Silence hung over the room. Then, somebody started clapping, followed by another and another until it was a storm breaking. 'Hear, hear.' Goopta knew he could ask for nothing. It would be churlish.

'Apology accepted.' Then, under his breath, so only Debraj could hear, he muttered, 'But you will pay for this one.'

Debraj saluted but as his hand went down, all the fingers curled in — except for the middle finger which stood straight. He smiled gently at Goopta, and walked out. Ahmed Hassan came up to Goopta. 'Thank you, Mr. Goopta. He will be reprimanded suitably. And now, I will have you escorted home.'

'Thank you. And all the best for the coming battle.'

Hassan paused, looking at him sharply. 'I beg your pardon?'

Goopta shook his head, made a placating gesture. 'Arre, Ahmed ji, don't worry, you can trust me. They say you go before the monsoons.'

'Rumours!' Ahmed smiled. 'Just like the rumour that you are perhaps loyal to the Congress?'

Gaffar, hovering close by with a tray of drinks, looked up sharply.

'My dear, Sir, I'm loyal only to a good bargain. Lain and dain… give and take…my two mistresses.'

'How wonderfully honest…of you.'

'Thank you, Sir. So it would be very helpful indeed to know when your Netaji is planning the offensive so we can conclude our business dealings accordingly.'

'Of course, I understand.'

The last guest had left. Debraj's impassioned speech had loosened many a cheque book and it had all concluded satisfactorily. Outside, it had become a bit foggy, a thick mist coming off the river, the moon a shimmering sickle behind the haze. Ahmed was sprawled in a chair, stroking a fat ginger tabby. It was his favourite, the one that calmed him the most. Netaji sat opposite. He wasn't fond of cats at all and merely suffered them for Ahmed's sake.

'He is a dangerous man. He has many secrets and many friends in different places, Sir.'

'More reason to make him our friend, yes?'

'He has no love for you, Sir.'

'Well, not many in the Party do.'

'Not just the Party. There's the League, the…'

'You don't have to remind me, I'm not very popular, god knows.'

'One thing I do know — the Party will help the British if it comes to a choice between you and them.'

'An acute observation, Ahmed.'

'You must not keep him close.'

'Goopta? I don't intend to. But because he is the crooked wretch he is, we can use him too. Misdirection, that's the trick. Like this mist. It hides everything…it makes you imagine shapes you want to see. A child sees dinosaurs and mammoths, monsters and dragons. But it's only a tree. We must make him see the things we want him to see.'

'He was asking whether the battle will be before the monsoons.'

'Tell him it will be during the monsoons, that we plan to use the terrain and the mud to trap their heavy artillery.'

They both laughed, good friends at the end of another day's slog.

In the tea shop, Haru jumps up incensed. 'Arre, why didn't Netaji get rid of this badmash fellow, Goopta? Anybody can see he's up to no good.'

'Ei, chup, silence.' Dulal da is curt. 'We can do without your expert comments.'

'But he's right. Netaji knew all about espionage and intelligence. Yet he allowed all kinds of people into his inner circle. He was remarkably…'

'Ah, Sudipto babu, there you go with all that analysis shanalysis again. How will we ever get to the end of the story?'

'But don't you want to know the why, the how, the facts behind the fiction, the truth behind the presumptions?'

'Arre baba, I just want to know how it all ends, who won and who lost. We are moddhobitto, middle-class people, we like our Star Plus serials, our Bollywood dishoom dishoom, a few songs, dances, some masala and happy endings. I don't want to think too much... gives me a headache.'

'But you know how it ends, don't you? You know the INA lost. So, what's the point of hearing this story?'

Dulal da scratches his armpit. 'Because I want to know what happens to all of them, to that Nishonko. Where the hell was he?'

'In Japan, remember? Training. But then he came back, just before Christmas,' says the old man.

The hospital lobby was being decked with streamers and bells. The British may have left Singapore but this equatorial city filled with Chinese and a dozen other races still wanted to celebrate Christmas, in spite of Japanese disapproval. Meenakshi was walking briskly through the lobby, carrying an armload of paper holly when she overheard a deep voice say, 'Where can I find Sister Aditi?'

She looked around. A tall man in uniform stood in front of the over-burdened nurse on duty. She shook her head. 'Out. On special duty' and turned away to deal with a woman holding a squalling infant.

Meenakshi, poised to leave, paused and called out over the din. 'Major Mitro?'

The man turned with a smile to see who was calling out his name. Meenakshi felt her breath catch. He had the most engaging smile, guileless. His teeth shone, white against the dark skin. He had long lashed very dark eyes, pretty as a girl's but everything else about him, his fit, whippet thin body, the luxuriant, nicely curling black moustache, was intensely masculine.

'Have we met?'

Meenakshi smiled back. 'No. But Aditi speaks of you. And I saw you with her, once. You didn't have the moustache then, did you?'

Nishonko looked pleased. 'I'll find her at home, I guess. Actually, the other reason I came here, could you find out if a patient got admitted here — a Captain Mookerji ?'

Meenakshi's eyes widened. 'Who?'

'Debraj Mookerji. Wounded in both legs.'

'You know him?'

'Oh, yes, very, very good friend of mine.'

'He was discharged.'

'Oh, that's great news. Any idea where he's now?'

'No, no… I…'

'Aditi? Would she know?'

'I…um…she might.'

'Well, you know Debraj…he'll leave a trail. Don't worry, I'll hunt him down. And your name, Sister?'

'Meena. Meenakshi.'

'Thank you, Sister Meenakshi. Nice meeting you.'

Meenakshi stood staring after him. Then she ran for the phone behind the nurse's desk, the fake holly spilling out of her arms.

The phone rang and rang in the empty house, sending the pigeons, fluttering in spirals into the clear blue winter sky. There was no one home.

They had gone driving into the countryside, a picnic basket in the back seat. Kabootar had discovered a secret lake at the eastern tip of the island, near Changi. It was a vast expanse of tidal inlets just off the coast, known only to the locals, providing a mix of sweet and salt water, a great place to fish. When they drove down the sandy road to the edge of the water, Kabootar disappeared down the shoreline carrying his fishing tackle, receding, until he was a mere mirage.

They opened up the wine and took off their clothes. Aditi was already in her single-piece swimsuit, still shy of wearing it in public. The wine was warm but it still tasted wonderful, with the briny, bracing tang of the open sea blowing in. The day had a strange translucent quality to it, a glow that touched everything, filling their eyes with a white light that left them dazzled. They both knew that time was running out, that the call would come any day. They snatched at moments together, each moment precious. It gave everything they did a clear, etched feeling, yet made it seem like gossamer, disappearing the moment they tried to grasp it. He lay with his head on her stomach, listening to the wine gurgle, the blood sighing like a river, the pulse started by her restless heart, echoing. When the wine was done, he waded into the lake, its waters sent scudding by the stiff, sharp wind. He slid in, stayed under long enough for her to sit up in alarm, then turned with a lazy, elegant movement of his long arms to swim to the far side. She was glad to see him so fit, his movements strong and assured. The cane was gone, the limp imperceptible. She had healed him, made him ready for battle, as commanded by her leader. Unbidden tears came to her salt-limned eyes. She knuckled them away. She walked into the lake, the dark blue waters an upside down sky speckled with the white of high cumulus clouds. The water claimed her inch by inch, climbing up her brown legs. When it reached her belly, she stopped. She turned full circle, scanning the horizon, the low hills behind, the long grass on the scrubby dunes, the far shore. Then she peeled off her swimsuit, and threw it on the shore. Now she let the water take her, cleaved through it strongly, feeling it resist her. It reminded her of the pond of her childhood and the big banyan tree with its branch overhanging the dark water. She would dive off it, terror stricken yet wildly exhilarated, as she went screaming and thrashing into the black depths and then emerge, spluttering, wet as a seal, the water pouring off her nut brown back. Nishonko da would still be sitting on the branch, his thin legs dangling, waiting for her to surface safely. Then he would jump, with a blood-curdling yell, which always made her giggle. He would cut clean through, hardly a splash, then emerge a few feet away, spitting out water, grinning, shaking his head, sending the water drops flying.

The pond had been their secret place, the hideout where they caught tadpoles and little snails' heads retreating into their shells as soon as they were touched. She swam now on her back, her naked body skimming through the water like a brown sleek fish, while the infinite sky filled her mouth and eyes with blue. A high cloud blanked out the sun, turning the world inside her eyes dark. He would be back, soon. The thought made her shiver. She treaded water, looked around for Debraj. He was a speck in the distance, far away. She raced back to shore, cold now. She wrapped herself in a towel, rubbing herself hard. Then she sat, brooding. Should she tell him about Debraj? Maybe he would just accept it and she was making a big thing out of nothing. Or maybe, he would do something bad. But if she just waited until the battle was over, so many things could happen. Maybe Nishonko da would be shipped out soon and there would be no need to talk. Maybe…no, that's horrible, how can you even imagine that. She reached for the wine bottle but it was empty. No, she would tell him. It was only fair. And maybe he would get along with Debraj, approve of him. Anyway, it wasn't as if he was really her big brother or that she was in any way answerable to him. Come on, he'll understand. She was just frightening herself, imagining the worst.

Debraj came panting out of the water, winded by the long swim, goose-pimpled. He saw her wrapped in the big towel, covered completely, her hair matted and wind blown, a loose strand straying across her lips, an enigmatic smile on her lips. He pulled the towel off her to dry himself, and stopped in his tracks. She was butt naked, sitting cross legged, a brown Buddha. He approached her, the towel falling, forgotten, on the sandy ground. He slowly kneeled in front of her, cupped those chocolate tipped breasts. She stared back at him, her eyes wet pools. He stared back, then cradling her sun-warmed hips, he brought his mouth to the shadowy place between her crossed legs. She shuddered, went back on her elbows, offering herself to him fully. Under that big sky, amongst the squawking of the wheeling gulls, her cries of abandonment were lost, torn away by the freshening wind.

Chhoto mashi was watering the plants in the verandah, when a voice just behind her made her jump. The small tin can went clattering on the stone flags.

'Hello, Ma'am.'

It was Nishonko, grinning. He had tiptoed up silently.

'Oh my god, you gave me such a fright.'

He laughed, his carefree mood evident. 'The main door was open. I'm so sorry. I wanted to surprise Jhilik. Is she home?'

'Oh dear, yes, I mean no…oh, I'm so flustered. You look different.'

'The moustache, perhaps?' he asked giving the ends a little twirl. 'I started growing it in Ja…at the place I was stationed and then just kept it. Do you think Jhilik will like it?'

'Jhilik has gone to…some special duty. Sit, sit.'

'What special duty?'

'Amah, some tea. So how long are you here?'

'I don't know. Depends on Netaji. But I thought — I might as well tell you — you're her family.'

Chhoto mashi frowned. What he was trying to say?

'I'm going to ask her…not that she needs to be asked, she knows, it's always been there, unsaid, you know.' He was stumbling over his words.

Chhoto mashi watched him, her expression blank, bland. 'Ask her what?'

He didn't hear her. 'But maybe you still have to come out and say the words. Maybe silence doesn't work always.'

'Ask her what?' Chhoto mashi's voice was edged with faint alarm.

'But I do have first right over her, she must know that.' He looked up now, emphatic.

Chhoto mashi finally understood. Her voice was sharp. 'Right? No one has a right over anybody, Nishonko'.

He looked at her, frowning, disagreeing. 'Even someone who has known her since childhood? I know her better than she knows herself.'

'Do you? So, what were you going to ask her?'

'I bought her this ring… found it in an old antique shop in Tok… Do you think she'll like it?' He held it out. It was an eternity ring, simple, made perhaps of silver.

'It's…pretty.'

He shrugged. 'It's the best I could do. She'll understand.'

'Hope you haven't left it too late.'

'Why…why do you say that?' He looked stricken for a moment.

She couldn't tell him. 'Well, the war…the uncertainty of the times…'

'We'll get through all this. Knowing we have each other. Well, I'm off. Have to report at HQ. Please tell Jhilik I'll be back.'

There was a flurry of activity at HQ. Netaji was leaving for Indonesia in the next few days for one final outreach to Indians in Japanese-occupied Asia before the final move. Nishonko had to wait for over an hour before he was ushered in. Netaji was dictating letters, aides were rushing in and out with lists. He stood to one side, waiting for Netaji to look up. When he did, he jumped up and hugged Nishonko.

'Nishonko, my dear fellow. Wonderful to see you finally.'

'Congratulations, Sir, on the go-ahead.'

'Shall we step outside for a moment. You can't think with the pandemonium here.'

'What's our strength, Sir? Do we have the numbers to make the offensive?

'Oh, almost 40,000. The Intelligence Wing, Debraj, in particular, has been doing a splendid job. He has turned entire units over to our cause. And he's very good at getting people to donate happily.'

'Yes, he's very good at charming the pants off people.'

'That's an asset, young man.'

'Really? I mean, we are the INA. Do we really need to resort to such...tactics?'

'Ah, my idealistic, serious-minded friend. Waging a war is expensive business. Do you know how much a Howitzer costs? Each of us must prepare in our own ways for the final push. And Major Mookerji is playing his role magnificently.'

'Major? When did that happen?'

'Recently.' Netaji gave him a sharp glance. 'You should be proud of your friend.'

'Of course. I'm glad for his promotion. '

There was a little silence.

'Where do I find him, Sir?'

'Division will help you. And now, if you'll excuse me, I have so much to finish.'

'Of course. And my reports?'

'Leave them on my desk. I'll be in touch.'

Nishonko stood outside the gate, feeling strangely left out. The campaign was buzzing but instead of being in the thick of things, he felt marginalised, irrelevant. Netaji was obviously very busy but, surely, he could have spared a little more time. He had thought he would come back to a hero's welcome after Japan but, instead, Debraj seemed to have got the upper hand. He felt at a loose end. He looked at the piece of paper the clerk had given him, with the scrawled address. He hailed a rickshaw at the corner.

As Chhoto mashi stepped out through her front door, on her way to the free evening clinic she ran, a jeep drove up. Aditi, her hair windswept, cheeks flushed by the sun, got off. Her sandals were slung over her shoulder and she was bare foot and laughing. She blew a kiss at the man in the front seat – and then caught sight of Chhoto mashi. She went red, then pale, looking very flustered. The man in the jeep looked at them, then stepped out. Dressed in rumpled linen, his hair mussed by the wind, the beard, he still managed to look very elegant. He bowed very low, sweeping the straw boater he had in his hand.

'Sister Aditi, won't you introduce us?'

'Yes, of course,' Aditi stammered, 'Chhoto mashi, Debraj, my patient…Debraj, my aunt, Suchandra Swaminathan.'

'Major Debraj Mookerji, at your service, Ma'am. Very honoured to meet you finally. I have heard so much about you.'

Chhoto mashi took Debraj in, the startling good looks, the light eyes, the easy, loose-limbed charm. She nodded at him politely. 'And I about you. When did the Major bit happen?'

Debraj stared at her, then burst into laughter. 'I can see where Aditi's candour comes from. The Major bit happened last week, Ma'am. Though what difference it makes, I have no idea.'

'I'm sure you will figure it out. And now if you will excuse me, I have to run.'

'Oh, we can't have that. I've waited far too long to meet you. Aditi has done her utmost to keep us apart. I insist on a cup of your famous Darjeeling.'

Chhoto mashi looked startled, then gave a grudging smile. 'Please do come in. Aditi, could you stop gaping and get us some tea? Amah is out.'

Aditi gulped, nodded.

They sat in the verandah, in the fading warmth of the sunlight. Debraj spoke of his days in England, the college pranks and about the English sense of humour. Chhoto mashi found herself laughing. He was witty, unpretentious, candid. He was able to make jokes about himself, about lawyering and the English weather.

'You like them, don't you? The English?' Chhoto mashi asked.

He paused. 'Yes, I do. Amazing what such a tiny island nation has achieved, its spirit of exploration, its enterprise, its ideas and social sytems. I have no problems acknowledging that. But they need to be stopped. It is wrong what they are doing to our country.'

'Do you really think this little adventure of Netaji's is going to work?'

Aditi interrupted, embarrassed. 'Chhoto mashi!'

'No, Aditi, let her speak. That is the first thing about freedom, isn't it — the freedom to think. More important than all the other freedoms.'

'Well put, Major. So what do *you* think?'

'Honestly, I too have my moments of doubt. But we can't carry on not doing anything, sitting on our hands, thinking that somehow, miraculously, the British will just leave this embarrassment of riches called India and walk away.'

'Why should they? They believe they have a divine right to it.'

'Precisely. This is what all colonials do. They enter a country on some pretext — trade, aid, converting the bloody heathens to their god — and then, boom, they take it over through force of arms, superior technology. They build their wonderful railways and canals and roads to carry the goods they loot from the country. They build their educational institutes to train the people who will be their puppets in governance. They build their monuments to greed, to trade. And then they say, hands off, chaps, all this belongs to us, you have no rights here.'

'Very eloquent, Major.'

'So yes, I think it's time we reclaimed our land. That's why I'll put my money on Netaji.'

He started to sing in a soft, deep voice a snatch of a Bengali song, a song about their beautiful, incomparable country, their homeland.

'Emon deshti kothao khuje pabena ko tumi…'

Both Aditi and Chhoto mashi joined in. 'You won't ever find another land like this, she's the queen of all lands, she's my motherland…'

'Shokol desher rani shey jey aamar janmobhumi, shey je…'

Chhoto mashi had sudden tears in her eyes. She stood up abruptly and said, 'I have to be at the clinic.'

Debraj stood up immediately. 'Hope to meet you again, Ma'am… before we leave.'

Chhoto mashi turned to leave, then stopped. 'Jhilik, there was…' Should she tell Aditi about Nishonko's return? She looked at them, so perfect together, and couldn't bear to destroy the moment. It could wait. She waved to them, left.

Inside, Aditi jumped onto Debraj's lap and hugged him. 'She likes you.'

'I like you. I like you, Aditi Sen, my odd, odd…what's that your aunt called you?'

She stopped him with a long deep kiss, then jumped off his lap and disappeared through the door. It remained empty for a few seconds. He frowned, not sure what she wanted him to do. Then she stepped back in, leaning against the door frame, coquettish, a pretend vamp, summoning him with a cocked finger. He laughed.

'Really? In the lion's den?'

She pouted, strutted, then gave a small shriek as he suddenly jumped up and gave chase. Their laughter echoed through the house.

Nishonko walked through the throngs in Chinatown. He had gone hunting for Debraj's house, found a ramshackle, dilapidated, almost derelict bungalow. He couldn't imagine that Debraj, of all people, would stay in such a dump and decided the clerk had given him the wrong address. But then he had found a handwritten sign saying 'Mookerji' taped to the side of the door. So he left a scrawled note and stuck it into the latch. He decided to walk, feeling restless. The late evening sun lit up the smoke pluming from the chop joints and gave everything a soft pastel wash. As he arrived at the riverside, he came across one of those small street markets that would spring up in the evenings at street corners, in defiance of the Japanese police. A gap-toothed Chinese woman selling floral lapel buttons at a street corner, called out to Nishonko. She pinned a white flower to his uniform shirt. A man selling INA flags called out, 'Buy one for our boys. Buy one for Netaji.'

By the time he turned into the street where Aditi lived, dusk was falling. Twinkling lights and little Christmas trees with fake cotton wool snow had been put up in some houses in a brave attempt to show solidarity for the Christians in the occupied city. A chilly wind came out of nowhere, swirling up the debris, making him shiver. He felt a moment of unease, a churning of the stomach. He realised he hadn't eaten anything the whole day in the flurry of coming back home. He would take Jhilik out for dinner, perhaps. Isn't that what Debraj had told him, to go down on his knees and declare his undying love? Mad idiot. Where was he? He touched the box with the ring in his pocket. The street was deserted at this hour, except for a lone jeep, parked a few yards down from Chhoto mashi's house. He went up to the door, checked the time. She should be back by now from whatever special duty she was doing. He climbed the stairs.

Kabootar, slouched in the jeep, just the top of his head visible, saw the man walking up to the door. In the dusk, he couldn't make out who it was. A moustachioed man in uniform. He closed his eyes.

Nishonko went to knock but the door opened under his hand. He shook his head. Terrible habit, Chhoto mashi had, never closed the door. The small hallway was in darkness. He stepped in, calling her name softly. 'Jhilik…' The corridor stretched empty in front of him. A creaky fan somewhere made a clicking sound. He looked in through a half open door into the modest living room. It too was empty. 'Jhilik??' Then, from somewhere ahead, he thought he heard a soft moan. He frowned. It sounded like someone in pain. 'Chhoto mashi?' he called out, a little louder. Another soft moan whispered out, making his hair stand on end. He padded to the last door in the corridor. It was shut but under the tentative pressure of his hand, it silently gave way. He peered in. A small anteroom, at the entrance, led to the main room, which opened up, out of sight, to his left. It was in semi darkness, also empty, the bamboo blinds pulled, silent. He would have gone, never seen anything but then, in the last moment, his eyes fell on a large antique mirror angled on the wall running on his right. It reflected, framed, like a painting, the unseen part of the room — a bed, darkened dressers, a lamp with a thin gossamer scarf thrown over it, scattered clothes. Lying back on the bed, half propped up on elbows, was a shadowy figure, a man, bare bodied, his hip outthrust. The moan broke out again, the man shuddered, arched his back. The Judas lamplight fell on his face. It was…Debraj?

Thinner, bearded but Debraj. What was happening? Why was...? Then another figure slid into the mirror's treacherous rectangle. A woman, slender bodied, full breasted. Her hair, curly, unruly, hung around her face, hiding it. She pushed the man, Debraj, how could it be Debraj, down and straddled him. And then, by a strange trick of light, the sleight of hand of the fates, the woman was caught in an errant golden beam of the last sunlight coming through some gap in the blinds as she threw back her head, her eyes glazed over, panting raggedly...it was Aditi, naked, luminous, undone. Their bodies began to move together in a familiar rhythm, both in thrall. It was Aditi. And Debraj.

Nishonko stood, rigid with shock, unable to move for what seemed an eternity. His brain was numb, his body stone. Then the slowly building crescendo of cries and whispers pierced the fog. Shame, corruscating shame, galvanised him, gave life to his legs. He backed out, silent as the Nishachar he was known as, melting back into the dusk of the corridor, gone like a swirl of grey smoke. He didn't know how he got to the main door, still half open. No one witnessed his blind flight. He stumbled out, almost fell down the stone stairs, sprawled on the pavement and threw up. Kabootar, still lounging in the jeep, heard the sounds of retching and sat up. Nishonko, on all fours on the street, looked up, the thin stream of puke trailing from his mouth. He saw a man's feet running towards him and covered his face. He didn't want to be seen, to be known, to have any evidence of having been here. The feet ran up, then waited as he cowered behind the fragile cover of his arms. Finally, Nishonko looked up. A street lamp that had just come on lit the man's face. There was a shock of recognition. They stared at each other. Nishonko staggered to his feet.

'You...you...'

A glare of pure malevolence, of murderous rage, and then he whirled and ran. Kabootar stared after him, then turned away. He saw the front door ajar, looked up and down the street, then mounted the stairs and pulled the door shut.

He ran pell mell...lights...blurs...laughing faces...painted women... hands reaching out...glitter of Christmas decorations...voices swirling…silent night, holy night, all is calm, all is bright…a candle-lit procession…nuns with round faces…orphans in new clothes… all laughing at him. Panic stricken, he hunted for cover. A small church with wide open doors, the light spilling out, beckoned. He stumbled in, looked wildly around. Two old women were at the far end, working on a Nativity tableau. An old man, a tattered wino, sprawled in one of the pews, sleeping.

He stumbled into a confessional, his face streaked with tears. The image of them, joined in ecstasy, seared his brain. He howled, like a dog, run over, unable to comprehend what had hit him. The mask of the soldier, the revolutionary and the commander of men was stripped away. Behind it was revealed the boy, the vulnerable, untried boy with his buried childhood, his fragile sense of self, the wound of this most grievous betrayal ripping him apart.

The partition in the booth slid back. A shadowy form leaned in. 'How long has it been since your last confession, my child?'

Nishonko gasped for air. The words tumbled out, a disjointed torrent. 'They…they were…like a bitch in heat…'

'Hush, my child, you are in…'

'I'll kill him…'

'Talk not of killing. Ask for the Lord's forgiveness…'

'Forgiveness!!?' His voice broke. 'I would have given my life for her. How could she…a fake...'

Through the latticed screen, Father Unnikrishnan could see the man, hugging himself, rocking back and forth.

'She's…fell for his glib talk. Swayed by…his wealth…his… Oh Jhilik, Jhilik, what have you done?' He gasped, dry retching, heaving.

'Easy son, easy…deep breaths.'

A whimper. 'I gave her everything. She's mine, God, promised to me by life itself.' It came out as an anguished shout. The two old ladies looked up, alarmed, whispered, a sound like rustling leaves. The old wino looked around blearily, then went back to sleep.

'Let us pray to alleviate your pain, my…'

'Damn your prayers!'

Nishonko flailed his way out of the booth. In his rage, he knocked down a brass stand with red votive candles. They fell, little circles of light, bouncing on the stone floor. Father Unnikrishnan fell to his knees, swatting out the little flames, somebody's prayers flickering out. He looked up but the church door stood empty, the troubled man gone.

He drove through the night, a bat out of hell. He had gone rushing to Netaji, hoping for, he knew not what, desperate for some salve, some comfort to soothe the unbearable pain, to still the burning pyre of his heart. He had never in his young life felt so disintegrated, had no idea what to do with himself. But Netaji had left for his tour, the Meyer Road residence empty, shuttered. On a blind curve, a buffalo standing stock still in the middle of the road sent the jeep skidding, an unbearable desire to let go, to crash into the rushing wall of trees. But the jeep skidded to a stop, raising dust silver in the moonlight. He sat clutching the wheel with bone white knuckles, a vast empty uncaring sky above his bare, unprotected head, the difficult tears squeezing out of his dark, dark eyes.

'Did Nishonko get in touch with you?' Chhoto mashi asked Aditi on one of the rare mornings when she bumped into her, already rushing out.

'No, is he here? Is he back?' Aditi skidded to a stop, her voice guarded.

'He came to see you. Just before Christmas. Didn't you meet him?'

'Oh, I'm sorry to have missed him.' Relief, mixed with guilt, made her voice a little high, a bit sharp.

'He seems to have...some deep feelings for you.'

Aditi gave an impatient shake of her head, the stubborn pout whenever she was thwarted, appearing unconsciously. 'Why doesn't he grow up?'

Chhoto mashi thought of the little eternity ring in the small unassuming box, wrapped up inexpertly in some cheap wrapping paper, holding in its tiny circle the fragile hopes and dreams of a very young man. She didn't know Nishonko too well but had sensed depths and complex currents underneath the surface calm. Would he, with his inexperience and rigidity and yet his unquestionable loyalty and honesty be a better man for Aditi than the vastly more seductive, yet unstable Debraj? Did she have the right to judge? It would have to be Aditi's choice. She thought of the disappointment that would sear Nishonko's heart when Aditi turned him down but with the practicality of someone who had lived two score and some years, she hoped he would get over it and move on. He was young, there would be others. So she did not tell Aditi about the ring and changed the subject to more mundane matters.

And the note left on the doorstep of Debraj's house? Gone, taken by Kabootar, crumpled and thrown away so Debraj knew nothing of Nishonko's visit. Nishonko had sent orders to have Kabootar arrested for desertion. But Kabootar had long anticipated this and had got himself officially appointed as Debraj's aide de camp. But the last thing he wanted was trouble. So, finding the small, easy-to-miss scrap of paper on the doorstep, he had thought it wise to destroy the evidence.

Finding himself thwarted here too, Nishonko's rage spilled over onto the unit. Any transgression was met with severe penalties far outstripping the original sin. The news of his behaviour filtered down to Singapur. Colonel Matthews, one of the senior officers close to him, bumped into Debraj one day as the year was drawing to a close.

'By the way, have you been in touch with Major Mitro?'

'Unfortunately, I have been rather amiss. Got taken up with all this recruiting and fundraising stuff. Where on earth is he? Haven't seen him or heard from him in months.'

'He was here, a week or so ago. Didn't he get in touch with you?'

'No. Strange. Must have been busy.' Debraj felt absurdly hurt. Nishonko had made no effort to find out where he was after he was wounded, or whether he was even alive. And now he had come to Singapur after such a long time and yet not even tried to call him. Nishonko was his *mitro*, his friend. What the hell was wrong with him?

'And then he just left, in the middle of the night. Have been getting some disquieting reports. He's pushing the men hard. Beat up one of the subedars for wearing the wrong socks. Something's wrong ...'

'I'll give him a call.'

Debraj slammed down the phone. Kabootar looked up in surprise. 'Damn Mitro, he's just not taking my calls.'

'Maybe, Sir, he doesn't wish to speak with you?'

'Why? What did I do to him?'

'Maybe he thinks you have taken something from him?'

'You mean my promotion? But he has his own command. No, he's not such a small man. Maybe he's just pissed off that I've got a cushy job here while he's slogging it out.'

'Maybe he is angry with you…for some reason?'

'No, he's behaving weirdly with everybody. He's hell bent on getting into fights, apparently. It's like he has some crazy death wish.'

'That day, at Missy baba's house…' Kabootar began in a low voice but stopped as Aditi entered, holding a bunch of flowers she had gathered from the run down little garden at the back.

'Who's got a death wish?'

'I'm really worried about him.'

'Who's this mystery person?'

'A friend. My best friend. The friend who got me to Singapore, who is probably responsible for bringing us together.'

'Really? Why haven't we met?'

'His name is Mitro…Major Nishonko Mitro. And you haven't met because…what's the matter? You look like you've seen a ghost.'

Aditi was looking at him, a deer caught in the headlights. The flowers fell from her nerveless fingers. Her hand flew to her throat, as if to still the flutter of fear there. Then she recovered, shaking her head.

'Nishonko? The…the man they call Nishachar?'

'Good lord, are you scared of him, you silly girl? He's a great guy.'

She shook her head, sat down abruptly.

'I've…he's legend.'

'Oh, I must tell him that. If he takes my call, of course?'

He turned to try the phone again. Aditi opened her mouth to say something but Kabootar stepped into her line of vision, shook his head. So she remained silent. But her heart quaked.

Chhoto mashi was in her small prayer room. She loved this time of the day, this hour of devotion. The smell of the incense, the ringing of the bell, the childish pleasure of dressing up the idols, giving them a bath, as if they were favourite dolls — it was soothing, giving her a sense of sanctuary in the midst of the turmoil of the times. Ever since she had lost her husband, a gentle, slow-moving man who believed implicitly in the existence and glory of the Almighty, she had found herself pulled more and more into these moments of private devotion. Brought up in the Brahmo tradition, which eschewed ritual and rites, celebrating instead the divine in all men, she had felt guilty at first. But, there was comfort to be had in these repeated actions, small, personal, and not worry about abstract ideas about who created what or the grand plans of the divine. Her thoughts were rudely interrupted by the door flying open. Aditi stood there, pale and panting. Alarm flared through Chhoto mashi's heart, making it shrink. She scrambled to her feet.

'What is it, child?'

Aditi did a quick pranam, her fingers flying to her forehead and breast, a brief gesture of prayer, then hugged her aunt fiercely.

'You're trembling. What has happened?'

'Debraj...'

'Oh dear, has something happened to him?'

'He...he will find out everything.'

'About what? Stop speaking in riddles, child.'

'They are friends...Debraj and Nishonko.'

Chhoto mashi sighed in relief. 'Is that all? Why are you so upset?'

Aditi started to cry, keening in despair. 'I'm so scared, Chhoto mashi. He'll do something terrible.'

'Who, Jhilik? Get a hold of yourself.'

'I can't tell Deb about Nishonko da. He will think I have been lying to him.'

'But there has been nothing between you and Nishonko, has there? Anything that you think you should have confessed?'

'No, nothing at all. He...he's...he's never even held my hand. He's so stiff, shy.'

'And Debraj? You care about him?'

'More...more than my life.'

'Then tell him the truth.'

'No! You don't understand Deb. He has such strong feelings about being betrayed. He will never understand.'

'Frankly, I think you should be more concerned what will happen when Nishonko finds out.'

Aditi shivered, her head hurting.

'When does Netaji return?' Chhoto mashi took a sip of tea as she sat back. The Club was crowded. The new year was approaching and there was a festive spirit in the air. Geeta too was in a relaxed mood, enjoying the slanting afternoon sun.

'Soon. He's landed in Port Blair. Remember, he had told Japan to hand over the Andaman Nicobar Islands before the year's end as the first piece of free India. It's happening. Why? Is there something you need from him?'

'And when do they march?'

'Come on, Suchandra, you know I can't tell you that. What is the problem?'

'Jhilik. Aditi. Her future. I know you will find this strange but I really want her to get engaged before she goes off.'

'Really? Is there someone who…'

Chhoto mashi looked at her, her expression enigmatic. Then she sighed. 'Debraj. Your Major Mookerji. I know, I know, I thought I would not approve of him. But he has Aditi's heart. And he's not so bad once you get to know him.'

'Ah, he's got you in his thrall.'

'Oh, don't be ridiculous, Geeta. I have a rhinoceros' hide when it comes to the blandishments of young men. But Aditi, she is vulnerable. If she's engaged, she will feel more stable. She will have something to keep her rooted. And he, he too will have something to come home to.'

'And what does the young man think of all this? Has he spoken?'

'No. But he will.' Chhoto mashi's face was grim. 'Maybe Netaji can speak to him?'

'What a little schemer you are, my dear. Why on earth should Netaji intervene in the private affairs of one of his men? And how would he know what this young man really wants? Is Debraj ready to propose? Is Aditi sure?'

'You just have to look at them. See them when they are together. They just light up in each other's presence. You know, I thought we had lost the old Jhilik, the imp with her curiosity and her peals of laughter and her appetitite for life. She had put up so many barricades, battened herself down. But he… he has set her free.'

'How poetic.'

'I'm sorry if all this sounds maudlin. I'm not sentimental, as you know well. But I see her…them…and I want to somehow protect that fragile bond they have created in the midst of all this violence and destruction.'

'I can't promise you anything but I will try and broach the subject.'

'At ease Major. Take a seat.'

Nishonko sat down in the hard wooden chair in front of Colonel Matthews' cluttered desk. He stared straight at the large map behind the Colonel's head, with its tiny coloured flags marking troop concentrations and thick lines in red ink. It all seemed remote, these preparations for an imagined war, some esoteric game. That blue flag, it stood for a unit, a cluster of real men, waiting to die, real men with real families back in India, homes with champa trees blooming in the courtyard, coal fires being fanned into life at dawn, the hot, dusty smell of chapatis being roasted, the tolling of temple bells at dusk…

'…heard a word I've said?' the Colonel's voice echoed, breaking his reverie. Nishonko looked up, his gaze calm. The Colonel was staring at him, his brows beetling, smoke curling up from a cigarette clamped in his lips.

'Sorry, Sir, you were saying?'

'I called you back to Singapur, Major because — some strange stuff we are hearing about you. Your behaviour at camp is drawing a lot of comment.'

'Really, Sir? And what might they be saying?'

'That you've been trying to get into fights, that you are behaving like a maniac, trying to get yourself killed.'

'Oh, I thought that was the general idea…to kill or be killed.'

'Nishonko, has something happened…personal stuff I should know?'

'Oh, we brave men of the INA never let anything personal stop us from carrying on the good fight, do we, Sir? Hearts of steel, Sir. Can't let anything damp those spirits, Sir.'

'I can smell it when a man goes AWOL. I want you to stick around at HQ for a while.'

'I don't much fancy Singapur, Sir. Rather be with the boys than traipse around looking pretty and meeting rich, fat men and sipping fancy drinks.'

'That's an order, soldier.'

Nishonko strode down the riverside path, cold rage like a steel bayonet inside him. He lived with this pain, this icy spike in his heart all the time. At times, he felt like cutting himself open to get the cold sliver out, to thaw out his insides, to feel some warmth. But it was out of his reach. The thought of being in the same city, on the same streets as her, was claustrophobic. He couldn't bear it, literally. He could bump into her, any time. What would he do if he did? Slap. Pummel. Crush. Slash. The flicker of images, the violent, clear rush of thoughts, the lucidity of his hatred shocked him, brought him to a stumbling halt. He leaned on a lamp post, taking deep breaths. The cold of the iron against his forehead steadied him. Should he just go, confront her? What would he say? That he had seen her in her moment of shame? That he wished he could undo the seeing, just wanted it all to have never happened, to rewind and take things back to the way they had been before? Tears threatened, gulped back fiercely. He slammed his head on the lamp post, hard, trying to clear the numbness.

They had finished dinner, fish and rice done in the Straits way, and now they were sprawled around the verandah of the Meyer Road bungalow, sipping home-made wine, obtained by Gaffar by some nefarious means. It was New Year's eve, and they waited for the hour, the coming of the new, the ship horns to herald in the most important year of their lives. It had been a quiet evening, muted conversation, a time for reflection. All of them had much on their minds. When the doorbell chimed, mere minutes before the midnight hour, echoing around the darkened house lit by candles, they looked up surprised. It was Debraj and Aditi. She was resplendent in a white and gold sari that set off her honey brown skin, red hibiscus flowers in her hair, her dark, kohl-lined eyes a little heavy-lidded with the afterglow of their lovemaking earlier that evening. They had come here, to this place of joined dreams, to wish their leader. There was a flurry of greetings, a passing around of wine, toasts. They all stood, as the sound of drums and a few church bells echoed up the hill from the streets below. Aditi, in her slightly broken voice, that little catch in her throat, began to sing softly. It was the Bengali version of the song 'Auld Lang Syne'. 'Purano shei deener katha…lest old acquaintance be forgotten…' Netaji joined in, his voice low but powerful.

When the fireworks exploded across the velvet canopy of the sky, they all stood, transfixed, war forgotten for a while. Debraj's arm stole around Aditi's waist. She lifted her head, fearless in that moment, kissed him.

'Such an attractive couple. And so obviously in love. You should advice them to get engaged, Sir.' Geeta chose her moment in a quiet voice.

'Really?' Netaji smiled. 'And why would I interfere in any of my men's personal lives?'

'I thought you were already playing Cupid?'

'Oh, I think the arrow had struck long before. And anyway, with the big offensive coming up, isn't it better not to let emotional entanglements distract them?'

Saito, who had been quietly smoking in the dark, spoke up. 'On the contrary, it might turn out to be a morale booster, Sir. Debraj is very popular. They have become the darlings of the force — symbols of hope. Getting engaged right before we launch into battle — ah, that would say much about our chances of success.'

Geeta smiled. 'I agree with the Brigadier. It would be so good to have something to celebrate, something life-affirming. Who knows when we will find occasion again.'

Netaji smiled, clapped Saito on the shoulder.

'Okay, Brigadier, let's have a grand celebration then at a regimental scale. Though what we can celebrate with at these times of war and rationing, I have no idea.'

'Ah, leave that to me. Being part of Japanese command in Singapore does have its advantages.'

'That's settled then. And let's do it on the eve of the troops' departure. Give them all a send-off they will remember.'

The jeep drove up to the old bungalow. Debraj and Aditi spilled out, laughing, tipsy, oops, careful, holding on to each other. Debraj fumbled for the key but it was nowhere to be found. He swore under his breath, pushed at the door. It opened under his hand, making him stagger over the threshold.

Across the road, in the shadows of a grove of cotton trees, a tiny red light winked. Camouflaged by the moving tracery of leaf shadows, stood a dark figure, watching them. Motionless, the only movement his hand cupping a burning cigarette to his lips, taking a small drag now and then, the smoke curling. The ground was littered with stubs. He had been waiting long. And now, the jeep had brought them. She was drunk. His lip curled in distaste. The desire to confront them, to rub their betrayal in their faces, receded. He felt very tired suddenly, his legs almost buckling. He dropped the cigarette butt, ground it out with his heel.

Inside the house, Kabootar stood looking intently out of the window. He waited to see if the wink of red light would come back.

'Kabootar ji, guess what? We are going to get engaged! Netaji himself suggested it.' Aditi came up to him, her face alight.

Debraj threw his shoes off, smiled. 'Suggested?! He practically held us at gunpoint and ordered us!'

Aditi turned to him, suddenly uncertain. 'Would you…would you have done it… if he hadn't?'

'Not a chance!'

Aditi's face fell. She took a step back. 'I'm…I'm sorry, I thought we both…'

He walked up to her, caught her hands, which had begun to twist the tassels on the end of her sari pallu in soft agitation and held them still. He looked at her, at the wide mouth with the merest hint of a tremble, the nervous swallow. He knew that he could never go back from this moment, that the die would have to be cast, the blind hand exposed. He took a deep breath.

'Aditi, my love, I'm not the marrying kind. I might as well tell you that right now. I had no plans to get engaged to you and I don't even have a ring to declare my troth. If Netaji had not asked me tonight, would I have proposed to you?' A smile of great tenderness softened the lines of his face. 'No. Instead, I would have run away, eloped and got married to you, you dope.'

Her face cracked into a huge smile, delight and relief making her jump. She punched him, making him wince. Now his face turned grave. 'No, seriously, I want to just take you away from all this. I don't want this stupid war. I can happily desert the INA this moment and spend the rest of my...'

He saw the look of shame in her downcast eyes and stumbled to a stop.

'Okay, okay, you want to see this through. I'll see it through. We will get engaged. We will march into India. And then we'll run away and get married. How does that sound, my love?'

Out in the grove, Nishonko pulled up the collar of his jacket, rubbed his face. The faint happy sounds of a Dixie band striking up came pouring out from the open windows of the lit house. The pale light of the dawn of 1944 appeared, a faint blush on the horizon.

It was still early when Gaffar slipped out of the house on Meyer Road. The city was very quiet, the streets empty in the aftermath of the previous night's celebrations. He was made to cool his heels for over an hour and was then summoned to the dining room where Goopta, pink and bathed, sat at the head of a long table with pristine white damask covers and expensive crockery, licking honey from a spoon, his hands sticky.

'Gaffar bhai! Any news, my good fellow?'

'Happy New Year, Sir.'

'Yes, yes.'

'They'll go as soon as they have Tojo's final go-ahead.'

'Are you sure? I was told they will wait till just before the monsoons.'

'No, it will be sooner. They will have a big party to celebrate Major Debraj's engagement to Sister Sen just before the troops' departure.'

Goopta frowned. 'How romantic. So we will know to the day when the movement will start?'

'Yes, Sir.'

'Excellent. And what will the staging point be?'

'KL or Rangoon.'

'Oh, can you not be more specific, Gaffar? We will be running all over South East Asia, chasing them.'

'I can't help it, Sir, they are dividing up the forces. I have no idea which is the diversion, which the actual thrust. Netaji is being very tight-lipped.'

Goopta sighed deeply. He had grand designs but, alas, small men to do his bidding. 'It's alright, Gaffar. We just have to prepare for all eventualities. I will supply you with codes. You will relay everything to me on a daily basis. Troop positions, artillery placements, your leader's movements — nothing is too trivial. I will remove myself to the other side of the border. I will be in touch.'

Gaffar stood, looking irresolute, his face heavy. 'Is there no way that Netaji could be spared? I owe him much.'

'Alas, Gaffar bhai, the exigencies of war. You are beside him 24 hours, you make sure he makes it through in one piece, what do you say, eh? None of us want him harmed. We just want the British to win, right?'

Gaffar nodded. 'Yes, Sir. That makes sense.'

Goopta sat brooding after Gaffar left, cracking walnuts. Noshir bhai poured him another cup of tea.

'G..g..gaf..far.'

'Yes, Noshir bhai, I know. A man of divided loyalties. Can't trust them, can you?'

'N..no, Sir.'

'But we must use the clay we have, yes? He will be useful, one way or another. And if he proves to be too much of a weak link, we will just…' He split open a particularly tough walnut shell with a loud crack and looked with satisfaction at the two perfect hemispheres nestling inside. He blew on it and popped them into his mouth.

'Let us prepare once more for our travels, Noshir bhai. Rangoon, first and then across the border.'

The next few days passed in a whirl for Aditi. When she broke the news to Chhoto mashi, her normally unflappable aunt went into a tizzy. In spite of repeated assurances from Geeta that all the arrangements would be taken care of by the INA, Chhoto mashi worried about everything — the venue, the guest list, Jhilik's trousseau, the food, the ring, oh my god the ring, did they need flowers, a band — it drove Aditi wild. Debraj had been ordered to get back into fighting shape and sent back to the tender mercies of Pandey ji for the next couple of weeks. Aditi felt suddenly at a loose end, marooned. She went for long walks, alone but felt very restless. She had a disquieting feeling that someone was watching her, following her. She would scan the crowds on the streets, turn suddenly on the riverside path at the sound of distant footsteps. But there was no one. She put it down to pre-engagement nerves and went back to work. When she shared her news with Meenakshi, 'Don't tell anyone, it's still unofficial,' Meenakshi screamed with delight and promptly told everyone the good news. People needed to hear something that would bring them joy, help them to hang on to the dream. The news spread like wildfire.

And then, one windy night, the big dried rubber tree leaves skittering across the pavement, Meenakshi, walking home past the small smoky bar near the hospital, saw something through the grimy window. A moment of hesitation, then she slipped in. The place was almost empty. At the far end, a shape sat, hunched over a drink.

'Hello. Nishonko?'

Nishonko looked over his shoulder. His eyes were bleary, his face heavy. He had an almost empty glass in front of him and looked as if he had not slept. He frowned at the dark, pretty girl in the nurse's uniform, trying to place her.

'Sister Meenakshi. From the hospital. Aditi's friend, remember?'

He grunted, turned away. He rapped the bar twice. The bartender poured out another shot. She hesitated a fraction of a moment, then settled herself on the next bar stool. She also rapped the bar twice and smiled at the bar tender.

'Please, one more of the same?'

Nishonko glowered at her. Unperturbed, she looked around at the seedy walls, the peanut shell debris on the floor, took off her nurse's cap and shook out her hair.

'How have you been? Did you meet Aditi finally?'

He growled something under his breath.

'Have you heard the good news?'

He knocked back the dregs of his drink and stood up, counting out some change on the top of the bar.

'She's getting engaged.'

He froze, the coins falling out of his fingers. One went rolling down the bar and came to a stop, spinning, spinning, till it fell on the counter.

'Who?' The single syllable came out, dry, hardly heard, as if he had not spoken in a long time.

'Your friend, Debraj.'

A hoarse, tortured whisper broke out of him, full of entreaty. 'No!'

She was startled. The desolation in that sound made her choke. Suddenly, her little flirtatious expedition seemed very trivial. He was a wounded animal, softly whimpering, bent over the bar.

'I'm so sorry, I didn't realise it meant so much to you.'

'She's mine, she's mine, she's mine.' A litany, a prayer, as if the repetition itself would make it real. Now she felt a little flare of anger, at him, at Aditi.

'No, I don't think she felt that way. She was quite scared of you.'

He looked at her, bemused. He couldn't understand what she was saying. His eyes were so dark, like pools of soot. And his mouth, underneath the masculine handlebar moustache, so vulnerable, so tender. She leaned forward and gently moved a lock of hair from his forehead, barely touching his skin, feeling the heat of his fevered thoughts burning her fingertips.

'Would you like to come with me…home? Just rest a bit?'

Suddenly, as if exhausted, he slumped. He accepted her caress like a dog, beaten, submissive.

Her bedsit was tiny, barely a bed, a sofa, an old chevalier mirror in the corner, a counter with a hot top and a kettle. An ancient fridge gurgled and rumbled in the corner. A groaning wooden fan and a shaded lamp came on at the touch of the switches. As she stepped in, wary of the formidable battleaxe who was her landlady, he stumbled, cursed. She shushed him, hurriedly battening the door. She led him to the single lumpy sofa, and he collapsed into it, muttering under his breath. She stood over him, looking at him, the coiled power in his shoulders, the black crop of his hair, springy, like fresh grass to her touch, as she gently stroked his bent head. He became still, trying to make sense of the gesture, the stranger's hand on his unprotected neck, the slither of the fingers down his back. He leaned forward, like a supplicant, and buried his head in her, into the musty shadowed triangle under her crumpled nurse's dress. She closed her eyes, her hips tilting forward, her hands pressing his cupped head deep into her belly. He reached for her blindly, as if he was drowning. The force of it brought her to her knees, their heads now level. They stared at each other across vast, immeasurable distances. What did he see? Not her, not her. With a sharp jerk, he pushed her back on the threadbare carpet, rolled over on top of her. She raised her head to be kissed but he flinched from the intimacy. He pulled down her underclothes roughly, awkwardly, fumbling, his inexperience and ignorance evident. She tried to slow him down, guide him but he was in a frenzy of impatience. He ground against her, flailed against her, all the anger and humiliation of the last few weeks pouring out in the violence with which he laid siege to her body. She winced but stifled the protest. He entered her finally, somehow, blind but her unexpected wetness, the hot cauldron inside her shocked him. He stopped, frightened. She reached for him but he batted her hand away. He moved again but when she moved with him, he stopped, unmade, unmanned. He withdrew from her, rolled over, curling up, his face turned away.

'It's okay, Nishonko.'

'I'm sorry, I can't betray her, she's the only one I can love.'

She was hopping mad, humiliated. Spite made her voice sharp. 'Well, you can't have her. She's going to marry Deb.'

He sat up. 'She can't. I won't let her.'

'Well, you better hurry. The party is ten days away.'

'What party?'

'She hasn't told you? It's going to be the social event of the year. Seems like everyone in Singapur is talking about it — you know, the love story between the "prince and princess of the INA." I'm sure you will be invited.'

His face crumpled, like someone had sucked the air out of him. He squinched his eyes shut, put his fingers to his ears. Slowly, like that, he stood up, then like a blind man, reached his hand out and walked towards the door. She went to call out to him, contrite but he was gone.

Aditi walked into the house, arms laden with groceries. She backed in through the main door, again open — when would Chhoto mashi learn — and as she turned, she bumped into someone. She turned to look and let out a scream. The bags dropped from her arms. It was Nishonko. His face was haggard, pasty, unhealthy in its pallor. His clothes looked like he had slept in them. She backed away.

'Don't…you don't have to be afraid of me.'

'What are you doing here?'

'Please Jhilik, you can't marry Debraj. Remember, that day in Bolpur, the day you were leaving?' He reached into his pocket and pulled out a small bracelet, cheap red beads, frayed at the edges. He had saved it, this little relic from the past.

'We promised each other? I kept it. It was the one thing that got me through all the bad things that won't stop happening.'

Aditi had recovered from her fright. She started collecting the fallen groceries, refusing to look at him.

'We were just kids.'

'You're all I have.'

'And you are my oldest friend. I thought you would be happy for me.'

'Happy! He'll never love you the way I…he's just a playboy, a womanising good-for-nothing.'

'He's your friend'.

'And he's betrayed me.'

'He knows nothing about you.'

'Oh, I'll teach him a few things about me.' Nishonko slammed his fist into the wall. Aditi flinched.

'Teach who?' Chhoto mashi entered from behind them, through the open door.

Nishonko stared at her. It took a few moments for the red haze to pass, for him to recognise her. He took a shuddering breath. 'Good evening, Ma'am.'

'Jhilik, go to your room.'

Aditi backed away, her face strained, her eyes pleading.

Chhoto mashi waited for her to leave, then turned to Nishonko. 'It's too late.'

'I'm sorry, I didn't realise the time.'

'It's too late. Let it go, Nishonko.'

He realised what she was saying, left without a word.

Chhoto mashi breathed out slowly.

Netaji sipped on his coffee. He needed it badly. He had not slept well the previous night. Tojo had not yet called. The days were just running out, sand trickling down in an hourglass. There was a small window of time in which the campaign could happen and Tokyo was dragging its feet. Saito had been constantly following up but Netaji was afraid the High Command was developing cold feet. His dark thoughts were interrupted by the sound of raised voices.

'Sorry, Sir, you can't go in there now. Let me...'

Nishonko barged in. He looked disordered, somehow, on the edge of coming apart, as if he had walked through a high wind. He came to attention and saluted untidily, his movements jerky, awkward. His words tumbled out in a rush, bumping into each other.

'Sorry. Disturbing, very...disturbing you, Sir Something important...can I speak?'

'Nishonko, my boy, you just disappeared without a word.'

'It's about Major Debraj Mookerji.'

'Oh. What's it now? All the arrangements for the party going well? Sit down, Nishonko, you're making me dizzy with all your striding around.'

'Yes, Sir. I had to come to you because there's no one else I can go to... for justice. It's about the rule. In every army rule book across the world. The INA must have it too. It's called "stealing the affections of a brother officer's wife or fiancé". It's a major crime, Sir. The offender must face court martial.'

'What on earth are you talking about?'

'Debraj has seduced my fiancé.'

'What!! Who is she?'

'Aditi Sen, Sir.'

Netaji stared at him, flabbergasted. He saw the feverish look in Nishonko's eyes, the glitter in those dark holes, the slick wet of sweat on his forehead.

'But he's getting engaged to her.'

'Precisely, Sir. She's already engaged to me.' Nishonko sat down, glad to have got it across to Netaji. Now, Netaji would put things right. He drew in a shuddering breath.

'Gaffar, could you please get Geeta Madam?'

Gaffar nodded grimly, stepped out. Netaji paced up and down, lighting up another cigarette. Nishonko suddenly looked lost, forlorn. He went to say something but Netaji silenced him with one look. The grandfather clock on the wall ticked away. Far away, some car backfired, like a distant gun shot. The wooden beams of the house creaked, settling in for the night. After an interminable wait, Geeta walked in, followed by Gaffar.

'What is it? I was just about to leave.'

'Geeta, I'm sorry to hold you up but we seem to have a situation here.'

'Oh hello, Nishonko, we've been worried about you. Where were you?'

'Geeta, a strange dilemma is upon us. Nishonko here is telling us that Debraj…how do I put it? That Debraj can't get engaged to Aditi because Nishonko here in fact is already engaged to Aditi.'

'Nonsense!' Geeta's tone was impatient, sharp. It had been a long day.

'We are.' The words came out strangled. Geeta heard the thin sound of exhaustion in his voice.

'I'm sorry, that was rude of me. But surely there's some misunderstanding?'

Nishonko opened his fist, which had been clenched all this time. The small ball of red beads sat crumpled in his palm, offered as evidence, as witness.

'We exchanged…vows…as children.'

'And now that you're both grown up, is it still valid?'

'They were sacred vows. She promised.' His mouth set in a hard line, his jaw working.

'Well, let's ask her ourselves, shall we?'

He was alarmed. Up on his feet, shaking his head. 'No no no… she will…'

'Deny it? You're not just making this up, are you, Nishonko?' Netaji decided this had gone on long enough.

'It's real…' Nishonko's voice was almost a whisper.

Netaji came to him, put his arm round his shoulder. 'What's also real is that we have the biggest moment in history about to unfold — and we can't have division in the ranks, Nishonko. You of all people…'

Nishonko flinched, moved away from the comfort of the arm. 'Yes, me of all people. I have never questioned you… I have sacrificed…'

Netaji threw up his hands. 'Then don't start now. I'm exhausted. What with planning the campaign, negotiating with the Japanese, constantly soothing frayed tempers and working so hard to smooth all our little communal differences!'

He flopped down at the table, knuckled his face. 'The INA has to be a true band of brothers. How can you let something so…so insignificant push the two of you apart? You're commanding officers.'

Nishonko looked at him, bereft, his arms hanging uselessly, helpless.

'I love her.' His voice was a mere whisper.

'More than you love India? More than you love our cause? Our freedom?'

'She's the only thing in my life that has mattered to me, the only person who can make me happy. Please don't ask me to give her up.'

Netaji saw the naked pain in the young man's face and his heart trembled. He too had stood at such a crossroad and had made his choices. Caged in the cramped confines of the U boat as it moved through the dark oily waters of the Indian Ocean taking him towards Japan, he had again and again gone over the moment of parting from the one he loved so dearly, the knowledge that he might never see her again, the loneliness like a cold desert wind howling wordlessly inside. He knew the anger that could ravage a man's brain, wondering why me, why me. He knew. Yet, he knew he must ask this of this young man.

'Yes, Nishonko. I must ask that of you. She has chosen. She has said so to me. She must have the freedom to choose. So, yes I ask you to carry out this sacrifice. I need you to back down. Do it. For me.'

Nishonko stumbled to the door, the wound mortal.

'Strong, Nishonko, strong. This is not the time for weakness. There will be other women, other loves. Now you have work to do.

Go to the engagement party. Show your support. That's an order. Not a word of this to anyone.'

Nishonko shook his head, wiping his cheeks with the back of his hand, a futile little childhood gesture. Gaffar opened the door silently, his head lowered. Geeta too stood, looking away, as if sparing him the indignity of being a witness to his loss. Nishonko paused at the door, caught in the shadow of the no man's land of the threshold. Then he was gone, the doorway yawned, empty. Gaffar closed it behind him without a sound as he too stepped outside tactfully. There was silence in the room, the ticking of the clock unnaturally loud. Then it rang the half hour, a lonely, plaintive reminder of time slipping by. Netaji stirred, coming slowly back from the reverie he had been in. He cleared his throat. Geeta looked up.

'Are you sure you aren't overestimating his loyalty, his devotion?'

Netaji yawned. It had been a long day.

'Nishonko? He's a good man. And he's still young. A little heartbreak at this age is very salutary for one's character.' His voice had a tinge of bitterness. He was very tired.

'Good night, Geeta.'

The sharp peremptory knocking on her door made Meenakshi poke her wet head out of the bathroom door.

'Who's it?'

The knocking came again, more insistent. Muttering unladylike words under her breath, she came out, wrapping a robe around her wet body. It must be that old battleaxe, the landlady come to complain about the water running. She opened the door a crack, then hastily closed it. It was Nishonko outside. He had come, why had he come. She stood with her back against the door, shaking. Not out of fear. Excitement coursed through her veins. She suddenly realised how much she was attracted to him, how she had thought of him ceaselessly ever since she had seen him first, thinking of his hands, his long bony fingers. There was another sharp ratatat. She whirled, quickly opened the door. The robe had fallen apart, revealing the coffee brown slope of her breasts, the tiny rivulets of water slithering down from the long wet column of her throat. Silently, they stared at each other, like two hunting cats sizing each other up, pupils distended. Then he stepped in wordlessly. He was carrying a brown paper wrapped bottle. He grabbed a glass off the counter, sloshed the contents of the bottle into the glass, something dark, pungent. He stared at her, at the bare legs, the long wet rope of hair, the parted lips. He began to circle around her, keeping his distance, deliberation in the slow pacing steps. She stood there, now defenceless, fear and heat making her heart hammer. He took a long sip, licking his lips. He came up behind her, on her blind side, traced the line of her bare shoulder, the swoop of it, with a forefinger, travelled down the cobbled street of her spine. She trembled, closed her eyes, scared to move, lest she spook him. He murmured, 'They're both from Cambridge, part of an old boys' network.'

Her eyes flew open. She was bewildered, not knowing what he was saying. She started to turn to him but he roughly, almost violently, spun her away. 'Natural that they stick together, isn't it, Sister Meena Meenakshi? And so the betrayal goes on...'

He held the nape of her neck and slowly forced her down, till she was bent over awkwardly. 'I loved him, you know. I loved...Deb. Like a brother.' It was a guttural whisper.

Meenakshi whimpered softly. 'Please. Let me go. You're hurting me.'

He let her go, his face close to hers, suffused with a rage that was the more frightening in its quietness, its iron control.

'Isn't this what you were asking for, Sister? Following me around, throwing yourself at me? Isn't this what you wanted? All of you, flaunting your...'

Meenakshi's eyes flashed. She grabbed his hand and peeling off her robe, placed it on her bare breast. 'Yes, Major, this is what I want. What are you going to do about it?'

He stared at her, his face clenched, his hand motionless, spread-eagled across the cool, ebony, perfect sphere of flesh, unable to embrace it, to own it, yet reluctant to let go, ashamed yet aroused. She reached for him. He was ready. Both drew a ragged breath. Then, he scooped her up in his arms and threw her on the bed and without removing his clothes or the robe snarled up underneath her, he mounted her from behind, his face impassive. The intimacy of bare skin, shared warmth, the tenderness of a kiss was all denied. He used his hands only to hold her steady, clasping the swell of her hips from behind, like controlling a horse. She cried out. It goaded him on. He rode her, roughly, long cruel plunges that knocked the breath out of her, punishing her, punishing himself. She tried to turn to face him but he didn't want to see her, see the face that didn't belong to another. He kept her face pinned to the bed, his hand hard on her neck, her long matted hair obliterating her mouth and eyes, the dark skeins like seaweed across the face of some drowned underwater creature. In mere moments, he came, joylessly, collapsing on her, his face contorted with pain. She lay, abandoned, a rag doll, on the rumpled bed, slow tears trickling down her neck. He got up finally buttoned himself up and flopping down on the broken springed sofa, drank from the open bottle.

The old man pauses, shakes his head in bewilderment, looks down. There is a long silence in Dulal da's tea shop.

'And then Tojo gave his approval, right?' Sudipto prompts. The old man starts, looks up.

'She was very beautiful, in her own way,' he says. 'He could have found happiness, a kind of negotiated peace, with her. She loved him, unconditionally, I think, the only one who did not betray him. Pity.' He turns to Sudipto.

'Yes, Tojo did it. Finally, word had come from the Diet, the Japanese Parliament, giving the go-ahead for the Burma campaign. There was great jubilation. Everybody was in a celebratory mood.' The old man's smile is bitter.

'Why did they drag their feet so long?'

'Well, their strategic aims were quite different from ours. They just wanted to stop the British from reconquering Burma. So, they didn't think the campaign was time sensitive. We...we knew we had to get into India before the monsoon broke. And everything had built up to such a fever pitch, we couldn't afford to let the momentum go. It was now or never.'

Things started moving fast from the day the official go-ahead came. The campaign, code named U Go, was now a reality. No one seemed to know where they were headed, it was all hush

hush. Part of the force was being sent to Malay, a small part up towards Arakan, and part to Rangoon. Uncertainty, excitement, fear — their thoughts were in a whirl. The pace at the training camps intensified. Both the divisions of the Rani Jhansi went into overdrive. Field hospitals would need to be set up. Supply lines had to be built fast. There were setbacks also. Espionage networks, carefully planned months in advance, developed cracks. Ismail Channia, a Gujarati who knew the Kathiawar coast, gave himself up and their entire network was compromised. On the North West Frontier, Bharat Ram was passing on information received from Netaji to the Communist Party leadership for transmission to the British authorities. On the other hand, radio contact was successfully established with Bengal. One of the earliest messages did not contain any vital military intelligence. Debraj found Netaji sitting in the radio room, his head bowed. It was evening but he had not turned on the lights.

'You look tired, Sir. Can I get you something?'

Netaji shook his head. 'No, I'm not tired, Debraj. Just that I… How are the preparations coming along for the engagement?'

'Excellent, Sir.'

'No last minute jitters?'

'Well, I told Aditi she just has a week to change her mind. But she seems bent on making an honest man of me.'

'Take good care of her, Debraj. She has no parents to be with her at such a time.'

'Oh, I wish my mother was here. She was famed for her parties and…'

'I… I got news, over the radio today, that Prabhabati Bose has passed away.'

'Oh, I'm sorry, Sir. Related to you?'

'My mother.'

Debraj's face froze. He stared at Netaji, trying to make sense of those three syllables. 'I'm so, so sorry, Sir. Are you planning to… no, I suppose not.'

'No, I can't, can I, Debraj? We don't even have this basic right, to mourn for our dead. My brother, Sisir, he sits behind bars in a jail in Coonoor. The British have turned down his request to attend the funeral. I am denied the right every son has to honour the passing of the one who gave him life. If I go back, it will have to be like a thief, under cover of darkness. The police will be at the funeral. And if the British get wind of it, it's my funeral all of you will have to conduct.'

'Is all this, this campaign, this...is it worth such sacrifice?'

'We will have to make it worth it. We must win, we must achieve what we have set out to do.'

Debraj felt his eyes smart. Thoughts of his own mother, his impossible, wayward, eccentric mother, came crowding into his heart, filling him with deep regret. He had done so little for his mother, just taken her for granted, demanded her attention and condemned her for its lack. An image surfaced. His tenth or maybe eleventh birthday. It was the year he had had measles. He had been quarantined. He had woken up in that dark hour before dawn, thirsty, hot, claustrophobic. Throwing off his damp bedclothes, he had gone padding barefoot, down the corridor, rebellious. Passing his mother's bedroom, he had seen the door ajar, a thin sliver of light. He had peeped in. The room had looked empty, no one in the four-poster bed with its pink flounces and lace. He had pushed open the door, the well-oiled hinges silent. The bedside light had been on, a gleaming silk robe thrown carelessly on the rich pile carpet, the bathroom door ajar. When he had poked his head to look into the bathroom, smelling of lavender and soap and powder and something else, something heavy, cloying, that had made his head swim, he had found her sitting on the floor, her bare legs drawn up, white against the white marble tiles, her head thrown back, resting against the rim of the bathtub, the eyes closed. Alarm had flared in his mind and he had called out. She had opened her eyes, slowly, as if she had been dreaming. She had looked at him, through him, somewhere far away. Then, in that broken, raspy voice he loved so much, she had whispered, 'Happy birthday, my darling one, kiss kiss.' Tears, like little diamond drops, had rolled down her pale cheeks, making her eyes glitter with unearthly fire. With a pang, he realised how lost, abandoned she had been, how alone in her confusion and hungers. Standing there, thousands of miles away in a strange land, in front of this man bowed by grief, he felt tears welling up in his eyes. He realised why strangers cried at funerals. They were reminded of their own loss, their own regrets of unfinished business. He would have given anything that moment to go home and sit at the feet of his inattentive mother, her careless hand playing with the hair on the back of his neck. He looked at Netaji, wanting to put his arm around him, to give him the solace of some human contact. But he didn't have the nerve.

'Shall I get you a cup of tea, Sir?'

'Yes, my friend, that would be nice.'

And so the day arrived. It was calm with a little breeze, not still and humid like normal Singapur evenings, almost cool. The breeze came sweeping in from the sea, sending the white Japanese paper lanterns, which had been strung up across the palms and hydrangeas, dancing and bobbing. The dome of the old whitewashed Victorian mansion, with its faded grandeur, glowed mauve and blue in the twilight. Tall French windows led to an open terrace where the Palm Court Orchestra played popular hits on a small wooden stage, decorated with tropical flowers. Couples, the men in uniform mostly, the women dressed in all the variety that this melting pot of a city in the middle of a world war could offer, danced to the music. Chinese boys balancing trays with hard-to-get wines and beers, procured through the offices of Saito, were weaving through the crowds. There were bursts of laughter, flushed faces, the tinkling of glasses touched in a toast, the steady murmur of the surf crashing and ebbing in the sea nearby.

Debraj and Aditi were centre stage, dancing. He was an elegant dancer, assured, masterful, guiding her, his hand round her tiny waist, she as light as a will o' the wisp. She looked resplendent in an antique blood red sari, her hair like a soft cumulus cloud around her, tinged by the dying orange glow of the setting sun, her mouth, that wide mouth, laughing, delighted by this good fortune, this blessing of love in the time of war. Looking at her as she was whirled round and round, so achingly beautiful, Chhoto mashi whispered a silent prayer to her gods. Geeta, sitting across the table from her, smiled, gave her hand a quick squeeze.

A flurry near the entrance made them all turn to look. Netaji entered, followed by the usual entourage of photographers and Gaffar and bodyguards. The band played a fanfare. When the guests realised who it was, wild applause rang out, cheers and hurrahs. They came and surrounded their leader, encircling him like ripples. He looked at them, at face after eager face, shining, and his heart was full.

'My comrades,' his voice rang out, stilling the cheering, bringing the murmurs to a halt.

'My dear compatriots of the INA, our friends from Japan and all the people gathered here in support of our magnificent dream, today we have come together to celebrate the vows of constancy to be exchanged by two of your comrades, Major Debraj Mookerji and Sister Aditi Sen.'

Whoops and cheers rang out again, making Aditi smile. Debraj held out his hand. They stepped forward.

'My god, what is he doing here? Who asked him here?' Chhoto mashi's voice was an alarmed hiss. Geeta turned to see the cause of her unease. Through the sea of heads, she spotted Nishonko. He was moving along the sides of the terrace, keeping to the shadows, his face hard, impassive. Meenakshi trailed behind him.

'He was invited by Netaji,' Geeta whispered. 'Don't worry, Suchandra, he won't be any trouble. Now, hush.'

Chhoto mashi turned back to see Netaji take Debraj and Aditi's hands and join them together.

'Will you, Debraj and Aditi, pledge your troth to each other, to honour and respect each other as comrades, to cherish each other as man and woman, to fight side by side for the cause of India's independence and not rest till she is free?'

There was a moment of silence, broken only by the cries of seagulls returning home and the sound of church bells ringing out the vespers in the distant city. It was as if the city held its breath. Then, clear as a bell, she spoke. 'Yes!' Another tiny heartbeat. Chhoto mashi turned to look at Nishonko through the crowd. He was leaning against the balustrade, his head down, his arms crossed, looking at his feet. She looked back. Aditi, her face upturned, was looking at Debraj. Debraj opened his mouth, then gulped and merely nodded. A shout went up. 'Speak up! Speak up! Come on Major, let's hear it from you, man!' He looked around, smiling yet grave, then, in a quiet voice that carried to the edges of the garden, 'I will.' Then Debraj took out the ring, an antique emerald from Burma, and put it on Aditi's finger. Her mouth was an 'O' of delight. She jumped in excitement, the finger and hand outstretched for all the world to admire.

As cheering rang out again, Chhoto mashi turned back. Through the waving hands and smiling faces, she saw Nishonko once more. He stood, his face like stone, a wall, a cliff, completely still. For a second, Chhoto mashi felt the hahakar, the desolate cry of his soul. Then, he looked at her directly, and it was as if she had been stung, slapped, electrocuted, annihilated. She found herself shaking and had to sit down. Surrounded by a wall of people standing around her, she could no longer see Netaji but his voice boomed out.

'And there could have been no more perfect timing for this most auspicious event. For in the act of making this commitment, these two young people are declaring their belief in the future, and planting the seeds of hope in our hearts. This is what we all need right now — this beacon of hope. This celebration is not only for Aditi and Debraj — it is a send-off for all our brave men and women.'

A buzz, a murmur, like the sound of a hive. Speculation, questions, looking at each other. And then came the words they had all waited for.

'We march this Thursday!'

A gasp, a moment to let it sink in, then there was an explosion of cheering, a roar like cannon fire.

'Jai Hind!'

'Chalo Delhi!!'

A thousand throats joined in.

Chhoto mashi sat stunned. So soon, so soon. She had thought there would be a little more time. Near the bar, Gaffar nodded. He would tell them tonight.

Ahmed nodded at Saito.

'Thank god, that's final. All this waiting was getting on my nerves.'

'It's going to be a race against time.'

The band struck up. Debraj scooped Aditi into his arms, twirled her around. As he turned, the faces around him whirling, one face jumped out. He stopped abruptly, bumping into Aditi, who was giddy, laughing. He steadied her with one hand, then walked off the dance floor, leaving her there. He strode to the edge of the crowd, heading straight towards Nishonko, his face grim. Nishonko slowly straightened up, staring back at him, his face unreadable. Debraj walked right up to him.

'Bastard!'

Aditi had come to a stop, swaying. She looked for Debraj, saw him walking towards...her heart jumped, stopped, then hammered at her rib cage. She almost stopped breathing. Nishonko da stood there, a strange look on his face. She felt cold. She stumbled towards Chhoto mashi.

Nishonko and Debraj stared at each other. And then, Debraj broke into a huge guffaw, threw his arms out and pulled Nishonko into a bear hug.

'Look at your face! Priceless! God, am I glad to see you! I've missed you, you idiot.'

He pulled Nishonko to the bar, rapped the counter twice. 'Where the hell have you been? I've been hunting and hunting for you.'

Nishonko leaned away, a little stiff. 'Really? I didn't hear from you.'

'I called and called. Why didn't you take my calls?'

Nishonko shrugged. 'Been busy.'

'Me too.'

'Yes, you have been, haven't you?' Nishonko knocked back his drink, rapped twice for another.

'I wanted to share it all with you. How did you get to know about it?'

Nishonko looked at his hands, his face calm.

'Oh, the whole town is speaking about the prince and princess of INA.'

'Have you met her? Has anyone introduced you? You'll love her.' He looked around for Aditi, saw her standing beside Chhoto mashi.

'Remember what you said on the ship? That I would know the one, when I met her? You were right. Though how a reprobate like me had the incredible good fortune to have won her, I'll never know. Don't run away.'

He ran across the dance floor and grabbed hold of Aditi's hand. She came, her feet dragging.

'This is Aditi. Aditi, my best friend Nishonko Mitro. The one they call Nishachar.'

Aditi spoke, almost inaudible, her eyes lowered, her fingers clutching Debraj's hand fiercely. 'I...we have heard so much about you.'

Nishonko looked at her bowed head, the flowers in her hair, the downturned eyes. 'And I know nothing about you. Debraj has kept it such a wonderful secret.'

Debraj chuckled. 'And what about your little secret? When are we to meet her?'

He turned to Aditi with a wink. 'Nish here has someone he adores and worships, the love of his life...but he's hidden her away.'

Aditi looked up. Finally, her eyes met Nishonko's. She opened her mouth to say something, to explain, to plead, to say sorry, sorry Nishonko da, I didn't want it to be this way, anything to stem this nightmare but fell silent. His face was unaccusing, expressionless, as he looked down at her. Then he looked away with a jerk.

'No, that didn't work out.'

Debraj's face fell. God, he could really be a chump. Damn tactless, bringing up the whole thing, especially on this occasion. It was like rubbing poor Nishonko's face in it. He gave Nishonko's arm a little shake. 'Hey, sorry to hear that, man. Her loss. Doesn't know what she's missing out on.'

He turned to Aditi. 'This man, when you get to know him, he's one in a million, the gold-plated works. I would do anything for him.'

Aditi opened her mouth again, on the brink of the abyss, wanting to jump, to confess, to let it all come out. And then she felt a squeeze on her arm. It was Meenakshi. Under cover of hugging her, she whispered fiercely.

'Smile! It's going to be okay!'

A small sound, a gulped word, escaped from Aditi's lips. The moment was lost, the lie was sealed. Debraj turned with a big smile to Meenakshi.

'Hey, gorgeous, you must meet Nishonko. Nish, this is...'

'Sister Meena Meenakshi. We have met.' He put his arm around Meenakshi's waist, pulled her towards him with an air of entitlement, of possession.

'You know each other? Capital! We must get together before we all run off to...' He saw Aditi's stunned expression.

'Darling, did this little minx keep you in the dark also?'

'We all have our little secrets, don't we?' Nishonko's voice was silken.

And then, they were surrounded by a bunch of officers, back slapping, shouting out tipsy congratulations. They pulled Debraj away, sweeping him up in their ribald merriment, their sly jokes. Nishonko's forehead knotted with pain. He let go of Meenakshi, turned away, rubbing his face, as if the very bones had turned bitter. Aditi's face had gone white. She stared at Nishonko, who ignored her completely.

'Nishonko da, I…'

'Shut up, Jhilik. Not a cheep out of you.' His voice was a savage rasp, unequivocal, a slap across her face. Meenakshi gently led her away, to the safety of a chair, made her sit.

'Meena, I…'

'Shh, it's okay, give it time.'

'Is it true, the two of you...?'

'Is it so inconceivable that he should want me?'

'No, Meena, I didn't mean that. Why did he come?'

'Netaji ordered him to.'

And now a conga line of guests came weaving through the crowd. They swept up Meenakshi and Aditi, Debraj and the officers. Nishonko stepped aside. He knocked back his drink, slipped away into the shadowed garden. Abruptly, the band stuttered to a halt, cymbals clashing, a stray trumpet note. A howl of protest went up. Then, scattered shouts as they saw someone talking to the band. The band leader called out a count. A roll of drums, a thudding, heart pounding beat and a roar from the crowd. Chairs were upturned in the haste to stand up. Like a crashing wave, the singing started. It was their favourite anthem, 'Kadam Kadam Badhaye Ja' played to a quick tempo. Arms joined arms, shoulders leaned on shoulders. Faces shone with fervour. The singing rose to a crescendo, carrying far beyond the terrace, across the beach and out over the sea — perhaps, reverberating in the imperial corridors, heralding an end to colonial rule.

ACT V

BURMA

And so, by the beginning of February, the historic march began. The INA HQ had already shifted to Rangoon by then. Part of the INA's first division joined the diversionary Ha Go Offensive and the others were committed to the U Go Offensive directed towards Manipur. They would protect the Japanese flanks against Chin and Kashin guerrillas as Mataguchi's men crossed the Chindwin River and the Naga Hills. They would then be directed towards the main offensive through Tamu in the direction of Imphal and Kohima.

Billows of dust hung in the early morning light as the troop transports rolled out. At the station, the black engines idled, belching out clouds of steam, their impatient whistles summoning the troops from miles around. The steady tramp of marching feet resounded through the city. 'Jana Gana Mana Adinayaka Jaya He', the simple Hindi translation of Tagore's ode to his country, now their anthem, was sung out in full throat. A stiff breeze sent the tricolour snapping on the bonnet of Netaji's jeep as he stood, his back ramrod straight, taking the salute from platoon after platoon as they marched by, their flags held high. As the trains carrying his soldiers left Rangoon for Mandalay and Prome, tears streamed down Netaji's face. He wept, unashamed of his deep emotion, as he sent his boys into battle. He knew that many of them, countless numbers of them, would fall in battle, that he would never see their smiling faces again. Each was dear to him and he cried, thinking of what he was asking of them.

Ahmed Hassan stood beside him, silent. Later, much later, he would say, 'What a group we were. I felt proud that I belonged to the INA. Baluchis were there amongst us, and Assamese, Kashmiris and Malayalis, Pathans and Sikhs and Gujaratis, proud members of classes called the martial and those till then denied reputation for martial valour but who proved in battle that they could, by their deeds, claim equal honour. Every region in India was represented and every religion and every caste, mixed inseparably together, even in the small platoons and sections, each unit being a living tribute to the unity of India. We had our different private faiths and we had our different languages but in our purpose and in our political belief, we were a well-knit, determined and indivisible whole.'

An open jeep drove up to an intersection with the main avenue. Aditi was at the wheel, her face drawn. As Kabootar started unloading kits and arms, Debraj leaned in and kissed Aditi passionately, to a roar of approval from the departing soldiers. Aditi was going to follow later with the medical force. Their parting the night before had been tender, the lovemaking quiet, the hours spent just holding each other tightly, as if to imprint each other's skin and flesh with the sense memory of the beloved. She had promised herself fiercely that she would not shed tears when the time came to let him go. She had vowed to keep all the imagined catastrophes locked in some iron chamber inside her heart, so she would not weaken him with her terrors. So she smiled, brightly, her eyelashes sparkling with unshed tears, drinking in every plane of his face, clutching the front of his uniform, like it was her lifeline and she was drowning. But now his men were coming up along the avenue.

Debraj unclasped her fingers, picked up his kit. But she still leaned forward, reaching out for him, her hands, her body, seeking a little more, one last-time contact. But it was as if some invisible current was pulling him away, implacable, leaving her marooned. She pulled herself back, her arms resting on the rim of the jeep's windshield, watching him fall into step with the men, slapping shoulders, shaking hands, grinning, already lost to her.

Across the road, Nishonko sat in a parked jeep, watching her, his face impassive. Nawaz in the driver's seat, saw his look. 'She was the one, wasn't she?'

Nishonko was silent.

'I told you and told you. Don't trust that snake. But you wouldn't listen to me.'

Nishonko was still silent, just a tiny tic near his cheek betraying the seething inner turmoil.

'Why are you letting him get away with murder? You should destroy him.' Nawaz's long simmering rage at Deb spilled over, vitriolic.

Nishonko shrugged. 'Have the food trucks rolled out as yet?'

'What? Yes. Yes, they have. But where are we going, Major? It's all under wraps.'

'Oh, you'll know in good time. And Nawaz, don't worry. He won't get away with it.'

That night, as the trains carrying them to their tryst with destiny thundered through the dark countryside, the moon scudding to stay alongside, they remembered their leader's words to them the day before.

'The hour of truth is here. The dream that I have been selling to millions of my countrymen and the world is now going to become a reality. Everything leading upto this hour…it's been just skirmishes… the real war awaits the warriors of the INA now. There are 40,000 of us. We need early victories, quick victories. That's what's going to galvanise the demoralised, timid masses of India. The British outstrip us in arms, armament as well as manpower. So we will avoid set-piece battles. We will harass them, outflank them. We know the terrain and the locality like the back of our hands. We will preempt every move of the British. We will use stealth, secrecy, the night, the mist at dawn, and the cover of the forest. We must move fast…so fast that the British will have no idea where we are.'

And so, India's war of independence was formally launched. Their brigade was placed under the command of the Japanese General Headquarters in Burma with Brigadier Saito in charge. Saito briefed them at the railhead, before they set out.

'The key in battle is timing. You heard Netaji. The final push to India will be fast. Very, very fast. Speed is the key. Speed is surprise. And surprise wins battles. More than guns, tanks or planes. Now, what is an army?'

He looked at them, his eyes bright, at the dozens of hands that came up. He shook his head at each of the answers.

'No. Look around you. An army is simply thousands of hungry stomachs.'

He rubbed his belly, smiled at the laughter.

'I'm serious. An army is a collection of thousands of hard-working men who need to be regularly fed, thousands of rumbling stomachs. Napoleon said that an army marches on its stomach… and it is the biggest truth of any military operation. What slows down an army? Eh? It is its long supply line. That is, the distance from its stores to its soldiers. That's why we need to set up stores at various points along our route. We need to build stockpiles close to the Indian border for the advancing INA and Japanese troops. So start building those supply points. Start making friends with the local populations.'

Nishonko, listening grimly, nodded. He understood Saito's tactics but hated the thought of being placed under the Japanese man's command. Hell, he should have got his own command. He deserved it. And on top of everything, Debraj and his men had also been placed under Saito. And, to make matters worse, Saito, damn him, had ordered Debraj's unit to go as the advance party, keeping them small and tight so they could move fast. Nishonko, with a larger contingent, carrying extra ammo and equipment, was ordered to follow. Pretty boy would get all the kudos for being the first to set foot on Indian soil. Talk about favouritism. He brooded about it as they marched, weighed down by his dark thoughts.

But then, the country they traversed took up all their attention. The 200-mile belt of hills and jungles which made up the terrain along the Indo-Burmese border was described by General William Slim as 'some of the world's worst country, breeding the world's worst diseases, and having for half the year, the world's worst climate.' The jungles were steaming hot, infested with leeches, and thick with undergrowth which they had to hack through with machetes. The hillsides were steep, rocky, inhospitable. Great groves of bamboo grew, home to the most deadly snakes and scorpions.

Not only was food rationed but the land yielded little. The local villages they came across turned out to be hostile, already having suffered at the hands of the retreating British and Indian forces who had laid waste to their fields, poisoned their wells, slaughtered their livestock. Kabootar kept Debraj's Company supplied with wild birds so they ate well sometimes but most of the time it was beggar's rations.

Wild animals were aplenty — bison, leopards, bears. One evening, as they forded a small river at day's end, foot sore, exhausted, holding their guns aloft to keep them dry, Kabootar, in the lead, froze. He started to back up, bumping into the man behind him. Before the man could swear, Kabootar clamped his mouth and pointed with a jerk of his head at a small copse of beeches on the other bank. It was dusk and the light was falling fast. Then, the leaves shook and from the underbrush, a magnificent Royal Bengal tiger emerged, its sides tawny gold. Down the bank it came, flicking its tail, walking majestically down to the river's edge to drink. The men were frozen mid river, their guns held above their heads. One of them slowly began to bring his gun down but Kabootar, without looking back, grabbed his arm hard. The tiger lapped at the running water, a distinct sound heard over the river's warbling song. Then it looked up. 'Tiger, tiger, burning bright, in the forests of the night...' The words from his childhood lessons came unbidden to Debraj. He was filled with awe, with almost a holy sense of reverence. The tiger stared at them, then yawned and ambled off.

Another day, near Bamnank, they thought they had run into a herd of elephants, from the crashing sounds coming from up ahead. But it turned out to be a British column, heading back for their own lines, making no attempt at concealment, blissfully unaware that the INA had penetrated this far. Debraj hastily signalled Captain Pradhan. Pradhan caught on. They had used this tactic before. A handful of men moved up to attack the British rearguard, while the main force, stalked them, moving parallel to them, separated by only a few yards of dense jungle. The British would be fooled into fighting the rearguard attack and leave their flank exposed. What they failed to notice was that the jungle was thinning out. The first two soldiers tripped over rolls of concealed, razor-sharp barbed wire. They had run smack into the British lines. Screaming helplessly, they, and the next five men evaporated in a cloud of blood as the cemented ratatat of a dozen machine guns filled the air. The British were safely dug into bunkers and deep trenches while Debraj's unit was caught in the open. There had to be a way out! Then he saw it. The usual low boundary wall constructed of mud and stones on the outer periphery of the British lines. If they could reach it...

'Section I, smoke!'

Under cover of the thick fog from a couple of smoke grenades, the unit crawled to the low mud wall. But then, the heavy mortars opened up, shredding the ground behind them. No going back. No going forward either. What would Nishonko do? Debraj had traded heavy firepower for mobility. Move fast, hit hard. Shoot and scoot, that had been his mantra. Then through the thick bush, he saw a sudden burst of orange flame, smelt a whiff of burnt petroleum. My god, it's a flame thrower team...if only we could get our hands on it. He signalled to Sergeant Kirpal Singh. Four fingers, then again four fingers, a sharp point to the front.

'Covering fire!' he yelled. Debraj and Captain Pradhan stood up and let off a volley. Kirpal and eight of the men vaulted over the wall, zigzagged through the tall grass and amazingly almost reached the trench, before getting pinned down again. Four bodies lay still. They unleashed another fierce burst of covering fire, screaming obscenities at the top of their voices. Had Kirpal made it? Through his field glasses, he saw the foliage part. A hand came through and did a thumbs-up.

'Oh good show, Kirpal!'

They waited, holding their breaths. And then, an unearthly scream. They looked over the rim of the wall. A roaring column of fire had jumped through the air and burnt everything in its path for 30 yards. Kirpal was standing up, holding the flame thrower with both hands, spreading its deadly dragon breath across the enemy ranks. The dry bushes around combusted with a loud pop. Torched figures bolted from the enemy's trenches, trying to feebly beat out the flames engulfing them. It bought them those precious minutes of reprieve. The unit beat a rapid retreat to the cover of the forest. But it came at a price. Every enemy gun trained on Kirpal's men and opened up. Geysers of mud and stone shot out of the thick smoke. The ground shook with explosions. Nothing could survive that.

'Medic, Sir?' Captain Pradhan's voice was unsteady.

'No, hold it. Only if they signal. Keep moving the men. Fall back.'

Miraculously, Kirpal had survived. When he came to, he felt fine, except he couldn't feel his lower body. He tried to move his legs but they seemed stuck. The blackened earth of the trench was the same colour as the soil of his village, a deep red. Even the broken bamboo stalks looked like his sugarcane crop at harvest. Was he home? He heard a ragged groan. He twisted his head around. It was Wajid, his rifleman. He was badly shot up, great gaping wounds in his side. He couldn't see any of the others. Wajid's eyes darted from side to side. He whispered, 'Medic ko bula do...call out for the medic.'

'Yes, Wajid.' He was surprised that even his voice was coming out in a whisper. Kirpal knew that Major Mookerji would send in the medic if they signalled for him. But in the rescue attempt, his mates would die. So Kirpal kept silent.

'Medic bula do, Sir.' Again the feeble whisper.

With a herculean effort, Kirpal managed to drag his body towards Wajid, pulling at his useless legs till, panting, weeping, he rested against a rock beside him. He cradled the boy's head.

'Medic ko bula do.'

'Yes, they're coming.'

He saw Wajid's eyes lose focus. His own thoughts were also slip-sliding away. He held Wajid close. Underneath Wajid's shredded shirt, he saw a *tabiz*, an amulet, tied around his neck, still intact. He pulled Wajid's face towards him tenderly.

'Allah hu Akbar.'

Wajid looked confused. Kirpal spat out the blood-soaked foam filling up his mouth and kept repeating, like a lullaby, 'Allah hu Akbar' till he felt Wajid relax. Then Wajid opened his eyes wide, searching Kirpal's face. He took in the deep gash below the turban, oozing bright red blood, covering Kirpal's face like a grotesque mask. He saw Kirpal's right eye, swollen and almost dislodged from its socket. He saw the shattered stumps of his legs. Wajid took a deep breath. With superhuman effort, he raised his hand to Kirpal's shoulder and smiled.

'Satnaam wahe guru.' It was the Sikh prayer that Kirpal had grown up with.

They both chanted. 'Allah hu Akbar, Allah hu Akbar...Satnaam wahe guru, Satnaam.' The Muslim for the Sikh and the Sikh for the Muslim. And, for a long time, their voices were clear, before fading away. And in that moment, in a blasted, bloodied, nameless hole in the ground in Burma, within a few miles of their homeland, what Netaji had striven so hard for, was achieved.

The valley was clothed in mist, cloud upon cloud, all greys, whites and blacks, the colours leached out, the pines like vertical ink stains. The tops of the hills bled into the swirling fog, a water colour. It was very beautiful, a monochrome still life. It was quiet, the quietness of wild places where men had not muddied the pools or taken possession of the trees. From the mist emerged shapes, ghostly, like some misshapen monster. The shapes resolved into INA soldiers in full battle gear, camouflage branches stuck in helmets and straps. They crept up, crouching, trying to see through the mist. A tree trunk loomed. A shape detached itself from it, held an open palm up in warning. It was Nishonko. They froze. A twig cracked. In front of them, suddenly, other shapes loomed. Were they friends or the enemy? Nishonko gave his soft birdcall. It was answered from their right. Nishonko called again. Again, they were answered from the right. No answer from the front. Nishonko brought up his gun carefully, the men followed. He stepped gingerly forward. Suddenly, in a moment of whimsical theatrics that only nature is capable of, a wind came up out of nowhere, the mist shifted, the path ahead cleared. Right in front of them, mere yards away, stood a British patrol, crouching but facing away from them. There was a moment of suspended animation. They were too startled to do anything. Then Nishonko brought up his gun. And the white mist exploded in red. Firing erupted all along the line. Nishonko roared out, 'Grab earth.' The unit, trained by him, honed by him, dropped to the rock and scrub undergrowth as one man. It was as if they had just gone underwater. In the mist clinging to the ground, they were invisible even a few feet away. They all brought up their guns and in unison, started shooting. The British were cut down, like a scythe going through stalks of rice. They dropped like chopped trees, their screams and guttural cries damped by the mist, rendering them disembodied, unreal.

By the time the killing was over, by the time they had gone around, checking that each man sprawled on the ground was actually dead and dispatching them if they weren't, the sun was up, the mist a memory, the beauty of the valley desecrated. Nishonko was exhausted. He had not been sleeping well; the short breaks he managed on hard ground were filled with uneasy dreams. His sense of loss, of feeling emptied out, just wouldn't go away. He wanted to find meaning, feel that the things he was doing — the slaughter, the working out of strategy, the lives of his men — all of it had some purpose. He just felt inured, the impassive mask he had put on, real now. He sat alone, spooning out his rations, looking forward to the oblivion of the night and dreading it.

Chhoto mashi clung to Aditi's hand through the train window at the Rangoon station.

'Let me know when you reach, I'll be worrying.'

'Chhoto mashi! We are at a field station, miles from nowhere. I'm quite sure there are no phone lines where we are going. I'll call you once we reach India!'

Chhoto mashi could not hold back her tears.

'Come on, stop being such a crybaby. It will be over by the monsoons.'

'From your lips to God's ears. I shall pray for you.'

'Pray for all of us.'

'And eat, whatever you get but keep your strength up. And try and sleep. You have become too thin. Meena, you look after her for me, okay?'

Meenakshi, sitting opposite, nodded, patted her hand. The whistle blew, the flag waved. Chhoto mashi stood, a forlorn, suddenly old, figure on the station platform as the train pulled out, taking the medical team of the Rani Jhansi Regiment to the front. Aditi leaned out of the window, waving at Chhoto mashi until a curve in the train tracks took her away. She sat back. Her kit bag lay at her feet, with her rifle and a bag of food that the amah had packed for her carefully. She looked down at her hands, the nails cut short, the rough khaki trousers and bush shirt. The antique emerald ring was on her finger, where Debraj had placed it. Chhoto mashi, wonderful, practical

Chhoto mashi, had told her to leave it in her safe keeping but Aditi wanted it with her, a talisman to protect her. She had no idea when she would see Debraj again. It was possible that their paths would never cross during the offensive. So they had made plans. Wherever each might be, they would meet, exactly 30 days after Independence was declared, in Calcutta, at Nahoum's at 10 a.m. and have cheese sumboosucks. She rubbed her head, feeling the tight braid that she had coiled her hair in. The others had chopped off their hair as part of regulation before heading for the front but she had managed to keep hers, albeit tied up. She wondered if Debraj would have liked her in a short, modern crop.

'You should have cut it off, you would have looked fabulous.'

Meenakshi was smiling at her, pulling on the cigarette she had lit up as soon as the train had left the station, the smoke snatched away by the wind coming in through the opened window. She had put on dark aviator glasses, emulating Geeta, and looked very dashing with her short bobbed hair. Aditi admired her boldness but the acrid smoke made her cough and want to throw up. She was glad for Meenakshi's presence. No one knew what lay ahead. They had been trained rigorously by regulars from the Indian Army — physical training, classes in military tactics, strategy, map reading, Hindi, Political Science. And, of course, nursing and emergency surgery and medical procedures. But Aditi knew that whatever training they had received would never prepare them for the real battle, the actual horror of it all.

'Captain, get me a troop from that Gurkha unit which came over to our side last week.' Debraj had a wicked grin on his face.

'Yes, Sir, for sentry duty?'

'No, I want them for a really special op.' Debraj's eyes sparkled with mischief. Bands of dacoits had been terrorising the countryside around Mamit. The retreating, British had freed the inmates of the local prison and these criminals had taken to rape, pillage and highway robbery. They were difficult to track as they just melted back into the jungle after their sorties. Debraj had got an idea on how to stop them. He chose 20 of the Gurkhas, all short and slightly built. When he told them what he wanted them to do, they collapsed in laughter. Gurung, their sergeant, turned red. He was very fair and blushed easily.

'You're perfect, Gurung, you'll make a very pretty lan tal.'

The men guffawed even louder. 'Lan tal' was Burmese street lingo for a sexy girl. Debraj's idea was to dress them up as women and use them as bait. The unit barbers gave them close shaves and reddened their lips and darkened their eyes and they got into their glahngs and salows, the native skirts and jackets.

'Ummm...something's missing.'

They got hold of a crate of oranges and chucked two to each man. Then they were driven off, accompanied by whistles and lewd comments from the rest of the unit. At the local market, they drew a lot of attention, giggling, bargaining loudly. Then, armed with khukris under their salows and revolvers in their baskets, they boarded a local bus bound for one of the outlying villages. Three hours after being jostled on the potholed road, the 'girls' hanging on desperately to the shifting fruit under their dresses, the bus was stopped by a group of rough-looking, unshaven men, armed with traditional long knives and shotguns. Licking their lips, they lined up the 'girls' on one side of the road. The leader, grinning through stained teeth, spat out a long stream of tobacco juice as he made a beeline for Gurung, easily the prettiest. As he roughly felt up the sergeant's body, leering, his fetid breath smelling of cheap country liquor making Gurung almost gag, his hand fell on a most unlady-like appendage. Frowning in puzzlement, he gave it an exploratory squeeze. That did it. The khukri hidden inside Gurung's jacket came out in a bright, silver arc and the man's throat was slit from ear to ear. With a blood curdling cry of 'Ayo Gurkhali!', Gurung went into what the Gurkhas call 'divine frenzy'. With his pretty features distorted into a snarl of revulsion, he leapt and slashed the next man across the throat and pirouetted to plunge his khukri into the next dacoit's eye. Most armies of the world lacked the nerve to face a full-on Gurkha charge. This was just a gang of common criminals. With Gurung menacingly polishing his khukri, they spilled all their secrets about hideouts and spies in the villages. Legends grew about the fair-skinned, beautiful female spirit who lopped off the heads of evil doers. Children were cowed into eating up their food on threats of having her invoked. And no bus running along that road was ever stopped again.

The field station was just a clearing in the jungle with a rough muddy track running up to it and petering off as it met the teeming wilderness of the tropical forest. As the truck carrying the Rani Jhansi team came lurching and slipping along the track, they were stopped by a man waving a flag.

'You'll have to wait. A truck is stuck up front.'

Aditi swung over the tailgate, jumped down, stretched. It had been a hard ride and every muscle in her body was protesting. Then she paused, entranced. The forest was a riot of colours, wild flowers blooming in profusion, the trees, row upon sentinel row, forming a canopy that stretched endlessly. Bird song, deafening in its shrill interplay, filled the air, now that the truck engines had been switched off. She took off her boots, slung them on her shoulder, rolled up her trousers, and walked through the thick springy grass, taking deep breaths of the fragrant, rich loamy air. From up ahead, she heard singing, men's voices. She started walking along the track in the direction of the sound. As she came around a bend, she stopped dead. An army transport stood, off kilter, sunk up to its haunches in mud. Men in muddy trousers, bare bodied, heaved and pushed to get it going. 'Dum Lagake Haisha' they sang. Then one of them spotted the apparition, the forest nymph in her khakis. They straightened up, stared. Aditi felt a tiny frisson of fear. But then, she waved. This was her army, her comrades. They looked at her a long moment, then they smiled and waved back.

By the time they reached the field station, it was dusk. A gigantic banyan tree, probably over a hundred years old, stood, a vast canopy above the pitched tents with their painted red crosses. There was an OT, two wards that could take about a hundred men, a recovery room, some outlying stores, a small mess tent and cook house. Water came from a fast-flowing stream. It was all very basic. Kerosene lamps provided the only illumination, the generator kept only for medical work. They had cold rations, and then bundled up in their sleeping bags on the grass which was surprisingly soft. She lay beside Meenakshi, looking up at the stars, the moon not yet up.

'Has he been in touch?' Aditi asked, softly.

'Nishonko? No. He's off fighting a war. I don't expect him to hold my hand.' The darkness hid Meenakshi's bitter smile. Nishonko had avoided her since that strange, mixed-up night in Singapur. But deep inside her, a tiny flame of hope refused to die. Maybe they would bump into each other. Maybe, he would get over Aditi. Her body ached for him. She tried to still this wayward desire, this unreasonable yearning. He had used her, shamed her. But still, her treacherous heart would not listen to reason. She had been practical all her life, it was what had made her survive being alone. Her mother died giving birth to her, during the ship's passage to Malaysia, and her father went on a sea voyage from which he never returned. The nuns had brought her up, trained her in nursing, given her a vocation. She had been careful always not to get her heart entangled. She sighed deeply. Life was so contrary.

'Go to sleep. It will be a busy day tomorrow.'

Debraj spooned out the last of the dal chawal from his tin plate, the last precious bits and flakes, scraping the sides. It was the first hot meal they'd had in two days. He drank the sweet water they had filled their canteens with at the last waterfall, to wash the simple meal down. The old locomotive belched out thick smoke, let out its dragon roar. They had been lucky to have commandeered the train, standing abandoned at a goods station. He loosened the chinstrap of his helmet and leaned against the wooden slats of the open carriage as the train picked up speed. Kabootar sat a few feet away, smoking a bidi. The breeze, and the sun was like a healing hand on his face. He felt at peace with the world, for now. He took out the photograph of Aditi, taken the night of the engagement, as she showed off her ring, her joy shining off her like a lighthouse, laughing. God, he missed her. Had she left Rangoon yet? Part of him wanted to see her, the other part wanted her to stay as far away as possible from these killing fields. What would she make of the sound of mortar fire, that terrible thump that rattled the very bones of your skull, vibrating away hours later, its numbing assault a memory the brain couldn't let go of ever? The first time he heard it, he had pissed his pants. What would she make of the leeches hanging from your dick after a night of sleeping on the ground, plump, deep red, like an overripe, rotten fruit?

His thoughts were interrupted as one of the sepoys threw his head back and started to sing in a raw, soulful voice. Debraj couldn't understand the words but the yearning in his voice washed over him, pulled him in. Another voice, and then another joined in, hands clapping out a simple rhythm. As their voices soared and dipped, all their thoughts turned to homes and wives and sweethearts and the pain of separation. The sound of their song carried across the valley as the train lumbered, huffing and puffing on the steep gradient, towards the rainbow that was forming on a distant hill. They were nearing Chapki Bridge.

They stopped about five miles short of the bridge. Intelligence had said that the British had retreated so fast, they had not stopped to blow up the bridge. But Debraj was not taking chances. His was going to be the first train to cross and he wanted to make sure they hadn't booby-trapped the bridge. They marched along the tracks, stretching out, gleaming in the sun, carefully picking their way, the sound of the rushing river ahead their beacon. The riverbanks were dense with green bush and giant ferns and thick, impenetrable forest. The sappers followed, engineers who would inspect the bridge spans for hidden explosives. It was a tough job. To check the underside of the bridge, they had to suspend themselves from the railings on either side and walk the whole bridge like that. They were completely exposed and vulnerable. Debraj and the men stood guard, scanning the thick forest cover for any signs of movement.

'This is Naga territory, Major. Some of the tribes are friendly with the British,' Kabootar breathed into his ear.

'There may be a whole goddamn bunch hidden in the bush, watching us this moment. With their poisoned arrows.' Satnam Singh's voice shook.

'Steady soldier, steady.' Debraj's voice was quiet.

The British had persuaded many of the Nagas to harass the INA as they advanced, using their usual tactics of promising titles, handing out money and pitting one tribe against another. But there were rumours that many tribes were actually ready to support the INA.

'Sir, there, at 3 o' clock, under the rocky outcrop,' Satnam hissed.

Debraj looked where Satnam was pointing. What was it? A flash of yellow, then it was gone. Was it a leopard? The forest was infested with them.

'It's a Naga!'

Now Debraj could make out the feathered headdress, the painted face, the curved bow in one hand. The Naga was motionless, watching them.

'Hold your fire.' His voice was soft.

Silence, except for the rushing of the river. Then the Naga melted back into the forest. In a show of good faith, Debraj moved his men back to the edge of the forest, to signal to the unseen Nagas that it was they who had control over their hunting area. When the sappers gave the go-ahead, they got on the train and slowly chugged across the bridge, the air suddenly cool over the river, their eyes peeled for any hostile movement, and entered the foothills.

Nishonko had a more fruitful encounter with the Nagas of the Somra tribe. They had come unarmed, to the camp. The chief's youngest son, a boy of fifteen, was dying of malaria. Normally, English missionaries would supply them with quinine but, scared of the Japanese advance, they had all fled, taking their medicines with them. Nishonko ordered Captain Nawaz to accompany the Medical Officer to the village and treat the boy. The chief, full of gratitude, invited their 'chief' Nishonko, to dine with him. The Nagas came out in full strength, dressed in ceremonial headdresses made of hornbill feathers and shiny ornaments. The chief's headdress towered over the others as he came forward and enfolded Nishonko in a tight embrace, smelling of strong tobacco and woodsmoke. Small, thin, with a wizened face and a gap-toothed smile, he led them ceremoniously to a place of honour. Gourds full of bubbling zu, the native beer, were offered to them. The fiery taste made Nishonko gasp. 'It's killer stuff. I'm sure something's ruptured inside.'

The chief grinned as he refilled their cups, shouting encouragement with the only English words he knew.

'Jolly good! Chin chin!'

But by the time they had downed their second glass, Nishonko felt much more mellow. The zu was followed by a sumptuous meal

— smoked wild boar, river fish, steaming spicy curries, mountain rice. Nishonko offered the chief one of his cigarettes. The old man lit up, exhaling happily. Nishonko explained, in Hindi, Netaji's vision for the Nagas, how he regarded them as an integral part of India's culture and how he would always protect and nurture them as equals. The chief nodded away and grinned broadly without understanding a word. He suddenly lunged and planted a wet kiss on each of Nishonko's cheeks. Nishonko almost recoiled but stopped himself in time. The chief smiled, bobbed his head, then waited with open arms. A moment passed. He threw open his arms again. Nawaz gently nudged Nishonko. 'Kiss him back, Major.' Nishonko hesitated. He hated all this huggermugger stuff. Then, he saw the frowns beginning to appear on some of the warriors' faces. He shrugged, and with great formality, pecked the Naga chief back. A roar went up from the villagers. By the time Nishonko, Nawaz and the MO walked back, none too steady on their feet, to camp, the countryside flooded with the calm, silver light of a waxing moon, they were accompanied by a group of five — three young men and two women. In the days to come, this group proved to be invaluable as scouts. Knowing the terrain like their own backyards, they would lead them through the jungles by the shortest, easiest trails leading to the Indian border. It was critical that their journeys be conducted in extreme secrecy. The British, who had by now almost retreated behind the Indian lines, just couldn't get a whiff of the forces massing towards them. On the trails that these scouts opened up, tons of food, ammunition and other necessities started slowly moving up on the backs of hundreds of mules.

'Drink! Drink!' Captain Mishra, the medic in charge with Debraj's unit, piped in his high bird-like voice. They had broken camp before dawn, while it was still dark and cool. But by mid morning, the sun had turned the whole forest into a steaming tandoor. Dehydration on this kind of forced march could kill. The heat just sucked the moisture out and they had to stop to rest every couple of miles. Uniforms dripped with sweat and the straps of their packs and rifles chafed the skin raw. Kishore Pradhan took a sip from his bottle, and grimaced at the vile taste of the water purification tablets.

Other days, it rained, an unrelenting downpour, turning the ground to mush, the air so humid, you could hardly breathe, the water streaming into eyes. The jungle was like a wilful being, blocking their way maliciously, the vicious vines snaking around them and tripping them with unseen roots. It had to be hacked, foot by foot, to carve out a path for them. But the worst were the leeches. They came jumping and arcing out of the squelching mud, their blind, hungry mouths thirsty for blood. Cigarettes were cupped in hands, to burn the buggers off, and make sure they didn't get inside your jocks. They couldn't even sit down. The mud got into everything.

'This effing slush! It just gets into any bloody hole it can find,' Debraj muttered as he cleaned the inside of his rifle barrel.

'My hole is spick and span!' Kishore grinned.

'That's why you're such a perfect ass hole!'

They were too wet even to laugh. Debraj looked at his watch.

'Five minutes up. On your feet.'

Groaning, the men picked up their heavy kits. The long lines of heavily laden mules also twitched and shook their heads. Even they had begun to recognise his voice.

'Make sure your socks are clean,' Debraj called out. This wasn't the facetious comment it sounded like. Every few miles, they all had to stop to scrape and hack off the mud. Blisters caused by muddy socks could cripple a man. And this was no country for a cripple.

By nightfall, they were crawling and limping the last tortuous mile to complete the target of ten miles a day. From the Chindwin River, where they started the march towards India, they had to cover about 180 miles to reach Kohima. Saito and the other planners had set a target of 20 days to do it in. Anything more, and the British would get wind of where they were going to attack. They got to high ground, open ground where wild animals would not attack, and flopped down. A large moon was coming up and there was light enough to strike camp.

'We better camp down wind, Sir. The angrez will be able to smell us from miles.' Captain Pradhan growled.

The men grimaced. They were all dying to bathe, have a shave but it was against the rules to use water for washing until they were next to a river or waterhole. Debraj looked at the men, sweat stained, filthy with mud. He knew how important personal cleanliness was to Indians. 'What the hell, the next water should be a few miles ahead. Wash up, fellows!'

They whooped like kids. Debraj allowed them half a helmet of water to wash in. Reverently, they splashed a handful over their faces, heads, snorting with pleasure, not spilling a drop.

'I'd like to brush my teeth again… I mean properly, before I die,' Satnam Singh said.

'We'll do it at the Grand,' Debraj chortled.

'The Grand?'

'The Grand Hotel in Calcutta, you ignoramus!'

'We're going there?'

'You bet. Next stop, after Kohima. We'll take in a soak in their hot tubs, a glass of chilled champagne and a sizzling ham steak.'

'Can I order chilled beer and sarson da saag?'

'Yes, bless your Punjabi soul, you may. Mess Sergeant!' Debraj called to a man down the line, 'What's for dinner?'

'Glad you asked, Sir. We have shahi pulao, dal makhani, macchhi korma and masala chai malai marke.'

Everyone groaned. It had been the same food since they had started this march. The shahi pulao was actually unpolished brown rice barely boiled, the dal makhani was a watery lentil gruel, macchhi korma was a paste of smelly dried fish in tins that the Japanese had supplied in great quantities. And since this combination would make anyone gag, it was washed down by cups of black tea sweetened with a spoon of rationed sugar and milk powder, the only luxury.

After their frugal meal, they made themselves comfortable in nooks and crannies in the hard ground. Steel helmets were adjusted to double up as pillows. Debraj opened the map and in the light of a field lantern, marked it.

'This is your prize for today, men.'

They leaned forward to see the couple of inches crossed out from the pencil line on the map. The line was getting shorter. Faster than HQ had planned. Then blessed sleep came, even as swarms of bugs and mosquitoes descended on them. They would just pop in the quinine tablets and let the mosquitoes bite. No one had the strength to raise a hand to slap them off.

Corporal Willis, a slightly portly Liverpudlian in his thirties, was dying to light up a cigarette but it was strictly forbidden if you were on sentry duty. Sergeant would have his hide. He slapped his sunburnt neck and scratched furiously. Hell and damnation, the mosquitos were fierce tonight.

'Bloody, blood suckin' vampires!' he growled.

Private Mason hunkered inside his blanket. The night was cold here up in the hills, and it kept him from being eaten up alive by the friggin' mosquitoes. He had already had two bouts of malaria and did not look forward to spending another spell shivering till his teeth rattled. If only they could light a fire but pulling sentry duty meant sitting in the bloody dark, staring at the tree line, and the rusted barbed wire coils stretching to the horizon, counting the damn hours till the relief came. Who in bleedin' hell would come here, anyway, to the top of this blasted hill in the middle of friggin' nowhere? The Japs were miles away from this godforsaken stretch of scrub and forest which made up His Majesty's outpost no 462 on the Burma-India border.

'What's the time?' His voice was loud in the vast silence of the night.

Willis yawned as he peered at his watch. 'Going on to three. I could do with a bit of shut-eye, mate. You okay, holding the fort?'

'I've got it. I see any of those yellow bastards, I'll give you a shout.'

Willis grinned, curled up against a rock and pulled his helmet down over his eyes. Silence descended. Then Mason looked up, his ears pricking.

'You heard that?'

'What, mate?' Willis grumbled, sleepily.

'I don't know, a rustle…it was…'

Willis sat up, scratching his belly. He listened. There was nothing, just a soft birdcall, some frightened night bird.

'If you're going to be jumping up at every tiny sound, like my sainted Aunt Agatha, bless her soul, I'm not going to get much of a kip, Private.'

'Sorry, you go on and settle down, it must have been a fox or something.'

'This ain't the English countryside, sonny. No bleedin' foxes traipsin' around. More like a wild boar, I'd say.'

Another birdcall came from the right somewhere.

'As long as it's not some big animal.'

'Whatever. Keep your gun handy. Now don't you go calling me again until it's Mr Hirohito himself.'

Mason grinned. 'Okay, Corporal.'

Willis settled back into sleep. Mason pulled his rifle closer to him, just in case. The hours dragged by. Mason found himself dropping off. He rubbed his face, got up, stamped his feet, then went to a nearby bush for a piss. As he shook himself off, he choked. Something tightened round his throat, a noose, a garrotte? His legs thrashed soundlessly in the air as he was lifted off the ground. He tried to claw at the rigid arm cutting off his air, biting into his windpipe, his face turning blue. His last thought before he sank into oblivion was there would be merry hell to pay.

Nishonko silently laid the limp body of the young British soldier down on the ground. He straightened up. His face and arms were blackened and he really looked like the ghost that his nickname Nishachar stood for. He turned. Nawaz had taken care of the other soldier as swiftly and efficiently, wiping his wet blade on the man's chest, which bled black in the moonlight. He gestured to his men, and they set off at a low, swift lope towards the main British camp a quarter mile down the hill.

Nishonko's unit had made very good time because of the Naga guides who had used secret trails bypassing the main roads and a series of underground caverns. They had brought them within yards of the sentries. It had been like taking candy from a child. By the time they fell upon the unsuspecting isolated British border outpost and slaughtered them to the last man, the sun was coming up. They stood, breathing heavily, adrenaline pounding in their brains, soaked in blood, the dead bodies lying like cut rice stalks, row upon row, all around them. Then, Neelu ran up, unfurling the tricolour. Solemnly, they planted it in the rocky ground, saluted it, sang their anthem, their voices clear in the morning air. They hugged each other, ecstatic. Some wept openly. They now stood, free men, on the first piece of freed Indian soil.

'Sir, mission accomplished!'

Nishonko's voice came broken through the static on the field telephone but the message was clear. A roar of jubilation rang out at the HQ in Rangoon. Netaji rushed out of the radio room and out into the corridor.

'They have done it. Our men have set foot on the holy soil of our motherland and planted our flag!'

Cheering broke out, the news relayed from room to room. The Japanese press captured scenes of celebration and camaraderie. Photographs were taken of Indian and Japanese officers and staff embracing each other, faces wreathed in smiles, all talking at the same time. Netaji hurried back to the radio room and spoke into the mic.

'Major Mitro, we salute you and commend your brave men. Now, push forward the advantage. Meet up with the rest of the troops at the rendezvous point at the earliest. Close in on the target!'

'Yes, Sir!' Static drowned out the rest of his words.

Gaffar Khan came running down the corridor. He had heard the roar going up. When he heard the news, his face tightened. Goopta would be very, very unhappy. And angry. He had not foreseen such speed. He still had no clue where they had made their breakthrough or where they were headed. This was a disaster. He was about to stride off to get to a phone when he heard his name called. It was Netaji.

'Gaffar, please start packing up my things. I will be joining the Japanese Command very soon.'

'Oh, that's wonderful news, Sir. Where will we be going?'

'Maybe Shenam, maybe Kawlin. We will know soon. But, Gaffar, you will have to remain behind, I'm afraid. No civilians allowed on the front lines. Plus, my small plane won't really take so much freight.'

Gaffar's face fell. 'But...but, Sir, who will look after you? I'm needed there.'

Netaji looked at him keenly. 'Oh, I can look after myself well enough. I will truly miss your kind ministrations but we must all make sacrifices.'

Gaffar fell to his knees, pleading. Netaji looked embarrassed, helped him up. 'Thank you, Gaffar for your consideration. We will see what can be done. You may have to follow, by road.'

'Anything, Sir, anything, as long as I can be by your side.'

Brigadier Alan Whyte settled himself into the large wooden chair. He was not in uniform. His trousers were knife-creased, the shirt, a pale blue silk, the same arctic blue of his expressionless eyes, was sadly rumpled. He had arrived that very afternoon in Kohima after a patricularly nasty, singularly uncomfortable journey across the hot, humid plains of Assam. They had told him in Calcutta that he would do well to base himself in Chittagong instead but he had decided to come here. It placed him closer to the border. He steepled his fingers, looked around the room. Painted in that dispiriting, dull ochre that was the staple of all Government offices, with a picture of the King, hanging a little crookedly — he got up to straighten it, hated things not being ship shape — it was a dump. The table was scuffed, with circles of old tea stains. The chair was hard and the two visitors' chairs did not match. But it would do. He would be out of here, as soon as he had got a feel of the lay of the land and got an idea of their defences and resources. There was a knock on the door. His adjutant poked his head in. 'Bloke by the name of G.G. Native. Businessman. Wants an audience, Sir.'

'Oh. Yes, that will be Goopta. Show the blighter in.'

Goopta waddled in, shiny and hand washing as usual. 'Brigadier Whyte, Sir, good day to you kind Sir.'

'Glad you made it to this fair little town. And would you have any good news for me, Goopta?'

'Alas, nothing as yet from our usual source. An attack is coming, that's for sure but he doesn't know exactly where and when.'

'Well, we have to know exactly where and when, don't we Goopta, my man? We have to get the correct intel. Can't go traipsing all over the Indo-Burma border, shooting at phantoms, can we? To quote Mr. Churchill, "Nothing is more important than this battle. It's imperative to win." Either you deliver or our little association — it will be over. And all those sweet promises of making you the mayor and those deals with your pathetic Party and the timber contracts — down the bloody tube, gone, flushed away.'

'Ah, my esteemed friend, you are so impatient.'

'We are not friends, Goopta. Don't ever call me that again.'

'Yes, Sir, I understand fully, Sir. We will get the intel you so heartily desire. Just a few days, just a matter of time.'

The news reached the field hospital under the giant banyan tree too. The medical team was summoned.

'The army is almost in range. We have been ordered to move small medical units up to take position as mobile dressing stations and emergency care units. You will receive your assignments at the end of the meeting. Please pack everything up. Transports should arrive in the next four days. We have to be ready to move by then. This is what all of you have been training for. Any questions?'

Hands were raised, questions asked. Aditi sat, cradling her knees, pensive. Now that the moment had come, she felt pulled apart. In the few days she had been here, she had grown to love this secret place in the woods — the benediction of the great banyan tree like a huge temple above their heads, waking up to the excited chatter of birds and monkeys, the daily swim in the rushing river, hidden by a curve from prying eyes, the silence of the nights, the fecund smell of things growing, of earth and woodsmoke. It seemed like an oasis, a place of sanctuary. The hospital wasn't very busy yet but she knew things would get frantic as soon as the actual engagements started. But, for now, there was calm. Whenever she thought of the days ahead, she would feel that prickle of foreboding, that cramping sensation in the pit of her stomach. She would break into tears for no reason. On top of that, she had been feeling really under the weather ever since the campaign began. The food would just not agree with her. She felt nauseous all the time and the thought of getting back on those jolting trucks made her stomach turn. God, she was such a weakling. She looked at Meenakshi, at her eyes hidden behind her aviator glasses. Did she feel the same contradictions? She thought of Chhoto mashi and how she had scolded her for joining the Rani Jhansi Regiment. She suddenly missed her with a deep intensity that brought those silly tears again. She missed her mothering, her worrying, her nagging. She shook herself. Buck up, you stupid girl, you're a soldier. But the flicker of sadness wouldn't go.

Gaffar took a taxi, urging it to hurry. He had a small window of time before Netaji returned. He had left Gaffar behind – again. Increasingly, Netaji was isolating himself, surrounded only by his bodyguards. When he reached the Paradiso, he felt out of place in its luxuriously appointed lobby, too exposed. But he kept his head down and ran up the curving stairs with their beautifully carved solid teak balustrade, his sweaty palm leaving a damp telltale trail on its meticulously polished surface. Upto the third floor, a right turn along the open verandah overlooking a courtyard with dwarf palms. He knocked discreetly on the last door, waited for the order to go in, entered. The curtains were drawn, the man he had been instructed to meet a shadowy silhouette, sitting on the only armchair in the room. He had a panama hat on, which he kept on throughout their exchange, his face hidden. The man gestured silently at him, ordering him to speak. Gaffar gave him his news, in a voice that was slightly breathless.

'Are you sure of this?'

'Yes, Command is being moved to Shenam and Kawlin.'

'You have done well.'

'Can I have a glass of water?'

The man pointed at a clear carafe and two glasses near the window, the light passing through them, transparent, clean. Gaffar drank thirstily while the man picked up the phone and dialled. The whirr and click of the dialling was loud in the room. Somewhere, a tap dripped. The man spoke into the receiver, in a voice which was inaudible even a couple of feet away, a good telephone operator's voice, used to keeping confidences. When he finished, he shot his cuffs with a crisp gesture.

'He is satisfied.'

As Gaffar walked down the staircase, the marble steps a little slippery, he failed to notice a thin Japanese man in his fifties, a little bent, his face hidden behind a newspaper, who followed him with his eyes as Gaffar darted across the lobby and slipped out through the broad revolving doors.

The old man sits back, cracking his knuckles. His voice is hoarse but his milky eyes are bright. He remembers the promise of that moment of history. Nothing, not the passing of time, nor the distortions of events by lesser men later, nor the pointing fingers and slurs could dim what they felt that March of 1944.

'We began the offensive on March 8. On March 18, we, the Azad Hind Fauj, crossed the border and carried the armed struggle onto Indian soil. The INA moved into Northeastern India, one part towards Imphal, the other towards Kohima. The Gwalior Lancers became the first entire unit of the Indian Army to cross over to the INA's side.'

'But how did you do it? How come the British were caught unawares?' Dulal da is flabbergasted.

'Unawares?!!' The old man lets off a gleeful cackle. 'The British were caught with their pants down. They thought they had all the time in the world. But we pulled off the impossible. We marched from the Chindwin River — 180 miles across thick jungle and endless ridges to 8,000 feet above sea level — and reached Kohima on the 3rd of April…in just 20 fucking days.'

'Unthinkable!'

'No one could have expected an entire Japanese division and an INA regiment to cross such hostile terrain so fast. They were still licking their wounds from the retreat. They hadn't bothered to strengthen their defenses. They had no clue where we were going to hit them. Ahead of us lay Kohima, a sleepy, tiny town in Nagaland. But Kohima held the key to India's destiny. If we could break the British defences in Kohima, the way lay wide open. Within days, we would be able to pour into Bengal. We would reach Calcutta. The British had their hands full fighting on the European and African fronts. The road to Delhi lay undefended. It would be a walkover. The battle for Kohima was what the British today have confessed was 'their greatest battle'.

'The battle of Kohima is often referred to as the "Stalingrad of the East", right, Sir?' Sudipto looks at the old man, his eyebrows raised. The old man gives a big gap-toothed smile of approval. 'Very good. Excellent.'

'If you two are through with your mutual admiration society, maybe we can move on?' Dulal da's tone is caustic. He has already lost a few clients to this tale and now wants to cut to the chase. Sudipto and the old man grin at each other. Somewhere, in the telling of the tale, they have become fellow travellers, brothers in arms. The old man clears his throat.

'Yes, of course. So, the principal actors all came together on the final stage. They met at the rendezvous point, as planned.'

ACT VI

KOHIMA

A gust of wind hit them as they crested the rise. It was April 4, 1944. 4/4/44. Brigadier Saito and the other Division commanders, panting a little from the climb, breathed in the sharp, resinous perfume of pines. The land fell away towards a small valley, a dip really, a mere clearing in the forest. This was it — the point marked 'X' in red on their maps. Finally, after 20 days of sheer agony, they had arrived at their destination, the intersection of the Tamanthi-Kohima-Dimapur highway — if this narrow ribbon of tar, crowded by overgrown bushes, could be called that.

'Doesn't look like much,' Debraj said, as he watched the road through his glasses. Nishonko stood on one side. His men and mule train were parked near the river.

'But from here, Kohima is just 10 miles. And from Kohima...' Saito cracked open his map, spread it open on the ground. He ran a finger along the rough jute paper. 'Dimapur is only 45 miles. That's the rail head. A day's journey will get us to the Brahmaputra Valley, the gateway to Bengal. This road is the key to the Red Fort.'

'Until we actually get Kohima, that road to Delhi is going to remain a chimera.' Nishonko's voice was condescending.

'Distance is the time taken from disbelief to belief! Old samurai saying.' Saito's smile was frosty. 'That humble-looking track is the only metalled road that runs from the mountains to the Brahmaputra. It's the enemy's lifeline. Now this ridge running here...it overlooks the road and the town. Who commands the ridge, commands Kohima. Whoever controls Kohima, controls this road and those hills beyond.'

They all turned to look to the north, at the distant hills, blue, grey, mauve, purple, the foothills of the Himalayas.

'You know, back in the briefing room, those hills on the map didn't seem a big deal. But looking at them now — they are like frigging castles!' Debraj's face was grim.

'Frightened, Major?' Nishonko's dark eyes held a shadow of contempt.

Debraj flushed, looked at him, surprised. 'Not really.'

Nishonko smiled thinly. 'But then, this is going to be your first real battle, isn't it?'

'Well, we did have our skirmishes along the way — some quite hair-raising, I can tell you.' Debraj was defensive.

'The Bahadurs are no more a guerilla outfit. This is the real thing, a proper battle — brigade-sized engagements with heavy artillery and air force. Are you up to it…Major?'

Debraj frowned. What was with Nishonko? They hadn't met in weeks and here he was trying to show him up in front of the others. Did he really mind him becoming a Major so much? Saito too looked at the map, his face impassive. He had specifically chosen these two to be under his command because of their friendship. Disunity between unit commanders was the last thing he wanted at this critical stage.

'We'll find out if any of us are up to it, gentlemen. Set up camp. Get the men rested. We move exactly at 4 p.m. We have a long night ahead.'

They saluted and turned away towards their lines. Debraj paused as he looked down from the top of the rise at the massive force camped on both sides of the Imphal-Dimapur highway.

'So this is what a whole division looks like. It's amazing, the discipline of the Japanese.'

Saito's entire division, the 31st, had split into three brigades at the Chindwin River crossing. The three brigades had traversed the Chindwin Hills by different routes and had assembled at the Imphal highway remarkably at the same time. With the two units of the INA Bahadurs supporting them, they numbered over 12,000. Intelligence reports gave the British strength in Kohima at about 5,000. Now, they moved, row upon row, in precise orderly lines, to their positions.

'We are a pukka army now, aren't we?' Debraj's face was flushed with excitement.

'Sounds like you're enjoying it.' Nishonko's tone was dry. He too had paused.

Debraj smiled. 'Funnily, I am…it's what we've been training for, isn't it?'

'Oh, I thought you playboys were only interested in a lark.'

Debraj's face twisted. 'Nishonko, for heaven's sake, what's with you, man? Why are you shitting on me this way? What have I done to you?'

Nishonko shook his head, as if trying to clear it. 'Forget it, just tired.' He strode away towards his lines.

Debraj stared after him. Nishonko was his friend but he could be a real arse sometimes. He had stopped trying to figure the man out.

The battle room at Maymyo, a small hill town near Mandalay, was a flurry of frenzied activity. Large sectional maps were being unrolled and put up on the walls. A large square wooden object, mysteriously wrapped in burlap, was carried in carefully by four Japanese staff. They placed it on the table and swept off the cover. It was a cleverly wrought scale model of the terrain around Kohima, with exquisite detail. Radio communication was being set up, great reels of cables unspooling along the ground like a nest of snakes being let loose. The Japanese High Command, including General Mataguchi, had moved to Maymyo to be closer to the front. Outside, men toiled at carving out a rough airstrip out of the rocky ground. The 'Azad Hind', Netaji's small plane, was going to land in a few days.

The narrow country roads had been built for the odd buses and village carts; they had never seen so many vehicles, such a rush of movement. Aditi's convoy got caught in one of the snarls. The exhaust fumes and the cacophony of horns made Aditi gag. The military police, seeing the large red crosses on the sides of the trucks, waved them through. But it was still a crawl, taking them well into evening, before they drew clear and hit the open road. The hours were whiled away with songs in a medley of languages, for the nurses came from many places. They clapped their palms, their high thin voices floating back on the wind as they drove away, moving steadily west, closer and closer to the war zone.

'There, there in the distance, beyond that river, beyond those jungles, beyond those hills, lies the promised land — the soil from which we sprang, the land to which we shall now return. Hark! India is calling. Delhi is calling. Three hundred and eighty eight million of our countrymen are calling. Blood is calling out to blood. Get up, we have no time to lose. Take up your arms. There, in front of you, is the road that our pioneers have built. We shall march along that road. We shall carve our way through the enemy's ranks — or if God wills, we shall die a martyr's death. And in our last sleep, we will kiss the road that will bring our army to Delhi. The road to Delhi is the road to freedom. Chalo, Delhi!'

Thus their leader, their Netaji spoke, on the eve of their tryst with destiny.

The night mist swirled around them, and in the waning moon's light, they were just shifting shapes, ghostly in the dark of the forest road. An entire Japanese brigade and part of the Bahadurs were on the move but except for the sound of hundreds of footsteps shuffling, like the wind moving through the high pines, and the odd clinking of metal against metal, it was almost silent. The soft bird hoot of an owl punctuated the darkness, a beacon from the scouts a 100 yards ahead, signalling that the way was clear. The night was bitterly cold, the wind sweeping down from the highlands but the steady march made Debraj sweat. As he came round a bend, Kabootar and Kishore at his heels, they found Saito watching their passage. He was accompanied by Major Daiki, his constant shadow, and the ever-present radio man, wireless set strapped to his back, long antennae waving, making him look like a giant insect in the gloaming. Saito fell into step beside Debraj.

'Walk with you, Major?'

'Yes, Sir.'

They were formal with each other. Military decorum demanded that Saito, as the division commander, be at the head of the Japanese contingent. The strict hierarchical structure of the Japanese Army forbade much interaction with the troops. Because of his rank and his reputation, even Saito's closest officers kept a respectful distance. Saito probably just needed some company before the firing started. The two men strode together in silence. The ground started to slope uphill.

Suddenly, the owl hoots changed to the warble of a mountain partridge. Saito stopped. His hand shot up.

'My kitsune foxes — my scouts—have spotted something.'

To a man, the entire brigade stood still. Then out of the shadows, a strange shape materialised. It was one of the foxes, short even for a Japanese, heavily camouflaged with leaves and branches. Even by day, he could creep up within feet of the enemy before they realised that it wasn't a shrub.

Saito listened to his report intently, then barked off instructions in Japanese. The radio operator relayed them swiftly, softly, in Japanese and in English to the INA units.

'All units hold position.'

Saito spread out his map as Major Daiki lit it with a torch. 'Two enemy machine gun positions ahead, here and here. On the left here, is Jail Hill. The British will be there in strength. Here, on the other side of the road, is Detail Hill, another British stronghold. I want to attack both simultaneously and I want to take them by surprise. But if we attack these machine gun posts, they'll radio their HQ and we'll lose the advantage of surprise.'

'I could pick them off. I'm pretty good at long-distance sniping.'

'I know, Major Mookerji. But the rifle shots will also give us away.'

'Then why don't we go around them? Bypass them.'

'Not by the rulebook but what the hell, it could work. We'll leave just a couple of squads here. Then, when we get ready to move against Jail Hill and Detail Hill, we radio our men here to attack at the same time.'

'Sounds like a plan,' Debraj grinned. 'Of course, the whole hill could be full of machine gun trenches.'

'It's a calculated risk, yes. But I've fought them for three years now. They are creatures of habit. They don't like spreading their resources. They feel safe in strongholds, their little castles.'

'Ah, you can say that, Brigadier.'

They split up — Colonel Watanabe with two Japanese regiments and Debraj and his unit headed for Jail Hill while Colonel Akira took the remaining Japanese force and Nishonko and his men to take on Detail Hill. They moved out, their hearts on fire, for the first battle for Kohima. The moon had set, the only sounds the crunch of wet gravel, the rattle and clink of weapons, their harsh breathing, like a serpent's breath, as they trudged uphill. Debraj could sense the pressure and presence of the nameless others who followed behind, the body of the serpent curling and curving to follow the head. The entire hillside could be packed with bunkers and dugouts. They could stumble on one, any second, and the alarm would go off. So, they went in stealth, low on the ground, loping, wolves on the hunt, the 700-strong contingent moving from ridge to ridge, crossing nullahs and gullies as they moved closer to Jail Hill.

Maybe it was the darkness, the inability to see but Debraj found he could smell everything acutely — the acrid sweat of unwashed bodies, the clean alpine scent of the forest, the sweet cloying fragrance of rhododendron in bloom. And then he smelt something else. It sent his sixth sense tingling. What was it? Gun oil, cigarette smoke. No, something else. It was chocolate. His stomach swooped. He was sure there was something ahead of him in the blackness. He leaned back to touch the shoulder of the man behind him, chopped the flat of his hand down. Like a current, the signal to stop was passed down the line. The men behind him crouched, rifles and sub-machine guns ready. Debraj waited, bated breath, Sten gun cocked, straining to hear. He took out a grenade, groped his way forward. At that instant, a Very light arced across the sky, turning the sky a lurid red. And outlined against it, black silhouettes, like cut-out puppet figures, he saw them. Two of them were rising to their feet, turned away, looking at the other side of the hill where Colonel Watanabe must be. Mere yards ahead, to his right, he saw the humps of sand bags lining a bunker, the silhouette of helmets, the long ugly barrel of…HELL! It was a Browning, a bloody monster! The Brits saw them, at the same time, saw the line of men, bathed in red.

'To your right, lads!' a Welsh voice roared.

It would take them a few seconds to traverse the gun. Quick. Pull the pin. Lob short. Get down! There was the double thunder of explosions. Someone else had also chucked a grenade. Good man! Screams from the bunker and the deep thudthudthud of the Browning gun. Shit, he had missed! But, the orange tracer shells, like fat beads of fire, were arcing straight up to the sky. There was no one behind the gun — for now.

'Chalo! HAMLAA!'

Without knowing it, Debraj was on his feet, firing his gun, charging ahead. All around him, the pop pop of rifles, the thud of the Browning, howls, thumps. He was over the sand bags and inside the bunker before he realised it. He just pointed at the mass of bodies and kept on firing till his magazine ran out. A large beefy man, his face scarlet, teeth bared, lunged at him with his bayonet. Debraj, with all the elegance and grace of a seasoned dancer who had strutted his stuff at many a May Ball, swayed back, from the waist. The wicked edge of the bayonet almost kissed his face, missing it by a mere inch. He pirouetted, and in one fluid motion, hit the man on the back of his head with his gun stock. The man went down, poleaxed. Debraj turned. Another British soldier, his legs braced wide, had him in his sights, at point blank range, his finger curling round the trigger. Debraj hauled at his revolver but knew it was too late. Then the man's head exploded like a watermelon, blood spattering on to Debraj's front. The British soldier slowly toppled to the ground, revealing, directly behind him, Kabootar with his gun, eye to the sight, the barrel still smoking. Then, the rest of the unit came pouring over the sand bags. They fired and stabbed, butted and bashed, kicked, gouged, hacked, clawed. They rolled in the mud and blood, in hand-to-hand combat. No mercy shown, none expected. Finally, a kind of quiet descended. The bunker was knee-deep in bodies. The stench of blood and cordite caught at his throat. He swayed, looking around. A feather floated down. He stared at it, bemused. No, it wasn't a feather, it was a silver chocolate wrapper, slowly descending, till it landed gently on a fallen soldier's face, beside the red ragged hole of his empty eye socket.

Debraj hungrily pulled at his cigarette. He looked at his hand. There was a slight tremor but no noticeable shake. It had taken about five minutes from the first shot to the last, five minutes of sheer terror.

But he had made it. And then a dozen Very lights shot into the sky, from the north side of the hill. A surreal sight met their eyes. In the red glow, they could make out waves of khaki as Watanabe's men charged through swirling smoke, storming the enemy bunkers on Jail Hill. And, then came the houkou kougeki — the 'howling assault'. It was the chilling sound of hundreds of frenzied voices screaming 'BANZAI! ADVANCE!' followed by blood-curdling howls. The primitive, atavistic sound sent the hair on Debraj's neck prickling. Now he could understand why this tactic, perfected by the Japanese infantry, had worked so well. In the dark, it could shatter anyone's nerve. But tonight, it didn't seem to work. The steady, determined fire of the defenders rolled down hill, slicing through Watanabe's men. Then the heavy mortars joined in.

What the hell is wrong?

Wait! He could see. That was the difference, he could *see* clearly. It wasn't a night attack anymore. The houkou kougeki depended on darkness to mess with the defenders' minds. But the barrage of Very lights had turned the night into day. He could only watch helplessly as another attack was mowed down. He had to admire their courage. He had heard of an entire company getting wiped out and then the lone survivor calmly fixing his bayonet and charging. *We are fighting for our freedom. What the hell inspires them?* He remembered Saito's words. *'Ours is a holy cause, Deb san. It is nothing of this earth. It is not about empire or freedom. It is our duty to our god, the Emperor. Everyone, from the runner to the highest General believes in this.'* Saito was one of the most intelligent people he had ever met and even he worshipped the Emperor with blind devotion. But intelligent or not, he needed help right now. He radioed Saito and told him how the British were neutralising Watanabe. Saito got it in seconds. He thanked Debraj courteously and signed off.

There was a lull. Debraj waited, wondering what Saito would do. Then, another howl went up from the Japanese. The British fell for it. They set off a half dozen flares and in their waning light, fired. But the Japanese didn't charge. Darkness, a pause. And then the Japanese launched a dozen high-intensity white flares. The entire hill seemed to burst into light. It blinded everyone, except the attackers who knew they had to shield their eyes. It had the same effect as darkness. For a few minutes, it took away the defenders' sight. By the time they could react, a flanking wave swept upto the crest and took the position. As they raised the triangular yellow flag to signal the capture of Jail Hill, cheering broke out, in Punjabi, in Tamil, in Bengali, and in Japanese.

At the Garrison Hill HQ, there was pandemonium. Colonel Richards, the CO of the Kohima garrison, had been up most of the night. His voice was hoarse, his eyes blood-shot.

'Brigadier Whyte, I'm up to my eyeballs right now. Both Detail Hill and Jail Hill are under attack and I don't have the time to sit and chat with you, begging your pardon, Sir.'

Whyte, seated across the table, carried on tamping tobacco into his pipe, his movements precise, contained, economical. Everything about him was neat, from the knife crease in his uniform to the careful centre parting in his Brylcreemed ginger hair. A silk regimental scarf and shiny oxfords completed the look. Now, he looked up. Richards felt his heart squeeze. The man's blue-grey eyes had all the warmth of an arctic icefield in December. His eyelashes, a pale ginger, gave his eyes a pallid, naked look. When he spoke, his voice was low, unhurried.

'Quite, Colonel. But I'm afraid you will have to make some time to debrief me. I must know the details of this so-called attack. If you...'

He was interrupted by a soldier rushing in, carrying a wireless message. Richards' face went pale when he read it. 'There's no response from our Company at Jail Hill. Seems like they've been overrun. My god, what are we...'

Brigadier Whyte's voice was sharp as a cut-throat razor on a cold winter morning. 'Colonel! Deep breath. What is the strength of the Japanese force?'

'It's certainly more than a regiment — contrary to what your intelligence bods had told us.' Richards' voice was shaking, livid with indignation. Whyte pinched the bridge of his nose. He could feel one of his headaches starting. Very patiently, as if talking to a child, he spoke gently.

'And the intelligence was right. It can't be the main Japanese force. They are days from here, probably still muddling around somewhere in the Naga hills. The last we heard, some of them are headed for Imphal. This is probably a diversionary attack. It can't possibly be anything stronger than a regiment.'

The door flew open. Another wireless message had come in. Richards jumped up from his chair, overturning it. He grabbed the message, his mouth tightening as the news sunk in.

'A bloody regiment, eh? A Somerset rifles unit has just spotted a full brigade at Detail Hill. As usual, your intelligence spooks have got it arse backwards!'

Whyte's voice was naturally low from a lifetime of clandestine meetings in small bars, echoing railway stations, dark street corners. Now he dropped it by an octave, spoke in a whisper almost.

'Colonel, I handle intel at a level that is so stratospheric, it will make your silly little head spin. Your pay grade doesn't entitle you to question me. Do. You. Understand?'

Richards opened and then closed his mouth, a guppy starved for air. The phone rang shrilly. He lunged for it. His response was a mix of *yessirs* and *rightsirs.* He looked up to see Whyte light his pipe. Dammit, why couldn't the man step outside instead of adding to the fug in the room?

'That was Divison HQ, Sir, Major General Ward.'

Richards smoothened out the large map on his desk. His hands were trembling.

'Division says that the Japs have launched a massive strike against Imphal.'

'Expected.'

'They may be in fact also trying to capture Kohima.'

He rubbed his face tiredly.

'This is nothing more than a piddly little garrison town. Why in hell do they want it?'

Whyte frowned, spun the map towards himself.

Why indeed.

The dead and wounded started pouring into the field dressing station on mule back and stretchers. The sun was barely up and they came out of the mist like a procession from some Biblical holocaust. One came, then another and another…an endless line of suffering, young bodies, broken, ruined. On the far side of the field, they started to lay down the bodies of the ones who had not made it. Martyrs, they would be called. They would be cremated or buried, according to their gods. The bodies could not be sent home, to wives and mothers and chidren, for a last look, a farewell, a closure. For they had been branded traitors, exiles, men without a country. Most were mangled like they'd been fed to a giant meat grinder. Aditi felt tears pouring down, soaking her surgical mask. The sheer numbers were numbing. Her nerve endings felt sutured, like her brain. Even the doctors, both Indian and Japanese, looked helpless. They had so little to treat these men with. They needed a fully equipped hospital. The nearest field hospital was near Tantabin and the closest hospital was in Rangoon, 627 miles away. She just kept on doing what she could, patching up torn and bleeding flesh and injecting morphine to help them bear the unbearable. The worst were the burn victims. They needed to be isolated but out here in the forest, the infection would take them the fastest. She worked like a mad woman, her hands slippery with blood, till Meenakshi pulled her away, on the point of collapse. She made her sit, drink some over-sweetened tea. But Aditi threw it up almost instantly.

'Are you okay?'

'I keep thinking, what if the next man I turn over is Deb. Oh, Meena, I'm so afraid.'

'Come on, buck up, Aditi Sen. You're a warrior, remember? You'll paralyse yourself thinking that. And stop weeping like a kitten. The men need you to be strong. They need to see your face and get the conviction that they will make it.'

'And it will be a lie.'

'If it has to be.'

Brigadier Whyte stared at the map, his flint-coloured eyes like needles. General Mataguchi was nobody's fool. Why would he waste any resources on some irrelevant little outpost? Richards, idiot that he was, had a point. Why attack it in strength? Whyte walked around the table, trying to see beyond the obvious, the familiar. As he reached the other side of the table, Richards hurriedly moving out of the way of this man with the frozen eyes, his perspective changed. Then like a jigsaw puzzle falling suddenly into place, like cloud patterns in the sky suddenly resolving themselves into giant elephants and bears, the pieces made a pattern. Hills on the map, shown as flat lines, suddenly reared up in his mind's eye and became high towering slopes. Valleys fell away to the thin spider lines of rivers. Whyte frowned. So that's why the Japs were in Kohima. It was the highest point, commanding the countryside around. His finger, neatly manicured, pink around the cuticles, stabbed the map. With Kohima captured, they could move against Dimapur, capturing the massive supply depot there. But so what? What was so important about capturing a few stores and driving the British line back a few miles, even a hundred miles? Why commit so many forces when there were easier routes into India? No, there had to be something more. He pinched the bridge of his nose, trying to keep the shooting pain at bay. Then, his eyes fell on the innocent, inconspicuous black line, snaking from Kohima to Dimapur and beyond into the plains of Assam. *What if?* No, it couldn't be. He had sent the reports himself — Bose and the INA are supporting the Japanese advance. But what if it was the other way around? What if the Japanese Army was *supporting* the INA? From Dimapur, the way to Bengal lay open. Bose and his INA renegades could then pour into India. The Japs were opening a doorway for Bose. *That was their main mission!*

Whyte slammed his fist on the map, making Richards jump in alarm. Way to the south, the entire British 18th Division was waiting for the Japs at the Shenam Pass, the easiest and the fastest route into the plains. The route from where everyone expected them to come. The route fed to him by his spies. And all along...the Japs had taken the toughest route and turned up where they were least expected. The attack on Imphal, 86 miles away, was a ruse. The prize was actually Kohima.

Whyte sucked on his pipe furiously as he realised the extent of Mataguchi's deception. Should he tell Richards? No, the man was a dithering bundle of nerves. He had to speak to Calcutta. He swept out of the door as the radios crackled and signallers rushed in with more bad news. He heard Richards shout, his voice cracking, 'Stand fast, lad...' Poor man, poor, frightened man, trying desperately to play soldier. But, war was a giant chess game. Mataguchi had just executed a very clever move. And, if Whyte didn't counter, it could mean the end of the game.

On his way out, he leaned in close to the duty sergeant.

'Keep me informed, Sergeant.' The man had become his creature. He would keep him closely updated on every changing situation. He wanted a transfer to Calcutta. Something to do with a native girl.

'Especially on the situation in Detail Hill.'

The large stretches of open ground provided absolutely no cover for a force coming uphill. The soldiers remembered what Pandey ji had dinned into them — when you get to a new position, dig. And when you dig, throw the earth behind you, then throw the dirt in front of you, because that way you won't be silhouetted. But it wasn't working now. They had launched two assaults on Detail Hill already but the Somerset Rifles were dug into even stronger fortified positions. Every time they charged, the Vickers and Brownings chopped through their ranks. Every yard gained was paid in blood. And now, the mountain artillery guns had opened up, raining red hot shrapnel that could dismember bodies, deafening them with their deep, bone rattling thumps, making the ground tremble, till their heads were ready to burst. Even Nishonko was appalled. He was a veteran of many raids and skirmishes but they had all been guerilla warfare; fast, surgical strikes like leopard attacks. This was different. This was an earth-shaking, head-on ramming of two bull elephants. His men were exhausted. Morning had broken, the sun beginning to come up. He didn't know how long they would be able to cling to this perilously slim outcrop of rock for protection. Nawaz, his face blackened, a deep bleeding gash running across his cheek, looked back, crouching desperately.

'This is insane, Major. Why doesn't Brigadier Saito do something?'

Nishonko ducked as the earth to their right exploded, showering them with rocks, clanging on their helmets. Their radio man crawled forward on his belly, handed Nishonko the receiver. He listened, hand clamped on the other ear, nodding his head silently, the barrage roaring around him.

'Okay, Nawaz, here they come. Brigadier Saito heard you.'

Minutes later, the Japanese 75 mm mountain guns boomed out. As their armageddon roar filled the dawn sky, Nishonko felt himself getting hard. The full-throated raw power of the barrage made his blood sing. The sun was up by the time the guns fell silent but it shone pale, like the winter sun, through the thick pall of smoke that blanketed the whole hill. This was the time to move. A hundred yards ahead, through the thick blanket of smoke, Nishonko could make out, through his binoculars, what looked like barracks. Maybe it housed reinforcements, maybe guns or stores.

'Nawaz, get the men ready. We're going to take those barracks.'

'Sir, shouldn't we inform Brigadier Saito and HQ before we go in?'

'If we have to go around informing everyone every time we want to attack, we will be sitting on our asses, getting fat. Soon the smoke will clear and the opportunity will be lost.'

Nawaz started to point out the flaws in the plan, then thought the better of it. Nishonko had been behaving rather strangely lately, flaring up at small things, not brooking argument or discussion.

'Bring your sections here and form up behind me. And stay off the command channel.'

'Sir but that's ...!'

Nishonko turned slowly to look at Nawaz. His voice was silky. 'Have the big guns turned you deaf, Captain? Did you not hear my orders?'

Nawaz turned red. He looked at the open ground ahead. If the British artillery opened up again, they would be sitting ducks. But he had been a soldier too long.

'Yes, Sir!'

'Unit 1 and 2, split up to the left and right. Captain Hussein, set up all the Brens and light up the target on my command! The rest of you, follow me.'

He ran, dodging from side to side, zig and zag. A vicious burst of gunfire kicked up the dirt near his boots. With a whoosh that emptied the air from his lungs, he threw himself down behind a rock. They had only gained a few yards. But he had managed to distract them. The Somerset Rifles were looking straight ahead, trying to see through the fug. They had not spotted the units he had sent to flank them. Now, these men were upon them before they could react. Nishonko made for the barracks at a run. No mercy now! He chucked a handful of grenades through an open window of the barracks, hearing them rattle on the floor. Someone shouted in the room. There was thunder and glass as the windows blew outward. Men were screaming and groaning inside the barracks. Nawaz came charging out of the mist with his men. More grenades went sailing in through the windows and the room erupted in white flame. Ears ringing, Nishonko charged towards the door. Two men came out staggering, both covering their bleeding eyes. Nishonko shot them from such close range, the flame from his gun's muzzle scorched their chests. They were flung backwards onto two others who were crawling out. He turned his gun on them but before he could shoot, more of his men reached the spot and savagely bayoneted them. But something was wrong. Something was off. He charged into the room. Bilious smoke blanketed the place. Through the haze, he made out shapes. Then he realised they were beds. It was a fucking field hospital. Then he realised what had been wrong. The men staggering out, the men they had slaughtered, were all wounded, bandaged. As he stumbled through the roiling yellow smoke, he saw a makeshift OT, an upturned IV stand, a man, his bare legs bleeding, shattered, as he pulled himself along the ground, leaving a slick of red. A man wearing the fatigues of a doctor loomed up, waving a revolver in his hand. Training took over from the horror and he fired at the same time as the young doctor. A bullet glanced off the rim of Nishonko's helmet, jerking his head back, making him lose his balance. He slipped but kept his trigger finger pressed as he went down. The doctor's body twitched and convulsed as he was hit and he was dead before he hit the floor. Nishonko too was sprawled on the floor, his legs rubbery, his skin crawling with horror. Then through the mist, another shape loomed. It was a very young man, with the single star of a Lieutenant, very pink, obviously new to the tropics, his thin blond hair plastered to his skull. He was pointing the dark hole of a Sten gun at him. Again, the training kicked in. Nishonko drew his knife and held it out, his arm rigid, like a spear head. And in the same movement, he pulled the barrel of the callow lieutenant's gun towards him — so violently, the man was thrown off balance. The

Englishman fell on the knife, and his weight drove the knife deep into his belly, all the way up to the hilt. His expression was one of almost comical surprise. Up close, he smelt of mint and, surprisingly, eau de cologne. Then, he screamed, spraying Nishonko's face with blood flecked spittle. Nishonko twisted his arm. The man made a funny gurgling noise. Nishonko's elbow became slick with crimson. The man collapsed on him, his head resting on Nishonko's shoulder, twitching, gasping — and then he was still. Nishonko pushed at him frantically, trying to push the dead weight off his chest, trying to push away the horror, suffocating, panic stricken. The man rolled off finally, a rag doll. Nishonko scrambled away, leaving his knife sticking to the man's chest. He heard a noise and spun around. Another dark shape! He scrabbled at his revolver. Kill! Kill!

'It's me, Sir!' Nawaz's voice cut through the haze. He stared at Nishonko, at his arm masked in blood, at the wild eyes.

'My god, are you hit, Sir?'

Nishonko touched himself, the soaked shirt, his face.

'I'm okay.'

'We got them all.'

'They were wounded. It's a goddamn field hospital, Captain.'

'Yes, Sir but we got the guns, all the postions. Your gamble paid off, Sir.'

'Set up a perimeter. They may strike back.' Nishonko's voice was shaking.

'I don't think so, Sir, the survivors disappeared over the hill. They were running like they wanted to reach London!'

Nawaz smiled. But Nishonko's eyes were still haunted.

'He was a doctor. He went to shoot me. I had to kill him.'

'Yes, Major, just take it easy now. Easy there.'

Nishonko sank onto a shattered iron bed, its back broken. Something felt cracked inside him also, making his bones feel thin, his teeth like glass. It had been so close.

Whyte gunned the engine as he roared up the rough track leading to the bungalow. It was located on the edge of the hill and was the guesthouse for men who had business in this far corner of the mighty British Empire. It was a modest structure, with a wide open verandah running all around it, and screens on the doors and windows to keep out insects and other nocturnal predators. Cherry trees bloomed along the edges of the courtyard but Whyte had no eyes for such fragile, ephemeral beauty. His mind chopped through options, like a cleaver through meat, trying to find answers to the present threat. The surprise Jap attack meant that his intelligence apparatus had failed. Gaffar was just one cog in the wheel but he was his cog and he had failed. As he came striding up the stairs, he saw Goopta waiting patiently, his hands in his lap, clutching a manila envelope, perched in one of the easy chairs. A sudden image of whipping the man's fat, little naked body with a riding crop, flaying it open, flashed with enormous lucidity through his mind. He shook his head, trying to clear it. Goopta scrambled out of the chair, waddled towards him, his feet flat like a penguin's.

'Gaffar sent the wrong information.' Whyte's voice was curiously devoid of all inflection, not even the hint of an accusation, merely a flat announcement of a fact, like reading a weather report. Goopta stumbled to a halt, almost falling. His face turned red, then pale. The khansama who looked after the bungalow came hurrying out, offering his hospitality.

'Laymonsherbut, Sir? Geentoni? Kuppacha?'

It took Whyte a couple of seconds to decipher what the man was saying. He didn't want the lemon sherbet or the cup of tea. In fact, he was dying to have a drink but he needed to have a clear head. He waved the man away, strode inside. It was a disaster. Unless, of course, he found a way to turn the whole situation to his advantage, as he had done so many times before in his cat and mouse career. He needed to pull off an intelligence coup to counter this. The Japanese Army had not missed a single beat so far. Kohima would fall — he was convinced about it. But since he had figured out what the INA was trying to do, or he thought he had, he would try and use it. He would need eyes on the ground, real time, seat of the pants intelligence straight from the battlefield. Goopta came up, scuttling like a crab, trying to hush the sound of his shoes clipclopping on the wooden plank floor. Whyte flopped down on an armchair, lumpy through infrequent use, and lit a cigarette. He pinched the space between his eyebrows, an unconscious, automatic gesture, looking for loopholes. Goopta stood, shifting his weight from foot to foot, a schoolboy in front of a dreaded taskmaster.

'I don't think Gaffar has deliberately...'

A languid wave of the wrist silenced him. Very faint, almost like the buzzing of a wasp, the faraway sound of the battle, came through the forest. 'It doesn't matter now whether he's turned, become a double agent or just made a colossal balls up. Either way, we're in a spot. That small force we were expecting is at least a fuckin' division of 10,000. In a couple of days, it'll overrun this garrison. Then that precious file you carry around won't be worth a wart on your flabby black arse!'

Goopta clutched the loosely bound, buff-coloured manila file to his chest. It was the ticket to his dreams. It was a contract for the Naga Hills' teak and sal forests. The Brigadier had used his contacts to lean on the district collector to give him sole logging rights — if Goopta got him what he wanted. It was his pay-off for helping Whyte. And whether the British stayed in India or not, he would be assured of untold wealth. And that would guarantee his entry into the Congress, making him one of the new masters of India. This file was the key to a future this white maggot could not even dream of. But, if the Japanese Army occupied this area, that was the end of his timber!

'The irony is, the real danger may not be the Japs at all. The real nigger in the woodpile, as our American cousins would put it, could be the INA.'

'But Whyte sahab, what you fear from those rabbles and riff-raffs? They are small in numbers. Ingrej raja, your English king, has bahut paltan to crush this ragtag fauj.' Goopta's voice was shrill with indignation, his hard-learnt English deserting him in this moment of crisis.

'I think all of us have made the mistake of underestimating them.' Whyte stared through the window at the distant hills where men were dying to defend their many causes. 'The idea behind this Fauj is symbolic. As your Gandhi has demonstrated, it is nearly impossible to defeat a symbol. We've sent more than 3,00,000 of our best men overseas. We're running on empty. We don't have the forces to defend this country. At this moment, if it stands up to support the *idea* of these rabbles, as you call them, what they stand for...' Whyte shook his head. 'Bose may turn out to be a much worthier adversary than we had suspected. Who knows, ultimately we just may have to negotiate with him rather than your khadiwallas.'

Goopta choked. *Here he was,* chatoing *every* gaand, *licking this white hijra's ass to be in the good books of the khadi brigade and this, this abominable man who looked like he had crawled out of a grave, was actually saying that Netaji — impossible to do business with — was saying Netaji might just scuttle all his plans?*

'That must not happen, Whyte sahab. What you are saying?! How to stop them please?'

Whyte looked at him, nodded. 'Khansama! Some tea, please. Now, we need to go about this differently. Sit, Goopta, sit.' His tone was almost gentle.

'What we must do is find others to do our bidding. We will ask Richards to give us a list of all the Indian soldiers they capture alive. You will help me interrogate them. You will find their weak spots, their Achilles heels. And then we will make them our creatures. Will you help me do that, Goopta?'

Goopta, in a swift about turn, almost fell to his knees to express his gratitude to this man with the queer orange lashes and orange eyebrows and the coldest eyes he had ever seen, the one man who could perhaps turn the tide.

Gaffar hurried with a glass of butter milk towards one of the tents. It had been a really long, tedious journey from Rangoon to the railhead and then up these infernal roads. But he was finally here, in the thick of things, close to the high command, witness to everything. He had a slight smile on his face as he ran up to the entrance. It would be gold, the stuff he would supply now. Up till now, it had all been a little conjecture, overheard snippets, a file left carelessly around, a rumour of a rumour passed on by a secretary. He had felt a little under-appreciated, given the risks he was constantly taking. But now, now he woud come into his own. That Goopta, Omar bhai, and whoever their shadow masters were, they would all understand Gaffar Khan's true worth.

But as he reached the entrance, he was stopped by the guards outside. They were Japanese, hard-faced, sallow men. The man on the left, a patch covering his eye, gestured to him to hand over the tray.

'But Netaji has asked for me. You must let me through.'

The Japanese guards shook their heads, jabbered something to each other — a singularly unattractive language, nothing like the melodious cadences of his native Urdu — and again demanded the tray. Snatches of conversation drifted out to him from inside, the crackle of radio communication, a buzz in the air. He pushed again but this time, their looks turned ugly. He knew they had respect issues. He backed off, the butter milk spilling. Haramzada.

Inside, the Army top brass were briefing Netaji. Small flags in different colours dotted the large-scale maps, looking pretty, like a nice game.

'We have the British on the back foot. The idea is to take the ridge, pin the buggers down.'

'We then cut off their supply lines, starve them.'

'We've code-named it "Rolling Thunder".'

'Good, I like it.' Netaji nodded, then bent over the map. 'Maybe, you should leave them a bolt hole. You know what they say about cornered rats. Give them space to run, and they will run. Cut off their escape route and they could just dig in and wait for reinforcements.'

'It will take them time to bring up reinforcements through this jungle terrain. By then, it will be too late. We'll have broken through.'

'I sincerely hope you are right.'

It was early evening by the time Watanabe's regiment joined the main force at Detail Hill. Not a man in Debraj's battalion had known what it would be like to face such unrelenting bombardment, hour after hour. Under shell fire for the first time in their young lives, they cowered, blinded by the stinging smoke and deafened by the concussion of the blasts. The air, already thin in these high altitudes, was sizzling with acrid fumes, difficult to breathe, hurting their chests as they laboured to suck in air on the steep slopes. They came over a rise and staggered to a halt. In front of them stretched a wasteland, a scene from hell. Blasted earth, shattered trees, clawing at the sky, twisted iron and steel sticking out like spines from the bubbling pools of fire. The trench in front of them had taken a direct hit. As they stumbled forward, their feet unsteady, they saw men sitting in the trench, their shoulders slumped. For a moment, they thought that the men were just resting. Then they understood. They had died where they sat. It felt as if giant boots had slammed down to crush them like ants. Wails and cries of the wounded filled the air.

Debraj thought the few weeks of combat had toughened him but as he walked towards the blackened still-smoking trench, he gagged. The bodies were mangled and fused with the mud. And then, to his horror, he recognised a face. It was Mohan Singh. He sat, leaning against a rock, in profile, staring straight ahead, his bearded jaw jutting out, his face and body intact.

'Mohan Singh, hey man...'

But as Debraj stepped forward, he saw, his stomach clenching, that the entire right side of the man's face had been vaporised. Something snapped inside his brain.

Fucking hell, it doesn't matter how good you are or how rich or how lucky in love, I'm going to die in this hell hole. I'll never make it back. What the hell am I doing here in this godforsaken place?

The taste of bitter bile flooded his mouth. A sob bubbled up.

Let someone else fight this damn war. I need to take Aditi and get the hell out. GET OUT!

'Sorry, Sir.'

He spun around. His radio man was staring at him. Had he spoken aloud?

'Sir, Brigadier Saito wants you to join him in the HQ tent right away.'

The field station took the brunt of the wounded. They had set up in a village school, its roof still intact. Tents were being pitched in an adjoining field, where children even the previous week had played football and hopscotch on the dusty ground. The lines of their carefree games, drawn with brick on the hard ground, were obliterated under the hoof marks of the mules bringing in the battle torn survivors. A field generator provided power, hiccupping occasionally, the belching smoke making the eyes water. The work carried on late into the night, by the flickering light.

Aditi and Meenakshi, exhausted, slept on an empty hospital cot, in a bare room piled with boxes. It had been the school staffroom and library and office rolled into one, housing the two teachers who came on bicycles twice a week to teach the children of the nearby villages the mysteries of History and Arithmetic. They lay curled up, their arms outflung in the abandon of utter exhaustion. Their hips touched, their breath mingled, as if both sought the warmth of the other and the comfort of knowing the person next to them was alive. Aditi's eyes had deep blue shadows underneath, the lids thin and transparent. Meenakshi slept with her mouth open, a sibilant snore escaping her full lips now and then. They would have slept like that if the distant sound of thunder had not woken them. Aditi stirred, a twitch in the fingers, as if coming back from some unfathomable depth. When she opened her eyes, the lids heavy, she looked confused, not sure where she was. Meenakshi sat up, knuckling her eyes, yawning prodigiously. She was like a cat waking up, stretching, flexing her spine.

'There's a storm coming. I hope they get the tents up in time.' Aditi's voice was sluggish with sleep. Meenakshi scratched her stomach.

'It isn't a storm, my pet.'

Aditi listened. It wasn't intermittent, the thunder. The sound was a continuous growl. Slowly, it dawned on her. It was the roar of big mountain guns, the distant drone of planes, the muffled boom of mortars.

'It's very close,' she whispered.

Meenakshi closed her eyes. 'Yes, get some rest. Tomorrow will bring many more wounded men.'

Aditi lay back but sleep wouldn't come. Her mind whirled with thoughts. Where was Deb? She wanted to talk to him so badly, it was like her lips would explode. What would she tell him if she met him? That she was terrified? That she was counting each day now, her heart hammering with each passing day? That she was torn between hope and guilt? She touched her stomach gingerly, the hard muscle, the concave dip.

'Meena?'

'Hmm...?'

'Are you awake?'

'That's the stupidest question I have heard the whole day. What is it?'

'Can you…you know…' She paused, the words trembling at the edge of her throat, tumbling into her mouth, filling her cheeks, pushing against her lips. She knew if she said it, it would be real.

'I haven't been…'

The door to the storeroom crashed open. A senior nurse poked her head in.

'Come on, you two, move your butts now. Aditi, to surgery. Meenakshi in Emergency. Come on, come on, on your feet.'

They tumbled out of the cot, straightening their uniforms, clipping on their caps, the hair all mussed up, combed through with fingers. As they hurried out, Meenakshi turned to Aditi.

'What were you saying?'

'Later. It can wait.'

When Debraj entered Saito's tent, he immediately knew something was wrong. Nishonko was standing glowering, his mouth set mutinously. Colonel Watanabe and Colonel Akira stood to one side, their gazes lowered, their faces wooden, expressionless. Saito was pacing back and forth, his face grim in the dim light of the field lamps.

'Inexcusable, Major. You had no cover. A shelling would have wiped out half your men. So would an air strike. What the hell were you thinking of?'

Debraj had never heard Saito raise his voice like this. He started to back out.

'Major Mookerji, stay. I would be obliged if you also paid attention to this.'

'Yes, Sir.'

'I saw the opportunity and acted, Brigadier. There was no time to clear the attack with you. I thought the place was a storehouse.' Nishonko was defiant.

'Instead, it turned out to be a hospital. You put the life of your men at risk unnecessarily. And we need every man for the job ahead!'

'Risk, Brigadier, is how we win battles. You said so yourself.' Nishonko's tone was stony, controlled.

'HQ needs to know exactly what each unit is up to ALL THE TIME! That's the way we win battles. If every commander decides to act on his own, there would be chaos.'

Nishonko's fingers clenched and unclenched.

'HQ means you, doesn't it, Saito? You're pissed off that I defied your authority.'

Colonel Watanabe took a step forward, his face darkening.

'Watanabe!' Saito's tone was curt. Watanabe backed down.

Saito sighed. 'Nishonko, please, this is not personal. I am the division commander.'

'The INA doesn't need to take orders from you!' Nishonko's tone was clipped.

'Er...actually we do, Major Mitro.' Debraj intervened. This was going too far. 'We have been placed under Brigadier Saito's command for this op. Netaji's orders.'

Nishonko's face turned red.

'And you, of course, are a good boy who always follows Netaji's orders.'

'Actually, I do. That's the only way this is going to work. We, the INA and the Japanese, we have to work together.'

There was a long pause, pregnant, the tension in the tent palpable. Then Nishonko smiled. A cold smile, a rictus, a grimace almost.

'Of course, just like brothers. Indo-Japan bhai bhai, eh?'

'Yes, brothers in arms, on the same side.'

Nishonko looked at both of them, almost blank, as if he were thinking of something else. Then, his eyes focused. He clapped Debraj on the shoulder.

'Yup, on the same side. You said it, Major.' He bowed to Saito, a little mocking but not overtly so.

'My apologies, Brigadier, for going off the deep end. The pressures of battle, you know. Won't happen again.'

Saito shrugged. He was glad that they had sorted that out but still felt some unease. But he played along, bowing back with punctilious formality.

'How about some ocha, that rather fine Japanese green tea, to soothe all our unquiet minds? Daiki, will you do the honours?'

'Hai!'

'Now the reason I called you was to figure out a way around the hill.'

The boy was 12 years old. He came out of the forest, tentatively, a wiry child with a mop of unruly hair. Tangshang Suckhrie. He was like some forest creature, curious but skittish, frightened easily. He too had experienced the thunder of the barrage for the first time in his brief life. His village, tucked away in a small valley to the right of Detail Hill, had never seen anything like it before. The sky had lit up in the middle of the night, fire-red, and the bone-shaking rumble had sent the elders rushing to their shrines, to placate the dragon that had woken up, as prophesied by the shamans. They had barred their windows, praying in the darkness for the monstrous bellowing to stop. Tangshang, however, was driven by the insatiable curiosity of all boys of 12. When the morning brought silence, he and two of his cousins slipped away, to find the nature of this beast. Instead, they found the killing fields, and Japanese soldiers, hunched in trenches, their faces black, carved into stone by exhaustion. Tangshang observed them from the cover of the forest, fascinated by their eyes, so like his own. The village had spoken of them, these men from across the seas who had come to set India free, who were fighting against the hated British. He saw their parched lips, their fierce defence of the conquered patch of barren ground. So he and his cousins carried water to them. When they appeared, seemingly out of the very ground, one soldier, more shaken than the others, brought up his gun but another knocked the barrel away. 'They are children, Hasegawa.'

The soldiers drank noisily, their Adam's apples bobbing with the greediness with which they slaked their thirst and sent the boys for more. It was already afternoon and they shared their meagre rations with the three; not that Tangshang fancied the dried kelp or the smelly rice balls much but his mother had drilled it into him never to dishonour food offered in friendship. One soldier, seeing one of the boys eyeing a fallen helmet, chucked it at him. The boy wore the outsize helmet with glee, treasuring it for years to come, proudly telling all who would hear, of the impassive men who fought the battle for Detail Hill. Tangshang picked up spent bullet shells, water flasks, the twisted pin of a grenade, anything they could lay their small hands on, as souvenirs. Through some rudimentary sign language, they communicated.

Saito was marking positions on the map — imperial red for the Japanese and royal blue for the British. Despite two nights of harrowing combat, the reds on the map were just pinpricks compared to the large swathes of blue.

'Slow slow,' muttered Saito.

Debraj looked up. 'Well, two nights ago, it was all blue. Now here, it looks like they are retreating. The red stretches are growing. This bit, it's the last obstacle to taking the hill. The scouts say it's a system of trenches.'

'It's code-named Charing Cross according to one of the captured British officers.'

'Ask him what it means.'

'He swears he doesn't know.'

'I'm sure he can be persuaded.' Nishonko, who had been standing in the periphery, in the shadows, spoke up.

'Well, the Kempeitai questioned him. By now, he must have spilled his guts.' Colonel Akira was grim.

Nishonko nodded. No one there needed to be reminded of the secret police's ability to extract information.

'Charing Cross. Why Charing Cross?' Debraj scratched the bristle on his cheeks.

'Maybe, the trenches are in the shape of a cross,' Nishonko volunteered.

'No, no, too obvious. The British are much more subtle than that.' Debraj's tone was matter of fact but Nishonko stiffened. He retreated once more into the shadows, the humiliation he felt quickly masked.

'Cross, boss, toss, loss...maybe it's some Cockney rhyming slang.' Debraj was too caught up in breaking the code to notice Nishonko's reaction.

'It's near Trafalgar Square, right? Maybe, it has to do with a square formation.' Saito too was caught up in unravelling the mystery.

'Well, it's also a Tube station... Hello, what have we here?'

Three boys in village clothes, their eyes darting inquisitively around, were led in by a Japanese sergeant and one of the Naga guides. 'These boys helping, bring water,' he said in guttural Japanese.

Saito frowned. Why the hell had they got kids here? But before he could dismiss them, Debraj hunkered down face-to-face with them and greeted them. 'What's your name, mister?' The Naga guide translated.

'Tangshang Suokhrie.'

'Arre, what a big name. Are you badass warrior, Tangshang?'

The boy giggled.

'And what is this secret you want to tell us?' Debraj gently put his hand on the boy's thin shoulder, making contact. Tangshang spoke in rapid fire local dialect. The Naga guide translated. None of the Japanese had a clue what he was saying but the growing grin on Debraj's face made them also smile. Finally, Debraj sat back on his haunches and slapped his thigh.

'Told you, it was about the Tube.'

Saito looked flabbergasted. Nishonko explained, with a rare smile.

'The boys are saying that there's a secret network of underground tunnels, part of an ancient route, all the way up the hill. The British are holed up in them, ready to bite us, the moment we overrun their positions. It's a trap, waiting to be sprung.'

Saito grinned savagely. 'Can the boys show us the positions of these tunnels on the map?'

Debraj pulled out the heavy grease pencil they all kept in their breast pockets and gave it to the boy. With great gusto and excitement, arguing amongst themselves, the boys drew thick lines on the map. And an hour later, Saito's specially designed 'quartet' — a lethal artillery combination of two heavy 75mm and two lighter 37mm guns — opened up, precision bombarding the tunnels. The deep thumps of the 75s, mingled with the screeching whines of the 37s, went echoing across the pine forests and highlands, sending fresh waves of terror through the villagers' hearts. After the bombardment, which actually lasted mere minutes, the infantry went in. Japanese soldiers could move faster on their bellies than anyone else Debraj had seen. Two companies crawled up the side of the hill, up to the entrance of the tunnels. Before the dazed survivors of the Somerset Rifles, staggering out of the blasted ruins could react, a wave of Japanese led by Lieutenant Colonel Katsumi, Saito's firebrand commander, was on them, going through them like a tsunami, stabbing, shooting, beheading every enemy soldier they encountered. It was pure slaughter, an orgy of killing. Face masked with blood, Katsumi raised the yellow flag of victory. Detail Hill was theirs.

Back in the command tent, far from the brutal field of dead, Saito pinned a fresh red flag on the map. He was smiling, pleased as he turned to Debraj. 'We've done it!'

'You're too fucking good, Brigadier!'

'You are too kind, Major Mookerji.'

'No, you fucking well are.'

'Well, if you insist — I fickin well am!' Some English expressions were beyond Saito's powers of enunciation.

'Fickin yay!'

'Fickin yay!'

Hooting with laughter, caught up in the euphoria of victory, they grappled good naturedly. Even the normally reticent Japanese commanders were smiling broadly, shaking each other's hands. Nishonko watched them all, detached, alone. Their horseplay was broken when Major Daiki coughed politely. Saito broke off, smoothening out his uniform.

'The next phase is to outflank the British garrison at Kohima and cut the road from Kohima to Dimapur at this point. Colonel Akira's battalion will undertake this.'

'Hai!'

'Radio me when you're commanding that road. Base will be at Kigwema village for the duration of the siege. Major Mookerji and Major Mitro, come with me. Long Live the Emperor.'

'Jai Hind!' Nishonko said, a little too loudly.

Meenakshi poked her head into the tent.

'You coming? Dinner's up.'

Aditi was curled up on her sleeping mat, her back to Meenakshi, the little knobby bones running along the spine, like prayer beads.

She had lost a lot of weight lately. She wasn't eating well at all. Not that anyone could blame her. The food was just awful, some slop with everything thrown in and none of the spicy masala they were used to. But it kept you going and Meenakshi wasn't a fussy eater. Her time with the nuns had taught her hard life lessons — eat whatever's put in front of you. You never know when you'll eat again or what you'll get to eat.

'Come on, Aditi, come and have something.'

A small whimper. 'I don't want to.'

'Don't be such a crybaby. You need to eat.' Meenakshi crawled into the tent and pulled at Aditi, then frowned. Aditi's skin was hot and clammy at the same time.

'Don't tell me you have a fever. Let me see.'

'No, I'm okay. Don't worry.'

She turned Aditi towards her. Aditi was sweating, pale. She tried to sit up but started to retch almost immediately. She threw up in a small enamel bowl she had kept on the side, painfully heaving.

'How long has this been going on? You need to take something.'

'Meena, don't fuss. Seriously, it's just that the food is not agreeing with me. They'll just send me back to Rangoon for nothing. I just need to get used to it. I'm a soldier, Meena, I want to…' The rest of what she was going to say was drowned in another bout of dry retching. Meenakshi rubbed her back, then gave her some water. She looked at Aditi, a sudden thought making her frown.

'You're not…?'

Aditi stared back at her, her eyes very huge in her face. She shook her head wordlessly.

'Are you…?'

A small sob from Aditi. 'I don't know, oh god, what will I do? I don't know.'

Meenakshi put her arms round Aditi, hugged her, shush shush. When she calmed down, her breath even, Meenakshi sat back.

'Look at me, no, look at me. You have to find out if it's true, deal with it.'

A flash of the old temper sparked in Aditi's eyes. 'I am dealing with it. I'm puking my guts out but I haven't let it affect my work. It could be just a bug. Or malaria. I need to take some medicines and just hang on until we get to Assam. We are days away from breaking through. I can't now hold everyone up and create a fuss.'

'Hey, if you are actually…'

Aditi clapped her hand on Meenakshi's lips, shutting her up.

'Don't say it, don't say it. You'll make it come true.'

'Silly girl. But, don't you want it to be true?'

'Wrong time, wrong place.' Aditi shivered. 'Please don't talk about this with anyone, promise me.'

'Okay, I promise. If you are sure, when you are sure, there are ways to take care of the problem, you know.'

Aditi shook her head, sudden tears spilling out. 'No, no, I couldn't. How could I face him later? Oh, Meena, I miss him so much. And Chhoto mashi. She would know what to do. I hate this war. I hate this food and the blood and… you know, the smell of it can never be washed away. It clings to your clothes and hair, at night, till you think you will never again be able to breathe without the reminder of the slop pails and the blood-stained bandages and that sweet rotten smell of gangrene. Am I a coward, Meena? Am I?'

Meenakshi looked at her, then got up.

'I think you are just hungry and tired and you need to get some decent food inside you and then the world will look a whole lot different. And where's your comb? And your kajal? Come on, let's get you looking beautiful — you know, just in case Major Mookerji happens to drop in on us girls.'

Aditi smiled, a wan smile but a smile. What on earth would she have done without Meena?

Debraj stretched out under the camouflage net shelter, rolling a cigarette with satisfaction. That was the best meal he'd had since they started from the Chindwin River. Instead of the rice, dal and fish paste that was their staple diet, they had been given actual meat stew scooped out of tins, with hot chapatis, followed by tinned peaches and condensed milk, all taken from the captured British stores. He hoped to make the memory last. Thousands of hungry soldiers had wiped out the stocks in just one meal. The next one would depend on when they managed to capture another store like this. He lit up, taking a deep drag. His thoughts strayed to Aditi. Where was she?

Maybe Tantabin, that was the closest field hospital, maybe not. Was she well? Was she thinking about him? There was no way he could meet her, until he was wounded. Ironical. But if they managed to keep up this pace, they would be pushing into Assam within the week. And then they would be home. His mind drifted to Mookerji Baadi, to thoughts of his parents. So what if the house, the estate was gone? They would make a fresh start. He would earn good money in post independence India. He would make a good lawyer. They would build up their fortunes again. He was no longer that good-time guy who had got off that ship that rainy night, so long, long ago. Nishonko had taken him on this strange journey and it had changed him forever. Thoughts of Nishonko gave him a twinge of unease. What was the matter with his friend? Why was he behaving so strangely these days? Impulsive as always, he jumped up. He would find Nishonko and sort it out right now, before the next battle began. Kabootar, sitting a few yards away, whittling a piece of wood, looked up as Debraj headed towards Nishonko's unit. He got up, brushing the back of his trousers, and followed at a discreet distance.

Debraj found Nishonko beside the small little stream, alone. He flopped down beside him.

'Hey, want a peach. Saved it up for you.' Debraj held out the can.

Nishonko shook his head, shifted away.

'Sure? Because this is really good stuff.'

'Obviously. It's Churchill rations. Churchill ordered that only those who fight for the empire should expect to be fed well. So the best goes to their soldiers. That's what they did during the Bengal Famine. Instead of feeding the sick and starving, they siphoned off rice and wheat for their troops.'

'Then it's only fair that we get to fill our bellies with it and fart to our heart's content!'

'Everything is a joke for you, isn't it?'

'*"I commend mirth."* Ecclesiastes 8:15. And you know what Plato said? *"Even the gods love jokes."*'

Nishonko grimaced, his lips twisting. 'Yes...and all at our expense.'

Debraj let out a couple of smoke rings. 'What's wrong, Mitro? You've been going around like a bear with a boil on its arse!'

Nishonko was unsmiling, his eyes averted.

'I got into all this because I like you, admire you. But, lately I've been getting the feeling that you don't really approve of me. What did I do wrong?'

Nishonko got up jerkily, tossed his cigarette down, stamped on it.

'I really don't want to talk about this now.'

'But why? Is it they made me Major? Is it that Saito is friendly with me? Come on, Mitro, you are the only friend I have here.'

'Friend? *That's* a joke. You contradict me at every turn, you question my authority and make fun of my experience.'

'Hey, hey, hey…where's all this coming from?' Debraj was on his feet too, his hands reaching out to grab Nishonko's shoulders. Nishonko shoved him back, sending him stumbling. Hidden in the tree line, Kabootar stirred, took a step forward.

'Easy, my friend, easy. If that's the problem, know that I'll always be there for you. Saito is our commander. We are bound to follow his orders. But if you are in the right, I will always stand up for you.'

Nishonko turned away, helpless in his rage. The frustration of not being able to speak about the real cause of his anger, not being able to take Deb's treacherous little neck and snap it in his hands, made him feel like throwing up. He walked away, then stopped. No, this wouldn't do. He would bide his time, he would find the opportunity to speak to Aditi, to change her mind once this was all over. She would see, he would *make* her see what a slimeball Deb really was. She would come back and he would forgive her and take her back. And that would be his revenge. To make Deb feel what he was feeling, to experience the same numbing sense of loss, to feel the same terrifying loneliness. He forced his lips into a smile, then turned.

'Fine, fine. I'll be counting on you. We'll work together, back each other up. How's that?'

'That sounds ripping.'

Debraj watched him stride away. He somehow felt cheated, suspected that there were other subterranean currents he couldn't quite put his finger on. But, for the moment, it seemed things were back on an even keel.

The voice came broken, scratchy, faint. But the panic and fear came through loud and clear, even through the static: 'Japanese... roadblock...45th...Dimapur...highway...machine guns...and mortars... Shooting...that moves...sniper fire...reinforcements... now...can't hold...send help!'

Richards blanched. The only exit out of Kohima was blocked!

'Just hold on, son. Help on the way!'

'Hurry...can't...longer!'

Richards slammed the table. He had a few units of Kents, Somersets and part of the Assam Regiment. He needed every man jack to hold the line at Kohima. With growing dread, he realised another certainty. No one could get out of Kohima — but no supplies could reach them either!

He picked up the phone.

'Get me Brigadier Whyte. Now.'

The news went up the line pretty fast — from Whyte to General Slim, Commander of the eastern region and onwards to the Supreme Command, South East Asia office in Delhi

'You have all this on good authority, Slim?' the clipped voice asked.

'From the horse's mouth, Sir. Brigadier Whyte. MI6 fella. Man on the ground. '

'Well, those MI6 boys have pulled off some rather spectacular espionage stuff recently. Quite on the nose. I would take them seriously, wouldn't you?'

Slim concurred.

'So, let me get this right. He's saying Japan's offensive in the south has been just a diversion. An army twice as large is attacking Imphal and a full division has surrounded this little garrison town — what did you say the name was?'

'Kohima, Sir.'

'And the whole point of it all is to get Bose's INA brigade within shouting distance of Calcutta. Upon which, he feels, our Indian troops will desert us and fall in with him. Have I got it right up till now?'

'Yes, Sir.'

'And thence to Delhi.'

There was a brief silence, the phone line humming.

'Ingenious, I say.'

'Yes, Sir. The point is, we have to stop them at Kohima. If they break through, Bose's juggernaut may well prove to be unstoppable!'

'Hmm...so how can I help, General?'

'We need planes, Sir, to airdrop supplies. And bombers. And reinforcements as fast as possible.'

'Hmm...we may have to involve our transatlantic cousins, you know. Only they have bases close enough.'

Mountbatten put down the phone. What General Slim was envisioning was preposterous — but just audacious enough to succeed. He had always found Bose's antics theatrical — all that strutting around in uniform and those rabble-rousing, tear-jerking speeches on that banned Azad Hind Radio —but maybe, they were not all bunkum after all. Slim, or that fella Whyte, must have thought long and hard before making that call. He needed to bump it upstairs. He picked up the receiver.

'Operator, get me Number 10, please.'

Through the powerful glasses, Kohima looked close, within hailing distance. It was pretty, one of those picture postcard colonial hill stations that dotted the highlands of India. The same cluster of bungalows, the same sloping red roofs. He racked the focus. A line of barracks came into view. A club house, the steeple of a church, and the 'mall', a lovely tree-lined avenue, completed the picture. It looked like a miniature Darjeeling and suddenly he was overwhelmed by nostalgia. The summer holidays spent there as a boy, the winding pathways, cycling through the mist, the open-pit barbecue parties, the mixed doubles tennis matches, the dance parties at the club, the terraced lawns with a view of the snow-capped Kanchenjunga, pink at sunrise. The gorgeous Gurung sisters. Losing his virginity that summer. Andrew. He closed his eyes. The pain of Andrew's betrayal was still raw, undiluted by the passage of time. It was as much Andrew's treachery as Mitro's friendship, that had plummeted him down the rabbit hole to this rendezvous.

'There it is, gentlemen.' Saito's voice cut into his reverie. He opened his eyes. Saito was pointing to a saddle-shaped dip between two hills.

'That's where the British are dug in. That large bungalow belongs to their District Collector.'

Debraj scanned the hills till he found what Saito was talking about. The bungalow, nestled in a grove of pines, stood on one of the hills, surrounded by a profusion of lavender-coloured kewhi, orchids from which Kohima took its name. Further up, was a clay tennis court.

'And that mile-long stretch there is the Kohima Ridge. Once we cross that ridge, the road to the west is clear. Taking that ridge is the key.'

'Tough but doable, Sir.' Nishonko spoke quietly.

'I hope so. But that's going to be Colonel Watanabe and Colonel Akira's job. I have something else planned for you two gentlemen.'

He drew them aside, smiling at their quizzical looks. 'I have the greatest respect for your personal bravery. But I need to tap another ability, which both of you possess, which must take precedence today.'

Debraj and Nishonko were mystified.

'According to my scouts, there's a unit of the Assam Regiment parked on the flank of Kohima Ridge. It's the first Indian unit we have encountered around these parts. I need them on our side. We don't have much time. This is what you are good at. I want you to get out there, clandestine, behind the lines, and turn them. You will be on your own. If you're caught, I can't help you. Both of you will need to work together. Can you do it?'

Nishonko's eyes gleamed. This was Nishachar's territory. He felt a frisson of excitement.

'What about our units, Sir?' Debraj asked, tentatively.

'Both of them will be under my direct charge until you return.'

'When do we start?'

'As soon as we start the main offensive. It will provide you with the cover you need. They will be so busy dealing with us, they won't be looking for you.'

Nishonko looked at Debraj. The idea of partnering him was galling but the excitement of the chase took precedence. Any way, it would be a small diversion.

Meenakshi trudged up the winding mountain roads, climbing higher and higher, her heavy backpack biting into her shoulder, the sweat pouring off her. The medical staff had been ordered to move up, section by section, to set up advance field stations, a few miles behind the front, near the base. She had been sent ahead in the first unit. Aditi would follow with the next lot. As they came closer, the dull sound of the battle carried clearly down to them. They must be beyond the next line of hills. She wondered where Nishonko would be. In the thick of things, if she knew him. It would be lovely to bump into him, just like that, see the look of surprise on his face, see those dark eyes widen. Would he be pleased to see her? Would the absence have made a little place in his heart for her? She smiled to herself. Sister Meenakshi, his name for her, you are an incurable romantic, a sentimental fool under your hard-assed exterior. He's a man. What would have a greater pull, seduce him more — blood lust or the lure of her dark body? She knew the answer to that. But still, her heedless heart refused to listen. Still, it held an ember of hope.

At the base camp, Debraj and Nishonko pored over a detailed sketch of Kohima Ridge prepared by the scouts. The Assam Regiment trenches were in a little bowl-shaped valley, where two hills intersected, on the lower slopes. But the Kents and Somersets positions were just a few yards away. Nishonko frowned. 'I don't like it. Their positions are practically overlapping.'

'Stay low, get in really close. Speak only in Bengali or Ahomiya. Get out fast.'

'It's not the actual encounter that worries me, it's the in and out. We are completely exposed.'

'Why don't we ask Saito to get his snipers to cover us in case we need to scoot out of there? They can be our back-up if everything goes tits up!'

Saito's snipers were legendary, masters of camouflage and patience. They could wait, motionless, for hours, indistinguishable from a tree or a bush, for an enemy to show himself. All they needed was one shot.

'Good idea,' Nishonko agreed, grudgingly. 'Let's get cracking.'

Outside, a mule train disgorged wounded men. Five minutes later, and Nishonko would have missed them. But as he stepped out of the tent after the briefing, he saw Nawaz on a stretcher, bleeding, unconscious. He rushed with the medics carrying the stretcher to the field dressing station. These stations were set up just behind the front, highly mobile, shifting with the changing fortunes of the battle. They were chaotic places, dealing with the freshly wounded, the hard decisions of who to patch up and send back to the front and who to ship back to the command hospital, who to give that extra penicillin and who to amputate immediately, being taken moment to moment. Nishonko grabbed hold of an exhausted-looking young doctor, tending to another patient, and shouted at him to treat Nawaz immediately. The doctor, overworked, underslept, shouted out.

'Sister Menon, bleeder here, get a clamp on him.'

A nurse came running at his command. Nishonko, his hands clamped round Nawaz's calf, didn't even look at her.

'Come on, Nawaz, hang in there, my friend, you'll be okay.'

'Nishonko.' The nurse spoke quietly. He looked up, surprised. For a few seconds, he couldn't recognise her. She had short cropped hair now, and was wearing a medical orderly's overalls and her face was covered with a surgical mask. Then he recognised the eyes, the dark lashed, black eyes edged with kohl, the luminous intelligence of her steady gaze.

'Meena. Meenakshi.'

She smiled, a smile hidden under the mask but so broad, it crinkled the corners of her eyes, a smile so generous, it betrayed her delight. She couldn't believe her luck. He was here, he was alive. In spite of himself, in spite of the faint contempt he felt for her, he smiled back. It was a known face, and her smile was infectious. She got busy, her manner business like, isolating the vein, clamping it off in seconds but her smile lingered. When she had the bleeding under control, she sat back on her haunches and pulled her mask down.

'Hello, Nishonko. How are you?'

He took her to his tent, sticking to the periphery to avoid being seen. Tea, he asked. She nodded, not taking her eyes off him. The intimacy of the enclosed space made both suddenly breathless. He stared at her, at the chopped thick black hair which made her look very different, very bold, very alien, the dark skin of her tanned arms shining in the flicker of the keroscene lamp. The valley between her breasts, the curves of her body, had a mystery, made more potent by being hidden inside the bulky man's overalls. She too, seemed to be on edge, waiting, holding herself back, the knees pulled up to the chin, the mouth blowing on the hot liquid, the lips wet with the sip. When he pulled her roughly towards him, almost reluctantly as it were, in spite of himself as it were, she let out a soft cry, of triumph or joy, it was difficult to tell. He rode her, averting his face, shame and desire, twin riding crops, whipping him on. He couldn't have enough of her and yet the corruscating reproach, the self disgust that he was somehow betraying Aditi — these conflicting forces goaded him on, held him back, egged him on, pulled him back from the brink, bringing intense pleasure never felt before, prolonged beyond the point of bearing, till she was screaming, his hand clamping her mouth to still the cries, she bucking like a horse under him, his own insides exploding, the mouth pulled back, the teeth bared, in a rictus of pain and release. A brief hiatus, a collecting of breath, a cooling of limbs. Then, once more they joined, this time, even more intensely, both more demanding. He lay, spent, afterwards, his eyes closed, turned away from her, she behind him, her eyes drinking in his battle-scarred skin, the slabs of hard muscle, the faint dimple on the coccyx that she now traced with a fingertip.

'I missed you.'

A little jerk, a stiffening, a retreat. She felt it but thought it a tendency to be ticklish. It made her playful, confident, forward.

'I would stay up nights, thinking of you, your hands. Oh, how I ached for you. Did you miss me, Nish? Can I call you that? Nishonko is so formal, such a mouthful. Or Nishi. The night. That suits you.'

He lay, his eyes open, staring at the shadows moving on his tent wall, willing her to be silent, wanting her to cease to exist. But she prattled on, foolish girl, unaware of the gathering storm.

'I knew you were busy, you had to be. But Aditi kept asking if you...'

He sat up with a jerk, the name like a slap.

'Shut up. Just shut up.'

Her mouth froze.

'Even to hear you speak her name…how dare you?'

She turned cold, uncomprehending, the blood rushing down to her feet.

'What did I say, Nish? I… I don't understand, I thought you…'

'That just…just because we pleasure each other, I owe you something? You think you are somehow the same as Aditi, her equal?'

'She's my friend.' She was bewildered.

'She might have befriended you but that's the way she is. She takes pity on everyone – the maimed, the sick, the poor. You? You're not worth the dust on her feet, the way you've thrown yourself at me…'

His words were lashes, striking her unprotected heart. Their virulence stripped her bare, flayed her, left her bereft, undone. But then the steel, always under the surface, bred into her by having to fight for her own food, defend her own space on the floor from the older children, the bullies in the orphanage, came surging through. She turned on him and snarled.

'Yes, I pleasure you. But at my own free will. Yes, I have loved you and given myself to you. But you can't shame me, Nishonko Mitro. I'm a full- blooded woman, just like your precious Aditi. She's not some plaster saint you've put on a pedestal. She too finds pleasure with the man she loves.'

He took a step towards her in anger. But her straight back and the iron in her jaw gave him pause.

'You, on the other hand? You are mean of spirit and small of heart, in denial, too scared to feel, to love, too…too…' She stuttered to a halt, stared at his rigid back. She gathered her humble, work-stained overalls up with dignity, fiercely gulping back the tears that threatened to be her undoing. He spoke, very softly, as if trying to convince her — and himself.

'She does not love him. She was led astray. I know her. She would not rut like an animal. She's a child.'

Now, her blood boiled. The need to hurt him back, to sear his heart and scar him was fierce. She laughed, not a nice sound, the edge of hysteria tinging it.

'Oh, you really think she was conned into having sex, that it was against her will? That she just accidentally conceived? Or did you think it was an immaculate conception, that she's Saint bloody Aditi, our very own little Virgin Mary?'

He frowned, first not understanding, then he went white.

'Of course, you didn't know, you sad, poor thing. Your precious Aditi is pregnant, preggers, bun in the oven, baby on board.'

Now the blood rushed to his face. There was great satisfaction and immense sadness in knowing she had hit home. But now he lurched, staggered back. His mouth worked but no words came out. He was like a stranded fish, gasping for air. What had she done? She wanted to drag the words back. But it was too late. She had betrayed Aditi's trust, her friendship. And she wasn't even sure that it was true. She took a step towards him, contrite now, wanting to ease the hurt. He flung up his hand warding off the unimaginable, the evil thing she had said.

'I'm sorry, Nish, I'm so sorry.'

He whispered something, a prayer, maybe. She touched his arm.

'I just wanted…'

'SHUT UP!' It was a hiss, a roar. He flung off her hand so violently, she was catapulted onto the tent wall, sliding down in a tangle of arms and legs. She tried to get up, lost her balance. He advanced upon her, his face ugly, the killing light in his eyes, the words like gunshots.

'OUT! Out. Out. Out. Out.'

She scrabbled on all fours, retreating, trying to cover herself with the clutched overall, fear choking her. She tumbled out of the tent flap, on knees and hands, panting. It was night. Quickly, under the blanket of darkness, she hobbled into her clothes, then ran.

He lay, curled up, foetal, trying to make himself as tiny as possible, as people do when threatened with physical harm, his arms covering his head, in self-defence. Dry eyed, dry mouthed, there was not even the ease of release, the shanti jal, the holy water of tears. Thoughts went scuttling round his head like a rat on a treadmill, an endless circle of 'She's going to have a baby. Debraj's child. She's gone. She's going to have a child. Debraj's baby. She's gone. I've lost her. She's going to be a mother. Debraj's the father…' Hours passed or maybe minutes. From somewhere far away, a voice called.

'It's time, Sir.'

He slowly uncoiled, his body hurting, every fibre screaming as if he had been pummelled, beaten up.

'Who is it?' His voice was hoarse, and the words came out jumbled, sticky. He called out again.

'It's Neel, Sir. Major Mookerji is calling for you.'

An ice cold flare of murderous thought, then stillness.

'Tell him I will be joining him shortly.'

By the evening of April 8th, the attack on Kohima Ridge was well underway. Saito had formed a two-mile wide arc of infantry to start the sweep from the foot of the ridge. But, it was tough going. The British had recovered somewhat from the initial shock of the Japanese attack and dug in strongly. They were also better armed. Crawling in and out of thick bush, the Japanese and INA tried to push up the steep slopes, one bloody inch at a time. It was a frustrating see-saw battle. They would charge a bunker with bayonets, flame throwers, grenades, sometimes with nothing except sheer grit, and capture it. Then the British mortars would start up and they would be forced to retreat. The British would then counter attack and take back their precious trench, paying a heavy price themselves — only to have it wrested from them at night by a 'howling attack.' Instead of one large, cohesive, organised battle, it became scrappy, with little, isolated pockets of intense fighting. It became a contest to just maintain a gruesome status quo. But in this contest, numbers would ultimately prevail. And the British were badly outnumbered.

They slinked through the forest, in camouflage, faces darkened with black woodash, moving like ghosts through the undergrowth. Further away, the battle raged on fiercely. They could hear the constant barking of machine guns, punctuated by the deep thump of artillery. Kohima was slowly becoming an island, marooned in the middle of a raging sea of soldiers. As yard by murderous yard, they pushed back the British, Nishonko and Debraj moved to their 'insertion point'. They worked silently, both experts by now in the tradecraft, minute hand signals their only way of communication. Nishonko was preternaturally calm. He could wait. Finish the job on hand, then deal with the charlatan. He had a whole war to do it in. He even smiled thinly, relishing when it would happen, anticipating the cat-and-mouse game he so loved to play.

The contact happened quite smoothly. They came upon an outpost. By April of 1944, it was common knowledge that hundreds of Indian soldiers of the British Indian Army on the Burma front had joined the INA. Many waited for 'contact' to happen. Debraj went in alone, his hands raised. When he revealed his credentials, he was greeted with handshakes and a mug of hot tea. A tin plate of hard biscuits was being offered, when Nishonko materialised from the darkness, an apparition in the faint wash of moonlight.

'It's okay, he's with me. He's a great warrior of the INA.'

Nishonko spoke a smattering of Ahomiya. He asked about their families, their homes, the coming Rongali Bihu festival, the celebration of the coming of spring.

'Aren't men supposed to conduct it for the good of the village? But you men will miss that, won't you? Because here you are stuck, serving your British masters. They have made you landless, rootless. They have taken from you what is rightfully yours. They have taken you out of India to fight their war, like bhade ke tattoo — mere mules for hire. They made you traitors to your motherland.'

Nishonko's voice was quiet but compelling in its intensity. Debraj watched, his heart filling with pride. This was the man he had followed.

'But today, you have a choice. A great decisive battle is being fought right now, mere miles from here. You can help to turn the tide. You can make a real difference to the battle tonight itself. Will you fight on as someone's naukar, slave, or will you fight as a free man for India?'

There were a few murmurs, about having eaten the Angrez's salt, about loyalty to Army and the King.

'You speak of eating the Englishman's salt. But the Englishman has devoured everything else and not given you even a beggar's portion in return. You owe nothing.'

The talk flowed back and forth but softly. The British positions were very close. They needed to be discreet. But at the end, the entire company, including the junior officers were ready to abandon their post.

The civilian and military telephone lines were down and the only contact with the outside world was by wireless radio Brigadier Whyte paced the room, dragging on his cigarette. He had spent the larger part of the day, making calls to Command HQ. Richards looked at him, fuming inside. Whyte had virtually assumed command. Only four long-range sets were working and Whyte had monopolised one. But Richards' hands were tied. Eastern Command had earlier sent a wire ordering the Garrison Command of Kohima to 'XTND FUL ASSISTNCE BRIG. WHYTE. PRIORITY.' Command had done everything except officially put his garrison under Whyte. The bloody war was being run by fucking armchair experts! They were too busy with their schemes and stratagems to understand what it took to withstand a head-on bayonet charge at night by the demonic Japs. *Want to help, Brig. Whyte? Go out there and join the lads and stand in a trench and shoot down one of those slant-eyed devils!* He looked at the British perimeter on the map. It was shrinking imperceptibly. They were losing ground.The stench of stale cigarette smoke was suddenly strong. He knew Whyte was peering over his shoulder.

'These Assam Regiment units.'

He tapped on the map with a perfectly manicured finger, spilling ash from his lit cigarette, making Richards grit his teeth.

'What's the distance between them and our lads?'

'Couple of hundred yards, Sir.'

'Hmm, close. And can you trust these blokes?'

'Of course I can. They're my boys. I can vouch for them!!' Richards was livid.

'So did many commanders before they lost their men to INA propaganda. They are the only Indian unit here. The line is very fragile. We can't have any weak links.'

'Exactly. I cant pull them out. We need them to hold the line.' Richards swallowed hard.

'Send a patrol of the Kents down to their positions — any excuse will do. You want to resupply them, whatever. Do it again after a few hours. I'll feel a lot safer with those trenches in British hands.'

'But, Sir, they've been with us since the beginning of the war. They're cracking good soldiers! They've never let us down!'

Whyte fixed him with a baleful stare. 'These cracking good soldiers who we've all treated as our pet monkeys are rattling their cages now. They've all been trained to kill. They can easily train their guns on us. We've been using them to fight their countrymen for two hundred years. Maybe the poor buggers have woken up now! Send the Kents down to those trenches now...there's a good man.'

Richards nodded. No matter how irritating this man was, his logic was indisputable.

It was almost dawn, the sky overcast, the light steel grey, with a strange, electric blue tinge. The first tendrils of mist had begun to roll down, filling the little valley.

'Good. That will give us some cover.' Debraj spoke in a whisper. They were heading to another unit, lower down the slope. Lieutenant Saikia had given them a runner to guide them.

'They're waiting for you. Ask for Corporal Saikia. He's my younger brother.'

Now they crept towards the rendezvous, wraiths in the fog. Nishonko looked in the direction of the grove of willow trees across the valley. That's where Saito's snipers were supposed to be staked out. But now they were going to be useless. They wouldn't be able to see them either. If they ran into trouble, they were on their own. They floated through the white cloud, everything blurred, shapes looming out of nowhere, clawing at their clothes. The mist made their faces wet, clung to their eyelashes. Nishonko crouched. He had heard something. Ahead, through the drifting, swirling mist, he caught sight of Debraj pushing through the undergrowth. Even here, with the British probably behind the next large rock, the man strutted like a sahib. *Is that what she liked about him?* The thought slipped through the elaborate defences he had constructed since the previous evening. He had deadened his mind, numbed the gaping wound of the terrible thing Meenakshi had told him. He had inured his heart to everything — sorrow, pain, fatigue. But now it came roaring back, blinding him with its intensity. The bastard obviously knew. That's why he was going around in this cocksure manner, jumping from rock to rock, as if he were on a picnic. Everything was a game to him. Aditi was a game to him.

She had been pure, sacred, and he had defiled her. She had been his and he had taken her!

His mouth on hers, his hands all over her body, on her breasts, her legs entwined around him. The perfect O of her mouth as she moaned and moved with him, wild and wanton. And now she was pregnant...with his child! His seed in her. Growing inside her, like some incubus, some monster. Turning her obese, ugly. How dare he? How dare he, with that lazy drawl, that infuriating smile, the talk... always the fucking talk!

He felt cold steel in his hands. He was holding his revolver. He didn't know how it had got there. Unbidden, unconscious, without any volition, he found himself pointing it, ramrod straight, the sight trained on Debraj's back. Debraj too had stopped, his head cocked, as if he had heard something. He was a still, perfect target. Nishonko eased back the hammer and it cocked with a tiny click, muted by the fog. It would be so easy. No one would ever know. They were behind enemy lines. Do it! His brain screamed. His hand trembled as he squeezed the trigger gently. Sweat popped out all over his body, trickled down his forehead into his eyes, momentarily blinding him. He looked away, wiping his eyes on his sleeve, then lined up Debraj in his sights again. Do it! His hand shook like a man wracked with malaria. Shoot him, dammit! Pull the fucking trigger! His finger clenched on the trigger but he couldn't pull it. The gun in his hand trembled. The barrel crept down. And then Debraj was gone, swallowed up once more in the treacherous mist. With a shudder, Nishonko let the gun drop. Why can't you do it? You coward! You chutiya! You are not a man! With a trembling hand, he put it back in the holster. A great wracking sob tore through his chest but before he could give it voice, something hard and heavy smashed into the back of his neck and he went down like a felled ox.

When he came to, he was on the ground, a gun trained on him. A ring of Kents surrounded them, with a couple of Indian soldiers. He turned his head. Debraj lay on the ground, with a gash on his forehead, groaning. Nishonko looked in the direction of the willow trees but there was just the white blindness of the fog, an opaque curtain hiding them from the snipers. So carefully placed, utterly useless in this thick pea soup. *Where had the British come from? How the hell had they known?* Through the throbbing pain in his skull, he made out a British Sergeant and a young Indian corporal.

'Well done, Corporal Saikia, good job.'

Debraj and Nishonko stared at him.

'Saikia?! Your brother? Isn't he…'

The man nodded. 'My brother's a fool, a romantic. Also a traitor. He will be taken care of.'

'Take them away, Corporal. And report to Whyte as soon as you have them in the clink. He wants to know the name of each prisoner we take.'

And so it goes, thought Debraj, his head hurting like the blazes, his mind woozy from the crack on his skull. *The age old Indian story. Brother against brother.*

Outside, it was overcast and unseasonably warm. Summer was coming to the highlands. Whyte had come back for a bath, a luxury in these part of the hills, the claw-toothed large cast-iron tub having to be filled, pail by pail, by a khansama. It had been a long night and he needed to be refreshed, to have his wits about him for the night to come. Now, in a crisp, freshly laundered and ironed cotton shirt and a 'geentonee' in his hand, the tonic, with its strong dose of quinine essential to prevent malaria, he was feeling a tad more human. He sat back in the planter's chair, breathing in the pine-scented air. The smell of hydrangeas hung heavy and the balmy breeze felt good on Whyte's face. Strangely, he felt at peace.

But not for long. Goopta came waddling down the corridor, all wringing hands, huffing and puffing. Whyte winced. The man was really such a buffoon. He was half tempted to dispense with his services. He was becoming redundant, a liability.

Goopta shivered as he waddled towards Whyte. It was chilly. And look at this Whyte, sitting outside, without even a muffler. He hated the hills. He hated the poky little lodgings he was in. He hated the food. He couldn't wait to finish up here and get the hell back to the comforts of Calcutta. The mango would be in season and he preferred the heat of the plains to this cold, ghostly, misty landscape. On top of everything, the news was steadily getting worse.

'Good day, Whyte sahib. I believe the Japanese and the Azad Fauj are getting closer?'

'I believe they are too, Mr. Goopta. You should have left with the other traders and baniyaas when they evacuated and saved your sorry ass.'

Goopta's expression did not change. Water off a duck's back, he was fond of saying. He had learnt to take these kind of racial insults ever since his childhood. Why blame a firangi, for a system that was quintessentially Indian? Even now with wealth enough to control most of Calcutta's hundis, his low birth was thrown in his face all the time. The baniyaa's time will come, sahib.

'Is there a danger of getting trapped here, Sir? Can we not escape to Dimapur via the highway now, Sir?'

Whyte smiled, a sardonic, somewhat unkind smile.

'I'm not going anywhere in a hurry, my man. But you should scarper. Of course, you could get blown to smithereens on that highway.'

'Oh, that would not do, Whyte sahib. Then what would happen to our deal? And our avowed purpose of defeating Netaji?'

'You're really such a funny man, Goopta. I would have thought that you would value your hide more than anything else.'

Whyte was not wrong. It was not bravado or patriotism or self-interest or even the prospect of the forest deal that had kept Goopta here when the rest were downing shutters and deserting the town like rats. It was just that he had been taken by surprise. He had never bargained for the Japs and the INA to move this fast. That fool Gaffar was supposed to have given him adequate warning. And he, Goopta, had really believed in the ability of the British to repulse them. Stupid, stupid.

The phone rang inside. It was the corporal, informing Whyte that two prisoners had been taken, INA officers, while they were trying to sneak into the Assam Regiment trenches. Whyte grunted with satisfaction. He had been right.

'Names? Okay. And the other? What!!? Yes, thank you. Keep them in the lock-up. I'm coming to interrogate them right away.'

He looked at the names he had written down. His sleet grey eyes were snapping, crackling with excitement.

'Do you know who we have in custody, Goopta?' he drawled, almost purring. He didn't wait for a reply.

'Nishonko Mitro. I have been hunting him for a long time now and here he is, on a plate, waiting to be picked clean.'

He rubbed his hands. This was such a stroke of luck. It was a good sign.

'He is close to Netaji, a man in the know. He will be made to yield secrets. I will make sure of that. We will know their positions, their strength, at least. We will find our weak link. We are back in the game, Goopta.'

Goopta nodded. He had heard of Nishonko Mitro, had in fact been despatched to Singapur to track his whereabouts. But there was not much he could help there now.

'What are the other names?'

'Just one more. A Major Mookerji. Um…Debraj. Sounds oddly familiar.'

Goopta's black heart jumped. His voice was eager, high pitched, a hound baying at the sight of prey.

'Did you say Debraj? Mookerji?'

'Ah, yes, that's why he sounded familiar. You know him rather well, don't you?'

'Very well, Sir. His father…and I were business associates. The son is a complete waster.'

'Ah, but the son may have a lot of value to us, Goopta. I need eyes on the ground now. If we can bring him around to our side, or at least force him to work for us, we could still hold off the Japanese advance.'

'I don't know, Sir…the young man had been full of azadi talk, all that drivel about independence, when I met him in Singapur. A very bad-mannered, arrogant good for nothing, if I may say so.'

'No, you may not. I'm not interested in your personal opinions of him. If he holds an important position in the INA battalions surrounding Kohima, then he's more valuable than a hundred Gaffars. We don't need to beat the Japs. We only need to hold them off for a few days till our reinforcements arrive. For that, we need to know their every move.'

'I will do my utmost, Sir.'

'Do that, my little man. This is where you earn your keep. If you can somehow convince him, you will find me — and His Majesty — very grateful.'

Goopta's Machiavellian brain had already gone into overdrive. If he could pull this off, the British government would not be the only grateful ones. The Party would give an arm and a leg to stop Netaji in his tracks. If he could pull this off, his dream of becoming mayor of Calcutta would be in the bag. Once again, the fates had stepped in and handed him the key. His face was glowing with the revelation.

'Ah, I can see that twisted brain beginning to tick.'

Goopta nodded happily.

Water dripped down the wall of the tiny, damp room they were using as a cell. Debraj shivered, a violent spasm, his skin feeling as if it was on fire. He knew he was coming down with a fever, malaria perhaps. His head was aching abominably, from the crack to his skull, when they walked into that trap. He had heard something back there in the fog, had thought of stopping for Nishonko but, dammit, his impetuous nature had got the better of him. Always, it had got him into trouble. Think, Nishonko would have said, think before you jump in. But, as usual, he had dropped his guard and gone ahead. And now, here he was, stuck in this hellhole, with no idea where Nishonko was. He shouted. 'Mitro! Mitro, you there?'

There was silence, only the sound of a steady trickle of water. They must be beside a stream of sorts, or some sewage nullah. The cell stank of stale urine, shit, vomit, fear. In the basement, there were a few small, windowless cells where Nagas who were caught going against the British were imprisoned. For days, they were kept chained, naked, starving, delirious with fever, wallowing in their own filth. He could hear their shouts, the cry of the damned. He pulled on his chains, rattling them, the iron links cold against his skin. He shivered again.

In an adjoining cell, Nishonko sat, his back against the wall. He was furious with himself. You took your eyes off the ball, you nincompoop. Netaji would be scathing, if he heard how stupidly he had allowed himself to walk into that trap. You just stood there and got your chaddis, your bloody undies taken. And all because you let your stupid emotions get the better of you, let Deb distract you. It was all his fault, making him think of Aditi. He shivered, suddenly very, very afraid. He remembered his instructions to his men. *'And under no circumstances, get caught. They will torture you and wring out the last bit of intel from you, then shoot you in the head for treason.'* He had got caught. He was a big fish. The moment the British knew they had the Nishachar, they would take him apart. They would milk him for every bit of information lodged in his brain. He felt hollow, his mouth suddenly bitter with the rush of acid. Oh god, what was he going to do? All those years of training had not prepared him for the reality of this moment, the certainty of unbearable, maliciously inflicted, extreme physical pain. He curled up in a ball, keening softly.

The door to the cell crashed open. Two military policemen, large men with beefy hands, marched in and hauled Debraj to his feet. The chains went skittering across the floor, as they snapped them open and threw them across the room. He tried to break away but was clubbed down and dragged, feet trailing, to a tent pitched outside. Inside the tent, lit from an opening in the roof, his eyes dark pools, unreadable, sat a man. His ginger orange hair, neatly parted in a razor straight line, Brilliantined, flared in the errant sunlight. He was in a neatly pressed uniform, his fingers steepled, a gentle smile under the clipped moustache. He studied Debraj with open interest. Debraj straightened up, looked above the man's head. He opened his mouth but the man pre-empted him.

'Debraj Mookerji. Yes, we know of you.'

'Major Debraj Mookerji, Azad Hind Fauj, Bahadur Regiment, Serial no 1123465.' Debraj was punctilious. It was important to establish that he was a soldier and the rules of combat applied. 'How do you know my name?'

'Oh, we have a mutual acquaintance, I believe.'

From the shadows, a portly figure emerged.

'Debu, Debu, my son. At last I have found you,' he engulfed him in a bear hug. Debraj balked at the overwhelming smell of pomade.

Debraj reeled back. 'Goopta! What the devil? What are you doing here?'

'Arre ki bolbo, what to tell you? I was here on work but then I heard of your capture. How could I leave? I hope these rascals are treating you well!'

He rounded on the military policemen. 'Release him... he's my nephew.'

Whyte nodded at the policemen. They uncuffed Debraj, pushing him down roughly in a chair. Debraj tried to focus. Of all people, Goopta... here in Kohima? It didn't make sense at all.

'Well, I'm dealing in timber these days, as I believe I told you last time we met...but you were in no mood to listen, were you, young Debu? Anyway, I'm hoping the Brigadier can give me safe passage and a shot at the concessions...the hills here are a gold mine.'

Whyte interrupted Goopta.

'Tch tch, Goopta. We are forgetting our manners. Our business can wait. I'm sure our young friend here is very hungry. Would you like something to eat, Mr. Mookerji?'

An orderly soon trotted in with a generous helping of thick egg sandwiches and a steaming pot of milky tea. Whyte and Goopta watched, their expressions almost avuncular, as Debraj wolfed down the food. He was famished. They were constantly hungry on their meagre rations and it seemed forever since he had tasted eggs or even bread. Finally, with a long pull on his mug of hot, sweet tea, he sat back with a weak grin.

'That hit the spot.'

Whyte leaned forward, offering an open tin of Dunhills. 'Smoke?'

'Much obliged. I don't believe I've had the pleasure.' He held out his hand. Whyte shook it.

'Brigadier Whyte, of His Majesty's Armed Services.'

As Debraj lit up, Whyte sat back and observed him. He was intrigued by this young man, his accent, his bearing. This was not what he had expected. This was no subjugated, spineless darkie. He would have to tread carefully.

'So Goopta babu, we are all being very civil here. But you are aware, that we are at war with the Brigadier here?'

'Oh, I never see any profit in being at war with any one. I am very friendly with everybody — our imperial masters, our esteemed Congress...even you, my dear boy. I do care for you deeply, you know. And I would come to any arrangement to get you safely back home.'

'Of course. So, gentlemen, you have me. What happens now?'

'You see, Debu, Brigadier Whyte is an old friend.'

Whyte grimaced in distaste, an involuntary expression not lost on Debraj.

'He has very kindly agreed to help you out. You know, your offence here is bad, it's very bad. You do know the penalty for treason is death? But I've explained to him how you must have been brainwashed, maybe even held against your will, forced to work against the government.

Whyte cut in, speaking in his soft, almost inaudible voice, making Debraj strain to hear him.

'What happens now, Mr. Mookerji, largely depends on the choices you make here.'

'That's Major Mookerji to you, Brigadier.'

'Let me guess what you might be thinking right now. You believe that you are a prisoner of war. You believe that it was unfortunate that you got captured but under the Geneva Convention, you believe that you are guaranteed certain rights and are assured of good treatment.'

Whyte dragged on his cigarette, letting the pause linger.

'All these beliefs that you hold would be wrong. Let me explain why. The British government doesn't acknowledge the existence of the INA. It believes that you are all British subjects, civilians, carrying on an armed mutiny against the Crown. It believes that you are nothing better than terrorists. Ergo, I can't hold you as a POW. I have to charge you with treason.'

Debraj laughed, openly derisive.

'How specious an argument. The INA has fought under a duly constituted government which has declared war on yours and we have waged it in observance of international law. You have no right over me. How can I be a traitor when I owe you no allegiance?'

Whyte smiled but his eyes had become pinpricks, sharp as diamond chips.

'Listen carefully, young man. We can do what the hell we want to you. The garrison commander can have you shot by firing squad this very evening. In fact, if I shoot you right now, no one will question me. I will then burn your corpse and scatter the ashes in a latrine pit. There will be nothing to mark your passing. No one will ever know that you tried to be brave. No one will give a shit.'

'No, no Whyte sahib. Please give me a moment to bring him to his senses. Debu, Brigadier Whyte, kind soul, is offering you safe passage back to Calcutta…back to your parents. They are broken up. Your inexplicable betrayal…'

'My betrayal! You're the snake who…'

'Water under the bridge. Your Baba is sick. He may not last very long. He needs you, Debu. Your mother yearns to see you. Go back to them. Reclaim your inheritance.'

Debraj stared at him, dumbfounded.

'I know, I know, I did say you have no inheritance left. I do own it all. But we could rectify that. An alliance with my family…and you would be able to get back to the life that's your birthright. I have my own modest political ambitions and we could form a mutually beneficial alliance, what do you say? Set things right, Debu.'

The game had started. Debraj knew what they were doing. But his head was pounding again, his mouth hot with approaching fever.

'You're a maggot. Goopta, a fucking pimp! Anybody ever told you that?'

Goopta recoiled. For a second, he lost his composure and raised his hand to strike Debraj. But a sibilant hiss from Whyte stopped him in his tracks. Goopta swallowed. He took a deep breath and went in for the kill.

'And…and I know where Debi is holed up.'

Debraj's head snapped up.

'I do have my connections, you know. You could see her again, redeem yourself.'

Whyte picked up where he had left off, his voice clipped. 'You decide, boy. Do you want to die in this lonely, dank, dark armpit of the world? Or do you want your old life back?'

Whyte reached for Debraj's effects that had been placed on the table. He picked up the wallet and ran his fingers over the hand-tooled leather.

'Harrods, eh? What I don't fathom is this. You're more English than many of the blokes at Whitehall. Completely the product of the British Empire. What the devil are you doing waltzing around with people who want to tear it down?'

He whistled suddenly. He had found Aditi's picture, taken at the engagement, luminous even in the black and white print.

'I say, who's this?'

Goopta peered round his arm for a better look.

'Oh, that's his little squeeze. Met her once. Quite a little tigress. Though why you had to get yourself engaged, my son, I don't know. Everyone knows what these Rani Jhansi types are.'

Debraj's hands balling into fists, the fever turning his breath into fire.

'Rani Jhansi, eh, Bose's ridiculous idea of a woman's army? Could it be that she's here somewhere...somewhere in these hills?'

The icy blue eyes, like gimlets, bored into his, the way a snake mesmerises a rabbit. The tiniest flicker in Debraj's eyes gave him away.

'Oh, you don't have to say anything lad, I know she's close. Imagine, if she gets away, she can join you within hours and you could be on a train heading for Calcutta. You would get your life back...as if you've never been away, as if none of this had happened. You will never have to be apart again.' Whyte's quiet voice was a seductive murmur.

Debraj covered his face with his hands, his thoughts in a whirl. *Aditi…she deserves better...shame on me… I can set things right…last chance, take it and get out…train to Calcutta… Aditi…safe… Ma… Baba…Debi…find them… Safe…* The tent seemed to spin.

'What do you want from me?'

'Good boy. What is it they say, quid pro...? There's just one thing you have to do.'

'That's right. No free lunches.' Whyte's laugh was genuine; he was elated. This had proved to be easier than he had imagined.

'So, before getting out of this hellhole, you'll have to go back to the INA. You will be my pet monkey. Take this short wave radio. It's a brand new device, easy to operate and small enough to hide. It's perfect for communicating in secret. Get yourself transferred to the main operations centre, close to Command. Over the next few days, I want you to relay the actual positions and battle plans of all Japanese and INA units to us...real time. Short transmissions, no more than a minute, three to four times a day. Got all that?'

Debraj nodded, bone tired.

'You need to do this only for a few days. Once our reinforcements arrive, we will sweep the Japs back. In exchange, as soon as we have this lot mopped up, you will be allowed to walk away scot free and go wherever you wish.'

'And how do you know I won't turn? That I won't give up your little plot to the INA?'

'Now that would be silly. Look like an intelligent bod, you do. And a good son...wouldn't want any harm to come to your parents, now, would you?'

The threat was clear but Whyte's face was serene. Goopta looked at Debraj, nodded.

'And if you betray us, Debu, it will be a simple matter to grab that whore of yours and throw her to the Gurkhas. Or even better, the Nagas.'

Debraj lunged at Goopta but the fever had made him slow, dizzy. He tottered, then collapsed to the floor, sprawled on the dusty, rough coir matting. Goopta came over and stood over him, his face ugly with malice.

'Chhoto laath, got you now.'

Two orderlies dragged the unconscious Debraj off to the cell.

'Hold him for the night. Let him chew on it. By tomorrow, he'll fall into line. And get the doctor to give him some quinine and penicillin. We need him up on his feet.'

They left, the radio transmitter shoved into Debraj's backpack. Whyte turned to Goopta. He gave him a grudging nod.

'You were good there. Care to join me for Nishonko Mitro's interrogation?'

'Why do you need him? We have all we want.'

'You can never have enough intelligence. And I have a suspicion this man will be a veritable gold mine.'

It had been over 24 hours that there had been no word from Debraj and Nishonko. Kabootar paced up and down, restless, slapping the khukri against his thigh. He was getting a very bad feeling. Brigadier Saito's snipers had come back saying that the fog had literally swallowed up the two. Captain Pradhan, also feeling antsy about Debraj's absence had gone to Colonel Watanabe but got no joy there. Watanabe was too caught up with the flanking movement on the front line to bother about an insertion happening somewhere in the sidelines. Watanabe's English, pretty sketchy at the best of times, was rapidly breaking down under pressure. He let off a torrent of Japanese, most of which sounded extremely agitated and totally incomprehensible to Kishore. Kabootar hung around outside the tent for a while, then nodded to himself. He made his way to the perimeter and slipped out. He ran, once under cover of the jungle, towards the British lines.

Sergeant Williams was a past master at administering the third degree. He had been a copper before the war and had relished his job of breaking down thieves and robbers and sundry delinquents and malefactors and getting them to spill the beans. He had been known in the force as 'The Canary' for his ability to make the criminal underclasses sing. He had tried to suss out Nishonko. The swollen eyes, the tremble in the hands had told him one story. This one's going to blab soon, he had thought in the morning. But, now several hours later, he had found that the boy — and he was actually just out of his teens — was able to withstand his ministrations quite well. Steel inside, stern stuff. If they weren't running out of time, and the Brigadier not breathing down his neck for usable gen, he would have enjoyed breaking down this boy's will slowly. He looked at him, the dark face puffed up, the right eye a mess, a couple of ribs definitely gone, hanging in there. Nishonko had given out information, in steady tiny driblets and drablets, useless stuff, nothing new but just enough to stop them from going at him seriously. But Williams knew in his bones that this guy had stuff to share. He finished his cup of over-sweetened tea, liked it nice and sugary he did, and stood up as the door opened. The Brigadier came in followed by a gnome, a dark toady toad, with a muffler, for heaven's sake, in this heat. They came up to him, the Brigadier offering him a cigarette. They looked at the boy, suspended from his chains, the arms spread-eagled, the head hanging.

'Anything?'

'Nothing new, Sir. Confirming what we know, basically. Quite clever, well trained.'

'Let me speak to him.'

A pail of water was splashed on Nishonko. He came to, sputtering.

'Good evening, Nishonko Mitro. They call you the Nishachar, I believe. What exactly does it mean, I wonder?'

'The ghost who walks at night.' Goopta translated.

'So ghost, or whatever you call yourself, are you going to give me something? I'm in a bit of a hurry, as you will appreciate, so I need stuff sooner rather than later and if this is going to be a waste of time, I would rather we put a bullet in you and get on with it.'

'Major Nishonko Mitro, Azad Hind Fauj, Bahadur Regiment, No. 111567 under the supreme command of Netaji.' Nishonko's words were slurred but his intention was clear.

'Oh, for Pete's sake, you're not a POW... I just finished telling your friend out there that you're not even officially a prisoner!'

That brought Nishonko's head up. He looked at Whyte, out of his undamaged eye. 'Major Mookerji. He is alive?'

'Indeed, he is.'

Goopta suddenly stepped forward. 'You know him well?'

Nishonko shook his head, tiny drops of blood flying in the dank air, from his eye and the corner of his mouth. Williams looked at Goopta, frowning. Why was the Brigadier letting the greaseball butt in?

'Strange. I thought you were great friends.'

Goopta looked at Nishonko, his eyes narrowed. One of the reasons Goopta was so successful at what he did was because he could always spot a person's weakness, then prey on it. The high-born ladies who were his clients in Calcutta, the ones who called him G.G., giggling, each had that weak spot, that Achilles heel that he could exploit. Their hungers drove them to indiscretion and then they were his to control. In one, it was a weakness for young, pubescent boys, in another the siren call of the cards, the diamond rings and bangles tossed on the table in the eternal hope that this hand would see her fortunes change. He knew from the shift and tilt of her head at a regimental dinner that a particular newly wedded Captain's wife was having a torrid affair with the scion of a quite penniless North Bengal family and that Mrs. Newbury, the chaplain's widowed sister, had had a secret abortion a mere six months ago. So, now, he stared at Nishonko and saw the hatred, like a bright flame, flare up at the mention of Debraj's name, and get damped down. How interesting.

'Anyway, I think he will be most cooperative.'

Again that flicker of red, the rage like magma, surfacing, then dying down.

Whyte looked at Goopta, looked at Nishonko, back at Goopta. He smiled thinly.

'Yes, I do agree. He will most certainly spill his guts. A weak man, open to negotiation, I would say.'

Goopta watched Nishonko, expressionless. What was the chink in this man's armour, he wondered.

'So, make it easier for yourself. Your options are rather limited, I would guess. I could lock you up forever and throw away the key. You would disappear, without a trace. Or I could let you die a slow, painful death at the hands of the Sergeant here. Or put you in front of a firing squad and no one the wiser. Or you could sit down — would you like to sit down, take the weight off those chains, what do you say — and tell us the positions of all your different units and the battle plan.' Whyte's voice was kind. Nishonko hung his head, his chin dropping to his chest, his body slack. He didn't reply.

'Okay, Sergeant, have your way.'

Goopta raised his hand silently. Whyte felt a surge of irritation. But Goopta was staring at Nishonko, unaware of Whyte's displeasure.

'That Major Mookerji — Debraj, isn't that his name, king of the gods — he'll just get away with it. Smart fellow. He'll go for the deal — you know, his freedom for some friendly information.'

Nishonko stirred. The chains whispered, mice scrabbled in the walls.

'He'll be in Calcutta, safe and sound, while you, poor boy, will be rotting away in some hellhole. What a pity.'

Silence again. Dripping of water, a muted cry from the dungeons, the buzz of flies.

'You must be having family, parents, a woman you perhaps love.'

A shudder, and then stillness once more. Goopta smiled, oily, a self-satisfied smoothing of his moustache.

'It would be so sad, them never knowing what happened to you. That Major Mookerji. He has a girl, did you know? See, how beautiful she is.' He held up the photograph of Aditi, purloined.

Now the head came up, the bloodied eye peering.

'Leave her alone.'

Goopta grinned, a terrible, malicious, triumphant stretch of the lips.

'Ah, we wish we could, isn't it Brigadier? We wish we could. Had a slap bang engagement party.'

Whyte smiled. He loved this, this wonderful probing and touching of nerve endings, this exploration of weaknesses and chinks.

'And now, he, that little upstart, that laath shaheb, is going to go scot free with his little juicy fuckpot, in tow. Back to Calcutta, back to safety. The world is so unfair.'

Nishonko jerked upright. He strained at the chains, slipped on the bloody, muddy floor, slid to his knees in the filth.

'No, he can't, he mustn't, please!' A low howl, a trapped animal.

'Oh, but he can. And he will. Unless of course, you make it worth our while. Quid pro quo, my favourite English words.'

Silence again. Nishonko shook his head, his face drenched in sweat.

'Is that a no?'

A soft sob, a muttered curse. Then he shook his head again.

Whyte shrugged.

'Well, have it your way. Sergeant, get on with it.'

As they left, they heard Williams crooning, as if to a child.

'Come on lad, open up a bit here. Good boy.'

At the head of the stairs, they paused at the terrible cry of pain that floated up the dingy, ill-lit stairs, the cry of an animal in agony.

'Are you a betting man, Goopta?'

'Yes, Sir, I enjoy a little flutter. Now and then. Of course, my whole life is such a gamble.'

'So what would you give me on the other one, the pretty boy, breaking first?'

Goopta bobbed his head, smiling, considering the odds.

Sweat dripped into Aditi's eyes, blinding her for a moment. She used her sleeve to mop it up, her hands in blood-stained gloves, unequal to the task. Then she leaned forward and gently closed the eyes of the man on the stretcher.

'Anant, over here.' She tried to shout above the din.

One of the orderlies, a large, slow man with sleepy eyes, trundled over.

'This one's gone.'

Anant and another orderly took the stretcher away, not even a blanket to cover the indignity of death. The man would be dumped on one of the mules, transported to the burial ground by the riverside, a beautiful place, ringed by tall trees but already overcrowded, filling up. She moved to the next stretcher but sat back, shaking her head. He was a young Sikh, very good looking, his beard not yet fully grown. He reminded her of Subedar Singh from those days in Singapur. How weak she had been then, weeping, making a scene in front of Nishonko da. How was Nishonko da? She missed him, she realised. She missed their long conversations about planets and whales and what to do when you had snakebite. Would he ever forgive her? Her hands moved automatically, while her thoughts drifted, picking up scissors and hacking through the khaki trouser, stiff with blood. She ripped the fabric aside, exposing mangled flesh and bone, his vulnerable privates. She had seen too many men naked, wiped the blood and pus off too many genitalia to make her feel queasy. They were like children to her, to be bathed and kept whole. He was unconscious but she wiped his face clean, did up one button. These simple, unimportant actions, they were due to him. He was not going to make it, that was for sure but he was owed this little courtesy, this attention.

'Sister, send him outside. We need space.'

She looked up. Dr. Mishra stood there, his face haggard with lack of sleep.

'Yes, Sir. Sorry.'

'That's alright. It's hard to send them to die outside but there are more you can actually save.'

He was right. Aditi steadied herself and stood up.

'Medic…quickly…this man needs help…fast!'

A man stepped in through the tent flap. She turned. For a moment, her heart was in a vise. She couldn't breathe, she couldn't move. It was Satnam Singh from Debraj's battalion. *Not Deb, please don't let it be Deb.*

The stretcher was lowered. She kept her face turned away, not able to look.

'Sister!' Dr. Mishra's voice was a whiplash.

She forced herself to look. *Oh, my god, thank you, thank you, I'm so sorry, forgive me, God.*

It was Captain Pradhan. She looked at his shredded body. A thought came unbidden. His mother. How she would have massaged his fat little body with warm mustard oil when he was a child, kissed away the hurt when he fell, covered him at night when he lay, his limbs tender with sleep. How precious that flesh, that bone had been, how carefully protected, how jealously cherished from the knocks and blows of fate. She looked around the dark cavern of the field dressing station — at a wounded man, delirious with morphine, singing, a man holding another in his arms, rocking him. She had asked a soldier once, a man who knew he would be a cripple all his life, what he had got in return for all the suffering. His answer had been simple.

'Netaji embraced me.'

These mad, mad boys. She didn't know whether to yell at them, hug them or thank them. The place looked like a slaughter house, the ground slick with blood and gore, the stench of medicines and putrefaction and lye, like smoke in the air. But her heart sang with pride.

She gently wiped the caked blood and dirt from Kishore's face. He looked up. A half smile struggled to his lips but didn't quite make it. He closed his eyes, a soft breath out, the wind on a summer day. Very gently, she took his head in her lap. She broke open an ampoule of morphine and injected it. His eyes opened, glazed, the pain receding, like the tide going out on that little beach Debraj and she had made their own. Cradling Kishore, Aditi sang. Broken at first, the words catching at her throat, then loud and clear in her husky, raspy voice, all the hurt in the world, all the tears of mothers and lovers, distilled in it, she sang of loss and hope. Slowly, everyone gathered around, standing there, for a few minutes, the blood and bandages forgotten. When it ended, she looked down. His eyes were open and there was a little smile on his lips. She tenderly pulled the sheet over his face, tucking in his left hand that lay outside, lest it bump into anything.

Later, outside, in the air which smelled so sweet, she sat by Satnam Singh.

'Any news of Major Mookerji?'

Satnam shook his head, spat out a fleck of tobacco. 'You know I can't tell you, Sister. But pray for him. Just pray he is safe.'

Forlorn, she watched him go. She stood up, brushing the leaves and grass off her uniform. She thought of Meena but Meena was in one of the forward stations. She was going to join her soon, maybe tomorrow. Everything was so fluid, no surety, no certainty, things adrift, only the reality of the mule trains rolling in with their cargo of pain and mutilation in the early morning, the klaxon sounding the summons, the meals on the run, the exhausted sleep which itself was like death. She wanted a bath so so badly. She looked at the emerald on her finger, kissed it. Stay safe, my love, stay safe. I'm okay, I will be okay.

There was silence in the smoke-wreathed underground room of The Fortress, the Prime Minister's war office in London. It was quite late in the evening, past the dinner hour. But the heads of Britain's wartime intelligence outfits and some of the ministers had been summoned for a special meeting. They sat silently around the long table, their faces tense as they watched the large, rotund form of the Prime Minister pace up and down, majesterial in his deliberation.

'How did it happen so fast, gentlemen? Where was everybody? I mean, the man went back to Singapore a mere, what is it...'

'Just about...a year, Sir.' The Minister of Supplies' voice was low.

'Speak up, Mr. Lyttleton.'

'About 12 months, Sir.'

'Precisely. And in under a year, he has an army, he is knocking at the doors of India and you are telling me we may not be able to stop him. Preposterous!'

The PM champed on the cigar, his jaw working. 'I thought we had decided to be rid of him permanently.'

'He has proved elusive, Sir.'

'And India may prove to be elusive, if he succeeds. If you let him succeed. Gentlemen, I will not be the one to oversee the break up of the British Empire. No Sir, not on my watch. Inches!'

'Yes, Sir.' His aide stepped forward.

'Message to the Supreme Allied Commander South East Asia Command. The battle of Kohima must be won. Do whatever it takes. Whatever. Got that?'

'Yes, Prime Minister.'

There had been a shower in the morning in Maymyo and it was still cool out in the open. Ahmed Hassan was just back from the front and Netaji had decided to sit outside under a spreading gulmohur, which was much nicer than the stuffy confines of the command tent.

'Tell me, Ahmed, how is it going?'

'We have breached the enemy's lines and the way is open. We have taken them completely by surprise. All along the front, the British Army is falling back. We're within an ace of capturing both Kohima and Imphal. And we have word that the rest of the Bahadur group fought extraordinarily well in the Bishenpur sector.'

'I scribbled a few lines to Brahmachari Kailasam, you know, of the Ramakrishna Mission the other day, to tell him things were going rather well at the front and that spirits were very high. Just a quick note, since, once we cross the frontier, I'm not too sure when I would be able to write again.'

'Yes. But we really need to wrap it up fast. The Japanese have taken an enormous risk deciding to travel light. The supply lines connecting all of us to Rangoon are very thin. Limited supplies across these long distances, over such difficult and treacherous terrain — it's a bad combination.'

'They are counting on capturing "Churchill rations".'

'Iffy, Sir, depending totally on that. We don't want to be stranded on the wrong side of the hills and jungles.'

'And I'm sure the Americans will step in and start to airdrop supplies soon.'

'Correct. Once that starts, we will lose the advantage. And it could become a very long drawn out siege, not what we are looking forward to. We want to be done before the monsoons break.'

'Yes, absolutely but tell me about the men. How are they? How's the morale? I hear the casualties are high.'

'Well, we outnumber them, for now. But they are very well entrenched, they're better armed, they have vastly more fire power and they command the air.'

'Hmm, it's a battle between the human spirit on one side and steel and armour on the other.'

'So yes, the boys are taking quite a drubbing. I met a Japanese soldier, one of the walking wounded. He told me that the situation was "slightly not so very good".'

Ahmed laughed but the expression on Netaji's face sobered him up. He was pacing around, short, jerky steps, his large forehead knotted. He took off his glasses, his naked, short-sighted eyes looking suddenly vulnerable, and wiped them, as if they had fogged up.

'Are you okay, Sir?'

'Frustrated, Ahmed, so frustrated. I want to go to the front. I want to meet the men, face to face. They must know their Supreme Commander is willing to march beside them, to take the risks they are taking. But I'm not allowed that freedom.'

'With reason. We can't have you getting blown up prematurely. You need to be at the head of the INA when we march into Delhi. Patience, my friend.'

'Oh, it's all very well of you to spout all that. Can I at least go to the field hospitals? I could encourage the boys.'

'Well, I suppose that could be arranged.'

Gaffar too felt frustrated as he watched them from a distance. No one, not even he, was allowed to go near the command area. It had been very, very galling. He had been, virtually, off the grid. And he had not been able to get through to either Goopta or Omar. Apart from the intelligence he had sent from Rangoon, there was little else he could gather. Of course, he saw the troop movements, the trucks trundling by. He had pumped a few of the wounded going through and knew the action was happening somewhere near some place called Kohima.

But, of actual battle plans, he had no clue. He thought of the voice on the other end of the line, the anonymous shadow figure and felt a flicker of alarm. The voice was patient but it did not appreciate dithering and empty promises. There had already been rumours, warnings. The Kempeitai was sniffing around. They suspected moles, spies, double agents, traitors. Soon, he could lose whatever access he had to Netaji as well. He had to find something substantial to report — and soon.

Whyte was feeling quite mellow and at peace with the world. The fire was crackling in the grate, nice and cheery, just keeping the chill off. It turned quite cool towards the night in this part of the hills and anyway, a fire was always welcome, a kind of reminder of good old Blighty. He sipped the amber liquid, relishing it. He looked at Goopta on the other side of the fireplace, bundled up in a shawl, for heaven's sake and, what did they call it, a monkey cap, if you please, and laughed. Goopta smiled back at him, his eyes drowsy.

'You are happy, Brigadier?'

'Yes, it has been a rather fruitful day. You know, this may sound strange to you but, though I think you are a slimy toad with the morals of an alley cat, and the disposition of a hyena, and I wouldn't trust you to wash my arse for me, I confess I find you a man after my heart.'

Goopta was confused with all the rambling sentences. Was the Brigadier being insulting again or was he being nice? It was so difficult to understand the English. They all spoke such peculiar English. Far away, he could hear the thump of mortar fire. Did it sound closer?

'You actually seem to have a talent for the craft. I did think, mind you, for a bit at least, that you were a dud. Fssst!' He laughed again, amused at Goopta's look of incomprehension and his owlish stare. 'But you came through, my man. You came through.'

He was reaching for his glass, when there was a knock at the guesthouse door. Who could it be, so late at night? There was the murmur of conversation, then the khansama ushered in one of the military police fellas.

'Sorry to disturb you so late at night but the sergeant told me to report to you that one of the prisoners, the INA chappies, he's ready to talk, Sir.'

'Capital! Which one is it?' Whyte's normally pale skin, the curse of a redhead, was flushed, with the liquor or with the triumph, it was hard to say.

Goopta held up a hand, suddenly commanding.

'Wait. One minute, one minute. Before he spills the beans, ha, ha, shall we conduct our little wager, Brigadier? Which one are you putting your money on, Sir? Which one is going to break? Shall we?'

Whyte looked at him, the empty glass half raised.

'And why not Goopta, why indeed not?'

Just as the first hint of light was appearing on the hills, a pale mauve wash, a flight of four Sonya Japanese bombers winged its way towards Kohima. By the time it was light enough to see the tennis court and the hillside sloping away from it, Saito's scouts had relayed their instructions on the radio. The dark lethal shapes of the bombs, painted a delicate pink by the dawn light, came tumbling out of the plane's bellies, falling silently, acorns of death, towards the British positions. The silence of the dawn, when men are at their weakest, drowned in sleep, dreaming of home, was shattered, scattering the birds into the air like gunshot. Plumes of dust and gravel flew up. A single helmet shot up into the sky, turned lazily end on end, then plummeted, sucked down by gravity. Howls of triumph went up from the Japanese and INA trenches, the men jumping out, waving their guns, cheering loudly. But as the last Sonya banked to make its run, the release mechanism in its belly jammed, locking the bombs. The pilot, a young farmer's son from Hokadate, rocked and waggled his wings vigorously to set his lethal cargo free. The four 110-pound bombs finally broke free but by that time, the plane had overshot its target. The bombs plummeted straight towards the outskirts of the small town of Kohima.

Later, the same morning, an INA unit, trudging through the forest towards the front, came across a strange sight. A peg-legged man, small, wiry, in a Lance Naik's uniform, was practically carrying a tall, decrepit figure in tattered khaki pants, bare bodied, clutching his kit bag to his chest, his face, blackened, singed, an ugly gash on his forehead. They ran to help. Up close, they recognised Major Debraj Mookerji and Kabootar Singh. Debraj smiled but he was a bit woozy, his words garbled. When they tried to take the kit bag from him, he vehemently refused. So they let it go and got him to the field station. Meenakshi patched him up. He had a fever, he was dehydrated, there was the nasty gash, and he had superficial burns but was remarkably unhurt, considering his ordeal

'How is…Nishonko?' she asked, tentatively, her face guarded.

'I…I don't know. We were captured but I escaped. I don't know if he made it. The prison got bombed. I'm sorry.'

Her face crumpled for a moment but she got herself under control.

Back at base, looking human again after a wash and a hot meal, he was summoned by Saito.

'What on earth happened? You two just vanished. Where is Major Mitro?'

'Got a whole unit to turn but then we were betrayed.'

'What do you mean?'

'Assam Regiment guy. Sold us down the river.'

'And then what?'

Debraj's eyes were dark. He sat, staring at his hands, a long moment, lost in thought. Then he looked up to find Saito looking at him keenly.

'Come on Major, fill me in. This is important. What did you see? Who was there?' 'Sorry, Sir, a bit fuzzy. Crack on the head. They had a British guy, a man with red hair. Interrogated me but I just kept mum.'

'Did you get a name?'

'No, um, no, Sir.'

'And then?'

'Then they stuck me in a cell and left me there. I must have passed out um…because the next thing… I think they came back…ummm…'

He fell silent, his eyes glazed.

'It's all hazy…and then, from nowhere…this great big rumble and crash, dust flying, bricks tumbling through the air. And smoke, choking me, blinding. And then out of the smoke came this crazy man, naked, filthy, a Naga, screaming at me. And he was pulling this big wooden beam off me… I was probably trapped underneath…he was screaming and pulling and he got me out and we came out, absolute chaos, a big British guy, a Sergeant, was lying on the ground, with a chain wrapped around his neck, strangled, his face blue.'

Debraj's eyes were clouded, the horrors he had seen like fungus on his brain, his gaze far away. Saito waited. Debraj was in shock, he would have to deal with it in his own time. At least, he had escaped torture, lucky man. Nishonko might not have been so fortunate.

'And then Kabootar found you.'

'I know, he just came through the smoke, brandishing a gun, like some lunatic. What was Kabootar doing there?'

'Looking for you, he said. You need to get that man of yours under control. He just does anything he fancies.'

'But he got me back.'

There was a pause.

'Can I get some furlough, Sir? I need to meet Aditi… Sister Sen.'

'Of course. I understand.'

'I'll be back by the evening. Then, I won't leave your side.'

'Glad to hear that Major. My regards to Sister Sen.'

When Dr. Mishra told her there was someone to see her, she couldn't move. She held her breath. Please, please let it be good news.

'Go on, Sister, move it. Work to be done. Don't stand around, dreaming.'

She walked out, her heart hammering. He was standing outside, his face turned away, one arm resting on some packing crates, the legs crossed. There was a plaster on his forehead but otherwise, he seemed unhurt. Kabootar sat on the ground beside him, like a dog, looking straight ahead. She must have shouted out his name, for he turned to look at her. She ran to him, regardless of the stares, the turns of the heads, the rules, the regulations. He caught her up in his arms, enveloping her in that familiar, so comforting, so much missed mélange of smells — the sweat saltiness, the tobacco aroma clinging to his sleeves, the moss and green, smoke and earth, the man-smell of him. He crushed her, robbing her of breath, then suddenly let her go. She almost fell, so greatly had she committed her body into the circle of his arms. But he steadied her and bundled her towards the road leading downhill. They walked away from the hospital, into the forest. She held his hand fiercely, her short nails digging into his palms. He was silent, looking back at the road, curling out behind them, like a trail. As soon as there was no more traffic, he pulled her to him and kissed her like he might drown. He pushed his tongue into her mouth as if he would drink her very soul. She was frightened by the intensity, his desperation. Something had gone wrong.

'What is it, my love?'

He shook his head, glanced at Kabootar. Kabootar walked ahead, not looking back. They went down to the river, a bend of it, where the water slowed down to a long swell and lilies grew in profusion, and a flat large rock as large as a king-sized bed jutted out over the current. They lay on it, their faces warmed by the sun, the ripples forming and breaking in the shadow of the rock, mesmerising. He told her, the details sketchy, of what had happened, leaving out the whole interaction with Goopta and Whyte. She clung to his hand, her eyes wide, drinking in his words.

'You could have been killed?'

'I'm okay.'

'Your eyebrows are burnt.'

'They will grow back.'

He kissed her then, again, his body on top of her, the weight of him comforting.

'I want you to go back to Rangoon. Tomorrow.'

'Whhhat?'

'You'll be safe there. I won't have to worry about you. You must leave these jungles.'

'Why? Why do you want me to go?'

'You…are in danger.'

'Aren't we all, Deb? I can't leave now, when I'm needed the most. This is what I trained for.'

'Things are going to turn bad, Aditi. You can't be here, when all hell breaks loose.'

'How do you know this?'

'Trust me, I do.'

'And what about marching into Calcutta? To Delhi? Our cheese sumboosucks? Would you deprive me of all that?'

'Stop being childish, Aditi.'

'Then stop treating me like some fragile piece of porcelain.'

He looked at her, the stubborn set of her jaw, the calm confidence in her eyes. Something had happened to her, some subtle change. There was a surety about her, a new steel beginning to show. *She will be okay, Goopta won't really be able to get to her, it was just threats and bluster.* He thought of the radio, sitting like a coiled snake, inside his kit bag, hidden in his tent. He should destroy it, get rid of it. *But Goopta knows where Ma, Baba and Debi are. He still has the power to harm them. But will he be able to? This battle will be over before we know it. We will break through in days. They said they are at the end of their tether. And what if we don't? He thinks he has persuaded me. He will expect immediate news. Maybe I can…'*

'You seem very far away, my love.'

He came back to her. She was looking at him, her eyes shadowed with concern. She had lost weight, there were soft grey pockets under those eyes.

'I haven't asked you how you have been. Are you well?'

She smiled, a tiny smile, to herself but it was like a light came on.

'I am well. How's Nishonko da?'

'When did you start calling him Nishonko da? He's probably younger than me.'

She looked startled but recovered. 'Oh, it's an old habit. From Shantiniketan. We called all older boys dada.'

'Well, that's the thing. Nishonko is missing. He was there somewhere in that prison and when it got hit, I don't know what happened to him. Maybe I should have waited, got him out but I just bolted.'

'So, he could be...' Her voice trailed off. He looked at her, saw the tears fill her eyes, spill over.

'It's so unfair.'

'Why are you crying? You hardly know the man.'

'After what we've done to him...'

'What do you mean?'

She stopped aghast, suddenly aware of what she had said. Then she squared up her shoulders. It didn't matter now, the friend of her childhood was gone. She drew in a shuddering breath.

'The time... It never seemed right...'

'I don't understand...'

'Nishonko da...he loved...loves me...'

'Mitro? You? What are you...what about Meenakshi?'

He got up, pacing. She looked at him, drew her knees up.

'It was so long ago...we were friends...and then I met you...'

'When were you going to tell me?'

'There was nothing...nothing.'

'Jhilik...that's what your aunt called you...and on the boat... he said...'

'Would it have made a difference? Would you have walked away?'

'God, now I understand...the way he's been...I feel like such a cad. How could you have let me do this?'

'It *is* my fault.'

He looked at her, her head lowered, clasping her knees, penitent. *Would I have given her up, even if I knew about Nishonko? No. Nishonko had his chance. She chose me. He wouldn't have been able to hang on to her anyway, with his cold-blooded, prissy, goody-two-shoes manner, not a woman like her. And anyway, now it was too late for all that. She was his. And Nishonko? Gone...*

He hunkered down, held her.

'You should have told me. You should have trusted me.'

'I was so afraid I would lose you.'

They sat, holding each other. A cloud of dragonflies swept over the water, darting, the evening sun catching the shimmering wings. Far away, in some village, temple bells rang, carrying the prayers of men to the mountaintops where the gods sat, amused by the twists of fate they spun.

It was late in the evening, alerted by the barking of dogs, that a Japanese patrol stumbled upon him, the right eye swollen shut, the wrists and ankles lacerated, clutching his chest. He had no kit, no gun. He was wounded, shot in the shoulder, while escaping, he told them. He had crawled for hours, hiding from British patrols. They rushed him to the field hospital, informed Saito. Dr. Mishra got working on him immediately.

'Fortunately for him, it's just a surface flesh wound. The bullet has just grazed the shoulder. His eye will be okay in a couple of days but he's bust a couple of ribs, I suspect.'

'Tortured?' Saito frowned.

'Most probably. He's been chained. There's blunt force trauma. A couple of teeth missing.'

'Can I speak to him?'

Mishra nodded. 'I've given him a sedative. A few minutes.'

Saito walked up to the pallet. Through the mosquito net, he looked at Nishonko. The man's face was like a carved mask, dark ebony. He stared into nothingness.

'Major, good to have you back.'

The dark eyes with the long lashes flickered.

'Thank you, Sir.' It came out a bit mumbled, the face swollen from Williams' dentistry.

'Did you give them anything? There's no shame in it but I need to know exactly what you've told them.'

'Of course, Sir. But I stuck to basics, the known, observable facts. I gave old positions. I kept the numbers vague, contradictory. They didn't get anything that could make a difference, Sir.'

'Good man. Brave man. How did you get away?' Saito's eyes were sharp in the gloom of the room.

'Well, they finished questioning me at dawn, I think. I had drifted away and then there were some explosions and the prison was hit. I managed to escape but was shot by one of their chaps.'

'Hmmm. Where were you since then…all this time?'

'Just wandering through the jungle, I guess, trying to avoid their patrols. May have passed out.'

'Well, Major Mookerji made it back.'

There was the tiniest of pauses.

'Oh, did he? Was he hurt?'

'No, he was lucky.'

'Where is he?'

'Gone to the field station to meet his fiancé. You know her? Aditi Sen?'

Nishonko turned his head away. Saito patted his shoulder. He could see the man's eyes were getting drowsy.

'Rest, Major. It's been quite an adventure.'

Nishonko turned. He clutched Saito's hand in a surprisingly strong grip. 'Sir, I can't rest. I want to be at the front. I want to get back at them.'

Saito was touched. This is what made the INA the army it was. 'You won't be much good to me at the front, not with that eye and that shoulder, Major. But don't worry about it. I need a good man at Division HQ. Someone trained to assess reports coming in, understand the moment to moment changes in the situation, and give me a bird's eye view. Up to it, Major?'

Nishonko looked blank for a moment. Then his face cracked open in a smile — the smile of a boy who has got exactly the birthday gift he wanted.

'Thank you, Brigadier, thank you.'

As Saito left the field station, Meenakshi watched from the shadows, hidden behind the grey mosquito nets. She had stayed away, sending in another nurse but had hung around. She overheard their conversation. Part of her wanted to go to him — still, you stupid, stupid woman. But she was afraid to look into his eyes, see the hatred and the violence again, the volcano sleeping inside. She waited and when she knew he had drifted off, she crept up to the pallet, silent on her cloth shoes. He was lying on his side, foetal under the sheet, his knees drawn up. A soft groan escaped, a guttural sound, his good arm flailing at something unseen in the air. She swiftly put her hand on him, shush, shush, calmed his breathing. The bruises on his chest and back were turning purple. Poor Nishonko. His good left eye suddenly opened. He looked at her, his gaze unfocussed, for a long moment, then closed it with a sigh. She sat down, to keep vigil. She would leave as soon as he came to. He need never know.

All over the ridge, the British were slowly retreating, conceding ground, foot by foot. Every rock and bush seemed to hide an ambush. In many cases, there were only pockets of resistance, as small groups of Britishers were isolated and cut down brutally. The hillside was strewn with bodies of the dead. The Japanese had managed to capture most of the surrounding hills and controlled the two springs which were the only water supply in the area. A steady stream of Indian soldiers defected from the British side. Many who were unsure simply melted away into the night, thinning the British ranks. Very often, the American Dakota pilots missed their target and dropped stores behind the Japanese lines. The men tore open the packages greedily to find a veritable feast of tinned beans, rice and condensed milk. There were also packets of plasma and, sometimes, mortar shells. An hour later, the same shells were fired on the British positions. As they retreated, fresh positions were marked on a large-scale situation map, the Kaiga, named after Japanese ink paintings. It had different coloured markers to indicate friendlies, hostiles, infantry, artillery and battle zones. Saito stood in front of the Kaiga, watching the red markers inching forward. A smattering of applause made him turn. Nishonko had just walked in, the eye behind a patch, his shoulder bandaged. The men were on their feet, cheering him. Word had spread about his escape and his bravery. Saito walked up and shook his hand.

'Sure you're ready for this?'

Nishonko looked around. The division HQ was a large tent covered with camouflage nets. In the centre, there was a cluster of tables and chairs. A string of naked bulbs, hung by flex wire and powered by a small generator, bathed everything in a lurid yellow light. On the right, five radio operators sat hunched over their machines, gently adjusting dials, listening on headphones, jotting down co-ordinates, relaying them to two officers who kept updating it on the Kaiga. The place buzzed, electric with urgency and tension. Nishonko smiled broadly.

'Absolutely!' He pointed at the Kaiga. 'Who's that close to the DC's bungalow?'

'Kitsume. He's gained a lot of ground in the past few hours.' Kitsume was a big, lumpy, bull dog of a man. No one had ever seen him smile or laugh. He had lost his wife and two sons to the American bombing of Okinawa.

'He's like a battering ram, just hammering his way through.

'He seems crude and unrefined but he wasn't like this. Before the war, he was a marine biologist, an expert on firefly squid. But his whole life has become a single-minded crusade to defeat the hated gaikokujin — the forces of the West. He's become a byakko, a legend, with his men. They say he's invincible. They'll follow him anywhere.'

'And this red marker, who is that?'

'That's Watanabe and Major Mookerji. They are now taking up positions around Garrison Hill.'

Nishonko's brow furrowed, as if he had a headache. 'That's the big one.'

'That's the biggest. Garrison Hill is the highest point in Kohima. With that in our hands, it will take five British divisions to knock us off. By the time they muster that, we will be through and on the road to the railhead.'

They were interrupted by a burst of static and a Japanese voice speaking rapidly. Nishonko knew some Japanese but this was beyond him. He remembered the month he had spent in Tokyo. It seemed like a lifetime away. Things had been so uncomplicated. There was a freedom to be won, a leader to be followed. But now...

'Major Kitsume has surrounded the DC's bungalow,' the operator translated.

And so the battle for the bungalow began. The hillside was terraced. Each terrace had to be climbed, breached. About 300 soldiers of the Kent Regiment were dug in amidst the rhododendrons and cannas of the DC's garden. Saito's snipers occupied every tree still standing, picking off any British soldier who showed his mug, one by one. Twelve hundred British Indian and British soldiers died fighting the Japanese that day. It was called the Battle under the Cherry Tree. That cherry tree was a Japanese sniper post. Kitsume and Captain Swaran Singh, sharing command, led sweeping charges up the slope. The Kents counter attacked. By the evening, the bungalow had changed hands thrice. But late that night, by the darkness of moonset, Kitsume led another couple of squads up the northern, steeper side of the hill and fell on the British. The bungalow was finally theirs. There was only one casualty. Kitsume took a flame thrower burst in his chest and fell. His men wailed. True to the legend of the byakko, he had fallen only to fire! The invincible warrior, immune to bullets and shrapnel, was gone. They carried his body down the hill, fighting for the privilege of carrying the bier. Twice they ran into British units but both times, the Japanese tore their way through with blazing guns, making sure not to dishonour the warrior by letting the bier hit the ground.

'And so it raged through the next day. The tennis court area became the new perimeter.' The old man rubs his milky eyes, tiredly. His knees feel stiff, the ancient wound in his leg is hurting like hell and his bony butt is sore from sitting on that hard bench for so long. It has been a long telling but now they are nearing the end. Dulal da shakes his head.

'What kind of a battle was this anyway? You said it was Britain's fiercest battle? It wasn't even a battlefield, moshai. These men were all running around capturing bungalows and tennis courts and some flower gardens. Seriously!'

The old man sighs. 'What was fought on that tennis court was heroic. The ground was what, maybe about 20 yards wide? At one time, no man's land shrunk to just five yards. It was gruelling. All the rules of combat had broken down. It was truly *the* agnipariksha — trial by fire — for the INA.'

'Still, there are so many contradictory accounts of what happened in Kohima.' Sudipto looks up from his notebook where he has been scribbling stuff. 'I mean, if you read British military memoirs, they really pooh pooh the role of the INA.'

Anger flares in the the old man's rheumy eyes. He slaps the table, sending the empty tea cups rattling.

'You've read them, you've read them? Load of poppycock. If you get your hands on British intelligence reports — you can, they're in files you can access — there's absolutely no basis for the self-congratulatory tone and substance of those memoirs. Most of those memoirs, they were written years later, often by people who were nowhere in Kohima at the time. Lies, fabrications, rumours of rumours, to bolster the legend of the great British Indian Army. We were there. We were witness.'

The old man pauses, his anger ebbing. He looks at their faces, at the unconscious pity reflected there, the barely concealed impatience with which people look at the old who rant about the past.

'Anyone have a cigarette?' he rasps. Reluctantly, Dulal da hands him a packet of Wills Filter. The old man takes out one, hesitates, takes out another and drops it into his kurta pocket. He lights up, savouring the smoke.

'Thank you, Dulal babu. Hanh, where was I? Yes, on that hillside, eyeball to eyeball, on our feet, 48 hours non stop. And, by the way, no food. The British were lucky. They had a ten to one advantage over the Japs in Burma when it came to air power. Their Dakotas were dropping regular supplies to the garrison. So, they, at least, could eat. We? We were down to just one rice ball per meal. The Japanese had spread themselves too thin over the Pacific. They couldn't provide air cover or air drop supplies to their own troops. We were practically starving. No planes were coming to drop tinned beans for us, you understand. So we actually had to hunt for food. You know why there were no dogs in Nagaland?'

He laughs, a chuckle of malicious amusement, at the expression on their faces. 'At night, our patrols carried out surprise attacks. We were losing men in these strikes but those night raids were essential. They were made purely to get food.'

Sudipto blinks, then gestures to Haru. 'Talking of food, how about some hot radhaballabhi and chholar dal, Haru? For all of us? On me.'

'Thank you, writer babu, that would be nice.' The old man licks his lips.

Richards had other problems besides feeding his troops. Every hour, he had been getting desperate messages from his commanders, pleading for reinforcements. His repeated pleas to Slim were met with cockamamie replies, urging them to hold on, no matter what, you are making history, Colonel, bullshit on bullshit, relief coming soon, if you give up, we will lose India! *You fockin' deserve to lose India, you sanctimonious bastards, sitting on your fat asses, safe, while my men are just getting mowed down by these unholy savages.* He felt like weeping but was so sleep deprived that his eyes felt dusty as a dry nullah in summer. And the reports of the Assam Regiment defections were growing. If word got around, they would be in trouble. It would spread like wildfire, to other regiments, other disloyal bastards, malcontents and troublemakers. It would grow from a trickle to a flood, breaking apart the British Army in the east.

The Allies kept a tight lid on news leaking out about Netaji and the INA, while denouncing Bose as a traitor in broadcasts from London. On April 17, *Time* magazine, in an article titled 'Renegade's Revenge' wrote, *'Thoughtful men thought twice when they learned that sardonic, myopic Bose, traitor, was with the Japs around Imphal.'* News was filtering through about Bose's army. According to *Time,* its strength varied from 3,000 to 30,000. *'One explosive fact: an armed anti-British Indian stands today on Indian soil and calls upon his fellows to rebel against the Raj.'* And John W. Gerber wrote in *The Nation* on April 22, *'Bose is on the verge of achieving his goal'* and if he succeeded in doing so, it would be *'a major political and military victory'*. To quote him, *'He had begun to turn his words into action.'*

'Sir, we have to put a lid on this, I feel.' General Slim's voice was firm.

'What are you suggesting, General Slim?' the Commander in Chief asked, quietly.'

'A complete news blackout. It is vital that no information about the INA or the Japanese in Kohima or about our reverses is made available to the press. Any adverse reports may hasten the drain of our troops.'

'Complete censorship, eh? Let me run it past Auk.'

General Auchinleck, 'The Auk' as he was commonly called, was his forthright self.

'Well, I wouldn't want to sweep this issue under the carpet. I have never doubted the integrity of the Indian sepoy, not even during that "Quit India" dust up in '42, aye. But this INA business is a different kettle of fish. It's made our johnnies think thoughts that are frankly quite unsettling. I say we block all news. It can only help.'

That settled it. If 'The Auk', who had spent much of his career in India and knew everything there was to know about the Indian Army, felt that his johnnies, the jawans, were getting swayed by this INA, he would make sure no one got to know anything about them. It would be as if that battle out there in those hills had not happened. He called in his secretary.

'Send a message out, right away, addressed to all the presswallahs. Top priority: The government is imposing a complete ban on any reporting linked to either the INA or the Japanese Army in any sector in India with immediate effect. Any defaulter will face serious consequences, with charges of sedition. Keep the Home Office in the loop, and the PMO, will you?'

'Has he sent anything as yet?' Goopta was staring out of the window of Whyte's office, his face dark. It had been a couple of days and K — the codename they had given the man they had turned, K for Kohima, simple — K's radio had not let out a single cheep. Goopta was secretly worried. Did they have enough leverage? Could love, silly thing, love, really turn a man against country, nation, cause?

'No. Nothing. As yet. He will need time, to settle in. Make sure he's not seen, caught. It's reported that a Major Jiro, the Kempeitai spycatcher, is trying to trap a suspected spy close to Netaji. He has been questioning everyone he can lay his hands on, not sparing anyone. He has apparently also been sniffing around the front lines, digging into people who are close to Netaji. So K could be feeling vulnerable, exposed, alone. It's a big step, Goopta, betrayal. Tears you apart.'

Goopta looked at him in surprise.

'You speak as if you are on his side, as if you sympathise with him.'

'True. How perceptive of you, dear chap. I...I feel rather parental once a man becomes mine. Once I own him, I have to nurture him, feed that darkness, keep that flame of hatred alive. Know what Socrates said?'

'I'm not familiar with the man.'

'Ah, you wouldn't be, would you? Greek chap. Said: *"From the deepest desires often comes the deepest hate."*'

'That is good. Clever man. So, we need to provide him with cover, yes?'

'Ah, what is your devious little brain cooking up now?'

'Oh, a small deception, if I may. Gaffar.'

'Our Gaffar? The man who isn't there? Our empty handed, missing in action friendly neighbourhood spy?'

'The selfsame one. Why don't we present him to Major Shiro…'

'Jiro.'

'Yes, yes, why not present some irresistible bait? Give him his spy to catch?'

Whyte raised an eyebrow, a slow, delighted smile starting to curl his lips.

'A red herring?'

'What is this red herring, Sir?'

'It's a fish that…oh, never mind. It's okay, don't look so mystified. I've got it. He catches his spy, they relax and don't bother to look under any more rocks...at least for a while.'

'The heat will be off and K can make his move.'

'You know Goopta, you never cease to amaze me! I would bung you into the Service in a shot, if you were…you know…'

'I completely understand, Sir.' Goopta was glowing with pride. In spite of the complicated words Whyte liked to use, he knew a compliment when he got one.

'There is of course only one person we can use as bait.'

'I was thinking of the very same person, sahib.'

'But Omar? He won't be happy if we use his man as a sacrificial lamb.'

'Omar has one agenda, only, Sir — the formation of Pakistan. He is a League man. Not only will he understand, he will cooperate fully.'

Whyte nodded. He hadn't lived in India for long but he'd studied Indian history. It had helped him see patterns — the threads of betrayal and treachery woven into the complex fabric of changing dynasties. *How fickle are their alliances. How quick they are to discard their own to gain advantage.*

'Just one more question, Whyte Sir. How do we make sure Gaffar keeps his mouth shut and doesn't betray all of us? He will not be able to take the Kempeitai's third degree.'

'Don't worry your pretty little head about that.'

The web was spun. When Major Jiro, brandishing the warrant like a charm, marched, with all the parade ground grace that his thin body allowed him, into Gaffar's tent, he was a proud man. How quickly he had solved the case. He knew that, in the last few weeks, he had become a bit of a nuisance for everyone, going to the front lines, questioning possible suspects, in the middle of the battle. He was like a bloodhound, sniffing, digging, scratching away to find the stooge. But what gold it had yielded! A chance conversation, overheard in a bar, sheer luck, had led them finally to a godown in Rangoon's dockside. There, certain documents, letters, photographs, in a locked steel trunk had come to light, pointing the finger irrevocably to one man only. He took everything to the Chief of the Kempeitai in Burma who in turn confronted Netaji with the evidence. Netaji was extremely sensitive when it came to loyalty. He would often say that it was the treachery at Plassey in 1757 that had made the British colonisation of India possible in the first place. Though he was shocked at the news that it was Gaffar — Gaffar with whom he had shared so much, so many nights of exile — that it was Gaffar who was the traitor, he steeled himself. His orders were very clear. Arrest him, question him and punish him if there's proof he is a traitor. So, Major Jiro came strutting, a righteous spring in his step to carry out his mandate. But disappointment, cruel frustration awaited him inside. There was a note, typewritten, Gaffar's full confession, unsigned. *Yes, he had been helping the British. Yes, he had given out war plans. But he had done it for a reason. He had done it to secure the future of Muslims! Netaji's idea of an undivided India was wrong. Jinnah was right! What future would Mussalmaans have in a Hindu India! Pakistan was the only refuge for the Muslims. People would think he was a traitor but he was a shahid, a true martyr to his cause. This was his holy duty. He would not be taken prisoner.* His body, stiff in rigor, hung from the tent pole, suspended by a keffiyeh, the toes almost brushing the hard earth floor. There were no clear strangulation marks, strange for a hanging but it was impossible to carry out a full investigation in the jungle HQ of the joint forces. So Major Jiro sent the body back to Rangoon for an official post mortem, which would unfortunately take weeks, and tried to drown his frustration of the quarry slipping out of his fingers with a bottle of sake.

In the command tent, they absorbed the news in stunned silence.

'Well, looks like the tiresome Major Jiro finally found his spy.' Saito smiled.

'Unbelievable...Gaffar Khan!' Debraj shook his head. 'Are they sure...I mean, Gaffar has been with Netaji for donkey's ages.'

'Full confession, I believe.' Saito shrugged.

'Goes to show, you can't ever know what a man is really capable of. At least, that Jiro will stop breathing down all our necks.' It was Nishonko, from the shadows, sitting in a camp chair in front of one of the radios, his arm bandaged, his eye patch giving him a piratical look. But when Debraj nodded at him, Nishonko turned away abruptly. Debraj shrugged. He had thought of speaking to Nishonko many times but had felt awkward, knowing what he did now. Also, the fact that he had bolted from the prison without making any attempt to save Nishonko made him feel shame, an uncomfortable feeling he didn't particularly relish.

'But if he was ratting on us, how come we still surprised them at Kohima?'

'Because the orders to turn the whole Division towards Kohima was kept under wraps. Even in Netaji san's staff, only a select few knew. Gaffar wasn't one of them.' Saito explained.

Debraj nodded, walked slowly to the Kaiga, his eyes scanning the positions, memorising them, getting a mind picture for the coming attack.

Whyte came striding out of the room where he had set up his own operations centre. He had arm-twisted Richards into giving him radios and a couple of operators, and he had orderlies scurrying back and forth from a large-scale map of the region which they had spread out on the wooden floor. An unlikely conglomeration of objects made up the markers — angami necklace beads, cowrie shells, cane baskets, cups, saucers, even a rice beer mug.

'Goopta! Goopta, you old goat, get your arse down here!'

Goopta came trotting from the verandah, alarmed, his beringed hands flapping.

'Yes, Whyte sahab, what is it, what is it?'

'It worked. We've just got the first message from K! The radio transmissions are crystal clear.' Whyte's ice grey eyes were glittering with excitement, on fire.

Goopta leaned on the door jamb, panting. 'And his information is any good?'

'Any good? You bloody heathen, it's pure gold!' Whyte held a wire recording spool in his hand.

'What is that, Sir?'

'That...that is my ticket to the good life, Goopta. Now I know exactly where and with how many men the Japanese commander is going to attack Garrison Hill.'

'Wonderful, wonderful, Sir.' Goopta said, solemly. 'And all for the love of a woman. I will confess, I had little doubts. Have you ever felt such love, Brigadier?'

'Fortunately, for the Service, no. We men of the netherworld, we tellers of lies, we can't afford such mush. I like the ladies, mind you, don't get me wrong, not a poofter, me. But giving up my life, my country for something in skirts...that's piffle. Come on, let's get to work. It's a tiny sliver but it's a chance finally to turn the tables.'

They had practically surrounded Garrison Hill and were now in position to strike the final death blow at this last stronghold of the British garrison at Kohima. Saito knew the British would be dug inside deep trenches and bunkers and ready with everything they had to repulse them. Both were on a knife edge, the British down to their last men and Saito down to his last resources of arms, materials, food and medicine. Neither could afford to lose.

Saito laid out his elaborate assault plan at the commander's meeting in Divison HQ. He had set up a three-mile corridor around the base of the hill and stocked it with small ammunition and supply depots.

From the corridor, his strike teams could sally forth, ready to move in either direction. When they got fatigued, they could fall back on the corridor and fresh teams could take their place. The pressure on the British positions would have to be relentless, unforgiving. His plan was met with applause.

Debraj, his arms crossed, watched Saito bow ceremoniously.

'If I may, Sir?'

'Yes, Major Mookerji?'

'It's going to take time. We don't have time. I think we should launch a full scale attack on the hill straight away, not give them time to breathe. We should bring up the artillery, put them in your four-piece orchestra formation and shell the living daylights out of them. Pulverise them into rubble.'

'Ah, Major Mookerji, the orchestra must follow a score, a pattern. When all the instruments come in at the right time, it will all come together in a symphony.' He looked at the others around the table. Most looked blank. Saito smiled.

'In this symphony, the conductor doesn't want to start with a boom boom boom boom... No, Major, the big drum must come in at the right time, only when the conductor wants a big, loud sound. It must complement, highlight, counterpoint. Only then will there be poetry.'

Debraj shuffled his feet impatiently. *Okay, okay, got it, man, now let's get on with it.* His nerves were on edge, the prospect of the big battle, the face to face with the enemy making his mouth dry, his heart hammer. *All this bullshit glorification of war, of killing. In the end, it will be the business end of a bayonet and a guy in front of you. It will be blood pouring out of a bullet hole somewhere and your head exploding in a thousand tiny fragments of bone. Where's the poetry in that Saito san?* His stomach clenched.

'So when will you bring in the artillery?' From far away, he heard Nishonko's voice. He pulled himself together. Nishonko was standing at the back, beside the Kaiga.

'And where?' Debraj added.

'There's is no point firing shells from the base. They will fall short. Our guns need to be here and here, up on the hill.' He looked at Nishonko's raised eyebrow and smiled. He was enjoying this.

'Question: how the hell are we going to take those big guns up there? We dismantle them. That's right. Completely. Then we move them up the hill by night and re-assemble them. We dispense with all inessentials, the wheels, the carriage...'

'And how do we cart the guns up those slopes? Airlift them, Sir?' Debraj's tone was sardonic.

Watanabe bristled. 'We can use the Nagas. They are good coolies.'

'And they are unfriendly. They don't like working for us. They will probably drop the whole lot down the mountain side, to just spite us.' Debraj's voice was sharp. Saito looked at him, a puzzled frown. What was up with Debraj? Normally, he was very supportive.

'So we use our faithful friends...the mules. The British cannot know that we are moving the guns. It must come as a surprise. So, a little minor surgery on the vocal cords — I believe it's called debraying — and the mules will carry our special cargo, silently, all the way up. How does that sound?'

They let it sink in. Then there was a chorus of approval.

'Ingenious!'

'Those poor fucking mules,' Debraj protested. 'Don't they have any say in this?'

There was a shout of laughter.

'Quite a scheme,' whispered Nishonko.

The sun was low by the time the meeting finished. The officers gathered their bags and map cases and moved off in different directions to join their units.

Nishonko, walking back from the command HQ, saw Debraj duck into the jungle. He stared at him in the gathering darkness. Probably headed for his unit, taking a short cut. They had not spoken to each other since the night they had got captured. Nishonko had wanted to question Debraj, whether he had been interrogated, what they had said to him, that paled-faced bastard with the cold grey eyes and his fat Indian stooge. *Debraj had not been tortured, that was evident. Why not? Why had they spared him? How did he actually get away??* Nishonko wanted to know the answers desperately but he just couldn't bring himself to speak to that filth. Debraj also seemed to be avoiding him. *What did he know?* Doesn't matter, he would pay. He would pay for his arrogance and that sense of entitlement he just oozed. He would pay for trying to steal Aditi away from him. He would pay for turning Netaji against him. He would pay for violating Aditi, he would…

'Halt!'

With a shock, he realised he was pointing his gun, ramrod straight, towards the jungle where Debraj had disappeared. He slowly straightened up, *when had he pulled it out,* dropped the gun in his holster. He turned to the sentry, a pimply boy, brandishing his rifle nervously. Nishonko summoned a smile.

'Sorry, thought I spotted a hyena in the jungle. At ease, soldier, I'm Major Mitro.'

'Yes, Sir, sorry, Sir.'

'No, it's good you're alert.' Nishonko strode off, entered his tent. He sat down. He looked at his hands, at the faintest of trembles. He must get his rage under control. He rummaged in his knapsack, pulled out an old faded print. It was blurred, hazy, the sun in the lens, of a little girl, with pigtails, looking up at the camera with the curious, challenging look of the very young. In her skirt, held up like a basket, were mangoes, stolen or retrieved after a storm, who knew. He looked at her for a long moment, then touched the picture to his lips.

'Don't worry, my little one, I will make everything okay.'

He took a torch, stepped out of his tent, headed for the jungle. The pimply sentry turned to an older soldier.

'Aren't there hyenas in the jungle? Where's the Major off to?'

'And leopards and bears. But don't worry about the Major, he knows how to look after himself. Probably just going for a dump. He's a fastidious man, doesn't like shitting on his own doorstep.'

Debraj walked fast through the forest, the pine trees like sentinels all around him. In the twilight, the woods had an air of mystery. Birds called farewells to each other, before getting ready to tuck into their nests for the coming of the night. He always wondered how they remained in the midst of such fury and hellfire and greeted the coming of each day with song? Wouldn't they want to fly away somewhere safe? Every time the forest went up in flames, the birds would rise in thousands, like specks of ash, flurries, black smudges wheeling up into the sky. And next morning, they would be back, their avian chatter waking the exhausted soldiers hugging the cold earth. He kept his eyes peeled. Didn't want to bump into anyone in these part of the woods. He climbed swiftly, the sweat breaking out on his neck. He reached the little clearing where bluebells and wild flowers still grew inspite of the battle being waged a few hundred yards away. He got his bearings from the funny rabbit-shaped rock on the left of the clearing and took a right. He passed between two thorn bushes, then he was in the dip in the ground. He went down on his knees and scrabbled through a pile of leaves and unearthed the radio he had buried the night he returned. He squatted on the ground and looked at it in the half light. It sat, innocuous but deadly, a black box, its dials gleaming dully. They were waiting for intel. If he told them about Saito's plans for Garrison Hill, they would be waiting. His men would die, they would not be able to take Garrison Hill. But if he didn't transmit, and the attack went through, they would know he had deliberately not given them intel. And they would find his parents and Debi and…or maybe send a Naga in the night after Aditi. He shivered. Or he could give them some vague rubbish to keep them happy and pretend to be surprised himself. Or he could tell Saito to change his plans at the last minute, tell him why. But then, they would know he had lied. Or…or they could take Garrison Hill tonight and Whyte and Goopta would be swept away and his crisis would be over. He buried his face in his hands, then stiffened. A sound, a whisper of a sound. He crouched in the dip, feeling terribly exposed. The twilight was fading into purple night. What was it? Who was it? A leopard? A wild boar? He inched his eyes above the lip of the dip. A figure, a man in uniform had crept out of the far tree line. He almost blended in with the tree trunk but Debraj's trained sniper's eyes could make out his shape. He was just waiting, watching. Then he slowly hunkered down on the ground, hidden behind the trunk, concealed by the tall grass. What was he waiting for? Debraj slowly inched his way down. He couldn't move until the unknown soldier left. He sat, frozen for long minutes, the time crawling. Finally, he inched his way up. The clearing had now become darker, the tree line indistinct. He couldn't afford to take chances. He waited for several more minutes, fretting. He couldn't transmit now, even if he wanted to. Maybe later. After a few more agonising minutes, he hid the radio, covered it with leaves. Then he crawled out and disappeared into the forest. No one challenged him. A few seconds later, a shadow detached itself from a tree and stepped into the clearing, staring in the direction that Debraj had gone.

Meenakshi sat on a small rock, up the hill from the field station, smoking her cigarette, her packed kit bag and rifle at her feet. She knew the Senior Sister would have her hide, if she got caught. But she found a kind of daring pleasure in inhaling the pungent smell, the smoke catching at her throat, the momentary buzz. Geeta Ma'am did it, why couldn't she? It was easy to wangle cigarettes; she just had to smile at one of the soldiers and they would be falling over their muddy boots to offer her one, and for the privilege of lighting it up. The fact that she could blow smoke rings was a topic of much discussion in the trenches, with expert opinions bandied about whether or not it meant that she was good at infinitely more pleasurable pursuits. And yet, though the rumour was that she was a hell raiser, none of the men gave her any cause for concern. This was Netaji's army, and on the whole, a woman, especially from the Rani Jhansi Brigade, could feel safe, her dignity respected. She took a last drag and as she pinched out the remainder, keeping it for another smoke, the mule train rolled in. They were going to be moving to another forward position, in preparation of the battle for Garrison Hill. As she stood up, and hauled her kit bag onto her shoulder, she spotted Aditi, looking around, stretching her back. Meenakshi paused. She wasn't looking forward to meeting Aditi, after the whole disaster with Nishonko. The thought of that evening still rankled. It wasn't Aditi's fault that Nishonko wanted every bloody woman to fall at Aditi's feet in adoration and worship her as Mother Mary but...she started to giggle at the picture. It had hurt like hell then. But she would put it behind her and move on. Aditi didn't need to know that she had told Nish about...maybe it wasn't even true. She called out to Aditi, waving her hand. Aditi looked up and her face split in a delighted smile. She ran to meet Meenakshi They hugged, squealed, two teenagers, really, in the middle of a war, reclaiming their friendship.

'I've missed you so much.'

'You look good! Are you...did you find out...you know...'

Aditi's eyes shone. 'Yes. Yes. Yes.'

'Oh my god!'

'Aren't you happy, for me?'

'Yes but we are in the middle of a war, you idiot!'

'So he...or she...will be a warrior.'

'You could get hurt.'

'I could get hurt crossing the road in Bukhit.'

'Does Deb know?'

'No one must know. He will just worry. I'm feeling strong and good and it will be months before I show. The puking, thank heavens has stopped. And I'm eating well. And I have you, my darling, darling Meena to look after me. I've been assigned the same station as you.'

Meenakshi hugged her fiercely. Please god, let it be okay.

'And Colonel Richards, please be advised that, tonight itself, your positions will be attacked in strength. Prepare for heavy artillery from the right flank at roughly 2300 hours. Range 600 yards.'

Richards was incredulous. He almost laughed. Where did he get this balderdash from?

'Really Brigadier Whyte, that's a load of bollocks, pardon my French, Sir.'

The line went silent. Richards waited. Just the sound of soft breathing.

'Sir? You there?'

Still nothing. Richards felt a little prickle up his neck. Then, Whyte's voice came, silken, almost gentle.

'What exactly do you find so hard to believe, Colonel?'

'Oh, well, the exactitude of your predictions, Sir. The one thing those slant-eyed devils are known for is their unpredictability. How do you know this, Sir?'

'Oh Richards, if only I could tell you that. But, you are rather a babe in the woods here, aren't you, and you will just have to listen to your betters, like a good little boy. You think you can mange that, my dear fellow?'

Richards went apoplectic, red in the face. He was glad that Whyte couldn't see him. He clenched and unclenched his fists, took a couple of deep breaths.

'But it'll take the better part of the day to dig deeper trenches and dugouts on the lee side of the hill. If the Japs do come tonight, my men will be pooped.'

'Better pooped than past tense, Colonel.'

'But don't you find the idea that the Japs are planning to haul their guns up hill on mules absolutely preposterous? I mean, really!'

'Not half as preposterous as the idea that you may lose Garrison Hill because you didn't listen to good intel.'

Whyte could almost hear Richards' brain ticking away, trying to concoct a new objection. *You stupid git, just fucking pick up your gun and fight like I tell you!* Whyte's knuckles were white with the effort not to smash the phone down on the table but the iron control he prided himself on, held.

'And Richards, you do understand that I have carte blanche. Or would you rather take this up with the old man?' His voice was level, quiet, very civil.

'I'll get it done, Sir.'

'Tickety boo, Richards.'

Saito stood on the little knoll in front of the command tent, as he surveyed the preparations, and smiled. The British were teetering on the brink of total collapse. There were classic telltale signs — a constantly retreating line, too many blank spaces, the exhausted faces of prisoners, the droop of the shoulders of men who didn't give a damn any more, the disorder and filth of the abandoned trenches. But more than anything else, it was an animal instinct that told you that the enemy was done. Saito's intuition was very well honed, something he had learnt to listen to in all the different theatres of war he had been through. They were going to win this one. Now his voice rung out, clear on the evening air.

'Shuto! Kasai! Shoot! Fire!'

The first wave of the attack went well. Carrying out a classic frontal assault on Garrison Hill, they swept behind the retreating Kents and the Somersets, giving chase, their baying screams carrying all the way to the grassy knoll. The British and Indian soldiers fell back. But as Saito's forces reached higher ground, they hit a wall of murderous machine gun fire. The Somerset Rifles had taken cover in carefully placed trenches on the lee side of the hill. The pursuing INA soldiers were perfectly silhouetted against the sky and were mowed down in minutes. Their momentum petered out, forcing them to fall back, little groups taking cover behind whatever rock or tree they could find.

Saito grunted, poured in more platoons. They streamed up from his corridor, a wave of khaki but they too faltered. Something was going wrong. Listening to the units on the radio, Nishonko knew that the assault had run out of steam.

'Pinned down, pinned down...'

'Reinforcements...under heavy fire.'

'2nd company unable to advance.'

'Medics...send the medics.'

Saito paced up and down, his normally cheerful face hard. Nishonko saw beads of sweat on his temple, despite the chill of the night. He chopped his hand down twice. The order was relayed. The night reverberated to the thumps and shrieks of the heavy cannons as the heavy artillery opened up. The gunners fired till their barrels glowed red, till their hands got blisters. The artillery fired 300 shells. They all waited with bated breath for the first report from the hill. Then the crackling voice spelt it out.

'No joy. They're dug in just beyond our range.'

'How the hell did the Brits know that we've moved the guns uphill?'

'I'm sure we'll over run them in our next attack, Brigadier. Shall we send in Major Mookerji's unit?' Nishonko stood at Saito's elbow, looking through feld glasses at the battlefield.

Saito shook his head. Nishonko grimaced.

'As you wish, Sir. I'm sure you will figure out how to break through.'

'I better, Major Mitro.' Saito smiled grimly, taking out a message from his pocket. 'Gentlemen, this came from General Mataguchi today. "The divine emperor himself wishes you success in your attack on Garrison Hill. You, Brigadier Saito have, by the Emperor's grace, been promoted to Major General. The success of the campaign now lies entirely in your hands".'

There was a scattering of applause. Saito bowed deeply but his face was heavy, his heart cold.

Richards ran his fingers through the sweat streaked bristle on his scalp.

'Another one tonight!? For heaven's sake, Sir, what more do you want from my men? They're done. They've given their all. They don't have anything in the larder.'

Whyte had driven up to the Garrison HQ. There was too much riding on this night. Goopta was manning the guesthouse. If anything came in on the radio, he would call. He looked at Richards. The man was a wreck, eyes bloodshot, his skin stretched and pasty, a tic making the corner of his mouth convulse every now and then.

'We just don't have the strength, Sir. Not one more time.'

'You have to hold them back, Richards. There isn't any choice, is there?'

'Why don't they send the troops?' His voice was close to breaking.

Whyte gave him a long look, then put his arm round Richards' shoulders. His tone was suddenly gentler.

'The reinforcements will get here. Believe me, they are Slim's top priority. Till then, it's up to us.'

Richards looked at him with hollowed eyes. 'Sometimes, I wish I had never got this damned garrison.'

'I'm not in this rotten cesspool either because I needed a vacation. I'm here because the goddamn Goths are at the gates and somebody has to stop them! We have to stop them, Richards. You and I.'

Richards rubbed his face tiredly. 'I can hold a gun. I can fight. Till the end. That's all I can do, Sir.'

'You do that Richards and I'll see if we can win this battle.'

He pulled a hip flask from his pocket, handed it to Richards.

'Go on, knock back a bit of good old Irish courage.'

Richards took a long swig, then another. He cleared his throat.

'Well, we could train our guns on theirs. They don't have wheels, so they aren't going anywhere. They're sitting ducks really. It will be a herculean task to reposition our guns but we could try.'

'Good man. Maybe, I'll just send a case of Dunville's for the lads.'

Richards laughed, shakily.

'That would be splendid, it would.'

Something was terribly wrong. Saito felt his nerves fizz and crackle with alarm. In all the years of thrust and parry, he had never seen the Brits behave this way. When pushed, they always retreated. But now, whichever way they manoeuvered, the British seemed to be waiting for them. How the hell did they know? Maybe they were on the brink, just one more thrust and they would go over the edge. He ordered the guns to be moved up.

'But we don't have wheels, Sir!' Colonel Oyama's voice was thin and clear.

Saito took a deep breath. Of course. 'Then move them bodily, Colonel. Push them into position. We need those guns moved forward at least 200 hundred yards.'

There was a humming silence. All the officers on the knoll kept quiet. Then Colonel Akira's voice came back, steady, calm.

'Hai. Long Live the Emperor.'

They waited, for what seemed like hours. The men smoked, paced around. Nishonko and a couple of others slipped into the forest to relieve themselves. A sliver of paleness lit up the rims of the far hills. Dawn was not too far behind. Then, word came. They were almost in position. And then, with a roar of thunder, the artillery opened up. But it wasn't their own guns, it was the British artillery, pounding the Japanese guns! The hillside turned into a scene from hell. In the red afterglow, they could see the hollow shells of derelict buildings, the shattered slopes stripped of foliage, the few remaining trees leaning drunkenly against the sky, their charred twisted limbs reaching up, like a dying man's outstretched fingers frozen in rigor. They watched helplessly, as their guns were decimated, the bodies of men and mules flung up into the lightening sky. It seemed to carry on for hours but it must have been mere minutes. Neither side had the munitions to do a prolonged barrage. Then, a ringing silence fell. Smoke wreathed up from the ground, like pale ghosts. The ground was a mess of churned mud, blood, corpses and spent shells. The faint cries of men, like distant wails of children, came floating downhill. Saito turned away.

'All units, stand down. Maintain positions. Send in the medical teams.'

In the light of the same dawn, Whyte saw first hand the devastation the Kohima garrison had gone through. The barracks, even the verandahs were lined with the wounded. The medical staff, woefully short in number, sleepless themselves, struggled to cope. There was no one on secondary duties. Every clerk, cook and driver had been handed a rifle and ordered to join the frontlines. Dead bodies had been stacked in open pits, lime thrown on them, a white mountain of decomposing flesh, crawling with flies. Scavenger birds wheeled in the grey light, their cries shrill as they fought over the cornucopia of death. They didn't even have men to dig proper graves. Some friendly Nagas had come from the adjoining villages to help. They went around dragging the bodies into the pits, their faces covered by headcloths. The stench made him gag. *God, Richards is right. These men are at the end of their rope. They look like they're ready to throw in the towel.*

Richards had not slept the whole night. Often, it had seemed impossible that they would be able to hold out against the onslaught. Sitting on the tailgate of a jeep, he felt faint as he looked at the battle reports. They had lost half their men in the last attacks. He saw Whyte, picking his way fastidiously through the filth and the lines of the wounded, coming down the verandah. He didn't have the energy to stand up and salute.

'Sir, I have to inform you that we're hanging by a thread. In most trenches and bunkers, I have only a handful of men left alive.'

Whyte looked at him, his own eyes ringed with fatigue. He knew that, like his garrison, Richards was close to collapse.

'We just have to hold for another 48 hours.'

'I think it may be too late. One more attack like last night's is going to finish us off.'

'Hold fast, my friend, don't lose heart.'

Richards looked up, surprised at the Brigadier's warm tone. But he was past hoping. Or caring.

Saito sat outside his tent in the misty glow of dawn, praying. He kneeled on the small tatami mat, his head lowered in deep apology. His second attack had failed. This was the awful truth. He broke into a cold sweat. There was nothing new he could think of. He had planned his move in great detail, like a complicated chess manoeuvre — moving his pawns into positon, keeping his rooks on the sides, distracting with his castle. He had covered every eventuality. And he had failed.

The loud warbling of geese made him look up. High cumulus clouds, suffused with purple and pink, sailed like majestic ocean liners. It reminded him of Osaka harbour, home. He missed the rush and bustle of the fish market, the steam and clanging from the ship yard, the simple rice and fish broth his mother would make to start their day. He had risen from humble beginnings to become a general in the Imperial Army, the youngest General. And he had failed.

He lingered outside delaying the moment when he would have to go into the tent and radio the news of failure to Mataguchi.

How do they know where we will be? How are they always one step ahead? Is there a traitor in our midst still? Counter intelligence had said that a double agent, supposedly a close confidant of Netaji himself — a man code-named Silver — a man to whom Netaji unwittingly had revealed his plans, was feeding the troop movements, providing the enemy with advance knowledge. But they had caught Gaffar. Was there another mole, another traitor? How is Silver getting to know stuff? How can he know the daily decisions, the smallest changes of plans? Is he here, right now, amongst us? Who can I trust?

A raised voice made him turn with a frown. It was one of his sentries. In the pale morning light, he couldn't make out who it was. Then he heard the voice of Debraj.

'It's okay, let him come.'

Debraj walked towards him, his stride easy. Just watching him come made Saito feel lighter. He realised how alone he had been feeling, how close he had become to this young man.

'Thought you needed some cheering up.'

'Thank you. Would you like some tea?'

'I thought something a little stronger might be in order. And I believe we have something to celebrate after all.'

Saito nodded, his face grave. He clapped his hands. An orderly trotted up, something in Japanese was murmured and soon two small, exquisitely handmade ceramic bowls and a hand-crafted pale grey stone flagon, warm to the touch, were placed in front of them on the tatami mat. Debraj flopped down on the grass, his boots off, squiggling his toes in the grass as he watched the pale amber liquid being poured, its clear transparency catching the first light of the sun.

'Cheers,' he said, before taking a sip. 'And congratulations on becoming a General.'

Saito bowed, took a ceremonious sip. His eyes looked haunted.

'Why the sad face? You've just been promoted.'

'Ah, Deb san, our military culture is very complex. This is a promotion, yes. But…' He picked up a leather bound book from beside him, riffled through its pages, packed with dense ideograms.

'This is our military code book. If you asked me to turn to the page where you can find the word for surrender, I will not be able to oblige you. It simply does not exist! No Japanese general has ever surrendered to the enemy in the field. Mataguchi knows now…there will be no surrender at Kohima. *General* Saito is in charge. This is his way of ensuring victory.'

'But where's all this talk of surrender coming from?'

'You do realise that, from the way we've committed our Division, we can only go forward. Retreat would be catastrophic. We don't have supplies. And British reinforcements are on their way and will be here within a matter of days.'

'So then we won't retreat. We will go forward. And we will break through. "*That army is beaten which considers itself to be beaten,*" to quote Marshal Ferdinand Foch.' He suddenly grinned. 'Imagine going through life with a name like that. What the Foch! Fochin' hell! Here's to success!' Debraj raised his bowl of sake and drained it.

Saito smiled and raised his cup. 'Seiko!' he said, softly.

'Fochin' yay!' said Debraj.

'Fochin' yay!' echoed Saito but the smile didn't quite reach his troubled eyes.

They drank, watching the sun coming up over the ravaged landscape.

'Someone is giving them information, someone from our ranks.'

Debraj's face froze.

'What...what do you mean?'

'The British knew our every move.'

Debraj looked away, then stood up abruptly.

'How will you find him?'

'It will be someone with a radio. That's the only way they're getting through. I would start with all the radio operators.'

Debraj fidgeted, looking around nervously. 'Okay, will do. Will keep my eyes peeled.'

The sun was up by the time Debraj left Saito. He headed for the communal baths, stripped and bathed. Back in his tent, he was too restless to sleep. He paced up and down, agonising over what to do. The radio was sitting in the forest, hidden but potent evidence. It was too dangerous to go out into the forest in broad daylight. Too many eyes, too much risk of exposure. But anyone could stumble across it. He lay down on his bedroll, his mind in a turmoil. He thought of Aditi. What was she doing now? He wished he could have spoken to her, shared the searing conflicts going on in his mind, told her how much he wanted to protect her. But, of course, he couldn't. He could never tell her how they had threatened her, Debi, his parents.

When she got off the car, Debi was appalled. That her parents, Sir Harindranath and Lady Mookerji should be reduced to such circumstances, to such a neighbourhood, was so hard to accept. She had adjusted to much in the last year, to living in a village in the middle of nowhere, to bathing in a pond crowded with the green waxy leaves of water hyacinth, the tiny fish nibbling around her toes. She had worn rough, handloom cotton and learnt to grind masala, crouching on the cool, earthen floor made smooth with cow dung.

She had given birth in a lean to, the midwife bringing forth the wildly squalling little bundle, covered in mucus and blood, the eyes grey like Andy's but the face, oh, so much like her brother's. She had become a woman, a mother, an outcast, at age 16 and survived it all. When Khogen da came with word of her parents' exile, the fall of the house of the Chandernagore Mookerjis, she had felt little regret at first. Serves them right, for what they did to me. This is payback for what they did to Dada. But, when she looked at the child, suspended in a cradle made of an old sari belonging to Khogen da's wife, warbling, the tiny inquisitive eyes, his questing fingers, she knew she wanted her family, knew her parents would need her and the child to regain some solace, some joy, find some sense of redemption. It took time to track them down. She couldn't find any sign of Goopta; it seemed he had disappeared, gone abroad for his business dealings. But she did finally get through to Kumudini, the daughter. Under the girl's bovine and simpering exterior, she found kindness and loneliness. It was a loneliness she recognised, the loneliness of being brought up in the midst of luxury and plenty by hired help and governesses. They became unlikely friends and it was Kumudini who got her the address, who sent a car to fetch her from the village. She looked at the simple green door with the two steps and knew that once she knocked on it, her life would change forever. She thought of Debraj, alone in some battlefield. He had joined the INA, that's what Khogenda's son had informed them. *You mustn't die, Dada, you must find your way home*. She thought of the day he would finally come back, how she would run up to him and tell him she had taken care of everything. He would be proud of her. They would once again be together. And then it would be alright.

She shut the car door with a firm click. None of the neighbourhood ladies paid any attention to the young girl in a cheap cotton sari and a cloth bag who stepped up to the door. She looked like any middle-class daughter of impoverished parents, very pretty, lovely bones but unadorned, nothing uncommon, not worth gossiping about. She knocked. Silence. She knocked again, a little louder. From inside, came a faint, tremulous voice, raspy.

'Kaay? Who is it?'

'It's me. Debi.'

Later in the morning, when Saito entered the command tent, he found Nishonko waiting for him.

'General, Sir, congratulations.'

'Thank you, Major Mitro.'

'Have an idea I want to bounce off you, Sir. It might give us a way out.'

'Splendid. What is it, Major?'

Nishonko led him to the Kaiga. 'I went through all the field reports, General and here, behind Garrison Hill, there's this track. As you will observe, there are other tracks...this...this...and this, all branching off from it. All of them lead to British and Indian positions.'

'And why is that important?'

'Simple. This is their supply network. Notice how it's spread all over the hillside. They use these tracks to move men and supplies. My idea is to take a small but strong force and cut off that main track. If we cut their access to this track, we cut off their supplies, isolate them into small groups, corner them and mop each one up separately.'

Saito lit a cigarette, drawing deeply on it as he studied the map quietly for a while. 'You know, my instinct was to launch another all-out attack tonight. Not give them a chance to recover.'

'Begging your pardon, Sir but no guarantee it will work. Every chance an all-out assault will fail again. I think they are dug in pretty strong. We need to flank them and get behind them and make sure no further supplies or reinforcements can reach them. Cut off their blood supply, so to speak. They are focusing on the front, not looking behind. We bite them in the arse...as Deb would put it rather inelegantly but aptly.'

Saito laughed. 'Maybe. But we're spread pretty thin too. If we divert troops from the main force at Garrison Hill, our position there will definitely be weakened. If the British mount a counter attack, they'll blow a big hole in our lines...they could overrun us. It's too risky.'

'Not if it's just a small contingent of good men. The British wouldn't even realise they are gone. All they would need to do is move behind the lines, block this track, and hold it till the main force breaks through. Just a couple of days' work, really. Think about it, Sir. This has a high chance of success.'

'You know what, it's quite a brilliant idea.'

'And how about you give it to Major Mookerji? He can pull it off.' Nishonko's voice was very confident. 'He's trained to move behind the lines. He's perfect for the job. Send him. It's time he got independent charge. He's earned it.'

Saito gave him a long look. It was true but he hadn't expected it to come from Nishonko. The strained relations between the two had been quite evident for some time.

'You're right. But keep it under wraps. We will reveal it only at the last minute. Got that?'

'Sure, General.'

'I think we have a mole.'

Nishonko's eyes widened. 'One of our own men, Sir?'

Saito grimaced, rubbed his face tiredly. 'One of our own. Someone is feeding the British information. So keep your mouth zipped and your eyes peeled, especially for anyone with access to a radio transmitter.'

Nishonko nodded.

'And Sir, can I take a few hours off to get my arm seen to?'

Saito nodded. The man had done more than his bit.

Debraj and Colonel Akira were summoned to the command tent. As Debraj took his place at the table, his eyes fell on the empty seats. He remembered the faces from when this campaign had started. How eager and brimming with vigour they'd all been. It all seemed a lifetime ago. Then he looked at the calendar. There were 19 crosses on it. Only 19 days had passed.

'Where's everybody? Where's Major Mitro?'

'I needed to speak to you separately.'

Saito outlined Nishonko's proposal briefly. Debraj was indignant.

'But General, we've already cut the road to Dimapur. Now if we block this track, their only escape route, we're doing the very thing Netaji warned us not to.'

Saito shook his head. 'Countermanded by General Mataguchi, if you remember.'

'But we need to leave a door open for them to bolt. Cornered rats. You know what happens to them.' Debraj was vehement.

'Maybe. But we just have to become better rat catchers. If neither of you have a better plan, let's work out the nitty gritties'.

The final plan was a simple one. Some of the 2nd Bahadur Battalion would move out at dawn. Saito had sent his scouts to survey the route. They reported that most of the 12 odd miles they had to travel was over hills, gulleys and through thick forest and brush. There was just a two-mile stretch which had no cover — a small valley, in a gorge, with trees on one side and a steep rock face on the other.

'This is the only hitch...crossing this stretch. Your task force, Major, will be completely exposed.'

'My task force? Won't Colonel Akira be coming along, Sir?'

'No, you're going to do this on your own. Up to it?'

The tug and pull of warring thoughts sent Debraj's mind whirling but his face was calm.

'Won't let you down, Sir. This seems the shortest way. Should cross it in a jiffy. And what are the odds the British will even know we are there?'

'Absolutely. Their whole attention will be focused on the main force in front of them. They won't be wasting any troops guarding some small valley in the middle of nowhere behind their lines. You'll be fine.'

As they dispersed after the briefing, Saito gestured to Debraj to stay back.

'Nervous?'

'It's a dangerous gambit. I just hope we can pull it off.'

'I'm sure you will. As Major Mitro said, you're the best man for the job. You've earned it.'

'Nishonko? He said that?'

'It was his idea you lead the task force. He's...he admires you, you know.'

Debraj shook his head. Nishonko was such a hard man to figure out. Did he mean it? Did he really think Debraj deserved a shot at excelling himself? Or was he trying to get rid of him by sending him on what could well turn out to be a suicide mission? Or was it going to be just a fool's errand, a distraction, a useless detour? Nishonko was stuck in the command tent, poor chap. He was missing out on all the action. Maybe he was just trying to send Debraj away from the main battle. Damn it, it was all so confusing. He would just go and grab the track and get back as fast as possible and rejoin the main force. It didn't matter what Nishonko thought.

Whyte sat, gently tapping his manicured finger on the last spool of tape. Meticulous as ever, he had recorded every conversation with K, then numbered and dated them. The tapes sat in a small leather covered box on his table. This was the complete record of K's treachery — and also irrefutable proof that he, Whyte, had masterminded and pulled off this remarkable intelligence coup. Those spools were proof that it was he who had won the day at Kohima. God, whichever god looked after the spooks of MI6, protected the professional liars and dissemblers, the manipulators and circus men, God, let K deliver one final time! He knew how vulnerable he himself was, how utterly open to betrayal. He was not blind to the fact that K could be sleeping with the enemy, could have turned double agent. In which case, Whyte would be instrumental in dividing the British forces and sending them on a wild goose chase. He would be the guy who lost India. But he hung onto what Goopta had told him. K would never let them down. He had the highest motivation. He was a man in love. With a grim smile, he locked the box of tapes away in a safe. He'd told Goopta that the spools were a record but they were actually a key to unlock any door he desired. If he won this round, they would not, they could not, deny him anything. He'd always fancied the office of the Director of MI6 — and everything that went with it. Tomorrow would decide whether it all would be his — or he would die in this unknown guesthouse in the armpit of the world — or worse, in obscurity in some subterranean cell in the maze of MI6, a cypher, a clerk.

'Is this seat taken?'

She looked up with a start at the familiar voice. The midday meal, a slop of rice, dal and some indeterminate roots and leaves, with only salt and fiery chillies to season it, tasted like warmed-up vomit. She had been spooning it into her mouth, forcing herself to eat, forcing herself to take in this basic nourishment. Nishonko da was standing there, an enamel plate in his hand. He had really lost weight. His face had become thinner, drawn. He needed a haircut.

'What's happened to your eye?' she blurted out, lost for words, frightened and yet strangely glad to see him. He touched the eye, all purple and black but without the stupid eye patch now, smiled.

'Ran into an immovable object.'

'And your shoulder? How did you hurt it?'

'Oh, it's nothing, just a nick. The guy with the gun must have been an awful shot. How are you, Jhilik?'

He looked at her, those wide set eyes with their open gaze as if she were always seeking something on the far horizon. Her mouth, that obstinate pout, now softer, as if she had learnt that the world didn't always listen to her tantrums, was slightly open, the lips parted. He could see her breath, the unconscious rise and fall of it, as she drew in the cool mountain air, and let it out, warmed. A tiny pulse beat at the base of her throat, a metronome marking the passing of each moment of her life. And the life inside her. He veered away sharply from the thought. He saw the way the hair curled around the edges of her nurse's cap, always trying to escape, giving her an unbound look even when her hair was pulled back and tamed. He wanted to reach out and tuck one stray curl behind her ear. There she sat, Jhilik, his Jhilik, the same, yet so changed. There was something about her, he couldn't put his finger on it, a luminosity, an inner incandescence, that made his heart ache, she was so beautiful. He saw her drop her eyes, the red tide creep up her cheeks, discomfited by his regard.

'I'm well. How is the battle? Are we winning?'

'Who can tell with battles? All a man can do is fight where he stands.'

'Yes, that's what I tell myself. One day at a time, Aditi, just save the lives in front of you.'

'I prefer Jhilik.'

'Sorry?'

'Jhilik...to Aditi. In my head, you have always been Jhilik.'

'And to me, you have always been Nishonko da, my trusted friend, my anchor, my khoonti.'

'And I'll always be that, Jhilik, whatever happens. You must know you can always come to me and I'll make everything alright.'

She hesitated. In all these months, she had never spoken to him about Deb, never had the courage. But now, she looked at him, her gaze untroubled. She was no longer afraid.

'You will always be special to me. But I do love him, you know. I love Deb. There, I've said it. And it would mean so much to me if you liked him too.'

He frowned, rubbed his forehead, as if a headache was coming.

'Do you remember the day that bull escaped from the Choudhury Baadi barn?'

She blinked, her mind trying to grapple with the jump. Then, hazily, a memory from childhood, a memory so fearsome, it had been long buried, drifted to the surface. The big zamindar house with the stables and barns. The big lake where, once a year, they would let the villagers fish, the fins of the katla fish thrashing in the water, as big as dogs. The bull, a mythical creature, glimpsed only during festivals, otherwise fattened for years, the ageing sultan of a harem of docile cows, had been earmarked for boli, the ritual sacrifice to the goddess, on the eighth day of the Puja. The bull, sensing its impending doom, perhaps, had broken free, gone on the rampage. The women and children had been rushed to the terraces of the small one-storeyed bungalows which made up the enclave, in their crisp, new festival clothes, to keep them safe. There, they peeped over the rim of the brick wall, as if they would be gored if the bull caught sight of them. The men had come, with nets and prods and trucks and guns, just in case, driven the magnificent, corpulent creature, its manhood standing up like a spear, the mouth frothing, its stentorian bellow the stuff of nightmares for months to come, driven it back. It pawed the ground, charged, then retreated, shaking the massive head with its scimitar horns painted with sindoor for the ceremony, the tiny brass bells on it jangling. Slowly, inexorably, they had pushed it back towards the lake, till it found itself cornered, the massive rear hooves slipping on the loose red soil at the edge of the lake, stumbling, slipping, its uncomprehending beast eyes, blood flecked. And then in one final rush, one final charge, its massive hind quarters had given way. It had slipped, a battleship hitting the water. It had thrashed around, tried to swim, to scramble up the wet sides of the lakes, its eyes pleading, so vulnerable. But the men prodded it back, screaming like animals, till it lost its footing. It bellowed, the water shooting up like a fountain, from its cavernous nostrils, drowning under its own weight, till it sank, the beautiful perfectly symmetrical horns the last remnant, till all that was left was ripples. A cheer had gone up. Blood had not been shed but the sacrifice had been done. The bull had to die, was destined to die, for the good of all mankind. That was the legend of Goddess Durga, the Destroyer of the Evil bull Mahishashur so that good could triumph. The priests explained it was a good omen, the bull dying like that. The drums beat even louder that evening.

'I remember.' Aditi whispered.

She had been inconsolable, seeing only the bull's agony, tears streaming from her big, black eyes as it sank to its watery grave. Nishonko da had held her hand, sung the incantation of the goddess to her, told her how the bull had given its life to make the land rich again, how it would be reborn as a mighty whale. She looked now at him, at his inscrutable face, the one good eye calm as he stared at her.

'What are you saying, Nishonko da? I don't understand.'

'In time you will, little one. Everything I do, I do for you. I will sacrifice anything to make you happy.'

'Oh, Nishonko da, that's so sweet of you. But you mustn't give up anything for me. I don't want you to sacrifice your happiness.'

'But isn't that what love is, little one? *"The sun loved the moon so much, he died every night to let her breathe."* Annada mashi taught me that. Love, Jhilik, is such a hard, demanding thing.'

'But I don't want such love!' Her voice was hard, strained, a whiplash.

He stood up, cupped his hand gently on the crown of her head, blessing her.

'Can one choose how one will be loved? Stay safe, Jhilik.'

She jerked her head away but he had already gone, his kit bag slung on his good shoulder, walking away with an easy, purposeful stride. She watched him leave, unease like a trapped pigeon fluttering under her ribs, the fine hairs at the back of her neck rising.

'I know we thought we would go with just a small force but the more I've been thinking about it, the more it seems that this idea of Major Mitro's is just gold.'

Saito looked at the ring of faces around him. He had reconvened a meeting.

'They aren't expecting us. They definitely won't expect a large force. So, when we get to the track, we can take them from the rear and roger them right royally, as Major Mookerji would put it so eloquently.'

A ripple of laughter spread through the room.

'We may even wrap up the battle for Garrison Hill right then and there. So, I thought... I've decided that we will combine the Japanese 332nd Brigade and the INA 2nd Bahadur Battalion for this operation.'

'A whole brigade? Isn't that a lot to risk.' Colonel Akira was frowning.

'No risk, no gain. And I will lead this strike force myself to make sure we win.'

There was a gasp around the room. A Major General on the field, on a secret operation like this? It was unconventional. But then everything Saito did was unpredictable. That's what made him the success he was.

'It's as good a time as any to take up our weapons, right Major Mookerji? Major?'

Debraj jerked to attention, flustered.

'Yes, Sir. Whatever you say, General.'

Saito gave him a keen look. Was Debraj disappointed about having the command taken from him? No, he was a bigger man than that. But he was a bit distracted.

'Let's prep. And no one outside this room must know what we are planning. The lesser the people who know that a brigade is on the march, the better. The men will not know where we are headed till tomorrow morning. We will leave within four hours, as soon as night falls, under cover of darkness, not wait for the light of dawn. Minimum rations. It's just a day's march. And radio silence till I say otherwise. We can't let the British get a whiff of this.'

Debraj packed his gear, unable to sleep. He had only hours. This thing had become much larger than a small guerilla sortie. He had to get to the clearing where he had hidden the radio, take it out and do what had to be done. But every time he had tried to slip away, there had been someone coming to check something, some detail to be sorted out. He felt claustrophobic, breathless. The hours were just galloping by, coming closer and closer to the hour of reckoning. He raised the back flap of the tent, slipped out.

The sun was dropping over the far hills, as he ran up to the dip in the woods and scrambled down on all fours. He was panting, the sprint up the hill a punishing one. He scrabbled at the pile of leaves, pushed them aside, shoved away the loose pile of rocks under which he had hidden the radio. But there was nothing. He dug more, moving out earth, small stones, grit under his finger nails. There was no radio! Shit. Shit. Shit. Someone had found it. But they couldn't trace it back to him, could they? Where the hell was it?

'Looking for something, Sir?'

He swung around, his heart leaping in his chest, the world turning black for an instant. But, oh god, thank you god, it was only Kabootar. He stood there, listing to one side, his weight on his good leg, looking down into the hole at Debraj, his gaze calm, level. Sweet-smelling pines formed a dark canopy behind him. Debraj scrambled to his feet, almost falling over in his haste and relief.

'Kabootar, what the hell are you doing here? You startled me.'

'Major saab, what are *you* doing here?'

Debraj took a deep breath. He looked at this diminutive man, who had saved his life so often, whom he trusted unconditionally, who had become a friend, more than a friend, a brother. He took a step forward but Kabootar took one step back, then waited, not judging but not accepting either, his hand on his kukhri.

'It's…it's a bit complicated, Kabootar.'

'It's very simple, sa'ab. Are you a beimaan or not?'

Debraj flushed, stung by the word, the insult. But the next moment, looking into Kabootar's eyes, he realised that Kabootar was not trying to humiliate him. He just wanted the truth.

'I don't know, my friend. I wish I did.'

'Where did you get the radio? Did that red-haired, red-assed monkey give it to you?'

'Yes, how do you know about him? Where's the radio?'

'I saw them going into your jail that night. I was hiding in the woods. I saw them leave. Then the bombs fell. What did they want you to do?'

'Report on our movements, on Saito's plans.'

'And they hurt you?'

'No. They threatened Aditi.'

Kabootar let out a growl, a feral animal sound, deep in his throat.

'And my family.'

'So, you are the one who has been telling them everything?' Kabootar's face seemed carved from stone.

'NO! No, Kabootar, please listen to me. I have been so confused, torn apart, in agony. I didn't know what to do. Aditi…if anything happened to Aditi, I would…it would destroy me, Kabootar.'

'So why didn't you come to Kabootar?'

'And tell you what? Should I betray my country or my girl? Should I sacrifice my men, Saito or sacrifice my family? Do you understand what a mess I was in?'

'What have you told them?'

'Nothing. I haven't used the radio even once. I haven't been in touch.'

'How do I know you are not lying?'

'If I had the radio, I would show you.'

Kabootar looked at him without expression, then slung his backpack down to the forest floor. He yanked open the rope and pulled out the S radio.

'Show me.'

Debraj peered at the radio, then his face fell.

'See, see there was a seal here. It was brand new. It's broken now, I know but that's because I had buried it in the ground. It must have snapped. But I promise you this has not been used...'

Kabootar's face was still blank, his eyes like two pinholes.

'Don't you understand? God dammit, I didn't break the frigging seal. I never used this infernal machine. No messages went out. Kabootar, look at me. Me. You have to trust me.'

Kabootar looked at him for a long moment, an eternity, then nodded, put away his knife. It was that simple, that easy.

'Then who is the traitor?'

'Damned if I know. Saito thinks it's one of the radio operators. I have been in a tizz since yesterday, wondering if I would be discovered, if someone would find the radio.'

'No, I dug it out yesterday. Smash it, saab.'

'What? No, Kabootar. Supposing we need to send them messages… you know, disinformation…lies…to throw them off the scent?'

'It's the shaitan's box, the devil's work. Destroy it, saab. Remove the temptation.'

'And if they don't hear from me…if they take it out on Aditi?'

'If we cannot protect our zenana, our women folk, we are not men. We will not let any harm come to Missy sahiba.'

'Very noble, Kabootar but there's a war going on, in case you haven't noticed. We won't be around to protect her. I say we hang on to the damned thing. Just in case. For a while.'

He saw Kabootar stare at him, saw the doubts swim underneath the calm surface of his face, like shadowy fish moving under water, and knew that, as much as he wanted to keep the radio for insurance, as a lifeline, to get Whyte and Goopta to help them get back safe to Calcutta, there was no way he could hold on to it any more. Its very presence was an indictment, a proof of treachery. If he held on to it, Kabootar would always wonder if he was the beimaan who had sold them out. It had to go.

'Okay, okay…let's do it.'

Kabootar placed the radio on a rock, handed Debraj his rifle. Debraj stared at the box, the blind eyes of the dials, the unmoving needles, the small little silver buttons that, once flipped on, would send black waves of treason over the ether. He picked up the gun and brought the butt swooping down.

A storm was coming up, bending the tall bamboos, whipping the tops of the pines, the rising moon scudding behind clouds, as Nishonko walked fast in the night down the winding road to the camp. He felt at peace, having met Jhilik. She wouldn't understand, she never had. He had done all the thinking for her when she was small. The thing he said today, about sacrifice, she hadn't got it at all. The difference between vadh and hatya, between slaying something and murdering someone was immense. Slaying was holy, different from the selfish act of murder. It took a warrior to pick up the sword and destroy all that was evil. Murder was the act of the weak. He thought of the coming day, the things to be done. He would go and break the news to Aditi. After all, Debraj was his best friend. He would be there for her, her strength and anchor.

When he strode into the command tent, the first thing that hit him was the relative quietness. Normally, it was bedlam, a babble of voices, languages, despatches, orders flying about. Now, a few men were manning some of the radios, talking to HQ but most of the radios were silent. The tent was also quite empty. What the hell was happening? Where was everybody? He went to switch on his radio but Major Daiki, Saito's aide de camp, stepped up.

'Sorry Major, no radio till morning.'

'What the hell?'

'General Saito's orders.'

Then, he remembered. Saito must have told them to shut down, for fear of compromising the operation. But why now? The op wasn't supposed to start till dawn.

'Where's the General?'

Daiki looked at him, suspiciously. 'You not know?'

'Know what?' He disliked Daiki, with his moon glasses and habit of looking down his sharp little nose and his prissy little black moustache, a precise line drawn on his upper lip, always curled in disapproval.

'They leave.'

'Yes, I know the Bahadur Battalion is meant to leave. I want to know where your precious Saito is, you moron.'

Daiki wasn't sure what he had been called and most of the English went above his shaved head but the snarl on Nishonko's face made him think it couldn't be complimentary. This man was not a polite man. Daiki turned away, a flick of his wrist to indicate they were done. Nishonko cursed under his breath, then swiftly intercepted him. He put up his hands, placating, dipping his head in apology.

'Shitsurei shimashu, Major Daiki san, sorry, apologies. You were saying?'

Daiki, marginally mollified, allowed himself to be persuaded.

'They going. Already, bye bye.'

'When did they leave?'

'At moonrise. Bahadur Battalion, go.'

'Shit!'

'It is bad?'

'No, no...it's okay, they will probably reach the rendezvous a little early, maybe.'

'No, go slow. Whole brigade marching. Take time.'

'Whole brigade!!? What the fuck are you talking about?'

Daiki recoiled again at the harshness in Nishonko's voice. Really, this man was very discourteous indeed.

'General Saito lead brigade, chop chop, to rendezvous.'

Why the hell had Saito decided to go at the last minute? Damn the man and his seat of the pants tactics, keeping him in the dark like this. Now the whole brigade would be in danger, not just Debraj. Putting Debraj in the line of fire, risking his life was one thing; endangering the whole Kohima operation was something else.

'Get him on the line. We have to talk to him.'

'No can. Total radio silence. General Saito decide when to talk.'

Nishonko's mind was in a whirl. It was almost two hours since they had left. He didn't even know the precise route they would take. Did Daiki know?

'No, all hush hush. What wrong, Major?'

Daiki was getting worried, the wild look in Nishonko's eyes making him very uneasy. Nishonko paced around, snapping his fingers, trying to decide between all the different options. Finally, he whirled around and ran out, leaving Major Daiki open-mouthed. As Nishonko sprinted off, the pimply sentry, now on duty outside the command tent saw him running towards the dark woods. Baap re, the Major must be having a bad case of the craps. He turned away, grinning, and missed the other shadowy figure that followed the Major into the dark maw of the forest.

The storm that had threatened had lost its teeth but the wind was still high, swaying the tree tops, a sussuration, a great dragon breath sound, filling their ears. The brigade moved in the intermittent moonlight, a silvery dappled mighty snake of men, in a tight double file. Saito's scouts had fanned out ahead, their soft owl hoots floating back, giving them the 'all clear' as they moved silently. Progress was slow for Saito had chosen the harder, steeper route through the hills. They encountered no one, not even any nocturnal beasts. For most of the march, they were under a canopy of thick pines and teak. As they stepped into one of the deep nullahs, its shadows ink black, Debraj looked back along the shifting line. Where the hell was Kabootar? Normally, he would be a few feet behind him, almost invisible but always there. Except when he decided to skip things for his own weird reasons. He would get into trouble one of these days for going AWOL. Had he not joined the march? Had he gone off to keep an eye on Aditi? Hell, he should have at least told him.

'You said a company. Now you're telling me you want a battalion. Who in tarnation do you think you are?!'

Whyte patted Richards' arm but the man just jerked his hand off.

'Bugger off, Brigadier. Report me to whoever you want to. I'm not going to do this.'

Whyte took a deep breath. Patience, Alan, patience.

'Richards, the only thing I'll report is what a splendid, truly heroic job you've done. Truly, I applaud what you and your men have achieved.'

Richards frowned, looked at Whyte with weary suspicion. The man was such a snake, really. Fork tongued, Janus faced, he was.

'Nobody could have expected a small garrison to hold out against a Japanese divison. Why, even our full divisions have not been able to withstand them. You, my friend, are worthy of a Military Cross. And a Brigadier's pips on that staunch shoulder of yours. I shall see to that.'

In spite of himself, Richards felt a warm glow. Somebody, for the love of Mary, had finally acknowledged the impossible thing he had pulled off on that accursed hill.

'I'm what they call a "ghost". MI6, yes? So, poof, I'm going to disappear, once we wrap up this lot. You...you're the one who's going to bask in all the glory and get all the credit. You'd like that, wouldn't you?'

Richards nodded, shrugging at the same time, it's not that important, what the hell.

'But, to do that, to see the fruits of a victory here, we have to pull off this one last thing, my friend.' He smiled, a warm comforting smile. He saw Richards search his face for any signs of guile He saw the man struggle. He knew he had him.

'Okay, Sir...but are you very, very sure? It could be suicide, plain and simple.'

'Hasn't all my intel been spot on?'

Richards nodded.

'Then this is what I want you to do.' Whyte unrolled the map of Garrison Hill.

Most patients died in that darkest hour before dawn. It was when the body's defences were at their lowest ebb, when the mind itself was lost, in thrall to dreams and nightmares, when the thin line between sleep and death was its most fragile, most blurred. That's why Aditi would always keep vigil through those hostage hours, as if by staying awake, she could frighten away Yamraj, the Hindu God of Death. She walked through the pallets, the green mosquito nets cocooning each broken body. The night was silent, except for the shrill, dry trill of the cicadas, and the whispers and breath and soft cries of the wounded. She heard the sound from far away, like the crashing of surf. But there was no sea here. She hurried out, saw Meenakshi and another nurse step out of one of the other tents, their faces turned to the sky, lit by the waning moon. The sound was too close, too loud. Then the air raid sirens began to wail from the Japanese ammunition dump in the woods, their frantic alarm waking everyone up. Orderlies, Dr. Mishra, they all rushed out, shouting, get the wounded out. But it was too late.

In the dark, the RAF Hurribombers did not see the big Red Cross painted on the roof of the tent. It mistook the long main tent for the ammunition dump and dropped its deadly load. The whole world erupted, tree trunks and branches going up in flames. Geysers of mud and shrapnel shredded the tents. Aditi was blown off her feet by the force of the explosion. When she came to, ears ringing from the concussion, she was lying on the ground, Meenakshi bent over her, shielding her. The field station was engulfed in fire, completely razed. Through the thick billowing smoke, she saw the figures of men, on fire, stumbling torches, screaming. One of the mules lay upside down at the edge of huge crater which seemed to have been clawed out of the ground, belching fire. She stood up shakily, clinging to Meenakshi. Meenakshi was screaming at her but all she could see was her mouth moving silently through the bells ringing in her head. The water tank had toppled, forming a huge puddle of water. She saw the whole nightmare reflected in it, a lurid watercolour of hell. Dr. Mishra lay in the water, spread-eagled. She tried to run to him, calling out but was pulled away by Meenakshi.

'He's gone, you can't do anything, let's get the hell out of here, it's going to go up!'

They hobbled to the stream running beside the jungle track, the only place the fire had not spread. Three other people, two orderlies and another nurse waited there, coughing, retching as they laboured to clear their lungs. They huddled together, their faces streaked, red in the light of the inferno. One of the orderlies had managed to retrieve the radio from the shack. He raised Division HQ.

'Can you save any supplies?'

'No, everything has gone up in flames.'

'Start moving north west and we'll radio you back where to rendezvous.'

Nishonko woke with a start. He had fallen asleep, dammit. What time was it? He looked at his watch by the light of the kerosene lamp in his tent. 5 a.m. Shit, word should be coming through about the strike force any minute. He had done what had to be done in the forest, had got back to his tent and must have just crashed. But if he managed to get through to Saito, maybe he could persuade the man to bring back the brigade and let Debraj carry on, on his own. He had no fight with Saito. He was a good soldier. He washed his face quickly, ran his fingers through his hair. The face in the small, chipped mirror that stared back at him was calm, the eye clearer, less bloodshot. The sleep had cleared his head.

He walked into the command tent and settled himself in one of the folding chairs. He rested his arm on the long table. The skin beneath the sling itched and his arm was a bit stiff. But otherwise, no pain. The usual crackle and static of different units reporting back was missing. Only a couple of work stations were open, receiving calls.

'Any report from the strike force?' he called out to one of the operators.

'General Saito called. They are making good time.'

'Why the hell didn't you call me?'

'It was a very brief transmission, and the General disconnected.'

'Shit. Do we have a map reference of where they have reached?'

'I think they were still in the forest. But the General did not specify.'

'Get me General Saito.'

'Sorry, Sir but we'll have to wait for them to call us back.'

'Dammit, why is he doing this? I need to talk to him. Pass me all the notes.'

He looked at the large sheaf of yellow, blue and pink slips that made up all the signals sent to the HQ by every unit through the day. Most were routine positon reports or requisitions for supplies. He was about to put the bunch away when something caught his eye. It was a transcript of a radio call from one of the advance field dressing stations. The first time he read it, it didn't register. He was shoving it aside when it hit him. His heart jolted. He stood up, upturning the chair with a loud crash. The others looked up from their mikes, startled. Nishonko was breathing hard and couldn't speak.

'When did this...who took this?' he stuttered, holding up a blue slip. Sharma, one of the officers, came over and looked at the slip. One glance at Nishonko and he knew something was terribly wrong.

'I...I did, Sir.'

'Why didn't you tell me? Who ordered this?' Nishonko was yelling. The others stared at him. He looked like a man possessed.

'I looked for you, Sir but you were gone for a long time. I had to take a decision. I thought the best course was for the survivors to join the strike force. They are the closest. So when General Saito called, I ran it by him and he...agreed.'

'Bastard! Bastard! Oh god! Oh dear god! Where is the rendezvous?'

'I think somewhere at the bottom of this hill but I can't be sure, Sir. They are communicating directly.'

Nishonko whirled, then shot out of the tent like his life depended on it. The others looked at each other. What the hell was happening? The sentry at the tent, watched open mouthed, at the Major running like a bat out of hell, as if pursued by demons, running for the woods. This guy spent more time in the john than he did in the tent, thought the sentry. He really should get the doctor to do something about it.

Debraj took off his boots and put his feet gingerly in the water, letting them sink gently to the pebbled bottom of the mountain stream where they had halted for a short break at dawn. Aah, it was heaven. The cold water soothed his sore feet, the inflammed blisters. It had been tough going and Saito had driven them hard. The terrain was mountainous, steep, with thick thorny bushes and rocky paths strewn with flint and shale that could shred a man's boot. Each mile had been agony. He splashed water on the back of his neck, on his bronzed arms and drank deeply. From here, it would be easier going. They would start to descend soon.

'How much more to go, Major?' Neel, whose squad had been attached to the strike force and put under Debraj, was also splashing water on his head.

'Don't know, maybe a couple of hours. It all depends. I'll check with the General.'

'Just wanted to say, Sir, that it's good to march with you again. It's been a long time.'

'Ditto, young Neel. All well back home?'

'I have no idea, Sir.'

Debraj nodded. It was as if they were completely insulated from the outside world, from the battle. This remote, wild misty mountain land was their only reality.

A runner came up to them.

'General Saito has asked for you, Major.'

'You called, Sir?'

'Yes, Major, I've got a bit of bad news and a bit of good news.'

'Bad news first always, Sir.'

'The medical field station near Dainang got bombed by the Allies.'

Debraj swayed, his face turning white.

'Steady. Sister Sen survived. Only five of them got away. They are on their way here to join our force.'

'Why aren't they going back to the safety of HQ?' Debraj's voice shook.

'Safer this way. They are quite close to our route. Better they join us than try and make their way back to the INA lines on their own.'

'But General, we can't spare men to escort them back. And we've come too far to turn back. We'll have to take them with us.'

'Afraid so, Major. Anyway, they are Rani Jhansi, meant to be at the front. We could do with a couple of medical personnel, you know, in case we run into trouble.'

Debraj nodded. Of course it made sense. He was just being selfish. He didn't want Aditi anywhere near an operation like this. But at least, she would be there with him. He would be able to lock after her.

'And the good news?'

'You get to see her. Come on, secretly you are happy providence has thrown you together, aren't you?'

Oh god, she's going to be with him. With him!! Nishonko crashed through the forest glade, panting, his chest on fire. He slammed into a rock face, ricocheted off, the searing pain in his shoulder disregarded. He ducked, scrambled into a tiny cave underneath a stone bluff. It was dark inside but he couldn't afford a light. He went down on his knees, scrabbled in the dark. Where was it, oh god, where was it? His fingers clawed through the earth. Then they found the cold metal, the bulky headphones. Oh man, hurry, hurry. He pulled the box towards him, ran his fingers over the knobs and dials, found the small silver power switch, flipped it on.

'Come in, come in, come in! K calling Whyte. K calling Whyte. Emergency. Come in.'

He pulled on the earphones, went to turn the dial, then noticed the set had not come on. It was blank. No green light. He switched it off, switched it on again. Still nothing. No dials lit up, no needle quivered.

'DAMMIT! Come on, start!'

He shook the box. Something tinkled, fell with a little clatter on the stone floor. He froze. NO! No, it couldn't be broken. He placed the box on the ground, frantically hunted for his matches. Where the hell were they? There, they were in his breast pocket. Almost sobbing, he lit one up. The match flared, went out in a gust of wind. Darkness. Another one. He cupped the tiny flame, saw the radio lying on the ground, its back smashed in, the dials like blind eyes, the wires like spilled entrails. Who had done this, he would kill them, what the fuck was he going to do! He had to get through to Whyte.

Suddenly, the hair on his neck stood up. He didn't turn but his hand crept towards the gun on his hip.

'I wouldn't touch that, Sir.'

Something cold and hard and sharp dug into the back of his neck. A stab of pain. A powerful torch flicked on, lighting up the bare little cave with its earthen walls.

'That's better.'

The gruff, gravelly voice was familiar but he couldn't identify it. He stayed on the ground, crouching, his hand frozen in mid air.

'Now, very slowly, take out the gun and lay it on the floor.'

Nishonko did what he had been told. The gun, the stock with its leaping tiger carving, clattered on the stone floor, skittered to the edge of the light.

'Very good.'

A booted foot came out and kicked at the radio.

'It's quite useless, your little gift from your lal gaand malik, your new white boss. I made sure of that. You won't be able to pass on any more secrets, behnchod sala.'

Now, Nishonko knew the voice. It was that gimp, that langda toady of Deb's. Ice cold rage washed over him. He remembered with perfect recall that December evening outside Chhoto mashi's house, just after he came back from Tokyo, the horror of what he had witnessed inside making him puke on the road. The fucking cripple had been there, seen him, seen his humiliation.

'Badtameez, kya kiya tu? Tell me what you have done, you bastard.' Kabootar's voice was calm, no anger.

Nishonko hunched down, his head in his hands.

'I'm trying to save her, save Aditi.'

Kabootar's eyes flared. The kukhri dug a little deeper into Nishonko's neck, sending a thin line of blood trickling.

'You touch her, you're dead. No harm must come to her, at the hospital or anywhere else.'

Nishonko held his breath. The dimwit knew nothing of what had happened.

'She's in danger. Let me go, Kabootar, I'm the only one who can save her.'

'You're the only one who's a beimaan.'

'No. It's Deb. He is the traitor. Don't you see, he's the one who betrayed us. He spilled everything under interrogation.'

Kabootar laughed, a short bark, not amused.

'That's not going to work. I know they gave him a radio also. And I know he's already destroyed it.'

Nishonko's eyes narrowed. So, Whyte had hedged his bets. He had given *both* of them a radio. He must have offered Deb a deal… or most probably blackmailed him into it.

'Oh, he's got all of you fooled. He's already passed on all the information they need. He doesn't need the radio anymore. He's convinced Saito to go with him.The whole brigade is going down. He's going to turn at the last minute and go scot free. Let me go… we're running out of time!'

He could feel the uncertainty start to creep into Kabootar's hand, into the hold of the knife.

'No, Major sa'ab wouldn't, no way. And why did they give you a radio?'

'They beat me up. They tortured me. You saw. They said if I didn't spy for them, they would kill Aditi. But Deb? He returned without a scratch. The British won't harm him…he's one of theirs.'

The pressure on the knife eased up a little more. The point wavered. He could hear Kabootar breathing raggedly.

'Then why were you trying to get through to that white shaitan?'

'I've been lying to him, misdirecting him. To fool him, confuse him. But now, you've destroyed the radio, I can't get through to anymore. How am I going to warn Saito? Help me.'

Kabootar's shoulders slumped. He turned. The torch beam slanted away, plunging the inside of the cave in darkness. Nishonko silently reached for the gun, lying in the shadows. In the confines of the little cave, the sound of the gun shot was deafening. The torch clattered to the ground, its beam bouncing off the rough walls, till it rolled to a stop. Nishonko stood up slowly, gun pointed. He waited. A grunt. A slither. He tiptoed to the torch, picked it up. In its beam, he saw Kabootar trying to use the knife to haul himself up, his other hand trying to claw his back where a deep red patch, arterial blood, had started to spread. Nishonko spat on the floor.

'Nawaz was right, you *are* a laath shaheber kutta…and dogs like you need to be put down!'

He shot him again, in between the shoulder blades, three more shots, then walked out of the cave. Kabootar, lay spread-eagled. Three exquisitely carved tiny wooden birds had spilled out of his pocket onto the blood-stained rock floor. With his last breath, he whispered, 'Forgive me, Major.'

Aditi, Meenakshi and the other nurse, Rosie something, flopped down on the ground, dropping their heavy loads. They had picked up all the emergency medical supplies they could salvage, and were carrying their own packs, weighing some thirty-five odd pounds, along with their rifles, ammunition and hand grenades. They were drenched in sweat, in spite of the early morning cool air. Aditi in particular was in considerable pain. The fall she had taken coupled with the punishing pace at which they had moved through the last hours of that horrible night made every step an agony. She lay on the ground, soft grass tickling her face, staring up at the forest canopy beginning to turn a soft, pale green, the colour seeping in with the strengthening light. She wanted to lie down and just close her eyes and never get up again. Meenakshi too lay sprawled on the grass beside her, her eyes shut, her body inert. As Aditi turned to look at her, her ears popped. She sat up with a gasp, the sudden onrush of sound overwhelming. Birdsong filled her ears, mouth, throat with sweet music, setting her ears tingling. She moved towards Meenakshi, lay down beside her. Meenakshi turned, hugged her. Aditi winced.

'Are you hurting?' Meenakshi asked, her eyes still shut.

She nodded dumbly, though Meena couldn't see her. Meenakshi started to rub her back gently, crooning under her breath.

The radio crackled to life. Mutthuram, the orderly, quickly unloaded the bulky contraption and switched it on. The directions were faint but clear.

'Rendezvous at 0700 hours. Map co-ordinates 7338.'

'Come on, ladies, let's move. We have no time to waste.'

'Relax, Mutthu, give her a few minutes.' Meenakshi kept her eyes closed, her breath hot on the back of Aditi's neck. Her strong, healing fingers slowly eased the hard knot of pain in Aditi's lower back.

'Is the baby alright?' she whispered to Aditi.

'I hope so. Oh god, I hope so.'

'Ladies, let's go, I'm telling you.'

Nishonko ran. The strike force was also on foot, and had most probably taken the harder, longer route and they were moving slowly. But they had a big headstart. He barely had a couple of hours to catch up. He had no idea when Jhilik would connect with them. Please, god, let me be in time. He pounded through the forest, crashing through the undergrowth. It will be okay, nothing will happen to her. Fiercely holding on to the hope, he ran.

When they arrived at the rendezvous, a small clearing in the forest at the bottom of the hill, they were practically collapsing. But when she saw Debraj running towards her, her heart soared. How strange the fates were. Who would have known that joining up with Saito's force would lead her to Debraj, to the safety of his warm body against hers, to the kisses with which he covered her face and eyes, to the smile, so full of hope and gladness with which he held her fast? When she winced, his eyes clouded with such concern. They did not speak much, just sat, he feeding her some wood apples and berries he had picked. Had she seen Kabootar? No, she told him.

His mind slipped back to his last encounter with Kabootar. Really, Kabootar could be such an ass sometimes. After all his big talk, he had not even been able to protect Aditi at the field station.

Now the idiot was MIA. He was angry with him, angry with himself. Maybe he shouldn't have listened to Kabootar. Maybe he should have taken his chance. What had that man Whyte told him? '*You will get your life back...as if you've never been away, as if none of this had happened. You will never have to be apart again.*' They still had many miles to go and many battles to fight before they reached Delhi. How on earth would he protect her? Once they were back at Garrison Hill after this little diversion, he would make sure she went back to Burma somehow. He wasn't going to listen to her. He held her, gently, rocking her, kissing the top of her unprotected head.

'You better get yourself a helmet.'

He pounded up the trail, legs pumping, the forest a wet green blur. His lungs were bursting, the cracked ribs a sharp needle in his chest. He didn't know how long he had been running. He had stumbled upon two advance British scouts, at the edge of the woods and charged at them, shooting them down, their mouths big O's of surprise as they went down. On the dirt road behind them, camouflaged in the bushes, stood a lone jeep. Exultant, he had gunned the engine of the jeep, and taken off in a cloud of dust. He had made good time, made up the strike force's lead almost. He had raced down the hill, clinging to the narrow mountain roads, twisting and turning vertiginously. But then, the rough, stony track petered off towards the British lines. He had to go through the wall of thick forest, to get to the strike force. He had abandoned the jeep, struck out on foot. Now, he ran, the branches whipping him, the slap of his feet hitting the ground and his whistling breath the only sounds as the light started to seep in through the tracery of leaves.

It was early morning by the time they came out of the forest. The sun had come up but it was just a dull, diffused glow behind the clouds. The mist lay very heavily, smelling of sulphur and woodsmoke. It was cold, bone chilling. They were probably at 7,000 feet here. The tree line ended abruptly. Ahead, lay a vast expanse of open, grassy slopes and scrubland, unknown territory, shrouded in moving curtains of fog. At the far end, barely glimpsed, it narrowed into a gorge with thick forest on the left and a towering, precipitous rock face on the right. Further ahead, where the gorge opened up, would be the narrow red track that was the target. It wound tightly around the hills but from here, it was invisible. The hills were empty, brooding. They stood, watching the open field through their glasses.

'I don't like these mountains,' Aditi whispered to Meenakshi.

Up front, she could see Debraj's back, strong, broad, where he stood beside Saito. The scouts had come back. Saito raised his fist in the air, then brought it down with a snap. They moved out of the cover of the pine forest, out into the open, two abreast.

The pain in his chest was an iron forge on fire. His mouth was bone dry, the throat full of sand. Stupid, stupid, not getting his canteen. His legs were jelly. He stumbled, hit his shoulder against a tree trunk, screamed. Birds flew out of the bamboo grove to his left, scolding, chattering their disapproval. He slid down the trunk to the ground, drawing in huge gulps of air. *That Goopta, that snake, it was his idea to shoot him in the shoulder, just a surface wound, a mere nick, he had said, to give him the excuse to be in the command tent, near the radios spewing out positions and movements. Oh mother, it hurt.* A small sob escaped his clenched lips but he ruthlessly clamped down on it. *You don't have time for this weak shit. You have to stop them! You have to get to her! Come on, just one more burst. Get up! You're close.* He looked at his watch. Oh god, let me be in time, let me be in time, let me be in time. The words became a litany inside his head as he propelled himself off the ground and stood up, swaying, hanging on to the tree. Then, with a grunt, he pushed himself off and stumbled forward. Have to be in time, have to be in time. Move. Move!

They had almost reached the end of the field. Ahead lay the gorge, cut like a giant slash into the mountainside by the passage of wind and water over millions of years. Here, the forest, dense, dark, impenetrable, came right up to the lip of the gorge. Pines had given way to giant black mahogany and teak. The mist still hung heavily, clinging to the trees, obscuring the far end. Saito held up a fist. The column came to a halt, hundreds of feet shuffling to a stop, the rifles clasped loosely in the hands, A few soft coughs, sips taken from water canteens. The officers huddled around Saito.

'I don't like the look of this. It's the only way to reach the track but we'll be bunched together.' Saito's face was creased with worry.

'Going through that thick forest will set us back by at least an hour, Sir.'

'15 minutes — that's all we will need to cross the gorge.'

'With all due respect, who the hell will know we're here? There's not a soul within miles of here.'

'And the mist will hide us.'

The mouth of the gorge was in deep shadow. The mist hung in curtains, drifting, silent. There was a strange quietness as they entered. Even the occasional cry of a hornbill was missing. They marched, two abreast, their eyes peeled. They were more than halfway across, most of the column already inside the gorge, when, with a loud whoosh, an expelling of breath, a strange red glow zigzagged through the mist. It came from the high grass, at the edge of the dark forest on their left. It rose into the sky, disappeared, and then fell, fish tailing, the improbably bright red orb of a flare, dangling on the end of a small chute. Everyone watched mesmerised. Debraj was the first one to react. *'GET DOWN! IT'S AN AMBUSH!'*

He yanked Aditi by the hand, bringing her tumbling to the ground. 'Take cover! It's a trap!'

But there was no cover. The ground was hard shale, the grass tall in a few patches but mostly just scrub and small brush, barely high enough to cover a grown man. The men closest to them dived for the pitifully inadequate clumps dotting the stony floor. From the darkness of the trees came the twinkling of what seemed like fireflies and then the entire forest on the left erupted with hell fire, in a hundred pinpricks of light. A dozen heavy Vickers machine guns, and scores of light machine guns, cleverly placed to maximise killing ground, opened up. The lethal fusillade of lead scythed through the brigade. The very first volley downed a couple of hundred men within the first few minutes. The whistling of mortar shells joined in, drowning out the screams of the wounded.

The firing seemed to come from everywhere. Shell shocked, disoriented by the mist and the noise, the men in the front spun around, falling in a heap. The men following behind, started crashing into them and fell, struck by the indiscriminate hail of bullets. As the wave of men started turning in on itself, a great wounded snake, coiling upon its tail, it got pushed back towards the sheer rock face of the mountain on the right. Desperate, some of the men tried to climb the rock face but machine guns from hidden ledges opened up, pouring down their murderous fire. There was nowhere to run.

Debraj too was pinned down. He knew they had to organise themselves fast, counter attack now! But how? He couldn't see anything, his face pressed into the sharp shale ground. But he could hear the blunt thwack of bullets hitting flesh close, very close. The animal part of his brain was screaming, stay down, dig in but another part, the trained mind of the soldier, was saying, move, you bastard, you'll get mowed down in minutes. He catapulted up, his whole body bracing for a blow. Adrenaline flooded through his system, a hot red kick, sharpening all his senses, coiling his muscles. Aditi was shouting something at him, trying to pull him back into the grass. He whipped her to her feet and ran, his legs pumping like pistons, and dived behind the closest heap of the dead. Meenakshi arrived seconds later, panting, clutching her gun. He saw Saito a few yards away. He was also barricaded behind a pile of bodies.

'General!' Debraj roared out.

Saito looked up. He held up two fists and criss-crossed his hands in a scissoring gesture. Nothing more needed to be said between them. Good man! He was going to organise a running defence. One squad would crouch and fire while the other would retreat and then switch. It was one of the toughest things to do under heavy fire. But it was the only way out. They started organising the disorderly, struggling mass of men into squads.

'Bahadurs!' Debraj roared. 'Towards the nullah!'

They started moving right, heading for the rock face towards a nullah that coursed at its base. A grove of trees and some large boulders lined its sides. It wasn't much but it would provide cover.

Aditi and Meenakshi, in the centre of his squad, were also firing on the run. But for every yard gained, it seemed they lost a dozen men. And then, with a shriek, an artillery shell landed a hundred yards from them, churning up a big mushroom cloud of dust and deadly shrapnel, roiling the mist into angry, swirling clouds.

No! Sweet Mother of God, Ma Durga, no!

Through his glasses, through a gap in the fog, he saw them. The smoking barrel of a British 3.7 inches mountain gun and another being unhitched from a jeep. On the very track they had come to capture. His heart stopped.

This is the end. He dropped to his knees beside Aditi. He looked at her, his warrior woman, in her tattered battle dress, stained with cordite, gun in hand, a great steadfastness, shining in her eyes. Then, she pointed behind him. He turned. It was Saito, heaving great gulps of air, as he came sliding and crashing on all fours up to them. He nodded towards the grove of trees.

'Take your squad and the women and make for those trees. One Japanese squad will cover you. Move!!'

'What about you, Sir?'

'I'll take the remaining men and hold them.' He saw the stubborn set to Debraj's jaw and sighed. 'It's the only way, you know it.'

'Can't do it, Sir. You're too important to the force.'

'That's insubordination, Major. It's an order. If you make a run for the nullah, it will distract them. It will give me time to dig in. If Nishonko was here today with us, he would have understood.'

Debraj still looked mutinous but he knew Saito was right. He looked at his friend's face. Sweat stained, soot blackened, the wise eyes with the crow's feet of frequent laughter, the Buddha lips which now curved in a smile.

'I come from a long line of samurai, my friend. We have our code. We do not surrender. I would rather commit hara-kiri than give up in battle. I cannot dishonour my ancestors. Please do not ask me to.' Saito looked at the surrounding forest, the mist shrouded hills. 'This…this is as good a place as any to make my stand.

Travelling this road
No one knows how long or short

I find myself home.

'A haiku to remember me by, Deb san.'

Another artillery shell came whistling through the air, exploded with a crump, somewhere to their left. Those guns would find the range soon. Saito stood up, placed his hand on his sword and bowed deeply, every inch an officer of the Imperial Army.

'Long Live the Emperor!'

Debraj bowed back.

'Live long, my... ' His voice trailed off in a whisper. What did you say to a friend in, what could be, a final farewell? Saito slipped away into the mist.

Nishonko could see the final ridge, just yards away. Sweat poured down his forehead, flooding his eyes, turning the forest into a blurred watercolour. Come on, just another few...then he heard the thunder of the guns, an ominous drum roll. NO! His lungs on fire, his face and arms blood-caked from a dozen cuts and bruises, he crashed through the remaining trees and burst out in the open. He stood swaying, a lone stick figure high up on the ridge, almost a 1,000 feet above the swirling mist, the gorge spread out below him, a grandstand view of the massacre. At first, he could make out nothing, just pinpricks of light piercing the mist. Then a random shift of the wind parted the mist, the tendrils revealing the bodies, lying like winnowed wheat, sheaf upon sheaf. His hands trembling, he dragged the field glasses to his eyes. What he saw made him cry out. *Too late! No one can survive such slaughter.* Then incredibly, he could make out Debraj, running pell mell, nurses streaming behind him, Jhilik, yes, there she was, heading for a nullah, across the gorge, away from the killing field. *She was alive!* They were still far away, downhill. It was futile but he shouted, his voice hoarse, breaking, 'Hold on Jhilik, I'm coming, hold on, little one!'

He slid down the steep hillside, scrabbling for purchase, grabbing the short clumps of fern, falling, blindly rushing to reach her. 'Stop shooting, you bastards! Stop! Whyte's orders.' But his words were drowned by the stutter of the annihilating guns.

The small grove of trees under the great rock face was nearer, the nullah with its meandering snow melt closer, more visible. They were getting further and further away from the lethal guns hidden in the inky shadows of the forest on the left side of the gorge. Once they got there, they would be safe, out of range hopefully. *We can do it.*

'Come on!' he yelled, reaching for Aditi's arm. But she was pulling him back. He stumbled, cursing. Why had she stopped? Then he saw the others were also halting. The firing had petered out. There was a sudden silence on the battlefield. What was happening?

Nishonko lost his footing, landed heavily, searing agony lancing through his chest. His uniform was in tatters and his boots were shredded, his feet like jelly. He whimpered. *I didn't mean to hurt you, my love...never you. Run, run Jhilik, run.* He clutched at the rock face, looked down. They were almost there...but they had stopped. She was looking back at something. What was happening?

A pale, clear shaft of sunlight pierced the mist and lit up the middle of the gorge. Everything seemed to slow down, unreal, almost staged. From the centre, waves of khaki clad figures rose, their rifles held in front. At a sharp command, they fixed their bayonets, a thousand flashes of light, each reflecting the sun. In the vanguard, stood the thick-set figure of Saito, today looking ten-feet tall. With a rasp and a ring that could be heard across the silenced battlefield, he drew his sword from its ancient leather scabbard. Small, in the immensity of the gorge and the surrounding, brooding mountains, yet powerful, his voice rang out in command.

'Form on me!'

His flag bearer ran forward, the flowing banner of the rising sun unfurling, bobbing over the heads of the men as he took his place beside Saito. An INA soldier, ran forward, whipping out the tricolour, and took his stand on Saito's other side. A sudden gust of wind lifted both flags, sending them snapping and crackling. The men took position in an extended battleline.

Any warrior, no matter where his loyalties lay, would hold his breath in reverence. Debraj suddenly remembered an evening in a pub, a few drinks, a hoary old professor, four sheets to the wind, raising his pint and reciting Macaulay's poem and all of them joining in.

Then out spoke brave Horatius,
the captain of the gate:
To every man upon this earth
Death comes soon or late,
And how can man die better
Than facing fearful odds,
For the flags of his fathers,
And the temples of his gods

Now, he stood, staring across the expanse of gorge, at his friend. General Harada Saito. *How can man die better...*

Saito held up the sword, pointed.

'BANZAI!' It was the roar of a lion.

'BANZAI ! ADVANCE!' It was echoed in a thousand throats. Then, Neel, his face set with resolve, stepped out.

'JAI HIND!' The famous INA battle cry rung out. A thousand voices joined in.

Like the name of their mission, Kirimomi Sakusen, 'Rolling Thunder', they charged the British guns. There was a hundred yards of open ground between them. The British gunners, who had frozen, their jaws slack with disbelief, now scrambled for their guns. There was an edge of desperation in their shooting. If the charging horde reached the forest, they would be overrun. They held down the triggers of their machine guns till the barrels glowed red. Like a giant scythe slashing through a ripe wheat field, the bullets cut down ranks upon ranks of the charging warriors. But still they came, vaulting over their fallen comrades, the wave thinning but seemingly unstoppable. Debraj tensed. *It might just work*! They had almost reached the tree line, it was happening, they were almost upon the hidden guns. But then, in mid stride, a few feet from the guns, Saito faltered. The great sword came down. Even from a distance, they could see the red explosions on Saito's chest, the spill and splash and flight of blood from the side of his head as he was hit. He went down on his knees.

Go, brave Horatius, into the gentle night…

The front line crashed through into the forest, scattered now, thinner. Debraj, Aditi, all of them waited, breath bated. Then the flag bearer stumbled out, backwards, still clutching the banner. He reeled, half his face blown away, went down, the flag spinning out of his dead hands. More Japanese soldiers came running out. They were shot in the back, their bodies jerking like marionettes. Neel backed out, shooting, shooting. Then he ran out of ammo. He threw his rifle down, put his hands behind his head. A Gurkha came charging out, bayonetted him in the belly, the blade going in till the hilt.

Debraj's legs were trembling. He wheeled, pulled Aditi's arm.

'Move, move, dammit!'

They were very close to the nullah and safety. His heart was booming in his ears. Aditi ran beside him, her face streaming with tears.

'Fan out, fan out, don't bunch up,' he yelled at the squads. And then two thunderclaps went off on their left, almost blowing them off their feet. The other nurse and a couple of his men were flung up like rag dolls into the air.

'Mines!' Debraj yelled. *Oh god! Please not now…we're nearly through.* Aditi was sprawled on the ground where she had been thrown. He pulled her to her feet, rough in his urgency. But she was screaming something, her lips stretched, pointing. He turned. Meenakshi was lying there, her body at an odd angle.

'Meena!' Aditi had run to her, trying to pull her upright. Oh god, they didn't have the time for this.

'Leave her! We have to move.'

'No! I'm not leaving her.' Aditi's eyes were fever bright.

Cursing under his breath, he picked up Meenakshi. Holding her in his arms, he stumbled forward. She was moaning. Which way to go? The ground on the left was sown with deadly steel seeds which could mangle a body horribly. The ground on the right was carpeted with bush and wild shrub. He had no idea where they had planted the mines but watched for disturbed ground. He stepped gingerly forward, knowing he could step on one any minute, that quiet click his death knell. His skin crawled with the thought.

'Aditi?'

'Yes?' Her voice was calm, composed. She was behind him, half facing the other way, walking backwards, her gun held up, guarding his back.

'Stay right behind me. Walk in my footsteps.'

'Yes, my love. I'm right behind you.'

Nishonko slithered down the last of the rock face and fell on the gully floor. Gasping for breath, he looked around wildly. Where were they? Where was Jhilik? Then he saw them, more than a quarter of a mile away, to his right. Deb was carrying someone, Jhilik behind him, protecting his back. They splashed through the nullah, heading into the grove of trees. Thank you, God, thank you. She had made it through the minefield.

Debraj and Aditi and the handful of men who had survived the mad dash and the mines plunged into the grove of trees. His heart thudded. *We made it.* The grove was in the shadow of a great jut of stone. It was dark beneath the trees. As the men flopped down in the undergrowth, their mouths open, dragging in lungfuls of air, he laid Meenakshi down gently, propping her against a rock. As he slipped his hands out, he saw they were slick with blood. His heart jolted, then he realised it was Meenakshi's. Aditi was already kneeling, softly talking to Meenakshi, tearing up bandages, trying to staunch the dark red flood welling out of her side. Debraj looked around. They had to find a way out. The grove would provide temporary refuge. He stood up. Zapft! The flat crack of a bullet. And another. The bark on the tree behind his head exploded. He ducked, bringing up his gun. Bullets sliced through the grove, slamming into the men. Aditi's head came up. He frantically signalled to her to stay down. She crouched, covered Meenakshi's body with her own. He saw the muzzle flash from a ledge on the rock face behind. He slithered forward, found himself a clear line of sight. Then he waited, patient, a bead drawn on the ledge. Sure enough, they showed themselves, looking over the ledge for survivors. He picked off three of them, smoothly, in one continuous motion. Then he slithered away and found a new vantage point.

But no one else fired back. He looked at the sprawled bodies of the men. They were all gone. Only he, Aditi and Meenakshi were left. On one side, the fallen trunk of a large wild teak lay across a small ditch. They moved Meenakshi behind the trunk and took cover in the ditch, safe for the time being.

The flurry of shots brought Nishonko to a skidding stop as he headed towards the grove. He looked around wildly. In the distance, across the gorge, he could see figures beginning to emerge from the tree line. He had to stop them. He started to sprint across the gorge, towards the British lines, waving, calling out Whyte's name. But no sound came, just a dry croak, a thready whisper. He kept calling, waving his arms.

Wild white lilies grew in profusion along the nullah, their heads delicately swaying in the mist.

'How can they be everywhere, Deb?' Aditi's voice was subdued.

He drew a deep breath. From the moment the ambush had been sprung, he had known it in his bones.

'We've been betrayed, Aditi.'

She nodded. The British seemed to know every little detail about them. The way the ambush was organised, the way they had the gorge covered, had men placed at strategic points to cut off any escape, the fact that the mines had been planted beforehand…they had thought of everything. The plan had been made…Deb thought back, realised with a shock it was only the day before that Nishonko had come up with it. It had to be someone close, someone in the know.

He checked their weapons. They had his Sten gun and revolver and the two rifles belonging to Meenakshi and Aditi but only one magazine and a handful of bullets. He scrounged around, going through the dead men's possessions, emptying pockets. He picked up another revolver, four magazines and six rounds of bullets, three canteens of water and some dried fish. He looked at Aditi carefully emptying out their satchels and laying down their possessions: a bag of gram flour and jaggery, two canteens of water, a tricolour flag, a crumpled packet of cigarettes, his lighter, a picture of her parents, morphine, some medical supplies. Neatly laid out, the assortment seemed even more pathetic. They chewed on the fish, gave Meenakshi a shot.

Across the gorge, the British had slowly started to emerge from the dark safety of the forest. They gingerly stepped out, looking around the vast empty field. Ravens and crows, kites and scavengers, had already started to ride the thermals, gliding, black wings spread, their inquisitive cawing warning each other of intruders. Some of them, the bolder ones, had alighted on the stony ground, hopping sideways, black glassy eyes blinking, inching up closer to the line of fallen men. The soldiers began picking their way through the slaughterhouse, poking the wounded with their rifle barrels, dispatching them with a gunshot if they moved.

'Mop them up, make sure not a single one is alive, men.'

'Right, Sergeant.'

'Saito…Neelu…all gone…' she whispered. 'What would Netaji do?'

'When he saw us off at the railhead, he said, *"I have only one word of command to give you, and that is if you have to go down temporarily, then go down fighting with the national tricolour held aloft; go down as heroes; go down upholding the highest code of honour and discipline."*'

'How do you remember it, word for word?'

He grinned. 'Wrote it down. Mugged it up.'

It made her smile, her pixie, impish smile. God, how he loved that smile.

'But we, we have so much to live for, my love. I don't know about honour and discipline but I would settle for a small house, making love in the afternoons, Khogen da's prawn malai curry and…' He sighed. 'We don't have to die. We can step out there, surrender honourably. We will suffer imprisonment, beatings, worse but we will live. Don't you want to live, Aditi?'

Her hand went instinctively to her belly…

'Yes, Deb, of course I do.'

She stared at him. Should she tell him? She felt calm, almost dreamy. He stared back at her, his face unreadable. Then, he shrugged, his shoulders drooping a bit.

'But, on the other hand, might as well face it, they won't let us live. They will line me up against a wall and shoot me for treason. And you, you my pretty, they will throw you to...'

His voice broke. He held her fiercely. They looked through the trees. The line of men, searching, carrying out their mop up work, oblivious to their presence, had moved closer.

'We can make a last stand here, take as many of them as we can with us.' Aditi's voice was low, almost hushed, as if those far men would hear her.

'We won't be able to hold them off for long. They outnumber us. They can outwait us. Or let loose those mortars on us. We are trapped.' Debraj was matter of fact, analysing, appraising.

'There has to be a way out.' Her voice for the first time had a tiny edge of desperation to it. He held her hand, pointed through the tree trunks across the gorge, on the left of the slowly advancing soldiers.

'That far line of trees, there, on the left, diagonally across, can you see it? They don't have anyone there. We make a run for it, take our chances.'

'I can't leave Meena.'

They turned to look at her, pale, propped against the tree trunk, her eyes closed. The bandage Aditi had put on her was already seeped through with fresh blood.

'She won't make it. She'll just slow us down.' Debraj spoke in a whisper.

'She's my friend. I'm not leaving her to die alone.' Aditi's whisper was fiercer.

'He's right, Aditi.' Meena opened her eyes. 'I'm not going anywhere. Give me a rifle, I'll cover you. I'll draw their fire. At least, the two of you can... might...make it back to our lines.'

'No, I'll stay with you...we'll both cover Deb.'

'That's ridiculous, Aditi, it's both of us or nothing. I can't let you go, don't you know that, you silly aagdoom baagdoom idiot?'

Again, that smile. He held her hands, kissed her palms one by one. In the vast silence of the gorge with its circling crows, they could hear the flat echoing crack of shots being fired, singles, sometimes a burst, as the wounded and the survivors were picked off.

'And when we're down to our last bullet?'

'Ah yes, that Japanese death before dishonour stuff and blowing out your own brains? Not my style. I would rather go with the Azad Hind Fauj motto — *Fight to the last man, fight with the last bullet!* I'm going to take my chances, I'm going to run like the blazes and I'm going to take as many of them as I can while I'm doing it. Are you with me, Aditi Sen?'

Again, that fleeting touch of her belly, that faraway look. Meena looked at her.

'Tell him,' she mouthed, silently.

Aditi nodded.

'I'm with you, Debraj Mookerji.' She started packing their meagre possessions into one bag. 'And if we fall, we will be legend. They'll sing songs about us. They will remember this day of sorrow, these friends, these martyrs, lying out there. Their sacrifice…it must mean something. It must not be forgotten.'

'And who will tell our story, Aditi?'

'Nishonko da. He will find the betrayer, he will make sure the truth is known.'

'Why should he? Have we not betrayed him?'

'He will…because he loves us…all of us. And we love him, each in our own way. And because the truth matters.'

And so, it was time. Aditi hugged Meenakshi. They clung to each other. Then Debraj carried Meenakshi tenderly to the edge of the grove, settled her in, her back against a large rock. She was in shadow, hidden from the approaching scattered line of men. He gave her two canteens and some of the food, all the medicines, her gun, ammo.

'Look after her, Major.' Meenakshi's eyes were shining with unshed tears.

He saluted her. 'Yes, Ma'am!'

Debraj and Aditi looked at each other. He held her, this unlikely love of his. She etched every line, every curve of that beloved face into her memory. They kissed, a long kiss, thousand fathoms deep. He tucked an errant curl behind her ear. She smiled her heart-breaking smile and it was enough.

'Cheese sumboosucks at Flury's, remember?'

'I'll be there, my only love.'

They stood up, hand in hand.

No one, neither the three in the grove, nor the hunting line of British soldiers, noticed the single man, running towards them, his hands waving in the air, his mouth moving silently. Nishonko flew across the field, leaping over the broken bodies of the dead, sidestepping the fallen guns, the dismembered limbs. He had to get to the British line, get Whyte somehow. He had helped Whyte, Whyte must help him back. Jhilik's life for all of theirs, even his. They had no use for a woman's life, nothing to gain by striking her dead, shooting her. They would see, they would agree. A thin cry for help from a fallen soldier, another, a Japanese, a boy almost, pleading for water, a hand stretched out for succour… nothing stopped his headlong rush. The corpses lay, body upon body, limp, a carpet of mutilated flesh and bone. A canteen with a bullet hole in it, abandoned bags, crushed helmets, tattered flags flew by his dust-streaked boots. He was halfway across the gorge when he heard the stutter of a Sten gun from the direction of the grove. He spun around, almost falling.

The British soldiers had started turning back, their grisly job done. The last of the dead bodies had petered out here. Up ahead was the grove of trees but there had been no movement inside for a while. No one had fired upon them as they advanced. Chances were, they were all wiped out. He turned to the Gurkha NCO.

'Corporal Thapa, take a couple of the lads and go and give that little grove up there a decko. The rest of you, stand down. Head back to your lines, boys. It's over.'

And then the Sten gun stuttered. The birds took alarm, took wing in a swarm, swirled up from the floor of the gorge and filled the sky in a black swooping cloud.

She came charging out of the grove like a wounded tigress, eyes shining with defiance. Her mane of hair had escaped its moorings and streamed behind her, the sun a halo around her head. The tricolour unfurled behind her shoulders like a cape. She was a goddess. The revolvers in her two hands blazed. Next to her was her Deb, her consort, the Sten gun shuddering in his hands. Corporal Thapa and his men went down in the first burst, taken by surprise.

The Sergeant whirled round in disbelief. What the tarnation was this?

Debraj held the Sten gun steady, spewing lead as he roared, 'JAI HIND!' More bodies crashed down in front of them, jerking, spinning, flying in a dance of death.

Nishonko tried to get to his feet, his mouth slack with disbelief. What was she doing, oh god, Jhilik, go back, go back.

Debraj and Aditi went through another knot of soldiers, caught flat-footed, scrambling, trying to bring their guns up, fumbling. Now the two were in the open, the gorge in front of them suddenly empty, the men left behind. As one, they veered left, making for the dark mass of the tree line, dodging the dead bodies, the live bullets.

Private Limbu brought up his gun, took careful aim, his sight centred between Debraj's shoulder blades. 'Marta kuch bhi karta,' he muttered. The dead will try anything. Then the left side of his jaw exploded from a shot. He spun and fell to the ground. Through the shale cutting into his cheek as he lay on his side, with his dying eyes, he saw the apparition...a dark woman, her short black hair standing up stiff wth sweat and blood, the sun glancing off her aviator glasses. She stood, her legs braced, blood soaked bandages flapping in the breeze, taking aim, firing, again and again. It was Meenakshi, out in the open.

Nishonko didn't see her. He had eyes only for Aditi. He shouted out her name but it was a silent scream. She didn't hear, through the roar of blood in her head. The gun was hot in her hand. Her feet had wings.

Debraj was changing magazines on the run. 'Coming up on your right,' he roared.

She pirouetted, light as a feather, fired, ran. Closer now to the tree line...

Meenakshi watched them run, reloading with shaking hands. You'll make it, you'll make it. A bullet thwacked three inches from her head. She brought up her gun calmly, shot the Gurkha leaping towards her.

Nishonko too turned towards the tree line, rushing to intercept Debraj and Aditi, hot on their heels.

And now, a fusillade of bullets, pinpricks of fairy lights, came from the British lines inside the forest.

Nishonko saw them, screamed. 'Hold your fire! I'm Whyte's man.' But his parched throat could only produce a ragged whisper. No one heard. He drew his revolver, fired into the air. No one heard.

But, miraculously, they made it through the hail of bullets. Aditi reached the safety of the tree line. Debraj was a few paces behind her, half turned, emptying out his magazine.

And then, he stumbled.

Aditi, in her headlong rush, was already inside the cover of the trees. She whirled to cover Debraj, bringing up her gun, her eyes slit.

A bright red flower bloomed on his chest. Slowly, like a tall tree falling in the depths of the forest, he went down on his knees, the gun slipping out of his hand. He had a look of intense surprise on his face.

Aditi's face crumpled. She started to run back to him. He looked up, shook his head.

'No. Go. Run.' With each word, a tiny bubble of red appeared at the corner of his mouth.

She ran up to him. The scarlet flower had bloomed more, a magic ink blot spreading faster. She kneeled in front of him.

'It's both or nothing, remember? So, are you going to get up and come with me, Debraj Mookerji? Or are you going to make a lady wait?'

Debraj gave her his crooked smile. He was breathing raggedly.

'We almost made it.'

Aditi's eyes were dry as she smiled. They faced each other, kneeling in the long grass at the edge of the forest.

'Gave them a run for their money. Did you see the look on their faces? Gobsmacked.' He laughed, coughed. The bubbles became a steady trickle, bright red, heartblood. She wiped it with infinite gentleness, ran her fingers through his sweat wet hair.

Nishonko crashed to a halt a little distance from them. As he stood, swaying, his chest heaving, the empty gun hanging by his side, another fusillade of bullets chattered out. He ducked, hugged the ground, then scrambled up and ran to the two kneeling figures. Aditi looked up, her eyes widening.

'Jhilik...oh my god, Jhilik, are you okay?'

'Nishonko da, how...why are you here?'

'I wanted to save you. I...why did you have to come?'

'Can you help him? My Deb? Please Nishonko da, he's...' Her voice broke.

Nishonko looked at Debraj, at the blood now pulsing out steadily, and knew it was too late. This was what he had wanted, what he had spent so many nights imagining, conjuring a hundred deaths for this man. And now, a vast tiredness, the uselessness of it all, overwhelmed him. Jhilik, she had never been his. He saw it all now — the love that she had denied him shining like the light of a thousand suns for this doomed man, the emptiness and desolation of her grieving heart, laid bare, like a wound, that he could never heal, that luminous promise and hope that was her essence, going out like a flickering lamp from her eyes.

'No, Jhilik, no.' His voice was a soft moan.

Debraj stared at him, his mouth twisting. 'Someone gave us away... Who was it, Nishonko? What did you do?' A gurgling, undersea sound came with each breath, each word.

'Deb, I swear, I didn't want to put her in harm's way. It wasn't meant to be like this.'

Aditi looked at him, uncomprehending. He shook his head, turned away. At the other end of the gorge, near the grove of trees, near the nullah, something was going on. Through the mist, he heard a high scream — a woman's or was it an animal — the sound of men laughing. He saw them circling something, someone on the ground, hyenas on the prowl, shouting, stamping their feet. 'Give it to the bitch, give it to the bitch.'

'It was you.' Her voice was hard, clear, sure.

He turned. She was still kneeling, her gun cradled in her lap.

'You were the traitor...YOU.'

He nodded, willing her to shoot. But she sat there, looking at him, still not believing it.

'Why?'

'I loved you. I love you.'

She stared up at him through those wide set eyes, the clouded sky, the pale hidden sun reflected in them. An eternity went by. Disbelief, despair, contempt, pity and acceptance moved like cloud shadows across her face. But no love. She started to raise her gun. Another volley of shots rang out from behind them. He was hit, the pain coming seconds later, like a thunderclap, in his thigh. And then he saw her body jerk. She clutched her stomach. Her face crumpled, she shook her head. She took Deb's hand and placed it beside hers, cupping the unborn child in her womb. She whispered something to him. They slowly leaned towards each other, their hands clasped, their foreheads gently touched. They were still.

The old man sighs, a sound like a night wind through the pines. It is late afternoon, the tea shop running empty. They are all silent, Haru is weeping, a child's unabashed tears at the waste of it all. Ganesh babu's face is sombre. Sudipto looks at the old man, He clears his throat.

'So Debraj Mookerji died.'

'But Nishonko survived.' The old man's voice is dry and cracked, like an old phonograph record.

Tentacles of mist had begun to swirl between the trees. They moved, shifted, slowly enveloped the man and woman, kneeling so still, in the long grass. Nishonko stirred, came to. He was on his knees, hunched over, almost as if he had been praying. Had he passed out? Where was he? A vast silence hung around him. The world was grey. A soft drizzle started to fall. He stared at the useless gun in his hand, looked with bemusement at the big jagged wound in his thigh. The rude cawing of a black raven, harbinger of death, dragged him back to the moment. He looked up, full awareness suddenly flaring up in those big, dreamy eyes. A low, strangled wail of despair, the cry of the damned, came out of his dry throat. His knees sank deeper into the mud and the blood. His head fell back, raised to the unforgiving sky. He howled out her name to the gathering clouds. Behind him, shadowy figures came out through the mist, their guns cocked. A rifle was raised and then brought down sharply, clubbing him on the head. He went down, his punishment just beginning.

'It's done. The Japanese brigade and a whole battalion of the INA have been decimated.' Richards voice was faint.

Whyte rubbed his cheeks tiredly. He needed a shave. It had been a long night. 'Good. We have bought ourselves the time. Are you happy, Richards?'

'Yes, Sir, thank you, Sir.' Even over the crackling of the line, Richards' relief was clear. Whyte put down the phone, poured himself a drink, a stiff one.

'Made it by the skin of our teeth, Goopta.'

Goopta nodded, huddled in the armchair, as usual all wrapped up.

'Yes, Sir, except for that last-minute hiccup.'

'All in the game, my man.' Whyte was feeling expansive.

'And Debraj? What of him, Sir?'

'Dead. Shot. Pity, could have used him, if he had been a bit sensible. He would have done well in post-war India.'

'Yes. Pity. How soon will the roads open up, Sir? To the railhead?'

'Can't wait to get your sorry ass out of here, eh Goopta?'

'Well Sir, the world of commerce waits for no man. Up and running, I must be. I do hope you will expedite the paperwork, Sir. You know, our little agreement? Regarding the timber?

Whyte stared at him over the rim of his glass. Greedy bastard. But he had his uses. He would do well. He had mastered the art of bending to the wind, something this country seemed so good at doing. He nodded.

An orderly walked in.

'Colonel Richards on the phone, Sir.'

'Now what does he want?'

Goopta listened, without much interest, his eyes hooded, turning one of the rings on his finger. The gomedh recommended by that Chinese astrologer in Rangoon, had turned out to be a most fortunate investment. Everything was falling into place. He would call up the Party bosses in Calcutta today, report to them that Netaji's little adventure in Kohima was fizzling out. Oh, they would be ecstatic. That mayorship was in his pocket.

'Who? Speak up. Oh yes, Nishonko Mitro. What is he saying?' Whyte listened to Richards' voice on the other end, tapping his finger on his glass impatiently.

'You tell that treacherous bastard that we should shoot him down like a dog. He misinformed us about the strength of the strike force. What? Yes, he did tell us finally but last minute. Made sure we were outnumbered. We just about scraped through. Skin of teeth. No, he doesn't get to meet me. Ever. Tell him I've got his treachery on tape, every last bit of treachery. His hide belongs to us. Go ahead, Richards, just put him in the stockade. Shoot him, starve him to death, expunge him from the records. I want his very existence wiped out.'

He slammed down the phone, his face pink from the heat of his words.

'That was K, yes?'

Whyte nodded, flopped down in an armchair.

'The gall of him. He actually thinks we owe him something.'

'From that day, it all unravelled.' The old man taps the newspaper with his palsied fingers, his hand shaking. 'The British force, on its last legs in Kohima, was relieved by General Slim in the next 48 hours. Heavy artillery and tanks rolled in from Dimapur. The Japanese and the INA, already stretched to breaking point, started retreating, fighting every inch of the way. By the time reinforcements of INA forces reached Ukhrul, Japanese forces had begun their withdrawal from Kohima.'

'If only the Japanese had bypassed Kohima and taken the railhead at Dimapur!' Sudipto slaps the table with bitter frustration, sending the glasses rattling, toppling. Haru hurriedly grabs them. 'Netaji had demanded it but Mataguchi, he wanted to catch a big fish. He just ended up with a big fat crocodile instead.'

The old man looks at him, his rheumy eyes enlarged behind his taped glasses. 'Why does it upset you so much, young man? It was such a long time ago.'

'I…I've studied the subject in some detail. And it makes me angry that things could have been…different. A huge lie, a concocted narrative has become accepted as the truth. A myth has been foisted on the whole world about the INA and Netaji. It makes me see red.'

'Myth? And mythya?' Ganesh babu smiles with self satisfaction at the pun that has popped into his head. 'What is this unspeakable lie you have so cleverly stumbled upon, Sudipto babu?'

'We've all been told that England fought World War II to save Europe and rest of the world from the scourge of Nazi Germany, right? Did they do it to gain political and material advantage? Perish the thought. Did they do it simply to defend its assets? Oh no. No, they were the lonely heroes who threw down the challenge when others hesitated. Bravely, they stood up against the evil hordes and were almost defeated. But, hurrah, hurrah, they finally prevailed and brought the barbarians to their knees. This is the stuff of stories, spun out through expensively shot movies and romantic novels about the Raj and War comic books — till even a mere child believes it to be the honest truth. This was the proposition the whole world bought into. Didn't you, Ganesh babu? So they forced all of us to agree that any Indian who raised his hand against the noble saviours of the civilised world, the good old British, was to be condemned by all good men. By this one act, he forfeited the sympathy and respect of civilised mankind. He was dubbed a power hungry traitor, a man who went against everything decent, everything good. And so what if he was only trying to obtain the freedom that is every people's due?'

There is silence around the table. The old man lets out a sigh, rubs his face. Ganesh babu looks down at his hands.

'Anyway, sorry, I interrupted you, Sir.' Sudipto leans back, the fire in his eyes dying out slowly.

'Then the monsoon broke early. By the third week of May, torrential rains washed away all tracks. The entire terrain turned into rivers of green mud. Supply lines were deluged. The ferocious fighting gave way to skirmishes. Harassed by Allied air craft and local Burmese irregulars, thousands of Indians and Japanese were killed or taken prisoner. The rivers ran with blood.'

'You know what General Gracey would ask Prem Sahgal after his capture?'

The old man shakes his head tiredly and looks at Sudipto.

'No, Sudipto babu, what did he say?'

'He said, quote, "*What did you mean, you people, by going on fighting? We had armour, artillery. You chaps had nothing. But instead of surrendering, you fought. It was madness!"* But Sahgal said their determination to fight against the odds was "neither light-hearted nor born of hurrah-patriotism." It was a powerful resolve, taught by Netaji at the training camps.' He notices their expressions of strained patience.

'Okay, okay, sorry, you were talking about the rains coming.'

Netaji looked up as the jeep came careening into the INA camp at Maymyo. Captain Nawaz Hussein piled out. Netaji read through the brief message he handed over and his face crumpled. Nawaz ran into the tent and started hurriedly packing. Netaji stood outside, alone. The sky was swollen with dark rain clouds. A powerful wind came up. Big fat drops fell to the ground, onto his unprotected head, soaked through his uniform. Nawaz ran up with an umbrella but Netaji waved him away. They strode through the downpour towards the airstrip. The airfield, carved out of the jungle mere weeks ago, was already losing its battle with the invading weeds and tropical grass. The propellors of the small plane were turning, the engine idling. On its side, in a fine cursive script was written *Azad Hind*. Nawaz Hussein opened the door, threw in the luggage. Netaji stood, his legs braced, looking back at the hills. Far to the west, ominous grey clouds were piled up high, tinged with scarlet. Distant thunder boomed, growled. Was it the wrath of the gods pouring down from the heavens, or was it the killing machines of wrathful mortals? Nawaz waited, his eyes filled with pity. Netaji slowly turned away, looking very tired. Nawaz helped him up the two steps, then pulled them up and slammed the door shut. The plane wobbled on the rough runway, then took off in an ungainly fashion. It circled and then became a small speck which disappeared into the clouds, heading south east.

Chhoto mashi hurried down the driveway. The news that Netaji was back in Rangoon had spread like wildfire. The first anniversary of Netaji taking leadership was fast approaching. She went to the reception.

'I have an appointment with Netaji.'

As she was ushered in, Netaji rose to greet her. Her hair had turned grey. He was shocked by the sudden deterioration.

'Mrs. Swaminathan, how are you?'

'Please, is there any news from the front?'

'Well, it's slowed down, perhaps even stalled a bit but all this talk of impending calamity? Please set your mind at ease. The news about the Imphal campaign is still positive. Morale is still high, funds are pouring in.'

Chhoto mashi sat still. 'And her? Is there any news of my Aditi?'

He sat down beside her. 'I wish I could tell you for sure. Their field station got bombed, that we know. But her body was not amongst the wounded or dead. We can only pray.'

'But it's already over two months.' Her voice rose on a wail, her hands fluttered like wounded birds. 'I'm so afraid, Netaji, I'm so frightened for my little one.'

Netaji could only nod, his own heart heavy.

The old man sighs.

'But by July, they knew it was over. A harrowing retreat back into Burma began. Wounded, starving, diseased, ravaged by malaria with no medicines, our men perished in their thousands. With supply lines cut, they survived on jungle grass and small fish caught in streams with their mosquito nets. Netaji retreated on foot to Thailand with his soldiers along with the remnants of the Rani Jhansi, a dangerous trek under constant enemy fire. Still, they didn't lose hope. Netaji thought the INA would recuperate, regroup. But then, those bastards dropped the atom bomb and Japan surrendered, and it was all over. Netaji had to flee to Japan.'

'And that's when he disappeared.' Ganesh babu chips in.

'Or died.' Haru puts in. Even he knows about the controversy surrounding the plane crash and the conspiracy theories which refused to die down.

'They're still arguing about it.'

'And the dream ended.' The old man slumps in his seat. He is exhausted.

'Actually, it didn't. If I can quote one last thing… from Netaji.' Sudipto opens his notebook, rifles through the pages of dense notes.

'Ah, here it is. It will take two seconds. He says, "*I regret more than you do that your sufferings and sacrifices have not borne immediate fruit. But they have not gone in vain, because they have ensured the emancipation of our motherland and will serve as an undying inspiration to Indians all over the world. Posterity will bless your name and will talk with pride about your offerings at the altar of India's freedom."* Wow! So, though Debraj Mookerji didn't reach the Red Fort, though all those INA guys didn't ignite the revolt in Bengal they wanted, they fought! They didn't just lie down and get kicked and take the lathi charges, they didn't sit around holding meetings and passing resolutions. They bloody well took up arms and fought. Fought at the border, fought at Kohima, fought again at Irawaddy, fought till the bitter end. And when the survivors came back to India in handcuffs, India discovered who they were and what they had attempted.'

The old man nods, his head almost too heavy for the thin, brittle neck.

'Yes, yes, that's true. The INA lit the fuse — that's what led to the British finally leaving India. Not the Quit India Movement, not Ahimsa or Non-Cooperation or the Mahatma.'

He held up his hand to the mutterings of protest. 'Of course, azadi came in a large part by Satyagraha but not to the extent that...'

He saw their looks of disbelief, shook his head.

'You, all of you, you've always believed that India became free by turning the other cheek, didn't you? Everybody thinks our independence happened because the moral force of Gandhi worked on the English conscience. Not so. You know what actually happened? A cosmic joke. After the war, when thousands of prisoners arrived, the triumphant British decided to teach a demoralised nation a lesson. So, they dragged three INA officers to stand public trial at the Red Fort. And who did they choose?'

The old man chuckled, shaking his head, gently slapping his thigh in some mirth.

'A Hindu, a Muslim, a Sikh. Netaji himself could not have made a better choice. They were to be tried for high treason against King-Emperor. Idiots! The whole plan misfired. There was a massive outburst of public protest. The INA men became overnight heroes. The defence argued that they had a constitutional right to fight for Indian independence against the Raj. But the Raj refused to back down. It proved to be a catastrophic error on the part of the colonial masters. The whole country rose up in arms. This led to the Bombay Mutiny, and forced the British to pack their bags and bugger off. As Deb would have put it.' He has a small, bitter smile of remembrance.

'So, the INA's crusade actually speeded up the process of India finally becoming free. After that, no one was going to buy a policy of appeasement anymore. Even the promise of making the colonial administration more Indian was not going to work anymore. There was no way the desire for freedom could be postponed any longer. Nor could Britain think about using the British Indian Army against the Burmese or to help the French and Dutch against the Vietnamese and Indonesian freedom movements.The INA nixed any chances of reconquest in other parts of the colonial world.'

'Hang on, hang on.' Sudipto bangs on the table.

Ganesh babu frowns. Really, this young man is a bit of a pondpaka, an asshole, terribly rude and pushy. Young people nowadays, really! 'Arre, let him finish…'

But Sudipto sweeps on, his eyes ablaze. 'Sure, it forced the hand of the British and independence did come. But a different kind of independence from what Netaji had dreamt. Think about it, if..if Netaji had won, if on that fateful day, the INA and Saito had won, our history, what's happened to this country…everything would have been different.'

'Sudipto babu, how have you come to this glorious conclusion?' Ganesh babu's Bengali blood is up. He is now feeling quite argumentative.

'I'll tell you. Netaji would have given India true independence as well as the revolution she needed, deserved. He would have given us an undivided India. He would have given us a truly secular, caste-free India. And a government that would be ethical, responsible, willing to truly serve the people. Can you imagine — no coalition politics, no chair niye maramari, no horse trading in Parliament, no criminal-politician nexus, no dynastic rule, no Emergency, no Babri Masjid. If Netaji had won, there would be free education and…'

'Ifs…buts…castles in the air, heads in the clouds,' Ganesh babu scoffs. 'You young anari dreamers…'

'Yes, we young clueless dreamers. At least we've got our heads in the clouds and not tucked up some politician's ass. At least our minds are open, not locked in rigor mortis. We can imagine an alternate narrative. You? You just sit there, being cynical and perverse…isn't that your mantra? Can't be done, won't be done? You've sat on your hands so long, played with your balls and done nothing, that you've forgotten there's a shitload coming down!'

'No need to be ob..ob..obnoxious, young man!' Ganesh babu is incensed.

'Whoa whoa…you people still at it?' It's Dulal da, back from his mundane errands of vegetable shopping and paying the weekly hafta to the beat cop. He looks at them, Sudipto, his face pink with anger, Ganesh babu glowering, the old man quietly smiling.

'So, tell me, who was it, the beimaan?'

'That Nishonko Mitro, shala.' Haru is indignant.

'I knew it. Always seemed a bit cracked.'

'How could he do it? He loved Aditi, right?'

The old man shakes his head, a hopeless gesture.

'You can betray only those you love, Haru, my son. A truth you will understand the day your heart is broken.'

'Arre, enough with this love shove. So you betray everyone in the name of love, haan? Very selfish, baba.' Ganesh babu's lip curls.

The old man laughs, an acid sound.

'We all betrayed each other, didn't we? The so-called patriots sitting on their high horses in Calcutta and Delhi. The men who carved up the country, created the horror of Partition, the thousands of lives, destroyed, on both sides of the border. Gaffar, Goopta…no one was innocent.'

'Hanh, by the way, what happened to that bastard Goopta?'

'Ah, Goopta. Goopta did well. Goopta now runs our judiciary. Goopta is the shadow kingmaker in Parliament. He is the builder razing our land for profit. He is the industrialist poisoning our rivers. He is the slumlord who has the Government in his pocket. The Gooptas of the world have prospered.'

'Bas, chalo, end of story.' Dulal da gets up, cuffs Haru on the head. 'Now, Haru, if you don't mind, I have an establishment to run and those potatoes need your kind attention.'

Haru slouches off, rubbing his head, hitching up his baggy, hand-me-down cargo pants. Dulal da goes behind the cash counter and slips into the proprietor's chair. Ganesh babu too starts to pick up his possessions. The extra tuition he gives to some of the neighbourhood boys is starting in another 15 minutes. But, something still niggles. Who is this old codger, this mad hatter, who has held them in thrall for so many hours with his twisted tale of betrayal?

'Aar aapnar role ta ki, Dadu? What was your role? Jhherey kashoon na...just spit it out, man.'

The old man sighs. He slowly strokes, settles the sparse strands of hair on his head, his eyes meditative.

'I'm the one who lived to tell the tale. The survivor, doomed to carry the burden. The man who wasn't allowed to die because who would then tell the truth?'

The old man is lost in thought. Ganesh babu shakes his head, looks at his watch, and bustles away. Now there's only Sudipto left.

'And Nishonko? What became of him, Sir? Did he die in prison?'

'No, no, though sometimes, he must have wished it. No, he was released but his very existence had been wiped out. He was neiher fish nor fowl, neither INA nor British Indian. He went to the Delhi Fort trials but no one there wanted to hear his story. The only version the world heard was the British version...through dodgy memoirs and insincerely edited documentaries and heavily self-congratulatory public speeches. He wanted to prove that that was not the only narrative, that there was a different truth hidden in the story of the Forgotten Army. He went hunting for Whyte and found him in Delhi on the eve of his departure to England. He found out that those tapes did in fact exist and Whyte had used them to get his plum posting. Nishonko begged him for the tapes, not to wipe out the evidence against himself but to set up proof of how the British had won at Kohima. But Whtye of course refused. To no avail, as it would seem that he died of a brain aneurysm just a year later. The tapes went to Whyte's sister as part of his estate. She handed them over to the National Army Museum, where to this day, they lie. So every year, from 1949, on the 23rd of January, on Netaji's birthday, he wrote to the museum asking for the files and tapes to be released. But there was only silence. Till today. Today, they finally acknowledged how important this battle was, that it shouldn't be forgotten.'

'It was you, wasn't it? You are Nishonko, aren't you?'

'Nishonko is lost. Nishachar is gone. And what would you do if you found him? Hand him over to the cops? Punish him? Hang him? Make him pay? He already has, Sudipto babu. Paid dearly, every single day. For almost 70 years.'

'I would talk to him. I would ask him questions. There is someone who would want to speak to him. I'm a writer, a reporter. I can defend the truth.'

'Then do it. Find the tapes. Find the evidence. Ask for the files. I bequeath this quest to you. Come tomorrow to this address. You will find everything you need.' He scrawls an address shakily on a piece of paper. He pulls out a keychain and worries one key out of it, then places it carefully on the slip of paper while Sudipto watches, bemused. He pats the key gently.

'Let the truth be known, my young friend.'

EPILOGUE

Painfully, he totters up. The long hours of sitting have played havoc with his ancient legs. He waits, his hand resting on the back of the chair for the thin blood to flow back. Sudipto gets up to help but is dismissed by a short jab of the gnarled hand. He slowly makes his way through the tables and steps onto the road, the pale light from outside blurring the edges of his thin, stooping figure, turning him almost transparent, invisible. Then he's gone.

The grey afternoon is slipping into a grey evening. It is quite cold. He pulls the shawl tighter around him. His limp is heavier as he shuffles through the narrow lanes. There is the fragrance of incense wafting out from some house from the evening puja. The booming sea sound of a conch shell marks the time as sacred, an end to the day, the coming of night, the in-between light. He shuffles to a ramshackle two-storeyed house, its paint washed by many monsoons to a dirty speckled yellow. He climbs, one painful step at a time, the cold red-oxide paved cement staircase. The stairwell is cloudy with the clinging leftover smell of fish fried for lunch and Keo Karpin hair oil. He opens the ancient brass lock to his room. It's the cheap one on the mezzanine floor, the only thing he can afford on his Irrigation Department clerk's pension. But inside, what treasures await. It's a shrine, a temple to the INA, to Netaji. Hundreds of photographs, black and white and sepia and colour, and meticulously cut news clips spanning decades line the walls, crowd the spaces above the single-barred window, fill the ceiling, not an inch of clear space. The bed, the bedside table, they are all made of stacked books and fat bunches of papers and ancient, dog-eared files, a much slept on sheet thrown over the lot. The only pieces of furniture in the room are a small desk and a battered, taped together chair. A hot plate, some meagre provisions, bottles of Horlicks sit on a small low stool. He shuts the door, then shuffles to the desk. At the bottom of the drawer, lies an antique brown leather-covered camera and beside it, an old revolver with a curious brass inlay of a leaping tiger. It's Nishonko's old gun. He carefully places it on the bed of books, then looks up at a picture of Netaji on the wall.

'Sir, I never gave up, I never let up. I hunted for you. I went everywhere, followed every lead, however tenuous. I refused to believe you had died. I held on to hope. So I went after the British, the Indian government, the media — but no one would help. I became a true Nishachar, an invisible ghost no one wanted to acknowledge or see. But I didn't give up.'

From a battered tin trunk, he takes out a khaki uniform — a long ago tattered outfit with the insignia of an INA Major. He dusts it, then, with great ceremony, places it on the makeshift bed. He slowly strips down to his underpants, the bony, bare body revealed. Ancient scars crisscross his chest, back, arms, legs. It's a warrior's body devastated by age and war. He pants a bit with the exertion, his breath clouding in the cold air. Then, he sighs, pulls on the khaki trousers, his thin bony shins vulnerable. The shirt and jacket are too big for him now. They hang loosely on his scarecrow shoulders. He tucks the tail in, neat, meticulous. He places the cap, adjusts it precisely on his thin scraggly hair and checks himself in a fly-blown mirror hanging from a nail, all the while talking to himself, shambling around.

'But today, Sir, today the British finally admitted the truth about Kohima. They confessed they came this close to losing. You...you often used to say, "Wait for your enemy to admit that you were his greatest adversary. You've truly won only when your enemy admits it."'

He straightens up, squares his shoulders and salutes.

'Today, the enemy has finally accepted. Today, the truth came out. They acknowledged Kohima was the greatest battle the British ever fought. Mission accomplished, Sir.'

Then humming 'Kadam Kadam Badaye Ja' in a soft, bruised voice to himself, he picks up a small chocolate tin and opens it. Inside lies a strange collection of oddments. He moves them aside and unearths a photograph in two pieces, torn in half. It's of Aditi and Deb, on the evening of their engagement, all the hope and promise and imagined beauty of their young lives, their perfect future, shining, resplendent, in that sundered, faded image. The old man puts the photograph together, so now, they are joined. He gently touches the face of each, his gnarled, knotted fingers very tender.

'Forgive me, my love…forgive me, my brother.'

Sudipto hurries into the editorial office, his head teeming. He flops down at his untidy desk, sweeps away the clutter of untold stories. His softboard is crammed with pictures of WW2, and INA, amongst others, notes, scribbles, printouts. He pins the address the old man has given him on the board and suspends the key from the large drawing pin. He will go tomorrow morning itself. He switches on his comp, stares at a blank page.

What was it Cicero had said? *'The life of the dead is placed in the memory of the living.'* He types it out, stares at it. Then he nods, hits the keyboard again. *'In this mortal world, everything perishes and will perish,' Bose wrote in 1940, 'but ideas, ideals and dreams do not.' He was confident that the idea for which one individual was prepared to die, would incarnate itself in a thousand lives. That he believed was how the wheels of evolution turned and how ideas, ideals and dreams of one generation were bequeathed to the next. No idea has ever fulfilled itself in this world except through an ordeal of suffering and sacrifice.'* He sits back. It's up to him now to find the truth, to tell the old man's tale. But before that he must tell one person. He picks up the phone.

In the verandah of one of the old, airy houses still left in North Calcutta, a white-haired lady, in her 80s, sits in a wheelchair. She has fine bones, a calm serenity, yet young, inquisitive eyes. She must have been a looker in her youth. She is surrounded by a bunch of young girls, different ages, poorly clad, from the nearby slums, their hair in neat oiled plaits, sitting at her feet on woven bamboo mats.

The old lady is reading from a textbook, slowly, the girls making notes in lined exercise books, their heads bent to the task. The maid comes and hands her a phone.

'It's Chhoto babu, your grandson for you.'

'Yes, Dipu, my dear. Working late again?'

'Hey Amma, I had to call you. Something strange happened today. I was at this little tea shop near my office. And this weird, really batty old man who sits there every day, really ancient and rickety, he told us this crazy story… about Netaji and the INA.'

'Oh dear, one more theory about…'

'No, no, this was…it's about a man called Nishonko Mitro…a girl called Aditi Sen and a…brace yourself…a man called Debraj Mookerji.'

There's silence. The line hums. Sudipto waits.

'Amma? Are you there?'

'Yes, my child. He said…Debraj?'

'Yes, Amma…and I think he was speaking the truth…and yes, I think it was your Debraj, your lost brother.'

'Is he…alive? Is he well?' Her voice trembles.

The line crackles. Sudipto's silence hangs heavy on the air. Her face crumples. Then she pulls herself together, wipes her rheumy eyes. She has waited a lifetime to hear the truth.

'Come home, Dipu. I would like to hear the whole story,' says Debi Mookerji, gently closing the book. 'And can I meet this old man? Can I speak to him myself?'

'Do you really want to? I could…'

'I really want to.' Her voice is firm.

The sabziwalla from Bihar, curses as the old Fiat comes honking round the corner of the narrow street, trying to squeeze past him. The young man at the wheel pokes his head out and asks for directions, the address written shakily on a thin slip of paper. The sabziwalla points, then spits out beetle juice in the car's wake. When they reach the house, old, decrepit, indistinguishable from hundreds of other similar run-down relics of the past, she is daunted a bit by the stairs. But she has brought along her walker and Sudipto helps her climb those cold, red-paved stairs, one at a time. A maid, chattering away on a mobile as she hurries down the stairs, points to the door on the mezzanine. No one else intercepts them or questions them as Sudipto knocks softly. The door gives an inch. It is not locked.

Debi sways, her hand shaking on the walker. It has been such a long, long wait. Years of hunting records of the INA, scanning obit notices, questioning Goopta, and there had been nothing. Years of watching the hope slowly seep out of her parents' eyes. Her son Andy Mookerji, shortened from Anondo, not Andrew, called it her royal obsession. 'Let it go, Ma, it's history.' But she hadn't. She couldn't. It was an unhealed wound she was unable to leave alone. Her rise in academic life, her successes, becoming the Principal of a leading women's college, her doctoral thesis, her Fellowship at Oxford — nothing quite filled that yawning hole. Even the devastation of losing both Andy and Mitali, her lovely, lovely daughter-in-law, in that Rajdhani train accident has not made her lose hope. And now she is on the threshold of finding out what really happened from this person who had been there with him, with her Dada.

The room is cold, musty, dimly lit. An unfamiliar metallic smell hangs on the still air. They can make out the indistinct shape of a man on a lumpy bed, lying curled up on his side, facing the wall. Is he sleeping? Sudipto clears his throat. There's no response. He searches for the light switch. It comes on, a naked bulb festooned with dusty spider webs. The sleeping man is in some khaki uniform, his hair white. They stare in wonder at the walls, the ceilings, the incredible testimony to a time forgotten. Sudipto clears his throat again.

'Moshai?'

But now Debi has hobbled ahead. Beside the man lies an open, rusty chocolate tin box. She reaches for its contents tentatively. There's a torn bead bracelet, its red a pale-washed pink memory. A small velvet box with a tarnished but pretty eternity ring. Now she gasps. Her fingers pick up a pair of old-fashioned antique emerald cuff links.

'Amma, wait. Don't.'

But she's transported, staring at them but not there. Does she remember that long ago night, the storm coming, the record playing in Debraj's bedroom, her homecoming gift for Deb? Sudipto pulls the rickety chair quickly to her, worried she will fall, so white she has gone. She sits, stares blindly at faded photographs inside the box. Of a little girl with pigtails, of a couple in a faded black and white studio portrait, of a man sitting bare-bodied, laughing, on a Chinese junk, impossibly handsome.

'It's him,' she whispers. And finally a torn photograph of Dada and a woman, with wide set eyes and a full mouth, laughing into the camera, eyes shining across the span of space and time. So this was Aditi, the woman Dipu had told her about, late, late into the previous night, the woman he had loved.

She wants to know everything that happened. Tentatively, with a tremor of anticipation, she reaches to touch the shoulder of the sleeping man. It is so still, so cold. And now he rolls over, the movement revealing his hand clasped around a gun with a carving of a leaping tiger. His face is calm, peaceful. And there's a great, big hole, singed black, right in the middle of his heart.